THE
BELGARIAD
PART ONE

By David Eddings
Published by Ballantine Books:

THE BELGARIAD

Book One: *Pawn of Prophecy*
Book Two: *Queen of Sorcery*
Book Three: *Magician's Gambit*
Book Four: *Castle of Wizardry*
Book Five: *Enchanters' End Game*

THE MALLOREON

Book One: *Guardians of the West*
Book Two: *King of the Murgos*
Book Three: *Demon Lord of Karanda*
Book Four: *Sorceress of Darshiva*
Book Five: *The Seeress of Kell*

THE ELENIUM

Book One: *The Diamond Throne*
Book Two: *The Ruby Knight*
Book Three: *The Sapphire Rose*

THE TAMULI

Book One: *Domes of Fire*
Book Two: *The Shining Ones*
Book Three: *The Hidden City*

HIGH HUNT

THE LOSERS

THE
BELGARIAD
PART ONE

DAVID
EDDINGS

DEL REY

A DEL REY® BOOK
BALLANTINE BOOKS
NEW YORK

A Del Rey ® Book
Published by Ballantine Books

Copyright © 1982, 1983 by David Eddings
Endpaper map copyright © 1995 by Larry Schwinger

This work was originally published as three separate volumes by Ballantine Books as *Pawn of Prophecy* and *Queen of Sorcery* in 1982 and *Magician's Gambit* in 1983.

Library of Congress Cataloging-in-Publication Data:
Eddings, David.
  The Belgariad / David Eddings.
    p.   cm.
  "A Del Rey book."
  Contents: Pawn of prophecy—Queen of sorcery—Magician's gambit.
  ISBN 0-345-40004-6
  1. Fantastic fiction, American.   I. Title.
PS3555.D38B45   1995
813'.54—dc20   95-17587
                                                                      CIP

Text design by Holly Johnson
Maps by Shelly Shapiro

Manufactured in the United States of America

First Edition: October 1995

10 9 8 7 6 5 4 3 2 1

CONTENTS

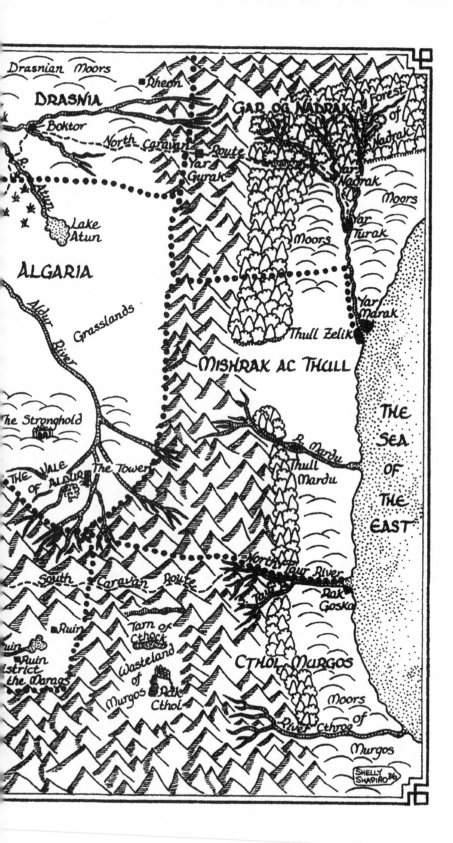

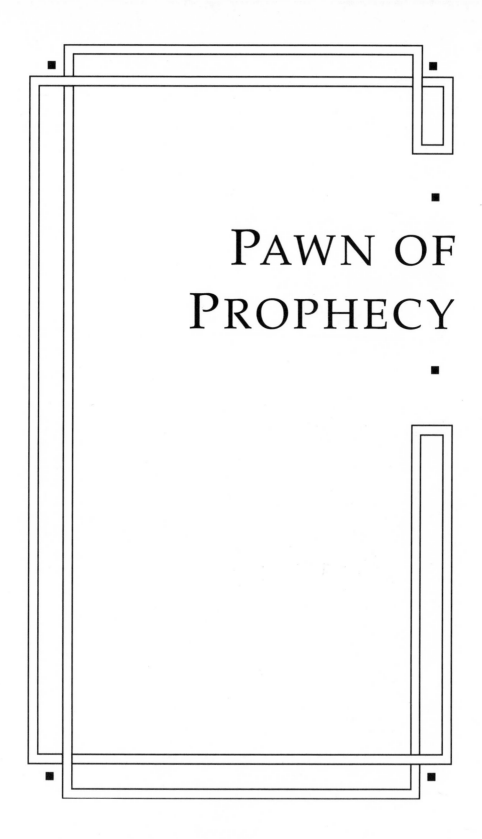

PAWN OF PROPHECY

For Theone,
  who told me stories but could not stay for
  mine—
and for Arthur,
  who showed me the way to become a man—
  and who shows me still.

PROLOGUE

Being a History of the War of the Gods and the Acts of Belgarath the Sorcerer

—ADAPTED FROM *THE BOOK OF ALORN*

When the world was new, the seven Gods dwelt in harmony, and the races of man were as one people. Belar, youngest of the Gods, was beloved by the Alorns. He abode with them and cherished them, and they prospered in his care. The other Gods also gathered peoples about them, and each God cherished his own people.

But Belar's eldest brother, Aldur, was God over no people. He dwelt apart from men and Gods, until the day that a vagrant child sought him out. Aldur accepted the child as his disciple and called him Belgarath. Belgarath learned the secret of the Will and the Word and became a sorcerer. In the years that followed, others also sought out the solitary God. They joined in brotherhood to learn at the feet of Aldur, and time did not touch them.

Now it happened that Aldur took up a stone in the shape of a globe, no larger than the heart of a child, and he turned the stone in his hand until it became a living soul. The power of the living jewel, which men called the Orb of Aldur, was very great, and Aldur worked wonders with it.

Of all the Gods, Torak was the most beautiful, and his people were the Angaraks. They burned sacrifices before him, calling him Lord of Lords, and Torak found the smell of sacrifice and the words of adoration sweet. The day came, however, when he heard of the Orb of Aldur, and from that moment he knew no peace.

Finally, in a dissembling guise, he went to Aldur. "My brother," he said, "it is not fitting that thou shouldst absent thyself from our company and counsel. Put aside this jewel which hath seduced thy mind from our fellowship."

Aldur looked into his brother's soul and rebuked him. "Why dost thou seek lordship and dominion, Torak? Is not Angarak enough for thee? Do not in thy pride seek to possess the Orb, lest it slay thee."

Great was Torak's shame at the words of Aldur, and he raised his hand and smote his brother. Taking the jewel, he fled.

The other Gods besought Torak to return the Orb, but he would not. Then the races of man rose up and came against the hosts of Angarak and made war on them. The wars of the Gods and of men raged across the land until, near the high places of Korim, Torak raised the Orb and forced its Will to join with his to split the earth asunder. The mountains were cast down, and the sea came in. But Belar and Aldur joined their Wills and set limits upon the sea. The races of man, however, were separated one from the others, and the Gods also.

Now when Torak raised the living Orb against the earth, it awoke and began to glow with holy flame. The face of Torak was seared by the blue fire. In pain he cast down the mountains; in anguish he cracked open the earth; in agony he let in the sea. His left hand flared and burned to ashes, the flesh on the left side of his face melted like wax, and his left eye boiled in its socket. With a great cry, he cast himself into the sea to quench the burning, but his anguish was without end.

When Torak rose from the water, his right side was still fair, but his left was burned and scarred hideously by the fire of the Orb. In endless pain, he led his people away to the east, where they built a great city on the plains of Mallorea, which they called *Cthol Mishrak*, City of Night, for Torak hid his maiming in darkness. The Angaraks raised an iron tower for their God and placed the Orb in an iron cask in the topmost chamber. Often Torak stood before the cask, then fled weeping, lest his yearning to look upon the Orb overpower him and he perish utterly.

The centuries rolled past in the lands of the Angarak, and they came to call their maimed God Kal-Torak, both King and God.

Belar had taken the Alorns to the north. Of all men, they were the most hardy and warlike, and Belar put eternal hatred for Angarak in their hearts. With cruel swords and axes they ranged the north, even to the fields of eternal ice, seeking a way to their ancient enemies.

Thus it was until the time when Cherek Bear-shoulders, greatest king of the Alorns, traveled to the Vale of Aldur to seek out Belgarath the Sorcerer. "The way to the north is open," he said. "The signs and the auguries are propitious. Now is the time ripe for us to discover the way to the City of Night and regain the Orb from One-eye."

Poledra, wife of Belgarath, was great with child, and he was reluctant to leave her. But Cherek prevailed. They stole away one night to join Cherek's sons, Dras Bull-neck, Algar Fleet-foot, and Riva Iron-grip.

Cruel winter gripped the northland, and the moors glittered beneath the stars with frost and steel-gray ice. To seek out their way, Belgarath cast an enchantment and took the shape of a great wolf. On silent feet, he slunk through the snow-floored forests where the trees cracked and shattered in the sundering cold. Grim frost silvered the ruff and shoulders of the wolf, and ever after the hair and beard of Belgarath were silver.

Through snow and mist they crossed into Mallorea and came at last to *Cthol Mishrak*. Finding a secret way into the city, Belgarath led them to the foot of the iron tower. Silently they climbed the rusted stairs which had known no step for twenty centuries. Fearfully they passed through the chamber where Torak tossed in pain-haunted slumber, his maimed face hidden by a steel mask. Stealthily they crept past the sleeping God in the smoldering darkness and came at last to the chamber where lay the iron cask in which rested the living Orb.

Cherek motioned for Belgarath to take the Orb, but Belgarath refused.

"I may not touch it," he said, "lest it destroy me. Once it welcomed the touch of man or God, but its Will hardened when Torak raised it against its mother. It will not be so used again. It reads our souls. Only one without ill intent, who is pure enough to take it and convey it in peril of his life, with no thought of power or possession, may touch it now."

"What man is without ill intent in the silence of his soul?" Cherek asked. But Riva Iron-grip opened the cask and took up the Orb. Its fire shone through his fingers, but he was not burned.

"So be it, Cherek," Belgarath said. "Your youngest son is pure. It shall be his doom and the doom of all who follow him to bear the Orb and protect it." And Belgarath sighed, knowing the burden he had placed upon Riva.

"Then his brothers and I will sustain him," Cherek said, "for so long as this doom is upon him."

Riva muffled the Orb in his cloak and hid it beneath his tunic. They crept again through the chambers of the maimed God, down the rusted stairs, along the secret way to the gates of the city, and into the wasteland beyond.

Soon after, Torak awoke and went as always into the Chamber of the Orb. But the cask stood open, and the Orb was gone. Horrible was the wrath of Kal-Torak. Taking his great sword, he went down from the iron tower and turned and smote it once, and the tower fell. To the Angaraks he cried out in a voice of thunder: "Because ye have become indolent and unwatchful and have let a thief steal that for which I paid so dearly, I will break your city and drive ye forth. Angarak shall wander the earth until *Cthrag Yaska*, the burning stone, is returned to me." Then he cast down the City of Night in ruins and drove the hosts of Angarak into the wilderness, and *Cthol Mishrak* was no more.

Three leagues off, Belgarath heard the wailing from the city and knew that Torak had awakened. "Now will he come after us," he said, "and only the power of the Orb can save us. When the hosts are upon us, Iron-grip, take the Orb and hold it so they may see it."

The hosts of Angarak came, with Torak himself in the forefront, but Riva held forth the Orb so that the maimed God and his hosts might behold it. The Orb knew its enemy. Its hatred flamed anew, and the sky became alight with its fury. Torak cried out and turned away. The front ranks of the Angarak hosts were consumed by fire, and the rest fled in terror.

Thus Belgarath and his companions escaped from Mallorea and passed again through the marches of the north, bearing the Orb of Aldur once more into the Kingdoms of the West.

Now the Gods, knowing all that had passed, held council, and Aldur advised them, "If we raise war again upon our brother Torak, our strife will destroy the world. Thus we must absent ourselves from the world so that our brother may not find us. No longer in flesh, but in spirit only may we remain to guide and protect our people. For the world's sake it must be so. In the day that we war again, the world will be unmade."

The Gods wept that they must depart. But Chaldan, Bull-God of the Arends, asked, "In our absence, shall not Torak have dominion?"

"Not so," Aldur replied. "So long as the Orb remains with the line of Riva Iron-grip, Torak shall not prevail."

So it was that the Gods departed, and only Torak remained. But the knowledge that the Orb in the hand of Riva denied him dominion cankered his soul.

Then Belgarath spoke with Cherek and his sons. "Here we must part, to guard the Orb and to prepare against the coming of Torak. Let each turn aside as I have instructed and make preparations."

"We will, Belgarath," vowed Cherek Bear-shoulders. "From this day, Aloria is no more, but the Alorns will deny dominion to Torak as long as one Alorn remains."

Belgarath raised his face. "Hear me, Torak One-eye," he cried. "The living Orb is secure against thee, and thou shalt not prevail against it. In the day that thou comest against us, I shall raise war against thee. I will maintain watch upon thee by day and by night and will abide against thy coming, even to the end of days."

In the wastelands of Mallorea, Kal-Torak heard the voice of Belgarath and smote about him in fury, for he knew that the living Orb was forever beyond his reach.

Then Cherek embraced his sons and turned away, to see them no more. Dras went north and dwelt in the lands drained by River Mrin. He built a city at Boktor and called his lands Drasnia. And he and his descendants stood athwart the northern marches and denied them to the enemy. Algar went south with his people and found horses on the broad plains drained by Aldur River. The horses they tamed and learned to ride and for the first time in the history of man, mounted warriors appeared. Their country they called Algaria, and they became nomads, following their herds. Cherek returned sadly to Val Alorn and renamed his kingdom Cherek, for now he was alone and without sons. Grimly he built tall ships of war to patrol the seas and deny them to the enemy.

Upon the bearer of the Orb, however, fell the burden of the longest journey. Taking his people, Riva went to the west coast of Sendaria. There he built ships, and he and his people crossed to the Isle of the Winds. They burned their ships and built a fortress and a walled city around it. The city they called Riva and the fortress the Hall of the Rivan King. Then Belar, God of the Alorns, caused two iron stars to fall from the sky, and Riva took up the stars and forged a blade from one and a hilt from the other, setting the Orb upon it as a pommel-stone. So large was the sword that none but Riva could wield it. In the wasteland of Mallorea, Kal-Torak felt in his soul the forging of the sword and he tasted fear for the first time.

The sword was set against the black rock that stood at the back of Riva's throne, with the Orb at the highest point, and the sword joined to the rock so that none but Riva could remove it. The Orb burned with cold fire when Riva sat upon the throne. And when he took down his sword and raised it, it became a great tongue of cold fire.

The greatest wonder of all was the marking of Riva's heir. In each generation, one child in the line of Riva bore upon the palm of his right hand the mark of the Orb. The child so marked was taken to the throne chamber, and his hand was placed upon the Orb, so that it might know him. With each infant touch, the Orb waxed in brilliance, and the bond between the living Orb and the line of Riva became stronger with each joining.

After Belgarath had parted from his companions, he hastened to the Vale of Aldur. But there he found that Poledra, his wife, had borne twin daughters, and then she had died. In sorrow he named the elder Polgara. Her hair was dark as the raven's wing. In the fashion of sorcerers, he stretched forth his hand to lay it upon her brow, and a single lock at her forehead turned frost-white at his touch. Then he was troubled, for the white lock was the mark of the sorcerers, and Polgara was the first female child to be so marked.

His second daughter, fair-skinned and golden-haired, was unmarked. He called her Beldaran, and he and her dark-haired sister loved her beyond all else and contended with each other for her affection.

Now when Polgara and Beldaran had reached their sixteenth year, the Spirit of Aldur came to Belgarath in a dream, saying, "My beloved disciple, I would join thy house with the house of the guardian of the Orb. Choose, therefore, which of thy daughters thou wilt give to the Rivan King to be his wife and the mother of his line, for in that line lies the hope of the world, against which the dark power of Torak may not prevail."

In the deep silence of his soul, Belgarath was tempted to choose Polgara. But, knowing the burden which lay upon the Rivan King, he sent Beldaran instead, and wept when she was gone. Polgara wept also, long and bitterly, knowing that her sister must fade and die. In time, however, they comforted each other and came at last to know each other.

They joined their powers to keep watch over Torak. And some men say that they abide still, keeping their vigil through all the uncounted centuries.

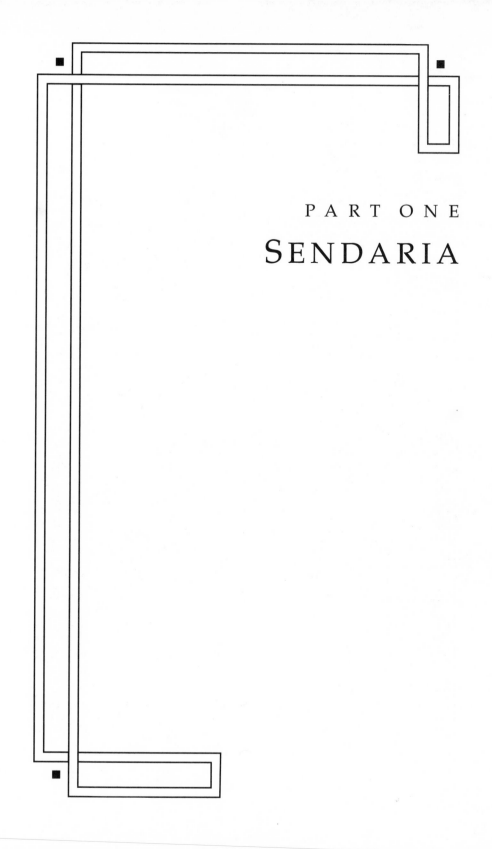

PART ONE

SENDARIA

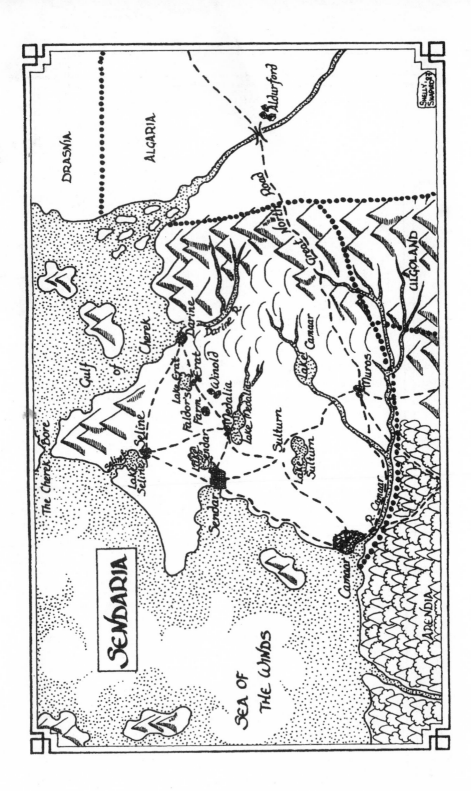

The first thing the boy Garion remembered was the kitchen at Faldor's farm. For all the rest of his life he had a special warm feeling for kitchens and those peculiar sounds and smells that seemed some-how to combine into a bustling seriousness that had to do with love and food and comfort and security and, above all, home. No matter how high Garion rose in life, he never forgot that all his memories began in that kitchen.

The kitchen at Faldor's farm was a large, low-beamed room filled with ovens and kettles and great spits that turned slowly in cavernlike arched fire-places. There were long, heavy worktables where bread was kneaded into loaves and chickens were cut up and carrots and celery were diced with quick, crisp rocking movements of long, curved knives. When Garion was very small, he played under those tables and soon learned to keep his fingers and toes out from under the feet of the kitchen helpers who worked around them. And sometimes in the late afternoon when he grew tired, he would lie in a corner and stare into one of the flickering fires that gleamed and re-flected back from the hundred polished pots and knives and long-handled spoons that hung from pegs along the whitewashed walls and, all bemused, he would drift off into sleep in perfect peace and harmony with all the world around him.

The center of the kitchen and everything that happened there was Aunt Pol. She seemed somehow to be able to be everywhere at once. The finishing touch that plumped a goose in its roasting pan or deftly shaped a rising loaf or garnished a smoking ham fresh from the oven was always hers. Though there were several others who worked in the kitchen, no loaf, stew, soup, roast, or vegetable ever went out of it that had not been touched at least once by Aunt Pol. She knew by smell, taste, or some higher instinct what each dish required, and she seasoned them all by pinch or trace or a negligent-seeming shake from earthenware spice pots. It was as if there was a kind of magic about her, a knowledge and power beyond that of ordinary people. And yet, even at her busiest, she always knew precisely where Garion was. In the very midst of crimping a pie crust or decorating a special cake or stitching up a freshly stuffed chicken she could, without looking, reach out a leg and hook him back out from under the feet of others with heel or ankle.

As he grew a bit older, it even became a game. Garion would watch until she seemed far too busy to notice him, and then, laughing, he would run on his sturdy little legs toward a door. But she would always catch him. And he would laugh and throw his arms around her neck and kiss her and then go back to watching for his next chance to run away again.

He was quite convinced in those early years that his Aunt Pol was quite the most important and beautiful woman in the world. For one thing, she was taller than the other women on Faldor's farm—very nearly as tall as a man—and her face was always serious—even stern—except with him, of course. Her hair was long and very dark—almost black—all but one lock just above her left brow which was white as new snow. At night when she tucked him into the little bed close beside her own in their private room above the kitchen, he would reach out and touch that white lock; she would smile at him and touch his face with a soft hand. Then he would sleep, content in the knowledge that she was there, watching over him.

Faldor's farm lay very nearly in the center of Sendaria, a misty kingdom bordered on the west by the Sea of the Winds and on the east by the Gulf of Cherek. Like all farmhouses in that particular time and place, Faldor's farmstead was not one building or two, but rather was a solidly constructed complex of sheds and barns and hen roosts and dovecotes all facing inward upon a central yard with a stout gate at the front. Along the second story gallery were the rooms, some spacious, some quite tiny, in which lived the farmhands who tilled and planted and weeded the extensive fields beyond the walls. Faldor himself lived in quarters in the square tower above the central dining hall where his workers assembled three times a day—sometimes four during harvest time—to feast on the bounty of Aunt Pol's kitchen.

All in all, it was quite a happy and harmonious place. Farmer Faldor was a good master. He was a tall, serious man with a long nose and an even longer jaw. Though he seldom laughed or even smiled, he was kindly to those who worked for him and seemed more intent on maintaining them all in health and well-being than extracting the last possible ounce of sweat from them. In many ways he was more like a father than a master to the sixty-odd people who lived on his freeholding. He ate with them—which was unusual, since many farmers in the district sought to hold themselves aloof from their workers—and his presence at the head of the central table in the dining hall exerted a restraining influence on some of the younger ones who tended sometimes to be boisterous. Farmer Faldor was a devout man, and he invariably invoked with simple eloquence the blessing of the Gods before each meal. The people of his farm, knowing this, filed with some decorum into the dining hall before each meal and sat in the semblance at least of piety before attacking the heaping platters and bowls of food that Aunt Pol and her helpers had placed before them.

Because of Faldor's good heart—and the magic of Aunt Pol's deft fingers—the farm was known throughout the district as the finest place to live and work for twenty leagues in any direction. Whole evenings were spent in the tavern in the nearby village of Upper Gralt in minute descriptions of the near-miraculous meals served regularly in Faldor's dining hall. Less fortunate men who worked at other farms were frequently seen, after several pots of ale, to weep openly at descriptions of one of Aunt Pol's roasted geese, and the fame of Faldor's farm spread wide throughout the district.

The most important man on the farm, aside from Faldor, was Durnik the smith. As Garion grew older and was allowed to move out from under Aunt Pol's watchful eye, he found his way inevitably to the smithy. The glowing iron that came from Durnik's forge had an almost hypnotic attraction for him. Durnik was an ordinary-looking man with plain brown hair and a plain face, ruddy from the heat of his forge. He was neither tall nor short, nor was he thin or stout. He was sober and quiet, and like most men who follow his trade, he was enormously strong. He wore a rough leather jerkin and an apron of the same material. Both were spotted with burns from the sparks which flew from his forge. He also wore tight-fitting hose and soft leather boots as was the custom in that part of Sendaria. At first Durnik's only words to Garion were warnings to keep his fingers away from the forge and the glowing metal which came from it. In time, however, he and the boy became friends, and he spoke more frequently.

"Always finish what you set your hand to," he would advise. "It's bad for the iron if you set it aside and then take it back to the fire more than is needful."

"Why is that?" Garion would ask.

Durnik would shrug. "It just is."

"Always do the very best job you can," he said on another occasion as he put a last few finishing touches with a file on the metal parts of a wagon tongue he was repairing.

"But that piece goes underneath," Garion said. "No one will ever see it."

"But I know it's there," Durnik said, still smoothing the metal. "If it isn't done as well as I can do it, I'll be ashamed every time I see this wagon go by—and I'll see the wagon every day."

And so it went. Without even intending to, Durnik instructed the small boy in those solid Sendarian virtues of work, thrift, sobriety, good manners, and practicality which formed the backbone of the society.

At first Aunt Pol worried about Garion's attraction to the smithy with its obvious dangers; but after watching from her kitchen door for a while, she realized that Durnik was almost as watchful of Garion's safety as she was herself, and she became less concerned.

"If the boy becomes pestersome, Goodman Durnik, send him away," she told the smith on one occasion when she had brought a large copper kettle to the smithy to be patched, "or tell me, and I'll keep him closer to the kitchen."

"He's no bother, Mistress Pol," Durnik said, smiling. "He's a sensible boy and knows enough to keep out of the way."

"You're too good-natured, friend Durnik," Aunt Pol said. "The boy is full of questions. Answer one and a dozen more pour out."

"That's the way of boys," Durnik said, carefully pouring bubbling metal into the small clay ring he'd placed around the tiny hole in the bottom of the kettle. "I was questionsome myself when I was a boy. My father and old Barl, the smith who taught me, were patient enough to answer what they could. I'd repay them poorly if I didn't have the same patience with Garion."

Garion, who was sitting nearby, had held his breath during this conversation. He knew that one wrong word on either side would have instantly banished him from the smithy. As Aunt Pol walked back across the hard-packed dirt of the yard toward her kitchen with the new-mended kettle, he noticed the way that Durnik watched her, and an idea began to form in his mind. It was a simple idea, and the beauty of it was that it provided something for everyone.

"Aunt Pol," he said that night, wincing as she washed one of his ears with a rough cloth.

"Yes?" she said, turning her attention to his neck.

"Why don't you marry Durnik?"

She stopped washing. "What?" she asked.

"I think it would be an awfully good idea."

"Oh, do you?" Her voice had a slight edge to it, and Garion knew he was on dangerous ground.

"He likes you," he said defensively.

"And I suppose you've already discussed this with him?"

"No," he said. "I thought I'd talk to you about it first."

"At least *that* was a good idea."

"I can tell him about it tomorrow morning, if you'd like."

His head was turned around quite firmly by one ear. Aunt Pol, Garion felt, found his ears far too convenient.

"Don't you so much as breathe one word of this nonsense to Durnik or anyone else," she said, her dark eyes burning into his with a fire he had never seen there before.

"It was only a thought," he said quickly.

"A very bad one. From now on leave thinking to grown-ups." She was still holding his ear.

"Anything you say," he agreed hastily.

Later that night, however, when they lay in their beds in the quiet darkness, he approached the problem obliquely.

"Aunt Pol?"

"Yes?"

"Since you don't want to marry Durnik, who *do* you want to marry?"

"Garion," she said.

"Yes?"

"Close your mouth and go to sleep."

"I think I've got a right to know," he said in an injured tone.

"*Garion!*"

"All right. I'm going to sleep, but I don't think you're being very fair about all this."

She drew in a deep breath. "Very well," she said. "I'm not thinking of getting married. I have never thought of getting married, and I seriously doubt that I'll ever think of getting married. I have far too many important things to attend to for any of that."

"Don't worry, Aunt Pol," he said, wanting to put her mind at ease. "When I grow up, *I'll* marry you."

She laughed then, a deep, rich laugh, and reached out to touch his face in the darkness. "Oh no, my Garion," she said. "There's another wife in store for you."

"Who?" he demanded.

"You'll find out," she said mysteriously. "Now go to sleep."

"Aunt Pol?"

"Yes?"

"Where's my mother?" It was a question he had been meaning to ask for quite some time.

There was a long pause, then Aunt Pol sighed. "She died," she said quietly.

Garion felt a sudden wrenching surge of grief, an unbearable anguish. He began to cry.

And then she was beside his bed. She knelt on the floor and put her arms around him. Finally, a long time later, after she had carried him to her own bed and held him close until his grief had run its course, Garion asked brokenly, "What was she like? My mother?"

"She was fair-haired," Aunt Pol said, "and very young and very beautiful. Her voice was gentle, and she was very happy."

"Did she love me?"

"More than you could imagine."

And then he cried again, but his crying was quieter now, more regretful than anguished.

Aunt Pol held him closely until he cried himself to sleep.

THERE WERE OTHER children on Faldor's farm, as was only natural in a community of sixty or so. The older ones on the farm all worked, but there were three other children of about Garion's age on the freeholding. These three became his playmates and his friends.

The oldest boy was named Rundorig. He was a year or two older than Garion and quite a bit taller. Ordinarily, since he was the eldest of the children, Rundorig would have been their leader; but because he was an Arend, his sense was a bit limited and he cheerfully deferred to the younger ones. The kingdom of Sendaria, unlike other kingdoms, was inhabited by a broad variety of racial stocks. Chereks, Algars, Drasnians, Arends, and even a substantial number of Tolnedrans had merged to form the elemental Sendar. Arends, of course, were very brave, but were also notoriously thick-witted.

Garion's second playmate was Doroon, a small, quick boy whose background was so mixed that he could only be called a Sendar. The most notable thing about Doroon was the fact that he was always running; he never walked if he could run. Like his feet, his mind seemed to tumble over itself, and his tongue as well. He talked continually and very fast and he was always excited.

The undisputed leader of the little foursome was the girl Zubrette, a golden-haired charmer who invented their games, made up stories to tell them, and set them to stealing apples and plums from Faldor's orchard for her. She ruled them as a little queen, playing one against the other and inciting them into fights. She was quite heartless, and each of the three boys at times hated her even while remaining helpless thralls to her tiniest whim.

In the winter they slid on wide boards down the snowy hillside behind the farmhouse and returned home, wet and snow-covered, with chapped hands and glowing cheeks as evening's purple shadows crept across the snow. Or, after Durnik the smith had proclaimed the ice safe, they would slide endlessly across the frozen pond that lay glittering frostily in a little dale just to the east of the farm buildings along the road to Upper Gralt. And, if the weather was too cold or on toward spring when rains and warm winds had made the snow slushy and the pond unsafe, they would gather in the hay barn and leap by the hour from the loft into the soft hay beneath, filling their hair with chaff and their noses with dust that smelled of summer.

In the spring they caught polliwogs along the marshy edges of the pond and climbed trees to stare in wonder at the tiny blue eggs the birds had laid in twiggy nests in the high branches.

It was Doroon, naturally, who fell from a tree and broke his arm one fine spring morning when Zubrette urged him into the highest branches of a tree near the edge of the pond. Since Rundorig stood helplessly gaping at his injured friend and Zubrette had run away almost before he hit the ground, it fell to Garion to make certain necessary decisions. Gravely he considered the situation for a few moments, his young face seriously intent beneath his shock of sandy hair. The arm was obviously broken, and Doroon, pale and frightened, bit his lip to keep from crying.

A movement caught Garion's eye, and he glanced up quickly. A man in a dark cloak sat astride a large black horse not far away, watching intently. When their eyes met, Garion felt a momentary chill, and he knew that he had seen the man before—that indeed that dark figure had hovered on the edge of his vision for as long as he could remember, never speaking, but always watching. There was in that silent scrutiny a kind of cold animosity curiously mingled with something that was almost, but not quite, fear. Then Doroon whimpered, and Garion turned back.

Carefully he bound the injured arm across the front of Doroon's body with his rope belt, and then he and Rundorig helped the injured boy to his feet.

"At least he could have helped us," Garion said resentfully.

"Who?" Rundorig said, looking around.

Garion turned to point at the dark-cloaked man, but the rider was gone.

"I didn't see anyone," Rundorig said.

"It hurts," Doroon said.

"Don't worry," Garion said. "Aunt Pol can fix it."

And so she did. When the three appeared at the door of her kitchen, she took in the situation with a single glance. "Bring him over here," she told them, her voice not even excited. She set the pale and violently trembling boy on a stool near one of the ovens and mixed a tea of several herbs taken from earthenware jars on a high shelf in the back of one of her pantries.

"Drink this," she instructed Doroon, handing him a steaming mug.

"Will it make my arm well?" Doroon asked, suspiciously eyeing the evil-smelling brew.

"Just drink it," she ordered, laying out some splints and linen strips.

"Ick! It tastes awful," Doroon said, making a face.

"It's supposed to," she told him. "Drink it all."

"I don't think I want any more," he said.

"Very well," she said. She pushed back the splints and took down a long, very sharp knife from a hook on the wall.

"What are you going to do with that?" he demanded shakily.

"Since you don't want to take the medicine," she said blandly, "I guess it'll have to come off."

"*Off?*" Doroon squeaked, his eyes bulging.

"Probably about right there," she said, thoughtfully touching his arm at the elbow with the point of the knife.

Tears coming to his eyes, Doroon gulped down the rest of the liquid and a few minutes later he was nodding, almost drowsing on his stool. He screamed once, though, when Aunt Pol set the broken bone, but after the arm had been wrapped and splinted, he drowsed again. Aunt Pol spoke briefly with the boy's frightened mother and then had Durnik carry him up to bed.

"You wouldn't really have cut off his arm," Garion said.

Aunt Pol looked at him, her expression unchanging. "Oh?" she said, and he was no longer sure. "I think I'd like to have a word with Mistress Zubrette now," she said then.

"She ran away when Doroon fell out of the tree," Garion said.

"Find her."

"She's hiding," Garion protested. "She always hides when something goes wrong. I wouldn't know where to look for her."

"Garion," Aunt Pol said, "I didn't ask you if you knew where to look. I told you to find her and bring her to me."

"What if she won't come?" Garion hedged.

"Garion!" There was a note of awful finality in Aunt Pol's tone, and Garion fled.

"I DIDN'T HAVE anything to do with it," Zubrette lied as soon as Garion led her to Aunt Pol in the kitchen.

"You," Aunt Pol said, pointing at a stool, "sit!"

Zubrette sank onto the stool, her mouth open and her eyes wide.

"You," Aunt Pol said to Garion, pointing at the kitchen door, "out!"

Garion left hurriedly.

Ten minutes later a sobbing little girl stumbled out of the kitchen. Aunt Pol stood in the doorway looking after her with eyes as hard as ice.

"Did you thrash her?" Garion asked hopefully.

Aunt Pol withered him with a glance. "Of course not," she said. "You don't thrash girls."

"*I* would have," Garion said, disappointed. "What did you do to her?"

"Don't you have anything to do?" Aunt Pol asked.

"No," Garion said, "not really." That, of course, was a mistake.

"Good," Aunt Pol said, finding one of his ears. "It's time you started to earn your way. You'll find some dirty pots in the scullery. I'd like to have them scrubbed."

"I don't know why you're angry with me," Garion objected, squirming. "It wasn't my fault that Doroon went up that tree."

"The scullery, Garion," she said. "Now."

The rest of that spring and the early part of the summer were quiet. Doroon, of course, could not play until his arm mended, and Zubrette had been so shaken by whatever it was that Aunt Pol had said to her that she avoided the two other boys. Garion was left with only Rundorig to play with, and Rundorig was not bright enough to be much fun. Because there was really nothing else to do, the boys often went into the fields to watch the hands work and listen to their talk.

As it happened, during that particular summer the men on Faldor's farm were talking about the Battle of Vo Mimbre, the most cataclysmic event in the history of the west. Garion and Rundorig listened, enthralled, as the men unfolded the story of how the hordes of Kal Torak had quite suddenly struck into the west some five hundred years before.

It had all begun in 4865, as men reckoned time in that part of the world, when vast multitudes of Murgos and Nadraks and Thulls had struck down across the mountains of the Nadrak Forest into Drasnia, and behind them in endless waves had come the uncountable numbers of the Malloreans.

After Drasnia had been brutally crushed, the Angaraks had turned southward onto the vast grasslands of Algaria and had laid siege to that enormous fortress called the Algarian Stronghold. The siege had lasted for eight years until finally, in disgust, Kal Torak had abandoned it. It was not until he turned his army westward into Ulgoland that the other kingdoms became aware that the Angarak invasion was directed not only against the Alorns but against all of the west. In the summer of 4875 Kal Torak had come down upon the Arendish plain before the city of Vo Mimbre, and it was there that the combined armies of the west awaited him.

The Sendars who participated in the battle were a part of the force under the leadership of Brand, the Rivan Warder. That force, consisting of Rivans, Sendars and Asturian Arends, assaulted the Angarak rear after the left had been engaged by Algars, Drasnians and Ulgos; the right by Tolnedrens and Chereks; and the front by the legendary charge of the Mimbrate Arends. For hours the battle had raged until, in the center of the field, Brand had met in a single combat with Kal Torak himself. Upon that duel had hinged the outcome of the battle.

Although twenty generations had passed since that titanic encounter, it was still as fresh in the memory of the Sendarian farmers who worked on Faldor's farm as if it had happened only yesterday. Each blow was described, and each feint and parry. At the final moment, when it seemed that he must inevitably be overthrown, Brand had removed the covering from his shield, and Kal Torak, taken aback by some momentary confusion, had lowered his guard and had been instantly struck down.

For Rundorig, the description of the battle was enough to set his Arendish blood seething. Garion, however, found that certain questions had been left unanswered by the stories.

"Why was Brand's shield covered?" he asked Cralto, one of the older hands.

Cralto shrugged. "It just was," he said. "Everyone I've ever talked with about it agrees on that."

"Was it a magic shield?" Garion persisted.

"It may have been," Cralto said, "but I've never heard anyone say so. All I know is that when Brand uncovered his shield, Kal Torak dropped his own shield, and Brand stabbed his sword into Kal Torak's head—through the eye, or so I am told."

Garion shook his head stubbornly. "I don't understand," he said. "How could something like that have made Kal Torak afraid?"

"I can't say," Cralto told him. "I've never heard anyone explain it."

Despite his dissatisfaction with the story, Garion quite quickly agreed to Rundorig's rather simple plan to re-enact the duel. After a day or so of posturing and banging at each other with sticks to simulate swords, Garion decided that they needed some equipment to make the game more enjoyable. Two kettles and two large pot lids mysteriously disappeared from Aunt Pol's kitchen; and Garion and Rundorig, now with helmets and shields, repaired to a quiet place to do war upon each other.

It was all going quite splendidly until Rundorig, who was older, taller and stronger, struck Garion a resounding whack on the head with his wooden sword. The rim of the kettle cut into Garion's eyebrow, and the blood began to flow. There was a sudden ringing in Garion's ears, and a kind of boiling exaltation surged up in his veins as he rose to his feet from the ground.

He never knew afterward quite what happened. He had only sketchy memories of shouting defiance at Kal Torak in words which sprang to his lips and which even he did not understand. Rundorig's familiar and somewhat foolish face was no longer the face before him but rather was replaced by something hideously maimed and ugly. In a fury Garion struck at that face again and again with fire seething in his brain.

And then it was over. Poor Rundorig lay at his feet, beaten senseless by the enraged attack. Garion was horrified at what he had done, but at the same time there was the fiery taste of victory in his mouth.

Later, in the kitchen, where all injuries on the farm were routinely taken, Aunt Pol tended their wounds with only minimal comments about them. Rundorig seemed not to be seriously hurt, though his face had begun to swell and turn purple in several places and he had difficulty focusing his eyes at first. A few cold cloths on his head and one of Aunt Pol's potions quickly restored him.

The cut on Garion's brow, however, required a bit more attention. She had Durnik hold the boy down and then she took needle and thread and sewed up the cut as calmly as she would have repaired a rip in a sleeve, all the while ignoring the howls from her patient. All in all, she seemed much more concerned about the dented kettles and battered pot lids than about the war wounds of the two boys.

When it was over, Garion had a headache and was taken up to bed.

"At least I beat Kal Torak," he told Aunt Pol somewhat drowsily.

She looked at him sharply. "Where did you hear about Torak?" she demanded.

"It's *Kal* Torak, Aunt Pol," Garion explained patiently.

"Answer me."

"The farmers were telling stories—old Cralto and the others—about Brand and Vo Mimbre and Kal Torak and all the rest. That's what Rundorig and I were playing. I was Brand and he was Kal Torak. I didn't get to uncover my shield, though. Rundorig hit me on the head before we got that far."

"I want you to listen to me, Garion," Aunt Pol said, "and I want you to listen carefully. You are never to speak the name of Torak again."

"It's *Kal* Torak, Aunt Pol," Garion explained again, "not just Torak."

Then she hit him—which she had never done before. The slap across his mouth surprised him more than it hurt, for she did not hit very hard. "You will *never* speak the name of Torak again. *Ever!*" she said. "This is important, Garion. Your safety depends on it. I want your promise."

"You don't have to get so angry about it," he said in an injured tone. "Promise."

"All right, I promise. It was only a game."

"A very foolish one," Aunt Pol said. "You might have killed Rundorig."

"What about *me?*" Garion protested.

"You were never in any danger," she told him. "Now go to sleep."

And as he dozed fitfully, his head light from his injury and the strange, bitter drink his aunt had given him, he seemed to hear her deep, rich voice saying, "Garion, my Garion, you're too young yet." And later, rising from deep sleep as a fish rises toward the silvery surface of the water, he seemed to hear her call, "Father, I need you." Then he plunged again into a troubled sleep, haunted by a dark figure of a man on a black horse who watched his every movement with a cold animosity and something that hovered very near the edge of fear; and behind that dark figure he had always known to be there but had never overtly acknowledged, even to Aunt Pol, the maimed and ugly face he had briefly seen or imagined in the fight with Rundorig loomed darkly, like the hideous fruit of an unspeakably evil tree.

CHAPTER TWO

Not long after in the endless noon of Garion's boyhood, the storyteller appeared once again at the gate of Faldor's farm. The storyteller, who seemed not to have a proper name as other men did, was a thoroughly disreputable old man. The knees of his hose were patched and his mismatched shoes were out at the toes. His long-sleeved woolen tunic was belted about the waist with a piece of rope, and his hood, a curious garment not normally worn in that part of Sendaria and one which Garion thought quite fine, with its loosely fitting yoke covering shoulders, back and chest, was spotted and soiled with spilled food and drink. Only his full cloak seemed relatively new. The old storyteller's white hair was cropped quite close, as was his beard. His face was strong, with a kind of angularity to it, and his features provided no clue to his background. He did not resemble Arend nor Cherek, Algar nor Drasnian, Rivan nor Tolnedran, but seemed rather to derive from some racial stock long since forgotten. His eyes were a deep and merry blue, forever young and forever full of mischief.

The storyteller appeared from time to time at Faldor's farm, and was always welcome. He was in truth a rootless vagabond who made his way in the world by telling stories. His stories were not always new, but there was in his telling of them a special kind of magic. His voice could roll like thunder or hush down into a zephyrlike whisper. He could imitate the voices of a dozen men at once; whistle so like a bird that the birds themselves would come to him to hear what he had to say; and when he imitated the howl of a wolf, the sound could raise the hair on the backs of his listeners' necks and strike a chill into their hearts like the depths of a Drasnian winter. He could make the sound of rain and of wind and even, most miraculously, the sound of snow falling. His stories were filled with sounds that made them come alive, and through the sounds and the words with which he wove the tales, sight and smell and the very *feel* of strange times and places seemed also to come to life for his spellbound listeners.

All of this wonder he gave freely in exchange for a few meals, a few tankards of ale, and a warm spot in the hay barn in which to sleep. He roamed about the world seemingly as free of possessions as the birds.

Between the storyteller and Aunt Pol there seemed to be a sort of hidden recognition. She had always viewed his coming with a kind of wry acceptance, knowing, it seemed, that the ultimate treasures of her kitchen were not safe so long as he lurked in the vicinity. Loaves and cakes had a way of disappearing when he was around, and his quick knife, always ready, could neatly divest the most carefully prepared goose of a pair of drumsticks and a generous slab of breast-meat with three swift slices when her back was turned. She called him "Old Wolf," and his appearance at the gate of Faldor's farm marked the resumption of a contest which had obviously been going on for years. He flattered her outrageously even as he stole from her. Offered cookies or dark brown bread, he would politely refuse and then steal half a plateful before the platter had moved out of his reach. Her beer pantry and wine cellar might as well have been delivered into his hands immediately upon his appearance at the gate. He seemed to delight in pilferage, and if she watched him with steely eye, he found quite easily a dozen confederates willing to sack her kitchen in exchange for a single story.

Lamentably, among his most able pupils was the boy Garion. Often, driven to distraction by the necessity of watching at once an old thief and a fledgling one, Aunt Pol would arm herself with a broom and drive them both from her kitchen with hard words and resounding blows. And the old storyteller, laughing, would flee with the boy to some secluded place where they would feast on the fruits of their pilferage and the old man, tasting frequently from a flagon of stolen wine or beer, would regale his student with stories out of the dim past.

The best stories, of course, were saved for the dining hall when, after the evening meal was over and the plates had been pushed back, the old man would rise from his place and carry his listeners off into a world of magical enchantment.

"Tell us of the beginnings, my old friend," Faldor, always pious, said one evening, "and of the Gods."

"Of the beginnings and the Gods," the old man mused. "A worthy subject, Faldor, but a dry and dusty one."

"I've noticed that you find all subjects dry and dusty, Old Wolf," Aunt Pol said, going to the barrel and drawing off a tankard of foamy beer for him.

He accepted the tankard with a stately bow. "It's one of the hazards of my profession, Mistress Pol," he explained. He drank deeply, then set the tankard aside. He lowered his head in thought for a moment, then looked directly, or so it seemed, at Garion. And then he did a strange thing which he had never before done when telling stories in Faldor's dining hall. He drew his cloak about him and rose to his full height.

"Behold," he said, his voice rich and sonorous, "at the beginning of days made the Gods the world and the seas and the dry land also. And cast they the stars across the night sky and did set the sun and his wife, the moon, in the heavens to give light unto the world.

"And the Gods caused the earth to bring forth the beasts, and the waters to bud with fish, and the skies to flower with birds.

"And they made men also, and divided men into Peoples.

"Now the Gods were seven in number and were all equal, and their names were Belar, and Chaldan, and Nedra, and Issa, and Mara, and Aldur, and Torak."

Garion knew the story, of course; everyone in that part of Sendaria was familiar with it, since the story was of Alorn origin and the lands on three sides of Sendaria were Alorn kingdoms. Though the tale was familiar, however, he had never before heard it told in such a way. His mind soared as in his imagination the Gods themselves strode the world in those dim, misty days when the world was first made, and a chill came over him at each mention of the forbidden name of Torak.

He listened intently as the storyteller described how each God selected a people—for Belar the Alorns, for Issa the Nyissans, for Chaldan the Arends, for Nedra the Tolnedrans, for Mara the Marags, which are no more, and for Torak the Angaraks. And he heard how the God Aldur dwelt apart and considered the stars in his solitude, and how some very few men he accepted as pupils and disciples.

Garion glanced at the others who were listening. Their faces were rapt with attention. Durnik's eyes were wide, and old Cralto's hands were clasped on the table in front of him. Faldor's face was pale, and tears stood in his eyes. Aunt Pol stood at the rear of the room. Though it was not cold, she too had drawn her mantle about her and stood very straight, her eyes intent.

"And it came to pass," the storyteller continued, "that the God Aldur caused to be made a jewel in the shape of a globe, and behold, in the jewel was captured the light of certain stars that did glitter in the northern sky. And great was the enchantment upon the jewel which men called the Orb of Aldur, for with the Orb could Aldur see that which had been, that which was, and that which was yet to be."

Garion realized he was holding his breath, for he was now completely caught up in the story. He listened in wonder as Torak stole the Orb and the other Gods made war on him. Torak used the Orb to sunder the earth and let in the sea to drown the land, until the Orb struck back against misuse by melting the left side of his face and destroying his left hand and eye.

The old man paused and drained his tankard. Aunt Pol, with her mantle still close about her, brought him another, her movements somehow stately and her eyes burning.

"I've never heard the story told so," Durnik said softly.

"It's *The Book of Alorn.** It's only told in the presence of kings," Cralto said, just as softly. "I knew a man once who had heard it at the king's court at Sendar, and he remembered some of it. I've never heard it all before, though."

The story continued, recounting how Belgarath the Sorcerer led Cherek and his three sons to regain the Orb two thousand years later, and how the western lands were settled and guarded against the hosts of Torak. The Gods removed from the world, leaving Riva to safeguard the Orb in his fortress on the Isle of the Winds. There he forged a great sword and set the Orb in its hilt. While the Orb remained there and the line of Riva sat on the throne, Torak could not prevail.

Then Belgarath sent his favorite daughter to Riva to be a mother to kings, while his other daughter remained with him and learned his art, for the mark of the sorcerers was upon her.

---

*Several shorter, less formal versions of the story existed, similar to the adaptation used here in the Prologue. Even *The Book of Alorn* was said to be an abridgment of a much older document.

The old storyteller's voice was now very soft as his ancient tale drew to its close. "And between them," he said, "did Belgarath and his daughter, the Sorceress Polgara, set enchantments to keep watch against the coming of Torak. And some men say they shall abide against his coming even though it be until the very end of days, for it is prophesied that one day shall maimed Torak come against the kingdoms of the west to reclaim the Orb which he so dearly purchased, and battle shall be joined between Torak and the fruit of the line of Riva, and in that battle shall be decided the fate of the world."

And then the old man fell silent and let his mantle drop from about his shoulders, signifying that his story was at an end.

There was a long silence in the hall, broken only by a few faint sputters from the dying fire and the endless song of frogs and crickets in the summer night outside.

Finally Faldor cleared his throat and rose, his bench scraping loudly on the wooden floor. "You have done us much honor tonight, my old friend," he said, his voice thick with emotion. "This is an event we will remember all our lives. You have told us a kingly story, not usually wasted on ordinary people."

The old man grinned then, his blue eyes twinkling. "I haven't consorted with many kings of late, Faldor." He laughed. "They all seem to be too busy to listen to the old tales, and a story must be told from time to time if it's not to be lost—besides, who knows these days where a king might be hiding?"

They all laughed at that and began to push back their benches, for it was growing late and time for those who must be up with the first light of the sun to seek their beds.

"Will you carry a lantern for me to the place where I sleep, boy?" the storyteller asked Garion.

"Gladly," Garion said, jumping up and running into the kitchen. He fetched down a square glass lantern, lighted the candle inside it from one of the banked kitchen fires, and went back into the dining hall.

Faldor was speaking with the storyteller. As he turned away, Garion saw a strange look pass between the old man and Aunt Pol, who still stood at the back of the hall.

"Are we ready then, boy?" the old man asked as Garion came up to him.

"Whenever you are," Garion replied, and the two of them turned and left the hall.

"Why's the story unfinished?" Garion asked, bursting with curiosity. "Why did you stop before we found out what happened when Torak met the Rivan King?"

"That's another story," the old man explained.

"Will you tell it to me sometime?" Garion pressed.

The old man laughed. "Torak and the Rivan King haven't as yet met," he said, "so I can't very well tell it, can I?—at least not until after their meeting."

"It's *only* a story," Garion objected. "Isn't it?"

"Is it?" The old man removed a flagon of wine from under his tunic and took a long drink. "Who's to say what's only a story and what's truth disguised as a story?"

"It's only a story," Garion said stubbornly, suddenly feeling very hardheaded and practical like any good Sendar. "It can't really be true. Why, Belgarath the Sorcerer would be—would be I don't know how old—and people don't live that long."

"Seven thousand years," the old man said.

"What?"

"Belgarath the Sorcerer is seven thousand years old—perhaps a bit older."

"That's impossible," Garion said.

"Is it? How old are you?"

"Nine—next Erastide."

"And in nine years you've learned everything that's both possible and impossible? You're a remarkable boy, Garion."

Garion flushed. "Well," he said, somehow not quite so sure of himself, "the oldest man I ever heard of is old Weldrik over on Mildrin's farm. Durnik says he's over ninety and that he's the oldest man in the district."

"And it's a very big district, of course," the old man said solemnly.

"How old are you?" Garion asked, not wanting to give up.

"Old enough, boy," the old man said.

"It's still only a story," Garion insisted.

"Many good and solid men would say so," the old man told him, looking up at the stars, "—good men who'll live out their lives believing only in what they can see and touch. But there's a world beyond what we can see and touch, and that world lives by its own laws. What may be impossible in this very ordinary world is very possible there, and sometimes the boundaries between the two worlds disappear, and then who can say what's possible and impossible?"

"I think I'd rather live in the ordinary world," Garion said. "The other one sounds too complicated."

"We don't always have that choice, Garion," the storyteller told him. "Don't be too surprised if that other world someday chooses you to do something that must be done—some great and noble thing."

"Me?" Garion said incredulously.

"Stranger things have happened. Go to bed, boy. I think I'll look at the stars for a while. The stars and I are very old friends."

"The stars?" Garion asked, looking up involuntarily. "You're a very strange old man—if you don't mind my saying so."

"Indeed," the storyteller agreed. "Quite the strangest you'll likely meet."

"I like you all the same," Garion said quickly, not wanting to give offense.

"That's a comfort, boy," the old man said. "Now go to bed. Your Aunt Pol will be worried about you."

Later, as he slept, Garion's dreams were troubled. The dark figure of maimed Torak loomed in the shadows, and monstrous things pursued him across twisted landscapes where the possible and the impossible merged and joined as that other world reached out to claim him.

CHAPTER THREE

Some few mornings later, when Aunt Pol had begun to scowl at his continued lurking in her kitchen, the old man made excuse of some errand to the nearby village of Upper Gralt.

"Good," Aunt Pol said, somewhat ungraciously. "At least my pantries will be safe while you're gone."

He bowed mockingly, his eyes twinkling. "Do you need anything, Mistress Pol?" he asked. "Some trifling thing I might purchase for you—as long as I'm going anyway?"

Aunt Pol thought a moment. "Some of my spice pots are a bit low," she said, "and there's a Tolnedran spice merchant in Fennel Lane just south of the Town Tavern. I'm sure you'll have no trouble finding the tavern."

"The trip's likely to be dry," the old man admitted pleasantly. "And lonely, too. Ten leagues with no one to talk to is a long way."

"Talk to the birds," Aunt Pol suggested bluntly.

"Birds listen well enough," the old man said, "but their speech is repetitious and quickly grows tiresome. Why don't I take the boy along for company?"

Garion held his breath.

"He's picking up enough bad habits on his own," Aunt Pol said tartly. "I'd prefer his not having expert instruction."

"Why, Mistress Pol," the old man objected, stealing a cruller almost absently, "you do me an injustice. Besides, a change'll do the boy good—broaden his horizons, you might say."

"His horizons are quite broad enough, thank you," she said.

Garion's heart sank.

"Still," she continued, "at least I can count on him not to forget my spices altogether or to become so fuddled with ale that he confuses peppercorns with cloves or cinnamon with nutmeg. Very well, take the boy along; but mind, I don't want you taking him into any low or disreputable places."

"Mistress Pol!" the old man said, feigning shock. "Would I frequent such places?"

"I know you too well, Old Wolf," she said dryly. "You take to vice and corruption as naturally as a duck takes to a pond. If I hear that you've taken the boy into any unsavory place, you and I will have words."

"Then I'll have to make sure that you don't hear of anything like that, won't I?"

Aunt Pol gave him a hard look. "I'll see which spices I need," she said.

"And I'll borrow a horse and cart from Faldor," the old man said, stealing another cruller.

In a surprisingly short time, Garion and the old man were bouncing along the rutted road to Upper Gralt behind a fast-trotting horse. It was a bright summer morning, and there were a few dandelion-puff clouds in the sky and deep blue shadows under the hedgerows. After a few hours, however, the sun became hot, and the jolting ride became tiresome. "Are we almost there?" Garion asked for the third time.

"Not for some time yet," the old man said. "Ten leagues is a goodly distance."

"I was there once before," Garion told him, trying to sound casual. "Of course I was only a child at the time, so I don't remember too much about it. It seemed to be quite a fine place."

The old man shrugged. "It's a village," he said, "much like any other." He seemed a bit preoccupied.

Garion, hoping to nudge the old man into a story to make the miles go faster, began asking questions.

"Why is it that you don't have a name—if I'm not being impolite in asking?"

"I have many names," the old man said, scratching his white beard. "Almost as many names as I have years."

"I've only got one," Garion said.

"So far."

"What?"

"You only have one name so far," the old man explained. "In time you may get another—or even several. Some people collect names as they go along through their lives. Sometimes names wear out—just like clothes."

"Aunt Pol calls you Old Wolf," Garion said.

"I know," the old man said. "Your Aunt Pol and I have known each other for a very long time."

"Why does she call you that?"

"Who can say why a woman such as your Aunt does anything?"

"May I call you Mister Wolf?" Garion asked. Names were quite important to Garion, and the fact that the old storyteller did not seem to have one had always bothered him. That namelessness had made the old man seem somehow incomplete, unfinished.

The old man looked at him soberly for a moment, and then he burst out laughing. "Mister Wolf indeed. How very appropriate. I think I like that name better than any I've had in years."

"May I then?" Garion asked. "Call you Mister Wolf, I mean?"

"I think I'd like that, Garion. I think I'd like that very much."

"Now would you *please* tell me a story, Mister Wolf?" Garion asked.

The time and distance went by much faster then as Mister Wolf wove for Garion tales of glorious adventure and dark treachery taken from those gloomy, unending centuries of the Arendish civil wars.

"Why are the Arends like that?" Garion asked after a particularly grim tale.

"The Arends are very noble," Wolf said, lounging back in the seat of the cart with the reins held negligently in one hand. "Nobility's a trait that's not always trustworthy, since it sometimes causes men to do things for obscure reasons."

"Rundorig's an Arend," Garion said. "He sometimes seems to be—well, not too quick of thought, if you know what I mean."

"It's the effect of all that nobility," Wolf said. "Arends spend so much time concentrating on being noble that they don't have time to think of other things."

They came over the crest of a long hill, and there in the next valley lay the village of Upper Gralt. To Garion the tiny cluster of gray stone houses with slate roofs seemed disappointingly small. Two roads, white with thick dust, intersected there, and there were a few narrow, winding streets besides. The houses were square and solid, but seemed almost like toys set down in the valley below. The horizon beyond was ragged with the mountains of eastern Sendaria, and, though it was summer, the tops of most of the mountains were still wrapped in snow.

Their tired horse plodded down the hill toward the village, his hooves stirring little clouds of dust with each step, and soon they were clattering along the cobblestoned streets toward the center of the village. The villagers, of course, were all too important to pay any attention to an old man and a small boy in a farm cart. The women wore gowns and high-pointed hats, and the men wore doublets and soft velvet caps. Their expressions seemed haughty, and they looked with obvious disdain at the few farmers in town who respectfully stood aside to let them pass.

"They're very fine, aren't they?" Garion observed.

"They seem to think so," Wolf said, his expression faintly amused. "I think it's time that we found something to eat, don't you?"

Though he had not realized it until the old man mentioned it, Garion was suddenly ravenous. "Where can we go?" he asked. "They all seem so splendid. Would any of them let strangers sit at their tables?"

Wolf laughed and shook a jingling purse at his waist. "We shouldn't have any trouble making acquaintances," he said. "There are places where one can buy food."

Buy food? Garion had never heard of such a thing before. Anyone who appeared at Faldor's gate at mealtime was invited to the table as a matter of course. The world of the villagers was obviously very different from the world of Faldor's farm. "But I don't have any money," he objected.

"I've got enough for us both," Wolf assured him, stopping their horse before a large, low building with a sign bearing a picture of a cluster of grapes hanging just above its door. There were words on the sign, but of course Garion could not read them.

"What do the words say, Mister Wolf?" he asked.

"They say that food and drink can be bought inside," Wolf told him, getting down from the cart.

"It must be a fine thing to be able to read," Garion said wistfully.

The old man looked at him, seemingly surprised. "You can't read, boy?" he asked incredulously.

"I've never found anyone to teach me," Garion said. "Faldor reads, I think, but no one else at the farm knows how."

"Nonsense," Wolf snorted. "I'll speak to your Aunt about it. She's been neglecting her responsibility. She should have taught you years ago."

"Can Aunt Pol read?" Garion asked, stunned.

"Of course she can," Wolf said, leading the way into the tavern. "She says she finds little advantage in it, but she and I had that particular argument out many years ago." The old man seemed quite upset by Garion's lack of education.

Garion, however, was far too interested in the smoky interior of the tavern to pay much attention. The room was large and dark with a low, beamed ceiling and a stone floor strewn with rushes. Though it was not cold, a fire burned in a stone pit in the center of the room, and the smoke rose errantly toward a chimney set above it on four square stone pillars. Tallow candles guttered in clay dishes on several of the long, stained tables, and there was a reek of wine and stale beer in the air.

"What have you to eat?" Wolf demanded of a sour, unshaven man wearing a grease-spotted apron.

"We've a bit of a joint left," the man said, pointing at a spit resting to one side of the fire pit. "Roasted only day before yesterday. And meat porridge fresh yesterday morning, and bread no more than a week old."

"Very well," Wolf said, sitting down. "And I'll have a pot of your best ale and milk for the boy."

"Milk?" Garion protested.

"Milk," Wolf said firmly.

"You have money?" the sour-looking man demanded.

Wolf jingled his purse, and the sour man looked suddenly less sour.

"Why's that man over there sleeping?" Garion asked, pointing at a snoring villager sitting with his head down on one of the tables.

"Drunk," Wolf said, scarcely glancing at the snoring man.

"Shouldn't someone take care of him?"

"He'd rather not be taken care of."

"Do you know him?"

"I know of him," Wolf said, "and many others like him. I've occasionally been in that condition myself."

"Why?"

"It seemed appropriate at the time."

The roast was dry and overdone, the meat porridge was thin and watery, and the bread was stale, but Garion was too hungry to notice. He carefully cleaned his plate as he had been taught, then sat as Mister Wolf lingered over a second pot of ale.

"Quite splendid," he said, more to be saying something than out of any real conviction. All in all he found that Upper Gralt did not live up to his expectations.

"Adequate." Wolf shrugged. "Village taverns are much the same the world over. I've seldom seen one I'd hurry to revisit. Shall we go?" He laid down a few coins, which the sour-looking man snatched up quickly, and led Garion back out into the afternoon sunlight.

"Let's find your Aunt's spice merchant," he said, "and then see to a night's lodging—and a stable for our horse." They set off down the street, leaving horse and cart beside the tavern.

The house of the Tolnedran spice merchant was a tall, narrow building in the next street. Two swarthy, thick-bodied men in short tunics lounged in the street at his front door near a fierce-looking black horse wearing a curious armored saddle. The two men stared with dull-eyed disinterest at passers-by in the lane.

Mister Wolf stopped when he caught sight of them.

"Is something wrong?" Garion asked.

"Thulls," Wolf said quietly, looking hard at the two men.

"What?"

"Those two are Thulls," the old man said. "They usually work as porters for the Murgos."

"What are Murgos?"

"The people of Cthol Murgos," Wolf said shortly. "Southern Angaraks."

"The ones we beat at the battle of Vo Mimbre?" Garion asked. "Why would they be here?"

"The Murgos have taken up commerce," Wolf said, frowning. "I hadn't expected to see one of them in so remote a village. We may as well go in. The Thulls have seen us, and it might look strange if we turned now and went back. Stay close to me, boy, and don't say anything."

They walked past the two heavyset men and entered the spice merchant's shop.

The Tolnedran was a thin, baldheaded man wearing a brown, belted gown that reached to the floor. He was nervously weighing several packets of pungent-smelling powder which lay on the counter before him.

"Good day to you," he said to Wolf. "Please have patience. I'll be with you shortly." He spoke with a slight lisp that Garion found peculiar.

"No hurry," Wolf said in a wheezy, cracking voice. Garion looked at him sharply and was astonished to see that his friend was stooped and that his head was nodding foolishly.

"See to their needs," the other man in the shop said shortly. He was a dark, burly man wearing a chain-mail shirt and a short sword belted to his waist. His cheekbones were high, and there were several savage-looking scars on his face. His eyes looked curiously angular, and his voice was harsh and thickly accented.

"No hurry," Wolf said in his wheezy cackle.

"My business here will take some time," the Murgo said coldly, "and I prefer not to be rushed. Tell the merchant here what you need, old man."

"My thanks, then," Wolf cackled. "I have a list somewhere about me." He began to fumble foolishly in his pockets. "My master drew it up. I do hope you can read it, friend merchant, for I cannot." He finally found the list and presented it to the Tolnedran.

The merchant glanced at the list. "This'll only take a moment," he told the Murgo.

The Murgo nodded and stood staring stonily at Wolf and Garion. His eyes narrowed slightly, and his expression changed. "You're a seemly appearing boy," he said to Garion. "What's your name?"

Until that moment, in his entire life, Garion had been an honest and truthful boy, but Wolf's manner had opened before his eyes an entire world of deception and subterfuge. Somewhere in the back of his mind he seemed to hear a warning voice, a dry, calm voice advising him that the situation was dangerous and that he should take steps to protect himself. He hesitated only an instant before telling his first deliberate lie. He allowed his mouth to drop open and his face to assume an expression of vacant-headed stupidity. "Rundorig, your Honor," he mumbled.

"An Arendish name," the Murgo said, his eyes narrowing even more. "You don't look like an Arend."

Garion gaped at him.

"Are you an Arend, Rundorig?" the Murgo pressed.

Garion frowned as if struggling with a thought while his mind raced. The dry voice suggested several alternatives.

"My father was," he said finally, "but my mother's a Sendar, and people say I favor her."

"You say *was*," the Murgo said quickly. "Is your father dead, then?" His scarred face was intent.

Garion nodded foolishly. "A tree he was cutting fell on him," he lied. "It was a long time ago."

The Murgo suddenly seemed to lose interest. "Here's a copper penny for you, boy," he said, indifferently tossing a small coin on the floor at Garion's feet. "It has the likeness of the God Torak stamped on it. Perhaps it will bring you luck—or at least more wit."

Wolf stooped quickly and retrieved the coin, but the coin he handed to Garion was a common Sendarian penny.

"Thank the good man, Rundorig," he wheezed.

"My thanks, your Honor," Garion said, concealing the penny tightly in his fist.

The Murgo shrugged and looked away.

Wolf paid the Tolnedran merchant for the spices, and he and Garion left the shop.

"You played a dangerous game, boy," Wolf said once they were out of ear-shot of the two lounging Thulls.

"You seemed not to want him to know who we were," Garion explained. "I wasn't sure why, but I thought I ought to do the same. Was what I did wrong?"

"You're very quick," Wolf said approvingly. "I think we managed to deceive the Murgo."

"Why did you change the coin?" Garion asked.

"Sometimes Angarak coins aren't what they seem," Wolf said. "It's better for you not to have any of them. Let's fetch our horse and cart. It's a long way back to Faldor's farm."

"I thought we were going to take lodgings for the night."

"That's changed now. Come along, boy. It's time for us to leave."

The horse was very tired, and he moved slowly up the long hill out of Upper Gralt as the sun went down ahead of them.

"Why wouldn't you let me keep the Angarak penny, Mister Wolf?" Garion persisted. The subject still puzzled him.

"There are many things in this world that seem to be one thing but are in fact another," Wolf said somewhat grimly. "I don't trust Angaraks, and I particularly don't trust Murgos. It'd be just as well, I think, if you never had anything in your possession that bears the likeness of Torak."

"But the war between the west and the Angaraks has been over for five hundred years now," Garion objected. "All men say so."

"Not *all* men," Wolf said. "Now take that robe out of the back of the cart and cover up. Your Aunt would never forgive me if I let you take a chill."

"I will if you think I should," Garion said, "but I'm not a bit cold and not at all sleepy. I'll keep you company as we go."

"That'll be a comfort, boy," Wolf said.

"Mister Wolf," Garion said after some time, "did you know my mother and father?"

"Yes," Wolf said quietly.

"My father's dead too, isn't he?"

"I'm afraid so."

Garion sighed deeply. "I thought so," he said. "I wish I'd known them. Aunt Pol says I was only a baby when—" He couldn't bring himself to say it. "I've tried to remember my mother, but I can't."

"You were very small," Wolf said.

"What were they like?" Garion asked.

Wolf scratched at his beard. "Ordinary," he said. "So ordinary you wouldn't look twice at either one of them."

Garion was offended by that. "Aunt Pol says my mother was very beautiful," he objected.

"She was."

"Then how can you say she was ordinary?"

"She wasn't prominent or important," Wolf said. "Neither was your father. Anyone who saw them thought that they were just simple village people—a young man with a young wife and their baby—that's all anyone ever saw. That's all anyone was ever supposed to see."

"I don't understand."

"It's very complicated."

"What was my father like?"

"Medium size," Wolf said. "Dark hair. A very serious young man. I liked him."

"Did he love my mother?"

"More than anything."

"And me?"

"Of course."

"What kind of place did they live in?"

"It was a small place," Wolf said, "a little village near the mountains, a long way from any main roads. They had a cottage at the end of the street. It was a small, solid little house. Your father built it himself—he was a stone-cutter. I used to stop by there once in a while when I was in the neighborhood." The old man's voice droned on, describing the village and the house and the two who lived there. Garion listened, not even realizing it when he fell asleep.

It must have been very late, almost on toward dawn. In a half drowse, the boy felt himself lifted from the cart and carried up a flight of stairs. The old man was surprisingly strong. Aunt Pol was there—he knew that without even opening his eyes. There was a particular scent about her that he could have found in a dark room.

"Just cover him up," Mister Wolf said softly to Aunt Pol. "Best not to wake him just now."

"What happened?" Aunt Pol asked, her voice as soft as the old man's.

"There was a Murgo in town—at your spice merchant's. He asked questions and he tried to give the boy an Angarak penny."

"In Upper Gralt? Are you certain he was only a Murgo?"

"It's impossible to tell. Not even I can distinguish between Murgo and Grolim with any certainty."

"What happened to the coin?"

"I was quick enough to get it. I gave the boy a Sendarian penny instead. If our Murgo was a Grolim, we'll let him follow me. I'm sure I can give him several months of entertainment."

"You'll be leaving, then?" Aunt Pol's voice seemed somehow sad.

"It's time," Wolf said. "Right now the boy's safe enough here, and I must be abroad. There are things afoot I must see to. When Murgos begin to appear in remote places, I begin to worry. We have a great responsibility and a great care placed upon us, and we mustn't allow ourselves to become careless."

"Will you be gone long?" Aunt Pol asked.

"Some years, I expect. There are many things I must look into and many people I'll have to see."

"I'll miss you," Aunt Pol said softly.

He laughed. "Sentimentality, Pol?" he said dryly. "That's hardly in character."

"You know what I mean. I'm not suited for this task you and the others have given me. What do I know about the raising of small boys?"

"You're doing well," Wolf said. "Keep the boy close, and don't let his nature drive you into hysterics. Be careful; he lies like a champion."

"Garion?" Her voice was shocked.

"He lied to the Murgo so well that even I was impressed."

"Garion?"

"He's also started asking questions about his parents," Wolf said. "How much have you told him?"

"Very little. Only that they're dead."

"Let's leave it at that for now. There's no point in telling him things he isn't old enough to cope with yet."

Their voices went on, but Garion drifted off into sleep again, and he was almost sure that it was all a dream.

But the next morning when he awoke, Mister Wolf was gone.

CHAPTER FOUR

The seasons turned, as seasons will. Summer ripened into autumn; the blaze of autumn died into winter; winter grudgingly relented to the urgency of spring; and spring bloomed into summer again. With the turning of the seasons the years turned, and Garion imperceptibly grew older.

As he grew, the other children grew as well—all except poor Doroon, who seemed doomed to be short and skinny all his life. Rundorig sprouted like a young tree and was soon almost as big as any man on the farm. Zubrette, of course, did not grow so tall, but she developed in other ways which the boys began to find interesting.

In the early autumn just before Garion's fourteenth birthday, he came very close to ending his career. In response to some primal urge all children have—given a pond and a handy supply of logs—they had built a raft that summer. The raft was neither very large nor was it particularly well-built. It had a tendency to sink on one end if the weight aboard it was improperly distributed and had an alarming habit of coming apart at unexpected moments.

Quite naturally it was Garion who was aboard the raft—showing off—on that fine autumn day when the raft quite suddenly decided once and for all to revert to its original state. The bindings all came undone, and the logs began to go their separate ways.

Realizing his danger only at the last moment, Garion made a desperate effort to pole for shore, but his haste only made the disintegration of his craft more rapid. In the end he found himself standing on a single log, his arms windmilling wildly in a futile effort to retain his balance. His eyes, desperately searching for some aid, swept the marshy shore. Some distance up the slope behind his playmates he saw the familiar figure of the man on the black horse. The man wore a dark robe, and his burning eyes watched the boy's plight. Then the spiteful log rolled under Garion's feet, and he toppled and fell with a resounding splash.

Garion's education, unfortunately, had not included instruction in the art of swimming; and while the water was not really very deep, it was deep enough.

The bottom of the pond was very unpleasant, a kind of dark, weedy ooze inhabited by frogs, turtles and a singularly unsavory-looking eel that slithered away snakelike when Garion plunged like a sinking rock into the weeds. Garion struggled, gulped water and launched himself with his legs toward the surface again. Like a broaching whale, he rose from the depths, gasped a couple of quick, sputtering breaths and heard the screams of his playmates. The dark figure on the slope had not moved, and for a single instant every detail of that bright afternoon was etched on Garion's mind. He even observed that, although the rider was in the open under the full glare of the autumn sun, neither man nor horse cast any shadow. Even as his mind grappled with that impossibility, he sank once more to the murky bottom.

It occurred to him as he struggled, drowning, amongst the weeds that if he could launch himself up in the vicinity of the log, he might catch hold of it and so remain afloat. He waved off a startled-looking frog and plunged upward again. He came up, unfortunately, directly under the log. The blow on the top of his head filled his eyes with light and his ears with a roaring sound, and he sank, no longer struggling, back toward the weeds which seemed to reach up for him.

And then Durnik was there. Garion felt himself lifted roughly by the hair toward the surface and then towed by that same convenient handle toward shore behind Durnik's powerfully churning strokes. The smith pulled the semiconscious boy out onto the bank, turned him over and stepped on him several times to force the water out of his lungs.

Garion's ribs creaked. "Enough, Durnik," he gasped finally. He sat up, and the blood from the splendid cut on top of his head immediately ran into his eyes. He wiped the blood clear and looked around for the dark, shadowless rider, but the figure had vanished. He tried to get up, but the world suddenly spun around him, and he fainted.

When he awoke, he was in his own bed with his head wrapped in bandages.

Aunt Pol stood beside his bed, her eyes blazing. "You stupid boy!" she cried. "What were you doing in that pond?"

"Rafting," Garion said, trying to make it sound quite ordinary.

"Rafting?" she said. "*Rafting?* Who gave you permission?"

"Well—" he said uncertainly. "We just—"

"You just what?"

He looked at her helplessly.

And then with a low cry she took him in her arms and crushed him to her almost suffocatingly.

Briefly Garion considered telling her about the strange, shadowless figure that had watched his struggles in the pond, but the dry voice in his mind that sometimes spoke to him told him that this was not the time for that. He seemed to know somehow that the business between him and the man on the black horse was something very private, and that the time would inevitably come when they would face each other in some kind of contest of will or deed. To speak of it now to Aunt Pol would involve her in the matter, and he did not want that. He was not sure exactly why, but he did know that the dark figure was an enemy, and though that thought was a bit frightening, it was also exciting. There was no question that Aunt Pol could deal with this stranger, but if she did, Garion knew that he would lose something very personal and for some reason very important. And so he said nothing.

"It really wasn't anything all that dangerous, Aunt Pol," he said instead, rather lamely. "I was starting to get the idea of how to swim. I'd have been all right if I hadn't hit my head on that log."

"But of course you *did* hit your head," she pointed out.

"Well, yes, but it wasn't that serious. I'd have been all right in a minute or two."

"Under the circumstances I'm not sure you *had* a minute or two," she said bluntly.

"Well—" he faltered, and then decided to let it drop.

That marked the end of Garion's freedom. Aunt Pol confined him to the scullery. He grew to know every dent and scratch on every pot in the kitchen intimately. He once estimated gloomily that he washed each one twenty-one times a week. In a seeming orgy of messiness, Aunt Pol suddenly could not even boil water without dirtying at least three or four pans, and Garion had to scrub every one. He hated it and began to think quite seriously of running away.

As autumn progressed and the weather began to deteriorate, the other children were also more or less confined to the compound as well, and it wasn't so bad. Rundorig, of course, was seldom with them anymore since his man's size had made him—even more than Garion—subject to more and more frequent labor.

When he could, Garion slipped away to be with Zubrette and Doroon, but they no longer found much entertainment in leaping into the hay or in the endless games of tag in the stables and barns. They had reached an age and size where adults rather quickly noticed such idleness and found tasks to occupy them. Most often they would sit in some out-of-the-way place and simply talk—which is to say that Garion and Zubrette would sit and listen to the endless flow of Doroon's chatter. That small, quick boy, as unable to be quiet as he was to sit still, could seemingly talk for hours about a half-dozen raindrops, and his words tumbled out breathlessly as he fidgeted.

"What's that mark on your hand, Garion?" Zubrette asked one rainy day, interrupting Doroon's bubbling voice.

Garion looked at the perfectly round, white patch on the palm of his right hand.

"I've noticed it too," Doroon said, quickly changing subjects in midsentence. "But Garion grew up in the kitchen, didn't you, Garion? It's probably a place where he burned himself when he was little—you know, reached out before anyone could stop him and put his hand on something hot. I'll bet his Aunt Pol really got angry about that, because she can get angrier faster than anybody else I've ever seen, and she can really—"

"It's always been there," Garion said, tracing the mark on his palm with his left forefinger. He had never really looked closely at it before. It covered the entire palm of his hand and had in certain light a faint silvery sheen.

"Maybe it's a birthmark," Zubrette suggested.

"I'll bet that's it," Doroon said quickly. "I saw a man once that had a big purple one on the side of his face—one of those wagoneers that comes by to pick up the turnip crop in the fall—anyway, the mark was all over the side of his face, and I thought it was a big bruise at first and thought that he must have been in an awful fight—those wagoneers fight all the time—but then I saw that it wasn't really a bruise but—like Zubrette just said—it was a birthmark. I wonder what causes things like that."

That evening, after he'd gotten ready for bed, he asked his Aunt about it. "What's this mark, Aunt Pol?" he asked, holding his hand up, palm out.

She looked up from where she was brushing her long, dark hair. "It's nothing to worry about," she told him.

"I wasn't worried about it," he said. "I just wondered what it was. Zubrette and Doroon think it's a birthmark. Is that what it is?"

"Something like that," she said.

"Did either of my parents have the same kind of mark?"

"Your father did. It's been in the family for a long time."

A sudden strange thought occurred to Garion. Without knowing why, he reached out with the hand and touched the white lock at his Aunt's brow. "Is it like that white place in your hair?" he asked.

He felt a sudden tingle in his hand, and it seemed somehow that a window opened in his mind. At first there was only the sense of uncountable years moving by like a vast sea of ponderously rolling clouds, and then, sharper than any knife, a feeling of endlessly repeated loss, of sorrow. Then, more recent, there was his own face, and behind it more faces, old, young, regal or quite ordinary, and behind them all, no longer foolish as it sometimes seemed, the face of Mister Wolf. But more than anything there was a knowledge of an unearthly, inhuman power, the certainty of an unconquerable will.

Aunt Pol moved her head away almost absently. "Don't do that, Garion," she said, and the window in his mind shut.

"What was it?" he asked, burning with curiosity and wanting to open the window again.

"A simple trick," she said.

"Show me how."

"Not yet, my Garion," she said, taking his face between her hands. "Not yet. You're not ready yet. Now go to bed."

"You'll be here?" he asked, a little frightened now.

"I'll always be here," she said, tucking him in. And then she went back to brushing her long, thick hair, humming a strange song as she did in a deep, melodious voice, and to that sound he fell asleep.

After that not even Garion himself saw the mark on his own palm very often. There suddenly seemed to be all kinds of dirty jobs for him to do which kept not only his hands, but the rest of him as well, very dirty.

The most important holiday in Sendaria—and indeed in the rest of the kingdoms of the west—was Erastide. It commemorated that day, eons before, when the seven Gods joined hands to create the world with a single word. The festival of Erastide took place in midwinter, and, because there was little to do on a farm like Faldor's at that season, it had by custom become a splendid two-week celebration with feasts and gifts and decorations in the dining hall and little pageants honoring the Gods. These last, of course, were a reflection of Faldor's piety. Faldor, though he was a good, simple man, had no illusions about how widely his sentiments were shared by others on the farm. He thought, however, that some outward show of devotional activity was in keeping with the season; and, because he was such a good master, the people on his farm chose to humor him.

It was also at this season, unfortunately, that Faldor's married daughter, Anhelda, and her husband, Eilbrig, made their customary annual visit to remain on speaking terms with her father. Anhelda had no intention of endangering her inheritance rights by seeming inattention. Her visits, however, were a trial to Faldor, who looked upon his daughter's somewhat overdressed and supercilious husband, a minor functionary in a commercial house in the capital city of Sendar, with scarcely concealed contempt.

Their arrival, however, marked the beginning of the Erastide festival at Faldor's farm; so, while no one cared for them personally, their appearance was always greeted with a certain enthusiasm.

The weather that year had been particularly foul—even for Sendaria. The rains had settled in early and were soon followed by a period of soggy snow—not the crisp, bright powder which came later in the winter, but a damp slush, always half-melting. For Garion, whose duties in the kitchen now prevented him from joining with his former playmates in their traditional preholiday orgy of anticipatory excitement, the approaching holiday seemed somehow flat and stale. He yearned back to the good old days and often sighed with regret and moped about the kitchen like a sandy-haired cloud of doom.

Even the traditional decorations in the dining hall, where Erastide festivities always took place, seemed decidedly tacky to him that year. The fir boughs festooning the ceiling beams were somehow not as green, and the polished apples carefully tied to the boughs were smaller and not as red. He sighed some more and reveled in his sullen moping.

Aunt Pol, however, was not impressed, and her attitude was firmly un-sympathetic. She routinely checked his brow with her hands for signs of fever and then dosed him with the foulest-tasting tonic she could concoct. Garion was careful after that to mope in private and to sigh less audibly. That dry, secret part of his mind informed him matter-of-factly that he was being ridic-ulous, but Garion chose not to listen. The voice in his mind was much older and wiser than he, but it seemed determined to take all the fun out of life.

On the morning of Erastide, a Murgo and five Thulls appeared with a wagon outside the gate and asked to see Faldor. Garion, who had long since learned that no one pays attention to a boy and that many interesting things may be learned by placing himself in a position to casually overhear conver-sations, busied himself with some small, unimportant chore near the gate.

The Murgo, his face scarred much like the face of the one in Upper Gralt, sat importantly on the wagon seat, his chain-mail shirt clinking each time he moved. He wore a black, hooded robe, and his sword was much in evidence. His eyes moved constantly, taking in everything. The Thulls, in muddy felt boots and heavy cloaks, lounged disinterestedly against the wagon, seemingly indifferent to the raw wind whipping across the snowy fields.

Faldor, in his finest doublet—it was after all Erastide—came across the yard, closely followed by Anhelda and Eilbrig.

"Good morrow, friend," Faldor said to the Murgo. "Joyous Erastide to you."

The Murgo grunted. "I take it you're the farmer Faldor?" he asked in his heavily accented voice.

"I am," Faldor replied.

"I understand you have a goodly number of hams on hand—well cured."

"The pigs did well this year," Faldor answered modestly.

"I'll buy them," the Murgo announced, jingling his purse.

Faldor bowed. "First thing tomorrow morning," he said.

The Murgo stared.

"This is a pious household," Faldor explained. "We don't offend the Gods by breaking the sanctity of Erastide."

"Father," Anhelda snapped, "don't be foolish. This noble merchant has come a long way to do business."

"Not on Erastide," Faldor said stubbornly, his long face firm.

"In the city of Sendar," Eilbrig said in his rather high-pitched, nasal voice, "we do not let such sentimentality interfere with business."

"This is not the city of Sendar," Faldor said flatly. "This is Faldor's farm, and on Faldor's farm we do no work and conduct no business on Erastide."

"Father," Anhelda protested, "the noble merchant has gold. Gold, father, gold!"

"I won't hear any more of it," Faldor announced. He turned to the Murgo. "You and your servants are welcome to join us in our celebration, friend," he said. "We can provide quarters for you and the promise of the fin-est dinner in all of Sendaria and the opportunity to honor the Gods on this special day. No man is made poorer by attending to his religious obligations."

"We do not observe this holiday in Cthol Murgos," the scar-faced man said coldly. "As the noble lady says, I've come a long way to do business and have not much time to tarry. I'm sure there are other farmers in the district with the merchandise I require."

"*Father!*" Anhelda wailed.

"I know my neighbors," Faldor said quietly. "Your luck today will be small, I fear. The observance of this day is a firm tradition in this area."

The Murgo thought for a moment. "It may be as you say," he said finally. "I'll accept your invitation, provided that we can do business as early as possible tomorrow."

Faldor bowed. "I'll place myself at your service at first light tomorrow if you so desire."

"Done, then," the Murgo said, climbing down from his wagon.

That afternoon the feast was laid in the dining hall. The kitchen helpers and a half-dozen others who had been pressed into service for the special day scurried from kitchen to hall bearing smoking roasts, steaming hams and sizzling geese all under the lash of Aunt Pol's tongue. Garion observed sourly as he struggled with an enormous baron of beef that Faldor's prohibition of work on Erastide stopped at the kitchen door.

In time, all was ready. The tables were loaded, the fires in the fireplaces burned brightly, dozens of candles filled the hall with golden light, and torches flared in their rings on the stone pillars. Faldor's people, all in their best clothes, filed into the hall, their mouths watering in anticipation.

When all were seated, Faldor rose from his bench at the head of the center table. "Dear friends," he said, lifting his tankard, "I dedicate this feast to the Gods."

"The Gods," the people responded in unison, rising respectfully.

Faldor drank briefly, and they all followed suit. "Hear me, O Gods," he prayed. "Most humbly we thank you for the bounty of this fair world which you made on this day, and we dedicate ourselves to your service for yet another year." He looked for a moment as if he were going to say more, but then sat down instead. Faldor always labored for many hours over special prayers for occasions such as this, but the agony of speaking in public invariably erased the words so carefully prepared from his mind. His prayers, therefore, were always very sincere and very short.

"Eat, dear friends," he instructed. "Don't let the food grow cold."

And so they ate. Anhelda and Eilbrig, who joined them all at this one meal only at Faldor's insistence, devoted their conversational efforts to the Murgo, since he was the only one in the room who was worthy of their attention.

"I have long thought of visiting Cthol Murgos," Eilbrig stated rather pompously. "Don't you agree, friend merchant, that greater contact between east and west is the way to overcome those mutual suspicions which have so marred our relationships in the past?"

"We Murgos prefer to keep to ourselves," the scar-faced man said shortly.

"But you are here, friend," Eilbrig pointed out. "Doesn't that suggest that greater contact might prove beneficial?"

"I'm here as a duty," the Murgo said. "I don't visit here out of preference." He looked around the room. "Are these then all of your people?" he asked Faldor.

"Every soul is here," Faldor told him.

"I was led to believe there was an old man here—with white hair and beard."

"Not here, friend," Faldor said. "I myself am the eldest here, and as you can see, my hair is far from white."

"One of my countrymen met such a one some years ago," the Murgo said. "He was accompanied by an Arendish boy—Rundorig, I believe his name was."

Garion, seated at the next table, kept his face to his plate and listened so hard that he thought his ears must be growing.

"We have a boy named Rundorig here," Faldor said. "That tall lad at the end of the far table over there." He pointed.

"No," the Murgo said, looking hard at Rundorig. "That isn't the boy who was described to me."

"It's not an uncommon name among the Arends," Faldor said. "Quite probably your friend met a pair from another farm."

"That must be it," the Murgo said, seeming to dismiss the affair. "This ham is excellent," he said, pointing at his plate with the point of the dagger with which he ate. "Are the ones in your smokehouse of similar quality?"

"Oh, no, friend merchant!" Faldor laughed. "You won't so easily trick me into talking business on this day."

The Murgo smiled briefly, the expression appearing strange on his scarred face. "One can always try," he said. "I would, however, compliment your cook."

"A compliment for you, Mistress Pol," Faldor said, raising his voice slightly. "Our friend from Cthol Murgos finds your cooking much to his liking."

"I thank him for his compliment," Aunt Pol said, somewhat coldly.

The Murgo looked at her, and his eyes widened slightly as if in recognition. "A noble meal, great lady," he said, bowing slightly in her direction. "Your kitchen is a place of magic."

"No," she said, her face suddenly very haughty, "not magic. Cooking's an art which anyone with patience may learn. Magic is quite something else."

"But magic is also an art, great lady," the Murgo said.

"There are many who think so," Aunt Pol said, "but true magic comes from within and isn't the result of nimble fingers which trick the eye."

The Murgo stared at her, his face hard, and she returned his gaze with steely eyes. To Garion, sitting nearby, it seemed as if something had passed between them that had nothing to do with the words they spoke—a kind of challenge seemed to hang in the air. And then the Murgo looked away almost as if he feared to take up that challenge.

When the meal was over, it was time for the rather simple pageant which traditionally marked Erastide. Seven of the older farmhands who had slipped away earlier appeared in the doorway wearing the long, hooded robes and carefully carved and painted masks which represented the faces of the Gods. The costumes were old and showed the wrinkles which were the result of having been packed away in Faldor's attic for the past year. With a slow step, the robed and masked figures paced into the hall and lined up at the foot of the table where Faldor sat. Then each in turn spoke a short piece which identified the God he represented.

"I am Aldur," Cralto's voice came from behind the first mask, "the God who dwells alone, and I command this world to be."

"I am Belar," came another familiar voice from behind the second mask, "Bear-God of the Alorns, and I command this world to be."

And so it went down the line, Chaldan, Issa, Nedra, Mara, and then finally the last figure, which, unlike the others, was robed in black and whose mask was made of steel instead of painted wood.

"I am Torak," Durnik's voice came hollowly from behind the mask, "Dragon-God of the Angaraks, and I command this world to be."

A movement caught Garion's eye, and he looked quickly. The Murgo had covered his face with his hands in a strange, almost ceremonial gesture. Beyond him, at the far table, the five Thulls were ashen-faced and trembling.

The seven figures at the foot of Faldor's table joined their hands. "We are the Gods," they said in unison, "and we command this world to be."

"Hearken unto the words of the Gods," Faldor declaimed. "Welcome are the Gods in the house of Faldor."

"The blessing of the Gods be upon the house of Faldor," the seven responded, "and upon all this company." And then they turned and, as slowly as they had come, they paced from the hall.

And then came the gifts. There was much excitement at this, for the gifts were all from Faldor, and the good farmer struggled long each year to provide the most suitable gift for each of his people. New tunics and hose and gowns and shoes were much in evidence, but Garion this year was nearly overwhelmed when he opened a smallish, cloth-wrapped bundle and found a neat, well-sheathed dagger.

"He's nearly a man," Faldor explained to Aunt Pol, "and a man always has need of a good knife."

Garion, of course, immediately tested the edge of his gift and quite promptly managed to cut his finger.

"It was inevitable, I suppose," Aunt Pol said, but whether she was speaking of the cut or the gift itself or the fact of Garion's growing up was not entirely clear.

The Murgo bought his hams the next morning, and he and the five Thulls departed. A few days later Anhelda and Eilbrig packed up and left on their return journey to the city of Sendar, and Faldor's farm returned to normal.

The winter plodded on. The snows came and went, and spring returned, as it always does. The only thing which made that spring any different from any other was the arrival of Brill, the new hand. One of the younger farmers had married and rented a small nearby croft and had left, laden down with practical gifts and good advice from Faldor to begin his life as a married man. Brill was hired to replace him.

Garion found Brill to be a definitely unattractive addition to the farm. The man's tunic and hose were patched and stained, his black hair and scraggly beard were unkempt, and one of his eyes looked off in a different direction from its fellow. He was a sour, solitary man, and he was none too clean. He seemed to carry with him an acrid reek of stale sweat that hung in his vicinity like a miasma. After a few attempts at conversation, Garion gave up and avoided him.

The boy, however, had other things to occupy his mind during that spring and summer. Though he had until then considered her to be more an inconvenience than a genuine playmate, quite suddenly he began to notice Zubrette. He had always known that she was pretty, but until that particular season that fact had been unimportant, and he had much preferred the company of Rundorig and Doroon. Now matters had changed. He noticed that the two other boys had also begun to pay more attention to her as well, and for the first time he began to feel the stirrings of jealousy.

Zubrette, of course, flirted outrageously with all three of them, and positively glowed when they glared at each other in her presence. Rundorig's duties in the fields kept him away most of the time, but Doroon was a serious worry to Garion. He became quite nervous and frequently found excuses to go about the compound to make certain that Doroon and Zubrette were not alone together.

His own campaign was charmingly simple—he resorted to bribery. Zubrette, like all little girls, was fond of sweets, and Garion had access to the entire kitchen. In a short period of time they had worked out an arrangement. Garion would steal sweets from the kitchen for his sunny-haired playmate, and in return she would let him kiss her. Things might perhaps have gone further if Aunt Pol had not caught them in the midst of such an exchange one bright summer afternoon in the seclusion of the hay barn.

"That's quite enough of that," she announced firmly from the doorway.

Garion jumped guiltily away from Zubrette.

"I've got something in my eye," Zubrette lied quickly. "Garion was trying to get it out for me."

Garion stood blushing furiously.

"Really?" Aunt Pol said. "How interesting. Come with me, Garion."

"I—" he started.

"*Now*, Garion."

And that was the end of that. Garion's time thereafter was totally occupied in the kitchen, and Aunt Pol's eyes seemed to be on him every moment. He mooned about a great deal and worried desperately about Doroon, who now appeared hatefully smug, but Aunt Pol remained watchful, and Garion remained in the kitchen.

CHAPTER FIVE

In midautumn that year, when the leaves had turned and the wind had showered them down from the trees like red and gold snow, when evenings were chill and the smoke from the chimneys at Faldor's farm rose straight and blue toward the first cold stars in a purpling sky, Wolf returned. He came up the road one gusty afternoon under a lowering autumn sky with the new-fallen leaves tumbling about him and his great, dark cloak whipping in the wind.

Garion, who had been dumping kitchen slops to the pigs, saw his approach and ran to meet him. The old man seemed travel-stained and tired, and his face under his gray hood was grim. His usual demeanor of happy-go-lucky cheerfulness had been replaced by a somber mood Garion had never seen in him before.

"Garion," Wolf said by way of greeting. "You've grown, I see."

"It's been five years," Garion said.

"Has it been that long?"

Garion nodded, falling into step beside his friend.

"Is everyone well?" Wolf asked.

"Oh yes," Garion said. "Everything's the same here—except that Breldo got married and moved away, and the old brown cow died last summer."

"I remember the cow," Wolf said. Then he said, "I must speak with your Aunt Pol."

"She's not in a very good mood today," Garion warned. "It might be better if you rested in one of the barns. I can sneak some food and drink to you in a bit."

"We'll have to chance her mood," Wolf said. "What I have to say to her can't wait."

They entered the gate and crossed the courtyard to the kitchen door.

Aunt Pol was waiting. "You again?" she said tartly, her hands on her hips. "My kitchen still hasn't recovered from your last visit."

"Mistress Pol," Wolf said, bowing. Then he did a strange thing. His fingers traced an intricate little design in the air in front of his chest. Garion was quite sure that he was not intended to see those gestures.

Aunt Pol's eyes widened slightly, then narrowed, and her face became grim. "How do you—" she started, then caught herself. "Garion," she said sharply, "I need some carrots. There are still some in the ground at the far end of the kitchen garden. Take a spade and a pail and fetch me some."

"But—" he protested, and then, warned by her expression, he left quickly. He got a spade and pail from a nearby shed and then loitered near the kitchen door. Eavesdropping, of course, was not a nice habit and was considered the worst sort of bad manners in Sendaria, but Garion had long ago concluded that whenever he was sent away, the conversation was bound to be very interesting and would probably concern him rather intimately. He had wrestled briefly with his conscience about it; but, since he really saw no harm in the practice—as long as he didn't repeat anything he heard—conscience had lost to curiosity.

Garion's ears were very sharp, but it took him a moment or two to separate the two familiar voices from the other sounds in the kitchen.

"He won't leave you a trail," Aunt Pol was saying.

"He doesn't have to," Wolf replied. "The thing itself will make its trail known to me. I can follow it as easily as a fox can scent out the track of a rabbit."

"Where will he take it?" she asked.

"Who can say? His mind's closed to me. My guess is that he'll go north to Boktor. That's the shortest route to Gar og Nadrak. He'll know that I'll be after him, and he'll want to cross into the lands of the Angaraks as soon as possible. His theft won't be complete so long as he stays in the west."

"When did it happen?"

"Four weeks ago."

"He could already be in the Angarak kingdoms."

"That's not likely. The distances are great; but if he is, I'll have to follow him. I'll need your help."

"But how can I leave here?" Aunt Pol asked. "I have to watch over the boy."

Garion's curiosity was becoming almost unbearable. He edged closer to the kitchen door.

"The boy'll be safe enough here," Wolf said. "This is an urgent matter."

"No," Aunt Pol contradicted. "Even this place isn't safe. Last Erastide a Murgo and five Thulls came here. He posed as a merchant, but he asked a few too many questions—about an old man and a boy named Rundorig who had been seen in Upper Gralt some years ago. He may also have recognized me."

"It's more serious than I thought, then," Wolf said thoughtfully. "We'll have to move the boy. We can leave him with friends elsewhere."

"No," Aunt Pol disagreed again. "If I go with you, he'll have to go along. He's reaching an age where he has to be watched most carefully."

"Don't be foolish," Wolf said sharply.

Garion was stunned. Nobody talked to Aunt Pol that way.

"It's my decision to make," Aunt Pol said crisply. "We all agreed that he was to be in my care until he was grown. I won't go unless he goes with me."

Garion's heart leaped.

"Pol," Wolf said sharply, "think where we may have to go. You can't deliver the boy into those hands."

"He'd be safer in Cthol Murgos or in Mallorea itself than he would be here without me to watch him," Aunt Pol said. "Last spring I caught him in the barn with a girl about his own age. As I said, he needs watching."

Wolf laughed then, a rich, merry sound. "Is that all?" he said. "You worry too much about such things."

"How would you like it if we returned and found him married and about to become a father?" Aunt Pol demanded acidly. "He'd make an excellent farmer, and what matter if we'd all have to wait a hundred years for the circumstances to be right again?"

"Surely it hasn't gone that far. They're only children."

"You're blind, Old Wolf," Aunt Pol said. "This is backcountry Sendaria, and the boy's been raised to do the proper and honorable thing. The girl's a bright-eyed little minx who's maturing much too rapidly for my comfort. Right now charming little Zubrette is a far greater danger than any Murgo could ever be. Either the boy goes along, or I won't go either. You have your responsibilities, and I have mine."

"There's no time to argue," Wolf said. "If it has to be this way, then so be it."

Garion almost choked with excitement. He felt only a passing, momentary pang at leaving Zubrette behind. He turned and looked exultantly up at the clouds scudding across the evening sky. And, because his back was turned, he did not see Aunt Pol approach through the kitchen door.

"The garden, as I recall, lies beyond the south wall," she pointed out.

Garion started guiltily.

"How is it that the carrots remain undug?" she demanded.

"I had to look for the spade," he said unconvincingly.

"Really? I see that you found it, however." Her eyebrows arched dangerously.

"Only just now."

"Splendid. Carrots, Garion—now!"

Garion grabbed his spade and pail and ran.

It was just dusk when he returned, and he saw Aunt Pol mounting the steps that led to Faldor's quarters. He might have followed her to listen, but a faint movement in the dark doorway of one of the sheds made him step instead into the shadow of the gate. A furtive figure moved from the shed to the foot of the stairs Aunt Pol had just climbed and silently crept up the stairs as soon as she went in Faldor's door. The light was fading, and Garion could not see exactly who followed his Aunt. He set down his pail and, grasping the spade like a weapon, he hurried quickly around the inner court, keeping to the shadows.

There came the sound of a movement inside the chambers upstairs, and the figure at the door straightened quickly and scurried down the steps. Garion slipped back out of sight, his spade still held at the ready. As the figure passed him, Garion briefly caught the scent of stale, musty clothing and rank sweat. As certainly as if he had seen the man's face, he knew that the figure that had followed his Aunt had been Brill, the new farmhand.

The door at the top of the stairs opened, and Garion heard his Aunt's voice. "I'm sorry, Faldor, but it's a family matter, and I must leave immediately."

"I would pay you more, Pol." Faldor's voice was almost breaking.

"Money has nothing to do with it," Aunt Pol replied. "You're a good man, Faldor, and your farm has been a haven to me when I needed one. I'm grateful to you—more than you can know—but I must leave."

"Perhaps when this family business is over, you can come back," Faldor almost pleaded.

"No, Faldor," she said. "I'm afraid not."

"We'll miss you, Pol," Faldor said with tears in his voice.

"And I'll miss you, dear Faldor. I've never met a better-hearted man. I'd take it kindly if you wouldn't mention my leaving until I've gone. I'm not fond of explanations or sentimental good-byes."

"Whatever you wish, Pol."

"Don't look so mournful, old friend," Aunt Pol said lightly. "My helpers are well-trained. Their cooking will be the same as mine. Your stomach will never know the difference."

"My heart will," Faldor said.

"Don't be silly," she said gently. "Now I must see to supper."

Garion moved quickly away from the foot of the stairs. Troubled, he put his spade back in the shed and fetched the pail of carrots he had left sitting by the gate. To reveal to his Aunt that he had seen Brill listening at the door would immediately raise questions about his own activities that he would prefer not to have to answer. In all probability Brill was merely curious, and there was nothing menacing or ominous about that. To observe the unsavory Brill duplicating his own seemingly harmless pastime, however, made Garion quite uncomfortable—even slightly ashamed of himself.

Although Garion was much too excited to eat, supper that evening seemed as ordinary as any meal on Faldor's farm had ever been. Garion covertly watched sour-faced Brill, but the man showed no outward sign of having in any way been changed by the conversation he had gone to so much trouble to overhear.

When supper was over, as was always the case when he visited the farm, Mister Wolf was prevailed upon to tell a story. He rose and stood for a moment deep in thought as the wind moaned in the chimney and the torches flickered in their rings on the pillars in the hall.

"As all men know," he began, "the Marags are no more, and the Spirit of Mara weeps alone in the wilderness and wails among the moss-grown ruins of Maragor. But also, as all men know, the hills and streams of Maragor are heavy with fine yellow gold. That gold, of course, was the cause of the destruction of the Marags. When a certain neighboring kingdom became aware of the gold, the temptation became too great, and the result—as it almost always is when gold is at issue between kingdoms—was war. The pretext for the war was the lamentable fact that the Marags were cannibals. While this habit is distasteful to civilized men, had there not been gold in Maragor it might have been overlooked.

"The war, however, was inevitable, and the Marags were slain. But the Spirit of Mara and the ghosts of all the slaughtered Marags remained in Maragor, as those who went into that haunted kingdom soon discovered.

"Now it chanced to happen that about that time there lived in the town of Muros in southern Sendaria three adventuresome men, and, hearing of all that gold, they resolved to journey down to Maragor to claim their share of it. The men, as I said, were adventuresome and bold, and they scoffed at the tales of ghosts.

"Their journey was long, for it is many hundreds of leagues from Muros to the upper reaches of Maragor, but the smell of the gold drew them on. And so it happened, one dark and stormy night, that they crept across the border into Maragor past the patrols which had been set to turn back just such as they. That nearby kingdom, having gone to all the expense and inconvenience of war, was quite naturally reluctant to share the gold with anyone who chanced to pass by.

"Through the night they crept, burning with their lust for gold. The Spirit of Mara wailed about them, but they were brave men and not afraid of spirits—and besides, they told each other, the sound was not truly a spirit, but merely the moaning of the wind in the trees.

"As dim and misty morning seeped amongst the hills, they could hear, not far away, the rushing sound of a river. As all men know, gold is most easily found along the banks of rivers, and so they made quickly toward that sound.

"Then one of them chanced to look down in the dim light, and behold, the ground at his feet was strewn with gold—lumps and chunks of it. Overcome with greed, he remained silent and loitered behind until his companions were out of sight; then he fell to his knees and began to gather up gold as a child might pick flowers.

"He heard a sound behind him and he turned. What he saw it is best not to say. Dropping all his gold, he bolted.

"Now the river they had heard cut through a gorge just about there, and his two companions were amazed to see him run off the edge of that gorge and even continue to run as he fell, his legs churning insubstantial air. Then they turned, and they saw what had been pursuing him.

"One went quite mad and leaped with a despairing cry into the same gorge which had just claimed his companion, but the third adventurer, the bravest and boldest of all, told himself that no ghost could actually hurt a living man and stood his ground. That, of course, was the worst mistake of all. The ghosts encircled him as he stood bravely, certain that they could not hurt him."

Mister Wolf paused and drank briefly from his tankard. "And then," the old storyteller continued, "because even ghosts can become hungry, they divided him up and ate him."

Garion's hair stood on end at the shocking conclusion of Wolf's tale, and he could sense the others at his table shuddering. It was not at all the kind of story they had expected to hear.

Durnik the smith, who was sitting nearby, had a perplexed expression on his plain face. Finally he spoke. "I would not question the truth of your story for the world," he said to Wolf, struggling with the words, "but if they ate him—the ghosts, I mean—where did it go? I mean—if ghosts are insubstantial, as all men say they are, they don't have stomachs, do they? And what would they bite with?"

Wolf's face grew sly and mysterious. He raised one finger as if he were about to make some cryptic reply to Durnik's puzzled question, and then he suddenly began to laugh.

Durnik looked annoyed at first, and then, rather sheepishly, he too began to laugh. Slowly the laughter spread as they all began to understand the joke.

"An excellent jest, old friend," Faldor said, laughing as hard as any of the others, "and one from which much instruction may be gained. Greed is bad, but fear is worse, and the world is dangerous enough without cluttering it with imaginary hobgoblins." Trust Faldor to twist a good story into a moralistic sermon of some kind.

"True enough, good Faldor," Wolf said more seriously, "but there *are* things in this world which can't be explained away or dismissed with laughter."

Brill, seated near the fire, had not joined in the laughter. "I've never seen a ghost," he said sourly, "nor ever met anyone who has, and I for one don't believe in any kind of magic or sorcery or such childishness." And he stood up and stamped out of the hall almost as if the story had been a kind of personal insult.

Later, in the kitchen, when Aunt Pol was seeing to the cleaning up and Wolf lounged against one of the worktables with a tankard of beer, Garion's struggle with his conscience finally came into the open. That dry, interior voice informed him most pointedly that concealing what he had seen was not merely foolish, but possibly dangerous as well. He set down the pot he was scrubbing and crossed to where they were. "It might not be important," he said carefully, "but this afternoon, when I was coming back from the garden, I saw Brill following you, Aunt Pol."

She turned and looked at him. Wolf set down his tankard. "Go on, Garion," Aunt Pol said.

"It was when you went up to talk with Faldor," Garion explained. "He waited until you'd gone up the stairs and Faldor had let you in. Then he sneaked up and listened at the door. I saw him up there when I went to put the spade away."

"How long has this man Brill been at the farm?" Wolf asked, frowning.

"He came just last spring," Garion said, "after Breldo got married and moved away."

"And the Murgo merchant was here at Erastide some months before?"

Aunt Pol looked at him sharply. "You think—" She did not finish.

"I think it might not be a bad idea if I stepped around and had a few words with friend Brill," Wolf said grimly. "Do you know where his room is, Garion?"

Garion nodded, his heart suddenly racing.

"Show me." Wolf moved away from the table against which he had been lounging, and his step was no longer the step of an old man. It was curiously as if the years had suddenly dropped away from him.

"Be careful," Aunt Pol warned.

Wolf chuckled, and the sound was chilling. "I'm always careful. You should know that by now."

Garion quickly led Wolf out into the yard and around to the far end where the steps mounted to the gallery that led to the rooms of the farmhands. They went up, their soft leather shoes making no sound on the worn steps.

"Down here," Garion whispered, not knowing exactly why he whispered.

Wolf nodded, and they went quietly down the dark gallery.

"Here," Garion whispered, stopping.

"Step back," Wolf breathed. He touched the door with his fingertips.

"Is it locked?" Garion asked.

"That's no problem," Wolf said softly. He put his hand to the latch, there was a click, and the door swung open. Wolf stepped inside with Garion close behind.

It was totally dark in the room, and the sour stink of Brill's unwashed clothes hung in the air.

"He's not here," Wolf said in a normal tone. He fumbled with something at his belt, and there was the scrape of flint against steel and a flare of sparks. A wisp of frayed rope caught the sparks and began to glow. Wolf blew on the spark for a second, and it flared into flame. He raised the burning wisp over his head and looked around the empty room.

The floor and bed were littered with rumpled clothes and personal belongings. Garion knew instantly that this was not simple untidiness, but rather was the sign of a hasty departure, and he did not know exactly how it was that he knew.

Wolf stood for a moment, holding his little torch. His face seemed somehow empty, as if his mind were searching for something.

"The stables," he said sharply. "Quickly, boy!"

Garion turned and dashed from the room with Wolf close behind. The burning wisp of rope drifted down into the yard, illuminating it briefly after Wolf discarded it over the railing as he ran.

There was a light in the stable. It was dim, partially covered, but faint beams shone through the weathered cracks in the door. The horses were stirring uneasily.

"Stay clear, boy," Wolf said as he jerked the stable door open.

Brill was inside, struggling to saddle a horse that shied from his rank smell.

"Leaving, Brill?" Wolf asked, stepping into the doorway with his arms crossed.

Brill turned quickly, crouched and with a snarl on his unshaven face. His off-center eye gleamed whitely in the half-muffled light of the lantern hanging from a peg on one of the stalls, and his broken teeth shone behind his pulled-back lips.

"A strange time for a journey," Wolf said dryly.

"Don't interfere with me, old man," Brill said, his tone menacing. "You'll regret it."

"I've regretted many things in my life," Wolf said. "I doubt that one more's going to make all that much difference."

"I warned you." Brill snarled, and his hand dove under his cloak and emerged with a short, rust-splotched sword.

"Don't be stupid," Wolf said in a tone of overwhelming contempt.

Garion, however, at the first flash of the sword, whipped his hand to his belt, drew his dagger, and stepped in front of the unarmed old man.

"Get back, boy," Wolf barked.

But Garion had already lunged forward, his bright dagger thrust out ahead of him. Later, when he had time to consider, he could not have explained why he reacted as he did. Some deep instinct seemed to take over.

"Garion," Wolf said, "get out of the way!"

"So much the better," Brill said, raising his sword.

And then Durnik was there. He appeared as if from nowhere, snatched up an ox yoke and struck the sword from Brill's hand. Brill turned on him, enraged, and Durnik's second blow took the cast-eyed man in the ribs, a little below the armpit. The breath whooshed from Brill's lungs, and he collapsed, gasping and writhing to the straw-littered floor.

"For shame, Garion," Durnik said reproachfully. "I didn't make that knife of yours for this kind of thing."

"He was going to kill Mister Wolf," Garion protested.

"Never mind that," Wolf said, bending over the gasping man on the floor of the stable. He searched Brill roughly and pulled a jingling purse out from under the stained tunic. He carried the purse to the lantern and opened it.

"That's mine," Brill gasped, trying to rise. Durnik raised the ox yoke, and Brill sank back again.

"A sizable sum for an ordinary farmhand to have, friend Brill," Wolf said, pouring the jingling coins from the purse into his hand. "How did you manage to come by it?"

Brill glared at him.

Garion's eyes grew wide at the sight of the coins. He had never seen gold before.

"You don't really need to answer, friend Brill," Wolf said, examining one of the coins. "Your gold speaks for you." He dumped the coins back in the purse and tossed the small leather pouch back to the man on the floor. Brill grabbed it quickly and pushed it back inside his tunic.

"I'll have to tell Faldor of this," Durnik said.

"No," Wolf said.

"It's a serious matter," Durnik said. "A bit of wrestling or a few blows exchanged is one thing, but drawing weapons is quite another."

"There's no time for all of that," Wolf said, taking a piece of harness strap from a peg on the wall. "Tie his hands behind him, and we'll put him in one of the grain bins. Someone will find him in the morning."

Durnik stared at him.

"Trust me, good Durnik," Wolf said. "The matter's urgent. Tie him up and hide him someplace; then come to the kitchen. Come with me, Garion." And he turned and left the stable.

Aunt Pol was pacing her kitchen nervously when they returned. "Well?" she demanded.

"He was trying to leave," Wolf said. "We stopped him."

"Did you—?" She left it hanging.

"No. He drew a sword, but Durnik happened to be nearby and knocked the belligerence out of him. The intervention was timely. Your cub here was about to do battle. That little dagger of his is a pretty thing, but not really much of a match for a sword."

Aunt Pol turned on Garion, her eyes ablaze. Garion prudently stepped back out of reach.

"There's no time for that," Wolf said, retrieving the tankard he had set down before leaving the kitchen. "Brill had a pouchful of good red Angarak gold. The Murgos have set eyes to watching this place. I'd wanted to make our going less noticeable, but since we're already being watched, there's no point in that now. Gather what you and the boy are likely to need. I want a few leagues between us and Brill before he manages to free himself. I don't want to be looking over my shoulder for Murgos every place I go."

Durnik, who had just come into the kitchen, stopped and stood staring at them. "Things aren't what they seem here," he said. "What manner of folk are you, and how is it that you have such dangerous enemies?"

"That's a long story, good Durnik," Wolf said, "but I'm afraid there's no time to tell it now. Make our apologies to Faldor, and see if you can't detain Brill for a day or so. I'd like our trail to be quite cold before he or his friends try to find it."

"Someone else is going to have to do that," Durnik said slowly. "I'm not sure what this is all about, but I am sure that there's danger involved in it. It appears that I'll have to go with you—at least until I've gotten you safely away from here."

Aunt Pol suddenly laughed. "You, Durnik? You mean to protect *us?*"

He drew himself up. "I'm sorry, Mistress Pol," he said. "I will not permit you to go unescorted."

"*Will not permit?*" she said incredulously.

"Very well," Wolf said, a sly look on his face.

"Have you totally taken leave of your senses?" Aunt Pol demanded, turning on him.

"Durnik's shown himself to be a useful man," Wolf said. "If nothing else, he'll give me someone to talk with along the way. Your tongue's grown sharper with the years, Pol, and I don't relish the idea of a hundred leagues or more with nothing but abuse for companionship."

"I see that you've finally slipped into your dotage, Old Wolf," she said acidly.

"That's exactly the sort of thing I meant," Wolf replied blandly. "Now gather a few necessary things, and let's be away from here. The night's passing rapidly."

She glared at him a moment and then stormed out of the kitchen.

"I'll have to fetch some things, too," Durnik said. He turned and went out into the gusty night.

Garion's mind whirled. Things were happening far too fast.

"Afraid, boy?" Wolf asked.

"Well—" Garion said. "It's just that I don't understand. I don't understand any of this at all."

"You will in time, Garion," Wolf said. "For now it's better perhaps that you don't. There's danger in what we're doing, but not all that great a danger. Your Aunt and I—and good Durnik, of course—will see that no harm comes to you. Now help me in the pantry." He took a lantern into the pantry and began loading some loaves of bread, a ham, a round yellow cheese and several bottles of wine into a sack which he took down from a peg.

It was nearly midnight, as closely as Garion could tell, when they quietly left the kitchen and crossed the dark courtyard. The faint creak of the gate as Durnik swung it open seemed enormously loud.

As they passed through the gate, Garion felt a momentary pang. Faldor's farm had been the only home he had ever known. He was leaving now, perhaps forever, and such things had great significance. He felt an even sharper pang at the memory of Zubrette. The thought of Doroon and Zubrette together in the hay barn almost made him want to give the whole thing up altogether, but it was far too late now.

Beyond the protection of the buildings, the gusty wind was chill and whipped at Garion's cloak. Heavy clouds covered the moon, and the road seemed only slightly less dark than the surrounding fields. It was cold and lonely and more than a little frightening. He walked a bit closer to Aunt Pol.

At the top of the hill he stopped and glanced back. Faldor's farm was only a pale, dim blur in the valley behind. Regretfully, he turned his back on it. The valley ahead was very dark, and even the road was lost in the gloom before them.

CHAPTER SIX

They had walked for miles, how many Garion could not say. He nodded as he walked, and sometimes stumbled over unseen stones on the dark road. More than anything now he wanted to sleep. His eyes burned, and his legs trembled on the verge of exhaustion.

At the top of another hill—there always seemed to be another hill, for that part of Sendaria was folded like a rumpled cloth—Mister Wolf stopped and looked about, his eyes searching the oppressive gloom.

"We turn aside from the road here," he announced.

"Is that wise?" Durnik asked. "There are woods hereabout, and I've heard that there may be robbers hiding there. Even if there aren't any robbers, aren't we likely to lose our way in the dark?" He looked up at the murky sky, his plain face, dimly seen, troubled. "I wish there was a moon."

"I don't think we need to be afraid of robbers," Wolf said confidently, "and I'm just as happy that there isn't a moon. I don't think we're being followed yet, but it's just as well that no one happens to see us pass. Murgo gold can buy most secrets." And with that he led them into the fields that lay beside the road.

For Garion the fields were impossible. If he had stumbled now and then on the road, the unseen furrows, holes, and clumps in the rough ground seemed to catch at his feet with every step. At the end of a mile, when they reached the black edge of the woods, he was almost ready to weep with exhaustion. "How can we find our way in there?" he demanded, peering into the utter darkness of the woods.

"There's a woodcutter's track not far to this side," Wolf said, pointing. "We only have a little farther to go." And he set off again, following the edge of the dark woods, with Garion and the others stumbling along behind him. "Here we are," he said finally, stopping to allow them to catch up. "It's going to be very dark in there, and the track isn't wide. I'll go first, and the rest of you follow me."

"I'll be right behind you, Garion," Durnik said. "Don't worry. Everything'll be all right." There was a note in the smith's voice, however, that hinted that his words were more to reassure himself than to calm the boy.

It seemed warmer in the woods. The trees sheltered them from the gusty wind, but it was so dark that Garion could not understand how Wolf could possibly find his way. A dreadful suspicion grew in his mind that Wolf actually did not know where he was going and was merely floundering along blindly, trusting to luck.

"Stop," a rumbling voice suddenly, shockingly, said directly ahead of them. Garion's eyes, accustomed slightly now to the gloom of the woods, saw a vague outline of something so huge that it could not possibly be a man.

"A giant!" he screamed in a sudden panic. Then, because he was exhausted and because everything that had happened that evening had simply piled too much upon him all at one time, his nerve broke and he bolted into the trees.

"Garion!" Aunt Pol's voice cried out after him. "Come back!"

But panic had taken hold of him. He ran on, falling over roots and bushes, crashing into trees and tangling his legs in brambles. It seemed like some endless nightmare of blind flight. He ran full tilt into a low-hanging, unseen branch, and sparks flared before his eyes with the sudden blow to his forehead. He lay on the damp earth, gasping and sobbing, trying to clear his head.

And then there were hands on him, horrid, unseen hands. A thousand terrors flashed through his mind at once, and he struggled desperately, trying to draw his dagger.

"Oh, no," a voice said. "None of that, my rabbit." His dagger was taken from him.

"Are you going to eat me?" Garion babbled, his voice breaking.

His captor laughed. "On your feet, rabbit," he said, and Garion felt himself pulled up by a strong hand. His arm was taken in a firm grasp, and he was half-dragged through the woods.

Somewhere ahead there was a light, a winking fire among the trees, and it seemed that he was being taken that way. He knew that he must think, must devise some means of escape, but his mind, stunned by fright and exhaustion, refused to function.

There were three wagons sitting in a rough half-circle around the fire. Durnik was there, and Wolf, and Aunt Pol, and with them a man so huge that Garion's mind simply refused to accept the possibility that he was real. His tree-trunk-sized legs were wrapped in furs cross-tied with leather thongs, and he wore a chain-mail shirt that reached to his knees, belted at the waist. From the belt hung a ponderous sword on one side and a short-handled axe on the other. His hair was in braids, and he had a vast, bristling red beard.

As they came into the light, Garion was able to see the man who had captured him. He was a small man, scarcely taller than Garion himself, and his face was dominated by a long pointed nose. His eyes were small and squinted, and his straight, black hair was raggedly cut. The face was not the sort to inspire confidence, and the man's stained and patched tunic and short, wicked-looking sword did little to contradict the implications of the face.

"Here's our rabbit," the small, weasel-like man announced as he pulled Garion into the circle of the firelight. "And a merry chase he led me, too."

Aunt Pol was furious. "Don't you ever do that again," she said sternly to Garion.

"Not so quick, Mistress Pol," Wolf said. "It's better for him to run than to fight just yet. Until he's bigger, his feet are his best friends."

"Have we been captured by robbers?" Garion asked in a quavering voice.

"Robbers?" Wolf laughed. "What a wild imagination you have, boy. These two are our friends."

"Friends?" Garion asked doubtfully, looking suspiciously at the red-bearded giant and the weasel-faced man beside him. "Are you sure?"

The giant laughed then too, his voice rumbling like an earthquake. "The boy seems mistrustful," he boomed. "Your face must have warned him, friend Silk."

The smaller man looked sourly at his burly companion.

"This is Garion," Wolf said, pointing at the boy. "You already know Mistress Pol." His voice seemed to stress Aunt Pol's name. "And this is Durnik, a brave smith who's decided to accompany us."

"Mistress Pol?" the smaller man said, laughing suddenly for no apparent reason.

"I am known so," Aunt Pol said pointedly.

"It shall be my pleasure to call you so, then, great lady," the small man said with a mocking bow.

"Our large friend here is Barak," Wolf went on. "He's useful to have around when there's trouble. As you can see, he's not a Sendar, but a Cherek from Val Alorn."

Garion had never seen a Cherek before, and the fearful tales of their prowess in battle became suddenly quite believable in the presence of the towering Barak.

"And I," the small man said with one hand to his chest, "am called Silk—not much of a name, I'll admit, but it suits me—and I'm from Boktor in Drasnia. I'm a juggler and an acrobat."

"And also a thief and a spy," Barak rumbled good-naturedly.

"We all have our faults," Silk admitted blandly, scratching at his scraggly whiskers.

"And I'm called Mister Wolf in this particular time and place," the old man said. "I'm rather fond of the name, since the boy there gave it to me."

"Mister Wolf?" Silk asked, and then he laughed again. "What a merry name for you, old friend."

"I'm delighted that you find it so, old friend," Wolf said flatly.

"Mister Wolf it shall be, then," Silk said. "Come to the fire, friends. Warm yourselves, and I'll see to some food."

Garion was still uncertain about the oddly matched pair. They obviously knew Aunt Pol and Mister Wolf—and just as obviously by different names. The fact that Aunt Pol might not be who he had always thought she was was very disturbing. One of the foundation stones of his entire life had just disappeared.

The food which Silk brought was rough, a turnip stew with thick chunks of meat floating in it and crudely hacked off slabs of bread, but Garion, amazed at the size of his appetite, fell into it as if he had not eaten for days.

And then, his stomach full and his feet warmed by the crackling campfire, he sat on a log, half-dozing.

"What now, Old Wolf?" he heard Aunt Pol ask. "What's the idea behind these clumsy wagons?"

"A brilliant plan," Wolf said, "even if I do say it myself. There are, as you know, wagons going every which way in Sendaria at this time of year. Harvests are moving from field to farm, from farm to village and from village to town. Nothing is more unremarkable in Sendaria than wagons. They're so common that they're almost invisible. This is how we're going to travel. We're now honest freight haulers."

"We're *what*?" Aunt Pol demanded.

"Wagoneers," Wolf said expansively. "Hard-working transporters of the goods of Sendaria—out to make our fortunes and seek adventure, bitten by the desire to travel, incurably infected by the romance of the road."

"Have you any idea how long it takes to travel by wagon?" Aunt Pol asked.

"Six to ten leagues a day," he told her. "Slow, I'll grant you, but it's better to move slowly than to attract attention."

She shook her head in disgust.

"Where first, Mister Wolf?" Silk asked.

"To Darine," Wolf announced. "If the one we're following went to the north, he'll have to have passed through Darine on his way to Boktor and beyond."

"And what exactly are we carrying to Darine?" Aunt Pol asked.

"Turnips, great lady," Silk said. "Last morning my large friend and I purchased three wagonloads of them in the village of Winold."

"Turnips?" Aunt Pol asked in a tone that spoke volumes.

"Yes, great lady, turnips," Silk said solemnly.

"Are we ready, then?" Wolf asked.

"We are," the giant Barak said shortly, rising with his mail shirt clinking.

"We should look the part," Wolf said carefully, eyeing Barak up and down. "Your armor, my friend, is not the sort of garb an honest wagoneer would wear. I think you should change it for stout wool."

Barak's face looked injured. "I could wear a tunic over it," he suggested tentatively.

"You rattle," Silk pointed out, "and armor has a distinctive fragrance about it. From the downwind side you smell like a rusty ironworks, Barak."

"I feel undressed without a mail shirt," Barak complained.

"We must all make sacrifices," Silk said.

Grumbling, Barak went to one of the wagons, jerked out a bundle of clothes and began to pull off his mail shirt. His linen undertunic bore large, reddish rust stains.

"I'd change tunics as well," Silk suggested. "Your shirt smells as bad as the armor."

Barak glowered at him. "Anything else?" he demanded. "I hope, for decency's sake, you don't plan to strip me entirely."

Silk laughed.

Barak pulled off his tunic. His torso was enormous and covered with thick red hair.

"You look like a rug," Silk observed.

"I can't help that," Barak said. "Winters are cold in Cherek, and the hair helps me to stay warm." He put on a fresh tunic.

"It's just as cold in Drasnia," Silk said. "Are you absolutely sure your grandmother didn't dally with a bear during one of those long winters?"

"Someday your mouth is going to get you into a great deal of trouble, friend Silk," Barak said ominously.

Silk laughed again. "I've been in trouble most of my life, friend Barak."

"I wonder why," Barak said ironically.

"I think all this could be discussed later," Wolf said pointedly. "I'd rather like to be away from here before the week's out, if I can."

"Of course, old friend," Silk said, jumping up. "Barak and I can amuse each other later."

Three teams of sturdy horses were picketed nearby, and they all helped to harness them to the wagons.

"I'll put out the fire," Silk said and fetched two pails of water from a small brook that trickled nearby. The fire hissed when the water struck it, and great clouds of steam boiled up toward the low-hanging tree limbs.

"We'll lead the horses to the edge of the wood," Wolf said. "I'd rather not pick my teeth on a low branch."

The horses seemed almost eager to start and moved without urging along a narrow track through the dark woods. They stopped at the edge of the open fields, and Wolf looked around carefully to see if anyone was in sight.

"I don't see anybody," he said. "Let's get moving."

"Ride with me, good smith," Barak said to Durnik. "Conversation with an honest man is much preferable to a night spent enduring the insults of an over-clever Drasnian."

"As you wish, friend," Durnik said politely.

"I'll lead," Silk said. "I'm familiar with the back roads and lanes hereabouts. I'll put us on the high road beyond Upper Gralt before noon. Barak and Durnik can bring up the rear. I'm sure that between them they can discourage anyone who might feel like following us."

"All right," Wolf said, climbing up onto the seat of the middle wagon. He reached down his hand and helped up Aunt Pol.

Garion quickly climbed up onto the wagon bed behind them, a trifle nervous that someone might suggest that he ride with Silk. It was all very well for Mister Wolf to say that the two they had just met were friends, but the fright he had suffered in the wood was still too fresh in his mind to make him quite comfortable with them.

The sacks of musty-smelling turnips were lumpy, but Garion soon managed to push and shove a kind of half-reclining seat for himself among them just behind Aunt Pol and Mister Wolf. He was sheltered from the wind, Aunt Pol was close, and his cloak, spread over him, kept him warm. He was altogether comfortable, and, despite the excitement of the night's events, he soon drifted into a half-drowse. The dry voice in his mind suggested briefly that he had not behaved too well back in the wood, but it too soon fell silent, and Garion slept.

It was the change of sound that woke him. The soft thud of the horses' hooves on the dirt road became a clatter as they came to the cobblestones of a small village sleeping in the last chill hours of the autumn night. Garion opened his eyes and looked sleepily at the tall, narrow houses with their tiny windows all dark.

A dog barked briefly, then retreated back to his warm place under some stairs. Garion wondered what village it might be and how many people slept under those steep-peaked tile roofs, unaware of the passage of their three wagons.

The cobbled street was very narrow, and Garion could almost have reached out and touched the weathered stones of the houses as they passed.

And then the nameless village was behind them, and they were back on the road again. The soft sound of the horses' hooves lured him once more toward sleep.

"What if he hasn't passed through Darine?" Aunt Pol asked Mister Wolf in a low tone.

It occurred to Garion that in all the excitement he had never actually found out exactly what it was that they were seeking. He kept his eyes closed and listened.

"Don't start with the 'what ifs,' " Wolf said irritably. "If we sit around saying 'what if,' we'll never do anything."

"I was merely asking," Aunt Pol said.

"If he hasn't gone through Darine, we'll turn south—to Muros. He may have joined a caravan there to take the Great North Road to Boktor."

"And if he hasn't gone through Muros?"

"Then we go on to Camaar."

"And then?"

"We'll see when we get to Camaar." His tone was final, as if he no longer wished to discuss the matter.

Aunt Pol drew in a breath as if she were about to deliver some final retort, but apparently she decided against it and settled back instead on the wagon seat.

To the east, ahead of them, the faint stain of dawn touched the lowering clouds, and they moved on through the tattered, windswept end of the long night in their search for something which, though he could not yet even identify it, was so important that Garion's entire life had been uprooted in a single day because of it.

CHAPTER SEVEN

It took them four days to reach Darine on the north coast. The first day went quite well, since, though it was cloudy and the wind kept blowing, the air was dry and the roads were good. They passed quiet farmsteads and an occasional farmer bent to his labor in the middle of a field. Inevitably each man stopped his work to watch them pass. Some waved, but some did not.

And then there were villages, clusters of tall houses nestled in valleys. As they passed, the children came out and ran after the wagons, shouting with excitement. The villagers watched, idly curious, until it became obvious that the wagons were not going to stop, and then they sniffed and went back to their own concerns.

As afternoon of that first day lowered toward evening, Silk led them into a grove of trees at the roadside, and they made preparations for the night. They ate the last of the ham and cheese Wolf had filched from Faldor's pantry and then spread their blankets on the ground beneath the wagons. The ground was hard and cold, but the exciting sense of being on some great adventure helped Garion to endure the discomfort.

The next morning, however, it began to rain. It was a fine, misty rain at first, scattering before the wind, but as the morning wore on, it settled into a steady drizzle. The musty smell of the turnips in their wet sacks became stronger, and Garion huddled miserably with his cloak pulled tightly around him. The adventure was growing much less exciting.

The road became muddy and slick, and the horses struggled their way up each hill and had to be rested often. On the first day they had covered eight leagues; after that they were lucky to make five.

Aunt Pol became waspish and short-tempered. "This is idiocy," she said to Mister Wolf about noon on the third day.

"Everything is idiocy if you choose to look at it in the proper light," he replied philosophically.

"Why wagoneers?" she demanded. "There are faster ways to travel—a wealthy family in a proper carriage, for instance, or Imperial messengers on good horses—either way would have put us in Darine by now."

"And left a trail in the memories of all these simple people we've passed so wide that even a Thull could follow it," Wolf explained patiently. "Brill has long since reported our departure to his employers. Every Murgo in Sendaria's looking for us by now."

"Why are we hiding from the Murgos, Mister Wolf?" Garion asked, hesitant to interrupt, but impelled by curiosity to try to penetrate the mystery behind their flight. "Aren't they just merchants—like the Tolnedrans and the Drasnians?"

"The Murgos have no real interest in trade," Wolf explained. "Nadraks are merchants, but the Murgos are warriors. The Murgos pose as merchants for the same reason that we pose as wagoneers—so that they can move about more or less undetected. If you simply assumed that all Murgos are spies, you wouldn't be too far from the truth."

"Haven't you anything better to do than ask all these questions?" Aunt Pol asked.

"Not really," Garion said, and then instantly knew that he'd made a mistake.

"Good," she said. "In the back of Barak's wagon you'll find the dirty dishes from this morning's meal. You'll also find a bucket. Fetch the bucket and run to that stream ahead for water, then return to Barak's wagon and wash the dishes."

"In cold water?" he objected.

"*Now,* Garion," she said firmly.

Grumbling, he climbed down off the slowly moving wagon.

In the late afternoon of the fourth day they came over a high hilltop and saw below the city of Darine and beyond the city the leaden gray sea. Garion caught his breath. To his eyes the city looked very large. Its surrounding walls were thick and high, and there were more buildings within those walls than he had seen in all his life. But it was to the sea that his eyes were drawn. There was a sharp tang to the air. Faint hints of that smell had been coming to him on the wind for the past league or so, but now, inhaling deeply, he breathed in that perfume of the sea for the first time in his life. His spirit soared.

"Finally," Aunt Pol said.

Silk had stopped the lead wagon and came walking back. His hood was pulled back slightly, and the rain ran down his long nose to drip from its pointed tip. "Do we stop here or go on down to the city?" he asked.

"We go to the city," Aunt Pol said. "I'm not going to sleep under a wagon when there are inns so close at hand."

"Honest wagoneers would seek out an inn," Mister Wolf agreed, "and a warm taproom."

"I might have guessed that," Aunt Pol said.

"We have to try to look the part." Wolf shrugged.

They went on down the hill, the horses' hooves slipping and sliding as they braced back against the weight of the wagons.

At the city gate two watchmen in stained tunics and wearing rust-spotted helmets came out of the tiny watch house just inside the gate.

"What's your business in Darine?" one of them asked Silk.

"I'm Ambar of Kotu," Silk lied pleasantly, "a poor Drasnian merchant hoping to do business in your splendid city."

"Splendid?" one of the watchmen snorted.

"What have you in your wagons, merchant?" the other inquired.

"Turnips," Silk said deprecatingly. "My family's been in the spice trade for generations, but I'm reduced to peddling turnips." He sighed. "The world is a topsy-turvy place, is it not, good friend?"

"We're obliged to inspect your wagons," the watchman said. "It'll take some time, I'm afraid."

"And a wet time at that," Silk said, squinting up into the rain. "It'd be much more pleasant to devote the time to wetting one's inside in some friendly tavern."

"That's difficult when one doesn't have much money," the watchman suggested hopefully.

"I'd be more than pleased if you'd accept some small token of friendship from me to aid you in your wetting," Silk offered.

"You're most kind," the watchman replied with a slight bow.

Some coins changed hands, and the wagons moved on into the city uninspected.

From the hilltop Darine had looked quite splendid, but Garion found it much less so as they clattered through the wet streets. The buildings all seemed the same with a kind of self-important aloofness about them, and the streets were littered and dirty. The salt tang of the sea was tainted here with the smell of dead fish, and the faces of the people hurrying along were grim and unfriendly. Garion's first excitement began to fade.

"Why are the people all so unhappy?" he asked Mister Wolf.

"They have a stern and demanding God," Wolf replied.

"Which God is that?" Garion asked.

"Money," Wolf said. "Money's a worse God than Torak himself."

"Don't fill the boy's head with nonsense," Aunt Pol said. "The people aren't really unhappy, Garion. They're just all in a hurry. They have important affairs to attend to and they're afraid they'll be late. That's all."

"I don't think I'd like to live here," Garion said. "It seems like a bleak, unfriendly kind of place." He sighed. "Sometimes I wish we were all back at Faldor's farm."

"There are worse places than Faldor's," Wolf agreed.

The inn Silk chose for them was near the docks, and the smell of the sea and the rank detritus of the meeting of sea and land was strong there. The inn, however, was a stout building with stables attached and storage sheds for the wagons. Like most inns, the main floor was given over to the kitchen and the large common room with its rows of tables and large fireplaces. The upper floors provided sleeping chambers for the guests.

"It's a suitable place," Silk announced as he came back out to the wagons after speaking at some length with the innkeeper. "The kitchen seems clean, and I didn't see any bugs when I inspected the sleeping chambers."

"I'll inspect it," Aunt Pol said, climbing down from the wagon.

"As you wish, great lady," Silk said with a polite bow.

Aunt Pol's inspection took much longer than Silk's, and it was nearly dark when she returned to the courtyard. "Adequate," she sniffed, "but only barely."

"It's not as if we planned to settle in for the winter, Pol," Wolf said. "At most we'll only be here a few days."

She ignored that. "I've ordered hot water sent up to our chambers," she announced. "I'll take the boy up and wash him while you and the others see to the wagons and horses. Come along, Garion." And she turned and went back into the inn.

Garion wished fervently that they would all stop referring to him as "the boy." He did, after all, he reflected, have a name, and it was not that difficult a name to remember. He was gloomily convinced that even if he lived to have a long gray beard, they would still speak of him as "the boy."

After the horses and wagons had been attended to and they had all washed up, they went down again to the common room and dined. The meal certainly didn't match up to Aunt Pol's, but it was a welcome change from turnips. Garion was absolutely certain that he'd never be able to look a turnip in the face again for the rest of his life.

After they had eaten, the men loitered over their ale pots, and Aunt

Pol's face registered her disapproval. "Garion and I are going up to bed now," she said to them. "Try not to fall down too many times when you come up."

Wolf, Barak and Silk laughed at that, but Durnik, Garion thought, looked a bit shamefaced.

The next day Mister Wolf and Silk left the inn early and were gone all day. Garion had positioned himself in a strategic place in hopes that he might be noticed and asked to go along, but he was not; so when Durnik went down to look after the horses, he accompanied him instead.

"Durnik," he said after they had fed and watered the animals and the smith was examining their hooves for cuts or stone bruises, "does all this seem strange to you?"

Durnik carefully lowered the leg of the patient horse he was checking. "All what, Garion?" he asked, his plain face sober.

"Everything," Garion said rather vaguely. "This journey, Barak and Silk, Mister Wolf and Aunt Pol—all of it. They all talk sometimes when they don't think I can hear them. This all seems terribly important, but I can't tell if we're running away from someone or looking for something."

"It's confusing to me as well, Garion," Durnik admitted. "Many things aren't what they seem—not what they seem at all."

"Does Aunt Pol seem different to you?" Garion asked. "What I mean is, they all treat her as if she were a noble-woman or something, and she acts differently too, now that we're away from Faldor's farm."

"Mistress Pol is a great lady," Durnik said. "I've always known that." His voice had that same respectful tone it always had when he spoke of her, and Garion knew that it was useless to try to make Durnik perceive anything unusual about her.

"And Mister Wolf," Garion said, trying another tack. "I always thought he was just an old storyteller."

"He doesn't seem to be an ordinary vagabond," Durnik admitted. "I think we've fallen in with important people, Garion, on important business. It's probably better for simple folk such as you and I not to ask too many questions, but to keep our eyes and ears open."

"Will you be going back to Faldor's farm when this is all over?" Garion asked carefully.

Durnik considered that, looking out across the rainswept courtyard of the inn. "No," he said finally in a soft voice. "I'll follow as long as Mistress Pol allows me to."

On an impulse Garion reached out and patted the smith's shoulder. "Everything's going to turn out for the best, Durnik."

Durnik sighed. "Let's hope so," he said and turned his attention back to the horses.

"Durnik," Garion asked, "did you know my parents?"

"No," Durnik said. "The first time I saw you, you were a baby in Mistress Pol's arms."

"What was she like then?"

"She seemed angry," Durnik said. "I don't think I've ever seen anyone quite so angry. She talked with Faldor for a while and then went to work in the kitchen—you know Faldor. He never turned anyone away in his whole life. At first she was just a helper, but that didn't last too long. Our old cook was getting fat and lazy, and she finally went off to live with her youngest daughter. After that, Mistress Pol ran the kitchen."

"She was a lot younger then, wasn't she?" Garion asked.

"No," Durnik said thoughtfully. "Mistress Pol never changes. She looks exactly the same now as she did that first day."

"I'm sure it only seems that way," Garion said. "Everybody gets older."

"Not Mistress Pol," Durnik said.

That evening Wolf and his sharp-nosed friend returned, their faces somber. "Nothing," Wolf announced shortly, scratching at his snowy beard.

"I might have told you that," Aunt Pol sniffed.

Wolf gave her an irritated look, then shrugged. "We had to be certain," he said.

The red-bearded giant, Barak, looked up from the mail shirt he was polishing. "No trace at all?" he asked.

"Not a hint," Wolf said. "He hasn't gone through here."

"Where now, then?" Barak asked, setting his mail shirt aside.

"Muros," Wolf said.

Barak rose and went to the window. "The rain's slacking," he said, "but the roads are going to be difficult."

"We won't be able to leave tomorrow anyway," Silk said, lounging on a stool near the door. "I have to dispose of our turnips. If we carry them out of Darine with us, it'll seem curious, and we don't want to be remembered by anyone who might have occasion to talk to any wandering Murgo."

"I suppose you're right," Wolf said. "I hate to lose the time, but there's no help for it."

"The roads'll be better after a day's drying," Silk pointed out, "and wagons travel faster empty."

"Are you sure you can sell them, friend Silk?" Durnik asked.

"I'm a Drasnian," Silk replied confidently. "I can sell anything. We might even make a good profit."

"Don't worry about that," Wolf said. "The turnips have served their purpose. All we need to do now is to get rid of them."

"It's a matter of principle," Silk said airily. "Besides, if I don't try to strike a hard bargain, that'd be remembered, too. Don't be concerned. The business won't take long and won't delay us."

"Could I go along with you, Silk?" Garion asked hopefully. "I haven't seen any part of Darine except for this inn."

Silk looked inquiringly at Aunt Pol.

She considered for a moment. "I don't suppose it'd do any harm," she said, "and it'll give me time to attend to some things."

The next morning after breakfast Silk and Garion set out with Garion carrying a bag of turnips. The small man seemed to be in extraordinarily good spirits, and his long, pointed nose seemed almost to quiver. "The whole point," he said as they walked along the littered, cobblestoned streets, "is not to appear too eager to sell—and to know the market, of course."

"That sounds reasonable," Garion said politely.

"Yesterday I made a few inquiries," Silk went on. "Turnips are selling on the docks of Kotu in Drasnia for a Drasnian silver link per hundredweight."

"A what?" Garion asked.

"It's a Drasnian coin," Silk explained, "about the same as a silver imperial—not quite, but close enough. The merchant will try to buy our turnips for no more than a quarter of that, but he'll go as high as half."

"How do you know that?"

"It's customary."

"How many turnips do we have?" Garion asked, stepping around a pile of refuse in the street.

"Thirty hundredweight," Silk said.

"That would be—" Garion's face contorted in an effort to make the complex calculation in his head.

"Fifteen imperials," Silk supplied. "Or three gold crowns."

"Gold?" Garion asked. Because gold coins were so rare in country dealings, the word seemed to have an almost magic quality.

Silk nodded. "It's always preferable," he said. "It's easier to carry. The weight of silver becomes burdensome."

"And how much did we pay for the turnips?"

"Five imperials," Silk said.

"The farmer gets five, we get fifteen, and the merchant gets thirty?" Garion asked incredulously. "That hardly seems fair."

Silk shrugged. "It's the way things are," he said. "There's the merchant's house." He pointed at a rather imposing building with broad steps. "When we go in, he'll pretend to be very busy and not at all interested in us. Later, while he and I are bargaining, he'll notice you and tell you what a splendid boy you are."

"Me?"

"He'll think that you're some relation of mine—a son or a nephew perhaps—and he'll think to gain advantage over me by flattering you."

"What a strange notion," Garion said.

"I'll tell him many things," Silk went on, talking very rapidly now. His eyes seemed to glitter, and his nose was actually twitching. "Pay no attention to what I say, and don't let any surprise show on your face. He'll be watching us both very closely."

"You're going to lie?" Garion was shocked.

"It's expected," Silk said. "He'll lie too. The one of us who lies the best will get the better of the bargain."

"It all seems terribly involved," Garion said.

"It's a game," Silk said, his ferretlike face breaking into a grin. "A very exciting game that's played all over the world. Good players get rich, and bad players don't."

"Are you a good player?" Garion asked.

"One of the best," Silk replied modestly. "Let's go in." And he led Garion up the broad steps to the merchant's house.

The merchant wore an unbelted, fur-trimmed gown of a pale green color and a close-fitting cap. He behaved much as Silk had predicted that he would, sitting before a plain table and leafing through many scraps of parchment with a busy frown on his face while Silk and Garion waited for him to notice them.

"Very well, then," he said finally. "You have business with me?"

"We have some turnips," Silk said somewhat deprecatingly.

"That's truly unfortunate, friend," the merchant said, assuming a long face. "The wharves at Kotu groan with turnips just now. It'd hardly pay me to take them off your hands at any price."

Silk shrugged. "Perhaps the Chereks or the Algars, then," he said. "Their markets may not yet be as glutted as yours." He turned. "Come along, boy," he said to Garion.

"A moment, good friend," the merchant said. "I detect from your speech that you and I are countrymen. Perhaps as a favor I'll look at your turnips."

"Your time's valuable," Silk said. "If you aren't in the market for turnips, why should we trouble you further?"

"I might still be able to find a buyer somewhere," the merchant protested, "if the merchandise is of good quality." He took the bag from Garion and opened it.

Garion listened with fascination as Silk and the merchant fenced politely with each other, each attempting to gain the advantage.

"What a splendid boy this is," the merchant said, suddenly seeming to notice Garion for the first time.

"An orphan," Silk said, "placed in my care. I'm attempting to teach him the rudiments of business, but he's slow to learn."

"Ah," the merchant said, sounding slightly disappointed.

Then Silk made a curious gesture with the fingers of his right hand.

The merchant's eyes widened slightly, then he too gestured.

After that, Garion had no idea of what was going on. The hands of Silk and the merchant wove intricate designs in the air, sometimes flickering so rapidly that the eye could scarce follow them. Silk's long, slender fingers seemed to dance, and the merchant's eyes were fixed upon them, his forehead breaking into a sweat at the intensity of his concentration.

"Done, then?" Silk said finally, breaking the long silence in the room.

"Done," the merchant agreed somewhat ruefully.

"It's always a pleasure doing business with an honest man," Silk said.

"I've learned much today," the merchant said. "I hope you don't intend to remain in this business for long, friend. If you do, I might just as well give you the keys to my warehouse and strongroom right now and save myself the anguish I'll experience every time you appear."

Silk laughed. "You've been a worthy opponent, friend merchant," he said.

"I thought so at first," the merchant said, shaking his head, "but I'm no match for you. Deliver your turnips to my warehouse on Bedik wharf tomorrow morning." He scratched a few lines on a piece of parchment with a quill. "My overseer will pay you."

Silk bowed and took the parchment. "Come along, boy," he said to Garion, and led the way from the room.

"What happened?" Garion asked when they were outside in the blustery street.

"We got the price I wanted," Silk said, somewhat smugly.

"But you didn't say anything," Garion objected.

"We spoke at great length, Garion," Silk said. "Weren't you watching?"

"All I saw was the two of you wiggling your fingers at each other."

"That's how we spoke," Silk explained. "It's a separate language my countrymen devised thousands of years ago. It's called the secret language, and it's much faster than the spoken one. It also permits us to speak in the presence of strangers without being overheard. An adept can conduct business while discussing the weather, if he chooses."

"Will you teach it to me?" Garion asked, fascinated.

"It takes a long time to learn," Silk told him.

"Isn't the trip to Muros likely to take a long time?" Garion suggested.

Silk shrugged. "As you wish," he said. "It won't be easy, but it'll help pass the time, I suppose."

"Are we going back to the inn now?" Garion asked.

"Not right away," Silk said. "We'll need a cargo to explain our entry into Muros."

"I thought we were going to leave with the wagons empty."

"We are."

"But you just said—"

"We'll see a merchant I know," Silk explained. "He buys farm goods all over Sendaria and has them held on the farms until the markets are right in Arendia and Tolnedra. Then he arranges to have them freighted either to Muros or Camaar."

"It sounds very complicated," Garion said doubtfully.

"It's not really," Silk assured him. "Come along, my boy, you'll see."

The merchant was a Tolnedran who wore a flowing blue robe and a disdainful expression on his face. He was talking with a grim-faced Murgo as Silk and Garion entered his counting room. The Murgo, like all of his race Garion had ever seen, had deep scars on his face, and his black eyes were penetrating.

Silk touched Garion's shoulder with a cautionary hand when they entered and saw the Murgo, then he stepped forward. "Forgive me, noble merchant," he said ingratiatingly. "I didn't know you were occupied. My porter and I'll wait outside until you have time for us."

"My friend and I'll be busy for most of the day," the Tolnedran said. "Is it something important?"

"I was just wondering if you might have a cargo for me," Silk replied.

"No," the Tolnedran said shortly. "Nothing." He started to turn back to the Murgo, then stopped and looked sharply at Silk. "Aren't you Ambar of Kotu?" he asked. "I thought you dealt in spices."

Garion recognized the name Silk had given the watchmen at the gates of the city. It was evident that the little man had used the name before.

"Alas," Silk sighed. "My last venture lies at the bottom of the sea just off the hook of Arendia—two full shiploads bound for Tol Honeth. A sudden storm and I'm a pauper."

"A tragic tale, worthy Ambar," the Tolnedran master merchant said, somewhat smugly.

"I'm now reduced to freighting produce," Silk said morosely. "I have three rickety wagons, and that's all that's left of the empire of Ambar of Kotu."

"Reverses come to us all," the Tolnedran said philosophically.

"So this is the famous Ambar of Kotu," the Murgo said, his harshly accented voice quite soft. He looked Silk up and down, his black eyes probing. "It was a fortunate chance that brought me out today. I am enriched by meeting so illustrious a man."

Silk bowed politely. "You're too kind, noble sir," he said.

"I am Asharak of Rak Goska," the Murgo introduced himself. He turned to the Tolnedran. "We can put aside our discussion for a bit, Mingan," he said. "We'll accrue much honor by assisting so great a merchant to begin recouping his losses."

"You're too kind, worthy Asharak," Silk said, bowing again.

Garion's mind was shrieking all kinds of warnings, but the Murgo's sharp eyes made it impossible for him to make the slightest gesture to Silk. He kept his face impassive and his eyes dull even as his thoughts raced.

"I'd gladly help you, my friend," Mingan said, "but I have no cargo in Darine at the moment."

"I'm already committed from Darine to Medalia," Silk said quickly. "Three wagonloads of Cherek iron. And I also have a contract to move furs from Muros to Camaar. It's the fifty leagues from Medalia to Muros that concerns me. Wagons traveling empty earn no profit."

"Medalia." Mingan frowned. "Let me examine my records. It seems to me that I do have something there." He stepped out of the room.

"Your exploits are legendary in the kingdoms of the east, Ambar," Asharak of Rak Goska said admiringly. "When last I left Cthol Murgos there was still a kingly price on your head."

Silk laughed easily. "A minor misunderstanding, Asharak," he said. "I was merely investigating the extent of Tolnedran intelligence gathering activities in your kingdom. I took some chances I probably shouldn't have, and the Tolnedrans found out what I was up to. The charges they leveled at me were fabrications."

"How did you manage to escape?" Asharak asked. "The soldiers of King Taur Urgas nearly dismantled the kingdom searching for you."

"I chanced to meet a Thullish lady of high station," Silk said. "I managed to prevail upon her to smuggle me across the border into Mishrak ac Thull."

"Ah," Asharak said, smiling briefly. "Thullish ladies are notoriously easy to prevail upon."

"But most demanding," Silk said. "They expect full repayment for any favors. I found it more difficult to escape from her than I did from Cthol Murgos."

"Do you still perform such services for your government?" Asharak asked casually.

"They won't even talk to me," Silk said with a gloomy expression. "Ambar the spice merchant is useful to them, but Ambar the poor wagoneer is quite another thing."

"Of course," Asharak said, and his tone indicated that he obviously did not believe what he had been told. He glanced briefly and without seeming interest at Garion, and Garion felt a strange shock of recognition. Without knowing exactly how it was that he knew, he was instantly sure that Asharak of Rak Goska had known him for all of his life. There was a familiarity in that glance, a familiarity that had grown out of the dozen times or more that their eyes had met while Garion was growing up and Asharak, muffled always in a black cloak and astride a black horse, had stopped and watched and then moved on. Garion returned the gaze without expression, and the faintest hint of a smile flickered across Asharak's scarred face.

Mingan returned to the room then. "I have some hams on a farm near Medalia," he announced. "When do you expect to arrive in Muros?"

"Fifteen or twenty days," Silk told him.

Mingan nodded. "I'll give you a contract to move my hams to Muros," he offered. "Seven silver nobles per wagonload."

"Tolnedran nobles or Sendarian?" Silk asked quickly.

"This is Sendaria, worthy Ambar."

"We're citizens of the world, noble merchant," Silk pointed out. "Transactions between us have always been in Tolnedran coin."

Mingan sighed. "You were ever quick, worthy Ambar," he said. "Very well, Tolnedran nobles—because we're old friends, and I grieve for your misfortunes."

"Perhaps we'll meet again, Ambar," Asharak said.

"Perhaps," Silk said, and he and Garion left the counting room.

"Skinflint," Silk muttered when they reached the street. "The rate should have been *ten*, not seven."

"What about the Murgo?" Garion asked. Once again there was the familiar reluctance to reveal too much about the strange, unspoken link that had existed between him and the figure that now at least had a name.

Silk shrugged. "He knows I'm up to something, but he doesn't know exactly what—just as I know that he's up to something. I've had dozens of meetings like that. Unless our purposes happen to collide, we won't interfere with each other. Asharak and I are both professionals."

"You're a very strange person, Silk," Garion said.

Silk winked at him.

"Why were you and Mingan arguing about the coins?" Garion asked.

"Tolnedran coins are a bit purer," Silk told him. "They're worth more."

"I see," Garion said.

The next morning they all mounted the wagons again and delivered their turnips to the warehouse of the Drasnian merchant. Then, their wagons rumbling emptily, they rolled out of Darine, bound toward the south.

The rain had ceased, but the morning was overcast and blustery. On the hill outside town Silk turned to Garion, who rode beside him. "Very well," he said, "let's begin." He moved his fingers in front of Garion's face. "This means 'Good morning.'"

CHAPTER EIGHT

After the first day the wind blew itself out, and the pale autumn sun reappeared. Their route southward led them along the Darine River, a turbulent stream that rushed down from the mountains on its way to the Gulf of Cherek. The country was hilly and timbered but, since the wagons were empty, their horses made good time.

Garion paid scant attention to the scenery as they trundled up the valley of the Darine. His attention was riveted almost totally on Silk's flickering fingers.

"Don't shout," Silk instructed as Garion practiced.

"Shout?" Garion asked, puzzled.

"Keep your gestures small. Don't exaggerate them. The idea is to make the whole business inconspicuous."

"I'm only practicing," Garion said.

"Better to break bad habits before they become too strong," Silk said. "And be careful not to mumble."

"Mumble?"

"Form each phrase precisely. Finish one before you go on to the next. Don't worry about speed. That comes with time."

By the third day their conversations were half in words and half in gestures, and Garion was beginning to feel quite proud of himself. They pulled off the road into a grove of tall cedars that evening and formed up their usual half-circle with the wagons.

"How goes the instruction?" Mister Wolf asked as he climbed down.

"It progresses," Silk said. "I expect it'll go more rapidly when the boy outgrows his tendency to use baby talk."

Garion was crushed.

Barak, who was also dismounting, laughed. "I've often thought that the secret language might be useful to know," he said, "but fingers built to grip a sword aren't nimble enough for it." He held out his huge hand and shook his head.

Durnik lifted his face and sniffed at the air. "It's going to be cold tonight," he said. "We'll have frost before morning."

Barak also sniffed, and then he nodded. "You're right, Durnik," he rumbled. "We'll need a good fire tonight." He reached into the wagon and lifted out his axe.

"There are riders coming," Aunt Pol announced, still seated on the wagon.

They all stopped talking and listened to the faint drumming sound on the road they had just left.

"Three at least," Barak said grimly. He handed the axe to Durnik and reached back into the wagon for his sword.

"Four," Silk said. He stepped to his own wagon and took his own sword out from under the seat.

"We're far enough from the road," Wolf said. "If we stay still, they'll pass without seeing us."

"That won't hide us from Grolims," Aunt Pol said. "They won't be searching with their eyes." She made two quick gestures to Wolf which Garion did not recognize.

No, Wolf gestured back. Let us instead— He also made an unrecognizable gesture.

Aunt Pol looked at him for a moment and then nodded.

"All of you stay quite still," Wolf instructed them. Then he turned toward the road, his face intent.

Garion held his breath. The sound of the galloping horses grew nearer.

Then a strange thing happened. Though Garion knew he should be fearful of the approaching riders and the threat they seemed to pose, a kind of dreamy lassitude fell over him. It was as if his mind had quite suddenly gone to sleep, leaving his body still standing there watching incuriously the passage of those dark-mantled horsemen along the road.

How long he stood so he was not able to say; but when he roused from his half-dream, the riders were gone and the sun had set. The sky to the east had grown purple with approaching evening, and there were tatters of sun-stained clouds along the western horizon.

"Murgos," Aunt Pol said quite calmly, "and one Grolim." She started to climb down from the wagon.

"There are many Murgos in Sendaria, great lady," Silk said, helping her down, "and on many different missions."

"Murgos are one thing," Wolf said grimly, "but Grolims are quite something else. I think it might be better if we moved off the well-traveled roads. Do you know a back way to Medalia?"

"Old friend," Silk replied modestly, "I know a back way to every place."

"Good," Wolf said. "Let's move deeper into these woods. I'd prefer it if no chance gleam from our fire reached the road."

Garion had seen the cloaked Murgos only briefly. There was no way to be sure if one of them had been that same Asharak he had finally met after all the years of knowing him only as a dark figure on a black horse, but somehow he was almost certain that Asharak had been among them. Asharak would follow him, would be there wherever he went. It was the kind of thing one could count on.

Durnik had been right when he had spoken of frost. The ground was white with it the next morning, and the horses' breath steamed in the chill air as they set out. They moved along lanes and little-used tracks that were partially weed-choked. The going was slower than it might have been on the main road, but they all felt much safer.

It took them five more days to reach the village of Winold, some twelve leagues to the north of Medalia. There, at Aunt Pol's insistence, they stopped overnight at a somewhat run-down inn. "I refuse to sleep on the ground again," she announced flatly.

After they had eaten in the dingy common room of the inn, the men turned to their ale pots, and Aunt Pol went up to her chamber with instructions that hot water be brought to her for bathing. Garion, however, made some pretext about checking the horses and went outside. It was not that he was in the habit of being deliberately deceptive, but it had occurred to him in the last day or so that he had not had a single moment alone since they had left Faldor's farm. He was not by nature a solitary boy, but he had begun to feel quite keenly the restriction of always being in the presence of his elders.

The village of Winold was not a large one, and he explored it from one end to the other in less than half an hour, loitering along its narrow, cobblestoned streets in the crispness of the early evening air. The windows of the houses glowed with golden candlelight, and Garion suddenly felt a great surge of homesickness.

Then, at the next corner of the crooked street, in the brief light from an opening door, he saw a familiar figure. He could not be positive, but he shrank back against a rough stone wall anyway.

The man at the corner turned in irritation toward the light, and Garion caught the sudden white gleam from one of his eyes. It was Brill. The unkempt man moved quickly out of the light, obviously not wishing to be seen, then he stopped.

Garion hugged the wall, watching Brill's impatient pacing at the corner. The wisest thing would have been to slip away and hurry back to the inn, but Garion quickly dismissed that idea. He was safe enough here in the deep shadow beside the wall, and he was too caught up by curiosity to leave without seeing exactly what Brill was doing here.

After what seemed hours, but was really only a few more minutes, another shadowy shape came scurrying down the street. The man was hooded, so it was impossible to see his face, but the outline of his form revealed a figure dressed in the tunic, hose and calf-length boots of an ordinary Sendar. There was also, when he turned, the outline of a sword belted at his waist, and that was far from ordinary. While it was not precisely illegal for Sendars of the lower classes to bear arms, it was uncommon enough to attract notice.

Garion tried to edge close enough to hear what Brill said to the man with the sword, but they spoke only briefly. There was a clink as some coins changed hands, and then the two separated. Brill moved quietly off around the corner, and the man with the sword walked up the narrow, crooked street toward the spot where Garion stood.

There was no place to hide, and as soon as the hooded man came close enough, he would be able to see Garion. To turn and run would be even more dangerous. Since there was no alternative, Garion put on a bold front and marched determinedly toward the oncoming figure.

"Who's there?" the hooded man demanded, his hand going to his sword-hilt.

"Good evening, sir," Garion said, deliberately forcing his voice up into the squeaky registers of a much younger boy. "Cold night, isn't it?"

The hooded man grunted and seemed to relax.

Garion's legs quivered with the desire to run. He passed the man with the sword, and his back prickled as he felt that suspicious gaze follow him.

"Boy," the man said abruptly.

Garion stopped. "Yes, sir?" he said, turning.

"Do you live here?"

"Yes, sir," Garion lied, trying to keep his voice from trembling.

"Is there a tavern hereabouts?"

Garion had just explored the town, and he spoke confidently. "Yes, sir," he said. "You go on up this street to the next corner and turn to your left. There are torches out front. You can't miss it."

"My thanks," the hooded man said shortly, and walked on up the narrow street.

"Good night, sir," Garion called after him, made bold by the fact that the danger seemed past.

The man did not answer, and Garion marched on down to the corner, exhilarated by his brief encounter. Once he was around the corner, however, he dropped the guise of a simple village boy and ran.

He was breathless by the time he reached the inn and burst into the smoky common room where Mister Wolf and the others sat talking by the fire.

At the last instant, realizing that to blurt out his news in the common room where others might overhear would be a mistake, he forced himself to walk calmly to where his friends sat. He stood before the fire as if warming himself and spoke in a low tone. "I just saw Brill in the village," he said.

"Brill?" Silk asked. "Who's Brill?"

Wolf frowned. "A farmhand with too much Angarak gold in his purse to be entirely honest," he said. Quickly he told Silk and Barak about the adventure in Faldor's stable.

"You should have killed him," Barak rumbled.

"This isn't Cherek," Wolf said. "Sendars are touchy about casual killings." He turned to Garion. "Did he see you?" he asked.

"No," Garion said. "I saw him first and hid in the dark. He met another man and gave him some money, I think. The other man had a sword." Briefly he described the whole incident.

"This changes things," Wolf said. "I think we'll leave earlier in the morning than we'd planned."

"It wouldn't be hard to make Brill lose interest in us," Durnik said. "I could probably find him and hit him on the head a few times."

"Tempting." Wolf grinned. "But I think it might be better just to slip out of town early tomorrow and leave him with no notion that we've ever been here. We don't really have time to start fighting with everyone we run across."

"I'd like a closer look at this sword-carrying Sendar, however," Silk said, rising. "If it turns out that he's following us, I'd rather know what he looks like. I don't like being followed by strangers."

"Discreetly," Wolf cautioned.

Silk laughed. "Have you ever known me to be otherwise?" he asked. "This won't take long. Where did you say that tavern was, Garion?"

Garion gave him directions.

Silk nodded, his eyes bright and his long nose twitching. He turned, went quickly across the smoky common room and out into the chill night.

"I wonder," Barak considered. "If we're being followed this closely, wouldn't it be better to discard the wagons and this tiresome disguise, buy good horses and simply make straight for Muros at a gallop?"

Wolf shook his head. "I don't think the Murgos are all that certain where we are," he said. "Brill could be here for some other dishonesty, and we'd be foolish to start running from shadows. Better just to move on quietly. Even if Brill's still working for the Murgos, I'd rather just slip away and leave them all beating the bushes here in central Sendaria." He stood up. "I'm going to step upstairs and let Pol know what's happened." He crossed the common room and mounted the stairs.

"I still don't like it," Barak muttered, his face dark.

They sat quietly then, waiting for Silk's return. The fire popped, and Garion started slightly. It occurred to him as he waited that he had changed a great deal since they'd left Faldor's farm. Everything had seemed simple then with the world neatly divided into friends and enemies. In the short time since they'd left, however, he'd begun to perceive complexities that he hadn't imagined before. He'd grown wary and distrustful and listened more frequently to that interior voice that always advised caution if not outright guile. He'd also learned not to accept anything at face value. Briefly he regretted the loss of his former innocence, but the dry voice told him that such regret was childish.

Then Mister Wolf came back down the stairs and rejoined them.

After about a half hour Silk returned. "Thoroughly disreputable-looking fellow," he said, standing in front of the fire. "My guess is that he's a common footpad."

"Brill's seeking his natural level," Wolf observed. "If he's still working for the Murgos, he's probably hiring ruffians to watch for us. They'll be looking for four people on foot, however, rather than six in wagons. If we can get out of Winold early enough in the morning, I think we can elude them altogether."

"I think Durnik and I should stand watch tonight," Barak said.

"Not a bad idea," Wolf agreed. "Let's plan to leave about the fourth hour after midnight. I'd like to have two or three leagues of back roads between us and this place when the sun comes up."

Garion scarcely slept that night; when he did, there were nightmares about a hooded man with a cruel sword chasing him endlessly down dark, narrow streets. When Barak woke them, Garion's eyes felt sandy, and his head was thick from the exhausting night.

Aunt Pol carefully drew the shutters in their chamber before lighting a single candle. "It's going to be colder now," she said, opening the large bundle she'd had him carry up from the wagons. She took out a pair of heavy woolen hose and winter boots lined with lambswool. "Put these on," she instructed Garion, "and your heavy cloak."

"I'm not a baby anymore, Aunt Pol," Garion said.

"Do you enjoy being cold?"

"Well, no, but—" He stopped, unable to think of any words to explain how he felt. He began to dress. He could hear the faint murmur of the others talking softly in the adjoining chamber in that curious, hushed tone that men always assume when they rise before the sun.

"We're ready, Mistress Pol," Silk's voice came through the doorway.

"Let's leave, then," she said, drawing up the hood of her cloak.

The moon had risen late that night and shone brightly on the frost-silvered stones outside the inn. Durnik had hitched the horses to the wagons and had led them out of the stable.

"We'll lead the horses out to the road," Wolf said very quietly. "I don't see any need for rousing the villagers as we pass."

Silk again took the lead, and they moved slowly out of the innyard.

The fields beyond the village were white with frost, and the pale, smoky-looking moonlight seemed to have leeched all color from them.

"As soon as we're well out of earshot," Wolf said, climbing up into his wagon, "let's put some significant distance between us and this place. The wagons are empty, and a little run won't hurt the horses."

"Truly," Silk agreed.

They all mounted their wagons and set off at a walk. The stars glittered overhead in the crisp, cold sky. The fields were very white in the moonlight, and the clumps of trees back from the road very dark.

Just as they went over the first hilltop, Garion looked back at the dark cluster of houses in the valley behind. A single flicker of light came from a window somewhere, a lone, golden pinpoint that appeared and then vanished.

"Someone's awake back there," he told Silk. "I just saw a light."

"Some early riser perhaps," Silk suggested. "But then again, perhaps not." He shook the reins slightly, and the horses increased their pace. He shook them again, and they began to trot.

"Hang on, boy," he instructed, reached forward and slapped the reins down smartly on the rumps of the horses.

The wagon bounced and clattered fearfully behind the running team, and the bitterly chill air rushed at Garion's face as he clung to the wagon seat.

At full gallop the three wagons plunged down into the next valley, rushing between the frost-white fields in the bright moonlight, leaving the village and its single light far behind.

By the time the sun rose, they had covered a good four leagues, and Silk reined in his steaming horses. Garion felt battered and sore from the wild ride over the iron-hard roads and was glad for the chance to rest. Silk handed him the reins and jumped down from the wagon. He walked back and spoke briefly to Mister Wolf and Aunt Pol, then returned to the wagon.

"We turn off at that lane just ahead," he told Garion as he massaged his fingers.

Garion offered him the reins.

"You drive," Silk told him. "My hands are frozen stiff. Just let the horses walk."

Garion clucked at the horses and shook the reins slightly. Obediently, the team started out again.

"The lane circles around to the back of that hill," Silk said, pointing with his chin since his hands were tucked inside his tunic. "On the far side there's a copse of fir trees. We'll stop there to rest the horses."

"Do you think we're being followed?" Garion asked.

"This'll be a good time to find out," Silk said.

They rounded the hill and drove on down to where the dark firs bordered the road. Then Garion turned the horses and moved in under the shadowy trees.

"This'll do fine," Silk said, getting down. "Come along."

"Where are we going?"

"I want to have a look at that road behind us," Silk said. "We'll go up through the trees to the top of the hill and see if our back trail has attracted any interest." And he started up the hill, moving quite rapidly but making absolutely no sound as he went. Garion floundered along behind him, his feet cracking the dead twigs underfoot embarrassingly until he began to catch the secret of it. Silk nodded approvingly once, but said nothing.

The trees ended just at the crest of the hill, and Silk stopped there. The valley below with the dark road passing through it was empty except for two deer who had come out of the woods on the far side to graze in the frosty grass.

"We'll wait awhile," Silk said. "If Brill and his hireling are following, they shouldn't be far behind." He sat on a stump and watched the empty valley.

After a while, a cart moved slowly along the road toward Winold. It looked tiny in the distance, and its pace along the scar of the road seemed very slow.

The sun rose a bit higher, and they squinted into its full morning brightness.

"Silk," Garion said finally in a hesitant tone.

"Yes, Garion?"

"What's this all about?" It was a bold question to ask, but Garion felt he knew Silk well enough to ask it.

"All what?"

"What we're doing. I've heard a few things and guessed a few more, but it doesn't really make any sense to me."

"And just what have you guessed, Garion?" Silk asked, his small eyes very bright in his unshaven face.

"Something's been stolen—something very important—and Mister Wolf and Aunt Pol—and the rest of us—are trying to get it back."

"All right," Silk said. "That much is true."

"Mister Wolf and Aunt Pol are not at all what they seem to be," Garion went on.

"No," Silk agreed, "they aren't."

"I think they can do things that other people can't do," Garion said, struggling with the words. "Mister Wolf can follow this thing—whatever it is—without seeing it. And last week in those woods when the Murgos passed, they did something—I don't even know how to describe it, but it was almost as if they reached out and put my mind to sleep. How did they do that? And why?"

Silk chuckled. "You're a very observant lad," he said. Then his tone became more serious. "We're living in momentous times, Garion. The events of a thousand years and more have all focused on these very days. The world, I'm told, is like that. Centuries pass when nothing happens, and then in a few short years events of such tremendous importance take place that the world is never the same again."

"I think that if I had my choice, I'd prefer one of those quiet centuries," Garion said glumly.

"Oh, no," Silk said, his lips drawing back in a ferretlike grin. "Now's the time to be alive—to see it all happen, to be a part of it. That makes the blood race, and each breath is an adventure."

Garion let that pass. "What is this thing we're following?" he asked.

"It's best if you don't even know its name," Silk told him seriously, "or the name of the one who stole it. There are people trying to stop us; and what you don't know, you can't reveal."

"I'm not in the habit of talking to Murgos," Garion said stiffly.

"It's not necessary to talk to them," Silk said. "There are some among them who can reach out and pick the thoughts right out of your mind."

"That isn't possible," Garion said.

"Who's to say what's possible and what isn't?" Silk asked. And Garion remembered a conversation he had once had with Mister Wolf about the possible and the impossible.

Silk sat on the stump in the newly risen sun looking thoughtfully down into the still-shadowy valley, an ordinary-looking little man in ordinary-looking tunic and hose and a rough brown shoulder cape with its hood turned up over his head. "You were raised as a Sendar, Garion," he said, "and Sendars are solid, practical men with little patience for such things as sorcery and magic and other things that can't be seen or touched. Your friend, Durnik, is a perfect Sendar. He can mend a shoe or fix a broken wheel or dose a sick horse, but I doubt that he could bring himself to believe in the tiniest bit of magic."

"I *am* a Sendar," Garion objected. The hint implicit in Silk's observation struck at the very center of his sense of his own identity.

Silk turned and looked at him closely. "No," he said, "you aren't. I know a Sendar when I see one—just as I can recognize the difference between an Arend and a Tolnedran or a Cherek and an Algar. There's a certain set of the head, a certain look about the eyes of Sendars that you don't have. You're not a Sendar."

"What am I, then?" Garion challenged.

"I don't know," Silk said with a puzzled frown, "and that's very unusual, since I've been trained to know what people are. It may come to me in time, though."

"Is Aunt Pol a Sendar?" Garion asked.

"Of course not." Silk laughed.

"That explains it, then," Garion said. "I'm probably the same thing she is."

Silk looked sharply at him.

"She's my father's sister, after all," Garion said. "At first I thought it was my mother she was related to, but that was wrong. It was my father; I know that now."

"That's impossible," Silk said flatly.

"Impossible?"

"Absolutely out of the question. The whole notion's unthinkable."

"Why?"

Silk chewed at his lower lip for a moment. "Let's go back to the wagons," he said shortly.

They turned and went down through the dark trees with the bright morning sunlight slanting on their backs in the frosty air.

They rode the back lanes for the rest of the day. Late in the afternoon when the sun had begun to drop into a purple bank of clouds toward the west, they arrived at the farm where they were to pick up Mingan's hams. Silk spoke with the stout farmer and showed him the piece of parchment Mingan had given them in Darine.

"I'll be glad to get rid of them," the farmer said. "They've been occupying storage space I sorely need."

"That's frequently the case when one has dealings with Tolnedrans," Silk observed. "They're gifted at getting a bit more than they pay for—even if it's only the free use of someone else's storage sheds."

The farmer glumly agreed.

"I wonder," Silk said as if the thought had just occurred to him, "I won-der if you might have seen a friend of mine—Brill by name? A medium-sized man with black hair and beard and a cast to one eye?"

"Patched clothes and a sour disposition?" the stout farmer asked.

"That's him," Silk said.

"He's been about the area," the farmer said, "looking—or so he said—for an old man and a woman and a boy. He said that they stole some things from his master and that he'd been sent to find them."

"How long ago was that?" Silk asked.

"A week or so," the farmer said.

"I'm sorry to have missed him," Silk said. "I wish I had the leisure to look him up."

"I can't for my life think why," the farmer said bluntly. "To be honest with you, I didn't much care for your friend."

"I'm not overfond of him myself," Silk agreed, "but the truth is that he owes me some money. I could quite easily do without Brill's companionship, but I'm lonesome for the money, if you take my meaning."

The farmer laughed.

"I'd take it as a kindness if you happened to forget that I asked after him," Silk said. "He'll likely be hard enough to find even if he isn't warned that I'm looking for him."

"You can depend on my discretion," the stout man said, still laughing. "I have a loft where you and your wagoneers can put up for the night, and I'd take it kindly if you'd sup with my workers in the dining hall over there."

"My thanks," Silk said, bowing slightly. "The ground's cold, and it's been some time since we've eaten anything but the rough fare of the road."

"You wagoneers lead adventuresome lives," the stout man said almost en-viously. "Free as birds with always a new horizon just beyond the next hilltop."

"It's much overrated," Silk told him, "and winter's a thin time for birds and wagoneers both."

The farmer laughed again, clapped Silk on the shoulder and then showed him where to put up the horses.

The food in the stout farmer's dining hall was plain, but there was plenty; and the loft was a bit drafty, but the hay was soft. Garion slept soundly. The farm was not Faldor's, but it was familiar enough, and there was that comforting sense of having walls about him again that made him feel secure.

The following morning, after a solid breakfast, they loaded the wagons with the Tolnedran's salt-crusted hams and bade the farmer a friendly good-bye.

The clouds that had begun to bank up in the west the evening before

had covered the sky during the night, and it was cold and gray as they set
out for Muros, fifty leagues to the south.

CHAPTER NINE

The almost two weeks it took them to reach Muros were the most
uncomfortable Garion had ever spent. Their route skirted the edge
of the foothills through rolling and sparsely settled country, and the sky hung
gray and cold overhead. There were occasional spits of snow, and the mountains loomed black against the skyline to the east.

It seemed to Garion that he would never be warm again. Despite
Durnik's best efforts to find dry firewood each night, their fires always seemed
pitifully small, and the great cold around them enormously large. The ground
upon which they slept was always frozen, and the chill seemed actually to
seep in Garion's bones.

His education in the Drasnian secret language continued and he became,
if not adept, at least competent by the time they passed Lake Camaar and began the long, downhill grade that led to Muros.

The city of Muros in south-central Sendaria was a sprawling, unattractive place that had been since time immemorial the site of a great annual
fair. Each year in late summer, Algar horsemen drove vast cattle herds
through the mountains along the Great North Road to Muros where cattle
buyers from all over the west gathered to await their coming. Huge sums
changed hands, and, because the Algar clansmen also commonly made their
yearly purchases of useful and ornamental articles at that time, merchants
from as far away as Nyissa in the remote south gathered to offer their wares.
A large plain which lay to the east of the city was given over entirely to the
cattle pens that stretched for miles but were still inadequate to contain the
herds which arrived at the height of the season. Beyond the pens to the east
lay the more or less permanent encampment of the Algars.

It was to this city one midmorning at the tag end of the fair, when the
cattle pens were nearly empty and most of the Algars had departed and only
the most desperate merchants remained, that Silk led the three wagons laden
with the hams of Mingan the Tolnedran.

The delivery of the hams took place without incident, and the wagons
soon drew into an innyard near the northern outskirts of the city.

"This is a respectable inn, great lady," Silk assured Aunt Pol as he helped
her down from the wagon. "I've stopped here before."

"Let's hope so," she said. "The inns of Muros have an unsavory
reputation."

"Those particular inns lie along the eastern edge of town," Silk assured her delicately. "I know them well."

"I'm certain you do," she said with an arched eyebrow.

"My profession sometimes requires me to seek out places I might otherwise prefer to avoid," he said blandly.

The inn, Garion noted, was surprisingly clean, and its guests seemed for the most part to be Sendarian merchants. "I thought there'd be many different kinds of people here in Muros," he said as he and Silk carried their bundles up to the chambers on the second floor.

"There are," Silk said, "but each group tends to remain aloof from the others. The Tolnedrans gather in one part of town, the Drasnians in another, the Nyissans in yet another. The Earl of Muros prefers it that way. Tempers sometimes flare in the heat of the day's business, and it's best not to have natural enemies housed under the same roof."

Garion nodded. "You know," he said as they entered the chambers they had taken for their stay in Muros, "I don't think I've ever seen a Nyissan."

"You're lucky," Silk said with distaste. "They're an unpleasant race."

"Are they like Murgos?"

"No," Silk said. "The Nyissans worship Issa, the Snake-God, and it's considered seemly among them to adopt the mannerisms of the serpent. I don't find it at all attractive myself. Besides, the Nyissans murdered the Rivan King, and all Alorns have disliked them since then."

"The Rivans don't have a king," Garion objected.

"Not anymore," Silk said. "They did once, though—until Queen Salmissra decided to have him murdered."

"When was that?" Garion asked, fascinated.

"Thirteen hundred years ago," Silk said, as if it had only been yesterday.

"Isn't that sort of a long time to hold a grudge?" Garion asked.

"Some things are unforgivable," Silk said shortly.

Since there was still a good part of the day left, Silk and Wolf left the inn that afternoon to search the streets of Muros for those strange, lingering traces that Wolf could apparently see or feel and which would tell him whether the object they sought had passed this way. Garion sat near the fire in the chamber he shared with Aunt Pol, trying to bake the chill out of his feet. Aunt Pol also sat by the fire, mending one of his tunics, her shining needle flickering in and out of the fabric.

"Who was the Rivan King, Aunt Pol?" he asked her.

She stopped sewing. "Why do you ask?" she said.

"Silk was telling me about Nyissans," he said. "He told me that their queen murdered the Rivan King. Why would she do that?"

"You're full of questions today, aren't you?" she asked, her needle moving again.

"Silk and I talk about a lot of things as we ride along," Garion said, pushing his feet even closer to the fire.

"Don't burn your shoes," she told him.

"Silk says that I'm not a Sendar," Garion said. "He says that he doesn't know what I am, but that I'm not a Sendar."

"Silk talks too much," Aunt Pol observed.

"You never tell me anything, Aunt Pol," he said in irritation.

"I tell you everything you need to know," she said calmly. "Right now it's not necessary for you to know anything about Rivan kings or Nyissan queens."

"All you want to do is keep me an ignorant child," Garion said petulantly. "I'm almost a man, and I don't even know what I am—or who."

"I know who you are," she said, not looking up.

"Who am I, then?"

"You're a young man who's about to catch his shoes on fire," she said. He jerked his feet back quickly. "You didn't answer me," he accused.

"That's right," she said in that infuriatingly calm voice.

"Why not?"

"It's not necessary for you to know yet. When it's time, I'll tell you, but not until."

"That's not fair," he objected.

"The world's full of injustice," she said. "Now, since you're feeling so manly, why don't you fetch some more firewood? That'll give you something useful to think about."

He glared at her and stamped across the room.

"Garion," she said.

"What?"

"Don't even *think* about slamming the door."

That evening when Wolf and Silk returned, the usually cheerful old man seemed impatient and irritable. He sat down at the table in the common room of the inn and stared moodily at the fire. "I don't think it passed this way," he said finally. "There are a few places left to try, but I'm almost certain that it hasn't been here."

"Then we go on to Camaar?" Barak rumbled, his thick fingers combing his bristling beard.

"We must," Wolf said. "Most likely we should have gone there first."

"There was no way to know," Aunt Pol told him. "Why would he go to Camaar if he's trying to carry it to the Angarak kingdoms?"

"I can't even be certain where he's going," Wolf said irritably. "Maybe he wants to keep the thing for himself. He's always coveted it." He stared into the fire again.

"We're going to need some kind of freight for the trip to Camaar," Silk said.

Wolf shook his head. "It slows us too much," he said. "It's not unusual for wagons to return to Camaar from Muros without freight, and it's reaching the point where we'll have to gamble our disguise for the sake of speed. It's forty leagues to Camaar, and the weather's turning bad. A heavy snowstorm could stop the wagons entirely, and I don't have time to spend the whole winter mired down in a snowbank."

Durnik dropped his knife suddenly and started to scramble to his feet. "What's amiss?" Barak asked quickly.

"I just saw Brill," Durnik said. "He was in that doorway."

"Are you sure?" Wolf demanded.

"I know him," Durnik said grimly. "It was Brill, all right."

Silk pounded his fist down on the table. "Idiot!" he accused himself. "I underestimated the man."

"That doesn't matter now," Mister Wolf said, and there was almost a kind of relief in his voice. "Our disguise is useless now. I think it's time for speed."

"I'll see to the wagons," Durnik said.

"No," Wolf said. "The wagons are too slow. We'll go to the camp of the Algars and buy good horses." He stood up quickly.

"What of the wagons?" Durnik persisted.

"Forget them," Wolf said. "They're only a hindrance now. We'll ride the wagon horses to the camp of the Algars and take only what we can conveniently carry. Let's get ready to leave immediately. Meet me in the innyard as soon as you can." He went quickly to the door and out into the cold night.

It was only a few minutes later that they all met near the door to the stable in the cobblestoned innyard, each carrying a small bundle. Hulking Barak jingled as he walked, and Garion could smell the oiled steel of his mail shirt. A few flakes of snow drifted down through the frosty air and settled like tiny feathers to the frozen ground.

Durnik was the last to join them. He came breathlessly out of the inn and pressed a small handful of coins upon Mister Wolf. "It was the best I could do," he apologized. "It's scarce half the worth of the wagons, but the innkeeper sensed my haste and bargained meanly." He shrugged then. "At least we're rid of them," he said. "It's not good to leave things of value behind. They nag at the mind and distract one from the business at hand."

Silk laughed. "Durnik," he said, "you're the absolute soul of a Sendar."

"One must follow one's nature," Durnik said.

"Thank you, my friend," Wolf said gravely, dropping the coins in his purse. "Let's lead the horses," he went on. "Galloping through these narrow streets at night would only attract attention."

"I'll lead," Barak announced, drawing his sword. "If there's any trouble, I'm best equipped to deal with it."

"I'll walk along beside you, friend Barak," Durnik said, hefting a stout cudgel of firewood.

Barak nodded, his eyes grimly bright, and led his horse out through the gate with Durnik closely at his side.

Taking his lead from Durnik, Garion paused momentarily as he passed the woodpile and selected a good oak stick. It had a comforting weight, and he swung it a few times to get the feel of it. Then he saw Aunt Pol watching him, and he hurried on without any further display.

The streets through which they passed were narrow and dark, and the snow had begun to fall a bit more heavily now, settling almost lazily through the dead calm air. The horses, made skittish by the snow, seemed to be fearful and crowded close to those who led them.

When the attack came, it was unexpected and swift.

There was a sudden rush of footsteps and a sharp ring of steel on steel as Barak fended off the first blow with his sword.

Garion could see only shadowy figures outlined against the falling snow, and then, as once before when in his boyhood he had struck down his friend Rundorig in mock battle, his ears began to ring; his blood surged boilingly in his veins as he leaped into the fight, ignoring the single cry from Aunt Pol.

He received a smart rap on the shoulder, whirled and struck with his stick. He was rewarded with a muffled grunt. He struck again—and then again, swinging his club at those parts of his shadowy enemy which he instinctively knew were most sensitive.

The main fight, however, surged around Barak and Durnik. The ring of Barak's sword and the thump of Durnik's cudgel resounded in the narrow street along with the groans of their assailants.

"There's the boy!" a voice rang out from behind them, and Garion whirled. Two men were running down the street toward him, one with a sword and the other with a wicked-looking curved knife. Knowing it was hopeless, Garion raised his club, but Silk was there. The small man launched himself from the shadows directly at the feet of the two, and all three crashed to the street in a tangle of arms and legs. Silk rolled to his feet like a cat, spun and kicked one of the floundering men solidly just below the ear. The man sank twitching to the cobblestones. The other scrambled away and half rose just in time to receive both of Silk's heels in his face as the rat-faced Drasnian leaped into the air, twisted and struck with both legs. Then Silk turned almost casually.

"Are you all right?" he asked Garion.

"I'm fine," Garion said. "You're awfully good at this kind of thing."

"I'm an acrobat," Silk said. "It's simple once you know how."

"They're getting away," Garion told him.

Silk turned, but the two he had just put down were dragging themselves into a dark alley.

There was a triumphant shout from Barak, and Garion saw that the rest of the attackers were fleeing.

At the end of the street in the snow-speckled light from a small window was Brill, almost dancing with fury. "Cowards!" he shouted at his hirelings. "Cowards!" And then Barak started for him, and he too turned and ran.

"Are you all right, Aunt Pol?" Garion said, crossing the street to where she stood.

"Of course I am," she snapped. "And don't do that again, young man. Leave street brawling to those better suited for it."

"I was all right," he objected. "I had my stick here."

"Don't argue with me," she said. "I didn't go to all the trouble of raising you to have you end up dead in a gutter."

Durnik dropped his knife suddenly and started to scramble to his feet. "What's amiss?" Barak asked quickly.

"I just saw Brill," Durnik said. "He was in that doorway."

"Are you sure?" Wolf demanded.

"I know him," Durnik said grimly. "It was Brill, all right."

Silk pounded his fist down on the table. "Idiot!" he accused himself. "I underestimated the man."

"That doesn't matter now," Mister Wolf said, and there was almost a kind of relief in his voice. "Our disguise is useless now. I think it's time for speed."

"I'll see to the wagons," Durnik said.

"No," Wolf said. "The wagons are too slow. We'll go to the camp of the Algars and buy good horses." He stood up quickly.

"What of the wagons?" Durnik persisted.

"Forget them," Wolf said. "They're only a hindrance now. We'll ride the wagon horses to the camp of the Algars and take only what we can conveniently carry. Let's get ready to leave immediately. Meet me in the innyard as soon as you can." He went quickly to the door and out into the cold night.

It was only a few minutes later that they all met near the door to the stable in the cobblestoned innyard, each carrying a small bundle. Hulking Barak jingled as he walked, and Garion could smell the oiled steel of his mail shirt. A few flakes of snow drifted down through the frosty air and settled like tiny feathers to the frozen ground.

Durnik was the last to join them. He came breathlessly out of the inn and pressed a small handful of coins upon Mister Wolf. "It was the best I could do," he apologized. "It's scarce half the worth of the wagons, but the innkeeper sensed my haste and bargained meanly." He shrugged then. "At least we're rid of them," he said. "It's not good to leave things of value behind. They nag at the mind and distract one from the business at hand."

Silk laughed. "Durnik," he said, "you're the absolute soul of a Sendar."

"One must follow one's nature," Durnik said.

"Thank you, my friend," Wolf said gravely, dropping the coins in his purse. "Let's lead the horses," he went on. "Galloping through these narrow streets at night would only attract attention."

"I'll lead," Barak announced, drawing his sword. "If there's any trouble, I'm best equipped to deal with it."

"I'll walk along beside you, friend Barak," Durnik said, hefting a stout cudgel of firewood.

Barak nodded, his eyes grimly bright, and led his horse out through the gate with Durnik closely at his side.

Taking his lead from Durnik, Garion paused momentarily as he passed the woodpile and selected a good oak stick. It had a comforting weight, and he swung it a few times to get the feel of it. Then he saw Aunt Pol watching him, and he hurried on without any further display.

The streets through which they passed were narrow and dark, and the snow had begun to fall a bit more heavily now, settling almost lazily through the dead calm air. The horses, made skittish by the snow, seemed to be fearful and crowded close to those who led them.

When the attack came, it was unexpected and swift.

There was a sudden rush of footsteps and a sharp ring of steel on steel as Barak fended off the first blow with his sword.

Garion could see only shadowy figures outlined against the falling snow, and then, as once before when in his boyhood he had struck down his friend Rundorig in mock battle, his ears began to ring; his blood surged boilingly in his veins as he leaped into the fight, ignoring the single cry from Aunt Pol.

He received a smart rap on the shoulder, whirled and struck with his stick. He was rewarded with a muffled grunt. He struck again—and then again, swinging his club at those parts of his shadowy enemy which he instinctively knew were most sensitive.

The main fight, however, surged around Barak and Durnik. The ring of Barak's sword and the thump of Durnik's cudgel resounded in the narrow street along with the groans of their assailants.

"There's the boy!" a voice rang out from behind them, and Garion whirled. Two men were running down the street toward him, one with a sword and the other with a wicked-looking curved knife. Knowing it was hopeless, Garion raised his club, but Silk was there. The small man launched himself from the shadows directly at the feet of the two, and all three crashed to the street in a tangle of arms and legs. Silk rolled to his feet like a cat, spun and kicked one of the floundering men solidly just below the ear. The man sank twitching to the cobblestones. The other scrambled away and half rose just in time to receive both of Silk's heels in his face as the rat-faced Drasnian leaped into the air, twisted and struck with both legs. Then Silk turned almost casually.

"Are you all right?" he asked Garion.

"I'm fine," Garion said. "You're awfully good at this kind of thing."

"I'm an acrobat," Silk said. "It's simple once you know how."

"They're getting away," Garion told him.

Silk turned, but the two he had just put down were dragging themselves into a dark alley.

There was a triumphant shout from Barak, and Garion saw that the rest of the attackers were fleeing.

At the end of the street in the snow-speckled light from a small window was Brill, almost dancing with fury. "Cowards!" he shouted at his hirelings. "Cowards!" And then Barak started for him, and he too turned and ran.

"Are you all right, Aunt Pol?" Garion said, crossing the street to where she stood.

"Of course I am," she snapped. "And don't do that again, young man. Leave street brawling to those better suited for it."

"I was all right," he objected. "I had my stick here."

"Don't argue with me," she said. "I didn't go to all the trouble of raising you to have you end up dead in a gutter."

"Is everyone all right?" Durnik asked anxiously, coming back to them.

"Of course we are," Aunt Pol snapped peevishly. "Why don't you see if you can help the Old Wolf with the horses?"

"Certainly, Mistress Pol," Durnik said mildly.

"A splendid little fight," Barak said, wiping his sword as he joined them. "Not much blood, but satisfying all the same."

"I'm delighted you found it so," Aunt Pol said acidly. "I don't much care for such encounters. Did they leave anyone behind?"

"Regrettably no, dear lady," Barak said. "The quarters were too narrow for good strokes, and these stones too slippery for good footing. I marked a couple of them quite well, however. We managed to break a few bones and dent a head or two. As a group, they were much better at running than at fighting."

Silk came back from the alley where he had pursued the two who had tried to attack Garion. His eyes were bright, and his grin was vicious. "Invigorating," he said, and then laughed for no apparent reason.

Wolf and Durnik had managed to calm their wild-eyed horses and led them back to where Garion and the others stood. "Is anyone hurt?" Wolf demanded.

"We're all intact," Barak rumbled. "The business was hardly worth drawing a sword for."

Garion's mind was racing; in his excitement, he spoke without stopping to consider the fact that it might be wiser to think the whole thing through first. "How did Brill know we were in Muros?" he asked.

Silk looked at him sharply, his eyes narrowing. "Perhaps he followed us from Winold," he said.

"But we stopped and looked back," Garion said. "He wasn't following when we left, and we've kept a watch behind us every day."

Silk frowned. "Go on, Garion," he said.

"I think he knew where we were going," Garion blurted, struggling against a strange compulsion not to speak what his mind saw clearly now.

"And what else do you think?" Wolf asked.

"Somebody told him," Garion said. "Somebody who knew we were coming here."

"Mingan knew," Silk said, "but Mingan's a merchant, and he wouldn't talk about his dealings to somebody like Brill."

"But Asharak the Murgo was in Mingan's counting room when Mingan hired us." The compulsion was so strong now that Garion's tongue felt stiff.

Silk shrugged. "Why should it concern him? Asharak didn't know who we were."

"But what if he did?" Garion struggled. "What if he isn't just an ordinary Murgo, but one of those others—like the one who was with those ones who passed us a couple days after we left Darine?"

"A Grolim?" Silk said, and his eyes widened. "Yes, I suppose that if Asharak's a Grolim, he'd have known who we are and what we're doing."

"And what if the Grolim who passed us that day was Asharak?" Garion fought to say. "What if he wasn't really looking for us, but just coming south to find Brill and send him here to wait for us?"

Silk looked very hard at Garion. "Very good," he said softly. "Very, very good." He glanced at Aunt Pol. "My compliments, Mistress Pol. You've raised a rare boy here."

"What did this Asharak look like?" Wolf asked quickly.

"A Murgo." Silk shrugged. "He said he was from Rak Goska. I took him to be an ordinary spy on some business that didn't concern us. My mind seems to have gone to sleep." Silk seemed oddly evasive.

"It happens when one deals with Grolims," Wolf told him.

"Someone's watching us," Durnik said quietly, "from that window up there."

Garion looked up quickly and saw a dark shape at a second-story window outlined by a dim light. The shape was hauntingly familiar.

Mister Wolf did not look up, but his face turned blank as if he were looking inward, or his mind were searching for something. Then he drew himself up and looked at the figure in the window, his eyes blazing. "A Grolim," he said shortly.

"A dead one perhaps," Silk said. He reached inside his tunic and drew out a long, needle-pointed dirk. He took two quick steps away from the house where the Grolim stood watching, spun and threw the dirk with a smooth, overhand cast.

The dirk crashed through the window. There was a muffled shout, and the light went out. Garion felt a strange pang in his left arm.

"Marked him," Silk said with a grin.

"Good throw," Barak said admiringly.

"One has picked up certain skills," Silk said modestly. "If it was Asharak, I owed him that for deceiving me in Mingan's counting room."

"At least it'll give him something to think about," Wolf said. "There's no point in trying to creep through town now. They know we're here. Let's mount and ride." He climbed onto his horse and led the way down the street at a quick walk.

The compulsion was gone now, and Garion wanted to tell them about Asharak, but there was no chance for that as they rode.

Once they reached the outskirts of the city, they nudged their horses into a fast canter. The snow was falling more seriously now, and the hoof-churned ground in the vast cattle pens was already faintly dusted with white.

"It's going to be a cold night," Silk shouted as they rode.

"We could always go back to Muros," Barak suggested. "Another scuffle or two might warm your blood."

Silk laughed and put his heels to his horse again.

The encampment of the Algars was three leagues to the east of Muros. It was a large area surrounded by a stout palisade of poles set in the ground. The snow by now was falling thickly enough to make the camp look hazy and indistinct. The gate, flanked by hissing torches, was guarded by two fierce-looking warriors in leather leggings, snow-dusted jerkins of the same material, and pot-shaped steel helmets. The points of their lances glittered in the torchlight.

"Halt," one of the warriors commanded, leveling his lance at Mister Wolf. "What business have you here at this time of night?"

"I have urgent need of speaking with your herd master," Wolf replied politely. "May I step down?"

The two guards spoke together briefly.

"You may come down," one of them said. "Your companions, however, must withdraw somewhat—but not beyond the light."

"Algars!" Silk muttered under his breath. "Always suspicious."

Mister Wolf climbed down from this horse, and, throwing back his hood, approached the two guards through the snow.

Then a strange thing happened. The elder of the two guards stared at Mister Wolf, taking in his silver hair and beard. His eyes suddenly opened very wide. He quickly muttered something to his companion, and the two men bowed deeply to Wolf.

"There isn't time for that," Wolf said in annoyance. "Convey me to your herd master."

"At once, Ancient One," the elder guard said quickly and hurried to open the gate.

"What was that about?" Garion whispered to Aunt Pol.

"Algars are superstitious," she said shortly. "Don't ask so many questions."

They waited with snow settling down upon them and melting on their horses. After about a half hour, the gate opened again and two dozen mounted Algars, fierce in their rivet-studded leather vests and steel helmets, herded six saddled horses out into the snow.

Behind them Mister Wolf walked, accompanied by a tall man with his head shaved except for a flowing scalp lock.

"You have honored our camp by your visit, Ancient One," the tall man was saying, "and I wish you all speed on your journey."

"I have little fear of being delayed with Algar horses under us," Wolf replied.

"My riders will accompany you along a route they know which will put you on the far side of Muros within a few hours," the tall man said. "They will then linger for a time to be certain you are not followed."

"I cannot express my gratitude, noble herd master," Wolf said, bowing.

"It is I who am grateful for the opportunity to be of service," the herd master said, also bowing.

The change to their new horses took only a minute. With half of their contingent of Algars leading and the other half bringing up the rear, they turned and rode back toward the west through the dark, snowy night.

CHAPTER TEN

Gradually, almost imperceptibly, the darkness became paler as the softly falling snow made indistinct even the arrival of morning. Their seemingly inexhaustible horses pounded on through the growing light, the sound of their hooves muffled by the snow now lying fetlock-deep on the broad surface of the Great North Road. Garion glanced back once and saw the jumbled tracks of their passage stretching behind them and, already at the hazy gray limit of his vision, beginning to fill with concealing snow.

When it was fully light, Mister Wolf reined in his steaming horse and proceeded at a walk for a time. "How far have we come?" he asked Silk.

The weasel-faced man who had been shaking the snow out of the folds of his cloak looked around, trying to pick out a landmark in the misty veil of dropping flakes. "Ten leagues," he said finally. "Perhaps a bit more."

"This is a miserable way to travel," Barak rumbled, wincing slightly as he shifted his bulk in the saddle.

"Think of how your horse must feel." Silk grinned at him.

"How far is it to Camaar?" Aunt Pol asked.

"Forty leagues from Muros," Silk told her.

"We'll need shelter, then," she said. "We can't gallop forty leagues without rest, no matter who's behind us."

"I don't think we need to worry about pursuit just now," Wolf said. "I think we can count on the Algars to detain Brill and his hirelings or even Asharak if they try to follow us."

"At least there's something Algars are good for," Silk said dryly.

"If I remember correctly, there should be an imperial hostel about five leagues farther to the west," Wolf said. "We ought to reach it by noon."

"Will we be allowed to stay there?" Durnik asked doubtfully. "I've never heard that Tolnedrans are noted for hospitality."

"Tolnedrans sell anything for a price," Silk said. "The hostel would be a good place to stop. Even if Brill or Asharak evade the Algars and follow us there, the legionnaires won't permit any foolishness within their walls."

"Why should there be Tolnedran soldiers in Sendaria?" Garion asked, feeling a brief surge of patriotic resentment at the thought.

"Wherever the great roads are, you'll find the legions," Silk said. "Tolnedrans are even better at writing treaties than they are at giving short weight to their customers."

Mister Wolf chuckled. "You're inconsistent, Silk," he said. "You don't object to their highways, but you dislike their legions. You can't have the one without the other."

"I've never pretended to be consistent," the sharp-nosed man said airily. "If we want to reach the questionable comfort of the imperial hostel by noon, hadn't we better move along? I wouldn't want to deny His Imperial Majesty the opportunity to pick my pocket."

"All right," Wolf said, "let's ride." And he put his heels to the flanks of the Algar horse which had already begun to prance impatiently under him.

The hostel, when they reached it in the full light of snowy noon, proved to be a series of stout buildings surrounded by an even stouter wall. The legionnaires who manned it were not the same sort of men as the Tolnedran merchants Garion had seen before. Unlike the oily men of commerce, these were hard-faced professional fighting men in burnished breastplates and plumed helmets. They carried themselves proudly, even arrogantly, each bearing the knowledge that the might of all Tolnedra was behind him.

The food in the dining hall was plain and wholesome, but dreadfully expensive. The tiny sleeping cubicles were scrupulously clean, with hard, narrow beds and thick woolen blankets, and were also expensive. The stables were neat, and they too reached deeply into Mister Wolf's purse. Garion wondered at the thought of how much their lodging was costing, but Wolf paid for it all with seeming indifference as if his purse were bottomless.

"We'll rest here until tomorrow," the white-bearded old man announced when they had finished eating. "Maybe it'll snow itself out by morning. I'm not happy with all this plunging blindly through a snowstorm. Too many things can hide in our path in such weather."

Garion, who by now was numb with exhaustion, heard these words gratefully as he half-drowsed at the table. The others sat talking quietly, but he was too tired to listen to what they said.

"Garion," Aunt Pol said finally, "why don't you go to bed?"

"I'm all right, Aunt Pol," he said, rousing himself quickly, mortified once more at being treated like a child.

"*Now*, Garion," she said in that infuriating tone he knew so well. It seemed that all his life she had been saying "*Now*, Garion," to him. But he knew better than to argue.

He stood up and was surprised to feel that his legs were trembling. Aunt Pol also rose and led him from the dining hall.

"I can find my way by myself," he objected.

"Of course," she said. "Now come along."

After he had crawled into bed in his cubicle, she pulled his blankets up firmly around his neck. "Stay covered," she told him. "I don't want you taking cold." She laid her cool hand briefly on his forehead as she had done when he was a small child.

"Aunt Pol?" he asked drowsily.

"Yes, Garion?"

"Who were my parents? I mean, what were their names?"

She looked at him gravely. "We can talk about that later," she said.

"I want to know," he said stubbornly.

"All right. Your father's name was Geran; your mother's was Ildera."

Garion thought about that. "The names don't sound Sendarian," he said finally.

"They're not," Aunt Pol said.

"Why was that?"

"It's a very long story," she said, "and you're much too tired to hear it just now."

On a sudden impulse he reached out and touched the white lock at her brow with the mark of the palm of his right hand. As had sometimes happened before, a window seemed to open in his mind at the tingling touch, but this time that window opened on something much more serious. There was anger, and a single face—a face that was strangely like Mister Wolf's, but was not his face, and all the towering fury in the world was directed at that face.

Aunt Pol moved her head away. "I've asked you not to do that, Garion," she said, her tone very matter-of-fact. "You're not ready for it yet."

"You're going to have to tell me what it is someday," he said.

"Perhaps," she said, "but not now. Close your eyes and go to sleep."

And then, as if that command had somehow dissolved his will, he fell immediately into a deep, untroubled sleep.

By the next morning it had stopped snowing. The world outside the walls of the imperial hostel was mantled in thick, unbroken white, and the air was filmy with a kind of damp haze that was almost—but not quite—fog.

"Misty Sendaria," Silk said ironically at breakfast. "Sometimes I'm amazed that the entire kingdom doesn't rust shut."

They traveled all that day at a mile-eating canter, and that night there was another imperial hostel, almost identical to the one they had left that morning—so closely identical in fact that it almost seemed to Garion that they had ridden all day and merely arrived back where they had started. He commented on that to Silk as they were putting their horses in the stable.

"Tolnedrans are nothing if not predictable," Silk said. "All their hostels are exactly the same. You can find these same buildings in Drasnia, Algaria, Arendia and any place else their great roads go. It's their one weakness—this lack of imagination."

"Don't they get tired of doing the same thing over and over again?"

"It makes them feel comfortable, I guess." Silk laughed. "Let's go see about supper."

It snowed again the following day, but by noon Garion caught a scent other than that faintly dusty odor snow always seemed to have. Even as he had done when they had approached Darine, he began to smell the sea, and he knew their journey was almost at an end.

Camaar, the largest city in Sendaria and the major seaport of the north, was a sprawling place which had existed at the mouth of the Greater Camaar River since antiquity. It was the natural western terminus of the Great North Road which stretched to Boktor in Drasnia and the equally natural northern end of the Great West Road which reached down across Arendia into Tolnedra and the imperial capital at Tol Honeth. With some accuracy it could be said that all roads ended at Camaar.

Late on a chill, snowy afternoon, they rode down a gradual hill toward the city. Some distance from the gate, Aunt Pol stopped her horse. "Since we're no longer posing as vagabonds," she announced, "I see no further need for selecting the most disreputable inns, do you?"

"I hadn't really thought about it," Mister Wolf said.

"Well, I have," she said. "I've had more than enough of wayside hostels and seedy village inns. I need a bath, a clean bed and some decent food. If you don't mind, I'll choose our lodging this time."

"Of course, Pol," Wolf said mildly. "Whatever you say."

"Very well, then," she said and rode on toward the city gate with the rest of them trailing behind her.

"What's your business in Camaar?" one of the fur-mantled guards at the broad gate asked rather rudely.

Aunt Pol threw back her hood and fixed the man with a steely gaze. "I am the Duchess of Erat," she announced in ringing tones. "These are my retainers, and my business in Camaar is my own affair."

The guard blinked and then bowed respectfully. "Forgive me, your Grace," he said. "I didn't intend to give offense."

"Indeed?" Aunt Pol said, her tone still cold and her gaze still dangerous.

"I didn't recognize your Grace," the poor man floundered, squirming under that imperious stare. "May I offer any assistance?"

"I hardly think so," Aunt Pol said, looking him up and down. "Which is the finest inn in Camaar?"

"That would be the Lion, my Lady."

"And—?" she said impatiently.

"And what, my Lady?" the man said, confused by her question.

"Where is it?" she demanded. "Don't stand there gaping like a dolt. Speak up."

"It lies beyond the customs houses," the guard replied, flushing at her words. "Follow this street until you reach Customs Square. Anyone there can direct you to the Lion."

Aunt Pol pulled her hood back up. "Give the fellow something," she said over her shoulder and rode on into the city without a backward glance.

"My thanks," the guard said as Wolf leaned down to hand him a small coin. "I must admit that I haven't heard of the Duchess of Erat before."

"You're a fortunate man," Wolf said.

"She's a great beauty," the man said admiringly.

"And has a temper to match," Wolf told him.

"I noticed that," the guard said.

"We noticed you noticing," Silk told him slyly.

They nudged their horses and caught up with Aunt Pol.

"The Duchess of Erat?" Silk asked mildly.

"The fellow's manner irritated me," Aunt Pol said loftily, "and I'm tired of putting on a poor face in front of strangers."

At Customs Square Silk accosted a busy-looking merchant trudging across the snow-covered paving. "You—fellow," he said in the most insulting way possible, pulling his horse directly in front of the startled merchant. "My mistress, the Duchess of Erat, requires directions to an inn called the Lion. Be so good as to provide them."

The merchant blinked, his face flushing at the rat-faced man's tone. "Up that street," he said softly, pointing. "Some goodly way. It'll be on your left. There's a sign of a lion at the front."

Silk sniffed ungraciously, tossed a few coins into the snow at the man's feet and whirled his horse in a grand manner. The merchant, Garion noted, looked outraged, but he *did* grope in the snow for the coins Silk had thrown.

"I doubt that any of these people will quickly forget our passage," Wolf said sourly when they were some ways up the street.

"They'll remember the passage of an arrogant noblewoman," Silk said. "This is as good a disguise as any we've tried."

When they arrived at the inn, Aunt Pol commanded not just the usual sleeping chambers but an entire apartment. "My chamberlain there will pay you," she said to the innkeeper, indicating Mister Wolf. "Our baggage horses are some days behind with the rest of my servants, so I'll require the services of a dressmaker and a maid. See to it." And she turned and swept imperially up the long staircase that led to her apartment, following the servant who scurried ahead to show her the way.

"The duchess has a commanding presence, doesn't she?" the innkeeper ventured as Wolf began counting out coins.

"She has indeed," Wolf agreed. "I've discovered the wisdom of not countering her wishes."

"I'll be guided by you, then," the innkeeper assured him. "My youngest daughter is a serviceable girl. I'll dispatch her to serve as her Grace's maid."

"Many thanks, friend," Silk told him. "Our Lady becomes most irritable when those things she desires are delayed, and we're the ones who suffer most from her displeasure."

They trooped up the stairs to the apartments Aunt Pol had taken and stepped into the main sitting room, a splendid chamber far richer than any Garion had seen before. The walls were covered by tapestries with intricate pictures woven into the fabric. A wealth of candles—real wax instead of smoky tallow—gleamed in sconces on the walls and in a massive candelabra on the polished table. A good warm fire danced merrily on the hearth, and a large carpet of curious design lay on the floor.

Aunt Pol was standing before the fire, warming her hands. "Isn't this better than some shabby, wharfside inn reeking of fish and unwashed sailors?" she asked.

"If the Duchess of Erat will forgive my saying so," Wolf said somewhat tartly, "this is hardly the way to escape notice, and the cost of these lodgings would feed a legion for a week."

"Don't grow parsimonious in your dotage, Old Wolf," she replied. "No one takes a spoiled noblewoman seriously, and your wagons weren't able to keep that disgusting Brill from finding us. This guise is at least comfortable, and it permits us to move more rapidly."

Wolf grunted. "I only hope we won't regret all this," he said.

"Stop grumbling, old man," she told him.

"Have it your way, Pol." He sighed.

"I intend to," she said.

"How are we to behave, Mistress Pol?" Durnik asked hesitantly. Her sudden regal manner had obviously confused him. "I'm not familiar with the ways of the gentry."

"It's quite simple, Durnik," she said. She eyed him up and down, noting his plain, dependable face and his solid competence. "How would you like to be chief groom to the Duchess of Erat? And Master of her stables?"

Durnik laughed uncomfortably. "Noble titles for work I've done all my life," he said. "I could manage the work easily enough, but the titles might grow a bit heavy."

"You'll do splendidly, friend Durnik," Silk assured him. "That honest face of yours makes people believe anything you choose to tell them. If I had a face like yours, I could steal half the world." He turned to Aunt Pol. "And what role am I to play, my Lady?" he asked.

"You'll be my reeve," she said. "The thievery usually associated with the position should suit you."

Silk bowed ironically.

"And I?" Barak said, grinning openly.

"My man-at-arms," she said. "I doubt that any would believe you to be a dancing master. Just stand around looking dangerous."

"What about me, Aunt Pol?" Garion asked. "What do I do?"

"You can be my page."

"What does a page do?"

"You fetch things for me."

"I've always done that. Is that what it's called?"

"Don't be impertinent. You also answer doors and announce visitors; and when I'm melancholy, you may sing to me."

"Sing?" he said incredulously. "Me?"

"It's customary."

"You wouldn't make me do that, would you, Aunt Pol?"

"Your Grace," she corrected.

"You won't be very gracious if you have to listen to me sing," he warned. "My voice isn't very good."

"You'll do just fine, dear," she said.

"And I've already been appointed your Grace's chamberlain," Wolf said.

"My chief steward," she told him. "Manager of my estates and keeper of my purse."

"Somehow I knew that would be part of it."

There was a timid rap at the door.

"See who that is, Garion," Aunt Pol said.

When he opened the door, Garion found a young girl with light brown hair in a sober dress and starched apron and cap standing outside. She had very large brown eyes that looked at him apprehensively.

"Yes?" he asked.

"I've been sent to wait upon the duchess," she said in a low voice.

"Your maid has arrived, your Grace," Garion announced.

"Splendid," Aunt Pol said. "Come in, child."

The girl entered the room.

"What a pretty thing you are," Aunt Pol said.

"Thank you, my Lady," the girl answered with a brief curtsy and a rosy blush.

"And what is your name?"

"I am called Donia, my Lady."

"A lovely name," Aunt Pol said. "Now to important matters. Is there a bath on the premises?"

It was still snowing the next morning. The roofs of nearby houses were piled high with white, and the narrow streets were deep with it.

"I think we're close to the end of our search," Mister Wolf said as he stared intently out through the rippled glass of the window in the room with the tapestries.

"It's unlikely that the one we're after would stay in Camaar for long," Silk said.

"Very unlikely," Wolf agreed, "but once we've found his trail, we'll be able to move more rapidly. Let's go into the city and see if I'm right."

After Mister Wolf and Silk had left, Garion sat for a while talking with Donia, who seemed to be about his own age. Although she was not quite as pretty as Zubrette, Garion found her soft voice and huge brown eyes extremely attractive. Things were going along well between them until Aunt Pol's dressmaker arrived and Donia's presence was required in the chamber where the Duchess of Erat was being fitted for her new gowns.

Since Durnik, obviously ill at ease in the luxurious surroundings of their chambers, had adjourned to the stables after breakfast, Garion was left in the company of the giant Barak, who worked patiently with a small stone, polishing a nick out of the edge of his sword—a memento of the skirmish in Muros. Garion had never been wholly comfortable with the huge, red-bearded man. Barak spoke rarely, and there seemed to be a kind of hulking menace about him. So it was that Garion spent the morning examining the tapestries on the walls of the sitting room. The tapestries depicted knights in full armor and castles on hilltops and strangely angular-looking maidens moping about in gardens.

"Arendish," Barak said, directly behind him. Garion jumped. The huge man had moved up so quietly that Garion had not heard him.

"How can you tell?" Garion asked politely.

"The Arends have a fondness for tapestry," Barak rumbled, "and the weaving of pictures occupies their women while the men are off denting each other's armor."

"Do they really wear all that?" Garion asked, pointing at a heavily armored knight pictured on the tapestry.

"Oh yes." Barak laughed. "That and more. Even their horses wear armor. It's a silly way to make war."

Garion scuffed his shoe on the carpet. "Is this Arendish too?" he asked.

Barak shook his head. "Mallorean," he said.

"How did it get here all the way from Mallorea?" Garion asked. "I've heard that Mallorea's all the way on the other end of the world."

"It's a goodly way off," Barak agreed, "but a merchant would go twice as far to make a profit. Such goods as this commonly move along the North Caravan Route out of Gar og Nadrak to Boktor. Mallorean carpets are prized by the wealthy. I don't much care for them myself, since I'm not fond of anything that has to do with the Angaraks."

"How many kinds of Angaraks are there?" Garion asked. "I know there are Murgos and Thulls, and I've heard stories about the Battle of Vo Mimbre and all, but I don't know much about them really."

"There are five tribes of them," Barak said, sitting back down and resuming his polishing, "Murgos and Thulls, Nadraks and Malloreans, and of course the Grolims. They live in the four kingdoms of the east—Mallorea, Gar og Nadrak, Mishrak ac Thull and Cthol Murgos."

"Where do the Grolims live?"

"They have no special place," Barak replied grimly. "The Grolims are the priests of Torak One-eye and are everywhere in the lands of the Angaraks. They're the ones who perform the sacrifices to Torak. Grolim knives have spilled more Angarak blood than a dozen Vo Mimbres."

Garion shuddered. "Why should Torak take such pleasure in the slaughter of his own people?" he asked.

"Who can say?" Barak shrugged. "He's a twisted and evil God. Some believe that he was made mad when he used the Orb of Aldur to crack the world and the Orb repaid him by burning out his eye and consuming his hand."

"How could the world be cracked?" Garion asked. "I've never understood that part of the story."

"The power of the Orb of Aldur is such that it can accomplish anything," Barak told him. "When Torak raised it, the earth was split apart by its power, and the seas came in to drown the land. The story's very old, but I think that it's probably true."

"Where's the Orb of Aldur now?" Garion asked suddenly.

Barak looked at him, his eyes icy blue and his face thoughtful, but he didn't say anything.

"Do you know what I think?" Garion said on a sudden impulse. "I think that it's the Orb of Aldur that's been stolen. I think it's the Orb that Mister Wolf is trying to find."

"And I think it'd be better if you didn't think so much about such things," Barak warned.

"But I want to *know*," Garion protested, his curiosity driving him even in the face of Barak's words and the warning voice in his mind. "Everyone treats me like an ignorant boy. All I do is tag along with no idea of what we're doing. Who *is* Mister Wolf, anyway? Why did the Algars behave the way they did when they saw him? How can he follow something that he can't see? Please tell me, Barak."

"Not me." Barak laughed. "Your Aunt would pull out my beard whisker by whisker if I made that mistake."

"You're not afraid of her, are you?"

"Any man with good sense is afraid of her," Barak said, rising and sliding his sword into its sheath.

"Aunt Pol?" Garion asked incredulously.

"Aren't you afraid of her?" Barak asked pointedly.

"No," Garion said, and then realized that was not precisely true. "Well—not really afraid. It's more—" He left it hanging, not knowing how to explain it.

"Exactly," Barak said. "And I'm no more foolhardy than you, my boy. You're too full of questions I'd be far wiser not to answer. If you want to know about these things, you'll have to ask your Aunt."

"She won't tell me," Garion said glumly. "She won't tell me anything. She won't even tell me about my parents—not really."

Barak frowned. "That's strange," he said.

"I don't think they were Sendars," Garion said. "Their names weren't Sendarian, and Silk says that I'm not a Sendar—at least I don't look like one."

Barak looked at him closely. "No," he said finally. "Now that you mention it, you don't. You look more like a Rivan than anything else—but not quite that either."

"Is Aunt Pol a Rivan?"

Barak's eyes narrowed slightly. "I think we're getting to some more of those questions I hadn't better answer," he said.

"I'm going to find out someday," Garion said.

"But not today," Barak said. "Come along. I need some exercise. Let's go out into the innyard and I'll teach you how to use a sword."

"Me?" Garion said, all his curiosity suddenly melting away in the excitement of that thought.

"You're at an age where you should begin to learn," Barak said. "The occasion may someday arise when it'll be a useful thing for you to know."

Late that afternoon when Garion's arm had begun to ache from the effort of swinging Barak's heavy sword and the whole idea of learning the skills of a warrior had become a great deal less exciting, Mister Wolf and Silk returned. Their clothes were wet from the snow through which they had trudged all day, but Wolf's eyes were bright, and his face had a curiously exultant expression as he led them all back up the stairs to the sitting room.

"Ask your Aunt to join us," he told Garion as he removed his sodden mantle and stepped to the fire to warm himself.

Garion sensed quickly that this was not the time for questions. He hurried to the polished door where Aunt Pol had been closeted with her dressmaker all day and rapped.

"What is it?" her voice came from inside.

"Mister—uh—that is, your chamberlain has returned, my Lady," Garion said, remembering at the last moment that she was not alone. "He requests a word with you."

"Oh, very well," she said. After a minute she came out, firmly closing the door behind her.

Garion gasped. The rich, blue velvet gown she wore made her so magnificent that she quite took his breath away. He stared at her in helpless admiration.

"Where is he?" she asked. "Don't stand and gape, Garion. It's not polite."

"You're *beautiful*, Aunt Pol," he blurted.

"Yes, dear," she said, patting his cheek, "I know. Now where's the Old Wolf?"

"In the room with the tapestries," Garion said, still unable to take his eyes from her.

"Come along, then," she said and swept down the short hall to the sitting room. They entered to find the others all standing by the fireplace.

"Well?" she asked.

Wolf looked up at her, his eyes still bright. "An excellent choice, Pol," he said admiringly. "Blue has always been your best color."

"Do you like it?" she asked, holding out her arms and turning almost girlishly so that they all might see how fine she looked. "I hope it pleases you, old man, because it's costing you a great deal of money."

Wolf laughed. "I was almost certain it would," he said.

The effect of Aunt Pol's gown on Durnik was painfully obvious. The poor man's eyes literally bulged, and his face turned alternately very pale and then very red, then finally settled into an expression of such hopelessness that Garion was touched to the quick by it.

Silk and Barak in curious unison both bowed deeply and wordlessly to Aunt Pol, and her eyes sparkled at their silent tribute.

"It's been here," Wolf announced seriously.

"You're certain?" Aunt Pol demanded.

He nodded. "I could feel the memory of its passage in the very stones."

"Did it come by sea?" she asked.

"No. He probably came ashore with it in some secluded cove up the coast and then traveled here by land."

"And took ship again?"

"I doubt that," Wolf said. "I know him well. He's not comfortable on the sea."

"Besides which," Barak said, "one word to King Anheg of Cherek would have put a hundred warships on his trail. No one can hide on the sea from the ships of Cherek, and he knows that."

"You're right," Wolf agreed. "I think he'll avoid the domains of the Alorns. That's probably why he chose not to pass along the North Road through Algaria and Drasnia. The Spirit of Belar is strong in the kingdoms of the Alorns, and not even this thief is bold enough to risk a confrontation with the Bear-God."

"Which leaves Arendia," Silk said, "or the land of the Ulgos."

"Arendia, I think," Wolf said. "The wrath of UL is even more fearsome than that of Belar."

"Forgive me," Durnik said, his eyes still on Aunt Pol. "This is all most confusing. I've never heard just exactly who this thief is."

"I'm sorry, gentle Durnik," Wolf said. "It's not a good idea to speak his name. He has certain powers which might make it possible for him to know our every move if we alert him to our location, and he can hear his name spoken a thousand leagues away."

"A sorcerer?" Durnik asked unbelievingly.

"The word isn't one I'd choose," Wolf said. "It's a term used by men who don't understand that particular art. Instead let's call him 'thief,' though there are a few other names I might call him which are far less kindly."

"Can we be certain that he'll make for the kingdoms of the Angaraks?" Silk asked, frowning. "If that's the case, wouldn't it be quicker to take ship directly to Tol Honeth and pick up his trail on the South Caravan Route into Cthol Murgos?"

Wolf shook his head. "Better to stay with this trail now that we've found it. We don't know what he intends. Maybe he wants to keep the thing he's stolen for himself rather than deliver it over to the Grolims. He might even seek sanctuary in Nyissa."

"He couldn't do that without the connivance of Salmissra," Aunt Pol said.

"It wouldn't be the first time that the Queen of the Serpent People has tampered with things that are none of her concern," Wolf pointed out.

"If that turns out to be true," Aunt Pol said grimly, "I think I'll give myself the leisure to deal with the snakewoman permanently."

"It's too early to know," Wolf said. "Tomorrow we'll buy provisions and ferry across the river to Arendia. I'll take up the trail there. For the time being all we can do is follow that trail. Once we know for certain where it leads, we'll be able to consider our alternatives."

From the evening-darkened innyard outside there came suddenly the sound of many horses.

Barak stepped quickly to the window and glanced out. "Soldiers," he said shortly.

"Here?" Silk said, also hurrying to the window.

"They appear to be from one of the king's regiments," Barak said.

"They won't be interested in us," Aunt Pol said.

"Unless they aren't what they seem," Silk said. "Uniforms of one kind or another aren't that difficult to come by."

"They aren't Murgos," Barak said. "I'd recognize Murgos."

"Brill isn't a Murgo either," Silk said, staring down into the innyard.

"See if you can hear what they say," Wolf instructed.

Barak carefully opened one of the windows a crack, and the candles all flickered in the gust of icy wind. In the yard below the captain of the soldiers was speaking with the innkeeper. "He's a man of somewhat more than me-dium height, with white hair and a short white beard. He may be traveling with some others."

"There's such a one here, your Honor," the innkeeper said dubiously, "but I'm sure he isn't the one you seek. This one is chief steward to the Duchess of Erat, who honors my inn with her presence."

"The Duchess of where?" the captain asked sharply.

"Of Erat," the innkeeper replied. "A most noble lady of great beauty and a commanding presence."

"I wonder if I might have a word with her Grace," the captain said, climbing down from his horse.

"I'll ask her if she'll receive your Honor," the innkeeper replied.

Barak closed the window. "I'll deal with this meddlesome captain," he said firmly.

"No," Wolf said. "He's got too many soldiers with him, and if they're who they seem to be, they're good men who haven't done us any harm."

"There's the back stairs," Silk suggested. "We could be three streets away before he reached our door."

"And if he stationed soldiers at the back of the inn?" Aunt Pol sug-gested. "What then? Since he's coming to speak with the Duchess of Erat, why don't we let the duchess deal with him?"

"What have you got in mind?" Wolf asked.

"If the rest of you stay out of sight, I'll speak with him," she said. "I should be able to put him off until morning. We can be across the river into Arendia before he comes back."

"Perhaps," Wolf said, "but this captain sounds like a determined man."

"I've dealt with determined men before," she said.

"We'll have to decide quickly," Silk said from the door. "He's on the stairs right now."

"We'll try it your way, Pol," Wolf said, opening the door to the next chamber.

"Garion," Aunt Pol said, "you stay here. A duchess wouldn't be unattended."

Wolf and the others quickly left the room.

"What do you want me to do, Aunt Pol?" Garion whispered.

"Just remember that you're my page, dear," she said, seating herself in a large chair near the center of the room and carefully arranging the folds of her gown. "Stand near my chair and try to look attentive. I'll take care of the rest."

"Yes, my Lady," Garion said.

The captain, when he arrived behind the innkeeper's knock, proved to be a tall, sober-looking man with penetrating gray eyes. Garion, trying his best to sound officious, requested the soldier's name and then turned to Aunt Pol.

"There's a Captain Brendig to see you, your Grace," he announced. "He says that it's a matter of importance."

Aunt Pol looked at him for a moment as if considering the request. "Oh, very well," she said finally. "Show him in."

Captain Brendig stepped into the room, and the innkeeper left hurriedly.

"Your Grace," the captain said, bowing deferentially to Aunt Pol.

"What is it, Captain?" she demanded.

"I would not trouble your Grace if my mission were not of such urgency," Brendig apologized. "My orders are directly from the king himself, and you of all people will know that we must defer to his wishes."

"I suppose I can spare you a few moments for the king's business," she said.

"There's a certain man the king wishes to have apprehended," Brendig said. "An elderly man with white hair and beard. I'm informed that you have such a one among your servants."

"Is the man a criminal?" she asked.

"The king didn't say so, your Grace," he told her. "I was only told that the man was to be seized and delivered to the palace at Sendar—and all who are with him as well."

"I am seldom at court," Aunt Pol said. "It's most unlikely that any of my servants would be of such interest to the king."

"Your Grace," Brendig said delicately, "in addition to my duties in one of the king's own regiments, I also have the honor to hold a baronetcy. I've been at court all my life and must confess that I've never seen you there. A lady of your striking appearance would not be soon forgotten."

Aunt Pol inclined her head slightly in acknowledgment of the compliment. "I suppose I should have guessed, my Lord Brendig," she said. "Your manners are not those of a common soldier."

"Moreover, your Grace," he continued, "I'm familiar with all the holdings of the kingdom. If I'm not mistaken, the district of Erat is an earldom, and the Earl of Erat is a short, stout man—my great uncle incidentally. There has been no duchy in that part of Sendaria since the kingdom was under the dominion of the Wacite Arends."

Aunt Pol fixed him with an icy stare.

"My Lady," Brendig said almost apologetically, "the Wacite Arends were exterminated by their Asturian cousins in the last years of the third millennium. There has been no Wacite nobility for over two thousand years."

"I thank you for the history lesson, my Lord," Aunt Pol said coldly.

"All of that, however, is hardly the issue, is it?" Brendig continued. "I am bidden by my king to seek out the man of whom I spoke. Upon your honor, Lady, do you know such a man?"

The question hung in the air between them, and Garion, knowing in sudden panic that they were caught, almost shouted for Barak.

Then the door to the next chamber opened, and Mister Wolf stepped into the room. "There's no need to continue with this," he said. "I'm the one you're looking for. What does Fulrach of Sendaria want with me?"

Brendig looked at him without seeming surprise. "His Majesty did not see fit to take me into his confidence," he said. "He will explain it himself, I have no doubt, as soon as we reach the palace at Sendar."

"The sooner the better then," Wolf said. "When do we leave?"

"We depart for Sendar directly after breakfast in the morning," Brendig said. "I will accept your word that none of you will attempt to leave this inn during the night. I'd prefer not to subject the Duchess of Erat to the indignity of confinement at the local barracks. The cells there are most uncomfortable, I'm told."

"You have my word," Mister Wolf said.

"Thank you," Brendig said, bowing slightly. "I must also advise you that I am obliged to post guards about this inn—for your protection, of course."

"Your solicitude overwhelms us, my Lord," Aunt Pol said dryly.

"Your servant, my Lady," Brendig said with a formal bow. And then he turned and left the room.

The polished door was only wood; Garion knew that, but as it closed behind the departing Brendig it seemed to have that dreadful, final clang of the door to a dungeon.

CHAPTER ELEVEN

They were nine days on the coast road from Camaar to the capital at Sendar, though it was only fifty-five leagues. Captain Brendig measured their pace carefully, and his detachment of soldiers was arranged in such fashion that even the thought of escape was impossible. Although it had stopped snowing, the road was still difficult, and the wind which blew in off the sea and across the broad, snow-covered salt marshes was raw and chill. They stayed each night in the evenly spaced Sendarian hostels which stood like mileposts along that uninhabited stretch of coast. The hostels were not quite so well appointed as were their Tolnedran counterparts along the Great North Road, but they were at least adequate. Captain Brendig seemed solicitous about their comfort, but he also posted guards each night.

On the evening of the second day, Garion sat near the fire with Durnik, staring moodily into the flames. Durnik was his oldest friend, and Garion felt a desperate need for friendship just then.

"Durnik," he said finally.

"Yes, lad?"

"Have you ever been in a dungeon?"

"What could I have done to be put in a dungeon?"

"I thought that you might have seen one sometime."

"Honest folk don't go near such places," Durnik said.

"I've heard they're awful—dark and cold and full of rats."

"What's all this talk of dungeons?" Durnik asked.

"I'm afraid we may find out all about places like that very soon," Garion said, trying not to sound too frightened.

"We've done nothing wrong," Durnik said.

"Then why would the king have us seized like this? Kings don't do things like that without good reason."

"We haven't done anything wrong," Durnik repeated stubbornly.

"But maybe Mister Wolf has," Garion suggested. "The king wouldn't send all these soldiers after him without some reason—and we could all be thrown in the dungeon with him just because we happened to be his companions."

"Things like that don't happen in Sendaria," Durnik said firmly.

The next day the wind was very strong as it blew in off the sea; but it was a warm wind, and the foot-deep snow on the road began to turn slushy. By midday it had started to rain. They rode in sodden misery toward the next hostel.

"I'm afraid we'll have to delay our journey until this blows out," Captain Brendig said that evening, looking out one of the tiny windows of the hostel. "The road's going to be quite impassable by morning."

They spent the next day, and the next, sitting in the cramped main room of the hostel listening to the wind-driven rain slashing at the walls and roof, all the while under the watchful eyes of Brendig and his soldiers.

"Silk," Garion said on the second day, moving over to the bench where the rat-faced little man sat dozing.

"Yes, Garion?" Silk asked, rousing himself.

"What kind of man is the king?"

"Which king?"

"Of Sendaria."

"A foolish man—like all kings." Silk laughed. "The Sendarian kings are perhaps a bit more foolish, but that's only natural. Why do you ask?"

"Well—" Garion hesitated. "Let's suppose that somebody did something that the king didn't like, and there were some other people traveling with him, and the king had these people seized. Would the king just throw them all into the dungeon? Or would he let the others go and just keep the one who'd angered him?"

Silk looked at him for a moment and then spoke firmly. "That question's unworthy of you, Garion."

Garion flushed. "I'm afraid of dungeons," he said in a small voice, suddenly very ashamed of himself. "I don't want to be locked up in the dark forever when I don't even know what for."

"The kings of Sendaria are just and honest men," Silk told him. "Not too bright, I'm afraid, but always fair."

"How can they be kings if they aren't wise?" Garion objected.

"Wisdom's a useful trait in a king," Silk said, "but hardly essential."

"How do they get to be kings, then?" Garion demanded.

"Some are born to it," Silk said. "The stupidest man in the world can be a king if he has the right parents. Sendarian kings have a disadvantage because they started so low."

"Low?"

"They were elected. Nobody ever elected a king before—only the Sendars."

"How do you elect a king?"

Silk smiled. "Very badly, Garion. It's a poor way to select a king. The other ways are worse, but election is a very bad way to choose a king."

"Tell me how it was done," Garion said.

Silk glanced briefly at the rain-spattered window across the room and shrugged. "It's a way to pass the time," he said. And then he leaned back, stretched his feet toward the fire and began.

"It all started about fifteen hundred years ago," he said, his voice loud enough to reach the ears of Captain Brendig, who sat nearby writing on a piece of parchment. "Sendaria wasn't a kingdom then, nor even a separate country. It had belonged from time to time to Cherek, Algaria or the northern Arends—Wacite or Asturian, depending on the fortunes of the Arendish civil war. When that war finally came to an end and the Wacites were destroyed and the Asturians had been defeated and driven into the untracked reaches of the great forest in northern Arendia, the Emperor of Tolnedra, Ran Horb II, decided that there ought to be a kingdom here."

"How could a Tolnedran emperor make that kind of decision for Sendaria?" Garion asked.

"The arm of the Empire is very long," Silk said. "The Great North Road had been built during the Second Borune Dynasty—I think it was Ran Borune IV who started the construction, wasn't it, Captain?"

"The fifth," Brendig said somewhat sourly without looking up. "Ran Borune V."

"Thank you, Captain," Silk said. "I can never keep the Borune Dynasties straight. Anyway, there were already imperial legions in Sendaria to maintain the highway, and if one has troops in an area, one has a certain authority, wouldn't you say, Captain?"

"It's your story," Brendig said shortly.

"Indeed it is," Silk agreed. "Now it wasn't really out of any kind of generosity that Ran Horb made his decision, Garion. Don't misunderstand that. Tolnedrans never give anything away. It was just that the Mimbrate Arends had finally won the Arendish civil war—a thousand years of bloodshed and treachery—and Tolnedra couldn't afford to allow the Mimbrates to expand into the north. The creation of an independent kingdom in Sendaria would block Mimbrate access to the trade routes down out of Drasnia and prevent the seat of world power from moving to Vo Mimbre and leaving the imperial capital at Tol Honeth in a kind of backwater."

"It all sounds terribly involved," Garion said.

"Not really," Silk said. "It's only politics, and that's a very simple game, isn't it, Captain?"

"A game I do not play," Brendig said, not looking up.

"Really?" Silk asked. "So long at court and not a politician? You're a rare man, Captain. At any rate, the Sendars suddenly discovered that they had themselves a kingdom but that they had no genuine hereditary nobility. Oh, there were a few retired Tolnedran nobles living on estates here and there, assorted pretenders to this or that Wacite or Asturian title, a Cherek war chief or two with a few followers, but no genuine Sendarian nobility. And so it was that they decided to hold a national election—select a king, don't you see, and then leave the bestowing of titles up to him. A very practical approach, and typically Sendarian."

"How do you elect a king?" Garion asked, beginning to lose his dread of dungeons in his fascination with the story.

"Everybody votes," Silk said simply. "Parents, of course, probably cast the votes for their children, but it appears that there was very little cheating. The rest of the world stood around and laughed at all this foolishness, but the Sendars continued to cast ballot after ballot for a dozen years."

"Six years, actually," Brendig said with his face still down over his parchment. "3827 to 3833."

"And there were over a thousand candidates," Silk said expansively.

"Seven hundred and forty-three," Brendig said tightly.

"I stand corrected, noble Captain," Silk said. "It's an enormous comfort to have such an expert here to catch my errors. I'm but a simple Drasnian merchant with little background in history. Anyway, on the twenty-third ballot, they finally elected their king—a rutabaga farmer named Fundor."

"He raised more than just rutabagas," Brendig said, looking up with an angry face.

"Of course he did," Silk said, smacking his forehead with an open palm. "How could I have forgotten the cabbages? He raised cabbages, too, Garion. Never forget the cabbages. Well, everybody in Sendaria who thought he was important journeyed to Fundor's farm and found him vigorously fertilizing his fields, and they greeted him with a great cry, 'Hail, Fundor the Magnificent, King of Sendaria,' and fell on their knees in his august presence."

"Must we continue with this?" Brendig asked in a pained voice, looking up.

"The boy wants to know, Captain," Silk replied with an innocent face. "It's our duty as his elders to instruct him in the history of our past, wouldn't you say?"

"Say whatever you like," Brendig said in a stiff voice.

"Thank you for your permission, Captain," Silk said, inclining his head. "Do you know what the King of Sendaria said then, Garion?" he asked.

"No," Garion said. "What?"

" 'I pray you, your eminences,' the king said, 'have a care for your finery. I have just well manured the bed in which you are kneeling.' "

Barak, who was sitting nearby, roared with laughter, pounding his knee with one huge hand.

"I find this less than amusing, sir," Captain Brendig said coldly, rising to his feet. "I make no jokes about the King of Drasnia, do I?"

"You're a courteous man, Captain," Silk said mildly, "and a nobleman. I'm merely a poor man trying to make his way in the world."

Brendig looked at him helplessly and then turned and stamped from the room.

The following morning the wind had blown itself out and the rain had stopped. The road was very nearly a quagmire, but Brendig decided that they must continue. Travel that day was difficult, but the next was somewhat easier as the road began to drain.

Aunt Pol seemed unconcerned by the fact that they had been seized at the king's orders. She maintained her regal bearing even though Garion saw no real need to continue the subterfuge and wished fervently that she would abandon it. The familiar practical sensibility with which she had ruled her kitchen at Faldor's farm had somehow been replaced by a kind of demanding willfulness that Garion found particularly distressing. For the first time in his life he felt a distance between them, and it left a vacancy that had never been there before. To make matters worse, the gnawing uncertainty which had been steadily growing since Silk's unequivocal declaration on the hilltop outside Winold that Aunt Pol could not possibly be his Aunt sawed roughly at his sense of his own identity, and Garion often found himself staring at the awful question, "Who am I?"

Mister Wolf seemed changed as well. He seldom spoke either on the road nor at night in the hostels. He spent a great deal of time sitting by himself with an expression of moody irritability on his face.

Finally, on the ninth day after their departure from Camaar, the broad salt marshes ended, and the land along the coast became more rolling. They topped a hill about midday just as the pale winter sun broke through the clouds, and there in the valley below them the walled city of Sendar lay facing the sea.

The detachment of guards at the south gate of the city saluted smartly as Captain Brendig led the little party through, and he returned their salute crisply. The broad streets of the city seemed filled with people in the finest clothing, all moving about importantly as if their errands were the most vital in the world.

"Courtiers." Barak, who chanced to be riding beside Garion, snorted with contempt. "Not a real man amongst them."

"A necessary evil, my dear Barak," Silk said back over his shoulder to the big man. "Little jobs require little men, and it's the little jobs that keep a kingdom running."

After they had passed through a magnificently large square, they moved up a wide avenue to the palace. It was a very large building with many stories and broad wings extending out on each side of the paved courtyard. The entire structure was surmounted by a round tower that was easily the highest edifice in the whole city.

"Where do you suppose the dungeons are?" Garion whispered to Durnik when they stopped.

"I would take it most kindly, Garion," Durnik said with a pained look, "if you would not speak so much of dungeons."

Captain Brendig dismounted and went to meet a fussy-looking man in an embroidered tunic and feathered cap who came down the wide steps at the front of the palace to meet them. They spoke for a few moments and seemed to be arguing.

"My orders are from the king himself," Brendig said, his voice carrying to where they sat. "I am commanded to deliver these people directly to him immediately upon our arrival."

"My orders are also from the king," the fussy-looking man said, "and I am commanded to have them made presentable before they are delivered to the throne room. I'll take charge of them."

"They'll remain in my custody, Count Nilden, until they have been delivered to the king himself," Brendig said coldly.

"I won't have your muddy soldiers tracking through the halls of the palace, Lord Brendig," the Count replied.

"Then we'll wait here, Count Nilden," Brendig said. "Be so good as to fetch his Majesty."

"Fetch?" The Count's face was aghast. "I am Chief Butler to his Majesty's household, Lord Brendig. I do not fetch anything or anybody."

Brendig turned as if to remount his horse.

"Oh, very well," Count Nilden said petulantly, "if you must have it your own way. At least have them wipe their feet."

Brendig bowed coldly.

"I won't forget this, Lord Brendig," Nilden threatened.

"Nor shall I, Count Nilden," Brendig replied.

Then they all dismounted and, with Brendig's soldiers drawn up in close order about them, they crossed the courtyard to a broad door near the center of the west wing.

"Be so good as to follow me," Count Nilden said, glancing with a shudder at the mud-spattered soldiers, and he led them into the wide corridor which lay beyond the door.

Apprehension and curiosity struggled in Garion's mind. Despite the assurances of Silk and Durnik and the hopeful implications of Count Nilden's announcement that he was going to have them made presentable, the threat of some clammy, rat-infested dungeon, complete with a rack and a wheel and other unpleasant things, still seemed very real. On the other hand, he had never been in a palace before, and his eyes tried to be everywhere at once. That part of his mind which sometimes spoke to him in dry detachment told him that his fears were probably groundless and that his gawking made him appear to be a doltish country bumpkin.

Count Nilden led them directly to a part of the corridor where there were a number of highly polished doors. "This one is for the boy," he announced, pointing at one of them.

One of the soldiers opened the door, and Garion reluctantly stepped through, looking back over his shoulder at Aunt Pol.

"Come along now," a somewhat impatient voice said.

Garion whirled, not knowing what to expect.

"Close the door, boy," the fine-looking man who had been waiting for him said. "We don't have all day, you know." The man was waiting beside a large wooden tub with steam rising from it. "Quickly, boy, take off those filthy rags and get into the tub. His Majesty is waiting."

Too confused to object or even answer, Garion numbly began to unlace his tunic.

After he had been bathed and the knots had been brushed out of his hair, he was dressed in clothes which lay on a nearby bench. His coarse woolen hose of serviceable peasant brown were exchanged for ones of a much finer weave in a lustrous blue. His scuffed and muddy boots were traded for soft leather shoes. His tunic was soft white linen, and the doublet he wore over it was a rich blue, trimmed with a silvery fur.

"I guess that's the best I can do on short notice," the man who had bathed and dressed him said, looking him up and down critically. "At least I won't be totally embarrassed when you're presented to the king."

Garion mumbled his thanks and then stood, waiting for further instructions.

"Well, go along, boy. You mustn't keep his Majesty waiting."

Silk and Barak stood in the corridor, talking quietly. Barak was hugely splendid in a green brocade doublet, but looked uncomfortable without his sword. Silk's doublet was a rich black, trimmed in silver, and his scraggly whiskers had been carefully trimmed into an elegant short beard.

"What does all of this mean?" Garion asked as he joined them.

"We're to be presented to the king," Barak said, "and our honest clothes might have given offense. Kings aren't accustomed to looking at ordinary men."

Durnik emerged from one of the rooms, his face pale with anger. "That overdressed fool wanted to give me a bath!" he said in choked outrage.

"It's the custom," Silk explained. "Noble guests aren't expected to bathe themselves. I hope you didn't hurt him."

"I'm not a noble, and I'm quite able to bathe myself," Durnik said hotly. "I told him that I'd drown him in his own tub if he didn't keep his hands to himself. After that, he didn't pester me anymore, but he did steal my clothes. I had to put these on instead." He gestured at his clothes, which were quite similar to Garion's. "I hope nobody sees me in all this frippery."

"Barak says the king might be offended if he saw us in our real clothes," Garion told him.

"The king won't be looking at me," Durnik said, "and I don't like this business of trying to look like something I'm not. I'll wait outside with the horses if I can get my own clothes back."

"Be patient, Durnik," Barak advised. "We'll get this business with the king straightened out and then be on our way again."

If Durnik was angry, Mister Wolf was in what could best be described as a towering fury. He came out into the corridor dressed in a snowy white robe, deeply cowled at the back. "Someone's going to pay for this," he raged.

"It *does* become you," Silk said admiringly.

"Your taste has always been questionable, Master Silk," Wolf said in a frosty tone. "Where's Pol?"

"The lady has not yet made her appearance," Silk said.

"I should have known," Wolf said, sitting down on a nearby bench. "We may as well be comfortable. Pol's preparations usually take quite a while."

And so they waited. Captain Brendig, who had changed his boots and doublet, paced up and down as the minutes dragged by. Garion was totally baffled by their reception. They did not seem to be under arrest, but his imagination still saw dungeons, and that was enough to make him very jumpy.

And then Aunt Pol appeared. She wore the blue velvet gown that had been made for her in Camaar and a silver circlet about her head which set off the single white lock at her brow. Her bearing was regal and her face stern.

"So soon, Mistress Pol?" Wolf asked dryly. "I hope you weren't rushed."

She ignored that and examined each of them in turn. "Adequate, I suppose," she said finally, absently adjusting the collar of Garion's doublet. "Give me your arm, Old Wolf, and let's find out what the King of the Sendars wants with us."

Mister Wolf rose from his bench, extended his arm, and the two of them started down the corridor. Captain Brendig hastily assembled his soldiers and followed them all in some kind of ragged order. "If you please, my Lady," he called out to Aunt Pol, "permit me to show you the way."

"We know the way, Lord Brendig," she replied without so much as turning her head.

Count Nilden, the Chief Butler, stood waiting for them in front of two massive doors guarded by uniformed men-at-arms. He bowed slightly to Aunt Pol and snapped his fingers. The men-at-arms swung the heavy doors inward.

Fulrach, the King of Sendaria, was a dumpy-looking man with a short brown beard. He sat, rather uncomfortably it appeared, on a high-backed throne which stood on a dais at one end of the great hall into which Count Nilden led them. The throne room was vast, with a high, vaulted ceiling and walls covered with what seemed acres of heavy, red velvet drapery. There were candles everywhere, and dozens of people strolled about in fine clothes and chatted idly in the corners, all but ignoring the presence of the king.

"May I announce you?" Count Nilden asked Mister Wolf.

"Fulrach knows who I am," Wolf replied shortly and strode down the long scarlet carpet toward the throne with Aunt Pol still on his arm. Garion and the others followed, with Brendig and his soldiers close behind, through the suddenly quiet crowd of courtiers and their ladies.

At the foot of the throne they all stopped, and Wolf bowed rather coldly. Aunt Pol, her eyes frosty, curtsied, and Barak and Silk bowed in a courtly manner. Durnik and Garion followed suit, though not nearly as gracefully.

"If it please your Majesty," Brendig's voice came from behind them, "these are the ones you sought."

"I knew you could be depended upon, Lord Brendig," the King replied in a rather ordinary-sounding voice. "Your reputation is well deserved. You have my thanks." Then he looked at Mister Wolf and the rest of them, his expression indecipherable.

Garion began to tremble.

"My dear old friend," the king said to Mister Wolf. "It's been too many years since we met last."

"Have you lost your wits entirely, Fulrach?" Mister Wolf snapped in a voice which carried no further than the king's ears. "Why do you choose to interfere with me—now, of all times? And what possessed you to outfit me in this absurd thing?" He plucked at the front of his white robe in disgust. "Are you trying to announce my presence to every Murgo from here to the hook of Arendia?"

The king's face looked pained. "I was afraid you might take it this way," he said in a voice no louder than Mister Wolf's had been. "I'll explain when we can speak more privately." He turned quickly to Aunt Pol as if trying to preserve the appearance at least of dignity. "It's been much too long since we have seen you, dear Lady. Layla and the children have missed you, and I have been desolate in your absence."

"Your Majesty is too kind," Aunt Pol said, her tone as cold as Wolf's.

The king winced. "Pray, dear Lady," he apologized, "don't judge me too hastily. My reasons were urgent. I hope that Lord Brendig's summons did not too greatly inconvenience you."

"Lord Brendig was the soul of courtesy," Aunt Pol said, her tone unchanged. She glanced once at Brendig, who had grown visibly pale.

"And you, my Lord Barak," the king hurried on as if trying to make the best of a bad situation, "how fares your cousin, our dear brother king, Anheg of Cherek?"

"He was well when last I saw him, your Majesty," Barak replied formally. "A bit drunk, but that's not unusual for Anheg."

The king chuckled a bit nervously and turned quickly to Silk. "Prince Kheldar of the Royal House of Drasnia," he said. "We are amazed to find such noble visitors in our realm, and more than a little injured that they chose not to call upon us so that we might greet them. Is the King of the Sendars of so little note that he's not even worth a brief stop?"

"We intended no disrespect, your Majesty," Silk replied, bowing, "but our errand was of such urgency that there was no time for the usual courtesies."

The king flickered a warning glance at that and surprisingly wove his fingers in the scarce perceptible gestures of the Drasnian secret language. *Not here. Too many ears about.* He then looked inquiringly at Durnik and Garion.

Aunt Pol stepped forward. "This is Goodman Durnik of the District of Erat, your Majesty," she said, "a brave and honest man."

"Welcome, Goodman Durnik," the king said. "I can only hope that men may also one day call *me* a brave and honest man."

Durnik bowed awkwardly, his face filled with bewilderment. "I'm just a simple blacksmith, your Honor," he said, "but I hope all men know that I am your Honor's most loyal and devoted subject."

"Well-spoken, Goodman Durnik," the king said with a smile, and then he looked at Garion.

Aunt Pol followed his glance. "A boy, your Majesty," she said rather indifferently. "Garion by name. He was placed in my care some years ago and accompanies us because I didn't know what else to do with him."

A terrible coldness struck at Garion's stomach. The certainty that her casual words were in fact the bald truth came crashing down upon him. She had not even tried to soften the blow. The indifference with which she had destroyed his life hurt almost more than the destruction itself.

"Also welcome, Garion," the king said. "You travel in noble company for one so young."

"I didn't know who they were, your Majesty," Garion said miserably. "Nobody tells me anything."

The king laughed in tolerant amusement. "As you grow older, Garion," he said, "you'll probably find that during these days such innocence is the most comfortable state in which to live. I've been told things of late that I'd much prefer not to know."

"May we speak privately now, Fulrach?" Mister Wolf said, his voice still irritated.

"In good time, my old friend," the king replied. "I've ordered a banquet prepared in your honor. Let's all go in and dine. Layla and the children are waiting for us. There will be time later to discuss certain matters." And with that he rose and stepped down from the dais.

Garion, sunk in his private misery, fell in beside Silk. "Prince Kheldar?" he said, desperately needing to take his mind off the shocking reality that had just fallen upon him.

"An accident of birth, Garion," Silk said with a shrug. "Something over which I had no control. Fortunately I'm only the nephew of the King of Drasnia and far down in the line of succession. I'm not in any immediate danger of ascending the throne."

"And Barak is—?"

"The cousin of King Anheg of Cherek," Silk replied. He looked over his shoulder. "What is your exact rank, Barak?" he asked.

"The Earl of Trellheim," Barak rumbled. "Why do you ask?"

"The lad here was curious," Silk said.

"It's all nonsense anyway," Barak said, "but when Anheg became king, someone had to become Clan-Chief. In Cherek you can't be both. It's considered unlucky—particularly by the chiefs of the other clans."

"I can see why they might feel that way." Silk laughed.

"It's an empty title anyway," Barak observed. "There hasn't been a clan war in Cherek for over three thousand years. I let my youngest brother act in my stead. He's a simpleminded fellow and easily amused. Besides, it annoys my wife."

"You're married?" Garion was startled.

"If you want to call it that," Barak said sourly.

Silk nudged Garion warningly, indicating that this was a delicate subject.

"Why didn't you tell us?" Garion demanded accusingly. "About your ti-tles, I mean."

"Would it have made any difference?" Silk asked.

"Well—no," Garion admitted, "but—" He stopped, unable to put his feelings about the matter into words. "I don't understand any of this," he concluded lamely.

"It'll all become clear in time," Silk assured him as they entered the ban-quet hall.

The hall was almost as large as the throne room. There were long tables covered with fine linen cloth and once again candles everywhere. A servant stood behind each chair, and everything was supervised by a plump little woman with a beaming face and a tiny crown perched precariously atop her head. As they all entered, she came forward quickly.

"Dear Pol," she said, "you look just wonderful." She embraced Aunt Pol warmly, and the two began talking together animatedly.

"Queen Layla," Silk explained briefly to Garion. "They call her the Mother of Sendaria. The four children over there are hers. She has four or five others—older and probably away on state business, since Fulrach insists that his children earn their keep. It's a standard joke among the other kings that Queen Layla's been pregnant since she was fourteen, but that's probably because they're expected to send royal gifts at each new birth. She's a good woman, though, and she keeps King Fulrach from making too many mistakes."

"She knows Aunt Pol," Garion said, and that fact disturbed him for some reason.

"Everybody knows your Aunt Pol," Silk told him.

Since Aunt Pol and the queen were deep in conversation and already drifting toward the head of the table, Garion stayed close to Silk. *Don't let me make any mistakes,* he gestured, trying to keep the movements of his fin-gers inconspicuous.

Silk winked in reply.

Once they were all seated and the food began to arrive, Garion began to relax. He found that all he had to do was follow Silk's lead, and the in-tricate niceties of formal dining no longer intimidated him. The talk around him was dignified and quite incomprehensible, but he reasoned that no one was likely to pay much attention to him and that he was probably safe if he kept his mouth shut and his eyes on his plate.

An elderly nobleman with a beautifully curled silvery beard, however, leaned toward him. "You have traveled recently, I'm told," he said in a some-what condescending tone. "How fares the kingdom, young man?"

Garion looked helplessly across the table at Silk. *What do I say?* he gestured with his fingers.

Tell him that the kingdom fares no better nor no worse than might be anti-cipated under the present circumstances, Silk replied.

Garion dutifully repeated that.

"Ah," the old nobleman said, "much as I had expected. You're a very ob-servant boy for one so young. I enjoy talking with young people. Their views are so fresh."

Who is he? Garion gestured.

The Earl of Seline, Silk replied. *He's a tiresome old bore, but be polite to him. Address him as my Lord.*

"And how did you find the roads?" the earl inquired.

"Somewhat in disrepair, my Lord," Garion replied with Silk's prompting. "But that's normal for this time of year, isn't it?"

"Indeed it is," the earl said approvingly. "What a splendid boy you are."

The strange three-way conversation continued, and Garion even began to enjoy himself as the comments fed to him by Silk seemed to amaze the old gentleman.

At last the banquet was over, and the king rose from his seat at the head of the table. "And now, dear friends," he announced, "Queen Layla and I would like to visit privately with our noble guests, and so we pray you will excuse us." He offered his arm to Aunt Pol, Mister Wolf offered his to the plump little queen, and the four of them walked toward the far door of the hall.

The Earl of Seline smiled broadly at Garion and then looked across the table. "I've enjoyed our conversation, Prince Kheldar," he said to Silk. "I may indeed be a tiresome old bore as you say, but that can sometimes be an ad-vantage, don't you think?"

Silk laughed ruefully. "I should have known that an old fox like you would be an adept at the secret language, my Lord."

"A legacy from a misspent youth." The earl laughed. "Your pupil is most proficient, Prince Kheldar, but his accent is strange."

"The weather was cold while he was learning, my Lord," Silk said, "and our fingers were a bit stiff. I'll correct the problem when we have leisure."

The old nobleman seemed enormously pleased with himself at having outsmarted Silk. "Splendid boy," he said, patting Garion's shoulder, and then he went off chuckling to himself.

"You knew he understood all along," Garion accused Silk.

"Of course," Silk said. "Drasnian intelligence knows every adept at our secret speech. Sometimes it's useful to permit certain carefully selected mes-sages to be intercepted. Don't ever underestimate the Earl of Seline, however. It's not impossible that he's at least as clever as I am, but look how much he enjoyed catching us."

"Can't you ever do anything without being sly?" Garion asked. His tone was a bit grumpy, since he was convinced that somehow he had been the butt of the whole joke.

"Not unless I absolutely have to, my Garion." Silk laughed. "People like me continually practice deception—even when it's not necessary. Our lives sometimes depend on how cunning we are, and so we need to keep our wits sharp."

"It must be a lonely way to live," Garion observed rather shrewdly at the silent prompting of his inner voice. "You never really trust anyone, do you?"

"I suppose not," Silk said. "It's a game we play, Garion. We're all very skilled at it—at least we are if we intend to live very long. We all know each other, since we're members of a very small profession. The rewards are great, but after a while we play our game only for the joy of defeating each other. You're right, though. It *is* lonely, and sometimes disgusting—but most of the time it's a great deal of fun."

Count Nilden came up to them and bowed politely. "His Majesty asks that you and the boy join him and your other friends in his private apartments, Prince Kheldar," he said. "If you'll be so good as to follow me."

"Of course," Silk said. "Come along, Garion."

The king's private apartments were much simpler than the ornate halls in the main palace. King Fulrach had removed his crown and state robes and now looked much like any other Sendar in rather ordinary clothes. He stood talking quietly with Barak. Queen Layla and Aunt Pol were seated on a couch deep in conversation, and Durnik was not far away, trying his best to look inconspicuous. Mister Wolf stood alone near a window, his face like a thundercloud.

"Ah, Prince Kheldar," the king said. "We thought perhaps you and Garion had been waylaid."

"We were fencing with the Earl of Seline, your Majesty," Silk said lightly. "Figuratively speaking, of course."

"Be careful of him," the king cautioned. "It's quite possible that he's too shrewd even for one of your talents."

"I have a great deal of respect for the old scoundrel." Silk laughed.

King Fulrach glanced apprehensively at Mister Wolf, then squared his shoulders and sighed. "I suppose we'd better get this unpleasantness over with," he said. "Layla, would you entertain our other guests while I give our grim-faced old friend there and the Lady the opportunity to scold me. It's obvious that he's not going to be happy until they've said a few unkind things to me about some matters that weren't really my fault."

"Of course, dear," Queen Layla said. "Try not to be too long and please don't shout. The children have been put to bed and they need their rest."

Aunt Pol rose from the couch, and she and Mister Wolf, whose expression hadn't changed, followed the king into an adjoining chamber.

"Well, then," Queen Layla said pleasantly, "what shall we talk about?"

"I am instructed, your Highness, to convey the regards of Queen Porenn of Drasnia to you should the occasion arise," Silk said in a courtly manner. "She asks leave of you to broach a correspondence on a matter of some delicacy."

"Why, of course," Queen Layla beamed. "She's a dear child, far too pretty and sweet-natured for that fat old bandit, Rhodar. I hope he hasn't made her unhappy."

"No, your Highness," Silk said. "Amazing though it may seem, she loves my uncle to distraction, and he, of course, is delirious with joy over so young and beautiful a wife. It's positively sickening the way they dote on each other."

"Some day, Prince Kheldar, you will fall in love," the queen said with a little smirk, "and the twelve kingdoms will stand around and chortle over the fall of so notorious a bachelor. What is this matter Porenn wishes to discuss with me?"

"It's a question of fertility, your Highness," Silk said with a delicate cough. "She wants to present my uncle with an heir and she needs to seek your advice in the business. The entire world stands in awe of your gifts in that particular area."

Queen Layla blushed prettily and then laughed. "I'll write to her at once," she promised.

Garion by now had carefully worked his way to the door through which King Fulrach had taken Aunt Pol and Mister Wolf. He began a meticulous examination of a tapestry on the wall to conceal the fact that he was trying to hear what was going on behind the closed door. It took him only a moment to begin to pick up familiar voices.

"Exactly what does all this foolishness mean, Fulrach?" Mister Wolf was saying.

"Please don't judge me too hastily, Ancient One," the King said placatingly. "Some things have happened that you might not be aware of."

"You know that I'm aware of everything that happens," Wolf said.

"Did you know that we are defenseless if the Accursed One awakens? That which held him in check has been stolen from off the throne of the Rivan King."

"As a matter of fact, I was following the trail of the thief when your noble Captain Brendig interrupted me in my search."

"I'm sorry," Fulrach said, "but you wouldn't have gone much farther anyway. All the Kings of Aloria have been searching for you for three months now. Your likeness, drawn by the finest artists, is in the hands of every ambassador, agent and official of the five kingdoms of the north. Actually, you've been followed since you left Darine."

"Fulrach, I'm busy. Tell the Alorn Kings to leave me alone. Why are they suddenly so interested in my movements?"

"They want to have council with you," the king said. "The Alorns are preparing for war, and even my poor Sendaria is being quietly mobilized. If the Accursed One arises now, we're all doomed. The power that's been stolen can very possibly be used to awaken him, and his first move will be to attack the west—you know that, Belgarath. And you also know that until the return of the Rivan King, the west has no real defense."

Garion blinked and started violently, then tried to cover the sudden movement by bending to look at some of the finer detail on the tapestry. He told himself that he had heard wrong. The name King Fulrach had spoken could not have really been Belgarath. Belgarath was a fairy-tale figure, a myth.

"Just tell the Alorn Kings that I'm in pursuit of the thief," Mister Wolf said. "I don't have time for councils just now. If they'll leave me alone, I should be able to catch up with him before he can do any mischief with the thing he's managed to steal."

"Don't tempt fate, Fulrach," Aunt Pol advised. "Your interference is costing us time we can't afford to lose. Presently I'll become vexed with you."

The king's voice was firm as he answered. "I know your power, Lady Polgara," he said, and Garion jumped again. "I don't have any choice, however," the king continued. "I'm bound by my word to deliver you all up at Val Alorn to the Kings of Aloria, and a king can't break his word to other kings."

There was a long silence in the other room while Garion's mind raced through a dozen possibilities.

"You're not a bad man, Fulrach," Mister Wolf said. "Not perhaps as bright as I might wish, but a good man nonetheless. I won't raise my hand against you—nor will my daughter."

"Speak for yourself, Old Wolf," Aunt Pol said grimly.

"No, Polgara," he said. "If we have to go to Val Alorn, let's go with all possible speed. The sooner we explain things to the Alorns, the sooner they'll stop interfering."

"I think age is beginning to soften your brain, Father," Aunt Pol said. "We don't have the time for this excursion to Val Alorn. Fulrach can explain to the Alorn Kings."

"It won't do any good, Lady Polgara," the king said rather ruefully. "As your father so pointedly mentioned, I'm not considered very bright. The Alorn Kings won't listen to me. If you leave now, they'll just send someone like Brendig to apprehend you again."

"Then that unfortunate man may suddenly find himself living out the remainder of his days as a toad or possibly a radish," Aunt Pol said ominously.

"Enough of that, Pol," Mister Wolf said. "Is there a ship ready, Fulrach?"

"It lies at the north wharf, Belgarath," the king replied. "A Cherek vessel sent by King Anheg."

"Very well," Mister Wolf said. "Tomorrow then we'll go to Cherek. It seems that I'm going to have to point out a few things to some thickheaded Alorns. Will you be going with us?"

"I'm obliged to," Fulrach said. "The council's to be general, and Sendaria's involved."

"You haven't heard the last of this, Fulrach," Aunt Pol said.

"Never mind, Pol," Mister Wolf said. "He's only doing what he thinks is right. We'll straighten it all out in Val Alorn."

Garion was trembling as he stepped away from the door. It was impossible. His skeptical Sendarian upbringing made him at first incapable of even considering such an absurdity. Reluctantly, however, he finally forced himself to look the idea full in the face.

What if Mister Wolf really *was* Belgarath the Sorcerer, a man who had lived for over seven thousand years? And what if Aunt Pol was really his daughter, Polgara the Sorceress, who was only slightly younger? All the bits and pieces, the cryptic hints, the half-truths, fell together. Silk had been right; she could not be his Aunt. Garion's orphaning was complete now. He was adrift in the world with no ties of blood or heritage to cling to. Desperately he wanted to go home, back to Faldor's farm, where he could sink himself in unthinking obscurity in a quiet place where there were no sorcerers or strange searches or anything that would even remind him of Aunt Pol and the cruel hoax she had made of his life.

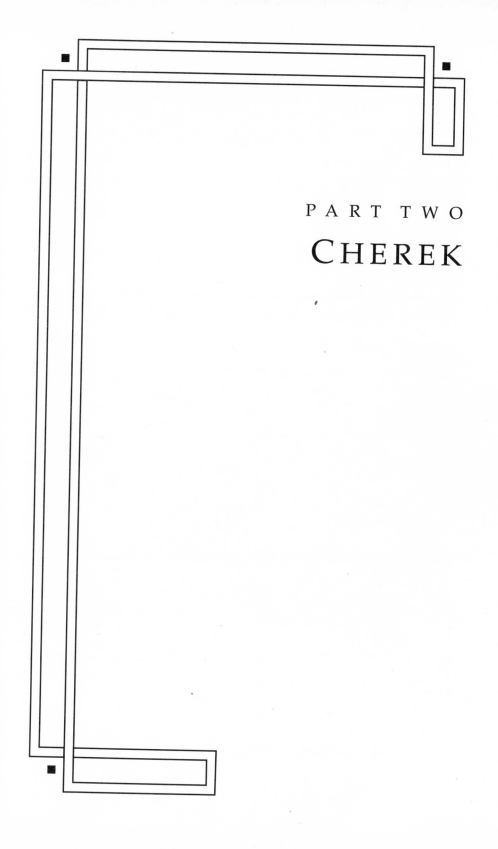

PART TWO

CHEREK

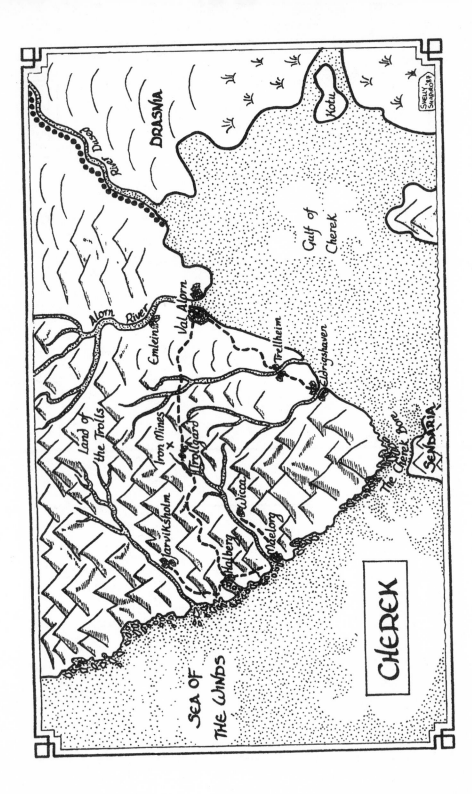

In the gray first light of early morning they rode through the quiet streets of Sendar to the harbor and their waiting ship. The finery of the evening before had been put aside, and they had all resumed their customary clothes. Even King Fulrach and the Earl of Seline had donned plain garb and now resembled nothing quite so much as two moderately prosperous Sendars on a business trip. Queen Layla, who was not to go with them, rode beside her husband, talking earnestly to him with an expression on her face that seemed almost to hover on the verge of tears. The party was accompanied by soldiers, cloaked against the raw, chill wind off the sea.

At the foot of the street which led down from the palace to the harbor, the stone wharves of Sendar jutted out into the choppy water, and there, rocking and straining against the hawsers which held her, was their ship. She was a lean vessel, narrow of beam and high-prowed, with a kind of wolfish appearance that did little to quiet Garion's nervousness about his first sea voyage. Lounging about on her deck were a number of savage-looking sailors, bearded and garbed in shaggy garments made of fur. With the exception of Barak, these were the first Chereks Garion had ever seen, and his first impression was that they would probably prove to be totally unreliable.

"Barak!" a burly man halfway up the mast shouted and dropped hand over hand down a steeply slanting rope to the deck and then jumped across to the wharf.

"Greldik!" Barak roared in response, swung down from his horse and clasped the evil-looking sailor in a bear hug.

"It would seem that Lord Barak is acquainted with our captain," the Earl of Seline observed.

"That's disquieting," Silk said wryly. "I was hoping for a sober, sensible captain of middle years and a conservative disposition. I'm not fond of ships and sea travel to begin with."

"I'm told that Captain Greldik is one of the finest seamen in all of Cherek," the earl assured him.

"My Lord," Silk said with a pained look, "Cherek definitions can be deceptive." Sourly he watched Barak and Greldik toasting their reunion with tankards of ale that had been passed down to them from the ship by a grinning sailor.

Queen Layla had dismounted and she embraced Aunt Pol. "Please watch out for my poor husband, Pol," she said with a little laugh that quivered a bit. "Don't let those Alorn bullies goad him into doing anything foolish."

"Of course, Layla," Aunt Pol said comfortingly.

"Now, Layla," King Fulrach said in an embarrassed voice. "I'll be all right. I'm a grown man, after all."

The plump little queen wiped her eyes. "I want you to promise to wear warm clothes," she said, "and not to sit up all night drinking with Anheg."

"We're on serious business, Layla," the king said. "There won't be time for any of that."

"I know Anheg too well," the queen sniffed. She turned to Mister Wolf, stood on her tiptoes and kissed his bearded cheek. "Dear Belgarath," she said. "When this is over, promise that you and Pol will come back for a long visit."

"I promise, Layla," Mister Wolf said gravely.

"The tide's turning, Lord King," Greldik said, "and my ship's growing restless."

"Oh dear," the queen said. She put her arms around the king's neck and buried her face in his shoulder.

"Now, now," Fulrach said awkwardly.

"If you don't go now, I'm going to cry right here in public," she said, pushing him away.

The stones of the wharf were slippery, and the slim Cherek ship bobbed and rolled in the chop. The narrow plank they had to cross heaved and swayed dangerously, but they all managed to board without accident. The sailors slipped the hawsers and took their places at the oars. The lean vessel leaped away from the wharf and moved swiftly into the harbor past the stout and bulky merchantmen anchored nearby. Queen Layla stood forlornly on the wharf, surrounded by tall soldiers. She waved a few times and then stood watching, her chin lifted bravely.

Captain Greldik took his place at the tiller with Barak by his side and signaled to a squat, muscular warrior crouched nearby. The squat man nodded and pulled a ragged square of sailcloth off a hide-topped drum. He began a slow beat, and the oarsmen immediately took up the rhythm. The ship surged ahead and made for the open sea.

Once they were beyond the protection of the harbor, the swells grew so ponderous that the ship no longer rocked but ran instead down the back of each wave and up the face of the next. The long oars, dipping to the rhythm of the sullen drum, left little swirls on the surface of the waves. The sea was lead-gray beneath the wintry sky, and the low, snow-covered coastline of Sendaria slid by on their right, bleak and desolate-looking.

Garion spent most of the day shivering in a sheltered spot near the high prow, moodily staring out at the sea. The shards and shambles into which his life had fallen the night before lay in ruins around him. The idea that Wolf was Belgarath and Aunt Pol was Polgara was of course an absurdity. He was convinced, however, that a part of the whole thing at least was true. She might not be Polgara, but she was almost certainly not his Aunt. He avoided looking at her as much as possible, and did not speak to anyone.

They slept that night in cramped quarters beneath the stern deck of the ship. Mister Wolf sat talking for a long time with King Fulrach and the Earl of Seline. Garion covertly watched the old man whose silvery hair and short-cropped beard seemed almost to glow in the light from a swinging oil lamp hanging from one of the low beams. He still looked the same as always, and Garion finally turned over and went to sleep.

The next day they rounded the hook of Sendaria and beat northeasterly with a good following wind. The sails were raised, and the oarsmen were able to rest. Garion continued to wrestle with his problem.

On the third day out the weather turned stormy and bitterly cold. The rigging crackled with ice, and sleet hissed into the sea around them.

"If this doesn't break, it'll be a rough passage through the Bore," Barak said, frowning into the sleet.

"The what?" Durnik asked apprehensively. Durnik was not at all comfortable on the ship. He was just recovering from a bout of seasickness, and he was obviously a bit edgy.

"The Cherek Bore," Barak explained. "It's a passage about a league wide between the northern tip of Sendaria and the southern end of the Cherek peninsula—riptides, whirlpools, that sort of thing. Don't be alarmed, Durnik. This is a good ship, and Greldik knows the secret of navigating the Bore. It may be a bit rough, but we'll be perfectly safe—unless we're unlucky, of course."

"That's a cheery thing to say," Silk observed dryly from nearby. "I've been trying for three days not to think about the Bore."

"Is it really that bad?" Durnik asked in a sinking voice.

"I make a special point of not going through it sober," Silk told him.

Barak laughed. "You ought to be thankful for the Bore, Silk," he said. "It keeps the Empire out of the Gulf of Cherek. All Drasnia would be a Tolnedran province if it wasn't there."

"I admire it politically," Silk said, "but personally I'd be much happier if I never had to look at it again."

On the following day they anchored near the rocky coast of northern Sendaria and waited for the tide to turn. In time it slackened and reversed, and the waters of the Sea of the Winds mounted and plunged through the Bore to raise the level of the Gulf of Cherek.

"Find something solid to hold on to, Garion," Barak advised as Greldik ordered the anchor raised. "With this following wind, the passage could be interesting." He strode along the narrow deck, his teeth gleaming in a broad grin.

It was foolish. Garion knew that, even as he stood up and began to follow the red-bearded man toward the prow, but four days of solitary brooding over a problem that refused to yield to any kind of logic made him feel almost belligerently reckless. He set his teeth together and took hold of a rusted iron ring embedded in the prow.

Barak laughed and clapped him a stunning blow on the shoulder. "Good boy," he said approvingly. "We'll stand together and look the Bore right down the throat."

Garion decided not to answer that.

With wind and tide behind her, Greldik's ship literally flew through the passage, yawing and shuddering as she was seized by the violent riptides. Icy spray stung their faces, and Garion, half-blinded by it, did not see the enormous whirlpool in the center of the Bore until they were almost upon it. He seemed to hear a vast roar and cleared his eyes just in time to see it yawning in front of him. "What's that?" he yelled over the noise.

"The Great Maelstrom," Barak shouted. "Hold on."

The Maelstrom was fully as large as the village of Upper Gralt and descended horribly down into a seething, mist-filled pit unimaginably far below. Incredibly, instead of guiding his vessel away from the vortex, Greldik steered directly at it.

"What's he doing?" Garion screamed.

"It's the secret of passing through the Bore," Barak roared. "We circle the Maelstrom twice to gain more speed. If the ship doesn't break up, she comes out like a rock from a sling, and we pass through the riptides beyond the Maelstrom before they can slow us down and drag us back."

"If the ship doesn't *what?*"

"Sometimes a ship is torn apart in the Maelstrom," Barak said. "Don't worry, boy. It doesn't happen very often, and Greldik's ship seems stout enough."

The ship's prow dipped hideously into the outer edges of the Maelstrom and then raced twice around the huge whirlpool with the oarsmen frantically bending their backs to the frenzied beat of the drum. The wind tore at Garion's face, and he clung to his iron ring, keeping his eyes averted from the seething maw gaping below.

And then they broke free and shot like a whistling stone through the churning water beyond the Maelstrom. The wind of their passage howled in the rigging, and Garion felt half-suffocated by its force.

Gradually the ship slowed in the swirling eddies, but the speed they had gained from the Maelstrom carried them on to calm water in a partially sheltered cove on the Sendarian side.

Barak was laughing gleefully and mopping spray from his beard. "Well, lad," he said, "what do you think of the Bore?"

Garion didn't trust himself to answer and concentrated on trying to pry his numb fingers from the iron ring.

A familiar voice rang out from the stern. "Garion!"

"Now you've gone and got me in trouble," Garion said resentfully, ignoring the fact that standing in the prow had been his own idea.

Aunt Pol spoke scathingly to Barak about his irresponsibility and then turned her attention to Garion.

"Well?" she said. "I'm waiting. Would you like to explain?"

"It wasn't Barak's fault," Garion said. "It was my own idea." There was no point in their both being in trouble, after all.

"I see," she said. "And what was behind that?"

The confusion and doubt which had been troubling him made him reckless. "I felt like it," he said, half-defiantly. For the first time in his life he felt on the verge of open rebellion.

"You what?"

"I felt like it," he repeated. "What difference does it make why I did it? You're going to punish me anyway."

Aunt Pol stiffened, and her eyes blazed.

Mister Wolf, who was sitting nearby, chuckled.

"What's so funny?" she snapped.

"Why don't you let me handle this, Pol?" the old man suggested.

"I can deal with it," she said.

"But not well, Pol," he said. "Not well at all. Your temper's too quick, and your tongue's too sharp. He's not a child anymore. He's not a man yet, but he's not a child either. The problem needs to be dealt with in a special way. I'll take care of it." He stood up. "I think I insist, Pol."

"You *what?*"

"I insist." His eyes hardened.

"Very well," she said in an icy voice, turned, and walked away.

"Sit down, Garion," the old man said.

"Why's she so mean?" Garion blurted.

"She isn't," Mister Wolf said. "She's angry because you frightened her. Nobody likes to be frightened."

"I'm sorry," Garion mumbled, ashamed of himself.

"Don't apologize to me," Wolf said. "I wasn't frightened." He looked for a moment at Garion, his eyes penetrating. "What's the problem?" he asked.

"They call you Belgarath," Garion said as if that explained it all, "and they call her Polgara."

"So?"

"It's just not possible."

"Didn't we have this conversation before? A long time ago?"

"Are you Belgarath?" Garion demanded bluntly.

"Some people call me that. What difference does it make?"

"I'm sorry," Garion said. "I just don't believe it."

"All right," Wolf shrugged. "You don't have to if you don't want to. What's that got to do with your being impolite to your Aunt?"

"It's just—" Garion faltered. "Well—" Desperately he wanted to ask Mister Wolf that ultimate, fatal question, but despite his certainty that there was no kinship between himself and Aunt Pol, he could not bear the thought of having it finally and irrevocably confirmed.

"You're confused," Wolf said. "Is that it? Nothing seems to be like it ought to be, and you're angry with your Aunt because it seems like it has to be her fault."

"You make it sound awfully childish," Garion said, flushing slightly.

"Isn't it?"

Garion flushed even more.

"It's your own problem, Garion," Mister Wolf said. "Do you really think it's proper to make others unhappy because of it?"

"No," Garion admitted in a scarcely audible voice.

"Your Aunt and I are who we are," Wolf said quietly. "People have made up a lot of nonsense about us, but that doesn't really matter. There are things that have to be done, and we're the ones who have to do them. That's what matters. Don't make things more difficult for your Aunt just because the world isn't exactly to your liking. That's not only childish, it's ill-mannered, and you're a better boy than that. Now, I really think you owe her an apology, don't you?"

"I suppose so," Garion said.

"I'm glad we had this chance to talk," the old man said, "but I wouldn't wait too long before making up with her. You wouldn't believe how long she can stay angry." He grinned suddenly. "She's been angry with me for as long as I can remember, and that's so long that I don't even like to think about it."

"I'll do it right now," Garion said.

"Good," Wolf approved.

Garion stood up and walked purposefully to where Aunt Pol stood staring out at the swirling currents of the Cherek Bore.

"Aunt Pol," he said.

"Yes, dear?"

"I'm sorry. I was wrong."

She turned and looked at him gravely. "Yes," she said, "you were."

"I won't do it again."

She laughed then, a low, warm laugh, and ran her fingers through his tangled hair. "Don't make promises you can't keep, dear," she said, and she embraced him, and everything was all right again.

After the fury of the tide through the Cherek Bore had abated, they sailed north along the snow-muffled east coast of the Cherek peninsula toward the ancient city which was the ancestral home of all Alorns, Algar and Drasnian as well as Cherek and Rivan. The wind was chill and the skies threatening, but the remainder of the voyage was uneventful. After three more days their ship entered the harbor at Val Alorn and tied up at one of the ice-shrouded wharves.

Val Alorn was unlike any Sendarian city. Its walls and buildings were so incredibly ancient that they seemed more like natural rock formations than the construction of human hands. The narrow, crooked streets were clogged with snow, and the mountains behind the city loomed high and white against the dark sky.

Several horse-drawn sleighs awaited them at the wharf with savage-looking drivers and shaggy horses stamping impatiently in the packed snow.

There were fur robes in the sleighs, and Garion drew one of them about him as he waited for Barak to conclude his farewells to Greldik and the sailors.

"Let's go," Barak told the driver as he climbed into the sleigh. "See if you can't catch up with the others."

"If you hadn't talked so long, they wouldn't be so far ahead, Lord Barak," the driver said sourly.

"That's probably true," Barak agreed.

The driver grunted, touched his horses with his whip, and the sleigh started up the street where the others had already disappeared.

Fur-clad Cherek warriors swaggered up and down the narrow streets, and many of them bellowed greetings to Barak as the sleigh passed. At one corner their driver was forced to halt while two burly men, stripped to the waist in the biting cold, wrestled savagely in the snow in the center of the street to the encouraging shouts of a crowd of onlookers.

"A common pastime," Barak told Garion. "Winter's a tedious time in Val Alorn."

"Is that the palace ahead?" Garion asked.

Barak shook his head. "The temple of Belar," he said. "Some men say that the Bear-God resides there in spirit. I've never seen him myself, though, so I can't say for sure."

Then the wrestlers rolled out of the way, and they continued.

On the steps of the temple an ancient woman wrapped in ragged woolen robes stood with a long staff clutched in one bony hand and her stringy hair wild about her face. "Hail, Lord Barak," she called in a cracked voice as they passed. "Thy Doom still awaits thee."

"Stop the sleigh," Barak growled at the driver, and he threw off his fur robe and jumped to the ground. "Martje," he thundered at the old woman. "You've been forbidden to loiter here. If I tell Anheg that you've disobeyed him, he'll have the priests of the temple burn you for a witch."

The old woman cackled at him, and Garion noted with a shudder that her eyes were milk-white blankness.

"The fire will not touch old Martje," she laughed shrilly. "That is not the Doom which awaits her."

"Enough of dooms," Barak said. "Get away from the temple."

"Martje sees what she sees," the old woman said. "The mark of thy Doom is still upon thee, great Lord Barak. When it comes to thee, thou shalt remember the words of old Martje." And then she seemed to look at the sleigh where Garion sat, though her milky eyes were obviously blind. Her expression suddenly changed from malicious glee to one strangely awestruck.

"Hail, greatest of Lords," she crooned, bowing deeply. "When thou comest into thine inheritance, remember that it was old Martje who first greeted thee."

Barak started toward her with a roar, but she scurried away, her staff tapping on the stone steps.

"What did she mean?" Garion asked when Barak returned to the sleigh.

"She's a crazy woman," Barak replied, his face pale with anger. "She's always lurking around the temple, begging and frightening gullible housewives with her gibberish. If Anheg had any sense, he'd have had her driven out of the city or burned years ago." He climbed back into the sleigh. "Let's go," he growled at the driver.

Garion looked back over his shoulder as they sped away, but the old blind woman was nowhere in sight.

CHAPTER THIRTEEN

The palace of King Anheg of Cherek was a vast, brooding structure near the center of Val Alorn. Huge wings, many of them crumbled into decay with unpaned windows staring emptily at the open sky through collapsed roofs, stretched out from the main building in all directions. So far as Garion could tell there was no plan to the palace whatsoever. It had, it seemed, merely grown over the three thousand years and more that the kings of Cherek had ruled there.

"Why is so much of it empty and broken down like that?" he asked Barak as their sleigh whirled into the snow-packed courtyard.

"What some kings build, other kings let fall down," Barak said shortly. "It's the way of kings." Barak's mood had been black since their encounter with the blind woman at the temple.

The others had all dismounted and stood waiting.

"You've been away from home too long if you can get lost on the way from the harbor to the palace," Silk said pleasantly.

"We were delayed," Barak grunted.

A broad, ironbound door at the top of the wide steps that led up to the palace opened then as if someone behind it had been waiting for them all to arrive. A woman with long flaxen braids and wearing a deep scarlet cloak trimmed with rich fur stepped out onto the portico at the top of the stairs and stood looking down at them. "Greetings, Lord Barak, Earl of Trellheim and husband," she said formally.

Barak's face grew even more somber. "Merel," he acknowledged with a curt nod.

"King Anheg granted me permission to greet you, my Lord," Barak's wife said, "as is my right and my duty."

"You've always been most attentive to your duties, Merel," Barak said. "Where are my daughters?"

"At Trellheim, my Lord," she said. "I didn't think it would be a good idea for them to travel so far in the cold." There was a faintly malicious note in her voice.

Barak sighed. "I see," he said.

"Was I in error, my Lord?" Merel asked.

"Let it pass," Barak said.

"If you and your friends are ready, my Lord," she said, "I'll escort you to the throne room."

Barak went up the stairs, briefly and rather formally embraced his wife, and the two of them went through the wide doorway.

"Tragic," the Earl of Seline murmured, shaking his head as they all went up the stairs to the palace door.

"Hardly that," Silk said. "After all, Barak got what he wanted, didn't he?"

"You're a cruel man, Prince Kheldar," the earl said.

"Not really," Silk said. "I'm a realist, that's all. Barak spent all those years yearning after Merel, and now he's got her. I'm delighted to see such steadfastness rewarded. Aren't you?"

The Earl of Seline sighed.

A party of mailed warriors joined them and escorted them through a maze of corridors, up broad stairs and down narrow ones, deeper and deeper into the vast pile.

"I've always admired Cherek architecture," Silk said sardonically. "It's so unanticipated."

"Expanding the palace gives weak kings something to do," King Fulrach observed. "It's not a bad idea, really. In Sendaria bad kings usually devote their time to street-paving projects, but all of Val Alorn was paved thousands of years ago."

Silk laughed. "It's always been a problem, your Majesty," he said. "How do you keep bad kings out of mischief?"

"Prince Kheldar," King Fulrach said, "I don't wish your uncle any misfortune, but I think it might be very interesting if the crown of Drasnia just happened to fall to you."

"Please, your Majesty," Silk said with feigned shock, "don't even suggest that."

"Also a wife," the Earl of Seline said slyly. "The prince definitely needs a wife."

"That's even worse," Silk said with a shudder.

The throne room of King Anheg was a vaulted chamber with a great fire pit in the center where whole logs blazed and crackled. Unlike the lushly draped hall of King Fulrach, the stone walls here were bare, and torches flared and smoked in iron rings sunk in stone. The men who lounged near the fire were not the elegant courtiers of Fulrach's court, but rather were bearded Cherek warriors, gleaming in chain mail. At one end of the room sat five thrones, each surmounted by a banner. Four of the thrones were occupied, and three regal-looking women stood talking nearby.

"Fulrach, King of Sendaria!" one of the warriors who had escorted them boomed, striking the butt of his spear hollowly on the rush-strewn floor.

"Hail, Fulrach," a large, black-bearded man on one of the thrones called, rising to his feet. His long blue robe was wrinkled and spotted, and his hair was shaggy and unkempt. The gold crown he wore was dented in a place or two, and one of its points had been broken off.

"Hail, Anheg," the King of the Sendars replied, bowing slightly.

"Thy throne awaits thee, my dear Fulrach," the shaggy-haired man said, indicating the banner of Sendaria behind the one vacant throne. "The Kings of Aloria welcome the wisdom of the King of Sendaria at this council."

Garion found the stilted, archaic form of address strangely impressive.

"Which king is which, friend Silk?" Durnik whispered as they approached the thrones.

"The fat one in the red robe with the reindeer on his banner is my uncle, Rhodar of Drasnia. The lean-faced one in black under the horse banner is Cho-Hag of Algaria. The big, grim-faced one in gray with no crown who sits beneath the sword banner is Brand, the Rivan Warder."

"Brand?" Garion interrupted, startled as he remembered the stories of the Battle of Vo Mimbre.

"All Rivan Warders are named Brand," Silk explained.

King Fulrach greeted each of the other kings in the formal language that seemed to be customary, and then he took his place beneath the green banner with its golden sheaf of wheat that was the emblem of Sendaria.

"Hail Belgarath, Disciple of Aldur," Anheg said, "and hail Lady Polgara, honored daughter of immortal Belgarath."

"There's little time for all this ceremony, Anheg," Mister Wolf said tartly, throwing back his cloak and striding forward. "Why have the Kings of Aloria summoned me?"

"Permit us our little ceremonies, Ancient One," Rhodar, the grossly fat King of Drasnia, said slyly. "We so seldom have the chance to play king. We won't be much longer at it."

Mister Wolf shook his head in disgust.

One of the three regal-looking women came forward then. She was a tall, raven-haired beauty in an elaborately cross-tied black velvet gown. She curtsied to King Fulrach and touched her cheek briefly to his. "Your Majesty," she said, "your presence honors our home."

"Your Highness," Fulrach replied, inclining his head respectfully.

·   "Queen Islena," Silk murmured to Durnik and Garion, "Anheg's wife." The little man's nose twitched with suppressed mirth. "Watch her when she greets Polgara."

The queen turned and curtsied deeply to Mister Wolf. "Divine Belgarath," she said, her rich voice throbbing with respect.

"Hardly divine, Islena," the old man said dryly.

"Immortal son of Aldur," she swept on, ignoring the interruption, "mightiest sorcerer in all the world. My poor house trembles at the awesome power you bring within its walls."

"A pretty speech, Islena," Wolf said. "A little inaccurate, but pretty all the same."

But the queen had already turned to Aunt Pol. "Glorious sister," she intoned.

"Sister?" Garion was startled.

"She's a mystic," Silk said softly. "She dabbles a bit in magic and thinks of herself as a sorceress. Watch."

With an elaborate gesture the queen produced a green jewel and presented it to Aunt Pol.

"She had it up her sleeve," Silk whispered gleefully.

"A royal gift, Islena," Aunt Pol said in a strange voice. "A pity that I can only offer this in return." She handed the queen a single deep red rose.

"Where did she get that?" Garion asked in amazement.

Silk winked at him.

The queen looked at the rose doubtfully and cupped it between her two hands. She examined it closely, and her eyes widened. The color drained out of her face, and her hands began to tremble.

The second queen had stepped forward. She was a tiny blonde with a beautiful smile. Without ceremony she kissed King Fulrach and then Mister Wolf and embraced Aunt Pol warmly. Her affection seemed simple and unselfconscious.

"Porenn, Queen of Drasnia," Silk said, and his voice had an odd note to it. Garion glanced at him and saw the faintest hint of a bitter, self-mocking expression flicker across his face. In that single instant, as clearly as if it had suddenly been illuminated by a bright light, Garion saw the reason for Silk's sometimes strange manner. An almost suffocating surge of sympathy welled up in his throat.

The third queen, Silar of Algaria, greeted King Fulrach, Mister Wolf and Aunt Pol with a few brief words in a quiet voice.

"Is the Rivan Warder unmarried?" Durnik asked, looking around for another queen.

"He had a wife," Silk said shortly, his eyes still on Queen Porenn, "but she died some years ago. She left him four sons."

"Ah," Durnik said.

Then Barak, grim-faced and obviously angry, entered the hall and strode to King Anheg's throne.

"Welcome home, cousin," King Anheg said. "I thought perhaps you'd lost your way."

"Family business, Anheg," Barak said. "I had to have a few words with my wife."

"I see," Anheg said and let it drop.

"Have you met our friends?" Barak asked.

"Not as yet, Lord Barak," King Rhodar said. "We were involved with the customary formalities." He chuckled, and his great paunch jiggled.

"I'm sure you all know the Earl of Seline," Barak said, "and this is Durnik, a smith and a brave man. The boy's name is Garion. He's in Lady Polgara's care—a good lad."

"Do you suppose we could get on with this?" Mister Wolf asked impatiently.

Cho-Hag, King of the Algars, spoke in a strangely soft voice. "Art thou aware, Belgarath, of the misfortune which hath befallen us? We turn to thee for counsel."

"Cho-Hag," Wolf said testily, "you sound like a bad Arendish epic. Is all this theeing and thouing really necessary?"

Cho-Hag looked embarrassed and glanced at King Anheg.

"My fault, Belgarath," Anheg said ruefully. "I set scribes to work to record our meetings. Cho-Hag was speaking to history as well as to you." His crown had slipped a bit and perched precariously over one ear.

"History's very tolerant, Anheg," Wolf said. "You don't have to try to impress her. She'll forget most of what we say anyway." He turned to the Rivan Warder. "Brand," he said, "do you suppose you could explain all this without too much embellishment?"

"I'm afraid it's my fault, Belgarath," the gray-robed Warder said in a deep voice. "The Apostate was able to carry off his theft because of my laxity."

"The thing's supposed to protect itself, Brand," Wolf told him. "I can't even touch it. I know the thief, and there's no way you could have kept him out of Riva. What concerns me is how he was able to lay hands on it without being destroyed by its power."

Brand spread his hands helplessly. "We woke one morning, and it was gone. The priests were only able to divine the name of the thief. The Spirit of the Bear-God wouldn't say any more. Since we knew who he was, we were careful not to speak his name or the name of the thing he took."

"Good," Wolf said. "He has ways to pick words out of the air at great distances. I taught him how to do that myself."

Brand nodded. "We knew that," he said. "It made phrasing our message to you difficult. When you didn't come to Riva and my messenger didn't return, I thought something had gone wrong. That's when we sent men out to find you."

Mister Wolf scratched at his beard. "I guess it's my own fault that I'm here, then," he said. "I borrowed your messenger. I had to get word to some people in Arendia. I suppose I should have known better."

Silk cleared his throat. "May I speak?" he asked politely.

"Certainly, Prince Kheldar," King Anheg said.

"Is it entirely prudent to continue these discussions in public?" Silk asked. "The Murgos have enough gold to buy ears in many places, and the arts of the Grolims can lift the thoughts out of the minds of the most loyal warriors. What isn't known can't be revealed, if you take my meaning."

"The warriors of Anheg aren't so easily bought, Silk," Barak said testily, "and there aren't any Grolims in Cherek."

"Are you also confident about the serving men and the kitchen wenches?" Silk suggested. "And I've found Grolims in some very unexpected places."

"There's something in what my nephew says," King Rhodar said, his face thoughtful. "Drasnia has centuries of experience in the gathering of information, and Kheldar is one of our best. If he thinks that our words might go further than we'd want them to, we might be wise to listen to him."

"Thank you, uncle," Silk said bowing.

"Could *you* penetrate this palace, Prince Kheldar?" King Anheg challenged.

"I already have, your Majesty," Silk said modestly, "a dozen times or more."

Anheg looked at Rhodar with one raised eyebrow.

Rhodar coughed slightly. "It was some time ago, Anheg. Nothing serious. I was just curious about something, that's all."

"All you had to do was ask," Anheg said in a slightly injured tone.

"I didn't want to bother you," Rhodar said with a shrug. "Besides, it's more fun to do it the other way."

"Friends," King Fulrach said, "the issue before us is too important to chance compromising it. Wouldn't it be better to be overcautious rather than take any risks?"

King Anheg frowned and then shrugged. "Whatever you wish," he said. "We'll continue in private, then. Cousin, would you clear old King Eldrig's hall for us and set guards in the hallways near it?"

"I will, Anheg," Barak said. He took a dozen warriors and left the hall.

The kings rose from their thrones—all except Cho-Hag. A lean warrior, very nearly as tall as Barak and with the shaved head and flowing scalp lock of the Algars, stepped forward and helped him up.

Garion looked inquiringly at Silk.

"An illness when he was a child," Silk explained softly. "It left his legs so weak that he can't stand unaided."

"Doesn't that make it kind of hard for him to be king?" Garion asked.

"Algars spend more time sitting on horses than they do standing on their feet," Silk said. "Once he's on a horse, Cho-Hag's the equal of any man in Algaria. The warrior who's helping him is Hettar, his adopted son."

"You know him?" Garion asked.

"I know everyone, Garion." Silk laughed softly. "Hettar and I have met a few times. I like him, though I'd rather he didn't know that."

Queen Porenn came over to where they stood. "Islena's taking Silar and me to her private quarters," she said to Silk. "Apparently women aren't supposed to be involved in matters of state here in Cherek."

"Our Cherek cousins have a few blind spots, your Highness," Silk said. "They're arch-conservatives, of course, and it hasn't occurred to them yet that women are human."

Queen Porenn winked at him with a sly little grin. "I'd hoped that we might get a chance to talk, Kheldar, but it doesn't look like it now. Did you get my message to Layla?"

Silk nodded. "She said she'd write to you immediately," he said. "If we'd known you were going to be here, I could have carried her letter myself."

"It was Islena's idea," she said. "She decided that it might be nice to have a council of queens while the kings were meeting. She'd have invited Layla too, but everyone knows how terrified she is of sea travel."

"Has your council produced anything momentous, Highness?" Silk asked lightly.

Queen Porenn made a face. "We sit around and watch Islena do tricks—disappearing coins, things up her sleeves, that kind of thing," she said. "Or she tells fortunes. Silar's too polite to object, and I'm the youngest, so I'm not supposed to say too much. It's terribly dull, particularly when she goes into trances over that stupid crystal ball of hers. Did Layla think she could help me?"

"If anyone can," Silk assured her. "I should warn you, though, that her advice is likely to be quite explicit. Queen Layla's an earthy little soul, and sometimes very blunt."

Queen Porenn giggled wickedly. "That's all right," she said. "I'm a grown woman, after all."

"Of course," Silk said. "I just wanted to prepare you, that's all."

"Are you making fun of me, Kheldar?" she asked.

"Would I do that, your Highness?" Silk asked, his face full of innocence.

"I think you would," she said.

"Coming, Porenn?" Queen Islena asked from not far away.

"At once, your Highness," the queen of Drasnia said. Her fingers flickered briefly at Silk. *What a bore.*

Patience, Highness, Silk gestured in reply.

Queen Porenn docilely followed the stately Queen of Cherek and the silent Queen of Algaria from the hall. Silk's eyes followed her, and his face had that same self-mocking expression as before.

"The others are leaving," Garion said delicately and pointed to the far end of the hall where the Alorn Kings were just going out the door.

"All right," Silk said and led the way quickly after them.

Garion stayed at the rear of the group as they all made their way through the drafty corridors toward King Eldrig's hall. The dry voice in his mind told him that if Aunt Pol saw him, she'd probably find a reason to send him away.

As he loitered along at the rear of the procession, a furtive movement flickered briefly far down one of the side corridors. He caught only one glimpse of the man, an ordinary-looking Cherek warrior wearing a dark green cloak, and then they had moved past that corridor. Garion stopped and stepped back to look again, but the man in the green cloak was gone.

At the door to King Eldrig's hall, Aunt Pol stood waiting with her arms crossed. "Where have you been?" she asked.

"I was just looking," he said as innocently as possible.

"I see," she said. Then she turned to Barak. "The council's probably going to last for a long time," she said, "and Garion's just going to get restless before it's over. Is there someplace where he can amuse himself until suppertime?"

"Aunt Pol!" Garion protested.

"The armory, perhaps?" Barak suggested.

"What would I do in an armory?" Garion demanded.

"Would you prefer the scullery?" Aunt Pol asked pointedly.

"On second thought, I think I might like to see the armory."

"I thought you might."

"It's at the far end of this corridor, Garion," Barak said. "The room with the red door."

"Run along, dear," Aunt Pol said, "and try not to cut yourself on anything."

Garion sulked slowly down the corridor Barak had pointed out to him, keenly feeling the injustice of the situation. The guards posted in the passageway outside Kind Eldrig's hall even made eavesdropping impossible. Garion sighed and continued his solitary way toward the armory.

The other part of his mind was busy, however, mulling over certain problems. Despite his stubborn refusal to accept the possibility that Mister Wolf and Aunt Pol were indeed Belgarath and Polgara, the behavior of the Alorn Kings made it obvious that they at least *did* believe it. Then there was the question of the rose Aunt Pol had given to Queen Islena. Setting aside the fact that roses do not bloom in the winter, how had Aunt Pol known that Islena would present her with that green jewel and therefore prepared the rose in advance? He deliberately avoided the idea that his Aunt had simply created the rose on the spot.

The corridor along which he passed, deep in thought, was dim, with only a few torches set in rings on the walls to light the way. Side passages branched out from it here and there, gloomy, unlighted openings that stretched back into the darkness. He had almost reached the armory when he heard a faint sound in one of those dark passages. Without knowing exactly why, he drew back into one of the other openings and waited.

The man in the green cloak stepped out into the lighted corridor and looked around furtively. He was an ordinary-looking man with a short, sandy beard, and he probably could have walked anywhere in the palace without attracting much notice. His manner, however, and his stealthy movements cried out louder than words that he was doing something he was not supposed to be doing. He hurried up the corridor in the direction from which Garion had come, and Garion shrank back into the protective darkness of his hiding place. When he carefully poked his head out into the corridor again, the man had disappeared, and it was impossible to know down which of those dark side passageways he had gone.

Garion's inner voice told him that even if he told anyone about this, they wouldn't listen. He'd need more than just an uneasy feeling of suspicion to report if he didn't want to appear foolish. All he could do for the time being was to keep his eyes open for the man in the green cloak.

CHAPTER FOURTEEN

It was snowing the following morning, and Aunt Pol, Silk, Barak, and Mister Wolf again met for council with the kings, leaving Garion in Durnik's keeping. The two sat near the fire in the huge hall with the thrones, watching the two dozen or so bearded Cherek warriors who lounged about or engaged in various activities to pass the time. Some of them sharpened their swords or polished their armor; others ate or sat drinking— even though it was still quite early in the morning; several were engaged in a heated dice game; and some simply sat with their backs against the wall and slept.

"These Chereks seem to be very idle people," Durnik said quietly to Garion. "I haven't seen anyone actually working since we arrived, have you?"

Garion shook his head. "I think these are the king's own warriors," he said just as quietly. "I don't think they're supposed to do anything except sit around and wait for the king to tell them to fight someone."

Durnik frowned disapprovingly. "It must be a terribly boring way to live," he said.

"Durnik," Garion asked after a moment, "did you notice the way Barak and his wife acted toward each other?"

"It's very sad," Durnik said. "Silk told me about it yesterday. Barak fell in love with her when they were both very young, but she was highborn and didn't take him very seriously."

"How does it happen that they're married, then?" Garion asked.

"It was her family's idea," Durnik explained. "After Barak became the Earl of Trellheim, they decided that a marriage would give them a valuable connection. Merel objected, but it didn't do her any good. Silk said that Barak found out after they were married that she's really a very shallow person, but of course it was too late by then. She does spiteful things to try to hurt him, and he spends as much time away from home as possible."

"Do they have any children?" Garion asked.

"Two," Durnik said. "Both girls—about five and seven. Barak loves them very much, but he doesn't get to see them very often."

Garion sighed. "I wish there was something we could do," he said.

"We can't interfere between a man and his wife," Durnik said. "Things like that just aren't done."

"Did you know that Silk's in love with his aunt?" Garion said without stopping to think.

"Garion!" Durnik's voice was shocked. "That's an unseemly thing to say."

"It's true all the same," Garion said defensively. "Of course she's not really his aunt, I guess. She's his uncle's second wife. It's not exactly like she was his real aunt."

"She's married to his uncle," Durnik said firmly. "Who made up this scandalous story?"

"Nobody made it up," Garion said. "I was watching his face when he talked to her yesterday. It's pretty plain the way he feels about her."

"I'm sure you just imagined it," Durnik said disapprovingly. He stood up. "Let's look around. That'll give us something better to do than sit here gossiping about our friends. It's really not the sort of thing decent men do."

"All right," Garion agreed quickly, a little embarrassed. He stood up and followed Durnik across the smoky hall and out into the corridor.

"Let's have a look at the kitchen," Garion suggested.

"And the smithy, too," Durnik said.

The royal kitchens were enormous. Entire oxen roasted on spits, and whole flocks of geese simmered in lakes of gravy. Stews bubbled in cart-sized cauldrons, and battalions of loaves were marched into ovens big enough to stand in. Unlike Aunt Pol's well-ordered kitchen at Faldor's farm, everything here was chaos and confusion. The head cook was a huge man with a red face who screamed orders which everyone ignored. There were shouts and threats and a great deal of horseplay. A spoon heated in a fire and left where an unsuspecting cook would pick it up brought shrieks of mirth, and one man's hat was stolen and deliberately thrown into a seething pot of stew.

"Let's go someplace else, Durnik," Garion said. "This isn't what I expected at all."

Durnik nodded. "Mistress Pol would never tolerate all of this foolishness," he agreed disapprovingly.

In the hallway outside the kitchen a maid with reddish-blond hair and a pale green dress cut quite low at the bodice loitered.

"Excuse me," Durnik said to her politely, "could you direct us to the smithy?"

She looked him up and down boldly. "Are you new here?" she asked. "I haven't seen you before."

"We're just visiting," Durnik said.

"Where are you from?" she demanded.

"Sendaria," Durnik said.

"How interesting. Perhaps the boy could run this errand for you, and you and I could talk for a while." Her look was direct.

Durnik coughed, and his ears reddened. "The smithy?" he asked again.

The maid laughed lightly. "In the courtyard at the end of this corridor," she said. "I'm usually around here someplace. I'm sure you can find me when you finish your business with the smith."

"Yes," Durnik said, "I'm sure I could. Come along, Garion."

They went on down the corridor and out into a snowy inner courtyard.

"Outrageous!" Durnik said stiffly, his ears still flaming. "The girl has no sense of propriety whatsoever. I'd report her if I knew to whom."

"Shocking," Garion agreed, secretly amused by Durnik's embarrassment. They crossed the courtyard through the lightly sifting snow.

The smithy was presided over by a huge, black-bearded man with fore-arms as big as Garion's thighs. Durnik introduced himself and the two were soon happily talking shop to the accompaniment of the ringing blows of the smith's hammer. Garion noticed that instead of the plows, spades, and hoes that would fill a Sendarian smithy, the walls here were hung with swords, spears, and war axes. At one forge an apprentice was hammering out arrow-heads, and at another, a lean, one-eyed man was working on an evil-looking dagger.

Durnik and the smith talked together for most of the remainder of the morning while Garion wandered about the inner courtyard watching the var-ious workmen at their tasks. There were coopers and wheelwrights, cobblers and carpenters, saddlers and candlemakers, all busily at work to maintain the huge household of King Anheg. As he watched, Garion also kept his eyes open for the sandy-bearded man in the green cloak he'd seen the night be-fore. It wasn't likely that the man would be here where honest work was be-ing done, but Garion stayed alert all the same.

About noon, Barak came looking for them and led them back to the great hall where Silk lounged, intently watching a dice game.

"Anheg and the others want to meet privately this afternoon," Barak said. "I've got an errand to run, and I thought you might want to go along."

"That might not be a bad idea," Silk said, tearing his eyes from the game. "Your cousin's warriors dice badly, and I'm tempted to try a few rolls with them. It'd probably be better if I didn't. Most men take offense at losing to strangers."

Barak grinned. "I'm sure they'd be glad to let you play, Silk," he said. "They've got just as much chance of winning as you do."

"Just as the sun has as much chance of coming up in the west as in the east," Silk said.

"Are you that sure of your skill, friend Silk?" Durnik asked.

"I'm sure of theirs." Silk chuckled. He jumped up. "Let's go," he said. "My fingers are starting to itch. Let's get them away from temptation."

"Anything you say, Prince Kheldar." Barak laughed.

They all put on fur cloaks and left the palace. The snow had almost stopped, and the wind was brisk.

"I'm a bit confused by all these names," Durnik said as they trudged to-ward the central part of Val Alorn. "I've been meaning to ask about it. You, friend Silk, are also Prince Kheldar and sometimes the merchant Ambar of Kotu, and Mister Wolf is called Belgarath, and Mistress Pol is also Lady Polgara or the Duchess of Erat. Where I come from, people usually have one name."

"Names are like clothes, Durnik," Silk explained. "We put on what's most suitable for the occasion. Honest men have little need to wear strange clothes or strange names. Those of us who aren't so honest, however, occa-sionally have to change one or the other."

"I don't find it amusing to hear Mistress Pol described as not being honest," Durnik said stiffly.

"No disrespect intended," Silk assured him. "Simple definitions don't apply to Lady Polgara; and when I say that we're not honest, I simply mean that this business we're in sometimes requires us to conceal ourselves from people who are evil as well as devious."

Durnik looked unconvinced but let it pass.

"Let's take this street," Barak suggested. "I don't want to pass the Temple of Belar today."

"Why?" Garion asked.

"I'm a little behind in my religious duties," Barak said with a pained look, "and I'd rather not be reminded of it by the High Priest of Belar. His voice is very penetrating, and I don't like being called down in front of the whole city. A prudent man doesn't give either a priest or a woman the opportunity to scold him in public."

The streets of Val Alorn were narrow and crooked, and the ancient stone houses were tall and narrow with overhanging second stories. Despite the intermittent snow and the crisp wind, the streets seemed full of people, most of them garbed in furs against the chill.

There was much good-humored shouting and the exchange of bawdy insults. Two elderly and dignified men were pelting each other with snowballs in the middle of one street to the raucous encouragement of the bystanders.

"They're old friends," Barak said with a broad grin. "They do this every day all winter long. Pretty soon they'll go to an alehouse and get drunk and sing old songs together until they fall off their benches. They've been doing it for years now."

"What do they do in the summer?" Silk asked.

"They throw rocks," Barak said. "The drinking and singing and falling off the benches stays the same, though."

"Hello, Barak," a green-eyed young woman called from an upper window. "When are you coming to see me again?"

Barak glanced up, and his face flushed, but he didn't answer.

"That lady's talking to you, Barak," Garion said.

"I heard her," Barak replied shortly.

"She seems to know you," Silk said with a sly look.

"She knows everyone," Barak said, flushing even more. "Shall we move along?"

Around another corner a group of men dressed in shaggy furs shuffled along in single file. Their gait was a kind of curious swaying from side to side, and people quickly made way for them.

"Hail, Lord Barak," their leader intoned.

"Hail, Lord Barak," the others said in unison, still swaying.

Barak bowed stiffly.

"May the arm of Belar protect thee," the leader said.

"All praise to Belar, Bear-God of Aloria," the others said.

Barak bowed again and stood until the procession had passed.

"Who were they?" Durnik asked.

"Bear-cultists," Barak said with distaste. "Religious fanatics."

"A troublesome group," Silk explained. "They have chapters in all the Alorn kingdoms. They're excellent warriors, but they're the instruments of the High Priest of Belar. They spend their time in rituals, military training, and interfering in local politics."

"Where's this Aloria they spoke of?" Garion asked.

"All around us," Barak said with a broad gesture. "Aloria used to be all the Alorn kingdoms together. They were all one nation. The cultists want to reunite them."

"That doesn't seem unreasonable," Durnik said.

"Aloria was divided for a reason," Barak said. "A certain thing had to be protected, and the division of Aloria was the best way to do that."

"Was this thing so important?" Durnik asked.

"It's the most important thing in the world," Silk said. "The Bear-cultists tend to forget that."

"Only now it's been stolen, hasn't it?" Garion blurted as that dry voice in his mind informed him of the connection between what Barak and Silk had just said and the sudden disruption of his own life. "It's this thing that Mister Wolf is following."

Barak glanced quickly at him. "The lad is wiser than we thought, Silk," he said soberly.

"He's a clever boy," Silk agreed, "and it's not hard to put it all together." His weasel face was grave. "You're right, of course, Garion," he said. "We don't know how yet, but somebody's managed to steal it. If Belgarath gives the word, the Alorn Kings will take the world apart stone by stone to get it back."

"You mean war?" Durnik said in a sinking voice.

"There are worse things than war," Barak said grimly. "It might be a good opportunity to dispose of the Angaraks once and for all."

"Let's hope that Belgarath can persuade the Alorn Kings otherwise," Silk said.

"The thing has to be recovered," Barak insisted.

"Granted," Silk agreed, "but there are other ways, and I hardly think a public street's the place to discuss our alternatives."

Barak looked around quickly, his eyes narrowing.

They had by then reached the harbor where the masts of the ships of Cherek rose as thickly as trees in a forest. They crossed an icy bridge over a frozen stream and came to several large yards where the skeletons of ships lay in the snow.

A limping man in a leather smock came from a low stone building in the center of one of the yards and stood watching their approach.

"Ho, Krendig," Barak called.

"Ho, Barak," the man in the leather smock replied.

"How does the work go?" Barak asked.

"Slowly in this season," Krendig said. "It's not a good time to work with wood. My artisans are fashioning the fittings and sawing the boards, but we won't be able to do much more until spring."

Barak nodded and walked over to lay his hand on the new wood of a ship prow rising out of the snow. "Krendig is building this for me," he said, patting the prow. "She'll be the finest ship afloat."

"If your oarsmen are strong enough to move her," Krendig said. "She'll be very big, Barak, and very heavy."

"Then I'll man her with big men," Barak said, still gazing at the ribs of his ship.

Garion heard a gleeful shout from the hillside above the shipyard and looked up quickly. Several young people were sliding down the hill on smooth planks. It was obvious that Barak and the others were going to spend most of the rest of the afternoon discussing the ship. While that might be all very interesting, Garion realized that he hadn't spoken with anyone his own age for a long time. He drifted away from the others and stood at the foot of the hill, watching.

One blond girl particularly attracted his eye. In some ways she reminded him of Zubrette, but there were some differences. Where Zubrette had been petite, this girl was as big as a boy—though she was noticeably not a boy. Her laughter rang out merrily, and her cheeks were pink in the cold afternoon air as she slid down the hill with her long braids flying behind her.

"That looks like fun," Garion said as her improvised sled came to rest nearby.

"Would you like to try?" she asked, getting up and brushing the snow from her woolen dress.

"I don't have a sled," he told her.

"I might let you use mine," she said, looking at him archly, "if you give me something."

"What would you want me to give you?" he asked.

"We'll think of something," she said, eyeing him boldly. "What's your name?"

"Garion," he said.

"What an odd name. Do you come from here?"

"No. I'm from Sendaria."

"A Sendar? Truly?" Her blue eyes twinkled. "I've never met a Sendar before. My name is Maidee."

Garion inclined his head slightly.

"Do you want to use my sled?" Maidee asked.

"I might like to try it," Garion said.

"I might let you," she said, "for a kiss."

Garion blushed furiously, and Maidee laughed.

A large red-haired boy in a long tunic slid to a stop nearby and rose with a menacing look on his face. "Maidee, come away from there," he ordered.

"What if I don't want to?" she asked.

The red-haired boy swaggered toward Garion. "What are you doing here?" he demanded.

"I was talking with Maidee," Garion said.

"Who gave you permission?" the red-haired boy asked. He was a bit taller than Garion and somewhat heavier.

"I didn't bother to ask permission," Garion said.

The red-haired boy glowered, flexing his muscles threateningly. "I can thrash you if I like," he announced.

Garion realized that the redhead was feeling belligerent and that a fight was inevitable. The preliminaries—threats, insults and the like—would probably go on for several more minutes, but the fight would take place as soon as the boy in the long tunic had worked himself up to it. Garion decided not to wait. He doubled his fist and punched the larger boy in the nose.

The blow was a good one, and the redhead stumbled back and sat down heavily in the snow. He raised one hand to his nose and brought it away bright red. "It's bleeding!" he wailed accusingly. "You made my nose bleed."

"It'll stop in a few minutes," Garion said.

"What if it doesn't?"

"Nosebleeds don't last forever," Garion told him.

"Why did you hit me?" the redhead demanded tearfully, wiping his nose. "I didn't do anything to you."

"You were going to," Garion said. "Put snow on it, and don't be such a baby."

"It's still bleeding," the boy said.

"Put snow on it," Garion said again.

"What if it doesn't stop bleeding?"

"Then you'll probably bleed to death," Garion said in a heartless tone. It was a trick he had learned from Aunt Pol. It worked as well on the Cherek boy as it had on Doroon and Rundorig. The redhead blinked at him and then took a large handful of snow and held it to his nose.

"Are all Sendars so cruel?" Maidee asked.

"I don't know all the people in Sendaria," Garion said. The affair hadn't turned out well at all, and regretfully he turned and started back toward the shipyard.

"Garion, wait," Maidee said. She ran after him and caught him by the arm. "You forgot my kiss," she said, threw her arms around his neck and kissed him soundly on the lips.

"There," she said, and she turned and ran laughing back up the hill, her blond braids flying behind her.

Barak, Silk and Durnik were all laughing when he returned to where they stood.

"You were supposed to chase her," Barak said.

"What for?" Garion asked, flushing at their laughter.

"She wanted you to catch her."

"I don't understand."

"Barak," Silk said. "I think that one of us is going to have to inform the Lady Polgara that our Garion needs some further education."

"You're skilled with words, Silk," Barak said. "I'm sure you ought to be the one to tell her."

"Why don't we throw dice for the privilege?" Silk suggested.

"I've seen you throw dice before, Silk." Barak laughed.

"Of course we could simply stay here a while longer," Silk said slyly. "I rather imagine that Garion's new playmate would be quite happy to complete his education, and that way we wouldn't have to bother Lady Polgara about it."

Garion's ears were flaming. "I'm not as stupid as all that," he said hotly. "I know what you're talking about, and you don't have to say anything to Aunt Pol about it." He stamped away angrily, kicking at the snow.

After Barak had talked for a while longer with his shipbuilder and the harbor had begun to darken with the approach of evening, they started back toward the palace. Garion sulked along behind, still offended by their laughter. The clouds which had hung overhead since their arrival in Val Alorn had begun to tatter, and patches of clear sky began to appear. Here and there single stars twinkled as evening slowly settled in the snowy streets. The soft light of candles began to glow in the windows of the houses, and the few people left in the streets hurried to get home before dark.

Garion, still loitering behind, saw two men entering a wide door beneath a crude sign depicting a cluster of grapes. One of them was the sandy-bearded man in the green cloak he had seen in the palace the night before. The other man wore a dark hood, and Garion felt a familiar tingle of recognition. Even though he couldn't see the hooded man's face, there was no need of that. They had looked at each other too often for there to be any doubt. As always before, Garion felt that peculiar restraint, almost like a ghostly finger touching his lips. The hooded man was Asharak, and, though the Murgo's presence here was very important, it was for some reason impossible for Garion to speak of it. He watched the two men only for a moment then hurried to catch up with his friends. He struggled with the compulsion that froze his tongue, and then tried another approach.

"Barak," he asked, "are there many Murgos in Val Alorn?"

"There aren't any Murgos in Cherek," Barak said. "Angaraks aren't allowed in the kingdom on pain of death. It's our oldest law. It was laid down by old Cherek Bear-shoulders himself. Why do you ask?"

"I was just wondering," Garion said lamely. His mind shrieked with the need to tell them about Asharak, but his lips stayed frozen.

That evening, when they were all seated at the long table in King Anheg's central hall with a great feast set before them, Barak entertained them with a broadly exaggerated account of Garion's encounter with the young people on the hillside.

"A great blow it was," he said in expansive tones, "worthy of the mightiest warrior and truly struck upon the nose of the foe. The bright blood flew, and the enemy was dismayed and overcome. Like a hero, Garion stood over the vanquished, and, like a true hero, did not boast nor taunt his fallen opponent, but offered instead advice for quelling that crimson flood. With simple dignity then, he quit the field, but the bright-eyed maid would not let him depart unrewarded for his valor. Hastily, she pursued him and fondly clasped her snowy arms about his neck. And there she lovingly bestowed that single kiss that is the true hero's greatest reward. Her eyes flamed with admiration, and her chaste bosom heaved with newly wakened passion. But modest Garion innocently departed and tarried not to claim those other sweet rewards the gentle maid's fond demeanor so clearly offered. And thus the adventure ended with our hero tasting victory but tenderly declining victory's true compensation."

The warriors and kings at the long table roared with laughter and pounded the table and their knees and each other's backs in their glee. Queen Islena and Queen Silar smiled tolerantly, and Queen Porenn laughed openly. Lady Merel, however, remained stony-faced, her expression faintly contemptuous as she looked at her husband.

Garion sat with his face aflame, his ears besieged with shouted suggestions and advice.

"Is that really the way it happened, nephew?" King Rhodar demanded of Silk, wiping tears from his eyes.

"More or less," Silk replied. "Lord Barak's telling was masterly, though a good deal embellished."

"We should send for a minstrel," the Earl of Seline said. "This exploit should be immortalized in song."

"Don't tease him," Queen Porenn said, looking sympathetically at Garion.

Aunt Pol did not seem amused. Her eyes were cold as she looked at Barak. "Isn't it odd that three grown men can't keep one boy out of trouble?" she asked with a raised eyebrow.

"It was only one blow, my Lady," Silk protested, "and only one kiss, after all."

"Really?" she said. "And what's it going to be next time? A duel with swords, perhaps, and even greater foolishness afterward?"

"There was no real harm in it, Mistress Pol," Durnik assured her.

Aunt Pol shook her head. "I thought you at least had good sense, Durnik," she said, "but now I see that I was wrong."

Garion suddenly resented her remarks. It seemed that no matter what he did, she was ready to take it in the worst possible light. His resentment flared to the verge of open rebellion. What right had she to say anything about what he did? There was no tie between them, after all, and he could do anything he wanted without her permission if he felt like it. He glared at her in sullen anger.

She caught the look and returned it with a cool expression that seemed almost to challenge him. "Well?" she asked.

"Nothing," he said shortly.

CHAPTER FIFTEEN

The next morning dawned bright and crisp. The sky was a deep blue, and the sunlight was dazzling on the white mountaintops that rose behind the city. After breakfast, Mister Wolf announced that he and Aunt Pol would again meet privately that day with Fulrach and the Alorn Kings.

"Good idea," Barak said. "Gloomy ponderings are good for kings. Unless one has regal obligations, however, it's much too fine a day to be wasted indoors." He grinned mockingly at his cousin.

"There's a streak of cruelty in you that I hadn't suspected, Barak," King Anheg said, glancing longingly out a nearby window.

"Do the wild boars still come down to the edges of the forest?" Barak asked.

"In droves," Anheg replied even more disconsolately.

"I thought I might gather a few good men and go out and see if we can thin their numbers a bit," Barak said, his grin even wider now.

"I was almost sure you had something like that in mind," Anheg said moodily, scratching at his unkempt hair.

"I'm doing you a service, Anheg," Barak said. "You don't want your kingdom overrun with the beasts, do you?"

Rhodar, the fat King of Drasnia, laughed hugely. "I think he's got you, Anheg," he said.

"He usually does," Anheg agreed sourly.

"I gladly leave such activities to younger and leaner men," Rhodar said. He slapped his vast paunch with both hands. "I don't mind a good supper, but I'd rather not have to fight with it first. I make too good a target. The blindest boar in the world wouldn't have much trouble finding me."

"Well, Silk," Barak said, "what do you say?"

"You're not serious," Silk said.

"You must go along, Prince Kheldar," Queen Porenn insisted. "Someone has to represent the honor of Drasnia in this venture."

Silk's face looked pained.

"You can be my champion," she said, her eyes sparkling.

"Have you been reading Arendish epics again, your Highness?" Silk asked acidly.

"Consider it a royal command," she said. "Some fresh air and exercise won't hurt you. You're starting to look dyspeptic."

Silk bowed ironically. "As you wish, your Highness," he said. "I suppose that if things get out of hand I can always climb a tree."

"How about you, Durnik?" Barak asked.

"I don't know much about hunting, friend Barak," Durnik said doubtfully, "but I'll come along if you like."

"My Lord?" Barak asked the Earl of Seline politely.

"Oh, no, Lord Barak." Seline laughed. "I outgrew my enthusiasm for such sport years ago. Thanks for the invitation, however."

"Hettar?" Barak asked the rangy Algar.

Hettar glanced quickly at his father.

"Go along, Hettar," Cho-Hag said in his soft voice. "I'm sure King Anheg will lend me a warrior to help me walk."

"I'll do it myself, Cho-Hag," Anheg said. "I've carried heavier burdens."

"I'll go with you, then, Lord Barak," Hettar said. "And thanks for asking me." His voice was deep and resonant, but very soft, much like that of his father.

"Well, lad?" Barak asked Garion.

"Have you lost your wits entirely, Barak?" Aunt Pol snapped. "Didn't you get him into enough trouble yesterday?"

That was the last straw. The sudden elation he'd felt at Barak's invitation turned to anger. Garion gritted his teeth and threw away all caution. "If Barak doesn't think I'll just be in the way, I'll be glad to go along," he announced defiantly.

Aunt Pol stared at him, her eyes suddenly very hard.

"Your cub's growing teeth, Pol." Mister Wolf chuckled.

"Be still, father," Aunt Pol said, still glaring at Garion.

"Not this time, Miss," the old man said with a hint of iron in his voice. "He's made his decision, and you're not going to humiliate him by unmaking it for him. Garion isn't a child now. You may not have noticed, but he's almost man high and filling out now. He'll soon be fifteen, Pol. You're going to have to relax your grip sometime, and now's as good a time as any to start treating him like a man."

She looked at him for a moment. "Whatever you say, father," she said at last with deceptive meekness. "I'm sure we'll want to discuss this later, though—in private."

Mister Wolf winced.

Aunt Pol looked at Garion then. "Try to be careful, dear," she said, "and when you come back, we'll have a nice long talk, won't we?"

"Will my Lord require my aid in arming himself for the hunt?" Lady Merel asked in the stilted and insulting manner she always assumed with Barak.

"That won't be necessary, Merel," Barak said.

"I would not neglect any of my duties," she said.

"Leave it alone, Merel," Barak said. "You've made your point."

"Have I my Lord's permission then to withdraw?" she asked.

"You have," he said shortly.

"Perhaps you ladies would like to join me," Queen Islena said. "We'll cast auguries and see if we can predict the outcome of the hunt."

Queen Porenn, who stood somewhat behind the Queen of Cherek, rolled her eyes upward in resignation. Queen Silar smiled at her.

"Let's go, then," Barak said. "The boars are waiting."

"Sharpening their tusks, no doubt," Silk said.

Barak led them down to the red door of the armory where they were joined by a grizzled man with enormously broad shoulders who wore a bullhide shirt with metal plates sewn on it.

"This is Torvik," Barak introduced the grizzled man, "Anheg's chief huntsman. He knows every boar in the forest by his first name."

"My Lord Barak is overkind," Torvik said, bowing.

"How does one go about this hunting of boars, friend Torvik?" Durnik asked politely. "I've never done it before."

"It's a simple thing," Torvik explained. "I take my huntsmen into the forest and we drive the beasts with noise and shouting. You and the other hunters wait for them with these." He gestured at a rack of stout, broad-headed boar spears. "When the boar sees you standing in his way, he charges you and tries to kill you with his tusks, but instead you kill him with your spear."

"I see," Durnik said somewhat doubtfully. "It doesn't sound very complicated."

"We wear mail shirts, Durnik," Barak said. "Our hunters are hardly ever injured seriously."

" 'Hardly ever' has an uncomfortable ring of frequency to it, Barak," Silk said, fingering a mail shirt hanging on a peg by the door.

"No sport is very entertaining without a certain element of risk." Barak shrugged, hefting a boar spear.

"Have you ever thought of throwing dice instead?" Silk asked.

"Not with your dice, my friend." Barak laughed.

They began pulling on mail shirts while Torvik's huntsmen carried several armloads of boar spears out to the sleighs waiting in the snowy courtyard of the palace.

Garion found the mail shirt heavy and more than a little uncomfortable. The steel rings dug at his skin even through his heavy clothes, and every time he tried to shift his posture to relieve the pressure of one of them, a half-dozen others bit at him. The air was very cold as they climbed into the sleighs, and the usual fur robes seemed hardly adequate.

They drove through the narrow, twisting streets of Val Alorn toward the great west gate on the opposite side of the city from the harbor. The breath of the horses steamed in the icy air as they rode.

The ragged old blind woman from the temple stepped from a doorway as they passed in the bright morning sun. "Hail, Lord Barak," she croaked. "Thy Doom is at hand. Thou shalt taste of it before this day's sun finds its bed."

Without a word Barak rose in his sleigh, took up a boar spear and cast it with deadly accuracy full at the old woman.

With surprising speed, the witch-woman swung her staff and knocked the spear aside in midair. "It will avail thee not to try to kill old Martje." She laughed scornfully. "Thy spear shall not find her, neither shall thy sword. Go thou, Barak. Thy Doom awaits thee." And then she turned toward the sleigh in which Garion sat beside the startled Durnik. "Hail, Lord of Lords," she intoned. "Thy peril this day shall be great, but thou shalt survive it. And it is thy peril which shall reveal the mark of the beast which is the Doom of thy friend Barak." And then she bowed and scampered away before Barak could lay his hands on another spear.

"What was that about, Garion?" Durnik asked, his eyes still surprised.

"Barak says she's a crazy old blind woman," Garion said. "She stopped us when we arrived in Val Alorn after you and the others had already passed."

"What was all that talk about Doom?" Durnik asked with a shudder.

"I don't know," Garion said. "Barak wouldn't explain it."

"It's a bad omen so early in the day," Durnik said. "These Chereks are a strange people."

Garion nodded in agreement.

Beyond the west gate of the city were open fields, sparkling white in the full glare of the morning sun. They crossed the fields toward the dark edge of the forest two leagues away with great plumes of powdery snow flying out behind their racing sleighs.

Farmsteads lay muffled in snow along their track. The buildings were all made of logs and had high-peaked wooden roofs.

"These people seem to be indifferent to danger," Durnik said. "I certainly wouldn't want to live in a wooden house—what with the possibility of fire and all."

"It's a different country, after all," Garion said. "We can't expect the whole world to live the way we do in Sendaria."

"I suppose not," Durnik sighed, "but I'll tell you, Garion, I'm not very comfortable here. Some people just aren't meant for travel. Sometimes I wish we'd never left Faldor's farm."

"I do too, sometimes," Garion admitted, looking at the towering mountains that seemed to rise directly out of the forest ahead. "Someday it'll be over, though, and we'll be able to go home again."

Durnik nodded and sighed once more.

By the time they had entered the woods, Barak had regained his temper and his good spirits, and he set about placing the hunters as if nothing had happened. He led Garion through the calf-deep snow to a large tree some distance from the narrow sleigh track. "This is a good place," he said. "There's a game trail here, and the boars may use it to try to escape the noise of Torvik and his huntsmen. When one comes, brace yourself and hold your spear with its point aimed at his chest. They don't see very well, and he'll run full into your spear before he even knows it's there. After that it's probably best to jump behind a tree. Sometimes the spear makes them very angry."

"What if I miss?" Garion asked.

"I wouldn't do that," Barak advised. "It's not a very good idea."

"I didn't mean that I was going to do it on purpose," Garion said. "Will he try to get away from me or what?"

"Sometimes they'll try to run," Barak said, "but I wouldn't count on it. More likely he'll try to split you up the middle with his tusks. At that point it's usually a good idea to climb a tree."

"I'll remember that," Garion said.

"I won't be far away if you have trouble," Barak promised, handing Garion a pair of heavy spears. Then he trudged back to his sleigh, and they all galloped off, leaving Garion standing alone under the large oak tree.

It was shadowy among the dark tree trunks, and bitingly cold. Garion walked around a bit through the snow, looking for the best place to await the boar. The trail Barak had pointed out was a beaten path winding back through the dark brush, and Garion found the size of the tracks imprinted in the snow on the path alarmingly large. The oak tree with low-spreading limbs began to look very inviting, but he dismissed that thought angrily. He was expected to stand on the ground and meet the charge of the boar, and he decided that he would rather die than hide in a tree like a frightened child.

The dry voice in his mind advised him that he spent far too much time worrying about things like that. Until he was grown, no one would consider him a man, so why should he go to all the trouble of trying to seem brave when it wouldn't do any good anyway?

The forest was very quiet now, and the snow muffled all sounds. No bird sang, and there was only the occasional padded thump of snow sliding from overloaded branches to the earth beneath. Garion felt terribly alone. What was he doing here? What business had a good, sensible Sendarian boy here in the endless forests of Cherek, awaiting the charge of a savage wild pig with only a pair of unfamiliar spears for company? What had the pig ever done to him? He realized that he didn't even particularly like the taste of pork.

He was some distance from the beaten forest track along which their sleighs had passed, and he set his back to the oak tree, shivered, and waited.

He didn't realize how long he had been listening to the sound when he became fully aware of it. It was not the stamping, squealing rush of a wild boar he had been expecting but was, rather, the measured pace of several horses moving slowly along the snow-carpeted floor of the forest, and it was coming from behind him. Cautiously he eased his face around the tree.

Three riders, muffled in furs, emerged from the woods on the far side of the sleigh-churned track. They stopped and sat waiting. Two of them were bearded warriors, little different from dozens of others Garion had seen in King Anheg's palace. The third man, however, had long, flaxen-colored hair and wore no beard. His face had the sullen, pampered look of a spoiled child, although he was a man of middle years, and he sat his horse disdainfully as if the company of the other two somehow offended him.

After a time, the sound of another horse came from near the edge of the forest. Almost holding his breath, Garion waited. The other rider slowly approached the three who sat their horses in the snow at the edge of the trees. It was the sandy-bearded man in the green cloak whom Garion had seen creeping through the passageways of King Anheg's palace two nights before.

"My Lord," the green-cloaked man said deferentially as he joined the other three.

"Where have you been?" the flaxen-haired man demanded.

"Lord Barak took some of his guests on a boar hunt this morning. His route was the same as mine, and I didn't want to follow too closely."

The nobleman grunted sourly. "We saw them deeper in the wood," he said. "Well, what have you heard?"

"Very little, my Lord. The kings are meeting with the old man and the woman in a guarded chamber. I can't get close enough to hear what they're saying."

"I'm paying you good gold to get close enough. I have to know what they're saying. Go back to the palace and work out a way to hear what they're talking about."

"I'll try, my Lord," the green-cloaked man said, bowing somewhat stiffly.

"You'll do more than try," the flaxen-haired man snapped.

"As you wish, my Lord," the other said, starting to turn his horse.

"Wait," the nobleman commanded. "Were you able to meet with our friend?"

"Your friend, my Lord," the other corrected with distaste. "I met him, and we went to a tavern and talked a little."

"What did he say?"

"Nothing very useful. His kind seldom do."

"Will he meet us as he said he would?"

"He told me that he would. If you want to believe him, that's your affair."

The nobleman ignored that. "Who arrived with the King of the Sendars?"

"The old man and the woman, another old man—some Sendarian noble, I think, Lord Barak and a weasel-faced Drasnian, and another Sendar—a commoner of some sort."

"That's all? Wasn't there a boy with them as well?"

The spy shrugged. "I didn't think the boy was important," he said.

"He's there, then—in the palace?"

"He is, my Lord—an ordinary Sendarian boy of about fourteen, I'd judge. He seems to be some kind of servant to the woman."

"Very well. Go back to the palace and get close enough to that chamber to hear what the kings and the old man are saying."

"That may be very dangerous, my Lord."

"It'll be more dangerous if you don't. Now go, before that ape Barak comes back and finds you loitering here." He whirled his horse and, followed by his two warriors, plunged back into the forest on the far side of the snowy track that wound among the dark trees.

The man in the green cloak sat grimly watching for a moment, then he too turned his horse and rode back the way he had come.

Garion rose from his crouched position behind the tree. His hands were clenched so tightly around the shaft of his spear that they actually ached. This had gone entirely too far, he decided. The matter must be brought to someone's attention.

And then, some way off in the snowy depths of the wood, he heard the sound of hunting horns and the steely clash of swords ringing rhythmically on shields. The huntsmen were coming, driving all the beasts of the forest before them.

He heard a crackling in the bushes, and a great stag bounded into view, his eyes wild with fright and his antlers flaring above his head. With three huge leaps he was gone. Garion trembled with excitement.

Then there was a squealing rush, and a red-eyed sow plunged down the trail followed by a half-dozen scampering piglets. Garion stepped behind his tree and let them pass.

The next squeals were deeper and rang less with fright than with rage. It was the boar—Garion knew that before the beast even broke out of the heavy brush. When the boar appeared, Garion felt his heart quail. This was no fat, sleepy porker, but rather a savage, infuriated beast. The horrid tusks jutting up past the flaring snout were yellow, and bits of twigs and bark clung to them, mute evidence that the boar would slash at anything in his path— trees, bushes or a Sendarian boy without sense enough to get out of his way.

Then a peculiar thing happened. As in the long-ago fight with Rundorig or in the scuffle with Brill's hirelings in the dark streets of Muros, Garion felt his blood begin to surge, and there was a wild ringing in his ears. He seemed to hear a defiant, shouted challenge and could scarcely accept the fact that it came from his own throat. He suddenly realized that he was stepping into the middle of the trail and crouching with his spear braced and leveled at the massive beast.

The boar charged. Red-eyed and frothing from the mouth, with a deep-throated squeal of fury, he plunged at the waiting Garion. The powdery snow sprayed up from his churning hooves like foam from the prow of a ship. The snow crystals seemed to hang in the air, sparkling in a single ray of sunlight that chanced just there to reach the forest floor.

The shock as the boar hit the spear was frightful, but Garion's aim was good. The broad-bladed spearhead penetrated the coarsely haired chest, and the white froth dripping from the boar's tusks suddenly became bloody foam. Garion felt himself driven back by the impact, his feet slipping out from under him, and then the shaft of his spear snapped like a dry twig and the boar was on him.

The first slashing, upward-ripping blow of the boar's tusks took Garion full in the stomach, and he felt the wind whoosh out of his lungs. The second slash caught his hip as he tried to roll, gasping, out of the way. His chain-mail shirt deflected the tusks, saving him from being wounded, but the blows were stunning. The boar's third slash caught him in the back, and he was flung through the air and crashed into a tree. His eyes filled with shimmering light as his head banged against the rough bark.

And then Barak was there, roaring and charging through the snow—but somehow it seemed not to be Barak. Garion's eyes, glazed from the shock of the blow to his head, looked uncomprehendingly at something that could not be true. It was Barak, there could be no doubt of that, but it was also something else. Oddly, as if somehow occupying the same space as Barak, there was also a huge, hideous bear. The images of the two figures crashing through the snow were superimposed, their movements identical as if in sharing the same space they also shared the same thoughts.

Huge arms grasped up the wriggling, mortally wounded boar and crushed in upon it. Bright blood fountained from the boar's mouth, and the shaggy, half-man thing that seemed to be Barak and something else at the same time raised the dying pig and smashed it brutally to the ground. The man-thing lifted its awful face and roared in earthshaking triumph as the light slid away from Garion's eyes and he felt himself drifting down into the gray well of unconsciousness.

There was no way of knowing how much time passed until he came to in the sleigh. Silk was applying a cloth filled with snow to the back of his neck as they flew across the glaring white fields toward Val Alorn.

"I see that you've decided to live." Silk grinned at him.

"Where's Barak?" Garion mumbled groggily.

"In the sleigh behind us," Silk said, glancing back.

"Is he—all right?"

"What could hurt Barak?" Silk asked.

"I mean—does he seem like himself?"

"He seems like Barak to me." Silk shrugged. "No, boy, lie still. That wild pig may have cracked your ribs." He placed his hands on Garion's chest and gently held him down.

"My boar?" Garion demanded weakly. "Where is it?"

"The huntsmen are bringing it," Silk said. "You'll get your triumphal entry. If I might suggest it, however, you should give some thought to the virtue of constructive cowardice. These instincts of yours could shorten your life."

But Garion had already slipped back into unconsciousness.

And then they were in the palace, and Barak was carrying him, and Aunt Pol was there, white-faced at the sight of all the blood.

"It's not his," Barak assured her quickly. "He speared a boar, and it bled on him while they were tussling. I think the boy's all right—a little rap on the head is all."

"Bring him," Aunt Pol said curtly and led the way up the stairs toward Garion's room.

Later, with his head and chest wrapped and a foul-tasting cup of Aunt Pol's brewing making him light-headed and sleepy, Garion lay in his bed listening as Aunt Pol finally turned on Barak. "You great overgrown dolt," she raged. "Do you see what all your foolishness has done?"

"The lad's very brave," Barak said, his voice low and sunk in a kind of bleak melancholy.

"Brave doesn't interest me," Aunt Pol snapped. Then she stopped. "What's the matter with you?" she demanded. She reached out suddenly and put her hands on the sides of the huge man's head. She looked for a moment into his eyes and then slowly released him. "Oh," she said softly, "it finally happened, I see."

"I couldn't control it, Polgara," Barak said in misery.

"It'll be all right, Barak," she said, gently touching his bowed head.

"It'll never be all right again," Barak said.

"Get some sleep," she told him. "It won't seem so bad in the morning." The huge man turned and quietly left the room.

Garion knew they were talking about the strange thing he had seen when Barak had rescued him from the boar and he wanted to ask Aunt Pol about it; but the bitter drink she had given him pulled him down into a deep and dreamless sleep before he could put the words together to ask the question.

CHAPTER SIXTEEN

The next day Garion was too stiff and sore to even think about getting out of bed. A stream of visitors, however, kept him too occupied to think about his aches and pains. The visits from the Alorn Kings in their splendid robes were particularly flattering, and each of them praised his courage. Then the queens came and made a great fuss over his injuries, offering warm sympathy and gentle, stroking touches to his forehead. The combination of praise, sympathy and the certain knowledge that he was the absolute center of attention was overwhelming, and his heart was full.

The last visitor of the day, however, was Mister Wolf, who came when evening was creeping through the snowy streets of Val Alorn. The old man wore his usual tunic and cloak, and his hood was turned up as if he had been outside.

"Have you seen my boar, Mister Wolf?" Garion asked proudly.

"An excellent animal," Wolf said, though without much enthusiasm, "but didn't anyone tell you it's customary to jump out of the way after the boar has been speared?"

"I didn't really think about it," Garion admitted, "but wouldn't that seem—well—cowardly?"

"Were you that concerned about what a pig might think of you?"

"Well," Garion faltered, "not really, I guess."

"You're developing an amazing lack of good sense for one so young," Wolf observed. "It normally takes years and years to reach the point you seem to have arrived at overnight." He turned to Aunt Pol, who sat nearby. "Polgara, are you quite certain that there's no hint of Arendish blood in our Garion's background? He's been behaving most Arendish lately. First he rides the Great Maelstrom like a rocking horse, and then he tries to break a wild boar's tusks with his ribs. Are you sure you didn't drop him on his head when he was a baby?"

Aunt Pol smiled, but said nothing.

"I hope you recover soon, boy," Wolf said, "and try to give some thought to what I've said."

Garion sulked, mortally offended by Mister Wolf's words. Tears welled up in his eyes despite all his efforts to control them.

"Thank you for stopping by, Father," Aunt Pol said.

"It's always a pleasure to call on you, my daughter," Wolf said and quietly left the room.

"Why did he have to talk to me like that?" Garion burst out, wiping his nose. "Now he's gone and spoiled it all."

"Spoiled what, dear?" Aunt Pol asked, smoothing the front of her gray dress.

"All of it," Garion complained. "The kings all said I was very brave."

"Kings say things like that," Aunt Pol said. "I wouldn't pay too much attention, if I were you."

"I *was* brave, wasn't I?"

"I'm sure you were, dear," she said. "And I'm sure the pig was very impressed."

"You're as bad as Mister Wolf is," Garion accused.

"Yes, dear," she said, "I suppose I probably am, but that's only natural. Now, what would you like for supper?"

"I'm not hungry," Garion said defiantly.

"Really? You probably need a tonic, then. I'll fix you one."

"I think I've changed my mind," Garion said quickly.

"I rather thought you might," Aunt Pol said. And then, without explanation, she suddenly put her arms around him and held him close to her for a long time. "What am I going to do with you?" she said finally.

"I'm all right, Aunt Pol," he assured her.

"This time perhaps," she said, taking his face between her hands. "It's a splendid thing to be brave, my Garion, but try once in a while to think a little bit first. Promise me."

"All right, Aunt Pol," he said, a little embarrassed by all this. Oddly enough she still acted as if she really cared about him. The idea that there could still be a bond between them even if they were not related began to dawn on him. It could never be the same, of course, but at least it was something. He began to feel a little better about the whole thing.

The next day he was able to get up. His muscles still ached a bit, and his ribs were somewhat tender, but he was young and was healing fast. About midmorning he was sitting with Durnik in the great hall of Anheg's palace when the silvery-bearded Earl of Seline approached them.

"King Fulrach wonders if you would be so kind as to join us in the council chamber, Goodman Durnik," he said politely.

"Me, your Honor?" Durnik asked incredulously.

"His Majesty is most impressed with your sensibility," the old gentleman said. "He feels that you represent the very best of Sendarian practicality. What we face involves all men, not just the Kings of the West, and so it's only proper that good, solid common sense be represented in our proceedings."

"I'll come at once, your Honor," Durnik said, getting up quickly, "but you'll have to forgive me if I say very little."

Garion waited expectantly.

"We've all heard of your adventure, my boy," the Earl of Seline said pleasantly to Garion. "Ah, to be young again," he sighed. "Coming, Durnik?"

"Immediately, your Honor," Durnik said, and the two of them made their way out of the great hall toward the council chamber.

Garion sat alone, wounded to the quick by his exclusion. He was at an age where his self-esteem was very tender, and inwardly he writhed at the lack of regard implicit in his not being invited to join them. Hurt and offended, he sulkily left the great hall and went to visit his boar, which hung in an ice-filled cooling room just off the kitchen. At least the boar had taken him seriously.

One can, however, spend only so much time in the company of a dead pig without becoming depressed. The boar did not seem nearly so big as he had when he was alive and charging, and the tusks were impressive but neither so long nor so sharp as Garion remembered them. Besides, it was cold in the cooling room and sore muscles stiffened quickly in chilly places.

There was no point in trying to visit Barak. The red-bearded man had locked himself in his chamber to brood in blackest melancholy and refused to answer his door, even to his wife. And so Garion, left entirely on his own, moped about for a while and then decided that he might as well explore this vast palace with its dusty, unused chambers and dark, twisting corridors. He walked for what seemed hours, opening doors and following hallways that sometimes ended abruptly against blank stone walls.

The palace of Anheg was enormous, having been, as Barak had explained, some three thousand years and more in construction. One southern wing was so totally abandoned that its entire roof had fallen in centuries ago. Garion wandered there for a time in the second-floor corridors of the ruin, his mind filled with gloomy thoughts of mortality and transient glory as he looked into rooms where snow lay thickly on ancient beds and stools and the tiny tracks of mice and squirrels ran everywhere. And then he came to an unroofed corridor where there were other tracks, those of a man. The footprints were quite fresh, for there was no sign of snow in them and it had snowed heavily the night before. At first he thought the tracks might be his own and that he had somehow circled and come back to a corridor he had already explored, but the footprints were much larger than his.

There were a dozen possible explanations, of course, but Garion felt his breath quicken. The man in the green cloak was still lurking about the palace, Asharak the Murgo was somewhere in Val Alorn, and the flaxen-haired nobleman was hiding somewhere in the forest with obviously unfriendly intentions.

Garion realized that the situation might be dangerous and that he was unarmed except for his small dagger. He retraced his steps quickly to a snowy chamber he had just explored and took down a rusty sword from a peg where it had hung forgotten for uncountable years. Then, feeling a bit more secure, he returned to follow the silent tracks.

So long as the path of the unknown intruder lay in that roofless and long-abandoned corridor, following him was simplicity itself; the undisturbed snow made tracking easy. But once the trail led over a heap of fallen debris and into the gaping blackness of a dusty corridor where the roof was still intact, things became a bit more difficult. The dust on the floor helped, but it was necessary to do a great deal of stooping and bending over. Garion's ribs and legs were still sore, and he winced and grunted each time he had to bend down to examine the stone floor. In a very short while he was sweating and gritting his teeth and thinking about giving the whole thing up.

Then he heard a faint sound far down the corridor ahead. He shrank back against the wall, hoping that no light from behind him would filter dimly through to allow him to be seen. Far ahead, a figure passed stealthily through the pale light from a single tiny window. Garion caught a momentary flicker of green and knew finally whom he was following. He kept close to the wall and moved with catlike silence in his soft leather shoes, the rusty sword gripped tightly in his hand. If it had not been for the startling nearness of the voice of the Earl of Seline, however, he would probably have walked directly into the man he had been following.

"Is it at all possible, noble Belgarath, that our enemy can be awakened before all the conditions of the ancient prophecy are met?" the earl was asking.

Garion stopped. Directly ahead of him in a narrow embrasure in the wall of the corridor, he caught sight of a slight movement. The green-cloaked man lurked there, listening in the dimness to the words that seemed to come from somewhere beneath. Garion shrank back against the wall, scarcely daring to breathe. Carefully he stepped backward until he found another embrasure and drew himself into the concealing darkness.

"A most appropriate question, Belgarath," the quiet voice of Cho-Hag of the Algars said. "Can this Apostate use the power now in his hands to revive the Accursed One?"

"The power's there," the familiar voice of Mister Wolf said, "but he might be afraid to use it. If it isn't done properly, the power will destroy him. He won't rush into such an act, and it's that hesitation that gives us the little bit of time we have."

Then Silk spoke. "Didn't you say that he might want the thing for himself? Maybe he plans to leave his Master in undisturbed slumber and use the power he's stolen to raise himself as king in the lands of the Angaraks."

King Rhodar of Drasnia chuckled. "Somehow I don't see the Grolim Priesthood so easily relinquishing their power in the lands of Angarak and bowing down to an outsider. The High Priest of the Grolims is no mean sorcerer himself, I'm told."

"Forgive me, Rhodar," King Anheg said, "but if the power's in the thief's hands, the Grolims won't have any choice but to accept his dominion. I've studied the power of this thing, and if even half of what I've read is true, he can use it to rip down Rak Cthol as easily as you'd kick apart an anthill. Then, if they still resist, he could depopulate all of Cthol Murgos from Rak Goska to the Tolnedran border. No matter what, however, whether it's the Apostate or the Accursed One who eventually raises that power, the Angaraks will follow and they'll come west."

"Shouldn't we inform the Arends and Tolnedrans—and the Ulgos as well—about what's happened, then?" Brand, the Rivan Warder, asked. "Let's not be taken by surprise again."

"I wouldn't be in too much hurry to rouse our southern neighbors," Mister Wolf said. "When Pol and I leave here, we'll be moving south. If Arendia and Tolnedra are mobilizing for war, the general turmoil would only hinder us. The Emperor's legions are soldiers. They can respond quickly when the need arises, and the Arends are always ready for war. The whole kingdom hovers on the brink of general warfare all the time."

"It's premature," Aunt Pol's familiar voice agreed. "Armies would just get in the way of what we're trying to do. If we can apprehend my father's old pupil and return the thing he pilfered to Riva, the crisis will be past. Let's not stir up the southerners for nothing."

"She's right," Wolf said. "There's always a risk in a mobilization. A king with an army on his hands usually starts to think of mischief. I'll advise the King of the Arends at Vo Mimbre and the Emperor at Tol Honeth of as much as they need to know as I pass through. But we should get word through to the Gorim of Ulgo. Cho-Hag, do you think you could get a messenger through to Prolgu at this time of the year?"

"It's hard to say, Ancient One," Cho-Hag said. "The passes into those mountains are difficult in the winter. I'll try, though."

"Good," Wolf said. "Beyond that, there's not much more we can do. For the time being it might not be a bad idea to keep this matter in the family—so to speak. If worse comes to worst and the Angaraks invade again, Aloria at least will be armed and ready. There'll be time for Arendia and the Empire to make their preparations."

King Fulrach spoke then in a troubled voice. "It's easy for the Alorn Kings to talk of war," he said. "Alorns are warriors; but my Sendaria is a peaceful kingdom. We don't have castles or fortified keeps, and my people are farmers and tradesmen. Kal Torak made a mistake when he chose the battlefield at Vo Mimbre; and it's not likely that the Angaraks will make the same mistake again. I think they'll strike directly across the grasslands of northern Algaria and fall upon Sendaria. We have a lot of food and very few soldiers. Our country would provide an ideal base for a campaign in the west, and I'm afraid that we'd fall quite easily."

Then, to Garion's amazement, Durnik spoke. "Don't cheapen the men of Sendaria so, Lord King," he said in a firm voice. "I know my neighbors, and they'll fight. We don't know very much about swords and lances, but we'll fight. If Angaraks come to Sendaria, they won't find the taking as easy as some might imagine, and if we put torches to the fields and storehouses there won't be all that much food for them to eat."

There was a long silence, and then Fulrach spoke again in a voice strangely humble. "Your words shame me, Goodman Durnik," he said. "Maybe I've been king for so long that I've forgotten what it means to be a Sendar."

"One remembers that there are only a few passes leading through the western escarpment into Sendaria," Hettar, the son of King Cho-Hag, said quietly. "A few avalanches in the right places could make Sendaria as inaccessible as the moon. If the avalanches took place at the right times, whole armies of Angaraks might find themselves trapped in those narrow corridors."

"Now that's an entertaining thought." Silk chuckled. "Then we could let Durnik put his incendiary impulses to a better use than burning turnip patches. Since Torak One-eye seems to enjoy the smell of burning sacrifices so much, we might be able to accommodate him."

Far down the dusty passageway in which he was hiding, Garion caught the sudden flicker of a torch and heard the faint jingling of several mail shirts. He almost failed to recognize the danger until the last instant. The man in the green cloak also heard the sounds and saw the light of the torch. He stepped from his hiding place and fled back the way he had come—directly past the embrasure where Garion had concealed himself. Garion shrank back, clutching his rusty sword; but as luck had it, the man was looking back over his shoulder at the twinkling torch as he ran by on soft feet.

As soon as he had passed, Garion also slipped out of his hiding place and fled. The Cherek warriors were looking for intruders, and it might be difficult to explain what he was doing in the dark hallway. He briefly considered following the spy again, but decided that he'd had enough of that for one day. It was time to tell someone about the things he'd seen. Someone had to be told—someone to whom the kings would listen. Once he reached the more frequented corridors of the palace, he firmly began to make his way toward the chamber where Barak brooded in silent melancholy.

CHAPTER SEVENTEEN

"**B**arak," Garion called through the door after he had knocked for several minutes without any answer.

"Go away," Barak's voice came thickly through the door.

"Barak, it's me, Garion. I have to talk with you."

There was a long silence inside the room, and finally a slow movement. Then the door opened.

Barak's appearance was shocking. His tunic was rumpled and stained. His red beard was matted, the long braids he usually wore were undone, and his hair was tangled. The haunted look in his eyes, however, was the worst. The look was a mixture of horror and self-loathing so naked that Garion was forced to avert his eyes.

"You saw it, didn't you, boy?" Barak demanded. "You saw what happened to me out there."

"I didn't really see anything," Garion said carefully. "I hit my head on that tree, and all I really saw were stars."

"You must have seen it," Barak insisted. "You must have seen my Doom."

"Doom?" Garion said. "What are you talking about? You're still alive."

"A Doom doesn't always mean death," Barak said morosely, flinging himself into a large chair. "I wish mine did. A Doom is some terrible thing that's fated to happen to a man, and death's not the worst thing there is."

"You've just let the words of that crazy old blind woman take over your imagination," Garion said.

"It's not only Martje," Barak said. "She's just repeating what everybody in Cherek knows. An augurer was called in when I was born—it's the custom here. Most of the time the auguries don't show anything at all, and nothing special is going to happen during the child's life. But sometimes the future lies so heavily on one of us that almost anyone can see the Doom."

"That's just superstition," Garion scoffed. "I've never seen any fortune-teller who could even tell for sure if it's going to rain tomorrow. One of them came to Faldor's farm once and told Durnik that he was going to die twice. Isn't that silly?"

"The augurers and soothsayers of Cherek have more skill," Barak said, his face still sunk in melancholy. "The Doom they saw for me was always the same—I'm going to turn into a beast. I've had dozens of them tell me the same thing. And now it's happened. I've been sitting here for two days now, watching. The hair on my body's getting longer, and my teeth are starting to get pointed."

"You're imagining things," Garion said. "You look exactly the same to me as you always have."

"You're a kind boy, Garion," Barak said. "I know you're just trying to make me feel better, but I've got eyes of my own. I know that my teeth are getting pointed and my body's starting to grow fur. It won't be long until Anheg has to chain me up in his dungeon so I won't be able to hurt anyone, or I'll have to run off into the mountains and live with the trolls."

"Nonsense," Garion insisted.

"Tell me what you saw the other day," Barak pleaded. "What did I look like when I changed into a beast?"

"All I saw were stars from banging my head on that tree," Garion said again, trying to make it sound true.

"I just want to know what kind of beast I'm turning into," Barak said, his voice thick with self-pity. "Am I going to be a wolf or a bear or some kind of monster no one even has a name for?"

"Don't you remember anything at all about what happened?" Garion asked carefully, trying to blot the strange double image of Barak and the bear out of his memory.

"Nothing," Barak said. "I heard you shouting, and the next thing I remember was the boar lying dead at my feet and you lying under that tree with his blood all over you. I could feel the beast in me, though. I could even smell him."

"All you smelled was the boar," Garion said, "and all that happened was that you lost your head in all the excitement."

"Berserk, you mean?" Barak said, looking up hopefully. Then he shook his head. "No, Garion. I've been berserk before. It doesn't feel at all the same. This was completely different." He sighed.

"You're not turning into a beast," Garion insisted.

"I know what I know," Barak said stubbornly.

And then Lady Merel, Barak's wife, stepped into the room through the still-open door. "I see that my Lord is recovering his wits," she said.

"Leave me alone, Merel," Barak said. "I'm not in the mood for these games of yours."

"Games, my Lord?" she said innocently. "I'm simply concerned about my duties. If my Lord is unwell, I'm obliged to care for him. That's a wife's right, isn't it?"

"Quit worrying so much about rights and duties, Merel," Barak said. "Just go away and leave me alone."

"My Lord was quite insistent about certain rights and duties on the night of his return to Val Alorn," she said. "Not even the locked door of my bedchamber was enough to curb his insistence."

"All right," Barak said, flushing slightly. "I'm sorry about that. I'd hoped that things had changed between us. I was wrong. I won't bother you again."

"Bother, my Lord?" she said. "A duty is not a bother. A good wife is obliged to submit whenever her husband requires it of her—no matter how drunk or brutal he may be when he comes to her bed. No one will ever be able to accuse me of laxity in that regard."

"You're enjoying this, aren't you?" Barak accused.

"Enjoying what, my Lord?" Her voice was light, but there was a cutting edge to it.

"What do you want, Merel?" Barak demanded bluntly.

"I want to serve my Lord in his illness," she said. "I want to care for him and watch the progress of his disease—each symptom as it appears."

"Do you hate me that much?" Barak asked with heavy contempt. "Be careful, Merel. I might take it into my head to insist that you stay with me. How would you like that? How would you like to be locked in this room with a raging beast?"

"If you grow unmanageable, my Lord, I can always have you chained to the wall," she suggested, meeting his enraged glare with cool unconcern.

"Barak," Garion said uncomfortably, "I have to talk to you."

"Not now, Garion," Barak snapped.

"It's important. There's a spy in the palace."

"A spy?"

"A man in a green cloak," Garion said. "I've seen him several times."

"Many men wear green cloaks," Lady Merel said.

"Stay out of this, Merel," Barak said. He turned to Garion. "What makes you think he's a spy?"

"I saw him again this morning," Garion said, "and I followed him. He was sneaking along a corridor that nobody seems to use. It passes above the hall where the kings are meeting with Mister Wolf and Aunt Pol. He could hear every word they said."

"How do you know what he could hear?" Merel asked, her eyes narrowing.

"I was up there too," Garion said. "I hid not far from him, and I could hear them myself—almost as if I were in the same room with them."

"What does he look like?" Barak asked.

"He has sandy-colored hair," Garion said, "and a beard and, as I said, he wears a green cloak. I saw him the day we went down to look at your ship. He was going into a tavern with a Murgo."

"There aren't any Murgos in Val Alorn," Merel said.

"There's one," Garion said. "I've seen him before. I know who he is." He had to move around the subject carefully. The compulsion not to speak about his dark-robed enemy was as strong as always. Even the hint he had given made his tongue seem stiff and his lips numb.

"Who is he?" Barak demanded.

Garion ignored the question. "And then on the day of the boar hunt I saw him in the forest."

"The Murgo?" Barak asked.

"No. The man in the green cloak. He met some other men there. They talked for a while not far from where I was waiting for the boar to come. They didn't see me."

"There's nothing suspicious about that," Barak said. "A man can meet with his friends anywhere he likes."

"I don't think they were friends exactly," Garion said. "The one in the green cloak called one of the other men 'my Lord,' and that one was giving him orders to get close enough so that he could hear what Mister Wolf and the kings were saying."

"That's more serious," Barak said, seeming to forget his melancholy. "Did they say anything else?"

"The flaxen-haired man wanted to know about us," Garion said. "You, me, Durnik, Silk—all of us."

"Flaxen-colored hair?" Merel asked quickly.

"The one he called 'my Lord,' " Garion explained. "He seemed to know about us. He even knew about me."

"Long, pale-colored hair?" Merel demanded. "No beard? A little older than Barak?"

"It couldn't be him," Barak said. "Anheg banished him on pain of death."

"You're a child, Barak," she said. "He'd ignore that if it suited him. I think we'd better tell Anheg about this."

"Do you know him?" Garion asked. "Some of the things he said about Barak weren't very polite."

"I can imagine," Merel said ironically. "Barak was one of those who said that he ought to have his head removed."

Barak was already pulling on his mail shirt.

"Fix your hair," Merel told him in a tone that oddly had no hint of her former rancor in it. "You look like a haystack."

"I can't stop to fool with it now," Barak said impatiently. "Come along, both of you. We'll go to Anheg at once."

There was no time for any further questions, since Garion and Merel almost had to run to keep up with Barak. They swept through the great hall, and startled warriors scrambled out of their way after one look at Barak's face.

"My Lord Barak," one of the guards at the door of the council hall greeted the huge man.

"One side," Barak commanded and flung open the door with a crash.

King Anheg looked up, startled at the sudden interruption. "Welcome, cousin," he began.

"Treason, Anheg!" Barak roared. "The Earl of Jarvik has broken his banishment and set spies on you in your own palace."

"Jarvik?" Anheg said. "He wouldn't dare."

"He dared, all right," Barak said. "He's been seen not far from Val Alorn, and some of his plotting has been overheard."

"Who is this Jarvik?" the Rivan Warder asked.

"An earl I banished last year," Anheg said. "One of his men was stopped, and we found a message on him. The message was to a Murgo in Sendaria, and it gave the details of one of our most secret councils. Jarvik tried to deny that the message was his, even though it had his own seal on it and his strongroom bulged with red gold from the mines of Cthol Murgos. I'd have had his head on a pole, but his wife's a kinswoman of mine and she begged for his life. I banished him to one of his estates on the west coast instead." He looked at Barak. "How did you find out about this?" he asked. "Last I heard, you'd locked yourself in your room and wouldn't talk to anybody."

"My husband's words are true, Anheg," Lady Merel said in a voice that rang with challenge.

"I don't doubt him, Merel," Anheg said, looking at her with a faintly surprised expression. "I just wanted to know how he learned about Jarvik, that's all."

"This boy from Sendaria saw him," Merel said, "and heard him talk to his spy. I heard the boy's story myself, and I stand behind what my husband said, if anyone here dares to doubt him."

"Garion?" Aunt Pol said, startled.

"May I suggest that we hear from the lad?" Cho-Hag of the Algars said quietly. "A nobleman with a history of friendship for the Murgos who chooses this exact moment to break his banishment concerns us all, I think."

"Tell them what you told Merel and me, Garion," Barak ordered, pushing Garion forward.

"Your Majesty," Garion said, bowing awkwardly, "I've seen a man in a green cloak hiding here in your palace several times since we came here. He creeps along the passageways and takes a lot of trouble not to be seen. I saw him the first night we were here, and the next day I saw him going into a tavern in the city with a Murgo. Barak says there aren't any Murgos in Cherek, but I know that the man he was with was a Murgo."

"How do you know?" Anheg asked shrewdly.

Garion looked at him helplessly, unable to say Asharak's name.

"Well, boy?" King Rhodar asked.

Garion struggled with the words, but nothing would come out.

"Maybe you know this Murgo?" Silk suggested.

Garion nodded, relieved that someone could help him.

"You wouldn't know many Murgos," Silk said, rubbing his nose with one finger. "Was it the one we met in Darine, perhaps—and later in Muros? The one known as Asharak?"

Garion nodded again.

"Why didn't you tell us?" Barak asked.

"I—I couldn't," Garion stammered.

"Couldn't?"

"The words wouldn't come out," Garion said. "I don't know why, but I've never been able to talk about him."

"Then you've seen him before?" Silk said.

"Yes," Garion said.

"And you've never told anybody?"

"No."

Silk glanced quickly at Aunt Pol. "Is this the sort of thing you might know more about than we would, Polgara?" he asked.

She nodded slowly. "It's possible to do it," she said. "It's never been very reliable, so I don't bother with it myself. It is possible, however." Her expression grew grim.

"The Grolims think it's impressive," Mister Wolf said. "Grolims are easily impressed."

"Come with me, Garion," Aunt Pol said.

"Not yet," Wolf said.

"This is important," she said, her face hardening.

"You can do it later," he said. "Let's hear the rest of his story first. The damage has already been done. Go ahead, Garion, What else did you see?"

Garion took a deep breath. "All right," he said, relieved to be talking to the old man instead of the kings. "I saw the man in the green cloak again that day we all went hunting. He met in the forest with a yellow-haired man who doesn't wear a beard. They talked for a while, and I could hear what they were saying. The yellow-haired man wanted to know what all of you were saying in this hall."

"You should have come to me immediately," King Anheg said.

"Anyway," Garion went on, "I had that fight with the wild boar. I hit my head against a tree and was stunned. I didn't remember what I'd seen until this morning. After King Fulrach called Durnik here, I went exploring. I was in a part of the palace where the roof is all fallen in, and I found some footprints. I followed them, and then after a while I saw the man in the green cloak again. That was when I remembered all this. I followed him, and he went along a corridor that passes somewhere over the top of this hall. He hid up there and listened to what you were saying."

"How much do you think he could hear, Garion?" King Cho-Hag asked.

"You were talking about somebody called the Apostate," Garion said, "and you were wondering if he could use some power of some kind to awaken an enemy who's been asleep for a long time. Some of you thought you ought to warn the Arends and the Tolnedrans, but Mister Wolf didn't think so. And Durnik talked about how the men of Sendaria would fight if the Angaraks came."

They appeared startled.

"I was hiding not far from the man in the green cloak," Garion said. "I'm sure he could hear everything that I could. Then some soldiers came, and the man ran away. That's when I decided that I ought to tell Barak about all this."

"Up there," Silk said, standing near one of the walls and pointing at a corner of the ceiling of the hall. "The mortar's crumbled away. The sound of our voices carries right up through the cracks between the stones into the upper corridor."

"This is a valuable boy you've brought with you, Lady Polgara," King Rhodar said gravely. "If he's looking for a profession, I think I might find a place for him. Gathering information is a rewarding occupation, and he seems to have certain natural gifts along those lines."

"He has some other gifts as well," Aunt Pol said. "He seems to be very good at turning up in places where he's not supposed to be."

"Don't be too hard on the boy, Polgara," King Anheg said. "He's done us a service that we may never be able to repay."

Garion bowed again and retreated from Aunt Pol's steady gaze.

"Cousin," Anheg said then to Barak, "it seems that we have an unwelcome visitor somewhere in the palace. I think I'd like to have a little talk with this lurker in the green cloak."

"I'll take a few men," Barak said grimly. "We'll turn your palace upside down and shake it and see what falls out."

"I'd like to have him more or less intact," Anheg cautioned.

"Of course," Barak said.

"Not too intact, however. As long as he's still able to talk, he'll serve our purposes."

Barak grinned. "I'll make sure that he's talkative when I bring him to you, cousin," he said.

A bleak answering grin touched Anheg's face, and Barak started toward the door.

Then Anheg turned to Barak's wife. "I'd like to thank you also, Lady Merel," he said. "I'm sure you had a significant part in bringing this to us."

"I don't need thanks, your Majesty," she said. "It was my duty."

Anheg sighed. "Must it always be duty, Merel?" he asked sadly.

"What else is there?" she asked.

"A very great deal, actually," the king said, "but you're going to have to find that out for yourself."

"Garion," Aunt Pol said, "come here."

"Yes, ma'am," Garion said and went to her a little nervously.

"Don't be silly, dear," she said. "I'm not going to hurt you." She put her fingertips lightly to his forehead.

"Well?" Mister Wolf asked.

"It's there," she said. "It's very light, or I'd have noticed it before. I'm sorry, Father."

"Let's see," Wolf said. He came over and also touched Garion's head with his hand. "It's not serious," he said.

"It could have been," Aunt Pol said. "And it was my responsibility to see that something like this didn't happen."

"Don't flog yourself about it, Pol," Wolf said. "That's very unbecoming. Just get rid of it."

"What's the matter?" Garion asked, alarmed.

"It's nothing to worry about, dear," Aunt Pol said. She took his right hand and touched it for a moment to the white lock at her brow.

Garion felt a surge, a welter of confused impressions, and then a tingling wrench behind his ears. A sudden dizziness swept over him, and he would have fallen if Aunt Pol had not caught him.

"Who is the Murgo?" she asked, looking into his eyes.

"His name is Asharak," Garion said promptly.

"How long have you known him?"

"All my life. He used to come to Faldor's farm and watch me when I was little."

"That's enough for now, Pol," Mister Wolf said. "Let him rest a little first. I'll fix something to keep it from happening again."

"Is the boy ill?" King Cho-Hag asked.

"It's not exactly an illness, Cho-Hag," Mister Wolf said. "It's a little hard to explain. It's cleared up now, though."

"I want you to go to your room, Garion," Aunt Pol said, still holding him by the shoulders. "Are you steady enough on your feet to get there by yourself?"

"I'm all right," he said, still feeling a little light-headed.

"No side trips and no more exploring," she said firmly.

"No, ma'am."

"When you get there, lie down. I want you to think back and remember every single time you've seen this Murgo—what he did, what he said."

"He never spoke to me," Garion said. "He just watched."

"I'll be along in a little while," she went on, "and I'll want you to tell me everything you know about him. It's important, Garion, so concentrate as hard as you can."

"All right, Aunt Pol," he said.

Then she kissed him lightly on the forehead. "Run along now, dear," she said.

Feeling strangely light-headed, Garion went to the door and out into the corridor.

He passed through the great hall where Anheg's warriors were belting on swords and picking up vicious-looking battle-axes in preparation for the search of the palace. Still bemused, he went through without stopping.

Part of his mind seemed half-asleep, but that secret, inner part was wide awake. The dry voice observed that something significant had just happened. The powerful compulsion not to speak about Asharak was obviously gone. Aunt Pol had somehow pulled it out of his mind entirely. His feeling about that was oddly ambiguous. That strange relationship between himself and dark-robed, silent Asharak had always been intensely private, and now it was gone. He felt vaguely empty and somehow violated. He sighed and went up the broad stairway toward his room.

There were a half-dozen warriors in the hallway outside his room, probably part of Barak's search for the man in the green cloak. Garion stopped. Something was wrong, and he shook off his half daze. This part of the palace was much too populated to make it very likely that the spy would be hiding here. His heart began racing, and step by step he began to back away toward the top of the stairs he had just climbed. The warriors looked like any other Chereks in the palace—bearded, dressed in helmets, mail shirts, and furs, but something didn't seem exactly right.

A bulky man in a dark, hooded cloak stepped through the doorway of Garion's room into the corridor. It was Asharak. The Murgo was about to say something, but then his eyes fell on Garion. "Ah," he said softly. His dark eyes gleamed in his scarred face. "I've been looking for you, Garion," he said in that same soft voice. "Come here, boy."

Garion felt a tentative tug at his mind that seemed to slip away as if it somehow could not get a sure grip. He shook his head mutely and continued to back away.

"Come along now," Asharak said. "We've known each other far too long for this. Do as I say. You know that you must."

The tug became a powerful grasp that again slipped away.

"Come here, Garion!" Asharak commanded harshly.

Garion kept backing away, step by step. "No," he said.

Asharak's eyes blazed, and he drew himself up angrily.

This time it was not a tug or a grasp, but a blow. Garion could feel the force of it even as it seemed somehow to miss or be deflected.

Asharak's eyes widened slightly, then narrowed. "Who did this?" he demanded. "Polgara? Belgarath? It won't do any good, Garion. I had you once, and I can take you again anytime I want to. You're not strong enough to refuse me."

Garion looked at his enemy and answered out of some need for defiance. "Maybe I'm not," he said, "but I think you'll have to catch me first."

Asharak turned quickly to his warriors. "That's the boy I want," he barked sharply. "Take him!"

Smoothly, almost as if it were done without thought, one of the warriors raised his bow and leveled an arrow directly at Garion. Asharak swung his arm quickly and knocked the bow aside just as the steel-pointed shaft was loosed. The arrow sang in the air and clattered against the stones of the wall a few feet to Garion's left.

"Alive, idiot," Asharak snarled and struck the bowman a crushing blow to the side of the head. The bowman fell twitching to the stone floor.

Garion spun, dashed back to the stairs and plunged down three steps at a time. He didn't bother to look back. The sound of heavy feet told him that Asharak and his men were after him. At the bottom of the stairs, he turned sharply to the left and fled down a long, dark passageway that led back into the maze of Anheg's palace.

CHAPTER EIGHTEEN

There were warriors everywhere, and the sounds of fighting. In the first instant of his flight, Garion's plan had been simple. All he had to do was to find some of Barak's warriors, and he would be safe. But there were other warriors in the palace as well. The Earl of Jarvik had led a small army into the palace by way of the ruined wings to the south, and fighting raged in the corridors.

Garion quickly realized that there was no way he could distinguish friend from enemy. To him, one Cherek warrior looked the same as another. Unless he could find Barak or someone else he recognized, he did not dare reveal himself to any of them. The frustrating knowledge that he was running from friends as well as enemies added to his fright. It was altogether possible— even quite likely—that he would run from Barak's men directly into the arms of Jarvik's.

The most logical thing to do would be to go directly back to the council hall, but in his haste to escape from Asharak, he had run down so many dim passageways and turned so many corners that he had no idea where he was or how to get back to the familiar parts of the palace. His headlong flight was dangerous. Asharak or his men could wait around any corner to seize him, and he knew that the Murgo could quickly re-establish that strange bond between them that Aunt Pol had shattered with her touch. It was that which had to be avoided at any cost. Once Asharak had him again, he would never let go. The only alternative left to him was to find some place to hide.

He dodged into another narrow passageway and stopped, panting and with his back pressed tightly against the stones of the wall. Dimly, at the far end of this hallway, he could see a narrow flight of worn stone steps twisting upward in the flickering light of a single torch. He quickly reasoned that the higher he went, the less likely he would be to encounter anyone. The fighting would most likely be concentrated on the lower floors. He took a deep breath and went swiftly to the foot of the stairs.

Halfway up he saw the flaw in his plan. There were no side passages on the stairs, no way to escape and no place to hide. He had to get to the top quickly or chance discovery and capture—or even worse.

"Boy!" a shout came from below.

Garion looked quickly over his shoulder. A grim-faced Cherek in mail and helmet was coming up the stairs behind him, his sword drawn.

Garion started to run, stumbling up the stairs.

There was another shout from above, and Garion froze. The warrior at the top was as grim as the one below and wielded a cruel-looking axe.

He was trapped between them. Garion shrank back against the stones, fumbling for his dagger, though he knew it would be of little use.

Then the two warriors saw each other. With ringing shouts they both charged. The one with the sword rushed up past Garion while the one with the axe lunged down.

The axe swung wide, missed and clashed a shower of sparks from the stones of the wall. The sword was more true. With his hair standing on end in horror, Garion saw it slide through the downward-plunging body of the axeman. The axe fell clattering down the stairs, and the axeman, still falling on top of his opponent, pulled a broad dagger from its sheath at his hip and drove it into the chest of his enemy. The impact as the two men came together tore them from their feet, and they tumbled, still grappled together down the stairs, their daggers flashing as each man struck again and again.

In helpless horror Garion watched as they rolled and crashed past him, their daggers sinking into each other with sickening sounds and blood spurting from their wounds like red fountains.

Garion retched once, clenched his teeth tightly, and ran up the stairs, trying to close his ears to the awful sounds coming from below as the two dying men continued their horrid work on each other.

He no longer even considered stealth; he simply ran—fleeing more from that hideous encounter on the stairs than from Asharak or the Earl of Jarvik. At last, after how long he could not have said, gasping and winded, he plunged through the partially open door of a dusty, unused chamber. He pushed the door shut and stood trembling with his back against it.

There was a broad, sagging bed against one wall of the room and a small window set high in the same wall. Two broken chairs leaned wearily in corners and an empty chest, its lid open, in a third, and that was all. The chamber was at least a place out of the corridors where savage men were killing each other, but Garion quickly realized that the seeming safety here was an illusion. If anyone opened this door, he would be trapped. Desperately he began to look around the dusty room.

Hanging on the bare wall across from the bed were some drapes; and thinking that they might conceal some closet or adjoining chamber, Garion crossed the room and pulled them aside. There was an opening behind the drapes, though it did not lead into another room but instead into a dark, narrow hall. He peered into the passageway, but the darkness was so total that he could only see a short distance into it. He shuddered at the thought of groping through that blackness with armed men pounding along at his heels.

He glanced up at the single window and then dragged the heavy chest across the room to stand on so that he could see out. Perhaps he might be able to see something from the window that would give him some idea of his location. He climbed up on the chest, stood on his tiptoes and looked out.

Towers loomed here and there amid the long slate roofs of the endless galleries and halls of King Anheg's palace. It was hopeless. He saw nothing that he could recognize. He turned back toward the chamber and was about to jump down from the chest when he stopped suddenly. There, clearly in the dust which lay heavily on the floor, were his footprints.

He hopped quickly down and grabbed up the bolster from the long-unused bed. He spread it out on the floor and dragged it around the room, erasing the footprints. He knew that he could not completely conceal the fact that someone had been in the room, but he could obliterate the footprints which, because of their size, would immediately make it obvious to Asharak or any of his men that whoever had been hiding here was not yet full-grown. When he finished, he tossed the bolster back on the bed. The job wasn't perfect, but at least it was better than it had been.

Then there was a shout in the corridor outside and the ring of steel on steel.

Garion took a deep breath and plunged into the dark passageway behind the drapes.

He had gone no more than a few feet when the darkness in the narrow passage become absolute. His skin crawled at the touch of cobwebs on his face, and the dust of years rose chokingly from the uneven floor. At first he moved quite rapidly, wanting more than anything to put as much distance between himself and the fighting in the corridor as possible, but then he stumbled, and for one heart-stopping instant it seemed that he would fall. The picture of a steep stairway dropping down into the blackness flashed through his mind, and he realized that at his present pace there would be no possible way to catch himself. He began to move more cautiously, one hand on the stones of the wall and the other in front of his face to ward off the cobwebs which hung thickly from the low ceiling.

There was no sense of time in the dark, and it seemed to Garion that he had been groping for hours in this dark hallway that appeared to go on forever. Then, despite his care, he ran full into a rough stone wall. He felt a moment of panic. Did the passageway end here? Was it a trap?

Then, flickering at one corner of his vision, he saw dim light. The passageway did not end, but rather made a sharp turn to the right. There seemed to be a light at the far end, and Garion gratefully followed it.

As the light grew stronger, he moved more rapidly, and soon he reached the spot that was the source of the light. It was a narrow slot low in the wall. Garion knelt on the dusty stones and peered out.

The hall below was enormous, and a great fire burned in a pit in the center with the smoke rising to the openings in the vaulted roof which lofted even above the place where Garion was. Though it looked much different from up here, he immediately recognized King Anheg's throne room. As he looked down, he saw the gross shape of King Rhodar and the smaller form of King Cho-Hag with the ever-present Hettar standing behind him. Some distance from the thrones, King Fulrach stood in conversation with Mister Wolf, and nearby was Aunt Pol. Barak's wife was talking with Queen Islena, and Queen Porenn and Queen Silar stood not far from them. Silk paced the floor nervously, glancing now and then at the heavily guarded doors. Garion felt a surge of relief. He was safe.

He was about to call down to them when the great door banged open, and King Anheg, mail-shirted and with his sword in his hand, strode into the hall, closely followed by Barak and the Rivan Warder, holding between them the struggling form of the flaxen-haired man Garion had seen in the forest on the day of the boar hunt.

"This treason will cost you dearly, Jarvik," Anheg said grimly over his shoulder as he strode toward his throne.

"Is it over, then?" Aunt Pol asked.

"Soon, Polgara," Anheg said. "My men are chasing the last of Jarvik's brigands in the furthest reaches of the palace. If we hadn't been warned, it might have gone quite differently, though."

Garion, his shout still hovering just behind his lips, decided at the last instant to stay silent for a few more moments.

King Anheg sheathed his sword and took his place on his throne. "We'll talk for a bit, Jarvik," he said, "before what must be done is done."

The flaxen-haired man gave up his hopeless struggle against Barak and the almost equally powerful Brand. "I don't have anything to say, Anheg," he said defiantly. "If the luck had gone differently, I'd be sitting on your throne right now. I took my chance, and that's the end of it."

"Not quite," Anheg said. "I want the details. You might as well tell me. One way or another, you're going to talk."

"Do your worst," Jarvik sneered. "I'll bite out my own tongue before I tell you anything."

"We'll see about that," Anheg said grimly.

"That won't be necessary, Anheg," Aunt Pol said, walking slowly toward the captive. "There's an easier way to persuade him."

"I'm not going to say anything," Jarvik told her. "I'm a warrior and I'm not afraid of you, witch-woman."

"You're a greater fool than I thought, Lord Jarvik," Mister Wolf said. "Would you rather I did it, Pol?"

"I can manage, Father," she said, not taking her eyes off Jarvik.

"Carefully," the old man cautioned. "Sometimes you go to extremes. Just a little touch is enough."

"I know what I'm doing, Old Wolf," she said tartly. She stared full into the captive's eyes.

Garion, still hidden, held his breath.

The Earl of Jarvik began to sweat and tried desperately to pull his eyes away from Aunt Pol's gaze, but it was hopeless. Her will commanded him, locking his eyes. He trembled, and his face grew pale. She made no move, no gesture, but merely stood before him, her eyes burning into his brain.

And then, after a moment, he screamed. Then he screamed again and collapsed, his weight sagging down in the hands of the two men who held him.

"Take it away," he whimpered, shuddering uncontrollably. "I'll talk, but please take it away."

Silk, now lounging near Anheg's throne, looked at Hettar. "I wonder what he saw," he said.

"I think it might be better not to know," Hettar replied.

Queen Islena had watched intently as if hoping to gain some hint of how the trick was done. She winced visibly when Jarvik screamed, pulling her eyes away.

"All right, Jarvik," Anheg said, his tone strangely subdued. "Begin at the beginning. I want it all."

"It was a little thing at first," Jarvik said in a shaking voice. "There didn't seem to be any harm in it."

"There never does," Brand said.

The Earl of Jarvik drew in a deep breath, glanced once at Aunt Pol and shuddered again. Then he straightened. "It started about two years ago," he said. "I'd sailed to Kotu in Drasnia, and I met a Nadrak merchant named Grashor there. He seemed to be a good enough fellow, and after we'd gotten to know each other he asked me if I'd be interested in a profitable venture. I told him that I was an earl and not a common tradesman, but he persisted. He said he was nervous about the pirates who live on the islands in the Gulf of Cherek and an earl's ship manned by armed warriors was not likely to be attacked. His cargo was a single chest—not very large. I think it was some jewels he'd managed to smuggle past the customs houses in Boktor, and he wanted them delivered to Darine in Sendaria. I said that I wasn't really interested, but then he opened his purse and poured out gold. The gold was bright red, I remember, and I couldn't seem to take my eyes off it. I did need money—who doesn't after all?—and I really couldn't see any dishonor in doing what he asked.

"Anyway, I carried him and his cargo to Darine and met his associate—a Murgo named Asharak."

Garion started at the name, and he heard Silk's low whistle of surprise.

"As we'd agreed," Jarvik continued, "Asharak paid me a sum equal to what Grashor had given me, and I came away from the affair with a whole pouch of gold. Asharak told me that I'd done them a great favor and that if I ever needed more gold, he'd be happy to find ways for me to earn it.

"I now had more gold than I'd ever had at one time before, but it somehow seemed that it wasn't enough. For some reason I felt that I needed more."

"It's the nature of Angarak gold," Mister Wolf said. "It calls to its own. The more one has, the more it comes to possess him. That's why Murgos are so lavish with it. Asharak wasn't buying your services, Jarvik; he was buying your soul."

Jarvik nodded, his face gloomy. "At any rate," he continued, "it wasn't long before I found an excuse to sail to Darine again. Asharak told me that since Murgos are forbidden to enter Cherek, he'd developed a great curiosity about us and our kingdom. He asked me many questions and he gave me gold for every answer. It seemed to me to be a foolish way to spend money, but I gave him the answers and took his gold. When I came back to Cherek, I had another pouch full. I went to Jarviksholm and put the new gold with that I already had. I saw that I was a rich man, and I still hadn't done anything dishonorable. But now it seemed that there weren't enough hours in the day. I spent all my time locked in my strongroom, counting my gold over and over, polishing it until it gleamed red as blood and filling my ears with the sound of its tinkling.

"But after a while it seemed that I didn't really have very much, and so I went back to Asharak. He said he was still curious about Cherek and that he'd like to know Anheg's mind. He told me that he'd give me as much gold as I already had if I sent him word of what was said in the high councils here in the palace for a year. At first I said no, because I knew it would be dishonorable; but then he showed me the gold, and I couldn't say no anymore."

From where he watched Garion could see the expressions of those in the hall below. Their faces had a curious mingling of pity and contempt as Jarvik's story continued.

"It was then, Anheg," he said, "that your men captured one of my messengers, and I was banished to Jarviksholm. At first I didn't mind, because I could still play with my gold. But again it wasn't long before it seemed that I didn't have enough. I sent a fast ship through the Bore to Darine with a message to Asharak begging him to find something else for me to do to earn more gold. When the ship came back, Asharak was aboard her, and we sat down and talked about what I could do to increase my hoard."

"You're doubly a traitor then, Jarvik," Anheg said in a voice that was almost sad. "You've betrayed me, and you've broken the oldest law in Cherek. No Angarak has set foot on Cherek soil since the days of Bear-shoulders himself."

Jarvik shrugged. "I didn't really care by then," he said. "Asharak had a plan, and it seemed like a good one to me. If we could get through the city a few at a time, we could hide an army in the ruined southern wings of the palace. With surprise and a bit of luck we could kill Anheg and the other Alorn Kings, and I could take the throne of Cherek and maybe of all Aloria as well."

"And what was Asharak's price?" Mister Wolf demanded, his eyes narrowing. "What did he want in return for making you king?"

"A thing so small that I laughed when he told me what he wanted," Jarvik said. "But he said that he'd not only give me the crown but a roomful of gold if I'd get it for him."

"What was it?" Wolf repeated.

"He said that there was a boy—about fourteen—in the party of King Fulrach of Sendaria. He told me that as soon as that boy was delivered to him, he'd give me more gold than I could count and the throne of Cherek as well."

King Fulrach looked startled. "The boy Garion?" he asked. "Why would Asharak want him?"

Aunt Pol's single frightened gasp carried even up to where Garion was concealed. "Durnik!" she said in a ringing voice, but Durnik was already on his feet and racing toward the door with Silk close behind him. Aunt Pol spun with eyes blazing and the white lock at her brow almost incandescent in the midnight of her hair. The Earl of Jarvik flinched as her glare fell on him.

"If anything's happened to the boy, Jarvik, men will tremble at the memory of your fate for a thousand years," she told him.

It had gone far enough. Garion was ashamed and a little frightened by the fury of Aunt Pol's reaction.

"I'm all right, Aunt Pol," he called down to her through the narrow slot in the wall. "I'm up here."

"Garion?" She looked up, trying to see him. "Where are you?"

"Up here near the ceiling," he said, "behind the wall."

"How did you get up there?"

"I don't know. Some men were chasing me, and I ran. This is where I ended up."

"Come down here at once."

"I don't know how, Aunt Pol," he said. "I ran so far and took so many turns that I don't know how to get back. I'm lost."

"All right," she said, regaining her composure. "Stay where you are. We'll think of a way to get you down."

"I hope so," he said.

CHAPTER NINETEEN

"Well, it has to come out someplace," King Anheg said, squinting up toward the spot where Garion waited nervously. "All he has to do is follow it."

"And walk directly into the arms of Asharak the Murgo?" Aunt Pol asked. "He's better off staying where he is."

"Asharak's fleeing for his life," Anheg said. "He's nowhere in the palace."

"As I recall, he's not even supposed to be in the kingdom," she said pointedly.

"All right, Pol," Mister Wolf said. He called up, "Garion, which way does the passage run?"

"It seems to go on toward the back of the hall where the thrones are," Garion answered. "I can't tell for sure if it turns off or not. It's pretty dark up here."

"We'll pass you up a couple torches," Wolf said. "Set one at the spot where you are now and then go on down the passage with the other. As long as you can see the first one, you'll be going in a straight line."

"Very clever," Silk said. "I wish I were seven thousand years old so I could solve problems so easily."

Wolf let that pass.

"I still think the safest way would be to get some ladders and break a hole in the wall," Barak said.

King Anheg looked pained. "Couldn't we try Belgarath's suggestion first?" he asked.

Barak shrugged. "You're the king."

"Thanks," Anheg said dryly.

A warrior fetched a long pole and two torches were passed up to Garion.

"If the line of the passageway holds straight," Anheg said, "he should come out somewhere in the royal apartments."

"Interesting," King Rhodar said with one raised eyebrow. "It would be most enlightening to know if the passage led *to* the royal chambers or *from* them."

"It's entirely possible that the passageway is just some long-forgotten escape route," Anheg said in an injured tone. "Our history, after all, hasn't been all that peaceful. There's no need to suspect the worst, is there?"

"Of course not," King Rhodar said blandly, "no need at all."

Garion set one of the torches beside the slot in the wall and followed the dusty passageway, looking back often to be sure that the torch was still in plain sight. Eventually he came to a narrow door which opened into the back of an empty closet. The closet was attached to a splendid-looking bedchamber, and outside there was a broad, well-lighted corridor.

Several warriors were coming down the corridor, and Garion recognized

Torvik the huntsman among them. "Here I am," he said, stepping out with a surge of relief.

"You've been busy, haven't you?" Torvik said with a grin.

"It wasn't my idea," Garion said.

"Let's get you back to King Anheg," Torvik said. "The lady, your Aunt, seems concerned about you."

"She's angry with me, I suppose," Garion said, falling into step beside the broad-shouldered man.

"More than likely," Torvik said. "Women are almost always angry with us for one reason or another. It's one of the things you'll have to get used to as you get older."

Aunt Pol was waiting at the door to the throne room. There were no reproaches—not yet, at any rate. For one brief moment she clasped him fiercely to her and then looked at him gravely. "We've been waiting for you, dear," she said almost calmly; then she led him to where the others waited.

"In my grandmother's quarters, you say?" Anheg was saying to Torvik. "What an astonishing thing. I remember her as a crotchety old lady who walked with a cane."

"No one's born old, Anheg," King Rhodar said with a sly look.

"I'm sure there are many explanations, Anheg," Queen Porenn said. "My husband's just teasing you."

"One of the men looked into the passage, your Majesty," Torvik said tactfully. "The dust is very thick. It's possible that it hasn't been used for centuries."

"What an astonishing thing," Anheg said again.

The matter was then delicately allowed to drop, though King Rhodar's sly expression spoke volumes.

The Earl of Seline coughed politely. "I think young Garion here may have a story for us," he said.

"I expect he has," Aunt Pol said, turning toward Garion. "I seem to remember telling you to stay in your room."

"Asharak was in my room," Garion said, "and he had warriors with him. He tried to make me come to him. When I wouldn't, he said that he'd had me once and could get me again. I didn't understand exactly what he meant, but I told him that he'd have to catch me first. Then I ran."

Brand, the Rivan Warder, chuckled. "I don't see how you can find much fault with that, Polgara," he said. "I think that if I found a Grolim priest in my room, I'd probably run away too."

"You're sure it was Asharak?" Silk asked.

Garion nodded. "I've known him for a long time," he said. "All my life, I guess. And he knew me. He called me by name."

"I think I'd like to have a long talk with this Asharak," Anheg said. "I want to ask him some questions about all the mischief he's been stirring up in my kingdom."

"I doubt if you'll find him, Anheg," Mister Wolf said. "He seems to be more than just a Grolim priest. I touched his mind once—in Muros. It's not an ordinary mind."

"I'll amuse myself with the search for him," Anheg said with a bleak expression. "Not even a Grolim can walk on water, so I believe I'll just seal off all the ports in Cherek and then put my warriors to work searching the mountains and forests for him. They get fat and troublesome in the wintertime anyway, and it'll give them something to do."

"Driving fat, troublesome warriors into the snow in the dead of winter isn't going to make you a popular king, Anheg," Rhodar observed.

"Offer a reward," Silk suggested. "That way you get the job done and stay popular as well."

"That's an idea," Anheg said. "What kind of reward would you suggest, Prince Kheldar?"

"Promise to equal the weight of Asharak's head in gold," Silk said. "That should lure the fattest warrior away from the dice cup and the ale keg."

Anheg winced.

"He's a Grolim," Silk said. "They probably won't find him, but they'll take the kingdom apart looking. Your gold is safe, your warriors get a bit of exercise, you get a reputation for generosity, and, with every man in Cherek looking for him with an axe, Asharak's going to be much too busy hiding to stir up any more mischief. A man whose head is more valuable to others than it is to himself has little time for foolishness."

"Prince Kheldar," Anheg said gravely, "you're a devious man."

"I try, King Anheg," Silk said with an ironic bow.

"I don't suppose you'd care to come to work for me?" the King of Cherek offered.

"Anheg!" Rhodar protested.

Silk sighed. "Blood, King Anheg," he said. "I'm committed to my uncle by our bonds of kinship. I'd be interested to hear your offer, though. It might help in future negotiations about compensation for my services."

Queen Porenn's laughter was like a small silver bell, and King Rhodar's face became tragic. "You see," he said. "I'm absolutely surrounded by traitors. What's a poor fat old man to do?"

A grim-looking warrior entered the hall and marched up to Anheg. "It's done, King," he said. "Do you want to look at his head?"

"No," Anheg said shortly.

"Should we put it on a pole near the harbor?" the warrior asked.

"No," Anheg said. "Jarvik was a brave man once and my kinsman by marriage. Have him delivered to his wife for a proper burial."

The warrior bowed and left the hall.

"This problem of the Grolim, Asharak, interests me," Queen Islena said to Aunt Pol. "Might we not between us, Lady Polgara, devise a way to locate him?" Her expression had a certain quality of self-importance to it.

Mister Wolf spoke quickly before Aunt Pol could answer. "Bravely spoken, Islena," he said. "But we couldn't allow the Queen of Cherek to take such a risk. I'm sure your skills are formidable, but such a search opens the mind completely. If Asharak felt you looking for him, he'd retaliate instantly. Polgara wouldn't be in any danger, but I'm afraid your mind could be blown out like a candle. It would be a great shame to have the Queen of Cherek live out the rest of her life as a raving lunatic."

Islena turned suddenly very pale and did not see the sly wink Mister Wolf directed at Anheg.

"I couldn't permit it," Anheg said firmly. "My queen is far too precious for me to allow her to take such a terrible risk."

"I must accede to the will of my Lord," Islena said in a relieved tone. "By his command I withdraw my suggestion."

"The courage of my queen honors me," Anheg said with an absolutely straight face.

Islena bowed and backed away rather quickly. Aunt Pol looked at Mister Wolf with one raised eyebrow, but let it pass.

Wolf's expression became more serious as he rose from the chair in which he had been sitting. "I think that the time has come to make some decisions," he said. "Things are beginning to move too fast for any more delay." He looked at Anheg. "Is there some place where we can speak without risk of being overheard?"

"There's a chamber in one of the towers," Anheg said. "I thought about it before our first meeting, but—" He paused and looked at Cho-Hag.

"You shouldn't have let it concern you," Cho-Hag said. "I can manage stairs if I have to, and it would have been better for me to have been a little inconvenienced than to have had Jarvik's spy overhear us."

"I'll stay with Garion," Durnik said to Aunt Pol.

Aunt Pol shook her head firmly. "No," she said. "As long as Asharak is on the loose in Cherek, I don't want him out of my sight."

"Shall we go, then?" Mister Wolf said. "It's getting late, and I want to leave first thing in the morning. The trail I was following is getting colder."

Queen Islena, still looking shaken, stood to one side with Porenn and Silar and made no effort to follow as King Anheg led the way from the throne room.

I'll let you know what happens, King Rhodar signaled to his queen.

Of course, Porenn gestured back. Her face was placid, but the snap of her fingers as they spoke betrayed her irritability.

Calmly, child, Rhodar's fingers told her. *We're guests here and have to obey local customs.*

Whatever my Lord commands, she replied with a tilt of her hands that spoke whole volumes of sarcasm.

With Hettar's help, King Cho-Hag managed the stairs, although his progress was painfully slow. "I apologize for this," he puffed, stopping halfway up to catch his breath. "It's as tiresome for me as it is for you."

King Anheg posted guards at the foot of the stairs, then came up and closed the heavy door behind him. "Light the fire, cousin," he said to Barak. "We might as well be comfortable."

Barak nodded and put a torch to the wood in the fireplace.

The chamber was round and not too spacious, but there was adequate room for them all and chairs and benches to sit on.

Mister Wolf stood at one of the windows, looking down at the twinkling lights of Val Alorn below. "I've always been fond of towers," he said, almost to himself. "My Master lived in one like this, and I enjoyed the time I spent there."

"I'd give my life to have known Aldur," Cho-Hag said softly. "Was he really surrounded by light as some say?"

"He seemed quite ordinary to me," Mister Wolf said. "I lived with him for five years before I even knew who he was."

"Was he really as wise as we're told?" Anheg asked.

"Probably wiser," Wolf said. "I was a wild and errant boy when he found me dying in a snowstorm outside his tower. He managed to tame me—though it took him several hundred years to do it." He turned from the window with a deep sigh. "To work, then," he said.

"Where will you go to take up the search?" King Fulrach asked.

"Camaar," Wolf said. "I found the trail there. I think it led down into Arendia."

"We'll send warriors with you," Anheg said. "After what's happened here, it looks like the Grolims may try to stop you."

"No," Wolf said firmly. "Warriors are useless in dealing with the Grolims. I can't move with an army underfoot, and I won't have time to explain to the King of Arendia why I'm invading his kingdom with a horde of troops at my back. It takes even longer to explain things to Arends than it does to Alorns—impossible as that sounds."

"Don't be uncivil, Father," Aunt Pol said. "It's their world too, and they're concerned."

"You wouldn't necessarily need an army, Belgarath," King Rhodar said, "but wouldn't it be prudent to take along a few good men?"

"There's very little that Polgara and I can't deal with by ourselves," Wolf said, "and Silk, Barak and Durnik are along to deal with more mundane problems. The smaller our group, the less attention we'll attract." He turned to Cho-Hag. "As long as we're on the subject, though, I'd like to have your son Hettar with us. We're likely to need his rather specialized talents."

"Impossible," Hettar said flatly. "I have to remain with my father."

"No, Hettar," Cho-Hag said. "I don't intend for you to live out your life as a cripple's legs."

"I've never felt any restriction in serving you, Father," Hettar said. "There are plenty of others with the same talents I have. Let the Ancient One choose another."

"How many Sha-Darim are there among the Algars?" Mister Wolf asked gravely.

Hettar looked at him sharply as if trying to tell him something with his eyes.

King Cho-Hag drew in his breath sharply. "Hettar," he asked, "is this true?"

Hettar shrugged. "It may be, Father," he said. "I didn't think it was important."

Cho-Hag looked at Mister Wolf.

Wolf nodded. "It's true," he said. "I knew it the first time I saw him. He's a Sha-Dar. He had to find out for himself, though."

Cho-Hag's eyes suddenly brimmed with tears. "My son!" he said proudly, pulling Hettar into a rough embrace.

"It's no great thing, Father," Hettar said quietly, as if suddenly embarrassed.

"What are they talking about?" Garion whispered to Silk.

"It's something the Algars take very seriously," Silk said softly. "They think that there are some people who can talk to horses with their thoughts alone. They call these people Sha-Darim—Clan-Chiefs of the horses. It's very rare—maybe only two or three in a whole generation. It's instant nobility for any Algar who has it. Cho-Hag's going to explode with pride when he gets back to Algaria."

"Is it that important?" Garion asked.

Silk shrugged. "The Algars seem to think so," he said. "All the clans gather at the Stronghold when they find a new Sha-Dar. The whole nation celebrates for six weeks. There are all kinds of gifts. Hettar'll be a rich man if he chooses to accept them. He may not. He's a strange man."

"You must go," Cho-Hag said to Hettar. "The pride of Algaria goes with you. Your duty is clear."

"As my father decides," Hettar said reluctantly.

"Good," Mister Wolf said. "How long will it take you to go to Algaria, pick up a dozen or so of your best horses and take them to Camaar?"

Hettar thought for a moment. "Two weeks," he said. "If there aren't any blizzards in the mountains of Sendaria."

"We'll all leave here in the morning, then," Wolf said. "Anheg can give you a ship. Take the horses along the Great North Road to the place a few leagues east of Camaar where another road strikes off to the south. It fords the Greater Camaar River and runs down to join the Great West Road at the ruins of Vo Wacune in northern Arendia. We'll meet you there in two weeks."

Hettar nodded.

"We'll also be joined at Vo Wacune by an Asturian Arend," Wolf went on, "and somewhat later by a Mimbrate. They might be useful to us in the south."

"And will also fulfill the prophecies," Anheg said cryptically.

Wolf shrugged, his bright blue eyes twinkling suddenly. "I don't object to fulfilling prophecies," he said, "as long as it doesn't inconvenience me too much."

"Is there anything we can do to help in the search?" Brand asked.

"You'll have enough to do," Wolf said. "No matter how our search turns out, it's obvious that the Angaraks are getting ready for some kind of major action. If we're successful, they might hesitate, but Angaraks don't think the way we do. Even after what happened at Vo Mimbre, they may decide to risk an all-out attack on the west. It could be that they're responding to prophecies of their own that we don't know anything about. In any event, I think you should be ready for something fairly major from them. You'll need to make preparations."

Anheg grinned wolfishly. "We've been preparing for them for five thousand years," he said. "This time we'll purge the whole world of this Angarak infection. When Torak One-eye awakes, he'll find himself as alone as Mara—and just as powerless."

"Maybe," Mister Wolf said, "but don't plan the victory celebration until the war's over. Make your preparations quietly, and don't stir up the people in your kingdoms any more than you have to. The west is crawling with Grolims, and they're watching everything we do. The trail I'll be following could lead me into Cthol Murgos, and I'd rather not have to deal with an army of Murgos massed on the border."

"I can play the watching game too," King Rhodar said with a grim look on his plump face. "Probably even better than the Grolims. It's time to send a few more caravans to the east. The Angaraks won't move without help from the east, and the Malloreans will have to cross over into Gar og Nadrak before they deploy south. A bribe or two here and there, a few barrels of strong ale in the right mining camps—who knows what a bit of diligent corruption might turn up? A chance word or two could give us several months' warning."

"If they're planning anything major, the Thulls will be building supply dumps along the eastern escarpment," Cho-Hag said. "Thulls aren't bright, and it's easy to observe them without being seen. I'll increase my patrols along those mountains. With a little luck, we might be able to anticipate their invasion route. Is there anything else we can do to help you, Belgarath?"

Mister Wolf thought for a moment. Suddenly he grinned. "I'm certain that our thief is listening very hard, waiting for one of us to speak his name or the name of the thing he stole. Sooner or later someone's bound to make a slip; and once he locates us, he'll be able to hear every word we say. Instead of trying to gag ourselves, I think it might be better if we gave him something to listen to. If you can arrange it, I'd like to have every minstrel and storyteller in the north start retelling certain old stories—you know the ones. When those names start sounding in every village marketplace north of the Camaar River, it'll set up a roaring in his ears like a thunderstorm. If nothing else, it'll give us freedom to speak. In time he'll get tired of it and stop listening."

"It's getting late, Father," Aunt Pol reminded him.

Wolf nodded. "We're playing a deadly game," he told them all, "but our enemies are playing one just as deadly. Their danger's as great as ours, and right now no one can predict what will finally happen. Make your preparations and send out men you can trust to keep watch. Be patient and don't do anything rash. That could be more dangerous than anything else right now. At the moment, Polgara and I are the only ones who can act. You're going to have to trust us. I know that sometimes some of the things we've done have seemed a bit strange, but there are reasons for what we do. Please don't interfere again. I'll get word to you now and then about our progress; if I need you to do anything else, I'll let you know. All right?"

The kings nodded gravely, and everyone rose to his feet.

Anheg stepped over to Mister Wolf. "Could you come to my study in an hour or so, Belgarath?" he said quietly. "I'd like to have a few words with you and Polgara before your departure."

"If you wish, Anheg," Mister Wolf said.

"Come along, Garion," Aunt Pol said. "We have packing to take care of."

Garion, a little awed by the solemnity of the discussions, rose quietly and followed her to the door.

CHAPTER TWENTY

King Anheg's study was a large, cluttered room high in a square tower. Books bound in heavy leather lay everywhere, and strange devices with gears and pulleys and tiny brass chains sat on tables and stands. Intricately drawn maps with beautiful illuminations were pinned up on the walls, and the floor was littered with scraps of parchment covered with tiny writing. King Anheg, his coarse black hair hanging in his eyes, sat at a slanted table in the soft glow of a pair of candles studying a large book written on thin sheets of crackling parchment.

The guard at the door let them enter without a word, and Mister Wolf stepped briskly into the center of the room. "You wanted to see us, Anheg?"

The King of Cherek straightened from his book and laid it aside. "Belgarath," he said with a short nod of greeting. "Polgara." He glanced at Garion, who stood uncertainly near the door.

"I meant what I said earlier," Aunt Pol said. "I'm not going to let him out of my sight until I know for certain that he's out of the reach of the Grolim Asharak."

"Anything you say, Polgara," Anheg said. "Come in, Garion."

"I see that you're continuing your studies," Mister Wolf said approvingly, glancing at the littered room.

"There's so much to learn," Anheg said with a helpless gesture that included all the welter of books and papers and strange machines. "I have a feeling that I might have been happier if you'd never introduced me to this impossible task."

"You asked me," Wolf said simply.

"You could have said no." Anheg laughed. Then his brutish face turned serious. He glanced once at Garion and began to speak in an obviously oblique manner. "I don't want to interfere," he said, "but the behavior of this Asharak concerns me."

Garion moved away from Aunt Pol and began to study one of the strange little machines sitting on a nearby table, being careful not to touch it.

"We'll take care of Asharak," Aunt Pol said.

But Anheg persisted. "There have been rumors for centuries that you and your father have been protecting—" He hesitated, glanced at Garion, then continued smoothly. "—A certain thing that must be protected at all costs. Several of my books speak of it."

"You read too much, Anheg," Aunt Pol said.

Anheg laughed again. "It passes the time, Polgara," he said. "The alternative is drinking with my earls, and my stomach's getting a little delicate for that—and my ears as well. Have you any idea of how much noise a hall full of drunk Chereks can make? My books don't shout or boast and they don't fall down or slide under the tables and snore. They're much better company, really."

"Foolishness," Aunt Pol said.

"We're all foolish at one time or another," Anheg said philosophically. "But let's go back to this other matter. If those rumors I mentioned are true, aren't you taking some serious risks? Your search is likely to be very dangerous."

"No place is really safe," Mister Wolf said.

"Why take chances you don't have to?" Anheg asked. "Asharak isn't the only Grolim in the world, you know."

"I can see why they call you Anheg the sly," Wolf said with a smile.

"Wouldn't it be safer to leave this certain thing in my care until you return?" Anheg suggested.

"We've already found that not even Val Alorn is safe from the Grolims, Anheg," Aunt Pol said firmly. "The mines of Cthol Murgos and Gar og Nadrak are endless, and the Grolims have more gold at their disposal than you could even imagine. How many others like Jarvik have they bought? The Old Wolf and I are very experienced at protecting this certain thing you mentioned. It'll be safe with us."

"Thank you for your concern, however," Mister Wolf said.

"The matter concerns us all," Anheg said.

Garion, despite his youth and occasional recklessness, was not stupid. It was obvious that what they were talking about involved him in some way and quite possibly had to do with the mystery of his parentage as well. To conceal the fact that he was listening as hard as he could, he picked up a small book bound in a strangely textured black leather. He opened it, but there were neither pictures nor illuminations, merely a spidery-looking script that seemed strangely repulsive.

Aunt Pol, who always seemed to know what he was doing, looked over at him. "What are you doing with that?" she said sharply.

"Just looking," he said. "I can't read."

"Put it down immediately," she told him.

King Anheg smiled. "You wouldn't be able to read it anyway, Garion," he said. "It's written in Old Angarak."

"What are you doing with that filthy thing anyway?" Aunt Pol asked Anheg. "You of all people should know that it's forbidden."

"It's only a book, Pol," Mister Wolf said. "It doesn't have any power unless it's permitted to."

"Besides," Anheg said, rubbing thoughtfully at the side of his face, "the book gives us clues to the mind of our enemy. That's always a good thing to know."

"You can't know Torak's mind," Aunt Pol said, "and it's dangerous to open yourself to him. He can poison you without your even knowing what's happening."

"I don't think there's any danger of that, Pol," Wolf said. "Anheg's mind is well-trained enough to avoid the traps in Torak's book. They're pretty obvious, after all."

Anheg looked across the room at Garion and beckoned to him. Garion crossed and stood in front of the King of Cherek.

"You're an observant young man, Garion," Anheg said gravely. "You've done me a service today, and you can call on me at any time for service in return. Know that Anheg of Cherek is your friend." He extended his right hand, and Garion took it in his own without thinking.

King Anheg's eyes grew suddenly wide, and his face paled slightly. He turned Garion's hand over and looked down at the silvery mark on the boy's palm.

Then Aunt Pol's hands were also there, firmly closing Garion's fingers and removing him from Anheg's grip.

"It's true, then," Anheg said softly.

"Enough," Aunt Pol said. "Don't confuse the boy." Her hands were still firmly holding Garion's. "Come along, dear," she said. "It's time to finish packing." And she turned and led him from the room.

Garion's mind was racing. What was there about the mark on his hand that had so startled Anheg? The birthmark, he knew, was hereditary. Aunt Pol had once told him that his father's hand had had the same mark, but why would that be of interest to Anheg? It had gone too far. His need to know became almost unbearable. He had to know about his parents, about Aunt Pol—about all of it. If the answers hurt, then they'd just have to hurt. At least he would know.

The next morning was clear, and they left the palace for the harbor quite early. They all gathered in the courtyard where the sleighs waited.

"There's no need for you to come out in the cold like this, Merel," Barak told his fur-robed wife as she mounted the sleigh beside him.

"I have a duty to see my Lord safely to his ship," she replied with an arrogant lift of her chin.

Barak sighed. "Whatever you wish," he said.

With King Anheg and Queen Islena in the lead, the sleighs whirled out of the courtyard and into the snowy streets.

The sun was very bright, and the air was crisp. Garion rode silently with Silk and Hettar.

"Why so quiet, Garion?" Silk asked.

"A lot of things have happened here that I don't understand," Garion said.

"No one can understand everything," Hettar said rather sententiously.

"Chereks are a violent and moody people," Silk said. "They don't even understand themselves."

"It's not just the Chereks," Garion said, struggling with the words. "It's Aunt Pol and Mister Wolf and Asharak—all of it. Things are happening too fast. I can't get it all sorted out."

"Events are like horses," Hettar told him. "Sometimes they run away. After they've run for a while, though, they'll start to walk again. Then there'll be time to put everything together."

"I hope so," Garion said dubiously and fell silent again.

The sleighs came around a corner into the broad square before the temple of Belar. The blind woman was there again, and Garion realized that he had been half-expecting her. She stood on the steps of the temple and raised her staff. Unaccountably, the horses which pulled the sleighs stopped, trembling, despite the urgings of the drivers.

"Hail, Great One," the blind woman said. "I wish thee well on thy journey."

The sleigh in which Garion was riding had stopped closest to the temple steps, and it seemed that the old woman was speaking to him. Almost without thinking he answered, "Thank you. But why do you call me that?"

She ignored the question. "Remember me," she commanded, bowing deeply. "Remember Martje when thou comest into thine inheritance."

It was the second time she'd said that, and Garion felt a sharp pang of curiosity. "What inheritance?" he demanded.

But Barak was roaring with fury and struggling to throw off the fur robe and draw his sword at the same time. King Anheg was also climbing down from his sleigh, his coarse face livid with rage.

"No!" Aunt Pol said sharply from nearby. "I'll tend to this." She stood up. "Hear me, witch-woman," she said in a clear voice, casting back the hood of her cloak. "I think you see too much with those blind eyes of yours. I'm going to do you a favor so that you'll no longer be troubled by the darkness and these disturbing visions which grow out of it."

"Strike me down if it please thee, Polgara," the old woman said. "I see what I see."

"I won't strike you, Martje," Aunt Pol said. "I'm going to give you a gift instead." She raised her hand in a brief and curious gesture.

Garion saw it happen quite plainly, so there was no way that he could later persuade himself that it had all been some trick of the eye. He was looking directly at Martje's face and saw the white film drain down off her eyes like milk draining down the inside of a glass.

The old woman stood frozen to the spot as the bright blue of her eyes emerged from the film which had covered them. And then she screamed. She held up her hands, looked at them and screamed again. There was in her scream a wrenching note of indescribable loss.

"What did you do?" Queen Islena demanded.

"I gave her back her eyes," Aunt Pol said, sitting down again and rearranging the fur robe about her.

"You can do that?" Islena asked, her face blanching and her voice weak.

"Can't you? It's a simple thing, really."

"But," Queen Porenn objected, "with her eyes restored, she'll lose that other vision, won't she?"

"I imagine so," Aunt Pol said, "but that's a small price to pay, isn't it?"

"She'll no longer be a witch, then?" Porenn pressed.

"She wasn't really a very good witch anyway," Aunt Pol said. "Her vision was clouded and uncertain. It's better this way. She won't be disturbing herself and others with shadows anymore." She looked at King Anheg, who sat frozen with awe beside his half-fainting queen. "Shall we continue?" she asked calmly. "Our ship is waiting."

The horses, as if released by her words, leaped forward, and the sleighs sped away from the temple, spraying snow from their runners.

Garion glanced back once. Old Martje stood on the steps of the temple looking at her two outstretched hands and sobbing uncontrollably.

"We've been privileged to witness a miracle, my friends," Hettar said.

"I gather, however, that the beneficiary was not very pleased with it," Silk said dryly. "Remind me not to offend Polgara. Her miracles seem to have two edges to them."

CHAPTER TWENTY-ONE

The low-slanting rays of the morning sun glittered on the icy waters of the harbor as their sleighs halted near the stone quays. Greldik's ship rocked and strained at her hawsers, and a smaller ship nearby also waited with seeming impatience.

Hettar stepped down and went over to speak with Cho-Hag and Queen Silar. The three of them talked together quietly and seriously, drawing a kind of shell of privacy about them.

Queen Islena had partially regained her composure, and sat in her sleigh straight-backed and with a fixed smile on her face. After Anheg had gone to speak with Mister Wolf, Aunt Pol crossed the icy wharf and stopped near the sleigh of the Queen of Cherek.

"If I were you, Islena," she said firmly, "I'd find another hobby. Your gifts in the arts of sorcery are limited, and it's a dangerous area for dabbling. Too many things can go wrong if you don't know what you're doing."

The queen stared at her mutely.

"Oh," Aunt Pol said, "one other thing. It would be best, I think, if you broke off your connections with the Bear-cult. It's hardly proper for a queen to have dealings with her husband's political enemies."

Islena's eyes widened. "Does Anheg know?" she asked in a stricken voice.

"I wouldn't be surprised," Aunt Pol said. "He's much more clever than he looks, you know. You're walking very close to the edge of treason. You ought to have a few babies. They'd give you something useful to do with your time and keep you out of trouble. That's only a suggestion, of course, but you might think it over. I've enjoyed our visit, dear. Thank you for your hospitality." And with that she turned and walked away.

Silk whistled softly. "That explains a few things," he said.

"Explains what?" Garion asked.

"The High Priest of Belar's been dabbling in Cherek politics lately. He's obviously gone a bit further than I'd thought in penetrating the palace."

"The queen?" Garion asked, startled.

"Islena's obsessed with the idea of magic," Silk said. "The Bear-cultists dabble in certain kinds of rituals that might look sort of mystical to someone as gullible as she is." He looked quickly toward where King Rhodar was speaking with the other kings and Mister Wolf. Then he drew in a deep breath. "Let's go talk to Porenn," he said and led the way across the wharf to where the tiny blond Queen of Drasnia stood looking out at the icy sea.

"Highness," Silk said deferentially.

"Dear Kheldar," she said, smiling at him.

"Could you give some information to my uncle for me?" he asked.

"Of course."

"It seems that Queen Islena's been a bit indiscreet," Silk said. "She's been involved with the Bear-cult here in Cherek."

"Oh dear," Porenn said. "Does Anheg know?"

"It's hard to say," Silk told her. "I doubt if he'd admit it if he did. Garion and I happened to hear Polgara tell her to stop it."

"I hope that puts an end to it," Porenn said. "If it went too far, Anheg would have to take steps. That could be tragic."

"Polgara was quite firm," Silk said. "I think Islena will do as she was told, but advise my uncle. He likes to be kept aware of this kind of thing."

"I'll tell him about it," she said.

"You might also suggest that he keep his eyes on the local chapters of the cult in Boktor and Kotu," Silk suggested. "This kind of thing isn't usually isolated. It's been about fifty years since the last time the cult had to be suppressed."

Queen Porenn nodded gravely. "I'll see to it that he knows," she said. "I've got some of my own people planted in the Bear-cult. As soon as we get back to Boktor, I'll talk with them and see what's afoot."

"Your people? Have you gone that far already?" Silk asked in a bantering tone. "You're maturing rapidly, my Queen. It won't be long until you're as corrupt as the rest of us."

"Boktor's full of intrigue, Kheldar," the queen said primly. "It isn't just the Bear-cult, you know. Merchants from all over the world gather in our city, and at least half of them are spies. I have to protect myself—and my husband."

"Does Rhodar know what you're up to?" Silk asked slyly.

"Of course he does," she said. "He gave me my first dozen spies himself—as a wedding present."

"How typically Drasnian," Silk said.

"It's only practical, after all," she said. "My husband's concerned with matters involving other kingdoms. I try to keep an eye on things at home to leave his mind free for that kind of thing. My operations are a bit more modest than his, but I manage to stay aware of things." She looked at him slyly from beneath her eyelashes. "If you ever decide to come home to Boktor and settle down, I might just be able to find work for you."

Silk laughed. "The world seems to be full of opportunities lately," he said.

The queen looked at him seriously. "When *are* you coming home, Kheldar?" she asked. "When will you stop being this vagabond, Silk, and come back where you belong? My husband misses you very much, and you could serve Drasnia more by becoming his chief adviser than by all this flitting about the world."

Silk looked away, squinting into the bright wintry sun. "Not just yet, your Highness," he said. "Belgarath needs me too, and this is a very important thing we're doing just now. Besides, I'm not ready to settle down yet. The game is still entertaining. Perhaps someday when we're all much older it won't be anymore—who knows?"

She sighed. "I miss you too, Kheldar," she said gently.

"Poor, lonely little queen," Silk said, half-mockingly.

"You're impossible," she said, stamping her tiny foot.

"One does one's best." He grinned.

Hettar had embraced his father and mother and leaped across to the deck of the small ship King Anheg had provided him. "Belgarath," he called as the sailors slipped the stout ropes that bound the ship to the quay, "I'll meet you in two weeks at the ruins of Vo Wacune."

"We'll be there," Mister Wolf replied.

The sailors pushed the ship away from the quay and began to row out into the bay. Hettar stood on the deck, his long scalp lock flowing in the wind. He waved once, then turned to face the sea.

A long plank was run down over the side of Captain Greldik's ship to the snow-covered stones.

"Shall we go on board, Garion?" Silk said. They climbed the precarious plank and stepped out onto the deck.

"Give our daughters my love," Barak said to his wife.

"I will, my Lord," Merel said in the same stiffly formal tone she always used with him. "Have you any other instructions?"

"I won't be back for quite some time," Barak said. "Plant the south fields to oats this year, and let the west fields lie fallow. Do whatever you think best with the north fields. And don't move the cattle up to the high pastures until all the frost is out of the ground."

"I'll be most careful of my husband's lands and herds," she said.

"They're yours too," Barak said.

"As my husband wishes."

Barak sighed. "You never let it rest, do you, Merel?" he said sadly.

"My Lord?"

"Forget it."

"Will my Lord embrace me before he leaves?" she asked.

"What's the point?" Barak said. He jumped across to the ship and immediately went below.

Aunt Pol stopped on her way to the ship and looked gravely at Barak's wife. She looked as if she were about to say something. Then, without warning, she suddenly laughed.

"Something amusing, Lady Polgara?" Merel asked.

"Very amusing, Merel," Aunt Pol said with a mysterious smile.

"Might I be permitted to share it?"

"Oh, you'll share it, Merel," Aunt Pol promised, "but I wouldn't want to spoil it for you by telling you too soon." She laughed again and stepped onto the plank that led to the ship. Durnik offered his hand to steady her, and the two of them crossed to the deck.

Mister Wolf clasped hands with each of the kings in turn and then nimbly crossed to the ship. He stood for a moment on the deck looking at the ancient, snow-shrouded city of Val Alorn and the towering mountains of Cherek rising behind.

"Farewell, Belgarath," King Anheg called.

Mister Wolf nodded. "Don't forget about the minstrels," he said.

"We won't," Anheg promised. "Good luck."

Mister Wolf grinned and then walked forward toward the prow of Greldik's ship. Garion, on an impulse, followed him. There were questions which needed answers, and the old man would know if anyone would.

"Mister Wolf," he said when they both reached the high prow.

"Yes, Garion?"

He was not sure where to start, so Garion approached the problem obliquely. "How did Aunt Pol do that to old Martje's eyes?"

"The Will and the Word," Wolf said, his long cloak whipping about him in the stiff breeze. "It isn't difficult."

"I don't understand," Garion said.

"You simply will something to happen," the old man said, "and then speak the word. If your will's strong enough, it happens."

"That's all there is to it?" Garion asked, a little disappointed.

"That's all," Wolf said.

"Is the word a magic word?"

Wolf laughed, looking out at the sun glittering sharply on the winter sea. "No," he said. "There aren't any magic words. Some people think so, but they're wrong. Grolims use strange words, but that's not really necessary. Any word will do the job. It's the Will that's important, not the Word. The Word's just a channel for the Will."

"Could I do it?" Garion asked hopefully.

Wolf looked at him. "I don't know, Garion," he said. "I wasn't much older than you are the first time I did it, but I'd been living with Aldur for several years. That makes a difference, I suppose."

"What happened?"

"My Master wanted me to move a rock," Wolf said. "He seemed to think that it was in his way. I tried to move it, but it was too heavy. After a while I got angry, and I told it to move. It did. I was a little surprised, but my Master didn't seem to think it so unusual."

"You just said, 'move'? That's all?" Garion was incredulous.

"That's all." Wolf shrugged. "It seemed so simple that I was surprised I hadn't thought of it before. At the time I imagined that anybody could do it, but men have changed quite a bit since then. Maybe it isn't possible anymore. It's hard to say, really."

"I always thought that sorcery had to be done with long spells and strange signs and things like that," Garion said.

"Those are just the devices of tricksters and charlatans," Wolf said. "They make a fine show and impress and frighten simple people, but spells and incantations have nothing to do with the real thing. It's all in the Will. Focus the Will and speak the Word, and it happens. Sometimes a gesture of some sort helps, but it isn't really necessary. Your Aunt always seems to want to gesture when she makes something happen. I've been trying to break her of that habit for hundreds of years now."

Garion blinked. "*Hundreds* of years?" he gasped. "How old is she?"

"Older than she looks," Wolf said. "It isn't polite to ask questions about a lady's age, however."

Garion felt a sudden, shocking emptiness. The worst of his fears had just been confirmed. "Then she isn't really my Aunt, is she?" he asked sickly.

"What makes you say that?" Wolf asked.

"She couldn't be, could she? I always thought that she was my father's sister, but if she's hundreds and thousands of years old, it'd be impossible."

"You're much too fond of that word, Garion," Wolf said. "When you get right down to it, nothing—or at least very little—is actually impossible."

"How could she be? My Aunt, I mean?"

"All right," Wolf said. "Polgara was not strictly speaking your father's sister. Her relationship to him is quite a bit more complex. She was the sister of his grandmother—his ultimate grandmother, if there is such a term—and of yours as well, of course."

"Then she'd be my great-aunt," Garion said with a faint spark of hope. It was something, at least.

"I don't know that I'd use that precise term around her." Wolf grinned. "She might take offense. Why are you so concerned about all of this?"

"I was afraid that maybe she'd just said that she was my Aunt, and that there wasn't really any connection between us at all," Garion said. "I've been afraid of that for quite a while now."

"Why were you afraid?"

"It's kind of hard to explain," Garion said. "You see, I don't really know who I am or what I am. Silk says I'm not a Sendar, and Barak says I look sort of like a Rivan—but not exactly. I always thought I was a Sendar—like Durnik—but I guess I'm not. I don't know anything about my parents or where they came from or anything like that. If Aunt Pol isn't related to me, then I don't have anybody in the world at all. I'm all alone, and that's a very bad thing."

"But now it's all right, isn't it?" Wolf said. "Your Aunt is really your Aunt—at least your blood and hers are the same."

"I'm glad you told me," Garion said. "I've been worried about it."

Greldik's sailors untied the hawsers and began to push the ship away from the quay.

"Mister Wolf," Garion said as a strange thought occurred to him.

"Yes, Garion?"

"Aunt Pol really is my Aunt—or my Great-Aunt?"

"Yes."

"And she's your daughter?"

"I have to admit that she is," Wolf said wryly. "I try to forget that sometimes, but I can't really deny it."

Garion took a deep breath and plunged directly into it. "If she's my Aunt and you're her father," he said, "wouldn't that sort of make you my Grandfather?"

Wolf looked at him with a startled expression. "Why yes," he said, laughing suddenly, "I suppose that in a way it does. I'd never thought of it exactly like that before."

Garion's eyes suddenly filled with tears, and he impulsively embraced the old man. "Grandfather," he said, trying the word out.

"Well, well," Wolf said, his own voice strangely thick. "What a remarkable discovery." Awkwardly he patted Garion's shoulder.

They were both a little embarrassed by Garion's sudden display of affection, and they stood silently, watching as Greldik's sailors rowed the ship out into the harbor.

"Grandfather," Garion said after a while.

"Yes?"

"What really happened to my mother and father? I mean, how did they die?"

Wolf's face became very bleak. "There was a fire," he said shortly.

"A fire?" Garion said weakly, his imagination lurching back from that awful thought—of the unspeakable pain. "How did it happen?"

"It's not very pleasant," Wolf said grimly. "Are you really sure you want to know?"

"I have to, Grandfather," Garion said quietly. "I have to know everything I can about them. I don't know why, but it's very important."

Mister Wolf sighed. "Yes, Garion," he said, "I guess it would be at that. All right, then. If you're old enough to ask the questions, you're old enough to hear the answers." He sat down on a sheltered bench out of the chilly wind. "Come over here and sit down." He patted the bench beside him.

Garion sat down and pulled his cloak around him.

"Let's see," Wolf said, scratching thoughtfully at his beard, "where do we start?" He pondered for a moment. "Your family's very old, Garion," he said finally, "and like so many old families, it has a certain number of enemies."

"Enemies?" Garion was startled. That particular idea hadn't occurred to him before.

"It's not uncommon," Wolf said. "When we do something someone else doesn't like, they tend to hate us. The hatred builds up over the years until it turns into something almost like a religion. They hate not only us, but everything connected with us. Anyway, a long time ago your family's enemies became so dangerous that your Aunt and I decided that the only way we could protect the family was to hide it."

"You aren't telling me everything," Garion said.

"No," Wolf said blandly, "I'm not. I'm telling you as much as it's safe for you to know for right now. If you knew certain things, you'd act differently, and people would notice that. It's safer if you stay ordinary for a while longer."

"You mean ignorant," Garion accused.

"All right, ignorant then. Do you want to hear the story, or do you want to argue?"

"I'm sorry," Garion said.

"It's all right," Wolf said, patting Garion's shoulder. "Since your Aunt and I are related to your family in a rather special way, we were naturally interested in your safety. That's why we hid your people."

"Can you actually hide a whole family?" Garion asked.

"It's never been that big a family," Wolf said. "It seems, for one reason or another, to be a single, unbroken line—no cousins or uncles or that kind of thing. It's not all that hard to hide a man and wife with a single child. We've been doing it for hundreds of years now. We've hidden them in Tolnedra, Riva, Cherek, Drasnia—all kinds of places. They've lived simple lives—artisans mostly, sometimes ordinary peasants—the kind of people nobody would ever look at twice. Anyway, everything had gone well until about twenty years ago. We moved your father, Geran, from a place in Arendia to a little village in eastern Sendaria, about sixty leagues southeast of Darine, up in the mountains. Geran was a stonecutter—didn't I tell you that once before?"

Garion nodded. "A long time ago," he said. "You said you liked him and used to visit him once in a while. Was my mother a Sendar, then?"

"No," Wolf said. "Ildera was an Algar, actually—the second daughter of a Clan-Chief. Your Aunt and I introduced her to Geran when they were about the right age. The usual sort of thing happened, and they got married. You were born a year or so afterward."

"When was the fire?" Garion asked.

"I'm getting to that," Wolf said. "One of the enemies of your family had been looking for your people for a long time."

"How long?"

"Hundreds of years, actually."

"That means that he was a sorcerer, too, doesn't it?" Garion asked. "I mean, only sorcerers live for that long, don't they?"

"He has certain capabilities along those lines," Wolf admitted. "Sorcerer is a misleading term, though. It's not the sort of thing we actually call ourselves. Other people do, but we don't exactly think of it that way. It's a convenient term for people who don't really understand what it's all about. Anyway, your Aunt and I happened to be away when this enemy finally tracked down Geran and Ildera. He came to their house very early one morning while they were still sleeping and he sealed up the doors and windows and then he set it on fire."

"I thought you said the house was made of stone."

"It was," Wolf said, "but you can make stone burn if you really want to. The fire just has to be hotter, that's all. Geran and Ildera knew that there was no way they could get out of the burning house, but Geran managed to knock one of the stones out of the wall, and Ildera pushed you out through the hole. The one who had set the fire was waiting for that. He picked you up and started out of the village. We could never be sure exactly what he had in mind—either he was going to kill you, or maybe he was going to keep you for some reason of his own. At any rate, that's when I got there. I put out the fire, but Geran and Ildera were already dead. Then I went after the one who'd stolen you."

"Did you kill him?" Garion demanded fiercely.

"I try not to do that any more than I have to," Wolf said. "It disrupts the natural course of events too much. I had some other ideas at the time—much more unpleasant than killing." His eyes were icy. "As it turned out, though, I never got the chance. He threw you at me—you were only a baby—and I had to try to catch you. It gave him time to get away. I left you with Polgara and then I went looking for your enemy. I haven't been able to find him yet, though."

"I'm glad you haven't," Garion said.

Wolf looked a little surprised at that.

"When I get older, *I'm* going to find him," Garion said. "I think I ought to be the one who pays him back for what he did, don't you?"

Wolf looked at him gravely. "It could be dangerous," he said.

"I don't care. What's his name?"

"I think that maybe I'd better wait a while before I tell you that," Wolf said. "I don't want you jumping into something before you're ready."

"But you will tell me?"

"When the time comes."

"It's very important, Grandfather."

"Yes," Wolf said. "I can see that."

"Do you promise?"

"If you insist. And if I don't, I'm sure your Aunt will. She feels the same way you do."

"Don't you?"

"I'm much older," Wolf said. "I see things a little differently."

"I'm not that old yet," Garion said. "I won't be able to do the kind of things you'd do, so I'll have to settle for just killing him." He stood up and began to pace back and forth, a rage boiling in him.

"I don't suppose I'll be able to talk you out of this," Wolf said, "but I really think you're going to feel differently about it after it's over."

"Not very likely," Garion said, still pacing.

"We'll see," Wolf said.

"Thank you for telling me, Grandfather," Garion said.

"You'd have found out sooner or later anyway," the old man said, "and it's better that I tell you than for you to get a distorted account from somebody else."

"You mean Aunt Pol?"

"Polgara wouldn't deliberately lie to you," Wolf said, "but she sees things in a much more personal way than I do. Sometimes that colors her perceptions. I try to take the long view of things." He laughed rather wryly. "I suppose that's the only view I could take—under the circumstances."

Garion looked at the old man whose white hair and beard seemed somehow luminous in the morning sun. "What's it like to live forever, Grandfather?" he asked.

"I don't know," Wolf said. "I haven't lived forever."

"You know what I mean."

"The quality of life isn't much different," Wolf said. "We all live as long as we need to. It just happened that I have something to do that's taken a very long time." He stood up abruptly. "This conversation's taken a gloomy turn," he said.

"This thing that we're doing is very important, isn't it, Grandfather?" Garion asked.

"It's the most important thing in the world right now," Wolf said.

"I'm afraid I'm not going to be very much help," Garion said.

Wolf looked at him gravely for a moment and then put one arm around his shoulders. "I think you may be surprised about that before it's all over, Garion," he said.

And then they turned and looked out over the prow of the ship at the snowy coast of Cherek sliding by on their right as the sailors rowed the ship south toward Camaar and whatever lay beyond.

QUEEN OF
SORCERY

For Helen,
   who gave me the most precious thing in
   my life,
and for Mike,
   who taught me how to play.

PROLOGUE

Being an Account of the Battle of the Kingdoms of the West against the Invasion of Kal Torak.

—BASED UPON *THE BATTLE OF VO MIMBRE*

BY DAVOUL THE LAME

In the youth of the world, Torak stole the Orb of Aldur and fled, seeking dominion. The Orb resisted, and its fire maimed him with a dreadful burning. But he would not give it up, for it was precious to him.

Then Belgarath, the sorcerer and disciple of the God Aldur, led forth the king of the Alorns and his three sons, and they reclaimed the Orb from the iron tower of Torak. Torak sought to pursue, but the wrath of the Orb repelled him and drove him back.

Belgarath set Cherek and his sons to be kings over four great kingdoms in eternal guard against Torak. The Orb he gave to Riva Iron-grip to keep, saying that so long as a descendant of Riva held the Orb the West would be safe.

Century followed century with no menace from Torak, until the spring of 4865, when Drasnia was invaded by a vast horde of Nadraks, Thulls, and Murgos. In the center of this sea of Angaraks was borne the huge iron pavilion of Kal Torak, which means King and God. Cities and villages were razed and burned, for Kal Torak came to destroy, not to conquer. Those of the people who lived were given to the steel-masked Grolim priests for sacrifice in the unspeakable rites of the Angaraks. None survived save those who fled to Algaria or were taken from the mouth of the Aldur River by Cherek warships.

Next the horde struck south at Algaria. But there they found no cities. The nomadic Algarian horsemen fell back before them, then struck in vicious hit-and-run attacks. The traditional seat of the Algarian kings was the Stronghold, a man-made mountain with stone walls thirty feet thick. Against this, the Angaraks hurled themselves in vain before settling down to besiege the place. The siege lasted for eight futile years.

This gave the West time to mobilize and prepare. The generals gathered at the Imperial War College at Tol Honeth and planned their strategy. National differences were set aside, and Brand, the Warder of Riva, was chosen to have full command. With him came two strange advisers: an ancient but vigorous man who claimed knowledge even of the Angarak kingdoms; and a strikingly handsome woman with a silver lock at her brow and an imperious manner. To these Brand listened, and to them he paid almost deferential respect.

In the late spring of 4875, Kal Torak abandoned his siege and turned west toward the sea, pursued still by Algar horsemen. In the mountains, the

Ulgos came forth from their caverns by night and wreaked fearful slaughter on the sleeping Angaraks. But still the forces of Kal Torak were beyond counting. After a pause to regroup, the host proceeded down the valley of the River Arend toward the city of Vo Mimbre, destroying all in its path. Early in the summer, the Angaraks deployed for the assault upon the city.

On the third day of the battle, a horn was heard to blow three times. Then the gates of Vo Mimbre opened, and the Mimbrate knights charged out to fall upon the front of the Angarak horde, the iron-shod hoofs of their chargers trampling living and dead. From the left came Algar cavalry, Drasnian pikemen, and veiled Ulgo irregulars. And from the right came the Cherek berserks and the legions of Tolnedra.

Attacked on three sides, Kal Torak committed his reserves. It was then that the gray-clad Rivans, the Sendars, and the Asturian archers came upon his forces from the rear. The Angaraks fell like mown wheat and were overcome by confusion.

Then the Apostate, Zedar the Sorcerer, went in haste to the black iron pavilion from which Kal Torak had not yet emerged. And to the Accursed One he said, "Lord, thine enemies have thee surrounded in great numbers. Yea, even the gray Rivans have come in their numbers to cast their defiance into thy teeth."

Kal Torak arose in anger and declared, "I will come forth, that the false keepers of Cthrag Yaska, the jewel which was mine, shall see me and know fear of me. Send to me my kings."

"Great Lord," Zedar told him, "thy kings are no more. The battle hath claimed their lives and those of a multitude of thy Grolim priests as well."

Kal Torak's wrath grew at these words, and fire flared in his right eye and from the eye that was not. He ordered his servants to bind his shield to the arm on which he had no hand and he took up his dread black sword. With this, he went forth to do war.

Then came a voice from the midst of the Rivans, saying, "In the name of Belar I defy thee, Torak. In the name of Aldur I cast my despite in thy teeth. Let the bloodshed be abated, and I will meet thee to decide the battle. I am Brand, Warder of Riva. Meet me or take thy stinking host away and come no more against the kingdoms of the West."

Kal Torak strode apart from the host and cried, "Where is he who dares pit his mortal flesh against the King of the World? Behold, I am Torak, King of Kings and Lord of Lords. I will destroy this loud-voiced Rivan. Mine enemies shall perish, and Cthrag Yaska shall again be mine."

Brand stood forth. He bore a mighty sword and a shield muffled with cloth. A grizzled wolf marched at his side, and a snowy owl hovered over his head. And he spake, saying, "I am Brand and I will contend with thee, foul and misshapen Torak."

When Torak saw the wolf, he said, "Begone, Belgarath. Flee if thou wouldst save thy life." And to the owl he said, "Abjure thy father, Polgara, and worship me. I will wed thee and make thee Queen of the World."

But the wolf howled defiance, and the owl screeched her scorn.

Torak raised his sword and smote down upon the shield of Brand. Long they fought, and many and grievous were the blows they struck. Those who stood near to see them were amazed. The fury of Torak grew great, and his sword battered the shield of Brand until the Warder fell back before the onslaught of the Accursed One. And then the wolf howled and the owl shrieked in one voice together, and the strength of Brand was renewed.

With a single motion, the Rivan Warder unveiled his shield, in the center of which stood a round jewel, in size like the heart of a child. As Torak gazed upon it, the stone began to glow and flame. The Accursed One drew back from it. He dropped his shield and sword and raised his arms before his face to ward away the dread fire of the stone.

Brand struck, and his sword pierced Torak's visor to strike into the eye which was not, and to plunge into the Accursed One's head. Torak fell back and gave a great cry. He plucked out the sword and threw off his helmet. Those who watched recoiled in terror, for his face was seared by some great fire and was horrible to behold. Weeping blood, Torak cried out again as he beheld the jewel which he had named Cthrag Yaska and for which he had brought his war into the West. Then he collapsed, and the earth resounded with his fall.

A great cry went up from the host of the Angaraks when they saw what had befallen Kal Torak, and they sought to flee in their panic. But the armies of the West pursued them and slew them, so that when the smoky dawn broke on the fourth day, the host was no more.

Brand asked that the body of the Accursed One be brought to him, that he might behold him who would be king of all the world. But the body was not to be found, for in the night, Zedar the Sorcerer had cast an enchantment and passed unseen through the armies of the West, bearing away the one he had chosen as Master.

Then Brand took counsel with his advisers. And Belgarath said to him, "Torak is not dead. He only sleeps, for he is a God and cannot be slain by any mortal weapon."

"When will he awaken?" Brand asked. "I must prepare the West against his return."

Polgara answered, "When once again a King of Riva's line sits on his northern throne, the Dark God will waken to do war with him."

Brand frowned, saying, "But that is never!" For all knew that the last Rivan King had been slain with his family in 4002 by Nyissan assassins.

Again the woman spoke. "In the fullness of time the Rivan King will rise to claim his own, as the ancient Prophecy foretells. More cannot be said."

Brand was content and set his armies to cleansing the battlefield of the wreckage of Angaraks. And when that was finished, the kings of the West gathered before the city of Vo Mimbre and held council. Many were the voices raised in praise of Brand.

Soon men began crying that Brand should henceforth be chosen as ruler of all the West. Only Mergon, ambassador of Imperial Tolnedra, protested in the name of his Emperor, Ran Borune IV. Brand refused the honor, and the proposal was dropped, so that there was again peace among those assembled in council. But in return for peace, a demand was made of Tolnedra.

The Gorim of the Ulgos spoke first in a loud voice. "In fulfillment of the Prophecy, there must be promised a princess of Tolnedra to be wife unto the Rivan King who will come to save the world. This the Gods require of us."

Again Mergon protested. "The Hall of the Rivan King is empty and desolate. No king sits upon the Rivan throne. How may a princess of Imperial Tolnedra be wed with a phantom?"

Then the woman who was Polgara replied. "The Rivan King will return to assume his throne and claim his bride. From this day forward, therefore, each princess of Imperial Tolnedra shall present herself in the Hall of the Rivan King upon her sixteenth birthday. She shall be clad in her wedding gown and shall abide there for three days against the coming of the King. If he comes not to claim her, then she shall be free to return to her father for whatever he may decree for her."

Mergon cried out. "All Tolnedra shall rise against this indignity. No! It shall not be!"

The wise Gorim of the Ulgos spoke again. "Tell your Emperor that this is the will of the Gods. Tell him also that in the day Tolnedra fails in this, the West shall rise against him and scatter the sons of Nedra to the winds and pull down the might of the Empire, until Imperial Tolnedra is no more."

At that, seeing the might of the armies before him, the ambassador submitted to the matter. All then agreed and were bound to it.

When that was done, the nobles of strife-torn Arendia came to Brand, saying, "The king of the Mimbrates is dead and the duke of the Asturians also. Who now shall rule us? For two thousand years has war between Mimbre and Asturia rent fair Arendia. How may we become one people again?"

Brand considered. "Who is heir to the Mimbrate throne?"

"Korodullin is crown prince of the Mimbrates," the nobles replied.

"And to whom descends the Asturian line?"

"Mayaserana is the daughter of the Asturian duke," they told him.

Brand said, "Bring them to me." And when they were brought before Brand, he said to them, "The bloodshed between Mimbre and Asturia must end. Therefore, it is my will that you be wed to each other and that the houses which so long have warred shall thus be joined."

The two cried against the judgment, for they were filled with ancient enmity and with the pride of their separate lines. But Belgarath took Korodullin aside and spoke in private with him. And Polgara withdrew Mayaserana to a separate place and was long in converse with her. No man learned then or later what was said to the two young people. But when they returned to where Brand waited, Mayaserana and Korodullin were content that they should be wed. And this was the final act of the council that met after the battle of Vo Mimbre.

Brand spoke to all the kings and nobles one final time before departing for the north.

"Much has been wrought here that is good and shall endure. Behold, we have joined together against the Angaraks and they have been overthrown. Torak is quelled, and the covenant we have made here among us prepares the West for the day of the Prophecy when the Rivan King shall return and Torak shall wake from his long sleep to contend again for empire and dominion. All that may be done in this day to prepare for the great and final war has been done. We can do no more. And here, perchance, the wounds of Arendia have been healed, and the strife of more than two thousand years may see its end. So far as may be, I am content with it all. "Hail, then, and farewell!"

He turned from them and rode north with the grizzled man who was Belgarath and the queenly woman who was Polgara by his side. They took ship at Camaar in Sendaria and set sail for Riva. And Brand returned no more to the kingdoms of the West.

But of his companions are many tales told. And of that telling, what may be true and what false few men may know.

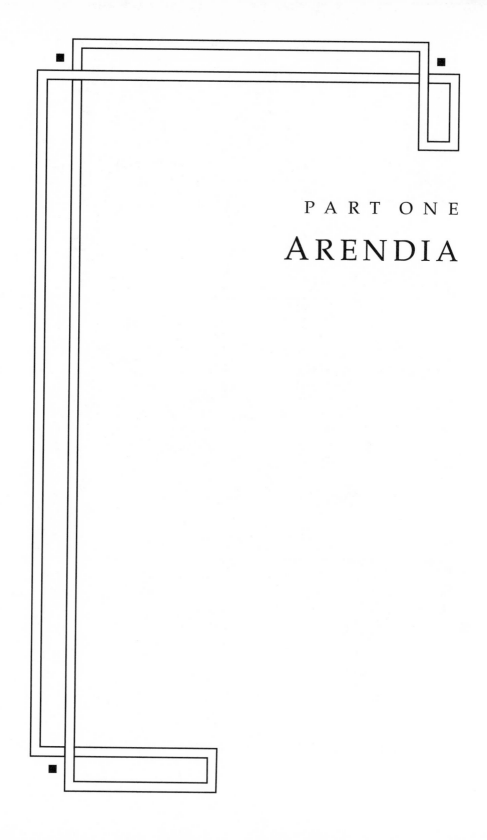

PART ONE
ARENDIA

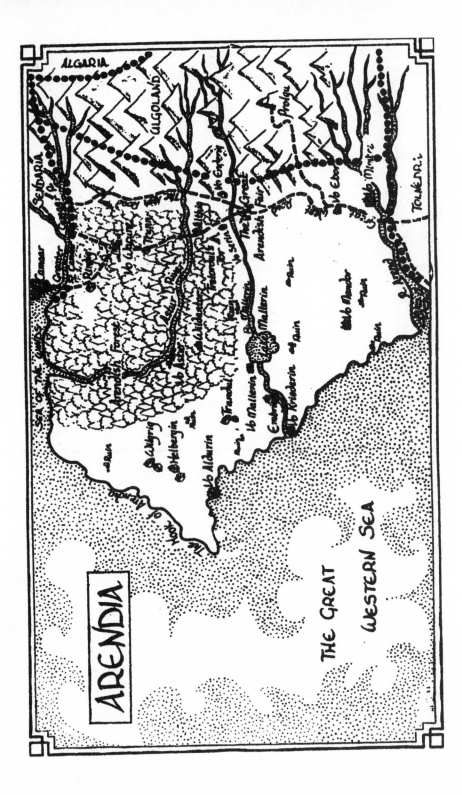

Vo Wacune was no more. Twenty-four centuries had passed since the city of the Wacite Arends had been laid waste, and the dark, endless forests of northern Arendia had reclaimed the ruins. Broken walls had toppled and been swallowed up in the moss and wet brown bracken of the forest floor, and only the shattered stumps of the once proud towers moldered among the trees and fog to mark the place where Vo Wacune had stood. Sodden snow blanketed the mist-shrouded ruins, and trickles of water ran down the faces of ancient stones like tears.

Garion wandered alone down the tree-choked avenues of the dead city, his stout gray wool cloak drawn tight against the chill, and his thoughts as mournful as the weeping stones around him. Faldor's farm with its green, sun-drenched fields was so far behind him that it seemed lost in a kind of receding haze, and he was desperately homesick. No matter how hard he tried to hold on to them, details kept escaping him. The rich smells of Aunt Pol's kitchen were only a faint memory; the ring of Durnik's hammer in the smithy faded like the dying echo of the last note of a bell, and the sharp, clear faces of his playmates wavered in his remembrance of them until he could no longer be sure that he would even recognize them. His childhood was slipping away, and try though he might, he could not hold on to it.

Everything was changing; that was the whole problem. The core of his life, the rock upon which his childhood had been built, had always been Aunt Pol. In the simple world of Faldor's farm she had been Mistress Pol, the cook, but in the world beyond Faldor's gate she was Polgara the Sorceress, who had watched the passage of three millennia with a purpose beyond mortal comprehension.

And Mister Wolf, the old vagabond storyteller, had also changed. Garion knew now that this old friend was in fact his great-great-grandfather—with an infinite number of additional "greats" added on for good measure—but that behind that roguish old face there had always been the steady gaze of Belgarath the Sorcerer, who had watched and waited as he had looked upon the folly of men and Gods for seven thousand years. Garion sighed and trudged on through the fog.

Their very names were unsettling. Garion had never wanted to believe in sorcery or magic or witchcraft. Such things were unnatural, and they violated his notion of solid, sensible reality. But too many things had happened to allow him to hold on to his comfortable skepticism any longer. In a single, shattering instant the last vestiges of his doubt had been swept away. As he had watched with stunned disbelief, Aunt Pol had erased the milky stains from the eyes of Martje the witch with a gesture and a single word, restoring the madwoman's sight and removing her power to see into the future with a brutal evenhandedness. Garion shuddered at the memory of Martje's despairing wail. That cry somehow marked the point at which the world had become less solid, less sensible, and infinitely less safe.

Uprooted from the only place he had ever known, unsure of the identities of the two people closest to him, and with his whole conception of the difference between the possible and the impossible destroyed, Garion found himself committed to a strange pilgrimage. He had no idea what they were doing in this shattered city swallowed up in trees, and not the faintest idea where they would go when they left. The only certainty that remained to him was the single grim thought to which he now clung: somewhere in the world there was a man who had crept through the predawn darkness to a small house in a forgotten village and had murdered Garion's parents; if it took him the rest of his life, Garion was going to find that man, and when he found him, he was going to kill him. There was something strangely comforting in that one solid fact.

He carefully climbed over the rubble of a house that had fallen outward into the street and continued his gloomy exploration of the ruined city. There was really nothing to see. The patient centuries had erased nearly all of what the war had left behind, and slushy snow and thick fog hid even those last remaining traces. Garion sighed again and began to retrace his steps toward the moldering stump of the tower where they had all spent the previous night.

As he approached, he saw Mister Wolf and Aunt Pol standing together some distance from the ruined tower, talking quietly. The old man's rust-colored hood was turned up, and Aunt Pol's blue cloak was drawn about her. There was a look of timeless regret on her face as she looked out at the foggy ruins. Her long, dark hair spilled down her back, and the single white lock at her brow seemed paler than the snow at her feet.

"There he is now," Mister Wolf said to her as Garion approached them.

She nodded and looked gravely at Garion. "Where have you been?" she asked.

"No place," Garion replied. "I was thinking, that's all."

"I see you've managed to soak your feet."

Garion lifted one of his sodden brown boots and looked down at the muddy slush clinging to it. "The snow's wetter than I thought," he apologized.

"Does wearing that thing really make you feel better?" Mister Wolf asked, pointing at the sword Garion always wore now.

"Everybody keeps saying how dangerous Arendia is," Garion explained. "Besides, I need to get used to it." He shifted the creaking new leather sword belt around until the wirebound hilt was not so obvious. The sword had been an Erastide present from Barak, one of several gifts he had received when the holiday had passed while they were at sea.

"It doesn't really suit you, you know," the old man told him somewhat disapprovingly.

"Leave him alone, father," Aunt Pol said almost absently. "It's his, after all, and he can wear it if he likes."

"Shouldn't Hettar be here by now?" Garion asked, wanting to change the subject.

"He may have run into deep snow in the mountains of Sendaria," Wolf replied. "He'll be here. Hettar's very dependable."

"I don't see why we just didn't buy horses in Camaar."

"They wouldn't have been as good," Mister Wolf answered, scratching at his short, white beard. "We've got a long way to go, and I don't want to have to worry about a horse foundering under me somewhere along the way. It's a lot better to take a little time now than to lose more time later."

Garion reached back and rubbed at his neck where the chain of the curiously carved silver amulet Wolf and Aunt Pol had given him for Erastide had chafed his skin.

"Don't worry at it, dear," Aunt Pol told him.

"I wish you'd let me wear it outside my clothes," he complained. "Nobody can see it under my tunic."

"It has to be next to your skin."

"It's not very comfortable. It looks nice enough, I suppose, but sometimes it seems cold, and other times it's hot, and once in a while it seems to be awfully heavy. The chain keeps rubbing at my neck. I guess I'm not used to ornaments."

"It's not entirely an ornament, dear," she told him. "You'll get used to it in time."

Wolf laughed. "Maybe it'll make you feel better to know that it took your aunt ten years to get used to hers. I was forever telling her to put it back on."

"I don't know that we need to go into that just now, father," Aunt Pol answered coolly.

"Do you have one, too?" Garion asked the old man, suddenly curious about it.

"Of course."

"Does it mean something that we all wear them?"

"It's a family custom, Garion," Aunt Pol told him in a tone that ended the discussion. The fog eddied around them as a chill, damp breeze briefly swirled through the ruins.

Garion sighed. "I wish Hettar would get here. I'd like to get away from this place. It's like a graveyard."

"It wasn't always this way," Aunt Pol said very quietly.

"What was it like?"

"I was happy here. The walls were high, and the towers soared. We all thought it would last forever." She pointed toward a rank patch of winter-browned brambles creeping over the broken stones. "Over there was a flower-filled garden where ladies in pale yellow dresses used to sit while young men sang to them from beyond the garden wall. The voices of the young men were very sweet, and the ladies would sigh and throw bright red roses over the wall to them. And down that avenue was a marble-paved square where the old men met to talk of forgotten wars and long-gone companions. Beyond that there was a house with a terrace where I used to sit with friends in the evening to watch the stars come out while a boy brought up chilled fruit and the nightingales sang as if their hearts were breaking." Her voice drifted off into silence. "But then the Asturians came," she went on, and there was a different note then. "You'd be surprised at how little time it takes to tear down something that took a thousand years to build."

"Don't worry at it, Pol," Wolf told her. "These things happen from time to time. There's not a great deal we can do about it."

"I *could* have done something, father," she replied, looking off into the ruins. "But you wouldn't let me, remember?"

"Do we have to go over that again, Pol?" Wolf asked in a pained voice. "You have to learn to accept your losses. The Wacite Arends were doomed anyway. At best, you'd have only been able to stall off the inevitable for a few months. We're not who we are and what we are in order to get mixed up in things that don't have any meaning."

"So you said before." She looked around at the filmy trees marching away in the fog down the empty streets. "I didn't think the trees would come back so fast," she said with a strange little catch in her voice. "I thought they might have waited a little longer."

"It's been almost twenty-five centuries, Pol."

"Really? It seems like only last year."

"Don't brood about it. It'll only make you melancholy. Why don't we go inside? The fog's beginning to make us all a bit moody."

Unaccountably, Aunt Pol put her arm about Garion's shoulders as they turned toward the tower. Her fragrance and the sense of her closeness brought a lump to his throat. The distance that had grown between them in the past few months seemed to vanish at her touch.

The chamber in the base of the tower had been built of such massive stones that neither the passage of centuries nor the silent, probing tendrils of tree roots had been able to dislodge them. Great, shallow arches supported the low stone ceiling, making the room seem almost like a cave. At the end of the room opposite the narrow doorway a wide crack between two of the rough-hewn blocks provided a natural chimney. Durnik had soberly considered the crack the previous evening when they had arrived, cold and wet, and then had quickly constructed a crude but efficient fireplace out of rubble. "It'll serve," the smith had said. "Not very elegant perhaps, but good enough for a few days."

As Wolf, Garion and Aunt Pol entered the low, cavelike chamber, a good fire crackled in the fireplace, casting looming shadows among the low arches and radiating a welcome warmth. Durnik, in his brown leather tunic, was stacking firewood along the wall. Barak, huge, red-bearded, and mail-shirted, was polishing his sword. Silk, in an unbleached linen shirt and black leather vest, lounged idly on one of the packs, toying with a pair of dice.

"Any sign of Hettar yet?" Barak asked, looking up.

"It's a day or so early," Mister Wolf replied, going to the fireplace to warm himself.

"Why don't you change your boots, Garion?" Aunt Pol suggested, hanging her blue cloak on one of the pegs Durnik had hammered into a crack in the wall.

Garion lifted his pack down from another peg and began rummaging through it.

"Your stockings, too," she added.

"Is the fog lifting at all?" Silk asked Mister Wolf.

"Not a chance."

"If I can persuade you all to move out from in front of the fire, I'll see about supper," Aunt Pol told them, suddenly very businesslike. She began setting out a ham, a few loaves of dark peasant bread, a sack of dried peas and a dozen or so leathery-looking carrots, humming softly to herself as she always did when she was cooking.

The next morning after breakfast, Garion pulled on a fleece-lined overvest, belted on his sword, and went back out into the fog-muffled ruins to watch for Hettar. It was a task to which he had appointed himself, and he was grateful that none of his friends had seen fit to tell him that it wasn't really necessary. As he trudged through the slush-covered streets toward the broken west gate of the city, he made a conscious effort to avoid the melancholy brooding that had blackened the previous day. Since there was absolutely nothing he could do about his circumstances, chewing on them would only leave a sour taste in his mouth. He was not exactly cheerful when he reached the low piece of wall by the west gate, but he was not precisely gloomy either.

The wall offered some protection, but the damp chill still crept through his clothes, and his feet were already cold. He shivered and settled down to wait. There was no point in trying to see any distance in the fog, so he concentrated on listening. His ears began to sort out the sounds in the forest beyond the wall, the drip of water from the trees, the occasional sodden thump of snow sliding from the limbs, and the tapping of a woodpecker working on a dead snag several hundred yards away.

"That's my cow," a voice said suddenly from somewhere off in the fog. Garion froze and stood silently, listening.

"Keep her in your own pasture, then," another voice replied shortly.

"Is that you, Lammer?" the first voice asked.

"Right. You're Detton, aren't you?"

"I didn't recognize you. How long's it been?"

"Four or five years, I suppose," Lammer judged.

"How are things going in your village?" Detton asked.

"We're hungry. The taxes took all our food."

"Ours too. We've been eating boiled tree roots."

"We haven't tried that yet. We're eating our shoes."

"How's your wife?" Detton asked politely.

"She died last year," Lammer answered in a flat, unemotional voice. "My lord took our son for a soldier, and he was killed in a battle somewhere. They poured boiling pitch on him. After that my wife stopped eating. It didn't take her long to die."

"I'm sorry," Detton sympathized. "She was very beautiful."

"They're both better off," Lammer declared. "They aren't cold or hungry anymore. Which kind of tree roots have you been eating?"

"Birch is the best," Detton told him. "Spruce has too much pitch, and oak's too tough. You boil some grass with the roots to give them a bit of flavor."

"I'll have to try it."

"I've got to get back," Detton said. "My lord's got me clearing trees, and he'll have me flogged if I stay away too long."

"Maybe I'll see you again sometime."

"If we both live."

"Good-bye, Detton."

"Good-bye, Lammer."

The two voices drifted away. Garion stood quite still for a long time after they were gone, his mind numb with shock and with tears of sympathy standing in his eyes. The worst part of it was the matter-of-fact way in which the two had accepted it all. A terrible anger began to burn in his throat. He wanted suddenly to hit somebody.

Then there was another sound off in the fog. Somewhere in the forest nearby someone was singing. The voice was a light, clear tenor, and Garion could hear it quite plainly as it drew closer. The song was filled with ancient wrongs, and the refrain was a call to battle. Irrationally, Garion's anger focused on the unknown singer. His vapid bawling about abstract injustices seemed somehow obscene in the face of the quiet despair of Lammer and Detton. Without thinking, Garion drew his sword and crouched slightly behind the shattered wall.

The song came yet nearer, and Garion could hear the step of a horse's hooves in the wet snow. Carefully he poked his head out from behind the wall as the singer appeared out of the fog no more than twenty paces away. He was a young man dressed in yellow hose and a bright red jerkin. His fur-lined cloak was tossed back, and he had a long, curved bow slung over one shoulder and a well-sheathed sword at his opposite hip. His reddish-gold hair fell smoothly down his back from beneath a pointed cap with a feather rising from it. Although his song was grim and he sang it in a voice throbbing with passion, there was about his youthful face a kind of friendly openness that no amount of scowling could erase. Garion glared at this empty-headed young nobleman, quite certain that the singing fool had never made a meal of tree roots or mourned the passing of a wife who had starved herself to death out of grief. The stranger turned his horse and, still singing, rode directly toward the broken arch of the gateway beside which Garion lurked in ambush.

Garion was not normally a belligerent boy, and under other circumstances he might have approached the situation differently. The gaudy young stranger, however, had presented himself at precisely the wrong time. Garion's quickly devised plan had the advantage of simplicity. Since there was nothing to complicate it, it worked admirably—up to a point. No sooner had the lyric young man passed through the gate than Garion stepped from his hiding place, grasped the back of the rider's cloak and yanked him bodily out of the saddle. With a startled outcry and a wet splat, the stranger landed unceremoniously on his back in the slush at Garion's feet. The second part of Garion's plan, however, fell completely apart. Even as he moved in to take the fallen rider prisoner at sword point, the young man rolled, came to his feet, and drew his own sword, seemingly all in one motion. His eyes were snapping with anger, and his sword weaved threateningly.

Garion was not a fencer, but his reflexes were good and the chores he had performed at Faldor's farm had hardened his muscles. Despite the anger which had moved him to attack in the first place, he had no real desire to hurt this young man. His opponent seemed to be holding his sword lightly, almost negligently, and Garion thought that a smart blow on the blade might very well knock it out of his hand. He swung quickly, but the blade flicked out of the path of his heavy swipe and clashed with a steely ring down on his own sword. Garion jumped back and made another clumsy swing. The swords rang again. Then the air was filled with clash and scrape and bell-like rattle as the two of them banged and parried and feinted with their blades. It took Garion only a moment to realize that his opponent was much better at this than he was, but that the young man had ignored several opportunities to strike at him. In spite of himself he began to grin in the excitement of their noisy contest. The stranger's answering grin was open, even friendly.

"All right, that's enough of that!" It was Mister Wolf. The old man was striding toward them with Barak and Silk close on his heels. "Just exactly what do you two think you're doing?"

Garion's opponent, after one startled glance, lowered his sword. "Belgarath—" he began.

"Lelldorin," Wolf's tone was scathing, "have you lost what little sense you had to begin with?"

Several things clicked into place in Garion's mind simultaneously as Wolf turned on him coldly. "Well, Garion, would you like to explain this?"

Garion instantly decided to try guile. "Grandfather," he said, stressing the word and giving the younger stranger a quick warning look, "you didn't think we were *really* fighting, did you? Lelldorin here was just showing me how you block somebody's sword when he attacks, that's all."

"Really?" Wolf replied skeptically.

"Of course," Garion said, all innocence now. "What possible reason could there be for us to be trying to hurt each other?"

Lelldorin opened his mouth to speak, but Garion deliberately stepped on his foot.

"Lelldorin's really very good," he rushed on, putting his hand in a friendly fashion on the young man's shoulder. "He taught me a lot in just a few minutes."

—Let it stand—Silk's fingers flickered at him in the minute gestures of the Drasnian secret language.—Always keep a lie simple—

"The lad is an apt pupil, Belgarath," Lelldorin said lamely, finally understanding.

"He's agile, if nothing else," Mister Wolf replied dryly. "What's the idea behind all the frippery?" He indicated Lelldorin's gaudy clothes. "You look like a maypole."

"The Mimbrates have started detaining honest Asturians for ques-, tioning," the young Arend explained, "and I had to pass several of their strongholds. I thought that if I dressed like one of their toadies I wouldn't be bothered."

"Maybe you've got better sense than I thought," Wolf conceded grudgingly. He turned to Silk and Barak. "This is Lelldorin, son of the Baron of Wildantor. He'll be joining us."

"I wanted to talk to you about that, Belgarath," Lelldorin put in quickly. "My father commanded me to come here and I can't disobey him, but I'm pledged in a matter of extremest urgency."

"Every young nobleman in Asturia's pledged in at least two or three such matters of urgency," Wolf replied. "I'm sorry, Lelldorin, but the matter we're involved in is much too important to be postponed while you go out to ambush a couple of Mimbrate tax collectors."

Aunt Pol approached them out of the fog then, with Durnik striding protectively at her side. "What are they doing with the swords, father?" she demanded, her eyes flashing.

"Playing," Mister Wolf replied shortly. "Or so they say. This is Lelldorin. I think I've mentioned him to you."

Aunt Pol looked Lelldorin up and down with one raised eyebrow. "A very colorful young man."

"The clothes are a disguise," Wolf explained. "He's not as frivolous as all that—not quite, anyway. He's the best bowman in Asturia, and we might need his skill before we're done with all this."

"I see," she said, somewhat unconvinced.

"There's another reason, of course," Wolf continued, "but I don't think we need to get into that just now, do we?"

"Are you still worried about that passage, father?" she asked with exasperation. "The Mrin Codex is very obscure, and none of the other versions say anything at all about the people it mentions. It could be pure allegory, you know."

"I've seen a few too many allegories turn out to be plain fact to start gambling at this point. Why don't we all go back to the tower?" he suggested. "It's a bit cold and wet out here for lengthy debates on textual variations."

Garion glanced at Silk, baffled by this exchange, but the little man returned his look with blank incomprehension.

"Will you help me catch my horse, Garion?" Lelldorin asked politely, sheathing his sword.

"Of course," Garion replied, also putting away his weapon. "I think he went that way."

Lelldorin picked up his bow, and the two of them followed the horse's tracks off into the ruins.

"I'm sorry I pulled you off your horse," Garion apologized when they were out of sight of the others.

"No matter." Lelldorin laughed easily. "I should have been paying more attention." He looked quizzically at Garion. "Why did you lie to Belgarath?"

"It wasn't *exactly* a lie," Garion replied. "We weren't really trying to hurt each other, and sometimes it takes hours trying to explain something like that."

Lelldorin laughed again, an infectious sort of laugh. In spite of himself, Garion could not help joining in.

Both laughing, they continued together down an overgrown street between the low mounds of slush-covered rubble.

CHAPTER TWO

Lelldorin of Wildantor was eighteen years old, although his ingenuous nature made him seem more boyish. No emotion touched him that did not instantly register in his expression, and sincerity shone in his face like a beacon. He was impulsive, extravagant in his declarations, and probably, Garion reluctantly concluded, not overly bright. It was impossible not to like him, however.

The following morning when Garion pulled on his cloak to go out and continue his watch for Hettar, Lelldorin immediately joined him. The young Arend had changed out of his garish clothing and now wore brown hose, a green tunic, and a dark brown wool cape. He carried his bow and wore a quiver of arrows at his belt; as they walked through the snow toward the broken west wall he amused himself by loosing arrows at targets only half-visible ahead of him.

"You're awfully good," Garion said admiringly after one particularly fine shot.

"I'm an Asturian," Lelldorin replied modestly. "We've been bowmen for thousands of years. My father had the limbs of this bow cut on the day I was born, and I could draw it by the time I was eight."

"I imagine you hunt a great deal," Garion said, thinking of the dense forest all around them and the tracks of game he had seen in the snow.

"It's our most common pastime." Lelldorin stopped to pull the arrow he had just shot from a tree trunk. "My father prides himself on the fact that beef or mutton are never served at his table."

"I went hunting once, in Cherek."

"Deer?" Lelldorin asked.

"No. Wild boars. We didn't use bows though. The Chereks hunt with spears."

"Spears? How can you get close enough to kill anything with a spear?"

Garion laughed a bit ruefully, remembering his bruised ribs and aching head. "Getting close isn't the problem. It's getting away after you've speared him that's the difficult part."

Lelldorin didn't seem to grasp that.

"The huntsmen form a line," Garion explained, "and they crash through the woods, making as much noise as they can. You take your spear and wait where the boars are likely to pass when they try to get away from the noise. Being chased makes them bad-tempered, and when they see you, they charge. That's when you spear them."

"Isn't that dangerous?" Lelldorin's eyes were wide.

Garion nodded. "I almost got all my ribs broken." He was not exactly boasting, but he admitted to himself that he was pleased by Lelldorin's reaction to his story.

"We don't have many dangerous animals in Asturia," Lelldorin said almost wistfully. "A few bears and once in a while a pack of wolves." He seemed to hesitate for a moment, looking closely at Garion. "*Some* men, though, find more interesting things to shoot at than wild stags." He said it with a kind of secretive sidelong glance.

"Oh?" Garion was not quite sure what he meant.

"Hardly a day goes by that some Mimbrate's horse doesn't come home riderless."

Garion was shocked at that.

"*Some* men think that there are too many Mimbrates in Asturia," Lelldorin explained with heavy emphasis.

"I thought that the Arendish civil war was over."

"There are many who don't believe that. There are many who believe that the war will continue until Asturia is free of the Mimbrate crown." Lelldorin's tone left no question as to where he stood in the matter.

"Wasn't the country unified after the Battle of Vo Mimbre?" Garion objected.

"Unified? How could anybody believe that? Asturia is treated like a subject province. The king's court is at Vo Mimbre; every governor, every tax collector, every bailiff, every high sheriff in the kingdom is a Mimbrate. There's not a single Asturian in a position of authority anywhere in Arendia. The Mimbrates even refuse to recognize our titles. My father, whose line extends back a thousand years, is called *landowner*. A Mimbrate would sooner bite out his tongue than call him Baron." Lelldorin's face had gone white with suppressed indignation.

"I didn't know that," Garion said carefully, not sure how to handle the young man's feelings.

"Asturia's humiliation is almost at an end, however," Lelldorin declared fervently. "There are some men in Asturia for whom patriotism is not dead, and the time is not far off when these men will hunt *royal* game." He emphasized his statement by snapping an arrow at a distant tree.

That confirmed the worst of Garion's fears. Lelldorin was a bit too familiar with the details not to be involved in this plot.

As if he had realized himself that he had gone too far, Lelldorin stared at Garion with consternation. "I'm a fool," he blurted with a guilty look around him. "I've never learned to control my tongue. Please forget what I just said, Garion. I know you're my friend, and I know you won't betray what I said in a moment of heat."

That was one thing Garion had feared. With that single statement, Lelldorin had effectively sealed his lips. He knew that Mister Wolf should be warned that some wild scheme was afoot, but Lelldorin's declaration of friendship and trust had made it impossible for him to speak. He wanted to grind his teeth with frustration as he stared full in the face of a major moral dilemma.

They walked on, neither of them speaking and both a little embarrassed, until they reached the bit of wall where Garion had waited in ambush the day before. For a time they stared out into the fog, their strained silence growing more uncomfortable by the moment.

"What's it like in Sendaria?" Lelldorin asked suddenly. "I've never been there."

"There aren't so many trees," Garion answered, looking over the wall at the dark trunks marching off in the fog. "It's an orderly kind of place."

"Where did you live there?"

"At Faldor's farm. It's near Lake Erat."

"Is this Faldor a nobleman?"

"Faldor?" Garion laughed. "No, Faldor's as common as old shoes. He's just a farmer—decent, honest, good-hearted. I miss him."

"A commoner, then," Lelldorin said, seeming ready to dismiss Faldor as a man of no consequence.

"Rank doesn't mean very much in Sendaria," Garion told him rather pointedly. "What a man does is more important than what he is." He made a wry face. "I was a scullery boy. It's not very pleasant, but somebody's got to do it, I suppose."

"Not a serf, certainly?" Lelldorin sounded shocked.

"There aren't any serfs in Sendaria."

"No serfs?" The young Arend stared at him uncomprehendingly.

"No," Garion said firmly. "We've never found it necessary to have serfs."

Lelldorin's expression clearly showed that he was baffled by the notion. Garion remembered the voices that had come to him out of the fog the day before, but he resisted the urge to say something about serfdom. Lelldorin would never understand, and the two of them were very close to friendship. Garion felt that he needed a friend just now and he didn't want to spoil things by saying something that would offend this likable young man.

"What sort of work does your father do?" Lelldorin asked politely.

"He's dead. So's my mother." Garion found that if he said it quickly, it didn't hurt so much.

Lelldorin's eyes filled in sudden, impulsive sympathy. He put his hand consolingly on Garion's shoulder. "I'm sorry," he said, his voice almost breaking. "It must have been a terrible loss."

"I was a baby." Garion shrugged, trying to sound offhand about it. "I don't even remember them." It was still too personal to talk about.

"Some pestilence?" Lelldorin asked gently.

"No," Garion answered in the same flat tone. "They were murdered."

Lelldorin gasped and his eyes went wide.

"A man crept into their village at night and set fire to their house," Garion continued unemotionally. "My grandfather tried to catch him, but he got away. From what I understand, the man is a very old enemy of my family."

"Surely you're not going to let it stand like that?" Lelldorin demanded.

"No," Garion replied, still looking out into the fog. "As soon as I'm old enough, I'm going to find him and kill him."

"Good lad!" Lelldorin exclaimed, suddenly catching Garion in a rough embrace. "We'll find him and cut him to pieces."

"We?"

"I'll be going with you, of course," Lelldorin declared. "No true friend could do any less." He was obviously speaking on impulse, but just as obviously he was totally sincere. He gripped Garion's hand firmly. "I swear to you, Garion, I won't rest until the murderer of your parents lies dead at your feet."

The sudden declaration was so totally predictable that Garion silently berated himself for not keeping his mouth shut. His feelings in the matter were very personal, and he was not really sure he wanted company in his search for his faceless enemy. Another part of his mind, however, rejoiced in Lelldorin's impulsive but unquestioning support. He decided to let the subject drop. He knew Lelldorin well enough by now to realize that the young man undoubtedly made a dozen devout promises a day, quickly offered in absolute sincerity, and just as quickly forgotten.

They talked then of other things, standing close together beside the shattered wall with their dark cloaks drawn tightly about them.

Shortly before noon Garion heard the muffled sound of horses' hooves somewhere out in the forest. A few minutes later, Hettar materialized out of the fog with a dozen wild-looking horses trailing after him. The tall Algar wore a short, fleece-lined leather cape. His boots were mud-spattered and his clothes travel-stained, but otherwise he seemed unaffected by his two weeks in the saddle.

"Garion," he said gravely by way of greeting, and Garion and Lelldorin stepped out to meet him.

"We've been waiting for you," Garion told him and introduced Lelldorin. "We'll show you where the others are."

Hettar nodded and followed the two young men through the ruins to the tower where Mister Wolf and the others were waiting. "Snow in the mountains," the Algar remarked laconically by way of explanation as he swung down from his horse. "It delayed me a bit." He pulled his hood back from his shaved head and shook out his long, black scalp lock.

"No harm's been done," Mister Wolf replied. "Come inside to the fire and have something to eat. We've got a lot to talk about."

Hettar looked at the horses, his tan, weathered face growing strangely blank as if he were concentrating. The horses all looked back at him, their eyes alert and their ears pointed sharply forward. Then they turned and picked their way off among the trees.

"Won't they stray?" Durnik wanted to know.

"No," Hettar answered. "I asked them not to."

Durnik looked puzzled, but he let it pass.

They all went into the tower and sat near the fireplace. Aunt Pol cut dark bread and pale, yellow cheese for them while Durnik put more wood on the fire.

"Cho-Hag sent word to the Clan-Chiefs," Hettar reported, pulling off his cape. He wore a black, long-sleeved horsehide jacket with steel discs riveted to it to form a kind of flexible armor. "They're gathering at the Stronghold for council." He unbelted the curved sabre he wore, laid it to one side and sat near the fire to eat.

Wolf nodded. "Is anyone trying to get through to Prolgu?"

"I sent a troop of my own men to the Gorim before I left," Hettar responded. "They'll get through if anyone can."

"I hope so," Wolf stated. "The Gorim's an old friend of mine, and I'll need his help before all this is finished."

"Aren't your people afraid of the land of the Ulgos?" Lelldorin inquired politely. "I've heard that there are monsters there that feed on the flesh of men."

Hettar shrugged. "They stay in their lairs in the wintertime. Besides, they're seldom brave enough to attack a full troop of mounted men." He looked over at Mister Wolf. "Southern Sendaria's crawling with Murgos. Or did you know that?"

"I could have guessed," Wolf replied. "Did they seem to be looking for anything in particular?"

"I don't talk with Murgos," Hettar said shortly. His hooked nose and fierce eyes made him look at that moment like a hawk about to swoop down to the kill.

"I'm surprised you weren't delayed even more," Silk bantered. "The whole world knows how you feel about Murgos."

"I indulged myself once," Hettar admitted. "I met two of them alone on the highway. It didn't take very long."

"Two less to worry about, then," Barak grunted with approval.

"I think it's time for some plain talk," Mister Wolf said, brushing crumbs off the front of his tunic. "Most of you have some notion of what we're doing, but I don't want anybody blundering into something by accident. We're after a man named Zedar. He used to be one of my Master's disciples— then he went over to Torak. Early last fall he somehow slipped into the throne room at Riva and stole the Orb of Aldur. We're going to chase him down and get it back."

"Isn't he a sorcerer too?" Barak asked, tugging absently at a thick red braid.

"That's not the term we use," Wolf replied, "but yes, he does have a certain amount of that kind of power. We all did—me, Beltira and Belkira, Belzedar—all the rest of us. That's one of the things I wanted to warn you about."

"You all seem to have the same sort of names," Silk noticed.

"Our Master changed our names when he took us as disciples. It was a simple change, but it meant a great deal to us."

"Wouldn't that mean that your original name was Garath?" Silk asked, his ferret eyes narrowing shrewdly.

Mister Wolf looked startled and then laughed. "I haven't heard *that* name for thousands of years. I've been Belgarath for so long that I'd almost completely forgotten Garath. It's probably just as well. Garath was a troublesome boy—a thief and a liar among other things."

"Some things never change," Aunt Pol observed.

"Nobody's perfect," Wolf admitted blandly.

"Why did Zedar steal the Orb?" Hettar asked, setting aside his plate.

"He's always wanted it for himself," the old man replied. "That could be it—but more likely he's trying to take it to Torak. The one who delivers the Orb to One-Eye is going to be his favorite."

"But Torak's dead," Lelldorin objected. "The Rivan Warder killed him at Vo Mimbre."

"No," Wolf said, "Torak isn't dead; only asleep. Brand's sword wasn't the one destined to kill him. Zedar carried him off after the battle and hid him someplace. Someday he'll awaken—probably someday fairly soon, if I'm reading the signs right. We've got to get the Orb back before that happens."

"This Zedar's caused a lot of trouble," Barak rumbled. "You should have dealt with him a long time ago."

"Possibly," Wolf admitted.

"Why don't you just wave your hand and make him disappear?" Barak suggested, making a sort of gesture with his thick fingers.

Wolf shook his head. "I can't. Not even the Gods can do that."

"We've got some big problems, then," Silk said with a frown. "Every Murgo from here to Rak Goska's going to try to stop us from catching Zedar."

"Not necessarily," Wolf disagreed. "Zedar's got the Orb, but Ctuchik commands the Grolims."

"Ctuchik?" Lelldorin asked.

"The Grolim High Priest. He and Zedar hate each other. I think we can count on him to try to keep Zedar from getting to Torak with the Orb."

Barak shrugged. "What difference does it make? You and Polgara can use magic if we run into anything difficult, can't you?"

"There are limitations on that sort of thing," Wolf said a bit evasively.

"I don't understand," Barak said, frowning.

Mister Wolf took a deep breath. "All right. As long as it's come up, let's go into that too. Sorcery—if that's what you want to call it—is a disruption of the natural order of things. Sometimes it has certain unexpected effects, so you have to be very careful about what you do with it. Not only that, it makes—" He frowned. "—Let's call it a sort of noise. That's not exactly what it is, but it serves well enough to explain. Others with the same abilities can hear that noise. Once Polgara and I start changing things, every Grolim in the West is going to know exactly where we are and what we're doing. They'll keep piling things in front of us until we're exhausted."

"It takes almost as much energy to do things that way as it does to do them with your arms and back," Aunt Pol explained. "It's very tiring." She sat beside the fire, carefully mending a small tear in one of Garion's tunics.

"I didn't know that," Barak admitted.

"Not many people do."

"If we have to, Pol and I can take certain steps," Wolf went on, "but we can't keep it up forever, and we can't simply make things vanish. I'm sure you can see why."

"Oh, of course," Silk professed, though his tone indicated that he did not.

"Everything that exists depends on everything else," Aunt Pol explained quietly. "If you were to unmake one thing, it's altogether possible that everything would vanish."

The fire popped, and Garion jumped slightly. The vaulted chamber seemed suddenly dark, and shadows lurked in the corners.

"That can't happen, of course," Wolf told them. "When you try to unmake something, your will simply recoils on you. If you say, 'Be not,' then *you* are the one who vanishes. That's why we're very careful about what we say."

"I can understand why," Silk said, his eyes widening slightly.

"Most of the things we'll encounter can be dealt with by ordinary means," Wolf continued. "That's the reason we've brought you together—at least that's one of the reasons. Among you, you'll be able to handle most of the things that get in our way. The important thing to remember is that Polgara and I have to get to Zedar before he can reach Torak with the Orb. Zedar's found some way to touch the Orb—I don't know how. If he can show Torak how it's done, no power on earth will be able to stop One-Eye from becoming King and God over the whole world."

They all sat in the ruddy, flickering light of the fire, their faces serious as they considered that possibility.

"I think that pretty well covers everything, don't you, Pol?"

"I believe so, father," she replied, smoothing the front of her gray, homespun gown.

Later, outside the tower as gray evening crept in among the foggy ruins of Vo Wacune and the smell of the thick stew Aunt Pol was cooking for supper drifted out to them, Garion turned to Silk. "Is it all really true?" he asked.

The small man looked out into the fog. "Let's act as if we believed that it is," he suggested. "Under the circumstances, I think it'd be a bad idea to make a mistake."

"Are you afraid too, Silk?" Garion asked.

Silk sighed. "Yes," he admitted, "but we can behave as if we believed that we aren't, can't we?"

"I guess we can try," Garion said, and the two of them turned to go back into the chamber at the foot of the tower where the firelight danced on the low stone arches, holding the fog and chill at bay.

CHAPTER THREE

The next morning Silk came out of the tower wearing a rich maroon doublet and a baglike black velvet cap cocked jauntily over one ear.

"What's all that about?" Aunt Pol asked him.

"I chanced across an old friend in one of the packs," Silk replied airily. "Radek of Boktor by name."

"What happened to Ambar of Kotu?"

"Ambar's a good enough fellow, I suppose," Silk said a bit deprecatingly, "but a Murgo named Asharak knows about him and may have dropped his name in certain quarters. Let's not look for trouble if we don't have to."

"Not a bad disguise," Mister Wolf agreed. "One more Drasnian merchant on the Great West Road won't attract any attention—whatever his name."

"Please," Silk objected in an injured tone. "The name's very important. You hang the whole disguise on the name."

"I don't see any difference," Barak asserted bluntly.

"There's all the difference in the world. Surely you can see that Ambar's a vagabond with very little regard for ethics, while Radek's a man of substance whose word is good in all the commercial centers of the West. Besides, Radek's always accompanied by servants."

"Servants?" One of Aunt Pol's eyebrows shot up.

"Just for the sake of the disguise," Silk assured her quickly. "You, of course, could never be a servant, Lady Polgara."

"Thank you."

"No one would ever believe it. You'll be my sister instead, traveling with me to see the splendors of Tol Honeth."

"Your sister?"

"You could be my mother instead, if you prefer," Silk suggested blandly, "making a religious pilgrimage to Mar Terrin to atone for a colorful past."

Aunt Pol gazed steadily at the small man for a moment while he grinned impudently at her. "Someday your sense of humor's going to get you into a great deal of trouble, Prince Kheldar."

"I'm always in trouble, Lady Polgara. I wouldn't know how to act if I weren't."

"Do you two suppose we could get started?" Mister Wolf asked.

"Just a moment more," Silk replied. "If we meet anyone and have to explain things, you, Lelldorin, and Garion are Polgara's servants. Hettar, Barak, and Durnik are mine."

"Anything you say," Wolf agreed wearily.

"There are reasons."

"All right."

"Don't you want to hear them?"

"Not particularly."

Silk looked a bit hurt.

"Are we ready?" Wolf asked.

"Everything's out of the tower," Durnik told him. "Oh—just a moment. I forgot to put out the fire." He went back inside.

Wolf glanced after the smith in exasperation. "What difference does it make?" he muttered. "This place is a ruin anyway."

"Leave him alone, father," Aunt Pol said placidly. "It's the way he is."

As they prepared to mount, Barak's horse, a large, sturdy gray, sighed and threw a reproachful look at Hettar, and the Algar chuckled.

"What's so funny?" Barak demanded suspiciously.

"The horse said something," Hettar replied. "Never mind."

Then they swung into their saddles and threaded their way out of the foggy ruins and along the narrow, muddy track that wound into the forest. Sodden snow lay under wet trees, and water dripped continually from the branches overhead. They all drew their cloaks about them to ward off the chill and dampness. Once they were under the trees, Lelldorin pulled his horse in beside Garion's, and they rode together. "Is Prince Kheldar always so—well—extremely complicated?" he asked.

"Silk? Oh yes. He's very devious. You see, he's a spy, and disguises and clever lies are second nature to him."

"A spy? Really?" Lelldorin's eyes brightened as his imagination caught hold of the idea.

"He works for his uncle, the King of Drasnia," Garion explained. "From what I understand, the Drasnians have been at this sort of thing for centuries."

"We've got to stop and pick up the rest of the packs," Silk was reminding Mister Wolf.

"I haven't forgotten," the old man replied.

"Packs?" Lelldorin asked.

"Silk picked up some wool cloth in Camaar," Garion told him. "He said it would give us a legitimate reason to be on the highway. We hid them in a cave when we left the road to come to Vo Wacune."

"He thinks of everything, doesn't he?"

"He tries. We're lucky to have him with us."

"Maybe we could have him show us a few things about disguises," Lelldorin suggested brightly. "It might be very useful when we go looking for your enemy."

Garion had thought that Lelldorin had forgotten his impulsive pledge. The young Arend's mind seemed too flighty to keep hold of one idea for very long, but he saw now that Lelldorin only seemed to forget things. The prospect of a serious search for his parents' murderer with this young enthusiast adding embellishments and improvisations at every turn began to present itself alarmingly.

By midmorning, after they had picked up Silk's packs and lashed them to the backs of the spare horses, they were back out on the Great West Road, the Tolnedran highway running through the heart of the forest. They rode south at a loping canter that ate up the miles.

They passed a heavily burdened serf clothed in scraps and pieces of sackcloth tied on with bits of string. The serf's face was gaunt, and he was very thin under his dirty rags. He stepped off the road and stared at them with apprehension until they had passed. Garion felt a sudden stab of compassion. He briefly remembered Lammer and Detton, and he wondered what would finally happen to them. It seemed important for some reason. "Is it really necessary to keep them so poor?" he demanded of Lelldorin, unable to hold it in any longer.

"Who?" Lelldorin asked, looking around.

"That serf."

Lelldorin glanced back over his shoulder at the ragged man.

"You didn't even see him," Garion accused.

Lelldorin shrugged. "There are so many."

"And they all dress in rags and live on the edge of starvation."

"Mimbrate taxes," Lelldorin replied as if that explained everything.

"*You* seem to have always had enough to eat."

"I'm not a serf, Garion," Lelldorin answered patiently. "The poorest people always suffer the most. It's the way the world is."

"It doesn't have to be," Garion retorted.

"You just don't understand."

"No. And I never will."

"Naturally not," Lelldorin said with infuriating complacency. "You're not Arendish."

Garion clenched his teeth to hold back the obvious reply.

By late afternoon they had covered ten leagues, and the snow had largely disappeared from the roadside. "Shouldn't we start to give some thought to where we're going to spend the night, father?" Aunt Pol suggested.

Mister Wolf scratched thoughtfully at his beard as he squinted at the shadows hovering in the trees around them.

"I have an uncle who lives not far from here," Lelldorin offered, "Count Reldegen. I'm sure he'll be glad to give us shelter."

"Thin?" Mister Wolf asked. "Dark hair?"

"It's gray now," Lelldorin replied. "Do you know him?"

"I haven't seen him for twenty years," Wolf told him. "As I recall, he used to be quite a hothead."

"Uncle Reldegen? You must have him confused with somebody else, Belgarath."

"Maybe," Wolf said. "How far is it to his house?"

"No more than a league and a half away."

"Let's go see him," Wolf decided.

Lelldorin shook his reins and moved into the lead to show them the way.

"How are you and your friend getting along?" Silk asked, falling in beside Garion.

"Fine, I suppose," Garion replied, not quite sure how the rat-faced little man intended the question. "It seems to be a little hard to explain things to him though."

"That's only natural," Silk observed. "He's an Arend, after all."

Garion quickly came to Lelldorin's defense. "He's honest and very brave."

"They all are. That's part of the problem."

"I like him," Garion asserted.

"So do I, Garion, but that doesn't keep me from realizing the truth about him."

"If you're trying to say something, why don't you just go ahead and say it?"

"All right, I will. Don't let friendship get the better of your good sense. Arendia's a very dangerous place, and Arends tend to blunder into disasters quite regularly. Don't let your exuberant young companion drag you into something that's none of your business." Silk's look was direct, and Garion realized that the little man was quite serious.

"I'll be careful," he promised.

"I knew I could count on you," Silk said gravely.

"Are you making fun of me?"

"Would I do that, Garion?" Silk asked mockingly. Then he laughed and they rode on together through the gloomy afternoon.

The gray stone house of Count Reldegen was about a mile back in the forest from the highway, and it stood in the center of a clearing that extended beyond bowshot in every direction. Although it had no wall, it had somehow the look of a fort. The windows facing out were narrow and covered with iron gratings. Strong turrets surmounted by battlements stood at each corner, and the gate which opened into the central courtyard of the house was made of whole tree trunks, squared off and strapped together with iron bands. Garion stared at the brooding pile as they approached in the rapidly fading light. There was a kind of haughty ugliness about the house, a grim solidity that seemed to defy the world. "It's not a very pleasant-looking sort of place, is it?" he said to Silk.

"Asturian architecture's a reflection of their society," Silk replied. "A strong house isn't a bad idea in a country where neighborhood disputes sometimes get out of hand."

"Are they all so afraid of each other?"

"Just cautious, Garion. Just cautious."

Lelldorin dismounted before the heavy gate and spoke to someone on the other side through a small grille. There was finally a rattling of chains and the grinding sound of heavy, iron-shod bars sliding back.

"I wouldn't make any quick moves once we're inside," Silk advised quietly. "There'll probably be archers watching us."

Garion looked at him sharply.

"A quaint custom of the region," Silk informed him.

They rode into a cobblestoned courtyard and dismounted.

Count Reldegen, when he appeared, was a tall, thin man with iron-gray hair and beard who walked with the aid of a stout cane. He wore a rich green doublet and black hose; despite the fact that he was in his own house, he carried a sword at his side. He limped heavily down a broad flight of stairs from the house to greet them.

"Uncle," Lelldorin said, bowing respectfully.

"Nephew," the count replied in polite acknowledgment.

"My friends and I found ourselves in the vicinity," Lelldorin stated, "and we thought we might impose on you for the night."

"You're always welcome, nephew," Reldegen answered with a kind of grave formality. "Have you dined yet?"

"No, uncle."

"Then you must all take supper with me. May I know your friends?"

Mister Wolf pushed back his hood and stepped forward. "You and I are already acquainted, Reldegen," he said.

The count's eyes widened, "Belgarath? Is it really you?"

Wolf grinned. "Oh, yes. I'm still wandering about the world, stirring up mischief."

Reldegen laughed then and grasped Wolf's upper arm warmly. "Come inside, all of you. Let's not stand about in the cold." He turned and limped up the steps to the house.

"What happened to your leg?" Wolf asked him.

"An arrow in the knee." The count shrugged. "The result of an old disagreement—long since forgotten."

"As I recall, you used to get involved in quite a few of those. I thought for a while that you intended to go through life with your sword half-drawn."

"I was an excitable youth," the count admitted, opening the broad door at the top of the steps. He led them down a long hallway to a room of imposing size with a large blazing fireplace at each end. Great curving stone arches supported the ceiling. The floor was of polished black stone, scattered with fur rugs, and the walls, arches, and ceiling were whitewashed in gleaming contrast. Heavy, carved chairs of dark brown wood sat here and there, and a great table with an iron candelabra in its center stood near the fireplace at one end. A dozen or so leather-bound books were scattered on its polished surface.

"Books, Reldegen?" Mister Wolf said in amazement as he and the others removed their cloaks and gave them to the servants who immediately appeared. "You *have* mellowed, my friend."

The count smiled at the old man's remark.

"I'm forgetting my manners," Wolf apologized. "My daughter, Polgara. Pol, this is Count Reldegen, an old friend."

"My Lady," the count acknowledged with an exquisite bow, "my house is honored."

Aunt Pol was about to reply when two young men burst into the room, arguing heatedly. "You're an idiot, Berentain!" the first, a dark-haired youth in a scarlet doublet, snapped.

"It may please thee to think so, Torasin," the second, a stout young man with pale, curly hair and wearing a green and yellow striped tunic, replied, "but whether it please thee or not, Asturia's future is in Mimbrate hands. Thy rancorous denouncements and sulfurous rhetoric shall not alter that fact."

"Don't thee me or thou me, Berentain," the dark-haired one sneered. "Your imitation Mimbrate courtesy turns my stomach."

"Gentlemen, that's enough!" Count Reldegen said sharply, rapping his cane on the stone floor. "If you two are going to insist on discussing politics, I'll have you separated—forcibly, if necessary."

The two young men scowled at each other and then stalked off to opposite sides of the room. "My son, Torasin," the count admitted apologetically, indicating the dark-haired youth, "and his cousin Berentain, the son of my late wife's brother. They've been wrangling like this for two weeks now. I had to take their swords away from them the day after Berentain arrived."

"Political discussion is good for the blood, my Lord," Silk observed, "especially in the winter. The heat keeps the veins from clogging up."

The count chuckled at the little man's remark.

"Prince Kheldar of the royal house of Drasnia," Mister Wolf introduced Silk.

"Your Highness," the count responded, bowing.

Silk winced slightly. "Please, my Lord. I've spent a lifetime running from that mode of address, and I'm sure that my connection with the royal family embarrasses my uncle almost as much as it embarrasses me."

The count laughed again with easy good nature. "Why don't we all adjourn to the dining table?" he suggested. "Two fat deer have been turning on spits in my kitchen since daybreak, and I recently obtained a cask of red wine from southern Tolnedra. As I recall, Belgarath has always had a great fondness for good food and fine wines."

"He hasn't changed, my Lord," Aunt Pol told him. "My father's terribly predictable, once you get to know him."

The count smiled and offered her his arm as they all moved toward the door on the far side of the room.

"Tell me, my Lord," Aunt Pol said, "do you by chance have a bathtub in your house?"

"Bathing in winter is dangerous, Lady Polgara," the count warned her.

"My Lord," she stated gravely, "I've been bathing winter or summer for more years than you could possibly imagine."

"Let her bathe, Reldegen," Mister Wolf urged. "Her temper deteriorates quite noticeably when she thinks she's getting dirty."

"A bath wouldn't hurt you either, Old Wolf," Aunt Pol retorted tartly. "You're starting to get a bit strong from the downwind side."

Mister Wolf looked a bit injured.

Much later, after they had eaten their fill of venison, gravy-soaked bread, and rich cherry tarts, Aunt Pol excused herself and went with a maidservant to oversee the preparation of her bath. The men all lingered at the table over their wine cups, their faces washed with the golden light of the many candles in Reldegen's dining hall.

"Let me show you to your rooms," Torasin suggested to Lelldorin and Garion, pushing back his chair and casting a look of veiled contempt across the table at Berentain.

They followed him from the room and up a long flight of stairs toward the upper stories of the house. "I don't want to offend you, Tor," Lelldorin said as they climbed, "but your cousin has some peculiar ideas."

Torasin snorted. "Berentain's a jackass. He thinks he can impress the Mimbrates by imitating their speech and by fawning on them." His dark face was angry in the light of the candle he carried to light their way.

"Why should he want to?" Lelldorin asked.

"He's desperate for some kind of holding he can call his own," Torasin replied. "My mother's brother has very little land to leave him. The fat idiot's all calf-eyed over the daughter of one of the barons in his district, and since the baron won't even consider a landless suitor, Berentain's trying to wheedle an estate from the Mimbrate governor. He'd swear fealty to the ghost of Kal Torak himself, if he thought it would get him land."

"Doesn't he realize that he hasn't got a chance?" Lelldorin inquired. "There are too many land-hungry Mimbrate knights around the governor for him to even think of granting an estate to an Asturian."

"I've told him the same thing myself," Torasin declared with scathing contempt, "but there's no reasoning with him. His behavior degrades our whole family."

Lelldorin shook his head commiseratingly as they reached an upper hall. He looked around quickly then. "I have to talk with you, Tor," he blurted, his voice dropping to a whisper.

Torasin looked at him sharply.

"My father's committed me to Belgarath's service in a matter of great importance," Lelldorin hurried on in that same hushed voice. "I don't know how long we'll be gone, so you and the others will have to kill Korodullin without me."

Torasin's eyes went wide with horror. "We're not alone, Lelldorin!" he said in a strangled voice.

"I'll go down to the other end of the hall," Garion said quickly.

"No," Lelldorin replied firmly, taking hold of Garion's arm. "Garion's my friend, Tor. I have no secrets from him."

"Lelldorin, please," Garion protested. "I'm not an Asturian—I'm not even an Arend. I don't want to know what you're planning."

"But you *will* know, Garion, as proof of my trust in you," Lelldorin declared. "Next summer, when Korodullin journeys to the ruined city of Vo Astur to hold court there for the six weeks that maintain the fiction of Arendish unity, we're going to ambush him on the highway."

"Lelldorin!" Torasin gasped, his face turning white.

But Lelldorin was already plunging on. "It won't be just a simple ambush, Garion. This will be a master stroke at Mimbre's heart. We're going to ambush him in the uniforms of Tolnedran legionnaires and cut him down with Tolnedran swords. Our attack will force Mimbre to declare war on the Tolnedran Empire, and Tolnedra will crush Mimbre like an eggshell. Mimbre will be destroyed, and Asturia will be free!"

"Nachak will have you killed for this, Lelldorin," Torasin cried. "We've all been sworn to secrecy on a blood oath."

"Tell the Murgo that I spit on his oath," Lelldorin said hotly. "What need have Asturian patriots for a Murgo henchman?"

"He's providing us with gold, you blockhead!" Torasin raged, almost beside himself. "We need his good red gold to buy the uniforms, the swords, and to strengthen the backbones of some of our weaker friends."

"I don't need weaklings with me," Lelldorin said intensely. "A patriot does what he does for love of his country—not for Angarak gold."

Garion's mind was moving quickly now. His moment of stunned amazement had passed. "There was a man in Cherek," he recalled. "The Earl of Jarvik. He also took Murgo gold and plotted to kill a king."

The two stared at him blankly.

"Something happens to a country when you kill its king," Garion explained. "No matter how bad the king is or how good the people are who kill him, the country falls apart for a while. Everything is confused, and there's nobody to point the country in any one direction. Then, if you start a war between that country and another one at the same time, you add just that much more confusion. I think that if I were a Murgo, that's exactly the kind of confusion I'd want to see in all the kingdoms of the West."

Garion listened to his own voice almost in amazement. There was a dry, dispassionate quality in it that he instantly recognized. From the time of his earliest memories that voice had always been there—inside his mind—occupying some quiet, hidden corner, telling him when he was wrong or foolish. But the voice had never actively interfered before in his dealings with other people. Now, however, it spoke directly to these two young men, patiently explaining.

"Angarak gold isn't what it seems to be," he went on. "There's a kind of power in it that corrupts you. Maybe that's why it's the color of blood. I'd think about that before I accepted any more red gold from this Murgo Nachak. Why do you suppose he's giving you gold and helping you with this plan of yours? He's not an Asturian, so patriotism couldn't have anything to do with it, could it? I'd think about that, too."

Lelldorin and his cousin looked suddenly troubled.

"I'm not going to say anything about this to anybody," Garion said. "You told me about it in confidence, and I really wasn't supposed to hear about it anyway. But remember that there's a lot more going on in the world right now than what's happening here in Arendia. Now I think I'd like to get some sleep. If you'll show me where my bed is, I'll leave you to talk things over all night, if you'd like."

All in all, Garion thought he'd handled the whole thing rather well. He'd planted a few doubts at the very least. He knew Arends well enough by now to realize that it probably wouldn't be enough to turn these two around, but it was a start.

CHAPTER FOUR

The following morning they rode out early while the mist still hung among the trees. Count Reldegen, wrapped in a dark cloak, stood at his gate to bid them farewell; and Torasin, standing beside his father, seemed unable to take his eyes off Garion's face. Garion kept his expression as blank as possible. The fiery young Asturian seemed to be filled with doubts, and those doubts might keep him from plunging headlong into something disastrous. It wasn't much, Garion realized, but it was the best he could manage under the circumstances.

"Come back soon, Belgarath," Reldegen said. "Sometime when you can stay longer. We're very isolated here, and I'd like to know what the rest of the world's doing. We'll sit by the fire and talk away a month or two."

Mister Wolf nodded gravely. "Maybe when this business of mine is over, Reldegen." Then he turned his horse and led the way across the wide clearing that surrounded Reldegen's house and back once again into the gloomy forest.

"The count's an unusual Arend," Silk said lightly as they rode along. "I think I actually detected an original thought or two in him last evening."

"He's changed a great deal," Wolf agreed.

"He sets a good table," Barak said. "I haven't felt this full since I left Val Alorn."

"You should," Aunt Pol told him. "You ate the biggest part of one deer by yourself."

"You're exaggerating, Polgara," Barak said.

"But not by very much," Hettar observed in his quiet voice.

Lelldorin had pulled his horse in beside Garion's, but he had not spoken. His face was as troubled as his cousin's had been. It was obvious that he wanted to say something and just as obvious that he didn't know how to begin.

"Go ahead," Garion said quietly. "We're good enough friends that I'm not going to be upset if it doesn't come out exactly right."

Lelldorin looked a little sheepish. "Am I really that obvious?"

"Honest is a better word for it," Garion told him. "You've just never learned to hide your feelings, that's all."

"Was it really true?" Lelldorin blurted. "I'm not doubting your word, but was there really a Murgo in Cherek plotting against King Anheg?"

"Ask Silk," Garion suggested, "or Barak, or Hettar—any of them. We were all there."

"Nachak isn't like that, though," Lelldorin said quickly, defensively.

"Can you be sure?" Garion asked him. "The plan was his in the first place, wasn't it? How did you happen to meet him?"

"We'd all gone down to the Great Fair, Torasin, me, several of the others. We bought some things from a Murgo merchant, and Tor made a few remarks about Mimbrates—you know how Tor is. The merchant said that he knew somebody we might be interested in meeting and he introduced us to Nachak. The more we talked with him, the more sympathetic he seemed to become to the way we felt."

"Naturally."

"He told us what the king is planning. You wouldn't believe it."

"Probably not."

Lelldorin gave him a quick, troubled look. "He's going to break up our estates and give them to landless Mimbrate nobles." He said it accusingly.

"Did you verify that with anybody but Nachak?"

"How could we? The Mimbrates wouldn't admit it if we confronted them with it, but it's the kind of thing Mimbrates *would* do."

"So you've only got Nachak's word for it? How did this plan of yours come up?"

"Nachak said that if he were an Asturian, he wouldn't let anybody take *his* land, but he said that it'd be too late to try to stop them when they came with knights and soldiers. He said that if he were doing it, he'd strike before they were ready and that he'd do it in such a way that the Mimbrates wouldn't know who'd done it. That's when he suggested the Tolnedran uniforms."

"When did he start giving you money?"

"I'm not sure. Tor handled that part of it."

"Did he ever say why he was giving you money?"

"He said it was out of friendship."

"Didn't that seem a little odd?"

"I'd give someone money out of friendship," Lelldorin protested.

"You're an Asturian," Garion told him. "You'd give somebody your life out of friendship. Nachak's a Murgo, though, and I've never heard that they were all that generous. What it comes down to, then, is that a stranger tells you that the king's planning to take your land. Then he gives you a plan to kill the king and start a war with Tolnedra; and to make sure you succeed with his plan, he gives you money. Is that about it?"

Lelldorin nodded mutely, his eyes stricken.

"Weren't any of you just the least bit suspicious?"

Lelldorin seemed almost about to cry. "It's such a *good* plan," he burst out finally. "It couldn't help but succeed."

"That's what makes it so dangerous," Garion replied.

"Garion, what am I going to do?" Lelldorin's voice was anguished.

"I don't think there's anything you can do right now," Garion told him. "Maybe later, after we've had time to think about it, we'll come up with something. If we can't, we can always tell my grandfather about it. He'll think of a way to stop it."

"We can't tell anybody," Lelldorin reminded him. "We're pledged to silence."

"We might have to break that pledge," Garion said somewhat reluctantly. "I don't see that either of us owes that Murgo anything, but it's going to have to be up to you. I won't say anything to anybody without your permission."

"*You* decide," Lelldorin pleaded then. "I can't do it, Garion."

"You're going to have to," Garion told him. "I'm sure that if you think about it, you'll see why."

They reached the Great West Road then, and Barak led them south at a brisk trot, cutting off the possibility of further discussion.

A league or so down the road they passed a muddy village, a dozen or so turf-roofed huts with walls made of wattles plastered over with mud. The fields around the village were dotted with tree stumps, and a few scrawny cows grazed near the edge of the forest. Garion could not control his indignation as he looked at the misery implicit in the crude collection of hovels. "Lelldorin," he said sharply, "look!"

"What? Where?" The blond young man came out of his troubled preoccupation quickly as if expecting some danger.

"The village," Garion told him. "Look at it."

"It's only a serfs' village," Lelldorin said indifferently. "I've seen hundreds like it." He seemed ready to return to his own inner turmoil.

"In Sendaria we wouldn't keep pigs in places like that." Garion's voice rang with fervor. If he could only make his friend *see!*

Two ragged serfs were dispiritedly hacking chunks of firewood from one of the stumps near the road. As the party approached, they dropped their axes and bolted in terror for the forest.

"Does it make you proud, Lelldorin?" Garion demanded. "Does it make you feel good to know that your own countrymen are so afraid of you that they run from the very sight of you?"

Lelldorin looked baffled. "They're *serfs*, Garion," he said as if that explained.

"They're men. They're not animals. Men deserve to be treated better."

"I can't do anything about it. They aren't *my* serfs." And with that Lelldorin's attention turned inward again as he continued to struggle with the dilemma Garion had placed upon him.

By late afternoon they had covered ten leagues and the cloudy sky was gradually darkening as evening approached. "I think we're going to have to spend the night in the forest, Belgarath," Silk said, looking around. "There's no chance of reaching the next Tolnedran hostel."

Mister Wolf had been half-dozing in his saddle. He looked up, blinking a bit. "All right," he replied, "but let's get back from the road a bit. Our fire could attract attention, and too many people know we're in Arendia already."

"There's a woodcutter's track right there." Durnik pointed at a break in the trees just ahead. "It should lead us back into the trees."

"All right," Wolf agreed.

The sound of their horses' hooves was muffled by the sodden leaves on the forest floor as they turned in among the trees to follow the narrow track. They rode silently for the better part of a mile until a clearing opened ahead of them.

"How about here?" Durnik asked. He indicated a brook trickling softly over mossy stones on one side of the clearing.

"It will do," Wolf agreed.

"We're going to need shelter," the smith observed.

"I bought tents in Camaar," Silk told him. "They're in the packs."

"That was foresighted of you," Aunt Pol complimented him.

"I've been in Arendia before, my Lady. I'm familiar with the weather."

"Garion and I'll go get wood for a fire, then," Durnik said, climbing down from his horse and untying his axe from his saddle.

"I'll help you," Lelldorin offered, his face still troubled.

Durnik nodded and led the way off into the trees. The woods were soaked, but the smith seemed to know almost instinctively where to find dry fuel. They worked quickly in the lowering twilight and soon had three large bundles of limbs and fagots. They returned to the clearing where Silk and the others were erecting several dun-colored tents. Durnik dropped his wood and cleared a space for the fire with his foot. Then he knelt and began striking sparks with his knife from a piece of flint into a wad of dry tinder he always carried. In a short time he had a small fire going, and Aunt Pol set out her pots beside it, humming softly to herself.

Hettar came back from tending the horses, and they all stood back watching Aunt Pol prepare a supper from the stores Count Reldegen had pressed on them before they had left his house that morning.

After they had eaten, they sat around the fire talking quietly. "How far have we come today?" Durnik asked.

"Twelve leagues," Hettar estimated.

"How much farther do we have to go to get out of the forest?"

"It's eighty leagues from Camaar to the central plain," Lelldorin replied.

Durnik sighed. "A week or more. I'd hoped that it'd be only a few days."

"I know what you mean, Durnik," Barak agreed. "It's gloomy under all these trees."

The horses, picketed near the brook, stirred uneasily. Hettar rose to his feet.

"Something wrong?" Barak asked, also rising.

"They shouldn't be—" Hettar started. Then he stopped. "Back!" he snapped. "Away from the fire. The horses say there are men out there. Many—with weapons." He jumped back from the fire, drawing his sabre.

Lelldorin took one startled look at him and bolted for one of the tents. Garion's sudden disappointment in his friend was almost like a blow to the stomach.

An arrow buzzed into the light and shattered on Barak's mail shirt. "Arm yourselves!" the big man roared, drawing his sword.

Garion grasped Aunt Pol's sleeve and tried to pull her from the light.

"Stop that!" she snapped, jerking her sleeve free. Another arrow whizzed out of the foggy woods. Aunt Pol flicked her hand as if brushing away a fly and muttered a single word. The arrow bounced back as if it had struck something solid and fell to the ground.

Then with a hoarse shout, a gang of rough, burly men burst from the edge of the trees and splashed across the brook, brandishing swords. As Barak and Hettar leaped forward to meet them, Lelldorin reemerged from the tent with his bow and began loosing arrows so rapidly that his hands seemed to blur as they moved. Garion was instantly ashamed that he had doubted his friend's courage.

With a choked cry, one of the attackers stumbled back, an arrow through his throat. Another doubled over sharply, clutching at his stomach, and fell to the ground, groaning. A third, quite young and with a pale, downy beard on his cheeks, dropped heavily and sat plucking at the feathers on the shaft protruding from his chest with a bewildered expression on his boyish face. Then he sighed and slumped over on his side with a stream of blood coming from his nose.

The ragged-looking men faltered under the rain of Lelldorin's arrows, and then Barak and Hettar were upon them. With a great sweep, Barak's heavy sword shattered an upflung blade and crunched down into the angle between the neck and shoulder of the black-whiskered man who had held it. The man collapsed. Hettar made a quick feint with his sabre, then ran it smoothly through the body of a pockmarked ruffian. The man stiffened, and a gush of bright blood burst from his mouth as Hettar pulled out his blade. Durnik ran forward with his axe, and Silk drew his long dagger from under his vest and ran directly at a man with a shaggy brown beard. At the last moment, he dived forward, rolled and struck the bearded man full in the chest with both feet. Without pausing he came up and ripped his dagger into his enemy's belly. The dagger made a wet, tearing sound as it sliced upward, and the stricken man clutched at his stomach with a scream, trying to hold in the blue-colored loops and coils of his entrails that seemed to come boiling out through his fingers.

Garion dived for the packs to get his own sword, but was suddenly grabbed roughly from behind. He struggled for an instant, then felt a stunning blow on the back of his head, and his eyes filled with a blinding flash of light.

"This is the one we want," a rough voice rasped as Garion sank into unconsciousness.

HE WAS BEING carried—that much was certain. He could feel the strong arms under him. He didn't know how long it had been since he had been struck on the head. His ears still rang, and he was more than a little sick to his stomach. He stayed limp, but carefully opened one eye. His vision was blurred and uncertain, but he could make out Barak's bearded face looming above him in the darkness, and merged with it, as once before in the snowy woods outside Val Alorn, he seemed to see the shaggy face of a great bear. He closed his eyes, shuddered, and started to struggle weakly.

"It's all right, Garion," Barak said, his voice sunk in a kind of despair. "It's me."

Garion opened his eyes again, and the bear seemed to be gone. He wasn't even sure he had ever really seen it.

"Are you all right?" Barak asked, setting him on the ground.

"They hit me on the head," Garion mumbled, his hand going to the swelling behind his ear.

"They won't do it again," Barak muttered, his tone still despairing. Then the huge man sank to the ground and buried his face in his hands. It was dark and difficult to see, but it looked as if Barak's shoulders were shaking with a kind of terrible suppressed grief—a soundless, wrenching series of convulsive sobs.

"Where are we?" Garion asked, looking around into the darkness.

Barak coughed and wiped at his face. "Quite a ways from the tents. It took me a little while to catch up to the two who were carrying you off."

"What happened?" Garion was still a bit confused.

"They're dead. Can you stand up?"

"I don't know." Garion tried to get up, but a wave of giddiness swept over him, and his stomach churned.

"Never mind. I'll carry you," Barak said in a now grimly practical voice. An owl screeched from a nearby tree, and its ghostly white shape drifted off through the trees ahead of them. As Barak lifted him, Garion closed his eyes and concentrated on keeping his stomach under control.

Before long they came out into the clearing and its circle of firelight. "Is he all right?" Aunt Pol asked, looking up from bandaging a cut on Durnik's arm.

"A bump on the head is all," Barak replied, setting Garion down. "Did you run them off?" His voice was harsh, even brutal.

"Those that could still run," Silk answered, his voice a bit excited and his ferret eyes bright. "They left a few behind." He pointed at a number of still shapes lying near the edge of the firelight.

Lelldorin came back into the clearing, looking over his shoulder and with his bow half-drawn. He was out of breath, his face was pale, and his hands were shaking. "Are you all right?" he asked as soon as he saw Garion.

Garion nodded, gently fingering the lump behind his ear.

"I tried to find the two who took you," the young man declared, "but they were too quick for me. There's some kind of animal out there. I heard it growling while I was looking for you—awful growls."

"The beast is gone now," Barak told him flatly.

"What's the matter with you?" Silk asked the big man.

"Nothing."

"Who were these men?" Garion asked.

"Robbers, most likely," Silk surmised, putting away his dagger. "It's one of the benefits of a society that holds men in serfdom. They get bored with being serfs and go out into the forest looking for excitement and profit."

"You sound just like Garion," Lelldorin objected. "Can't you people understand that serfdom's part of the natural order of things here? Our serfs couldn't take care of themselves alone, so those of us in higher station accept the responsibility of caring for them."

"Of course you do," Silk agreed sarcastically. "They're not so well-fed as your pigs nor as well-kenneled as your dogs, but you do care for them, don't you?"

"That'll do, Silk," Aunt Pol said coolly. "Let's not start bickering among ourselves." She tied a last knot on Durnik's bandage and came over to examine Garion's head. She touched her fingers gently to the lump, and he winced. "It doesn't seem too serious," she observed.

"It hurts all the same," he complained.

"Of course it does, dear," she said calmly. She dipped a cloth in a pail of cold water and held it to the lump. "You're going to have to learn to protect your head, Garion. If you keep banging it like this, you're going to soften your brains."

Garion was about to answer that, but Hettar and Mister Wolf came back into the firelight just then. "They're still running," Hettar announced. The steel discs on his horsehide jacket gleamed red in the flickering light, and his sabre was streaked with blood.

"They seemed to be awfully good at that part of it," Wolf said. "Is everyone all right?"

"A few bumps and bruises is about all," Aunt Pol told him. "It could have been much worse."

"Let's not start worrying about what could have been."

"Shall we remove those?" Barak growled, pointing at the bodies littering the ground near the brook.

"Shouldn't they be buried?" Durnik asked. His voice shook a little, and his face was very pale.

"Too much trouble," Barak said bluntly. "Their friends can come back later and take care of it—if they feel like it."

"Isn't that just a little uncivilized?" Durnik objected.

Barak shrugged. "It's customary."

Mister Wolf rolled one of the bodies over and carefully examined the dead man's gray face. "Looks like an ordinary Arendish outlaw," he grunted. "It's hard to say for sure, though."

Lelldorin was retrieving his arrows, carefully pulling them out of the bodies.

"Let's drag them all over there a ways," Barak said to Hettar. "I'm getting tired of looking at them."

Durnik looked away, and Garion saw two great tears standing in his eyes. "Does it hurt, Durnik?" he asked sympathetically, sitting on the log beside his friend.

"I killed one of those men, Garion," the smith replied in a shaking voice. "I hit him in the face with my axe. He screamed, and his blood splashed all over me. Then he fell down and kicked on the ground with his heels until he died."

"You didn't have any choice, Durnik," Garion told him. "They were trying to kill us."

"I've never killed anyone before," Durnik said, the tears now running down his face. "He kicked the ground for such a long time—such a terribly long time."

"Why don't you go to bed, Garion?" Aunt Pol suggested firmly. Her eyes were on Durnik's tear-streaked face.

Garion understood. "Good night, Durnik," he said. He got up and started toward one of the tents. He glanced back once. Aunt Pol had seated herself on the log beside the smith and was speaking quietly to him with one of her arms comfortingly about his shoulders.

CHAPTER FIVE

The fire had burned down to a tiny orange flicker outside the tent, and the forest around the clearing was silent. Garion lay with a throbbing head trying to sleep. Finally, long past midnight, he gave it up. He slid out from under his blanket and went searching for Aunt Pol.

Above the silvery fog a full moon had risen, and its light made the mist luminous. The air around him seemed almost to glow as he picked his way carefully through the silent camp. He scratched on the outside of her tent flap and whispered, "Aunt Pol?" There was no answer. "Aunt Pol," he whispered a bit louder, "it's me, Garion. May I come in?" There was still no answer, nor even the faintest sound. Carefully he pulled back the flap and peered inside. The tent was empty.

Puzzled, even a bit alarmed, he turned and looked around the clearing. Hettar stood watch not far from the picketed horses, his hawk face turned toward the foggy forest and his cape drawn about him. Garion hesitated a moment and then stepped quietly behind the tents. He angled down through the trees and the filmy, luminous fog toward the brook, thinking that if he bathed his aching head in the cold water it might help. He was about fifty yards from the tents when he saw a faint movement among the trees ahead. He stopped.

A huge gray wolf padded out of the fog and stopped in the center of a small open space among the trees. Garion drew in his breath sharply and froze beside a large, twisted oak. The wolf sat down on the damp leaves as if he were waiting for something. The glowing fog illuminated details Garion would not have been able to see on an ordinary night. The wolf's ruff and shoulders were silvery, and his muzzle was shot with gray. He carried his age with enormous dignity, and his yellow eyes seemed calm and very wise somehow.

Garion stood absolutely still. He knew that the slightest sound would instantly reach the sharp ears of the wolf, but it was more than that. The blow behind his ear had made him light-headed, and the strange glow of moon-drenched fog made this encounter seem somehow unreal. He found that he was holding his breath.

A large, snowy white owl swooped over the open space among the trees on ghosting wings, settled on a low branch and perched there, looking down at the wolf with an unblinking stare. The gray wolf looked calmly back at the perched bird. Then, though there was no breath of wind, it seemed somehow that a sudden eddy in the shimmering fog made the figures of the owl and the wolf hazy and indistinct. When it cleared again, Mister Wolf stood in the center of the opening, and Aunt Pol in her gray gown was seated rather sedately on the limb above him.

"It's been a long time since we've hunted together, Polgara," the old man said.

"Yes, it has, father." She raised her arms and pushed her fingers through the long, dark weight of her hair. "I'd almost forgotten what it was like." She seemed to shudder then with a strange kind of pleasure. "It's a very good night for it."

"A little damp," he replied, shaking one foot.

"It's very clear above the treetops, and the stars are particularly bright. It's a splendid night for flying."

"I'm glad you enjoyed yourself. Did you happen to remember what you were supposed to be doing?"

"Don't be sarcastic, father."

"Well?"

"There's no one in the vicinity but Arends, and most of them are asleep."

"You're sure?"

"Of course. There isn't a Grolim for five leagues in any direction. Did you find the ones you were looking for?"

"They weren't hard to follow," Wolf answered. "They're staying in a cave about three leagues deeper into the forest. Another one of them died on their way back there, and a couple more probably won't live until morning. The rest of them seemed a little bitter about the way things turned out."

"I can imagine. Did you get close enough to hear what they were saying?"

He nodded. "There's a man in one of the villages nearby who watches the road and lets them know when somebody passes by who might be worth robbing."

"Then they're just ordinary thieves?"

"Not exactly. They were watching for us in particular. We'd all been described to them in rather complete detail."

"I think I'll go talk to this villager," she said grimly. She flexed her fingers in an unpleasantly suggestive manner.

"It's not worth the time it'd take," Wolf told her, scratching thoughtfully at his beard. "All he'd be able to tell you is that some Murgo offered him gold. Grolims don't bother to explain very much to their hirelings."

"We should attend to him, father," she insisted. "We don't want him lurking behind us, trying to buy up every brigand in Arendia to send after us."

"After tomorrow he won't buy much of anything," Wolf replied with a short laugh. "His friends plan to lure him out into the woods in the morning and cut his throat for him—among other things."

"Good. I'd like to know who the Grolim is, though."

Wolf shrugged. "What difference does it make? There are dozens of them in northern Arendia, all stirring up as much trouble as they can. They know what's coming as well as we do. We can't expect them to just sit back and let us pass."

"Shouldn't we put a stop to it?"

"We don't have the time," he said. "It takes forever to explain things to Arends. If we move fast enough, maybe we can slip by before the Grolims are ready."

"And if we can't?"

"Then we'll do it the other way. I've got to get to Zedar before he crosses into Cthol Murgos. If too many things get in my way, I'll have to be more direct."

"You should have done that from the beginning, father. Sometimes you're too delicate about things."

"Are you going to start that again? That's always your answer to everything, Polgara. You're forever fixing things that would fix themselves if you'd just leave them alone, and changing things when they don't have to be changed."

"Don't be cross, father. Help me down."

"Why not fly down?" he suggested.

"Don't be absurd."

Garion slipped away among the mossy trees, trembling violently as he went.

When Aunt Pol and Mister Wolf returned to the clearing, they roused the others. "I think we'd better move on," Wolf told them. "We're a little vulnerable out here. It's safer on the highway, and I'd like to get past this particular stretch of woods."

The dismantling of their night's encampment took less than an hour, and they started back along the woodcutter's track toward the Great West Road. Though it was still some hours before dawn, the moon-bathed fog filled the night with misty luminosity, and it seemed almost as if they rode through a shining cloud that had settled among the dark trees. They reached the highway and turned south again.

"I'd like to be a good way from here when the sun comes up," Wolf said quietly, "but we don't want to blunder into anything, so keep your eyes and ears open."

They set off at a canter and had covered a good three leagues by the time the fog had begun to turn a pearly gray with the approach of morning. As they rounded a broad curve, Hettar suddenly raised his arm, signaling for a halt.

"What's wrong?" Barak asked him.

"Horses ahead," Hettar replied. "Coming this way."

"Are you sure? I don't hear anything."

"Forty at least," Hettar answered firmly.

"There," Durnik said, his head cocked to one side. "Hear that?"

Faintly they all heard a jingling clatter some distance off in the fog.

"We could hide in the woods until they've passed," Lelldorin suggested.

"It's better to stay on the road," Wolf replied.

"Let me handle it," Silk said confidently, moving into the lead. "I've done this sort of thing before." They proceeded at a careful walk.

The riders who emerged from the fog were encased in steel. They wore full suits of polished armor and round helmets with pointed visors that made them look strangely like huge insects. They carried long lances with colored pennons at their tips, and their horses were massive beasts, also encased in armor.

"Mimbrate knights," Lelldorin snarled, his eyes going flat.

"Keep your feelings to yourself," Wolf told the young man. "If any of them say anything to you, answer in such a way that they'll think you're a Mimbrate sympathizer—like young Berentain back at your uncle's house."

Lelldorin's face hardened.

"Do as he tells you, Lelldorin," Aunt Pol said. "This isn't the time for heroics."

"Hold!" the leader of the armored column commanded, lowering his lance until the steel point was leveled at them. "Let one come forward so that I may speak with him." The knight's tone was peremptory.

Silk moved toward the steel-cased man, his smile ingratiating. "We're glad to see you, Sir Knight," he lied glibly. "We were set upon by robbers last night, and we've been riding in fear of our lives."

"What is thy name?" the knight demanded, raising his visor, "and who are these who accompany thee?"

"I am Radek of Boktor, my Lord," Silk answered, bowing and pulling off his velvet cap, "a merchant of Drasnia bound for Tol Honeth with Sendarian woolens in hopes of catching the winter market."

The armored man's eyes narrowed suspiciously. "Thy party seems over-large for so simple an undertaking, worthy merchant."

"The three there are my servants," Silk told him, pointing at Barak, Hettar, and Durnik. "The old man and the boy serve my sister, a widow of independent means who accompanies me so that she might visit Tol Honeth."

"What of the other?" the knight pressed. "The Asturian?"

"A young nobleman traveling to Vo Mimbre to visit friends there. He graciously consented to guide us through this forest."

The knight's suspicion seemed to relax a bit. "Thou madest mention of robbers," he said. "Where did this ambush take place?"

"About three or four leagues back. They set upon us after we had made our night's encampment. We managed to beat them off, but my sister was terrified."

"This province of Asturia seethes with rebellion and brigandage," the knight said sternly. "My men and I are sent to suppress such offenses. Come here, Asturian."

Lelldorin's nostrils flared, but he obediently came forward.

"I will require thy name of thee."

"My name is Lelldorin, Sir Knight. How may I serve thee?"

"These robbers thy friends spoke of—were they commons or men of quality?"

"Serfs, my Lord," Lelldorin replied, "ragged and uncouth. Doubtless fled from lawful submission to their masters to take up outlawry in the forest."

"How may we expect duty and proper submission from serfs when nobles raise detestable rebellion against the crown?" the knight asserted.

"Truly, my Lord," Lelldorin agreed with a show of sadness that was a trifle overdone. "Much have I argued that selfsame point with those who speak endlessly of Mimbrate oppression and o'erweening arrogance. My appeals for reason and dutiful respect for His Majesty, our Lord King, however, are greeted with derision and cold despite." He sighed.

"Thy wisdom becomes thee, young Lelldorin," the knight approved. "Regrettably, I must detain thee and thy companions in order that we may verify certain details."

"Sir Knight!" Silk protested vigorously. "A change in the weather could destroy the value of my merchandise in Tol Honeth. I pray you, don't de-lay me."

"I regret the necessity, good merchant," the knight replied, "but Asturia is filled with dissemblers and plotters. I can permit none to pass without me-ticulous examination."

There was a stir at the rear of the Mimbrate column. In single file, re-splendent in burnished breastplates, plumed helmets and crimson capes, a half a hundred Tolnedran legionnaires rode slowly along the flank of the armored knights. "What seems to be the problem here?" the legion com-mander, a lean, leather-faced man of forty or so, asked politely as he stopped not far from Silk's horse.

"We do not require the assistance of the legions in this matter," the knight said coldly. "Our orders are from Vo Mimbre. We are sent to help re-store order in Asturia and we were questioning these travelers to that end."

"I have a great respect for order, Sir Knight," the Tolnedran replied, "but the security of the highway is *my* responsibility." He looked inquir-ingly at Silk.

"I am Radek of Boktor, Captain," Silk told him, "a Drasnian merchant bound for Tol Honeth. I have documents, if you wish to see them."

"Documents are easily forged," the knight declared.

"So they are," the Tolnedran agreed, "but to save time, I make it a prac-tice to accept all documents at face value. A Drasnian merchant with goods in his packs has a legitimate reason to be on an Imperial Highway, Sir Knight. There's no reason to detain him, is there?"

"We seek to stamp out banditry and rebellion," the knight asserted hotly.

"Stamp away," the captain said, "but *off* the highway, if you don't mind. By treaty the Imperial Highway is Tolnedran territory. What you do once you're fifty yards back in the trees is your affair; what happens on this road is *mine*. I'm certain that no true Mimbrate knight would want to humiliate his king by violating a solemn agreement between the Arendish crown and the Emperor of Tolnedra, would he?"

The knight looked at him helplessly.

"I think you should proceed, good merchant," the Tolnedran told Silk. "I know that all Tol Honeth awaits your arrival breathlessly."

Silk grinned at him and bowed floridly in his saddle. Then he gestured to the others and they all rode slowly past the fuming Mimbrate knight. After they had passed, the legionnaires closed ranks across the highway, ef-fectively cutting off any pursuit.

"Good man there," Barak said. "I don't think much of Tolnedrans ordi-narily, but that one's different."

"Let's move right along," Mister Wolf said. "I'd rather not have those knights doubling back on us after the Tolnedrans leave."

They pushed their horses into a gallop and rode on, leaving the knights behind, arguing heatedly with the legion commander in the middle of the road.

They stayed that night at a thick-walled Tolnedran hostel, and for per-haps the first time in his life Garion bathed without the insistence or even the suggestion of his aunt. Though he had not had the chance to become directly involved in the fight in the clearing the night before, he felt somehow as if he were spattered with blood or worse. He had not before realized how grotesquely men could be mutilated in close fighting. Watching a living man disemboweled or brained had filled him with a kind of deep shame that the ultimate inner secrets of the human body could be so grossly exposed. He felt unclean. He removed his clothing in the chilly bathhouse and even, without thinking, the silver amulet Mister Wolf and Aunt Pol had given him, and then he entered the steaming tub where he scrubbed at his skin with a coarse brush and strong soap, much harder than even the most meticulous obsession with personal cleanliness would have required.

For the next several days they moved southward at a steady pace, stopping each night at the evenly spaced Tolnedran hostels where the presence of the hard-faced legionnaires was a continual reminder that all the might of Imperial Tolnedra guaranteed the safety of travelers who sought refuge there.

On the sixth day after the fight in the forest, however, Lelldorin's horse pulled up lame. Durnik and Hettar, under Aunt Pol's supervision, spent several hours brewing poultices over a small fire by the roadside and applying steaming compresses to the animal's leg while Wolf fumed at the delay. By the time the horse was fit to continue, they all realized that there was no chance to reach the next hostel before dark.

"Well, Old Wolf," Aunt Pol said after they had remounted, "what now? Do we ride on at night, or do we try to take shelter in the forest again?"

"I haven't decided," Wolf answered shortly.

"If I remember right, there's a village not far ahead," Lelldorin, now mounted on an Algar horse, stated. "It's a poor place, but I think it has an inn—of sorts."

"That sounds ominous," Silk said. "What exactly do you mean by 'of sorts'?"

"The Lord of this demesne is notoriously greedy," Lelldorin replied. "His taxes are crushing, and his people have little left for themselves. The inn isn't good."

"We'll have to chance it," Wolf decided, and led them off at a brisk trot. As they approached the village, the heavy clouds began to clear off, and the sun broke through wanly.

The village was even worse than Lelldorin's description had led them to believe. A half-dozen ragged beggars stood in the mud on the outskirts, their hands held out imploringly and their voices shrill. The houses were nothing more than rude hovels oozing smoke from the pitiful fires within. Scrawny pigs rooted in the muddy streets, and the stench of the place was awful.

A funeral procession slogged through the mud toward the burial ground on the other side of the village. The corpse, carried on a board, was wrapped in a ragged brown blanket, and the richly robed and cowled priests of Chaldan, the Arendish God, chanted an age-old hymn that had much to do with war and vengeance, but little to do with comfort. The widow, a whimpering infant at her breast, followed the body, her face blank and her eyes dead.

The inn smelled of stale beer and half-rotten food. A fire had destroyed one end of the common room, charring and blackening the low-beamed ceiling. The gaping hole in the burned wall was curtained off with a sheet of rotting canvas. The fire pit in the center of the room smoked, and the hard-faced innkeeper was surly. For supper he offered only bowls of watery gruel—a mixture of barley and turnips.

"Charming," Silk said sardonically, pushing away his untouched bowl. "I'm a bit surprised at you, Lelldorin. Your passion for correcting wrongs seems to have overlooked this place. Might I suggest that your next crusade include a visit to the Lord of this demesne? His hanging seems long overdue."

"I hadn't realized it was so bad," Lelldorin replied in a subdued voice. He looked around as if seeing certain things for the first time. A kind of sick horror began to show itself in his transparent face.

Garion, his stomach churning, stood up. "I think I'll go outside," he declared.

"Not too far," Aunt Pol warned.

The air outside was at least somewhat cleaner, and Garion picked his way carefully toward the edge of the village, trying to avoid the worst of the mud.

"Please, my Lord," a little girl with huge eyes begged, "have you a crust of bread to spare?"

Garion looked at her helplessly. "I'm sorry." He fumbled through his clothes, looking for something to give her, but the child began to cry and turned away.

In the stump-dotted field beyond the stinking streets, a ragged boy about Garion's own age was playing a wooden flute as he watched a few scrubby cows. The melody he played was heartbreakingly pure, drifting unnoticed among the hovels squatting in the slanting rays of the pale sun. The boy saw him, but did not break off his playing. Their eyes met with a kind of grave recognition, but they did not speak.

At the edge of the forest beyond the field, a dark-robed and hooded man astride a black horse came out of the trees and sat watching the village. There was something ominous about the dark figure, and something vaguely familiar as well. It seemed somehow to Garion that he should know who the rider was, but, though his mind groped for a name, it tantalizingly eluded him. He looked at the figure at the edge of the woods for a long time, noticing without even being aware of it that though the horse and rider stood in the full light of the setting sun, there was no shadow behind them. Deep in his mind something tried to shriek at him, but, all bemused, he merely watched. He would not say anything to Aunt Pol or the others about the figure at the edge of the woods because there was nothing to say; as soon as he turned his back, he would forget.

The light began to fade, and, because he had begun to shiver, he turned to go back to the inn with the aching song of the boy's flute soaring toward the sky above him.

CHAPTER SIX

Despite the promise of the brief sunset, the next day dawned cold and murky with a chill drizzle that wreathed down among the trees and made the entire forest sodden and gloomy. They left the inn early and soon entered a part of the wood that seemed more darkly foreboding than even the ominous stretches through which they had previously passed. The trees here were enormous, and many vast, gnarled oaks lifted their bare limbs among the dark firs and spruces. The forest floor was covered with a kind of gray moss that looked diseased and unwholesome.

Lelldorin had spoken little that morning, and Garion assumed that his friend was still struggling with the problem of Nachak's scheme. The young Asturian rode along, wrapped in his heavy green cloak, his reddish-gold hair damp and dispirited-looking in the steady drizzle. Garion pulled in beside his friend, and they rode silently for a while. "What's troubling you, Lelldorin?" he asked finally.

"I think that all my life I've been blind, Garion," Lelldorin replied.

"Oh? In what way?" Garion said it carefully, hoping that his friend had finally decided to tell Mister Wolf everything.

"I saw only Mimbre's oppression of Asturia. I never saw our own oppression of our own people."

"I've been trying to tell you that," Garion pointed out. "What made you see it finally?"

"That village where we stayed last night," Lelldorin explained. "I've never seen so poor and mean a place—or people crushed into such hopeless misery. How can they bear it?"

"Do they have any choice?"

"My father at least looks after the people on his land," the young man asserted defensively. "No one goes hungry or without shelter—but those people are treated worse than animals. I've always been proud of my station, but now it makes me ashamed." Tears actually stood in his eyes.

Garion was not sure how to deal with his friend's sudden awakening. On the one hand, he was glad that Lelldorin had finally seen what had always been obvious; but on the other, he was more than a little afraid of what this newfound perception might cause his mercurial companion to leap into.

"I'll renounce my rank," Lelldorin declared suddenly, as if he had been listening to Garion's thoughts, "and when I return from this quest, I'll go among the serfs and share their lives—their sorrows."

"What good will that do? How would your suffering in any way make theirs less?"

Lelldorin looked up sharply, a half-dozen emotions chasing each other across his open face. Finally he smiled, but there was a determination in his blue eyes. "You're right, of course," he said. "You always are. It's amazing how you can always see directly to the heart of a problem, Garion."

"Just what have you got in mind?" Garion asked a little apprehensively.

"I'll lead them in revolt. I'll sweep across Arendia with an army of serfs at my back." His voice rang as his imagination fired with the idea.

Garion groaned. "Why is that always your answer to everything, Lelldorin?" he demanded. "In the first place, the serfs don't have any weapons and they don't know how to fight. No matter how hard you talk, you'd never get them to follow you. In the second place, if they did, every nobleman in Arendia would join ranks against you. They'd butcher your army; and afterward, things would be ten times worse. In the third place, you'd just be starting another civil war; and that's exactly what the Murgos want."

Lelldorin blinked several times as Garion's words sank in. His face gradually grew mournful again. "I hadn't thought of that," he confessed.

"I didn't think you had. You're going to keep making these mistakes as long as you keep carrying your brain in the same scabbard with your sword, Lelldorin."

Lelldorin flushed at that, and then he laughed ruefully. "That's a pointed way of putting it, Garion," he said reproachfully.

"I'm sorry," Garion apologized quickly. "Maybe I should have said it another way."

"No," Lelldorin told him. "I'm an Arend. I tend to miss things if they aren't said directly."

"It's not that you're stupid, Lelldorin," Garion protested. "That's a mistake everyone makes. Arends aren't stupid—they're just impulsive."

"All *this* was more than just impulsiveness," Lelldorin insisted sadly, gesturing out at the damp moss lying under the trees.

"This what?" Garion asked, looking around.

"This is the last stretch of forest before we come out on the plains of central Arendia," Lelldorin explained. "It's the natural boundary between Mimbre and Asturia."

"The woods look the same as all the rest," Garion observed, looking around.

"Not really," Lelldorin said somberly. "This was the favorite ground for ambush. The floor of this forest is carpeted with old bones. Look there." He pointed.

At first it seemed to Garion that what his friend indicated was merely a pair of twisted sticks protruding from the moss with the twigs at their ends entangled in a scrubby bush. Then, with revulsion, he realized that they were the greenish bones of a human arm, the fingers clutched at the bush in a last convulsive agony. Outraged, he demanded, "Why didn't they bury him?"

"It would take a thousand men a thousand years to gather all the bones that lie here and commit them to earth," Lelldorin intoned morbidly. "Whole generations of Arendia rest here—Mimbrate, Wacite, Asturian. All lie where they fell, and the moss blankets their endless slumber."

Garion shuddered and pulled his eyes away from the mute appeal of that lone arm rising from the sea of moss on the floor of the forest. The curious lumps and hummocks of that moss suggested the horror which lay moldering beneath. As he raised his eyes, he realized that the uneven surface extended as far as he could see. "How long until we reach the plain?" he asked in a hushed voice.

"Two days, probably."

"*Two days?* And it's all like *this?*"

Lelldorin nodded.

"*Why?*" Garion's tone was harsher, more accusing than he'd intended.

"At first for pride—and honor," Lelldorin replied. "Later for grief and revenge. Finally it was simply because we didn't know how to stop. As you said before, sometimes we Arends aren't very bright."

"But always brave," Garion answered quickly.

"Oh yes," Lelldorin admitted. "Always brave. It's our national curse."

"Belgarath," Hettar said quietly from behind them, "the horses smell something."

Mister Wolf roused himself from the doze in which he usually rode. "What?"

"The horses," Hettar repeated. "Something out there's frightening them."

Wolf's eyes narrowed and then grew strangely blank. After a moment he drew in a sharp breath with a muttered curse. "Algroths," he swore.

"What's an Algroth?" Durnik asked.

"A non-human—somewhat distantly related to Trolls."

"I saw a Troll once," Barak said. "A big ugly thing with claws and fangs."

"Will they attack us?" Durnik asked.

"Almost certainly." Wolf's voice was tense. "Hettar, you're going to have to keep the horses under control. We don't dare get separated."

"Where did they come from?" Lelldorin asked. "There aren't any monsters in this forest."

"They come down out of the mountains of Ulgo sometimes when they get hungry," Wolf answered. "They don't leave survivors to report their presence."

"You'd better do something, father," Aunt Pol said. "They're all around us."

Lelldorin looked quickly around as if getting his bearings. "We're not far from Elgon's tor," he offered. "We might be able to hold them off if we get there."

"Elgon's tor?" Barak said. He had already drawn his heavy sword.

"It's a high hillock covered with boulders," Lelldorin explained. "It's almost like a fort. Elgon held it for a month against a Mimbrate army."

"Sounds promising," Silk said. "It'd get us out of the trees at least." He looked nervously around at the forest looming about them in the drizzling rain.

"Let's try for it," Wolf decided. "They haven't worked themselves up to the point of attacking yet, and the rain's confusing their sense of smell."

A strange barking sound came from back in the forest. "Is that them?" Garion asked, his voice sounding shrill in his own ears.

"They're calling to each other," Wolf told him. "Some of them have seen us. Let's pick up the pace a bit, but don't start running until we see the tor."

They nudged their nervous horses into a trot and moved steadily along the muddy road as it began to climb toward the top of a low ridge. "Half a league," Lelldorin said tensely. "Half a league and we should see the tor."

The horses were difficult to hold in, and their eyes rolled wildly at the surrounding woods. Garion felt his heart pounding, and his mouth was suddenly dry. It started to rain a bit harder. He caught a movement out of the corner of his eye and looked quickly. A manlike figure was loping along parallel to the road about a hundred paces back in the forest. It ran half-crouched, its hands touching the ground. It seemed to be a loathsome gray color. "Over there!" Garion cried.

"I saw him," Barak growled. "Not quite as big as a Troll."

Silk grimaced. "Big enough."

"If they attack, be careful of their claws," Wolf warned. "They're venomous."

"That's exciting," Silk said.

"There's the tor," Aunt Pol announced quite calmly.

"Let's run!" Wolf barked.

The frightened horses, suddenly released, leaped forward and fled up the road, their hoofs churning. An enraged howl came from the woods behind them, and the barking sound grew louder all around them.

"We're going to make it!" Durnik shouted in encouragement. But suddenly a half-dozen snarling Algroths were in the road in front of them, their arms spread wide and their mouths gaping hideously. They were huge, with apelike arms and claws instead of fingers. Their faces were goatish, surmounted by short, sharp-pointed horns, and they had long, yellow fangs. Their gray skin was scaly, reptilian.

The horses screamed and reared, trying to bolt. Garion clung to his saddle with one hand and fought the reins with the other.

Barak beat at his horse's rump with the flat of his sword and kicked savagely at the animal's flanks until the horse, finally more afraid of him than the Algroths, charged. With two great sweeps, one to either side, Barak killed two of the beasts as he plunged through. A third, claws outstretched, tried to leap on his back, but stiffened and collapsed facedown in the mud with one of Lelldorin's arrows between its shoulders. Barak wheeled his horse and chopped at the three remaining creatures. "Let's go!" he bellowed.

Garion heard Lelldorin gasp and turned quickly. With sick horror he saw that a lone Algroth had crept out of the woods beside the road and was clawing at his friend, trying to hook him out of the saddle. Weakly, Lelldorin beat at the goat face with his bow. Garion desperately drew his sword, but Hettar, coming from behind, was already there. His curved sabre ran through the beast's body, and the Algroth shrieked and fell writhing to the ground beneath the pounding hoofs of the pack animals.

The horses, running now in sheer panic, scrambled toward the slope of the boulder-strewn tor. Garion glanced back over his shoulder and saw Lelldorin swaying dangerously in his saddle, his hand pressed to his bleeding side. Garion pulled in savagely on his reins and turned his horse.

"Save yourself, Garion!" Lelldorin shouted, his face deadly pale.

"No!" Garion sheathed his sword, pulled in beside his friend and took his arm, steadying him in the saddle. Together they galloped toward the tor with Garion straining to hold the injured young man.

The tor was a great jumble of earth and stone thrusting up above the tallest trees around it. Their horses scrambled and clattered up the side among the wet boulders. When they reached the small flat area at the top of the tor where the pack animals huddled together, trembling in the rain, Garion slid out of his saddle in time to catch Lelldorin, who toppled slowly to one side.

"Over here," Aunt Pol called sharply. She was pulling her small bundle of herbs and bandages out of one of the packs. "Durnik, I'll need a fire—at once."

Durnik looked around helplessly at the few scraps of wood lying in the rain at the top of the tor. "I'll try," he said doubtfully.

Lelldorin's breathing was shallow and very fast. His face was still a deadly white, and his legs would not hold him. Garion held him up, a sick fear in the pit of his stomach. Hettar took the wounded man's other arm, and between them they half-carried him to where Aunt Pol knelt, opening her bundle. "I have to get the poison out immediately," she told them. "Garion, give me your knife."

Garion drew his dagger and handed it to her. Swiftly she ripped open Lelldorin's brown tunic along his side, revealing the savage wounds the Algroth's claws had made. "This will hurt," she said. "Hold him."

Garion and Hettar took hold of Lelldorin's arms and legs, holding him down.

Aunt Pol took a deep breath and then deftly sliced open each of the puffy wounds. Blood spurted and Lelldorin screamed once. Then he fainted.

"Hettar!" Barak shouted from atop a boulder near the edge of the slope. "We need you!"

"Go!" Aunt Pol told the hawk-faced Algar. "We can handle this now. Garion, you stay here." She was crushing some dried leaves and sprinkling the fragments into the bleeding wounds. "The fire, Durnik," she ordered.

"It won't start, Mistress Pol," Durnik replied helplessly. "It's too wet."

She looked quickly at the pile of sodden wood the smith had gathered. Her eyes narrowed, and she made a quick gesture. Garion's ears rang strangely and there was a sudden hissing. A cloud of steam burst from the wood, and then crackling flames curled up from the sticks. Durnik jumped back, startled.

"The small pot, Garion," Aunt Pol instructed, "and water. Quickly." She pulled off her blue cloak and covered Lelldorin with it.

Silk, Barak, and Hettar stood at the edge of the slope, heaving large rocks over the edge. Garion could hear the clatter and clash of the rocks striking the boulders below and the barking of the Algroths, punctuated by an occasional howl of pain.

He cradled his friend's head in his lap, terribly afraid. "Is he going to be all right?" he appealed to Aunt Pol.

"It's too early to tell," she answered. "Don't bother me with questions just now."

"They're running!" Barak shouted.

"They're still hungry," Wolf replied grimly. "They'll be back."

From far off in the forest there came the sound of a brassy horn.

"What's that?" Silk asked, still puffing from the effort of heaving the heavy stones over the edge.

"Someone I've been expecting," Wolf answered with a strange smile. He raised his hands to his lips and whistled shrilly.

"I can manage now, Garion," Aunt Pol said, mashing a thick paste into a steaming pad of wet linen bandage. "You and Durnik go help the others."

Reluctantly Garion lowered Lelldorin's head to the wet turf and ran over to where Wolf stood. The slope below was littered with dead and dying Algroths, crushed by the rocks Barak and the others had hurled down on them.

"They're going to try again," Barak said, hefting another rock. "Can they get at us from behind?"

Silk shook his head. "No. I checked. The back of the hill's a sheer face."

The Algroths came out of the woods below, barking and snarling as they loped forward with their half-crouched gait. The first of them had already crossed the road when the horn blew again, very close this time.

And then a huge horse bearing a man in full armor burst out of the trees and thundered down upon the attacking creatures. The armored man crouched over his lance and plunged directly into the midst of the startled Algroths. The great horse screamed as he charged, and his iron-shod hoofs churned up big clots of mud. The lance crashed through the chest of one of the largest Algroths and splintered from the force of the blow. The splintered end took another full in the face. The knight discarded the shattered lance and drew his broadsword with a single sweep of his arm. With wide swings to the right and left he chopped his way through the pack, his warhorse trampling the living and the dead alike into the mud of the road. At the end of his charge he whirled and plunged back again, once more opening a path with his sword. The Algroths turned and fled howling into the woods.

"Mandorallen!" Wolf shouted. "Up here!"

The armored knight raised his blood-spattered visor and looked up the hill. "Permit me to disperse this rabble first, mine ancient friend," he answered gaily, clanged down his visor, and plunged into the rainy woods after the Algroths.

"Hettar!" Barak shouted, already moving.

Hettar nodded tersely, and the two of them ran to their horses. They swung into their saddles and plunged down the wet slope to the aid of the stranger.

"Your friend shows a remarkable lack of good sense," Silk observed to Mister Wolf, wiping the rain from his face. "Those things will turn on him any second now."

"It probably hasn't occurred to him that he's in any danger," Wolf replied. "He's a Mimbrate, and they tend to think they're invincible."

The fight in the woods seemed to last for a long time. There were shouts and ringing blows and shrieks of terror from the Algroths. Then Hettar, Barak, and the strange knight rode out of the trees and trotted up the tor. At the top, the armored man clanged down from his horse. "Well met, mine old friend," he boomed to Mister Wolf. "Thy friends below were most frolicsome." His armor gleamed wetly in the rain.

"I'm glad we found something to entertain you," Wolf said dryly.

"I can still hear them," Durnik reported. "I think they're still running."

"Their cowardice hath deprived us of an amusing afternoon," the knight observed, regretfully sheathing his sword and removing his helmet.

"We must all make sacrifices," Silk drawled.

The knight sighed. "All too true. Thou art a man of philosophy, I see." He shook the water out of the white plume on his helmet.

"Forgive me," Mister Wolf said. "This is Mandorallen, Baron of Vo Mandor. He'll be going with us. Mandorallen, this is Prince Kheldar of Drasnia and Barak, Earl of Trellheim and cousin to King Anheg of Cherek. Over there is Hettar, son of Cho-Hag, chief of the Clan-Chiefs of Algaria. The practical one is Goodman Durnik of Sendaria, and this boy is Garion, my grandson—several times removed."

Mandorallen bowed deeply to each of them. "I greet you, comrades all," he declaimed in his booming voice. "Our adventure hath seen a fortuitous beginning. And pray tell, who is this lady, whose beauty doth bedazzle mine eye?"

"A pretty speech, Sir Knight," Aunt Pol replied with a rich laugh, her hand going almost unconsciously to her damp hair. "I'm going to like this one, father."

"The legendary Lady Polgara?" Mandorallen asked. "My life hath now seen its crown." His courtly bow was somewhat marred by the creaking of his armor.

"Our injured friend is Lelldorin, son of the Baron of Wildantor," Wolf continued. "You may have heard of him."

Mandorallen's face darkened slightly. "Indeed. Rumor, which sometimes doth run before us like a barking dog, hath suggested that Lelldorin of Wildantor hath raised on occasion foul rebellion against the crown."

"That's of no matter now," Wolf stressed. "The business which has brought us together is much more serious than all that. You'll have to put it aside."

"It shall be as you say, noble Belgarath," Mandorallen declared immediately, though his eyes still lingered on the unconscious Lelldorin.

"Grandfather!" Garion called, pointing at a mounted figure that had suddenly appeared on the side of the stony hilltop. The figure was robed in black and sat a black horse. He pushed back his hood to reveal a polished steel mask cast in the form of a face that was at once beautiful and strangely repelling. A voice deep in Garion's mind told him that there was something important about the strange rider—something he should remember—but whatever it was eluded him.

"Abandon this quest, Belgarath." The voice was hollow behind the mask.

"You know me better than that, Chamdar," Mister Wolf said calmly, quite obviously recognizing the rider. "Was this childishness with the Algroths your idea?"

"And you should know *me* better than that," the figure retorted derisively. "When I come against you, you can expect things to be a bit more serious. For now, there are enough underlings about to delay you. That's all we really need. Once Zedar has carried Cthrag Yaska to my Master, you can try your power against the might and will of Torak, if you'd like."

"Are you running errands for Zedar, then?" Wolf asked.

"I run no man's errands," the figure replied with heavy contempt. The rider seemed solid, as real as any of them standing on the hilltop, but Garion could see the filmy drizzle striking the rocks directly beneath horse and man. Whatever the figure was, the rain was falling right through it.

"Why are you here, then, Chamdar?" Wolf demanded.

"Let's call it curiosity, Belgarath. I wanted to see for myself how you'd managed to translate the Prophecy into everyday terms." The figure looked around at the others on the hilltop. "Clever," it said with a certain grudging admiration. "Where did you find them all?"

"I didn't have to find them, Chamdar," Wolf answered. "They've been there all along. If any part of the Prophecy is valid, then it all has to be valid, doesn't it? There's no contrivance involved at all. Each one has come down to me through more generations than you can imagine."

The figure seemed to hiss with a sharp intake of its breath. "It isn't complete yet, old man."

"It will be, Chamdar," Wolf replied confidently. "I've already seen to that."

"Which is the one who will live twice?" the figure asked suddenly.

Wolf smiled coldly, but did not answer.

"Hail, my Queen," the figure said mockingly, then to Aunt Pol.

"Grolim courtesy always leaves me quite cold," she returned with a frosty look. "I'm not your queen, Chamdar."

"You will be, Polgara. My Master said that you are to become his wife when he comes into his kingdom. You'll be queen of all the world."

"That puts you at a bit of a disadvantage, doesn't it, Chamdar? If I'm to become your queen, you can't really cross me, can you?"

"I can work around you, Polgara, and once you've become the bride of Torak, his will becomes your will. I'm sure you won't hold any old grudges at that point."

"I think we've had about enough of this, Chamdar," Mister Wolf said. "Your conversation's beginning to bore me. You can have your shadow back now." He waved his hand negligently as if brushing away a troublesome fly. "Go," he commanded.

Once again Garion felt that strange surge and that hollow roaring in his mind. The horseman vanished.

"You didn't destroy him, did you?" Silk gasped in a shocked voice.

"No," Mister Wolf told him. "It was all just an illusion. It's a childish trick the Grolims find impressive. A shadow can be projected over quite some distance if you want to take the trouble. All I did was send his shadow back to him." He grinned suddenly with a sly twist to his lips. "Of course I selected a somewhat indirect route. It may take a few days to make the trip. It won't actually hurt him, but it's going to make him a bit uncomfortable— and extremely conspicuous."

"A most unseemly specter," Mandorallen observed. "Who was this rude shade?"

"It was Chamdar," Aunt Pol said, returning her attention to the injured Lelldorin, "one of the chief priests of the Grolims. Father and I have met him before."

"I think we'd getter get off this hilltop," Wolf stated. "How soon will Lelldorin be able to ride?"

"A week at least," Aunt Pol replied, "if then."

"That's out of the question. We can't stay here."

"He can't ride," she told him firmly.

"Couldn't we make a litter of some sort?" Durnik suggested. "I'm sure I can make something we can sling between two horses so we can move him without hurting him."

"Well, Pol?" Wolf asked.

"It might be all right," she said a little dubiously.

"Let's do it, then. We're much too exposed up here, and we've got to move on."

Durnik nodded and went to the packs for rope to use in building the litter.

CHAPTER SEVEN

Sir Mandorallen, Baron of Vo Mandor, was a man of slightly more than medium height. His hair was black and curly, his eyes were deep blue, and he had a resonant voice in which he expressed firmly held opinions. Garion did not like him. The knight's towering self-confidence, an egotism so pure that there was a kind of innocence about it, seemed to confirm the worst of Lelldorin's dark pronouncements about Mimbrates; and Mandorallen's extravagant courtesy to Aunt Pol struck Garion as beyond the bounds of proper civility. To make matters even worse, Aunt Pol seemed quite willing to accept the knight's flatteries at face value.

As they rode through the continuing drizzle along the Great West Road, Garion noted with some satisfaction that his companions appeared to share his opinion. Barak's expression spoke louder than words; Silk's eyebrows lifted sardonically at each of the knight's pronouncements; and Durnik scowled.

Garion, however, had little time to sort out his feelings about the Mimbrate. He rode close beside the litter upon which Lelldorin tossed painfully as the Algroth poison seared in his wounds. He offered his friend what comfort he could and exchanged frequent worried looks with Aunt Pol, who rode nearby. During the worst of Lelldorin's paroxysms, Garion helplessly held the young man's hand, unable to think of anything else to do to ease his pain.

"Bear thine infirmity with fortitude, good youth," Mandorallen cheerfully advised the injured Asturian after a particularly bad bout that left Lelldorin gasping and moaning. "This discomfort of thine is but an illusion. Thy mind can put it to rest if thou wouldst have it so."

"That's exactly the kind of comfort I'd expect from a Mimbrate," Lelldorin retorted from between clenched teeth. "I think I'd rather you didn't ride so close. Your opinions smell almost as bad as your armor."

Mandorallen's face flushed slightly. "The venom which doth rage through the body of our injured friend hath, it would seem, bereft him of civility as well as sense," he observed coldly.

Lelldorin half-raised himself in the litter as if to respond hotly, but the sudden movement seemed to aggravate his injury, and he lapsed into unconsciousness.

"His wounds are grave," Mandorallen stated. "Thy poultice, Lady Polgara, may not suffice to save his life."

"He needs rest," she told him. "Try not to agitate him so much."

"I will place myself beyond the reach of his eye," Mandorallen replied. "Through no fault of mine own, my visage is hateful to him and doth stir him to unhealthful choler." He moved his warhorse ahead at a canter until he was some distance in front of the rest of them.

"Do they all talk like that?" Garion asked with a certain rancor. "Thee's and thou's and doth's?"

"Mimbrates tend to be very formal," Aunt Pol explained. "You'll get used to it."

"I think it sounds stupid," Garion muttered darkly, glaring after the knight.

"An example of good manners won't hurt you all that much, Garion."

They rode on through the dripping forest as evening settled among the trees. "Aunt Pol?" Garion asked finally.

"Yes, dear?"

"What was that Grolim talking about when he said that about you and Torak?"

"It's something Torak said once when he was raving. The Grolims took it seriously, that's all." She pulled her blue cloak tighter about her.

"Doesn't it worry you?"

"Not particularly."

"What was that Prophecy the Grolim was talking about? I didn't understand any of that." The word "Prophecy" for some reason stirred something very deep in him.

"The Mrin Codex," she answered. "It's a very old version, and the writing's almost illegible. It mentions companions—the bear, the rat, and the man who will live twice. It's the only version that says anything about them. Nobody knows for certain that it really means anything."

"Grandfather thinks it does, doesn't he?"

"Your grandfather has a number of curious notions. Old things impress him—probably because he's so old himself."

Garion was going to ask her about this Prophecy that seemed to exist in more than one version, but Lelldorin moaned then and they both immediately turned to him.

They arrived shortly thereafter at a Tolnedran hostel with thick, white-washed walls and a red tile roof. Aunt Pol saw to it that Lelldorin was placed in a warm room, and she spent the night sitting by his bed caring for him. Garion padded worriedly down the dark hallway in his stocking feet a half-dozen times before morning to check on his friend, but there seemed to be no change.

By daybreak the rain had let up. They started out in the grayish dawn with Mandorallen still riding some distance ahead until they reached at last the edge of the dark forest and saw before them the vast, open expanse of the Arendish central plain, dun-colored and sere in the last few weeks of winter. The knight stopped there and waited for them to join him, his face somber.

"What's the trouble?" Silk asked him.

Mandorallen pointed gravely at a column of black smoke rising from a few miles out on the plain.

"What is it?" Silk inquired, his rat face puzzled.

"Smoke in Arendia can mean but one thing," the knight replied, pulling on his plumed helmet. "Abide here, dear friends. I will investigate, but I fear the worst." He set his spurs to the flanks of his charger and leaped forward at a thunderous gallop.

"Wait!" Barak roared after him, but Mandorallen rode on obliviously. "That idiot," the big Cherek fumed. "I'd better go with him in case there's trouble."

"It isn't necessary," Lelldorin advised weakly from his litter. "Not even an army would dare to interfere with him."

"I thought you didn't like him," Barak said, a little surprised.

"I don't," Lelldorin admitted, "but he's the most feared man in Arendia. Even in Asturia we've heard of Sir Mandorallen. No sane man would stand in his way."

They drew back into the shelter of the forest and waited for the knight to come back. When he returned, his face was angry. "It is as I feared," he announced. "A war doth rage in our path—a senseless war, since the two barons involved are kinsmen and the best of friends."

"Can we go around it?" Silk asked.

"Nay, Prince Kheldar," Mandorallen replied. "Their conflict is so widespread that we would be waylaid ere we had gone three leagues. I must, it would appear, buy us passage."

"Do you think they'll take money to let us pass?" Durnik asked dubiously.

"In Arendia there is another way to make such purchase, Goodman," Mandorallen responded. "May I prevail upon thee to obtain six or eight stout poles perhaps twenty feet in length and about as thick as my wrist at the butt?"

"Of course." Durnik took up his axe.

"What have you got in mind?" Barak rumbled.

"I will challenge them," Mandorallen announced calmly, "one or all. No true knight could refuse me without being called craven. Wilt thou be my second and deliver my challenge, my Lord?"

"What if you lose?" Silk suggested.

"*Lose?*" Mandorallen seemed shocked. "*I? Lose?*"

"Let it pass," Silk said.

By the time Durnik had returned with the poles, Mandorallen had finished tightening various straps beneath his armor. Taking one of the poles, he vaulted into his saddle and started at a rolling trot toward the column of smoke, with Barak at his side.

"Is this really necessary, father?" Aunt Pol asked.

"We have to get through, Pol," Mister Wolf replied. "Don't worry. Mandorallen knows what he's doing."

After a couple of miles they reached the top of a hill and looked down at the battle below. Two grim, black castles faced each other across a broad valley, and several villages dotted the plain on either side of the road. The nearest village was in flames, with a great pillar of greasy smoke rising from it to the lead-gray sky overhead, and serfs armed with scythes and pitchforks were attacking each other with a sort of mindless ferocity on the road itself. Some distance off, pikemen were gathering for a charge, and the air was thick with arrows. On two opposing hills parties of armored knights with bright-colored pennons on their lances watched the battle. Great siege engines lofted boulders into the air to crash down on the struggling men, killing, so far as Garion could tell, friend and foe indiscriminately. The valley was littered with the dead and the dying.

"Stupid," Wolf muttered darkly.

"No one I know of has ever accused Arends of brilliance," Silk observed.

Mandorallen set his horn to his lips and blew a shattering blast. The battle paused as the soldiers and serfs all stopped to stare up at him. He sounded his horn again, and then again, each brassy note a challenge in itself. As the two opposing bodies of knights galloped through the knee-high, winter-yellowed grass to investigate, Mandorallen turned to Barak. "If it please thee, my Lord," he requested politely, "deliver my challenge as soon as they approach us."

Barak shrugged. "It's your skin," he noted. He eyed the advancing knights and then lifted his voice in a great roar. "Sir Mandorallen, Baron of Vo Mandor, desires entertainment," he declaimed. "It would amuse him if each of your parties would select a champion to joust with him. If, however, you are all such cowardly dogs that you have no stomach for such a contest, cease this brawling and stand aside so that your betters may pass."

"Splendidly spoken, my Lord Barak," Mandorallen said with admiration.

"I've always had a way with words," Barak replied modestly.

The two parties of knights warily rode closer.

"For shame, my Lords," Mandorallen chided them. "Ye will gain no honor in this sorry war. Sir Derigen, what hath caused this contention?"

"An insult, Sir Mandorallen," the noble replied. He was a large man, and his polished steel helmet had a golden circlet riveted above the visor. "An insult so vile that it may not go unpunished."

"It was *I* who was insulted," a noble on the other side contended hotly.

"What was the nature of this insult, Sir Oltorain?" Mandorallen inquired.

Both men looked away uneasily, and neither spoke.

"Ye have gone to war over an insult which cannot even be recalled?" Mandorallen said incredulously. "I had thought, my Lords, that ye were serious men, but I now perceive my error."

"Don't the nobles of Arendia have anything better to do?" Barak asked in a voice heavy with contempt.

"Of Sir Mandorallen the bastard we have all heard," a swarthy knight in black-enameled armor sneered, "but who is this red-bearded ape who so maligns his betters?"

"You're going to take that?" Barak asked Mandorallen.

"It's more or less true," Mandorallen admitted with a pained look, "since there was some temporary irregularity about my birth which still raises questions about my legitimacy. This knight is Sir Haldorin, my third cousin— twice removed. Since it's considered unseemly in Arendia to spill the blood of kinsmen, he thus cheaply gains reputation for boldness by casting the matter in my teeth."

"Stupid custom," Barak grunted. "In Cherek kinsmen kill each other with more enthusiasm than they kill strangers."

"Alas," Mandorallen sighed. "This is not Cherek."

"Would you be offended if I dealt with this?" Barak asked politely.

"Not at all."

Barak moved closer to the swarthy knight. "I am Barak, Earl of Trellheim," he announced in a loud voice, "kinsman to King Anheg of Cherek, and I see that certain nobles in Arendia have even fewer manners than they have brains."

"The Lords of Arendia are not impressed by the self-bestowed titles of the pig-sty kingdoms of the north," Sir Haldorin retorted coldly.

"I find your words offensive, friend," Barak said ominously.

"And I find thy ape face and scraggly beard amusing," Sir Haldorin replied.

Barak did not even bother to draw his sword. He swung his huge arm in a wide circle and crashed his fist with stunning force against the side of the swarthy knight's helmet. Sir Haldorin's eyes glazed as he was swept from his saddle, and he made a vast clatter when he struck the ground.

"Would anyone else like to comment about my beard?" Barak demanded.

"Gently, my Lord," Mandorallen advised. He glanced down with a certain satisfaction at the unconscious form of his senseless kinsman twitching in the tall grass.

"Will we docilely accept this attack on our brave companion?" one of the knights in Baron Derigen's party demanded in a harshly accented voice. "Kill them all!" He reached for his sword.

"In the instant thy sword leaves its sheath thou art a dead man, Sir Knight," Mandorallen coolly advised him.

The knight's hand froze on his sword hilt.

"For shame, my Lords," Mandorallen continued accusingly. "Surely ye know that by courtesy and common usage my challenge, until it is answered, guarantees my safety and that of my companions. Choose your champions or withdraw. I tire of all this and presently will become irritable."

The two parties of knights pulled back some distance to confer, and several men-at-arms came to the hilltop to pick up Sir Haldorin.

"That one who was going to draw his sword was a Murgo," Garion said quietly.

"I noticed that," Hettar murmured, his dark eyes glittering.

"They're coming back," Durnik warned.

"I will joust with thee, Sir Mandorallen," Baron Derigen announced as he approached. "I doubt not that thy reputation is well-deserved, but I also have taken the prize in no small number of tourneys. I would be honored to try a lance with thee."

"And I too will try my skill against thine, Sir Knight," Baron Oltorain declared. "My arm is also feared in some parts of Arendia."

"Very well," Mandorallen replied. "Let us seek level ground and proceed. The day wears on, and my companions and I have business to the south."

They all rode down the hill to the field below where the two groups of knights drew up on either side of a course which had been quickly trampled out in the high, yellow grass. Derigen galloped to the far end, turned and sat waiting, his blunted lance resting in his stirrup.

"Thy courage becomes thee, my Lord," Mandorallen called, taking up one of the poles Durnik had cut. "I shall try not to injure thee too greatly. Art thou prepared to meet my charge?"

"I am," the baron replied, lowering his visor.

Mandorallen clapped down his visor, lowered his lance, and set his spurs to his warhorse.

"It's probably inappropriate under the circumstances," Silk murmured, "but I can't help wishing that our overbearing friend could suffer some humiliating defeat."

Mister Wolf gave him a withering look. "Forget it!"

"Is he *that* good?" Silk asked wistfully.

"Watch," Wolf told him.

The two knights met in the center of the course with a resounding crash, and their lances both shattered at the stunning impact, littering the trampled grass with splinters. They thundered past each other, turned and rode back, each to his original starting place. Derigen, Garion noticed, swayed somewhat in the saddle as he rode.

The knights charged again, and their fresh lances also shattered.

"I should have cut more poles," Durnik said thoughtfully.

But Baron Derigen swayed even more as he rode back this time, and on the third charge his faltering lance glanced off Mandorallen's shield. Mandorallen's lance, however, struck true, and the baron was hurled from his saddle by the force of their meeting.

Mandorallen reined in his charger and looked down at him. "Art thou able to continue, my Lord?" he asked politely.

Derigen staggered to his feet. "I do not yield," he gasped, drawing his sword.

"Splendid," Mandorallen replied. "I feared that I might have done thee harm." He slid out of his saddle, drew his sword and swung directly at Derigen's head. The blow glanced off the baron's hastily raised shield, and Mandorallen swung again without pause. Derigen managed one or two feeble swings before Mandorallen's broadsword caught him full on the side of the helmet. He spun once and collapsed facedown on the earth.

"My Lord?" Mandorallen inquired solicitously. He reached down, rolled over his fallen opponent and opened the dented visor of the baron's helmet. "Art thou unwell, my Lord?" he asked. "Dost thou wish to continue?"

Derigen did not reply. Blood ran freely from his nose, and his eyes were rolled back in his head. His face was blue, and the right side of his body quivered spasmodically.

"Since this brave knight is unable to speak for himself," Mandorallen announced, "I declare him vanquished." He looked around, his broadsword still in his hand. "Would any here gainsay my words?"

There was a vast silence.

"Will some few then remove him from the field?" Mandorallen suggested. "His injuries do not appear grave. A few months in bed should make him whole again." He turned to Baron Oltorain, whose face had grown visibly pale. "Well, my Lord," he said cheerfully, "shall we proceed? My companions and I are impatient to continue our journey."

Sir Oltorain was thrown to the ground on the first charge and broke his leg as he fell.

"Ill luck, my Lord," Mandorallen observed, approaching on foot with drawn sword. "Dost thou yield?"

"I cannot stand," Oltorain said from between clenched teeth. "I have no choice but to yield."

"And I and my companions may continue our journey?"

"Ye may freely depart," the man on the ground replied painfully.

"Not just yet," a harsh voice interrupted. The armored Murgo pushed his horse through the crowd of other mounted knights until he was directly in front of Mandorallen.

"I thought he might decide to interfere," Aunt Pol said quietly. She dismounted and stepped out onto the hoof-churned course. "Move out of the way, Mandorallen," she told the knight.

"Nay, my Lady," Mandorallen protested.

Wolf barked sharply, "Move, Mandorallen!"

Mandorallen looked startled and stepped aside.

"Well, Grolim?" Aunt Pol challenged, pushing back her hood.

The mounted man's eyes widened as he saw the white lock in her hair, and then he raised his hand almost despairingly, muttering rapidly under his breath.

Once again Garion felt that strange surge, and the hollow roaring filled his mind.

For an instant Aunt Pol's figure seemed surrounded by a kind of greenish light. She waved her hand indifferently, and the light disappeared. "You must be out of practice," she told him. "Would you like to try again?"

The Grolim raised both hands this time, but got no further. Maneuvering his horse carefully behind the armored man, Durnik had closed on him. With both hands he raised his axe and smashed it down directly on top of the Grolim's helmet.

"Durnik!" Aunt Pol shouted. "Get away!"

But the smith, his face set grimly, swung again, and the Grolim slid senseless from his saddle with a crash.

"You fool!" Aunt Pol raged. "What do you think you're doing?"

"He was attacking you, Mistress Pol," Durnik explained, his eyes still hot.

"Get down off that horse."

He slid down.

"Do you have any idea how dangerous that was?" she demanded. "He could have killed you."

"I *will* protect you, Mistress Pol," Durnik replied stubbornly. "I'm not a warrior or a magician, but I won't let anybody try to hurt you."

Her eyes widened in surprise for an instant, then narrowed, then softened. Garion, who had known her from childhood, recognized her rapid changes of emotion. Without warning she suddenly embraced the startled Durnik. "You great, clumsy, dear fool," she said. "*Never* do that again—never! You almost made my heart stop."

Garion looked away with a strange lump in his throat and saw the brief, sly smile that flickered across Mister Wolf's face.

A peculiar change had come over the knights lining the sides of the course. Several of them were looking around with the amazed expressions of men who had just been roused from some terrible dream. Others seemed suddenly lost in thought. Sir Oltorain struggled to rise.

"Nay, my Lord," Mandorallen told him, pressing him gently back down. "Thou wilt do thyself injury."

"What have we done?" the baron groaned, his face anguished.

Mister Wolf dismounted and knelt beside the injured man. "It wasn't your fault," he informed the baron. "Your war was the Murgo's doing. He twisted your minds and set you on each other."

"Sorcery?" Oltorain gasped, his face growing pale.

Wolf nodded. "He's not really a Murgo, but a Grolim priest."

"And the spell is now broken?"

Wolf nodded again, glancing at the unconscious Grolim.

"Chain the Murgo," the baron ordered the assembled knights. He looked back at Wolf. "We have ways of dealing with sorcerers," he said grimly. "We will use the occasion to celebrate the end of our unnatural war. This Grolim sorcerer hath cast his last enchantment."

"Good," Wolf replied with a bleak smile.

"Sir Mandorallen," Baron Oltorain said, wincing as he shifted his broken leg, "in what way may we repay thee and thy companions for bringing us to our senses?"

"That peace hath been restored is reward enough," Mandorallen replied somewhat pompously, "for, as all the world knows, I am the most peace-loving man in the kingdom." He glanced once at Lelldorin lying nearby on the ground in his litter, and a thought seemed to occur to him. "I would, however, ask a boon of thee. We have in our company a brave Asturian youth of noble family who hath suffered grievous injury. We would leave him, if we might, in thy care."

"His presence shall honor me, Sir Mandorallen," Oltorain assented immediately. "The women of my household will care for him most tenderly." He spoke briefly to one of his retainers, and the man mounted and rode quickly toward one of the nearby castles.

"You're not going to leave me behind," Lelldorin protested weakly. "I'll be able to ride in a day or so." He began to cough rackingly.

"I think not," Mandorallen disagreed with a cool expression. "The results of thy wounding have not yet run their natural course."

"I won't stay with Mimbrates," Lelldorin insisted. "I'd rather take my chances on the road."

"Young Lelldorin," Mandorallen replied bluntly, even harshly, "I know thy distaste for the men of Mimbre. Thy wound, however, will soon begin to abscess and then suppurate, and raging fever and delirium will afflict thee, making thy presence a burden upon us. We have not the time to care for thee, and thy sore need would delay us in our quest."

Garion gasped at the brutal directness of the knight's words. He glared at Mandorallen with something very close to hatred.

Lelldorin's face meanwhile had gone white. "Thank you for pointing that out to me, Sir Mandorallen," he said stiffly. "I should have considered it myself. If you'll help me to my horse, I'll leave immediately."

"You'll stay right where you are," Aunt Pol told him flatly.

Baron Oltorain's retainer returned with a group of household servants and a blonde girl of about seventeen wearing a rose-colored gown of stiff brocade and a velvet cloak of teal.

"My younger sister, Lady Ariana," Oltorain introduced her. "She's a spirited girl, and though she is young she is already well-versed in the care of the sick."

"I won't trouble her for long, my Lord," Lelldorin declared. "I'll be re-turning to Asturia within a week."

Lady Ariana laid a professional hand to his forehead. "Nay, good youth," she disagreed. "Thy visit, I think, will be protracted."

"I'll leave within the week," Lelldorin repeated stubbornly.

She shrugged. "As it please thee. I expect that my brother will be able to spare some few servants to follow after thee to provide thee that decent burial which, if I misjudge not, thou wilt require before thou hast gone ten leagues."

Lelldorin blinked.

Aunt Pol took Lady Ariana to one side and spoke with her at some length, giving her a small packet of herbs and certain instructions. Lelldorin motioned to Garion, and Garion went to him immediately and knelt beside the litter.

"So it ends," the young man murmured. "I wish I could go on with you."

"You'll be well in no time at all," Garion assured him, knowing that it wasn't true. "Maybe you can catch up with us later."

Lelldorin shook his head. "No," he disagreed, "I'm afraid not." He began to cough again, the spasms seeming to tear at his lungs. "We don't have much time, my friend," he gasped weakly, "so listen carefully."

Garion, near tears, took his friend's hand.

"You remember what we were talking about that morning after we left my uncle's house?"

Garion nodded.

"You said that I was the one who'd have to decide if we were to break our pledge to Torasin and the others to keep silent."

"I remember," Garion told him.

"All right," Lelldorin said. "I've decided. I release you from your pledge. Do what you have to do."

"It'd be better if you told my grandfather about it yourself, Lelldorin," Garion protested.

"I can't, Garion," Lelldorin groaned. "The words would stick in my throat. I'm sorry, but it's the way I am. I know that Nachak's only using us, but I gave the others my word. I'm an Arend, Garion. I'll keep my word even though I know it's wrong, so it's up to you. You're going to have to keep Nachak from destroying my country. I want you to go straight to the king himself."

"To the king? He'd never believe me."

"*Make* him believe you. Tell him everything."

Garion shook his head firmly. "I won't tell him your name," he declared, "or Torasin's. You know what he'd do to you if I did."

"We don't matter," Lelldorin insisted, coughing again.

"I'll tell him about Nachak," Garion said stubbornly, "but not about you. Where do I tell him to find the Murgo?"

"He'll know," Lelldorin replied, his voice very weak now. "Nachak's the ambassador to the court at Vo Mimbre. He's the personal representative of Taur Urgas, King of the Murgos."

Garion was stunned at the implications of that.

"He's got all the gold from the bottomless mines of Cthol Murgos at his command," Lelldorin continued. "The plot he gave my friends and me could be just one of a dozen or more all aimed at destroying Arendia. You've got to stop him, Garion. Promise me." The pale young man's eyes were feverish, and his grip on Garion's hand tightened.

"I'll stop him, Lelldorin," Garion vowed. "I don't know how yet, but one way or another, I'll stop him."

Lelldorin sank weakly back on the litter, his strength seeming to run out as if the necessity for extracting that promise had been the only thing sustaining him.

"Good-bye, Lelldorin," Garion said softly, his eyes filling with tears.

"Good-bye, my friend," Lelldorin barely more than whispered, and then his eyes closed, and the hand gripping Garion's went limp. Garion stared at him with a dreadful fear until he saw the faint flutter of his pulse in the hollow of his throat. Lelldorin was still alive—if only barely. Garion tenderly put down his friend's hand and pulled the rough gray blanket up around his shoulders. Then he stood up and walked quickly away with tears running down his cheeks.

The rest of the farewells were brief, and they remounted and rode at a trot toward the Great West Road. There were a few cheers from the serfs and pikemen as they passed, but in the distance there was another sound. The women from the villages had come out to search for their men among the bodies littering the field, and their wails and shrieks mocked the cheers.

With deliberate purpose, Garion pushed his horse forward until he drew in beside Mandorallen. "I have something to say to you," he said hotly. "You aren't going to like it, but I don't really care."

"Oh?" the knight replied mildly.

"I think the way you talked to Lelldorin back there was cruel and disgusting," Garion told him. "You might think you're the greatest knight in the world, but I think you're a loudmouthed braggart with no more compassion than a block of stone, and if you don't like it, what do you plan to do about it?"

"Ah," Mandorallen said. "That! I think that thou hast misunderstood, my young friend. It was necessary in order to save his life. The Asturian youth is very brave and so gives no thought to himself. Had I not spoken so to him, he would surely have insisted upon continuing with us and would soon have died."

"Died?" Garion scoffed. "Aunt Pol could have cured him."

"It was the Lady Polgara herself who informed me that his life was in danger," Mandorallen replied. "His honor would not permit him to seek proper care, but that same honor prevailed upon him to remain behind lest he delay us." The knight smiled wryly. "He will, I think, be no fonder of me for my words than thou art, but he will be alive, and that's what matters, is it not?"

Garion stared at the arrogant-seeming Mimbrate, his anger suddenly robbed of its target. With painful clarity he realized that he had just made a fool of himself. "I'm sorry," he apologized grudgingly. "I didn't realize what you were doing."

Mandorallen shrugged. "It's not important. I'm frequently misunderstood. As long as I know that my motives are good, however, I'm seldom very concerned with the opinions of others. I'm glad, though, that I had the opportunity to explain this to thee. Thou art to be my companion, and it ill-behooves companions to have misapprehensions about each other."

They rode on in silence as Garion struggled to readjust his thinking. There was, it seemed, much more to Mandorallen than he had suspected.

They reached the highway then and turned south again under a threatening sky.

CHAPTER EIGHT

The Arendish plain was a vast, rolling grassland only sparsely settled. The wind sweeping across the dried grass was raw and chill, and dirty-looking clouds scudded overhead as they rode. The necessity for leaving the injured Lelldorin behind had put them all into a melancholy mood, and for the most part they traveled in silence for the next several days. Garion rode at the rear with Hettar and the packhorses, doing his best to stay away from Mandorallen.

Hettar was a silent man who seemed undisturbed by hours of riding without conversation; but after two days of this, Garion made a deliberate effort to draw the hawk-faced Algar out. "Why is it that you hate Murgos so much, Hettar?" he asked for want of something better to say.

"All Alorns hate Murgos," Hettar answered quietly.

"Yes," Garion admitted, "but it seems to be something personal with you. Why is that?"

Hettar shifted in his saddle, his leather clothing creaking. "They killed my parents," he replied.

Garion felt a sudden shock as the Algar's words struck a responsive note. "How did it happen?" he asked before he realized that Hettar might prefer not to talk about it.

"I was seven," Hettar told him in an unemotional voice. "We were going to visit my mother's family—she was from a different clan. We had to pass near the eastern escarpment, and a Murgo raiding-party caught us. My mother's horse stumbled, and she was thrown. The Murgos were on us before my father and I could get her back on her horse. They took a long time to kill my parents. I remember that my mother screamed once, near the end." The

Algar's face was as bleak as rock, and his flat, quiet voice made his story seem that much more dreadful.

"After my parents were dead, the Murgos tied a rope around my feet and dragged me behind one of their horses," he continued. "When the rope finally broke, they thought I was dead, and they all rode off. They were laughing about it as I recall. Cho-Hag found me a couple of days later."

As clearly as if he had been there, Garion had a momentary picture of a child, dreadfully injured and alone, wandering in the emptiness of eastern Algaria with only grief and a terrible hatred keeping him alive.

"I killed my first Murgo when I was ten," Hettar went on in the same flat voice. "He was trying to escape from us, and I rode him down and put a javelin between his shoulders. He screamed when the javelin went through him. That made me feel better. Cho-Hag thought that if he made me watch the Murgo die, it might cure me of the hatred. He was wrong about that, though." The tall Algar's face was expressionless, and his wind-whipped scalp lock tossed and flowed out behind him. There was a kind of emptiness about him as if he were devoid of any feeling but that one driving compulsion.

For an instant Garion dimly understood what Mister Wolf had been driving at when he had warned about the danger of becoming obsessed with a desire for revenge, but he pushed the notion out of his mind. If Hettar could live with it, so could he. He felt a sudden fierce admiration for this lonely hunter in black leather.

Mister Wolf was deep in conversation with Mandorallen, and the two of them loitered until Hettar and Garion caught up with them. For a time they rode along together.

"It is our nature," the knight in his gleaming armor was saying in a melancholy voice. "We are over-proud, and it is our pride that dooms our poor Arendia to internecine war."

"That can be cured," Mister Wolf said.

"How?" Mandorallen asked. "It is in our blood. I myself am the most peaceful of men, but even I am subject to our national disease. Moreover, our divisions are too great, too buried in our history and our souls to be purged away. The peace will not last, my friend. Even now Asturian arrows sing in the forests, seeking Mimbrate targets, and Mimbre in reprisal burns Asturian houses and butchers hostages. War is inevitable, I fear."

"No," Wolf disagreed, "it's not."

"How may it be prevented?" Mandorallen demanded. "Who can cure our insanity?"

"I will, if I have to," Wolf told him quietly, pushing back his gray hood.

Mandorallen smiled wanly. "I appreciate thy good intentions, Belgarath, but that is impossible, even for thee."

"Nothing is actually impossible, Mandorallen," Wolf answered in a matter-of-fact voice. "Most of the time I prefer not to interfere with other people's amusements, but I can't afford to have Arendia going up in flames just now. If I have to, I'll step in and put a stop to any more foolishness."

"Hast thou in truth such power?" Mandorallen asked somewhat wistfully as if he could not quite bring himself to believe it.

"Yes," Wolf replied prosaically, scratching at his short white beard, "as a matter of fact, I do."

Mandorallen's face grew troubled, even a bit awed at the old man's quiet statement, and Garion found his grandfather's declaration profoundly disturbing. If Wolf could actually stop a war single-handedly, he'd have no difficulty at all thwarting Garion's own plans for revenge. It was something else to worry about.

Then Silk rode back toward them. "The Great Fair's just ahead," the rat-faced man announced. "Do we want to stop, or should we go around it?"

"We might as well stop," Wolf decided. "It's almost evening, and we need some supplies."

"The horses could use some rest, too," Hettar said. "They're starting to complain."

"You should have told me," Wolf said, glancing back at the pack train.

"They're not really in bad shape yet," Hettar informed him, "but they're starting to feel sorry for themselves. They're exaggerating, of course, but a little rest wouldn't hurt them."

"Exaggerating?" Silk sounded shocked. "You don't mean to say that horses can actually lie, do you?"

Hettar shrugged. "Of course. They lie all the time. They're very good at it."

For a moment Silk looked outraged at the thought, and then he suddenly laughed. "Somehow that restores my faith in the order of the universe," he declared.

Wolf looked pained. "Silk," he said pointedly, "you're a very evil man. Did you know that?"

"One does one's best," Silk replied mockingly.

The Arendish Fair lay at the intersection of the Great West Road and the mountain track leading down out of Ulgoland. It was a vast collection of blue, red, and yellow tents and broad-striped pavilions stretching for a league or more in every direction. It appeared like a brightly hued city in the midst of the dun-colored plain, and its brilliant pennons snapped bravely in the endless wind under a lowering sky.

"I hope I'll have time to do some business," Silk said as they rode down a long hill toward the Fair. The little man's sharp nose was twitching. "I'm starting to get out of practice."

A half-dozen mud-smeared beggars crouched miserably beside the road, their hands outstretched. Mandorallen paused and scattered some coins among them.

"You shouldn't encourage them," Barak growled.

"Charity is both a duty and a privilege, my Lord Barak," Mandorallen replied.

"Why don't they build houses here?" Garion asked Silk as they approached the central part of the Fair.

"Nobody stays here that long," Silk explained. "The Fair's always here, but the population's very fluid. Besides, buildings are taxed; tents aren't."

Many of the merchants who came out of their tents to watch the party pass seemed to know Silk, and some of them greeted him warily, suspicion plainly written on their faces.

"I see that your reputation's preceded you, Silk," Barak observed dryly.

Silk shrugged. "The price of fame."

"Isn't there some danger that somebody'll recognize you as that other merchant?" Durnik asked. "The one the Murgos are looking for?"

"You mean Ambar? It's not very likely. Ambar doesn't come to Arendia very often, and he and Radek don't look a bit alike."

"But they're the same man," Durnik objected. "They're both you."

"Ah," Silk said, raising one finger, "you and I both know that, but *they* don't. To you I always look like myself, but to others I look quite different."

Durnik looked profoundly skeptical.

"Radek, old friend," a bald Drasnian merchant called from a nearby tent.

"Delvor," Silk replied delightedly. "I haven't seen you in years."

"You look prosperous," the bald man observed.

"Getting by," Silk responded modestly. "What are you dealing in now?"

"I've got a few Mallorean carpets," Delvor told him. "Some of the local nobles are interested, but they don't like the price." His hands, however, were already speaking of other matters—*Your uncle sent out word that we were to help you if necessary. Do you need anything?*—"What are you carrying in your packs?" he asked aloud.

"Sendarian woolens," Silk answered, "and a few other odds and ends."—*Have you seen any Murgos here at the Fair?*—

—*One, but he left for Vo Mimbre a week ago. There are some Nadraks on the far side of the Fair, though*—

—*They're a long way from home*—Silk gestured.—*Are they really in business?*—

—*It's hard to say*—Delvor answered.

—*Can you put us up for a day or so?*—

—*I'm sure we can work something out*—Delvor replied with a sly twinkle in his eyes.

Silk's fingers betrayed his shock at the suggestion.

—*Business is business, after all*—Delvor gestured. "You must come inside," he said aloud. "Take a cup of wine, have some supper. We have years of catching up to do."

"We'd be delighted," Silk returned somewhat sourly.

"Could it be that you've met your match, Prince Kheldar?" Aunt Pol inquired softly with a faint smile as the little man helped her down from her horse in front of Delvor's brightly striped pavilion.

"Delvor? Hardly. He's been trying to get even with me for years—ever since a ploy of mine in Yar Gorak cost him a fortune. I'll let him think he's got me for a while, though. It'll make him feel good, and I'll enjoy it that much more when I pull the rug out from under him."

She laughed. "You're incorrigible."

He winked at her.

The interior of Delvor's main pavilion was ruddy in the light of several glowing braziers that put out a welcome warmth. The floor was covered with a deep blue carpet, and large red cushions were scattered here and there to sit upon. Once they were inside, Silk quickly made the introductions.

"I'm honored, Ancient One," Delvor murmured, bowing deeply to Mister Wolf and then to Aunt Pol. "What can I do to help?"

"Right now we need information more than anything," Wolf replied, pulling off his heavy cloak. "We ran into a Grolim stirring up trouble a few days north of here. Can you nose about and find out what's happening between here and Vo Mimbre? I'd like to avoid any more neighborhood squabbles if possible."

"I'll make inquiries," Delvor promised.

"I'll be moving around too," Silk said. "Between us, Delvor and I should be able to sift out most of the loose information in the Fair."

Wolf looked at him inquiringly.

"Radek of Boktor never passes up a chance to do business," the little man explained just a bit too quickly. "It'd look very strange if he stayed in Delvor's tent."

"I see," Wolf said.

"We wouldn't want anything to spoil our disguise, would we?" Silk asked innocently. His long nose, however, was twitching even more violently.

Wolf surrendered. "All right. But don't get exotic. I don't want a crowd of outraged customers outside the tent in the morning howling for your head."

Delvor's porters took the packs from the spare horses, and one of them showed Hettar the way to the horse pens on the outskirts of the Fair. Silk began rummaging through the packs. A myriad of small, expensive items began to pile up on Delvor's carpet as Silk's quick hands dipped into the corners and folds of the wool cloth.

"I wondered why you needed so much money in Camaar," Wolf commented dryly.

"Just part of the disguise," Silk replied. "Radek always has a few curios with him for trade along the way."

"That's a very convenient explanation," Barak observed, "but I wouldn't run it into the ground if I were you."

"If I can't double our old friend's money in the next hour, I'll retire permanently," Silk promised. "Oh, I almost forgot. I'll need Garion to act as a porter for me. Radek always has at least one porter."

"Try not to corrupt him too much," Aunt Pol said.

Silk bowed extravagantly and set his black velvet cap at a jaunty angle; with Garion at his heels, carrying a stout sack of his treasures, he swaggered out into the Great Arendish Fair like a man going into battle.

A fat Tolnedran three tents down the way proved troublesome and succeeded in getting a jeweled dagger away from Silk for only three times what it was worth, but two Arendish merchants in a row bought identical silver goblets at prices which, though widely different, more than made up for that setback. "I love to deal with Arends," Silk gloated as they moved on down the muddy streets between the pavilions.

The sly little Drasnian moved through the Fair, wreaking havoc as he went. When he could not sell, he bought; when he could not buy, he traded; and when he could not trade, he dredged for gossip and information. Some of the merchants, wiser than their fellows, saw him coming and promptly hid from him. Garion, swept along by the little man's enthusiasm, began to understand his friend's fascination with this game where profit was secondary to the satisfaction of besting an opponent.

Silk's predations were broadly ecumenical. He was willing to deal with anyone. He met them all on their own ground. Tolnedrans, Arends, Chereks, fellow Drasnians, Sendars—all fell before him. By midafternoon he had disposed of all of what he had bought in Camaar. His full purse jingled, and the sack on Garion's shoulder was still as heavy, but now it contained entirely new merchandise.

Silk, however, was frowning. He walked along bouncing a small, exquisitely blown glass bottle on the palm of his hand. He had traded two ivory-bound books of Wacite verse to a Rivan for the little bottle of perfume. "What's the trouble?" Garion asked him as they walked back toward Delvor's pavilions.

"I'm not sure who won," Silk told him shortly.

"What?"

"I don't have any idea what this is worth."

"Why did you take it, then?"

"I didn't want him to know that I didn't know its value."

"Sell it to somebody else."

"How can I sell it if I don't know what to ask for it? If I ask too much, nobody'll talk to me; and if I ask too little, I'll be laughed out of the Fair."

Garion started to chuckle.

"I don't see that it's all that funny, Garion," Silk said sensitively. He remained moody and irritable as they entered the pavilion. "Here's the profit I promised you," he told Mister Wolf somewhat ungraciously as he poured coins into the old man's hand.

"What's bothering you?" Wolf asked, eyeing the little man's grumpy face.

"Nothing," Silk replied shortly. Then he glanced over at Aunt Pol, and a broad smile suddenly appeared on his face. He crossed to her and bowed. "My dear Lady Polgara, please accept this trifling memento of my regard for you." With a flourish he presented the perfume bottle to her.

Aunt Pol's look was a peculiar mixture of pleasure and suspicion. She took the small bottle and carefully worked out the tightly fitting stopper. Then with a delicate gesture she touched the stopper to the inside of her wrist and raised the wrist to her face to catch the fragrance. "Why, Kheldar," she exclaimed with delight, "this is a princely gift."

Silk's smile turned a bit sickly, and he peered sharply at her, trying to determine if she were serious or not. Then he sighed and went outside, muttering darkly to himself about the duplicity of Rivans.

Delvor returned not long afterward, dropping his striped cloak in one corner and held out his hand to one of the glowing braziers. "As nearly as I was able to find out, things are quiet between here and Vo Mimbre," he reported to Mister Wolf, "but five Murgos just rode into the Fair with two dozen Thulls behind them."

Hettar looked up quickly, his hawk face alert.

Wolf frowned. "Did they come from the north or the south?"

"They claim to have come from Vo Mimbre, but there's red clay on the Thulls' boots. I don't think there's any clay between here and Vo Mimbre, is there?"

"None," Mandorallen declared firmly. "The only clay in the region is to the north."

Wolf nodded. "Get Silk back inside," he told Barak.

Barak went to the tent flap.

"Couldn't it just be a coincidence?" Durnik wondered.

"I don't think we want to take that chance," Wolf answered. "We'll wait until the Fair settles down for the night and then slip away."

Silk came back inside, and he and Delvor spoke together briefly.

"It won't take the Murgos long to find out we've been here," Barak rumbled, tugging thoughtfully at his red beard. "Then we'll have them dogging our heels every step of the way from here to Vo Mimbre. Wouldn't it simplify things if Hettar, Mandorallen, and I go pick a fight with them? Five dead Murgos aren't going to follow anybody."

Hettar nodded with a certain dreadful eagerness.

"I don't know if that would set too well with the Tolnedran legionnaires who police the Fair," Silk drawled. "Policemen seem to worry about unexplained bodies. It upsets their sense of neatness."

Barak shrugged. "It was a thought."

"I think I've got an idea," Delvor said, pulling on his cloak again. "They set up their tents near the pavilions of the Nadraks. I'll go do some business with them." He started toward the tent flap, then paused. "I don't know if it means anything," he told them, "but I found out that the leader is a Murgo named Asharak."

Garion felt a sudden chill at the mention of the name.

Barak whistled and looked suddenly very grim. "We're going to have to attend to that one sooner or later, Belgarath," he declared.

"You know him?" Delvor did not seem very surprised.

"We've met a time or two," Silk replied in an offhand way.

"He's starting to make a nuisance of himself," Aunt Pol agreed.

"I'll get started," Delvor said.

Garion lifted the tent flap to allow Delvor to leave; but as he glanced outside, he let out a startled gasp and jerked the flap shut again.

"What's the matter?" Silk asked him.

"I think I just saw Brill out there in the street."

"Let me see," Durnik said. His fingers parted the flap slightly, and he and Garion both peered out. A slovenly figure loitered in the muddy street outside. Brill had not changed much since they'd left Faldor's farm. His tunic and hose were still patched and stained; his face was still unshaven, and his cast eye still gleamed with a kind of unwholesome whiteness.

"It's Brill, all right," Durnik confirmed. "He's close enough for me to smell him."

Delvor looked at the smith inquiringly.

"Brill bathes irregularly," Durnik explained. "He's a fragrant sort of fellow."

"May I?" Delvor asked politely. He glanced out over Durnik's shoulder. "Ah," he said, "that one. He works for the Nadraks. I thought that was a little strange, but he didn't seem important, so I didn't bother to investigate."

"Durnik," Wolf said quickly, "step outside for a moment. Make sure he sees you, but don't let him know that you know he's there. After he sees you, come back inside. Hurry. We don't want to let him get away."

Durnik looked baffled, but he lifted the tent flap and stepped out.

"What are you up to, father?" Aunt Pol asked rather sharply. "Don't just stand there smirking, old man. That's very irritating."

"It's perfect," Wolf chortled, rubbing his hands together

Durnik came back in, his face worried. "He saw me," he reported. "Are you sure this is a good idea?"

"Of course," Wolf replied. "Asharak's obviously here because of us, and he's going to be looking all over the Fair for us."

"Why make it easy for him?" Aunt Pol asked.

"We won't," Wolf replied. "Asharak's used Brill before—in Muros, remember? He brought Brill down here because Brill would recognize you or me or Durnik or Garion—probably Barak too, and maybe Silk. Is he still out there?"

Garion peered out through the narrow opening. After a moment he saw the unkempt Brill half-hidden between two tents across the street. "He's still there," he answered.

"We'll want to keep him there," Wolf said. "We'll have to be sure that he doesn't get bored and go back to report to Asharak that he's found us."

Silk looked at Delvor, and they both began to laugh.

"What's funny?" Barak demanded suspiciously.

"You almost have to be a Drasnian to appreciate it," Silk replied. He looked at Wolf admiringly. "Sometimes you amaze me, old friend."

Mister Wolf winked at him.

"Thy plan still escapes me," Mandorallen confessed.

"May I?" Silk asked Wolf. He turned back to the knight. "It goes like this, Mandorallen. Asharak's counting on Brill to find us for him, but as long as we keep Brill interested enough, he'll delay going back to tell Asharak where we are. We've captured Asharak's eyes, and that puts him at quite a disadvantage."

"But will this curious Sendar not follow us as soon as we leave the tent?"

Mandorallen asked. "When we ride from the Fair, the Murgos will be immediately behind us."

"The back wall of the tent is only canvas, Mandorallen," Silk pointed
out gently. "With a sharp knife you can make as many doors in it as you
like."

Delvor winced slightly, then sighed. "I'll go see the Murgos," he said. "I
think I can delay them even more."

"Durnik and I'll go out with you," Silk told his bald friend. "You go one
way, and we'll go another. Brill will follow us, and we can lead him back
here."

Delvor nodded, and the three of them went out.

"Isn't all this unnecessarily complicated?" Barak asked sourly. "Brill
doesn't know Hettar. Why not just have Hettar slip out the back, circle
around behind him, and stick a knife between his ribs? Then we could stuff
him in a sack and drop him in a ditch somewhere after we leave the Fair."

Wolf shook his head. "Asharak would miss him," he replied. "I want him
to tell the Murgos that we're in this tent. With any luck, they'll sit outside
for a day or so before they realize that we're gone."

For the next several hours various members of the party went out into
the street in front of the tent on short and wholly imaginary errands to hold
the attention of the lurking Brill. When Garion stepped out into the gathering darkness, he put on a show of unconcern, although his skin prickled as
he felt Brill's eyes on him. He went into Delvor's supply tent and waited for
several minutes. The noise from a tavern pavilion several rows of tents over
seemed very loud in the growing stillness of the Fair as Garion waited nervously in the dark supply tent. Finally he drew a deep breath and went out
again, one arm tucked up as if he were carrying something. "I found it,
Durnik," he announced as he reentered the main pavilion.

"There's no need to improvise, dear," Aunt Pol remarked.

"I just wanted to sound natural," he replied innocently.

Delvor returned soon after that, and they all waited in the warm tent as
it grew darker outside and the streets emptied. Once it was fully dark,
Delvor's porters pulled the packs out through a slit in the back of the tent.
Silk, Delvor, and Hettar went with them to the horse pens on the outskirts
of the Fair while the rest remained long enough to keep Brill from losing interest. In a final attempt at misdirection, Mister Wolf and Barak went outside
to discuss the probable conditions of the road to Prolgu in Ulgoland.

"It might not work," Wolf admitted as he and the big red-bearded man
came back inside. "Asharak's sure to know that we're following Zedar south,
but if Brill tells him that we're going to Prolgu, it might make him divide his
forces to cover both roads." He looked around the inside of the tent. "All
right," he said, "let's go."

One by one they squeezed out through the slit in the back of the tent
and crept into the next street. Then, walking at a normal pace like serious
people on honest business, they proceeded toward the horse pens. They
passed the tavern pavilion where several men were singing. The streets were

mostly empty by now, and the night breeze brushed the city of tents, fluttering the pennons and banners.

Then they reached the edge of the Fair where Silk, Delvor, and Hettar waited with their mounts. "Good luck," Delvor said as they prepared to mount. "I'll delay the Murgos for as long as I can."

Silk shook his friend's hand. "I'd still like to know where you got those lead coins."

Delvor winked at him.

"What's this?" Wolf asked.

"Delvor's got some Tolnedran crowns stamped out of lead and gilded over," Silk told him. "He hid some of them in the Murgos' tent, and tomorrow morning he's going to go to the legionnaires with a few of them and accuse the Murgos of passing them. When the legionnaires search the Murgos' tent, they're sure to find the others."

"Money's awfully important to Tolnedrans," Barak observed. "If the legionnaires get excited enough about those coins, they might start hanging people."

Delvor smirked. "Wouldn't that be a terrible shame?"

They mounted then and rode away from the horse pens toward the highway. It was a cloudy night, and once they were out in the open the breeze was noticeably brisk. Behind them the Fair gleamed and twinkled under the night sky like some vast city. Garion drew his cloak about him. It was a lonely feeling to be on a dark road on a windy night when everyone else in the world had a fire and a bed and walls around him. Then they reached the Great West Road stretching pale and empty across the dark, rolling Arendish plain and turned south again.

CHAPTER NINE

The wind picked up again shortly before dawn and was blowing briskly by the time the sky over the low foothills to the east began to lighten. Garion was numb with exhaustion by then, and his mind had drifted into an almost dreamlike trance. The faces of his companions all seemed strange to him as the pale light began to grow stronger. At times he even forgot why they rode. He seemed caught in a company of grim-faced strangers pounding along a road to nowhere through a bleak, featureless landscape with their wind-whipped cloaks flying dark behind them like the clouds scudding low and dirty overhead. A peculiar idea began to take hold of him. The strangers were somehow his captors, and they were taking him away from his real friends. The idea seemed to grow stronger the farther they rode, and he began to be afraid.

Suddenly, without knowing why, he wheeled his horse and broke away, plunging off the side of the road and across the open field beside it.

"Garion!" a woman's voice called sharply from behind, but he set his heels to his horse's flanks and sped even faster across the rough field.

One of them was chasing him, a frightening man in black leather with a shaved head and a dark lock at his crown flowing behind him in the wind. In a panic Garion kicked at his horse, trying to make the beast run even faster, but the fearsome rider behind him closed the gap quickly and seized the reins from his hands. "What are you doing?" he demanded harshly.

Garion stared at him, unable to answer.

Then the woman in the blue cloak was there, and the others not far behind her. She dismounted quickly and stood looking at him with a stern face. She was tall for a woman, and her face was cold and imperious. Her hair was very dark, and there was a single white lock at her brow.

Garion trembled. The woman made him terribly afraid.

"Get down off that horse," she commanded.

"Gently, Pol," a silvery-haired old man with an evil face said.

A huge red-bearded giant rode closer, threatening, and Garion, almost sobbing with fright, slid down from his horse.

"Come here," the woman ordered. Falteringly, Garion approached her.

"Give me your hand," she said.

Hesitantly, he lifted his hand and she took his wrist firmly. She opened his fingers to reveal the ugly mark on his palm that he seemed to always have hated and then put his hand against the white lock in her hair.

"Aunt Pol," he gasped, the nightmare suddenly dropping away. She put her arms about him tightly and held him for some time. Strangely, he was not even embarrassed by that display of affection in front of the others.

"This is serious, father," she told Mister Wolf.

"What happened, Garion?" Wolf asked, his voice calm.

"I don't know," Garion replied. "It was as if I didn't know any of you, and you were my enemies, and all I wanted to do was run away to try to get back to my real friends."

"Are you still wearing the amulet I gave you?"

"Yes."

"Have you had it off at any time since I gave it to you?"

"Just once," Garion admitted. "When I took a bath in the Tolnedran hostel."

Wolf sighed. "You can't take if off," he said, "not ever—not for any reason. Take it out from under your tunic."

Garion drew out the silver pendant with the strange design on it.

The old man took a medallion out from under his own tunic. It was very bright and there was upon it the figure of a standing wolf so lifelike that it looked almost ready to lope away.

Aunt Pol, her one arm still about Garion's shoulders, drew a similar amulet out of her bodice. Upon the disc of her medallion was the figure of an owl. "Hold it in your right hand, dear," she instructed, firmly closing Garion's fingers over the pendant. Then, holding her amulet in her own right hand, she placed her left hand over his closed fist. Wolf, also holding his talisman, put his hand on theirs.

Garion's palm began to tingle as if the pendant were suddenly alive.

Mister Wolf and Aunt Pol looked at each other for a long moment, and the tingling in Garion's hand suddenly became very strong. His mind seemed to open, and strange things flickered before his eyes. He saw a round room very high up somewhere. A fire burned, but there was no wood in it. At a table there was seated an old man who looked somewhat like Mister Wolf but obviously was someone else. He seemed to be looking directly at Garion, and his eyes were kindly, even affectionate. Garion was suddenly over-whelmed with a consuming love for the old man.

"That should be enough," Wolf judged, releasing Garion's hand.

"Who was the old man?" Garion asked.

"My Master," Wolf replied.

"What happened?" Durnik asked, his face concerned.

"It's probably better not to talk about it," Aunt Pol said. "Do you think you could build a fire? It's time for breakfast."

"There are some trees over there where we can get out of the wind," Durnik suggested.

They all remounted and rode toward the trees.

After they had eaten, they sat by the small fire for a while. They were tired, and none of them felt quite up to facing the blustery morning again. Garion felt particularly exhausted, and he wished that he were young enough to sit close beside Aunt Pol and perhaps to put his head in her lap and sleep as he had done when he was very young. The strange thing that had hap-pened made him feel very much alone and more than a little frightened. "Durnik," he said, more to drive the mood away than out of any real curios-ity. "What sort of bird is that?" He pointed.

"A raven, I think," Durnik answered, looking at the bird circling above them.

"I thought so too," Garion said, "but they don't usually circle, do they?"

Durnik frowned. "Maybe it's watching something on the ground."

"How long has it been up there?" Wolf asked, squinting up at the large bird.

"I think I first saw it when we were crossing the field," Garion told him.

Mister Wolf glanced over at Aunt Pol. "What do you think?"

She looked up from one of Garion's stockings she had been mending. "I'll see." Her face took on a strange, probing expression.

Garion felt a peculiar tingling again. On an impulse he tried to push his own mind out toward the bird.

"Garion," Aunt Pol said without looking at him, "stop that."

"I'm sorry," he apologized quickly and pulled his mind back where it belonged.

Mister Wolf looked at him with a strange expression, then winked at him.

"It's Chamdar," Aunt Pol announced calmly. She carefully pushed her needle into the stocking and set it aside. Then she stood up and shook off her blue cloak.

"What have you got in mind?" Wolf asked.

"I think I'll go have a little chat with him," she replied, flexing her fingers like talons.

"You'd never catch him," Wolf told her. "Your feathers are too soft for this kind of wind. There's an easier way." The old man swept the windy sky with a searching gaze. "Over there." He pointed at a barely visible speck above the hills to the west. "You'd better do it, Pol. I don't get along with birds."

"Of course, father," she agreed. She looked intently at the speck, and Garion felt the tingle as she sent her mind out again. The speck began to circle, rising higher and higher until it disappeared.

The raven did not see the plummeting eagle until the last instant, just before the larger bird's talons struck. There was a sudden puff of black feathers, and the raven, screeching with fright, flapped wildly away with the eagle in pursuit.

"Nicely done, Pol," Wolf approved.

"It'll give him something to think about." She smiled. "Don't stare, Durnik."

Durnik was gaping at her, his mouth open. "How did you do that?"

"Do you really want to know?" she asked.

Durnik shuddered and looked away quickly.

"I think that just about settles it," Wolf said. "Disguises are probably useless now. I'm not sure what Chamdar's up to, but he's going to be watching us every step of the way. We might as well arm ourselves and ride straight on to Vo Mimbre."

"Aren't we going to follow the trail anymore?" Barak asked.

"The trail goes south," Wolf replied. "I can pick it up again once we cross over into Tolnedra. But first I want to stop by and have a word with King Korodullin. There are some things he needs to know."

"Korodullin?" Durnik looked puzzled. "Wasn't that the name of the first Arendish king? It seems to me somebody told me that once."

"All Arendish kings are named Korodullin," Silk told him. "And the queens are all named Mayaserana. It's part of the fiction the royal family here maintains to keep the kingdom from flying apart. They have to marry as closely within the bloodline as possible to maintain the illusion of the unification of the houses of Mimbre and Asturia. It makes them all a bit sickly, but there's no help for it—considering the peculiar nature of Arendish politics."

"All right, Silk," Aunt Pol said reprovingly.

Mandorallen looked thoughtful. "Could it be that this Chamdar who so dogs our steps is one of great substance in the dark society of the Grolims?" he asked.

"He'd like to be," Wolf answered. "Zedar and Ctuchik are Torak's disciples, and Chamdar wants to be one as well. He's always been Ctuchik's agent, but he may believe that this is his chance to move up in the Grolim hierarchy. Ctuchik's very old, and he spends all his time in the temple of Torak at Rak Cthol. Maybe Chamdar thinks it's time that someone else became High Priest."

"Is Torak's body at Rak Cthol?" Silk asked quickly.

Mister Wolf shrugged. "Nobody knows for sure, but I doubt it. After Zedar carried him away from the battlefield at Vo Mimbre, I don't think he'd have just handed him over to Ctuchik. He could be in Mallorea or somewhere in the southern reaches of Cthol Murgos. It's hard to say."

"But at the moment, Chamdar's the one we have to worry about," Silk concluded.

"Not if we keep moving," Wolf told him.

"We'd better get moving, then," Barak said, standing up.

By midmorning the heavy clouds had begun to break up and patches of blue sky showed here and there. Enormous pillars of sunlight stalked ponderously across the rolling fields that waited, damp and expectant, for the first touches of spring. With Mandorallen in the lead they had ridden hard and had covered a good six leagues. Finally they slowed to a walk to allow their steaming horses to rest.

"How much farther is it to Vo Mimbre, grandfather?" Garion asked, pulling his horse in beside Mister Wolf.

"Sixty leagues at least," Wolf answered. "Probably closer to eighty."

"That's a long way." Garion winced as he shifted in his saddle.

"Yes."

"I'm sorry I ran away like that back there," Garion apologized.

"It wasn't your fault. Chamdar was playing games."

"Why did he pick me? Couldn't he have done the same thing to Durnik—or Barak?"

Mister Wolf looked at him. "You're younger, more susceptible."

"That's not really it, is it?" Garion accused.

"No," Wolf admitted, "not really, but it's an answer, of sorts."

"This is another one of those things you aren't going to tell me, isn't it?"

"I suppose you could say that," Wolf answered blandly.

Garion sulked about that for a while, but Mister Wolf rode on, seemingly unconcerned by the boy's reproachful silence.

They stopped that night at a Tolnedran hostel, which, like all of them, was plain, adequate, and expensive. The next morning the sky had cleared except for billowy patches of white cloud scampering before the brisk wind. The sight of the sun made them all feel better, and there was even some bantering between Silk and Barak as they rode along—something Garion hadn't heard in all the weeks they'd spent traveling under the gloomy skies of northern Arendia.

Mandorallen, however, scarcely spoke that morning, and his face grew more somber with each passing mile. He was not wearing his armor, but instead a mail suit and a deep blue surcoat. His head was bare, and the wind tugged at his curly hair.

On a nearby hilltop a bleak-looking castle brooded down at them as they passed, its grim walls high and haughty-looking. Mandorallen seemed to avoid looking at it, and his face became even more melancholy.

Garion found it difficult to make up his mind about Mandorallen. He was honest enough with himself to admit that much of his thinking was still clouded by Lelldorin's prejudices. He didn't really want to like Mandorallen; but aside from the habitual gloominess which seemed characteristic of all Arends and the studied and involuted archaism of the man's speech and his towering self-confidence, there seemed little actually to dislike.

A half-league along the road from the castle, a ruin sat at the top of a long rise. It was not much more than a single wall with a high archway in the center and broken columns on either side. Near the ruin a woman sat on horseback, her dark red cape flowing in the wind.

Without a word, almost without seeming to think about it, Mandorallen turned his warhorse from the road and cantered up the rise toward the woman, who watched his approach without any seeming surprise, but also with no particular pleasure.

"Where's he going?" Barak asked.

"She's an acquaintance of his," Mister Wolf said dryly.

"Are we supposed to wait for him?"

"He can catch up with us," Wolf replied.

Mandorallen had stopped his horse near the woman and dismounted. He bowed to her and held out his hands to help her down from her horse. They walked together toward the ruin, not touching, but walking very close to each other. They stopped beneath the archway and talked. Behind the ruin, clouds raced in the windy sky, and their enormous shadows swept uncaring across the mournful fields of Arendia.

"We should have taken a different route," Wolf said. "I wasn't thinking, I guess."

"Is there some problem?" Durnik asked.

"Nothing unusual—in Arendia," Wolf answered. "I suppose it's my fault. Sometimes I forget the kind of things that can happen to young people."

"Don't be cryptic, father," Aunt Pol told him. "It's very irritating. Is this something we should know about?"

Wolf shrugged. "It isn't any secret," he replied. "Half of Arendia knows about it. A whole generation of Arendish virgins cry themselves to sleep every night over it."

"Father," Aunt Pol snapped exasperatedly.

"All right," Wolf said. "When Mandorallen was about Garion's age, he showed a great deal of promise—strong, courageous, not too bright—the qualities that make a good knight. His father asked me for advice, and I made arrangements for the young man to live for a while with the Baron of Vo Ebor—that's his castle back there. The baron had an enormous reputation, and he provided Mandorallen with the kind of instruction he needed. Mandorallen and the baron became almost like father and son, since the baron was quite a bit older. Everything was going along fine until the baron got married. His bride, however, was much younger—about Mandorallen's age."

"I think I see where this is going," Durnik remarked disapprovingly.

"Not exactly," Wolf disagreed. "After the honeymoon, the baron returned to his customary knightly pursuits and left a very bored young lady wandering around his castle. It's a situation with all kinds of interesting possibilities. Anyway, Mandorallen and the lady exchanged glances—then words—the usual sort of thing."

"It happens in Sendaria too," Durnik observed, "but I'm sure the name we have for it is different from the one they use here." His tone was critical, even offended.

"You're jumping to conclusions, Durnik," Wolf told him. "Things never went any further. It might have been better if they had. Adultery isn't really all that serious, and in time they'd have gotten bored with it. But, since they both loved and respected the baron too much to dishonor him, Mandorallen left the castle before things could get out of hand. Now they both suffer in silence. It's all very touching, but it seems like a waste of time to me. Of course, I'm older."

"You're older than everyone, father," Aunt Pol said.

"You didn't have to say that, Pol."

Silk laughed sardonically. "I'm glad to see that our stupendous friend at least has the bad taste to fall in love with another man's wife. His nobility was beginning to get rather cloying." The little man's expression had that bitter, self-mocking cast to it Garion had first seen in Val Alorn when they had spoken with Queen Porenn.

"Does the baron know about it?" Durnik asked.

"Naturally," Wolf replied. "That's the part that makes the Arends get all mushy inside about it. There was a knight once, stupider than most Arends, who made a bad joke about it. The baron promptly challenged him and ran a lance through him during the duel. Since then very few people have found the situation humorous."

"It's still disgraceful," Durnik said.

"Their behavior's above reproach, Durnik," Aunt Pol maintained firmly. "There's no shame in it as long as it doesn't go any further."

"Decent people don't allow it to happen in the first place," Durnik asserted.

"You'll never convince her, Durnik," Mister Wolf told the smith. "Polgara spent too many years associating with the Wacite Arends. They were as bad or worse than the Mimbrates. You can't wallow in that kind of sentimentality for that long without some of it rubbing off. Fortunately it hasn't *totally* blotted out her good sense. She's only occasionally girlish and gushy. If you can avoid her during those seizures, it's almost as if there were nothing wrong with her."

"My time was spent a little more usefully than yours, father," Aunt Pol observed acidly. "As I remember, *you* spent those years carousing in the waterfront dives in Camaar. And then there was that uplifting period you spent amusing the depraved women of Maragor. I'm certain those experiences broadened your concept of morality enormously."

Mister Wolf coughed uncomfortably and looked away.

Behind them, Mandorallen had remounted and begun to gallop back down the hill. The lady stood in the archway with her red cloak billowing in the wind, watching him as he rode away.

THEY WERE FIVE days on the road before they reached the River Arend, the boundary between Arendia and Tolnedra. The weather improved as they moved farther south, and by the morning when they reached the hill overlooking the river, it was almost warm. The sun was very bright, and a few fleecy clouds raced overhead in the fresh breeze.

"The high road to Vo Mimbre branches to the left just there," Mandorallen remarked.

"Yes," Wolf said. "Let's go down into that grove near the river and make ourselves a bit more presentable. Appearances are very important in Vo Mimbre, and we don't want to arrive looking like vagabonds."

Three brown-robed and hooded figures stood humbly at the crossroads, their faces down and their hands held out in supplication. Mister Wolf reined in his horse and approached them. He spoke with them briefly, then gave each a coin.

"Who are they?" Garion asked.

"Monks from Mar Terin," Silk replied.

"Where's that?"

"It's a monastery in southeastern Tolnedra where Maragor used to be," Silk told him. "The monks try to comfort the spirits of the Marags."

Mister Wolf motioned to them, and they rode on past the three humble figures at the roadside. "They say that no Murgos have passed here in the last two weeks."

"Are you sure you can believe them?" Hettar asked.

"Probably. The monks won't lie to anybody."

"Then they'll tell anybody who comes by that we've passed here?" Barak asked.

Wolf nodded. "They'll answer any question anybody puts to them."

"That's an unsavory habit," Barak grunted darkly.

Mister Wolf shrugged and led the way among the trees beside the river. "This ought to do," he decided, dismounting in a grassy glade. He waited while the others climbed down from their horses. "All right," he told them, "we're going to Vo Mimbre. I want you all to be careful about what you say there. Mimbrates are very touchy, and the slightest word can be taken as an insult."

"I think you should wear the white robe Fulrach gave you, father," Aunt Pol interrupted, pulling open one of the packs.

"Please, Pol," Wolf said, "I'm trying to explain something."

"They heard you, father. You tend to belabor things too much." She held up the white robe and looked at it critically. "You should have folded it more carefully. You've wrinkled it."

"I'm not going to wear that thing," he declared flatly.

"Yes, you are, father," she told him sweetly. "We might have to argue about it for an hour or two, but you'll wind up wearing it in the end anyway. Why not just save yourself all the time and aggravation?"

"It's silly," he complained.

"Lots of things are silly, father. I know the Arends better than you do. You'll get more respect if you look the part. Mandorallen and Hettar and Barak will wear their armor; Durnik and Silk and Garion can wear the doublets Fulrach gave them in Sendar; I'll wear my blue gown, and you'll wear the white robe. I insist, father."

"You *what*? Now listen here, Polgara—"

"Be still, father," she said absently, examining Garion's blue doublet. Wolf's face darkened, and his eyes bulged dangerously.

"Was there something else?" she asked with a level gaze.

Mister Wolf let it drop.

"He's as wise as they say he is," Silk observed.

An hour later they were on the high road to Vo Mimbre under a sunny sky. Mandorallen, once again in full armor and with a blue and silver pennon streaming from the tip of his lance, led the way with Barak in his gleaming mail shirt and black bearskin cape riding immediately behind him. At Aunt Pol's insistence, the big Cherek had combed the tangles out of his red beard and even rebraided his hair. Mister Wolf in his white robe rode sourly, muttering to himself, and Aunt Pol sat her horse demurely at his side in a short, fur-lined cape and with a blue satin headdress surmounting the heavy mass of her dark hair. Garion and Durnik were ill at ease in their finery, but Silk wore his doublet and black velvet cap with a kind of exuberant flair. Hettar's sole concession to formality had been the replacement of a ring of beaten silver for the leather thong which usually caught in his scalp lock.

The serfs and even the occasional knight they encountered along the way stood aside and saluted respectfully. The day was warm, the road was good, and their horses were strong. By midafternoon they crested a high hill overlooking the plain which sloped down to the gates of Vo Mimbre.

CHAPTER TEN

The City of the Mimbrate Arends reared almost like a mountain beside the sparkling river. Its thick, high walls were surmounted by massive battlements, and great towers and slender spires with bright banners at their tips rose within the walls, gleaming golden in the afternoon sun.

"Behold Vo Mimbre," Mandorallen proclaimed with pride, "queen of cities. Upon that rock the tide of Angarak crashed and recoiled and crashed again. Upon this field met they their ruin. The soul and pride of Arendia doth reside within that fortress, and the power of the Dark One may not prevail against it."

"We've been here before, Mandorallen," Mister Wolf said sourly.

"Don't be impolite, father," Aunt Pol told the old man. Then she turned to Mandorallen and to Garion's amazement she spoke in an idiom he had never heard from her lips before. "Wilt thou, Sir Knight, convey us presently into the palace of thy king? We must needs take council with him in matters of gravest urgency." She delivered this without the least trace of self-consciousness as if the archaic formality came quite naturally to her. "Forasmuch as thou art the mightiest knight on life, we place ourselves under the protection of thy arm."

Mandorallen, after a startled instant, slid with a crash from his warhorse and sank to his knees before her. "My Lady Polgara," he replied in a voice throbbing with respect—with reverence even, "I accept thy charge and will convey thee safely unto King Korodullin. Should any man question thy paramount right to the king's attention, I shall prove his folly upon his body."

Aunt Pol smiled at him encouragingly, and he vaulted into his saddle with a clang and led the way at a rolling trot, his whole bearing seething with a willingness to do battle.

"What was that all about?" Wolf asked.

"Mandorallen needed something to take his mind off his troubles," she replied. "He's been out of sorts for the last few days."

As they drew closer to the city, Garion could see the scars on the great walls where heavy stones from the Angarak catapults had struck the unyielding rock. The battlements high above were chipped and pitted from the impact of showers of steel-tipped arrows. The stone archway that led into the city revealed the incredible thickness of the walls, and the ironbound gate was massive. They clattered through the archway and into the narrow, crooked streets. The people they passed seemed for the most part to be commoners, who quickly moved aside. The faces of the men in dun-colored tunics and the women in patched dresses were dull and uncurious.

"They don't seem very interested in us," Garion commented quietly to Durnik.

"I don't think the ordinary people and the gentry pay much attention to each other here," Durnik replied. "They live side by side, but they don't know anything about each other. Maybe that's what's wrong with Arendia."

Garion nodded soberly.

Although the commoners were indifferent, the nobles at the palace seemed afire with curiosity. Word of the party's entrance into the city apparently had raced ahead of them through the narrow streets, and the windows and parapets of the palace were alive with people in brightly colored clothes.

"Abate thy pace, Sir Knight," a tall man with dark hair and beard, wearing a black velvet surcoat over his polished mail, called down from the parapet to Mandorallen as they clattered into the broad plaza before the palace. "Lift thy visor so I may know thee."

Mandorallen stopped in amazement before the closed gate and raised his visor. "What discourtesy is this?" he demanded. "I am, as all the world knows, Mandorallen, Baron of Vo Mandor. Surely thou canst see my crest upon the face of my shield."

"Any man may wear another's crest," the man above declared disdainfully.

Mandorallen's face darkened. "Art thou not mindful that no man on life would dare to counterfeit my semblance?" he asked in a dangerous tone.

"Sir Andorig," another knight on the parapet told the dark-haired man, "this is indeed Sir Mandorallen. I met him on the field of the great tourney last year, and our meeting cost me a broken shoulder and put a ringing in my ears which hath not yet subsided."

"Ah," Sir Andorig replied, "since thou wilt vouch for him, Sir Helbergin, I will admit that this is indeed the bastard of Vo Mandor."

"You're going to have to do something about that one of these days," Barak said quietly to Mandorallen.

"It would seem so," Mandorallen replied.

"Who, however, are these others with thee who seek admittance, Sir Knight?" Andorig demanded. "I will not cause the gates to open for foreign strangers."

Mandorallen straightened in his saddle. "Behold!" he announced in a voice that could probably be heard all over the city. "I bring you honor beyond measure. Fling wide the palace gates and prepare one and all to make obeisance. You look upon the holy face of Belgarath the Sorcerer, the Eternal Man, and upon the divine countenance of his daughter, the Lady Polgara, who have come to Vo Mimbre to consult with the King of Arendia on diverse matters."

"Isn't that a little overdone?" Garion whispered to Aunt Pol.

"It's customary, dear," she replied placidly. "When you're dealing with Arends, you have to be a little extravagant to get their attention."

"And who hath told thee that this is the Lord Belgarath?" Andorig asked with the faintest hint of a sneer. "I will bend no knee before an unproved vagabond."

"Dost thou question my word, Sir Knight?" Mandorallen returned in an ominously quiet voice. "And wilt thou then come down and put thy doubt to the test? Or is it perhaps that thou wouldst prefer to cringe doglike behind thy parapet and yap at thy betters?"

"Oh, that was *very* good," Barak said admiringly.

Mandorallen grinned tightly at the big man.

"I don't think we're getting anywhere with this," Mister Wolf muttered. "It looks like I'll have to prove something to this skeptic if we're ever going to get in to see Korodullin." He slid down from his saddle and thoughtfully removed a twig from his horse's tail, picked up somewhere during their journey. Then he strode to the center of the plaza and stood there in his gleaming white robe. "Sir Knight," he called up mildly to Andorig, "you're a cautious man, I see. That's a good quality, but it can be carried too far."

"I am hardly a child, old man," the dark-haired knight replied in a tone hovering on the verge of insult, "and I believe only what mine own eye hath confirmed."

"It must be a sad thing to believe so little," Wolf observed. He bent then and inserted the twig he'd been holding between two of the broad granite flagstones at his feet. He stepped back a pace and stretched his hand out above the twig, his face curiously gentle. "I'm going to do you a favor, Sir Andorig," he announced. "I'm going to restore your faith. Watch closely." And then he spoke a single soft word that Garion couldn't quite hear, but which set off the now-familiar surge and a faint roaring sound.

At first nothing seemed to be happening. Then the two flagstones began to buckle upward with a grinding sound as the twig grew visibly thicker and began to reach up toward Mister Wolf's outstretched hand. There were gasps from the palace walls as branches began to sprout from the twig as it grew. Wolf raised his hand higher, and the twig obediently grew at his gesture, its branches broadening. By now it was a young tree and still growing. One of the flagstones cracked with a sharp report.

There was absolute silence as every eye fixed in awed fascination on the tree. Mister Wolf held out both hands and turned them until the palms were up. He spoke again, and the tips of the branches swelled and began to bud. Then the tree burst into flower, its blossoms a delicate pink and white.

"Apple, wouldn't you say, Pol?" Wolf asked over his shoulder.

"It appears to be, father," she replied.

He patted the tree fondly and then turned back to the dark-haired knight who had sunk, white-faced and trembling, to his knees. "Well, Sir Andorig," he inquired, "what do you believe now?"

"Please forgive me, Holy Belgarath," Andorig begged in a strangled voice.

Mister Wolf drew himself up and spoke sternly, his words slipping into the measured cadences of the Mimbrate idiom as easily as Aunt Pol's had earlier. "I charge thee, Sir Knight, to care for this tree. It hath grown here to renew thy faith and trust. Thy debt to it must be paid with tender and loving attention to its needs. In time it will bear fruit, and thou wilt gather the fruit and give it freely to any who ask it of thee. For thy soul's sake, thou wilt refuse none, no matter how humble. As the tree gives freely, so shalt thou."

"That's a nice touch," Aunt Pol approved.

Wolf winked at her.

"I will do even as thou hast commanded me, Holy Belgarath," Sir Andorig choked. "I pledge my heart to it."

Mister Wolf returned to his horse. "At least he'll do *one* useful thing in his life," he muttered.

After that there was no further discussion. The palace gate creaked open, and they all rode into the inner courtyard and dismounted. Mandorallen led them past kneeling and even sobbing nobles who reached out to touch Mister Wolf's robe as he passed. At Mandorallen's heels they walked through the broad, tapestried hallways with a growing throng behind them. The door to the throne room opened, and they entered.

The Arendish throne room was a great, vaulted hall with sculptured buttresses soaring upward along the walls. Tall, narrow windows rose between the buttresses, and the light streaming through their stained-glass panels was jeweled. The floor was polished marble, and on the carpeted stone platform at the far end stood the double throne of Arendia, backed by heavy purple drapes. Flanking the draped wall hung the massive antique weapons of twenty generations of Arendish royalty. Lances, maces, and huge swords, taller than any man, hung among the tattered war banners of forgotten kings.

Korodullin of Arendia was a sickly-looking young man in a gold-embroidered purple robe, and he wore his large gold crown as if it were too heavy for him. Beside him on the double throne sat his pale, beautiful queen. Together they watched somewhat apprehensively as the throng surrounding Mister Wolf approached the wide steps leading up to the throne.

"My King," Mandorallen announced, dropping to one knee, "I bring into thy presence Holy Belgarath, Disciple of Aldur and the staff upon which the kingdoms of the West have leaned since time began."

"He knows who I am, Mandorallen," Mister Wolf said. He stepped forward and bowed briefly. "Hail Korodullin and Mayaserana," he greeted the king and queen. "I'm sorry we haven't had the chance to get acquainted before."

"The honor is ours, noble Belgarath," the young king replied in a voice whose rich timbre belied his frail appearance.

"My father spoke often of thee," the queen said.

"We were good friends," Wolf told her. "Allow me to present my daughter, Polgara."

"Great Lady," the king responded with a respectful inclination of his head. "All the world knows of thy power, but men have forgotten to speak of thy beauty."

"We'll get along well together," Aunt Pol answered warmly, smiling at him.

"My heart trembles at the sight of the flower of all womanhood," the queen declared.

Aunt Pol looked at the queen thoughtfully. "We must talk, Mayaserana," she said in a serious tone, "in private and very soon."

The queen looked startled.

Mister Wolf introduced the rest of them, and each bowed in turn to the young king.

"Welcome, gentles all," Korodullin said. "My poor court is overwhelmed by so noble a company."

"We don't have much time, Korodullin," Mister Wolf told him. "The courtesy of the Arendish throne is the marvel of the world. I don't want to offend you and your lovely queen by cutting short those stately observances which so ornament your court, but I have certain news which I have to present to you in private. The matter is of extreme urgency."

"Then I am at thine immediate disposal," the king replied, rising from his throne. "Forgive us, dear friends," he said to the assembled nobles, "but this ancient friend of our kingly line hath information which must be imparted to our ears alone with utmost urgency. I pray thee, let us go apart for a little space of time to receive this instruction. We shall return presently."

"Polgara," Mister Wolf said.

"Go ahead, father," she replied. "Just now I have to speak with Mayaserana about something that's very important to her."

"Can't it wait?"

"No, father, it can't." And with that she took the queen's arm, and the two left. Mister Wolf stared after her for a moment; then he shrugged, and he and Korodullin also left the throne room. An almost shocked silence followed their departure.

"Most unseemly," an old courtier with wispy white hair disapproved.

"A necessary haste, my Lord," Mandorallen informed him. "As the revered Belgarath hath intimated, our mission is the hinge-pin of the survival of all the kingdoms of the West. Our Ancient Foe may soon be abroad again. It will not be long, I fear, ere Mimbrate knights will again stand the brunt of titanic war."

"Blessed then be the tongue which brings the news," the white-haired old man declared. "I had feared that I had seen my last battle and would die abed in my dotage. I thank great Chaldan that I still have my vigor, and that my prowess is undiminished by the passage of a mere four-score years."

Garion drew off by himself to one side of the room to wrestle with a problem. Events had swept him into King Korodullin's court before he'd had the time to prepare himself for an unpleasant duty. He had given his word to Lelldorin to bring certain things to the king's attention, but he did not have the faintest idea how to begin. The exaggerated formality of the Arendish court intimidated him. This was not at all like the rough, good-natured court of King Anheg in Val Alorn or the almost homey court of King Fulrach in Sendar. This was Vo Mimbre, and the prospect of blurting out news of the wild scheme of a group of Asturian firebrands as he had blurted out the news of the Earl of Jarvik in Cherek now seemed utterly out of the question.

Suddenly the thought of that previous event struck him forcibly. The situation then was so similar to this one that it seemed all at once like some elaborate game. The moves on the board were almost identical, and in each case he had been placed in the uncomfortable position of being required to block that last crucial move where a king would die and a kingdom would collapse. He felt oddly powerless, as if his entire life were in the fingers of two faceless players maneuvering pieces in the same patterns on some vast board in a game that, for all he knew, had lasted for eternity. There was no question about what had to be done. The players, however, seemed content to leave it up to him to come up with a way to do it.

King Korodullin appeared shaken when he returned to the throne room with Mister Wolf a half hour later, and he controlled his expression with obvious difficulty. "Forgive me, gentles all," he apologized, "but I have had disturbing news. For the present time, however, let us put aside our cares and celebrate this historic visit. Summon musicians and command that a banquet be made ready."

There was a stir near the door, and a black-robed man entered with a half-dozen Mimbrate knights in full armor following him closely, their eyes narrow with suspicion and their hands on their sword hilts as if daring anyone to bar their leader's path. As the robed man strode nearer, Garion saw his angular eyes and scarred cheeks. The man was a Murgo.

Barak put a firm hand on Hettar's arm.

The Murgo had obviously dressed in haste and he seemed slightly breathless from his hurried trip to the throne room. "Your Majesty," he rasped, bowing deeply to Korodullin, "I have just been advised that visitors have arrived at thy court and have made haste here to greet them in the name of my king, Taur Urgas."

Korodullin's face grew cold. "I do not recall summoning thee, Nachak," he said.

"It is, then, as I had feared," the Murgo replied. "These messengers have spoken ill of my race, seeking to dissever the friendship which doth exist between the thrones of Arendia and of Cthol Murgos. I am chagrined to find that thou hast given ear to slanders without offering me opportunity to reply. Is this just, august Majesty?"

"Who is this?" Mister Wolf asked Korodullin.

"Nachak," the king replied, "the ambassador of Cthol Murgos. Shall I introduce thee to him, Ancient One?"

"That won't be necessary," Mister Wolf answered bleakly. "Every Murgo alive knows who I am. Mothers in Cthol Murgos frighten their children into obedience by mentioning my name."

"But I am not a child, old man," Nachak sneered. "I'm not afraid of you."

"That could be a serious failing," Silk observed.

The Murgo's name had struck Garion almost like a blow. As he looked at the scarred face of the man who had so misled Lelldorin and his friends, he realized that the players had once again moved their pieces into that last crucial position, and that who would win and who would lose once again depended entirely on him.

"What lies have you told the king?" Nachak was demanding of Mister Wolf.

"No lies, Nachak," Wolf told him. "Just the truth. That should be enough."

"I protest, your Majesty," Nachak appealed to the king. "I protest in the strongest manner possible. All the world knows of his hatred for my people. How can you allow him to poison your mind against us?"

"He forgot the thees and thous that time," Silk commented slyly.

"He's excited," Barak replied. "Murgos get clumsy when they're excited. It's one of their shortcomings."

"Alorns!" Nachak spat.

"That's right, Murgo," Barak said coldly. He was still holding Hettar's arm.

Nachak looked at them, and then his eyes widened as he seemed to see Hettar for the first time. He recoiled from the Algar's hate-filled stare, and his half-dozen knights closed protectively around him. "Your Majesty," he rasped, "I know that man to be Hettar of Algaria, a known murderer. I demand that you arrest him."

"*Demand*, Nachak?" the king asked with a dangerous glint in his eyes. "Thou wilt present demands to me in my own court?"

"Forgive me, your Majesty," Nachak apologized quickly. "The sight of that animal so disturbed me that I forgot myself."

"You'd be wise to leave now, Nachak," Mister Wolf recommended. "It's not really a good idea for a Murgo to be alone in the presence of so many Alorns. Accidents have a way of happening under such conditions."

"Grandfather," Garion said urgently. Without knowing exactly why, he knew that it was time to speak. Nachak must not be allowed to leave the throne room. The faceless players had made their final moves, and the game must end here. "Grandfather," he repeated, "there's something I have to tell you."

"Not now, Garion." Wolf was still looking with hard eyes at the Murgo.

"It's important, grandfather. *Very* important."

Mister Wolf turned as if to reply sharply, but then he seemed to see something—something that no one else in the throne room could see—and his eyes widened in momentary amazement. "All right, Garion," he said in a strangely quiet voice. "Go ahead."

"Some men are planning to kill the king of Arendia. Nachak's one of them." Garion had said it louder than he'd intended, and a sudden silence fell over the throne room at his words.

Nachak's face went pale, and his hand moved involuntarily toward his sword hilt, then froze. Garion was suddenly keenly aware of Barak hulking just behind him and Hettar, grim as death in black leather, towering beside him. Nachak stepped back and made a quick gesture to his steel-clad knights. Quickly they formed a protective ring around him, their hands on their weapons. "I won't stay and listen to such slander," the Murgo declared.

"I have not yet given thee my permission to withdraw, Nachak," Korodullin informed him coolly. "I require thy presence yet a while." The young king's face was stern, and his eyes bored into the Murgo's. Then he turned to Garion. "I would hear more of this. Speak truthfully, lad, and fear not reprisal from any man for thy words."

Garion drew a deep breath and spoke carefully. "I don't really know all the details, your Majesty," he explained. "I found out about it by accident."

"Say what thou canst," the king told him.

"As nearly as I can tell, your Majesty, next summer when you travel to Vo Astur, a group of men are going to try to kill you somewhere on the highway."

"Asturian traitors, doubtless," a gray-haired courtier suggested.

"They call themselves patriots," Garion answered.

"Inevitably," the courtier sneered.

"Such attempts are not uncommon," the king stated. "We will take steps to guard against them. I thank thee for this information."

"There's more, your Majesty," Garion added. "When they attack, they're going to be wearing the uniforms of Tolnedran legionnaires."

Silk whistled sharply.

"The whole idea is to make your nobles believe that you've been killed by the Tolnedrans," Garion continued. "These men are sure that Mimbre will immediately declare war on the Empire, and that as soon as that happens the legions will march in. Then, when everybody here is involved in the war, they're going to announce that Asturia's no longer subject to the Arendish throne. They're sure that the rest of Asturia will follow them at that point."

"I see," the king replied thoughtfully. " 'Tis a well-conceived plan, but with a subtlety uncharacteristic of our wild-eyed Asturian brothers. But I have yet heard nothing linking the emissary of Taur Urgas with this treason."

"The whole plan was his, your Majesty. He gave them all the details and the gold to buy the Tolnedran uniforms and to encourage other people to join them."

"He lies!" Nachak burst out.

"Thou shalt have opportunity to reply, Nachak," the king advised him. He turned back to Garion. "Let us pursue this matter further. How camest thou by this knowledge?"

"I can't say, your Majesty," Garion replied painfully. "I gave my word not to. One of the men told me about it to prove that he was my friend. He put his life in my hands to show how much he trusted me. I can't betray him."

"Thy loyalty speaks well of thee, young Garion," the king commended him, "but thine accusation against the Murgo ambassador is most grave. Without violating thy trust, canst thou provide corroboration?"

Helplessly, Garion shook his head.

"This is a serious matter, your Majesty," Nachak declared. "I am the personal representative of Taur Urgas. This lying urchin is Belgarath's creature, and his wild, unsubstantiated story is an obvious attempt to discredit me and to drive a wedge between the thrones of Arendia and Cthol Murgos. This accusation must not be allowed to stand. The boy must be forced to identify these imaginary plotters or to admit that he lies."

"He hath given his pledge, Nachak," the king pointed out.

"He says so, your Majesty," Nachak replied with a sneer. "Let us put him to the test. An hour on the rack may persuade him to speak freely."

"I've seldom had much faith in confessions obtained by torment," Korodullin said.

"If it please your Majesty," Mandorallen interjected, "it may be that I can help to resolve this matter."

Garion threw a stricken look at the knight. Mandorallen knew Lelldorin, and it would be a simple thing for him to guess the truth. Mandorallen, moreover, was a Mimbrate, and Korodullin was his king. Not only was he under no compulsion to remain silent, but his duty almost obliged him to speak.

"Sir Mandorallen," the king responded gravely, "thy devotion to truth and duty are legendary. Canst thou perchance identify these plotters?"

The question hung there.

"Nay, Sire," Mandorallen replied firmly, "but I know Garion to be a truthful and honest boy. I will vouch for him."

"That's scanty corroboration," Nachak asserted. "I declare that he lies, so where does that leave us?"

"The lad is my companion," Mandorallen said. "I will not be the instrument of breaking his pledge, since his honor is as dear to me as mine own. By our law, however, a cause incapable of proof may be decided by trial at arms. I will champion this boy. I declare before this company that this Nachak is a foul villain who hath joined with diverse others to slay my king." He pulled off his steel gauntlet and tossed it to the floor. The crash as it struck the polished stone seemed thunderous. "Take up my gage, Murgo," Mandorallen said coldly, "or let one of thy sycophant knights take it up for thee. I will prove thy villainy upon thy body or upon the body of thy champion."

Nachak stared first at the mailed gauntlet and then at the great knight standing accusingly before him. He licked his lips nervously and looked around the throne room. Except for Mandorallen, none of the Mimbrate nobles present were under arms. The Murgo's eyes narrowed with a sudden desperation. "Kill him!" he snarled at the six men in armor surrounding him.

The knights looked shocked, doubtful.

"Kill him!" Nachak commanded them. "A thousand gold pieces to the man who spills out his life!"

The faces of the six knights went flat at the words. As one man they drew their swords and spread out, moving with raised shields toward Mandorallen. There were gasps and cries of alarm as the nobles and their ladies scrambled out of the way.

"What treason is this?" Mandorallen demanded of them. "Are ye so enamored of this Murgo and his gold that ye will draw weapons in the king's presence in open defiance of the law's prohibitions? Put up your swords."

But they ignored his words and continued their grim advance.

"Defend thyself, Sir Mandorallen," Korodullin urged, half-rising from his throne. "I free thee of the law's constraint."

Barak, however, had already begun to move. Noting that Mandorallen had not carried his shield into the throne room, the red-bearded man jerked an enormous two-handed broadsword down from the array of banners and weapons at one side of the dais. "Mandorallen!" he shouted and with a great heave he slid the huge blade skittering and bouncing across the stone floor toward the knight's feet. Mandorallen stopped the sliding weapon with one mailed foot, stooped, and picked it up.

The approaching knights looked a bit less confident as Mandorallen lifted the six-foot blade with both hands.

Barak, grinning hugely, drew his sword from one hip and his war axe from the other. Hettar, his drawn sabre held low, was circling the clumsy knights on catlike feet. Without thinking, Garion reached for his own sword, but Mister Wolf's hand closed on his wrist. "You stay out of it," the old man told him and pulled him clear of the impending fight.

Mandorallen's first blow crashed against a quickly raised shield, shattering the arm of a knight with a crimson surcoat over his armor and hurling him into a clattering heap ten feet away. Barak parried a sword stroke from a burly knight with his axe and battered at the man's raised shield with his own heavy sword. Hettar toyed expertly with a knight in green-enameled armor, easily avoiding his opponent's awkward strokes and flicking the point of his sabre at the man's visored face.

The steely ring of sword on sword echoed through Korodullin's throne room, and showers of sparks cascaded from the clash of edge against edge. With huge blows, Mandorallen smashed at a second man. A vast sweep of his two-handed sword went under the knight's shield, and the man shrieked as the great blade bit through his armor and into his side. Then he fell with blood spouting from the sheared-in gash that reached halfway through his body.

Barak, with a deft backswing of his war axe, caved in the side of the burly knight's helmet, and the knight half-spun and fell to the floor. Hettar feinted a quick move, then drove his sabre point through a slot in the green-armored knight's visor. The stricken knight stiffened as the sabre ran into his brain.

As the mêlée surged across the polished floor, the nobles and ladies scurried this way and that to avoid being overrun by the struggling men. Nachak watched with dismay as his knights were systematically destroyed before his eyes. Then, quite suddenly, he turned and fled.

"He's getting away!" Garion shouted, but Hettar was already in pursuit, his dreadful face and blood-smeared sabre melting the courtiers and their screaming ladies out of his path as he ran to cut off Nachak's flight. The Murgo had almost reached the far end of the hall before Hettar's long strides carried him through the crowd to block the doorway. With a cry of despair, the ambassador yanked his sword from its scabbard, and Garion felt a strange, momentary pity for him.

As the Murgo raised his sword, Hettar flicked his sabre almost like a whip, lashing him once on each shoulder. Nachak desperately tried to raise his numbed arms to protect his head, but Hettar's blade dropped low instead. Then, with a peculiar fluid grace, the grim-faced Algar quite deliberately ran the Murgo through. Garion saw the sabre blade come out between Nachak's shoulders, angling sharply upward. The ambassador gasped, dropped his sword and gripped Hettar's wrist with both hands, but the hawk-faced man inexorably turned his hand, twisting the sharp, curved blade inside the Murgo's body. Nachak groaned and shuddered horribly. Then his hands slipped off Hettar's wrists and his legs buckled under him. With a gurgling sigh, he toppled backward, sliding limply off Hettar's blade.

CHAPTER ELEVEN

A moment of dreadful silence filled the throne room following the death of Nachak. Then the two members of his bodyguard who were still on their feet threw their weapons down on the blood-spattered floor with a sudden clatter. Mandorallen raised his visor and turned toward the throne. "Sire," he said respectfully, "the treachery of Nachak stands proved by reason of this trial at arms."

"Truly," the king agreed. "My only regret is that thine enthusiasm in pursuing this cause hath deprived us of the opportunity to probe more deeply into the full extent of Nachak's duplicity."

"I expect that the plots he hatched will dry up once word of what happened here gets around," Mister Wolf observed.

"Perhaps so," the king acknowledged. "I would have pursued the matter further, however. I would know if this villainy was Nachak's own or if I must look beyond him to Taur Urgas himself." He frowned thoughtfully, then shook his head as if to put certain dark speculations aside. "Arendia stands in thy debt, Ancient Belgarath. This brave company of thine hath forestalled the renewal of a war best forgotten." He looked sadly at the blood-smeared floor and the bodies littering it. "My throne room hath become as a battlefield. The curse of Arendia extends even here." He sighed. "Have it cleansed," he ordered shortly and turned his head so that he would not have to watch the grim business of cleaning up.

The nobles and ladies began to buzz as the dead were removed and the polished stone floor was quickly mopped to remove the pools of sticky blood.

"Good fight," Barak commented as he carefully wiped his axe blade.

"I am in thy debt, Lord Barak," Mandorallen said gravely. "Thine aid was fortuitous."

Barak shrugged. "It seemed appropriate."

Hettar rejoined them, his expression one of grim satisfaction.

"You did a nice job on Nachak," Barak complimented him.

"I've had a lot of practice," Hettar answered. "Murgos always seem to make that same mistake when they get into a fight. I think there's a gap in their training somewhere."

"That's a shame, isn't it?" Barak suggested with vast insincerity.

Garion moved away from them. Although he knew it was irrational, he nevertheless felt a keen sense of personal responsibility for the carnage he had just witnessed. The blood and violent death had come about as the result of his words. Had he not spoken, men who were now dead would still be alive. No matter how justified—how necessary—his speaking out had been, he still suffered the pangs of guilt. He did not at the moment trust himself to speak with his friends. More than anything he wished that he could talk with Aunt Pol, but she had not yet returned to the throne room, and so he was left to wrestle alone with his wounded conscience.

He reached one of the embrasures formed by the buttresses along the south wall of the throne room and stood alone in somber reflection until a girl, perhaps two years older than he, glided across the floor toward him, her stiff, crimson brocade gown rustling. The girl's hair was dark, even black, and her skin was creamy. Her bodice was cut quite low, and Garion found some difficulty in finding a safe place for his eyes as she bore down on him.

"I would add my thanks to the thanks of all Arendia, Lord Garion," she breathed at him. Her voice was vibrant with all kinds of emotions, none of which Garion understood. "Thy timely revelation of the Murgo's plotting hath in truth saved the life of our sovereign."

Garion felt a certain warmth at that. "I didn't do all that much, my Lady," he replied with a somewhat insincere attempt at modesty. "My friends did all the fighting."

"But it was *thy* brave denunciation which uncovered the foul plot," she persisted, "and virgins will sing of the nobility with which thou protected the identity of thy nameless and misguided friend."

Virgin was not a word with which Garion was prepared to deal. He blushed and floundered helplessly.

"Art thou in truth, noble Garion, the grandson of Eternal Belgarath?"

"The relationship is a bit more distant. We simplify it for the sake of convenience."

"But thou art in his direct line?" she persisted, her violet eyes glowing.

"He tells me I am."

"Is the Lady Polgara perchance thy mother?"

"My aunt."

"A close kinship nonetheless," she approved warmly, her hand coming to rest lightly on his wrist. "Thy blood, Lord Garion, is the noblest in the world. Tell me, art thou perchance as yet unbetrothed?"

Garion blinked at her, his ears growing suddenly redder.

"Ah, Garion," Mandorallen boomed in his hearty voice, striding into the awkward moment, "I had been seeking thee. Wilt thou excuse us, Countess?"

The young lady shot Mandorallen a look filled with sheer venom, but the knight's firm hand was already drawing Garion away.

"We will speak again, Lord Garion," she called after him.

"I hope so, my Lady," Garion replied back over his shoulder. Then he and Mandorallen merged with the crowd of courtiers near the center of the throne room.

"I wanted to thank you, Mandorallen," Garion said finally, struggling with it a little.

"For what, lad?"

"You knew whom I was protecting when I told the king about Nachak, didn't you?"

"Naturally," the knight replied in a rather offhand way.

"You could have told the king—actually it was your duty to tell him, wasn't it?"

"But thou hadst given thy pledge."

"You hadn't, though."

"Thou art my companion, lad. Thy pledge is as binding upon me as it is upon thee. Didst thou not know that?"

Garion was startled by Mandorallen's words. The exquisite involvement of Arendish ethics were beyond his grasp. "So you fought for me instead."

Mandorallen laughed easily. "Of course," he answered, "though I must confess to thee in all honesty, Garion, that my eagerness to stand as thy champion grew not entirely out of friendship. In truth I found the Murgo Nachak offensive and liked not the cold arrogance of his hirelings. I was inclined toward battle before thy need of championing presented itself. Perhaps it is I who should thank thee for providing the opportunity."

"I don't understand you at all, Mandorallen," Garion admitted. "Sometimes I think you're the most complicated man I've ever met."

"I?" Mandorallen seemed amazed. "I am the simplest of men." He looked around then and leaned slightly toward Garion. "I must advise thee to have a care in thy speech with the Countess Vasrana," he warned. "It was that which impelled me to draw thee aside."

"Who?"

"The comely young lady with whom thou wert speaking. She considers herself the greatest beauty in the kingdom and is seeking a husband worthy of her."

"Husband?" Garion responded in a faltering voice.

"Thou art fair game, lad. Thy blood is noble beyond measure by reason of thy kinship to Belgarath. Thou wouldst be a great prize for the countess."

"Husband?" Garion quavered again, his knees beginning to tremble. "Me?"

"I know not how things stand in misty Sendaria," Mandorallen declared, "but in Arendia thou art of marriageable age. Guard well thy speech, lad. The most innocent remark can be viewed as a promise, should a noble lady choose to take it so."

Garion swallowed hard and looked around apprehensively. After that he did his best to hide. His nerves, he felt, were not up to any more shocks.

The Countess Vasrana, however, proved to be a skilled huntress. With appalling determination she tracked him down and pinned him in another embrasure with smoldering eyes and heaving bosom. "Now perchance we may continue our most interesting discussion, Lord Garion," she purred at him.

Garion was considering flight when Aunt Pol, accompanied by a now-radiant Queen Mayaserana, reentered the throne room. Mandorallen spoke briefly to her, and she immediately crossed to the spot where the violet-eyed countess held Garion captive. "Garion, dear," she said as she approached. "It's time for your medicine."

"Medicine?" he replied, confused.

"A most forgetful boy," she told the countess. "Probably it was all the excitement, but he knows that if he doesn't take the potion every three hours, the madness will return."

"Madness?" the Countess Vasrana repeated sharply.

"The curse of his family," Aunt Pol sighed. "They all have it—all the male children. The potion works for a while, but of course it's only temporary. We'll have to find some patient and self-sacrificing lady soon, so that he can marry and father children before his brains begin to soften. After that his poor wife will be doomed to spend the rest of her days caring for him." She looked critically at the young countess. "I wonder," she said. "Could it be possible that *you* are as yet unbetrothed? You appear to be of a suitable age." She reached out and briefly took hold of Vasrana's rounded arm. "Nice and strong," she said approvingly. "I'll speak to my father, Lord Belgarath, about this immediately."

The countess began to back away, her eyes wide.

"Come back," Aunt Pol told her. "His fits won't start for several minutes yet."

The girl fled.

"Can't you ever stay out of trouble?" Aunt Pol demanded of Garion, leading him firmly away.

"But I didn't say anything," he objected.

Mandorallen joined them, grinning broadly. "I perceive that thou hast routed our predatory countess, my Lady. I should have thought she would prove more persistent."

"I gave her something to worry about. It dampened her enthusiasm for matrimony."

"What matter didst thou discuss with our queen?" he asked. "I have not seen her smile so in years."

"Mayaserana's had a problem of a female nature. I don't think you'd understand."

"Her inability to carry a child to term?"

"Don't Arends have anything better to do than gossip about things that don't concern them? Why don't you go find another fight instead of asking intimate questions?"

"The matter is of great concern to us all, my Lady," Mandorallen apologized. "If our queen does not produce an heir to the throne, we stand in danger of dynastic war. All Arendia could go up in flames."

"There aren't going to be any flames, Mandorallen. Fortunately I arrived in time—though it was very close. You'll have a crown prince before winter."

"Is it possible?"

"Would you like all the details?" she asked pointedly. "I've noticed that men usually prefer not to know about the exact mechanics involved in childbearing."

Mandorallen's face slowly flushed. "I will accept thine assurances, Lady Polgara," he replied quickly.

"I'm *so* glad."

"I must inform the king," he declared.

"You must mind your own business, Sir Mandorallen. The queen will tell Korodullin what he needs to know. Why don't you go clean off your armor? You look as if you just walked through a slaughterhouse."

He bowed, still blushing, and moved away.

"Men!" she said to his retreating back. Then she turned back to Garion. "I hear that you've been busy."

"I had to warn the king," he replied.

"You seem to have an absolute genius for getting mixed up in this sort of thing. Why didn't you tell me—or your grandfather?"

"I promised that I wouldn't say anything."

"Garion," she said firmly, "under our present circumstances, secrets are very dangerous. You knew that what Lelldorin told you was important, didn't you?"

"I didn't say it was Lelldorin."

She gave him a withering look. "Garion, dear," she told him bluntly, "don't ever make the mistake of thinking that I'm stupid."

"I didn't," he floundered. "I wasn't. I—Aunt Pol, I gave them my word that I wouldn't tell anybody."

She sighed. "We've got to get you out of Arendia," she declared. "The place seems to be affecting your good sense. The next time you feel the urge to make one of these startling public announcements, talk it over with me first, all right?"

"Yes, ma'am," he mumbled, embarrassed.

"Oh, Garion, what am I ever going to do with you?" Then she laughed fondly and put her arm about his shoulder and everything was all right again.

The evening passed uneventfully after that. The banquet was tedious, and the toasts afterward interminable as each Arendish noble arose in turn to salute Mister Wolf and Aunt Pol with flowery and formal speeches. They went to bed late, and Garion slept fitfully, troubled by nightmares of the hot-eyed countess pursuing him through endless, flower-strewn corridors.

They were up early the next morning, and after breakfast Aunt Pol and Mister Wolf spoke privately with the king and queen again. Garion, still nervous about his encounter with the Countess Vasrana, stayed close to Mandorallen. The Mimbrate knight seemed best equipped to help him avoid any more such adventures. They waited in an antechamber to the throne room, and Mandorallen in his blue surcoat explained at length an intricate tapestry which covered one entire wall.

About midmorning Sir Andorig, the dark-haired knight Mister Wolf had ordered to spend his days caring for the tree in the plaza, came looking for Mandorallen. "Sir Knight," he said respectfully, "the Baron of Vo Ebor hath arrived from the north accompanied by his lady. They have asked after thee and besought me that I should seek thee out for them."

"Thou art most kind, Sir Andorig," Mandorallen replied, rising quickly from the bench where he had been sitting. "Thy courtesy becomes thee greatly."

Andorig sighed. "Alas that it was not always so. I have this past night stood vigil before that miraculous tree which Holy Belgarath commended to my care. I thus had leisure to consider my life in retrospect. I have not been an admirable man. Bitterly I repent my faults and will strive earnestly for amendment."

Wordlessly, Mandorallen clasped the knight's hand and then followed him down a long hallway to a room where the visitors waited.

It was not until they entered the sunlit room that Garion remembered that the wife of the Baron of Vo Ebor was the lady to whom Mandorallen had spoken on that windswept hill beside the Great West Road some days before.

The baron was a solid-looking man in a green surcoat, and his hair and beard were touched with white. His eyes were deep-set, and there seemed to be a great sadness in them. "Mandorallen," he said, warmly embracing the younger knight. "Thou art unkind to absent thyself from us for so long."

"Duty, my Lord," Mandorallen replied in a subdued voice.

"Come, Nerina," the baron told his wife, "greet our friend."

The Baroness Nerina was much younger than her husband. Her hair was dark and very long. She wore a rose-colored gown, and she was beautiful— though, Garion thought, no more so than any of a half-dozen others he had seen at the Arendish court.

"Dear Mandorallen," she said, kissing the knight with a brief, chaste embrace, "we have missed thee at Vo Ebor."

"And the world is desolate for me that I must be absent from its well-loved halls."

Sir Andorig had bowed and then discreetly departed, leaving Garion standing awkwardly near the door.

"And who is this likely-appearing lad who accompanies thee, my son?" the baron asked.

"A Sendarian boy," Mandorallen responded. "His name is Garion. He and diverse others have joined with me in a perilous quest."

"Joyfully I greet my son's companion," the baron declared.

Garion bowed, but his mind raced, attempting to find some legitimate excuse to leave. The situation was terribly embarrassing, and he did not want to stay.

"I must wait upon the king," the baron announced. "Custom and courtesy demand that I present myself to him as soon as possible upon my arrival at his court. Wilt thou, Mandorallen, remain here with my baroness until I return?"

"I will, my Lord."

"I'll take you to where the king is meeting with my aunt and my grandfather, sir," Garion offered quickly.

"Nay, lad," the baron demurred. "Thou too must remain. Though I have no cause for anxiety, knowing full well the fidelity of my wife and my dearest friend, idle tongues would make scandal were they left together unattended. Prudent folk leave no possible foundation for false rumor and vile innuendo."

"I'll stay, then, sir," Garion replied quickly.

"Good lad," the baron approved. Then, with eyes that seemed somehow haunted, he quietly left the room.

"Wilt thou sit, my Lady?" Mandorallen asked Nerina, pointing to a sculptured bench near a window.

"I will," she said. "Our journey was fatiguing."

"It is a long way from Vo Ebor," Mandorallen agreed, sitting on another bench. "Didst thou and my Lord find the roads passable?"

"Perhaps not yet so dry as to make travel enjoyable," she told him.

They spoke at some length about roads and weather, sitting not far from each other, but not so close that anyone chancing to pass by the open door could have mistaken their conversation for anything less than innocent. Their eyes, however, spoke more intimately. Garion, painfully embarrassed, stood looking out a window, carefully choosing one that kept him in full view of the door.

As the conversation progressed, there were increasingly long pauses, and Garion cringed inwardly at each agonizing silence, afraid that either Mandorallen or the Lady Nerina might in the extremity of their hopeless love cross that unspoken boundary and blurt the one word, phrase, or sentence which would cause restraint and honor to crumble and turn their lives into disaster. And yet a certain part of his mind wished that the word or phrase or sentence might be spoken and that their love could flame, however briefly.

It was there, in that quiet sunlit chamber, that Garion passed a small crossroad. The prejudice against Mandorallen that Lelldorin's unthinking partisanship had instilled in him finally shattered and fell away. He felt a surge of feeling—not pity, for they would not have accepted pity, but compassion rather. More than that, there was the faint beginning of an understanding of the honor and towering pride which, though utterly selfless, was the foundation of that tragedy which had existed in Arendia for uncounted centuries.

For perhaps a half hour more Mandorallen and the Lady Nerina sat, speaking hardly at all now, their eyes lost in each other's faces while Garion, near to tears, stood his enforced watch over them. And then Durnik came to tell them that Aunt Pol and Mister Wolf were getting ready to leave.

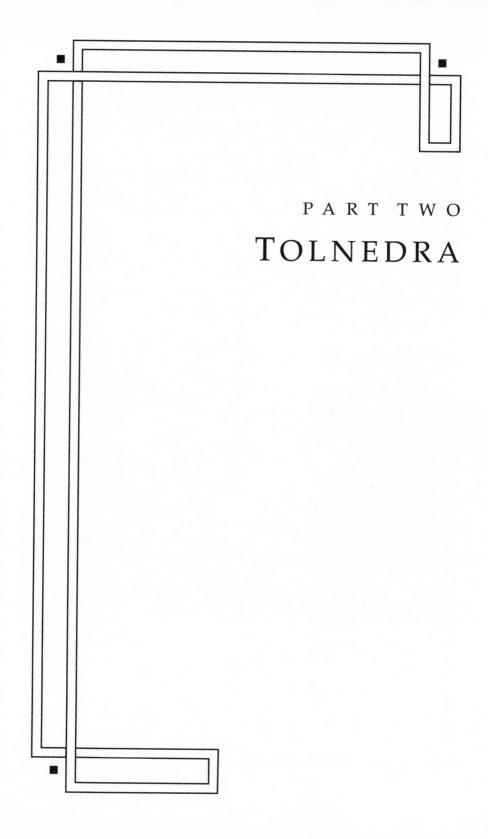

PART TWO

TOLNEDRA

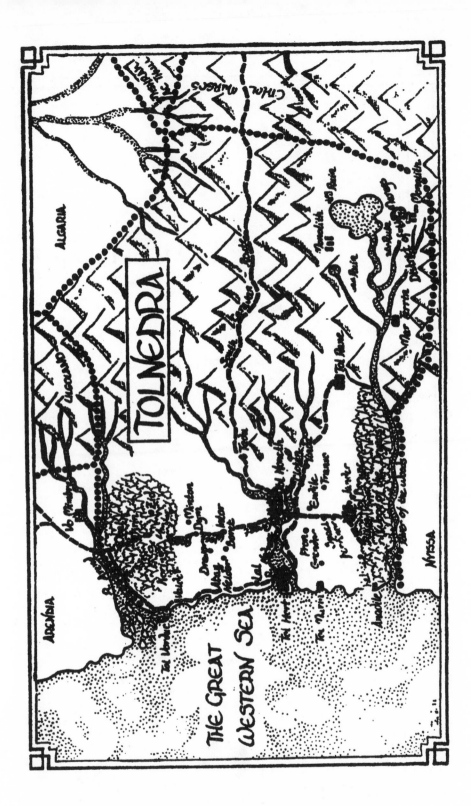

A brassy chorus of horns saluted them from the battlements of Vo Mimbre as they rode out of the city accompanied by two-score armored knights and by King Korodullin himself. Garion glanced back once and thought he saw the Lady Nerina standing upon the wall above the arched gate, though he could not be sure. The lady did not wave, and Mandorallen did not look back. Garion, however, very nearly held his breath until Vo Mimbre was out of sight.

It was midafternoon by the time they reached the ford which crossed the River Arend into Tolnedra, and the bright sun sparkled on the river. The sky was very blue overhead, and the colored pennons on the lances of the escorting knights snapped in the breeze. Garion felt a desperate urgency, an almost unbearable necessity to cross the river and leave Arendia and the terrible things that had happened there behind.

"Hail and farewell, Holy Belgarath," Korodullin said at the water's edge. "I will, as thou hast advised me, begin my preparations. Arendia will be ready. I pledge my life to it."

"And I'll keep you advised of our progress from time to time," Mister Wolf said.

"I will also examine the activities of the Murgos within my kingdom," Korodullin said. "If what thou hast told me should prove true, as I doubt not that it shall, then I will expel them from Arendia. I will seek them out, one and all, and harry them out of the land. I will make their lives a burden and an affliction to them for sowing discord and contention among my subjects."

Wolf grinned at him. "That's an idea that appeals to me. Murgos are an arrogant people, and a little affliction now and then teaches them humility." He reached out and took the king's hand. "Good-bye, Korodullin. I hope the world's happier next time we meet."

"I will pray that it may be so," the young king said.

Then Mister Wolf led the way down into the rippling water of the shallow ford. Beyond the river Imperial Tolnedra waited, and from the banks behind them the Mimbrate knights saluted with a great fanfare on their horns.

As they emerged on the far side of the river, Garion looked around, trying to see some difference in terrain or foliage which might distinguish Arendia from Tolnedra, but there seemed to be none. The land, indifferent to human boundaries, flowed on unchanged.

About a half-mile from the river they entered the forest of Vordue, an extensive tract of well-kept woodland which extended from the sea to the foothills of the mountains to the east. Once they were under the trees, they stopped and changed back into their traveling clothes. "I think we might as well keep the guise of merchants," Mister Wolf said, settling with obvious comfort back into his patched rust-colored tunic and mismatched shoes. "It won't fool the Grolims, of course, but it'll satisfy the Tolnedrans we meet along the way. We can deal with the Grolims in other ways."

"Are there any signs of the Orb about?" Barak rumbled as he stowed his bearskin cloak and helmet in one of the packs.

"A hint or two," Wolf said, looking around. "I'd guess that Zedar went through here a few weeks ago."

"We don't seem to be gaining on him much," Silk said, pulling on his leather vest.

"We're holding our own at least. Shall we go?"

They remounted and continued along the Tolnedran highway, which ran straight through the forest in the afternoon sun. After a league or so, they came to a wide place in the road where a single whitewashed stone building, low and red-roofed, stood solidly at the roadside. Several soldiers lounged indolently about, but their armor and equipment seemed less well-cared-for than that of the legionnaires Garion had seen before.

"Customs station," Silk said. "Tolnedrans like to put them far enough from the border so that they don't interfere with legitimate smuggling."

"Those are very slovenly legionnaires," Durnik said disapprovingly.

"They aren't legionnaires," Silk explained. "They're soldiers of the customs service—local troops. There's a great difference."

"I can see that," Durnik said.

A soldier wearing a rusty breastplate and carrying a short spear stepped into the road and held up his hand. "Customs inspection," he announced in a bored tone. "His Excellency will be with you in a moment or two. You can take your horses over there." He pointed to a kind of yard at the side of the building.

"Is trouble likely?" Mandorallen asked. The knight had removed his armor and now wore the mail suit and surcoat in which he customarily traveled.

"No," Silk said. "The customs agent will ask a few questions, and then we'll bribe him and be on our way."

"Bribe?" Durnik asked.

Silk shrugged. "Of course. That's the way things are in Tolnedra. Better let me do the talking. I've been through all this before."

The customs agent, a stout, balding man in a belted gown of a rusty brown color, came out of the stone building, brushing crumbs from the front of his clothes. "Good afternoon," he said in a businesslike manner.

"Good day, your Excellency," Silk replied with a brief bow.

"And what have we here?" the agent asked, looking appraisingly at the packs.

"I'm Radek of Boktor," Silk replied, "a Drasnian merchant. I'm taking

Sendarian wool to Tol Honeth." He opened the top of one of the packs and pulled out a corner of woven gray cloth.

"Your prospects are good, worthy merchant," the customs agent said, fingering the cloth. "It's been a chilly winter this year, and wool's bringing a good price."

There was a brief clinking sound as several coins changed hands. The customs agent smiled then, and his manner grew more relaxed. "I don't think we'll need to open all the packs," he said. "You're obviously an honorable man, worthy Radek, and I wouldn't want to delay you."

Silk bowed again. "Is there anything I should know about the road ahead, your Excellency?" he asked, tying up the pack again. "I've learned to rely on the advice of the customs service."

"The road's good," the agent said with a shrug. "The legions see to that."

"Of course. Any unusual conditions anywhere?"

"It might be wise if you kept somewhat to yourselves on your way south," the stout man advised. "There's a certain amount of political turmoil in Tolnedra just now. I'm sure, though, that if you show that you're tending strictly to business, you won't be bothered."

"Turmoil?" Silk asked, sounding a bit concerned. "I hadn't heard about that."

"It's the succession. Things are a bit stirred up at the moment."

"Is Ran Borune ill?" Silk asked with surprise.

"No," the stout man said, "only old. It's a disease no one recovers from. Since he doesn't have a son to succeed him, the Borune Dynasty hangs on his feeblest breath. The great families are already maneuvering for position. It's all terribly expensive, of course, and we Tolnedrans get agitated when there's money involved."

Silk laughed briefly. "Don't we all? Perhaps it might be to my advantage to make a few contacts in the right quarters. Which family would you guess is in the best position at the moment?"

"I think we have the edge over the rest of them," the agent said rather smugly.

"We?"

"The Vorduvians. I'm distantly related on my mother's side to the family. The Grand Duke Kador of Tol Vordue's the only logical choice for the throne."

"I don't believe I know him," Silk said.

"An excellent man," the agent said expansively. "A man of force and vigor and foresight. If the selection were based on simple merit, Grand Duke Kador would be given the throne by general consent. Unfortunately, though, the selection's in the hands of the Council of Advisers."

"Ah!"

"Indeed," the agent agreed bitterly. "You wouldn't believe the size of the bribes some of those men are asking for their votes, worthy Radek."

"It's an opportunity that comes only once in a lifetime, I suppose," Silk said.

"I don't begrudge any man the right to a decent, reasonable bribe," the stout agent complained, "but some of the men on the council have gone mad with greed. No matter what position I get in the new government, it's going to take me years to recoup what I've already been obliged to contribute. It's the same all over Tolnedra. Decent men are being driven to the wall by taxes and all these emergency subscriptions. You don't dare let a list go by that doesn't have your name on it, and there's a new list out every day. The expense is making everyone desperate. They're killing each other in the streets of Tol Honeth."

"That bad?" Silk asked.

"Worse than you can imagine," the customs man said. "The Horbites don't have the kind of money it takes to conduct a political campaign, so they've started to poison off council members. We spend millions to buy a vote, and the next day our man turns black in the face and falls over dead. Then we have to raise more millions to buy up his successor. They're absolutely destroying me. I don't have the right kind of nerves for politics."

"Terrible," Silk sympathized.

"If Ran Borune would only *die*," the Tolnedran complained desperately. "We're in control now, but the Honeths are richer than we are. If they unite behind one candidate, they'll be able to buy the throne right out from under us. And all the while Ran Borune sits in the palace doting on that little monster he calls a daughter and with so many guards around that we can't persuade even the bravest assassin to make an attempt on him. Sometimes I think he intends to live forever."

"Patience, Excellency," Silk advised. "The more we suffer, the greater the rewards in the end."

The Tolnedran sighed. "I'll be very rich someday then. But I've kept you long enough, worthy Radek. I wish you good speed and cold weather in Tol Honeth to bring up the price of your wool."

Silk bowed formally, remounted his horse and led the party a trot away from the customs station. "It's good to be back in Tolnedra again," the weasel-faced little man said expansively once they were out of earshot. "I love the smell of deceit, corruption, and intrigue."

"You're a bad man, Silk," Barak said. "This place is a cesspool."

"Of course it is." Silk laughed. "But it isn't dull, Barak. Tolnedra's never dull."

They approached a tidy Tolnedran village as evening fell and stopped for the night in a solid, well-kept inn where the food was good and the beds were clean. They were up early the next morning; after breakfast they clattered out of the innyard and onto the cobblestoned street in that curious silver light that comes just before the sun rises.

"A proper sort of place," Durnik said approvingly, looking around at the white stone houses with their red-tiled roofs. "Everything seems neat and orderly."

"It's a reflection of the Tolnedran mind," Mister Wolf explained. "They pay great attention to details."

"That's not an unseemly trait," Durnik observed.

Wolf was about to answer that when two brown-robed men ran out of a shadowy side street. "Look out!" the one in the rear yelled. "He's gone mad!"

The man running in front was clutching at his head, his face contorted into an expression of unspeakable horror. Garion's horse shied violently as the madman ran directly at him, and Garion raised his right hand to try to push the bulging-eyed lunatic away. At the instant his hand touched the man's forehead, he felt a surge in his hand and arm, a kind of tingling as if the arm were suddenly enormously strong, and his mind filled with a vast roaring. The madman's eyes went blank, and he collapsed on the cobblestones as if Garion's touch had been some colossal blow.

Then Barak nudged his horse between Garion and the fallen man. "What's this all about?" he demanded of the second robed man who ran up, gasping for breath.

"We're from Mar Terrin," the man answered. "Brother Obor couldn't stand the ghosts anymore, so I was given permission to bring him home until his sanity returned." He knelt over the fallen man. "You didn't have to hit him so hard," he accused.

"I didn't," Garion protested. "I only touched him. I think he fainted."

"You must have hit him," the monk said. "Look at the mark on his face."

An ugly red welt stood on the unconscious man's forehead.

"Garion," Aunt Pol said, "can you do exactly what I tell you to do without asking any questions?"

Garion nodded. "I think so."

"Get down off your horse. Go to the man on the ground and put the palm of your hand on his forehead. Then apologize to him for knocking him down."

"Are you sure it's safe, Polgara?" Barak asked.

"It will be all right. Do as I told you, Garion."

Garion hesitantly approached the stricken man, reached out, and laid his palm on the ugly welt. "I'm sorry," he said, "and I hope you get well soon." There was a surge in his arm again, but quite different from the first one.

The madman's eyes cleared, and he blinked. "Where am I?" he asked. "What happened?" His voice sounded very normal, and the welt on his forehead was gone.

"It's all right now," Garion told him, not knowing exactly why he said it. "You've been sick, but you're better now."

"Come along, Garion," Aunt Pol said. "His friend can care for him now."

Garion went back to his horse, his thoughts churning.

"A miracle!" the second monk exclaimed.

"Hardly that," Aunt Pol said. "The blow restored your friend's mind, that's all. It happens sometimes." But she and Mister Wolf exchanged a long glance that said quite plainly that something else had happened—something unexpected.

They rode on, leaving the two monks in the middle of the street.

"What happened?" Durnik asked, a stunned look on his face.

Mister Wolf shrugged. "Polgara had to use Garion," he said. "There wasn't time to do it any other way."

Durnik looked unconvinced.

"We don't do it often," Wolf explained. "It's a little cumbersome to go through someone else like that, but sometimes we don't have any choice."

"But Garion healed him," Durnik objected.

"It has to come from the same hand as the blow, Durnik," Aunt Pol said. "Please don't ask so many questions."

The dry awareness in Garion's mind, however, refused to accept any of their explanations. It told him that nothing had come from outside. With a troubled face he studied the silvery mark on his palm. It seemed different for some reason.

"Don't think about it, dear," Aunt Pol said quietly as they left the village and rode south along the highway. "It's nothing to worry about. I'll explain it all later." Then, to the caroling of birds that greeted the rising sun, she reached across and firmly closed his hand with her fingers.

CHAPTER THIRTEEN

It took them three days to pass through the forest of Vordue. Garion, remembering the dangers of the Arendish forest, was apprehensive at first and watched the shadows beneath the trees nervously, but after a day or so with nothing out of the ordinary occurring, he began to relax. Mister Wolf, however, seemed to grow increasingly irritable as they rode south. "They're planning something," he muttered. "I wish they'd get on with it. I hate to ride with one eye over my shoulder every step of the way."

Garion had little opportunity along the way to speak with Aunt Pol about what had happened to the crazy monk from Mar Terrin. It seemed almost as if she were deliberately avoiding him; when he finally did manage to ride briefly beside her and question her about the incident, her answers were vague and did little to quiet his unease about the whole affair.

It was the middle of the morning on the third day when they emerged from the trees and rode out into open farmland. Unlike the Arendish plain where vast tracts of land seemed to lie fallow, the ground here was extensively cultivated, and low stone walls surrounded each field. Although it was still far from being warm, the sun was very bright, and the well-turned earth in the fields seemed rich and black as it lay waiting for sowing. The highway was broad and straight, and they encountered frequent travelers along the way. Greetings between the party and these travelers were restrained but polite, and Garion began to feel more at ease. This country appeared to be much too civilized for the kind of dangers they had encountered in Arendia.

About midafternoon they rode into a sizable town where merchants in variously colored mantles called to them from booths and stalls which lined the streets, imploring them to stop and look at merchandise. "They sound almost desperate," Durnik said.

"Tolnedrans hate to see a customer get away," Silk told him. "They're greedy."

Ahead, in a small square, a disturbance suddenly broke out. A half-dozen slovenly, unshaven soldiers had accosted an arrogant-looking man in a green mantle. "Stand aside, I say," the arrogant man protested sharply.

"We just want a word or two with you, Lembor," one of the soldiers said with an evil-looking leer. He was a lean man with a long scar down one side of his face.

"What an idiot," a passerby observed with a callous laugh. "Lembor's gotten so important that he doesn't think he has to take any precautions."

"Is he being arrested, friend?" Durnik inquired politely.

"Only temporarily," the passerby said dryly.

"What are they going to do to him?" Durnik asked.

"The usual."

"What's the usual?"

"Watch and see. The fool should have known better than to come out without his bodyguards."

The soldiers had surrounded the man in the green mantle, and two of them took hold of his arms roughly.

"Let me go," Lembor protested. "What do you think you're doing?"

"Just come along quietly, Lembor," the scar-faced soldier ordered. "It'll be a lot easier that way." They began pulling him toward a narrow alleyway.

"Help!" Lembor shouted, desperately trying to struggle.

One of the soldiers smashed the captive in the mouth with his fist, and they pulled him into the alley. There was a single, short scream and the sounds of a brief scuffle. There were other sounds as well, a few grunts and the grating sound of steel on bone, then a long, sighing moan. A wide rivulet of bright blood trickled out of the mouth of the alley and ran into the gutter. A minute or so later, the soldiers came back out into the square, grinning and wiping their swords.

"We've got to do something," Garion said, sick with outrage and horror.

"No," Silk said bluntly. "What we have to do is mind our own business. We're not here to get involved in local politics."

"Politics?" Garion objected. "That was deliberate murder. Shouldn't we at least see if he's still alive?"

"Not too likely," Barak said. "Six men with swords can usually do a pretty thorough job."

A dozen other soldiers, as shabby-looking as the first group, ran into the square with drawn swords.

"Too late, Rabbas." The scar-faced soldier laughed harshly to the leader of the newcomers. "Lembor doesn't need you anymore. He just came down with a bad case of dead. It looks like you're out of work."

The one called Rabbas stopped, his expression dark. Then a look of brutal cunning spread across his face. "Maybe you're right, Kragger." His voice was also harsh. "But then again we might be able to create a few vacancies in Elgon's garrison. I'm sure he'd be happy to hire good replacements." He began to move forward again, his short sword swinging in a low, dangerous arc.

Then there came the sound of a jingling trot, and twenty legionnaires in a double column came into the square, their feet striking the cobblestones in unison. They carried short lances, and they stopped between the two groups of soldiers. Each column turned to face one group, their lances leveled. The breastplates of the legionnaires were brightly burnished, and their equipment was spotless.

"All right, Rabbas, Kragger, that's enough," the sergeant in charge said sharply. "I want both of you off the street immediately."

"These swine killed Lembor, Sergeant," Rabbas protested.

"That's too bad," the sergeant said without much sympathy. "Now clear the street. There's not going to be any brawling while I'm on duty."

"Aren't you going to do something?" Rabbas demanded.

"I am," the legionnaire said. "I'm clearing the street. Now get out of here."

Sullenly, Rabbas turned and led his men out of the square.

"That goes for you too, Kragger," the sergeant ordered.

"Of course, Sergeant," Kragger said with an oily smirk. "We were just leaving anyway."

A crowd had gathered, and there were several boos as the legionnaires herded the sloppy-looking soldiers out of the square.

The sergeant looked around, his face dangerous, and the boos died immediately.

Durnik hissed sharply. "Over there on the far side of the square," he said to Wolf in a hoarse whisper. "Isn't that Brill?"

"Again?" Wolf's voice held exasperation. "How does he keep getting ahead of us like this?"

"Let's find out what he's up to," Silk suggested, his eyes bright.

"He'd recognize any of us if we tried to follow him," Barak warned.

"Leave that to me," Silk said, sliding out of his saddle.

"Did he see us?" Garion asked.

"I don't think so," Durnik said. "He's talking to those men over there. He isn't looking this way."

"There's an inn near the south end of town," Silk said quickly, pulling off his vest and tying it to his saddle. "I'll meet you there in an hour or so." Then the little man turned and disappeared into the crowd.

"Get down off your horses," Mister Wolf ordered tersely. "We'll lead them."

They all dismounted and led their mounts slowly around the edge of the square, staying close to the buildings and keeping the animals between them and Brill as much as possible.

Garion glanced once up the narrow alleyway where Kragger and his men had dragged the protesting Lembor. He shuddered and looked away quickly.

A green-mantled heap lay in a grimy corner, and there was blood splashed thickly on the walls and the filthy cobblestones in the alley.

After they had moved out of the square, they found the entire town seething with excitement and in some cases consternation. "Lembor, you say?" an ashen-faced merchant in a blue mantle exclaimed to another shaken man. "Impossible."

"My brother just talked to a man who was there," the second merchant said. "Forty of Elgon's soldiers attacked him in the street and cut him down right in front of the crowd."

"What's going to happen to us?" the first man asked in a shaking voice.

"I don't know about you, but I'm going to hide. Now that Lembor's dead, Elgon's soldiers are probably going to try to kill us all."

"They wouldn't dare."

"Who's going to stop them? I'm going home."

"Why did we listen to Lembor?" the first merchant wailed. "We could have stayed out of the whole business."

"It's too late now," the second man said. "I'm going to go home and bar my doors." He turned and scurried away.

The first man stared after him and then he too turned and fled.

"They play for keeps, don't they?" Barak observed.

"Why do the legions allow it?" Mandorallen asked.

"The legions stay neutral in these affairs," Wolf said. "It's part of their oath."

The inn to which Silk had directed them was a neat, square building surrounded by a low wall. They tied their horses in the courtyard and went inside. "We might as well eat, father," Aunt Pol said, seating herself at a table of well-scrubbed oak in the sunny common room.

"I was just—" Wolf looked toward the door which led into the taproom.

"I know," she said, "but I think we should eat first."

Wolf sighed. "All right, Pol."

The serving-man brought them a platter of smoking cutlets and heavy slabs of brown bread soaked in butter. Garion's stomach was still a bit shaky after what he had witnessed in the square, but the smell of the cutlets soon overcame that. They had nearly finished eating when a shabby-looking little man in a linen shirt, leather apron, and a ragged hat came in and plunked himself unceremoniously at the end of their table. His face looked vaguely familiar somehow. "Wine!" he bawled at the serving-man, "and food." He squinted around in the golden light streaming through the yellow glass windows of the common room.

"There are other tables, friend," Mandorallen said coldly.

"I like this one," the stranger said. He peered at each of them in turn, and then he suddenly laughed. Garion stared in amazement as the man's face relaxed, the muscles seeming to shift under his skin back into their normal positions. It was Silk.

"How did you do that?" Barak asked, startled.

Silk grinned at him and then reached up to massage his cheeks with his fingertips. "Concentration, Barak. Concentration and lots of practice. It makes my jaws ache a bit, though."

"Useful skill, I'd imagine—under the right circumstances," Hettar said blandly.

"Particularly for a spy," Barak said.

Silk bowed mockingly.

"Where did you get the clothes?" Durnik asked.

"Stole them." Silk shrugged, peeling off the apron.

"What's Brill doing here?" Wolf asked.

"Stirring up trouble, the same as always," Silk replied. "He's telling people that a Murgo named Asharak is offering a reward for any information about us. He describes you quite well, old friend—not very flatteringly, but quite well."

"I expect we'll have to deal with this Asharak before long," Aunt Pol said. "He's beginning to irritate me."

"There's another thing." Silk started on one of the cutlets. "Brill's telling everyone that Garion is Asharak's son—that we've stolen him and that Asharak's offering a huge reward for his return."

"Garion?" Aunt Pol asked sharply.

Silk nodded. "The kind of money he's talking about is bound to make everyone in Tolnedra keep his eyes open." He reached for a piece of bread.

Garion felt a sharp pang of anxiety. "Why me?" he asked.

"It would delay us," Wolf said. "Asharak—whoever he is—knows that Polgara would stop to look for you. So would the rest of us, most likely. That would give Zedar time to get away."

"Just who *is* Asharak?" Hettar asked, his eyes narrowing.

"A Grolim, I expect," Wolf said. "His operations are a little too wide-spread for him to be an ordinary Murgo."

"How can one tell the difference?" Durnik asked.

"You can't," Wolf answered. "They look very much the same. They're two separate tribes, but they're much more closely related to each other than they are to other Angaraks. Anyone can tell the difference between a Nadrak and a Thull or a Thull and a Mallorean, but Murgos and Grolims are so much alike that you can't tell them apart."

"I've never had any problem," Aunt Pol said. "Their minds are quite different."

"That will make it much easier," Barak commented dryly. "We'll just chop open the head of the next Murgo we meet, and you can point out the differences to us."

"You've been spending too much time with Silk lately," Aunt Pol said acidly. "You're starting to talk like him."

Barak looked over at Silk and winked.

"Let's finish up here and see if we can't get out of town quietly," Wolf said. "Is there a back alley out of this place?" he asked Silk.

"Naturally," Silk said, still eating.

"Are you familiar with it?"

"Please!" Silk looked a little offended. "Of course I'm familiar with it."

"Let it pass," Wolf said.

The alleyway Silk led them through was narrow, deserted, and smelled quite bad, but it brought them to the town's south gate, and they were soon on the highway again.

"A little distance wouldn't hurt at this point," Wolf said. He thumped his heels to his horse's flanks and started off at a gallop. They rode until well after dark. The moon, looking swollen and unhealthy, rose slowly above the horizon and filled the night with a pale light that seemed to leech away all trace of color. Wolf finally pulled to a stop. "There's really no point in riding all night," he said. "Let's move off the road and get a few hours' sleep. We'll start out again early. I'd like to stay ahead of Brill this time if we can."

"Over there?" Durnik suggested, pointing at a small copse of trees looming black in the moonlight not far from the road.

"It'll do," Wolf decided. "I don't think we'll need a fire." They led the horses in among the trees and pulled their blankets out of the packs. The moonlight filtered in among the trees and dappled the leaf-strewn ground. Garion found a fairly level place with his feet, rolled up in his blankets and, after squirming around a bit, he fell asleep.

He awoke suddenly, his eyes dazzled by the light of a half-dozen torches. A heavy foot was pushed down on his chest, and the point of a sword was set firmly, uncomfortably against his throat.

"Nobody move!" a harsh voice ordered. "We'll kill anybody who moves."

Garion stiffened in panic, and the sword point at his throat dug in sharply. He rolled his head from side to side and saw that all of his friends were being held down in the same way he was. Durnik, who had been standing guard, was held by two rough-looking soldiers, and a piece of rag was stuffed in his mouth.

"What does this mean?" Silk demanded of the soldiers.

"You'll find out," the one in charged rasped. "Get their weapons." As he gestured, Garion saw that a finger was missing from his right hand.

"There's a mistake here," Silk said. "I'm Radek of Boktor, a merchant, and my friends and I haven't done anything wrong."

"Get on your feet," the three-fingered soldier ordered, ignoring the little man's objections. "If any one of you tries to get away, we'll kill all the rest."

Silk rose and crammed on his cap. "You're going to regret this, Captain," he said. "I've got powerful friends here in Tolnedra."

The soldier shrugged. "That doesn't mean anything to me," he said. "I take my orders from Count Dravor. He told me to bring you in."

"All right," Silk said. "Let's go see this Count Dravor, then. We'll get this cleared up right now, and there's no need for waving your swords around. We'll come along quietly. None of us is going to do anything to get you excited."

The three-fingered soldier's face darkened in the torchlight. "I don't like your tone, merchant."

"You're not being paid to like my tone, friend," Silk said. "You're being paid to escort us to Count Dravor. Now suppose we get moving. The quicker we get there, the quicker I can give him a full report about your behavior."

"Get their horses," the soldier growled.

Garion had edged over to Aunt Pol. "Can't you do anything?" he asked her quietly.

"No talking!" the soldier who had captured him barked.

Garion stood helplessly, staring at the sword leveled at his chest.

CHAPTER FOURTEEN

The house of Count Dravor was a large white building set in the center of a broad lawn with clipped hedges and formal gardens on either side. The moon, fully overhead now, illuminated every detail as they rode slowly up a white-graveled, curving road that led to the house.

The soldiers ordered them to dismount in the courtyard between the house and the garden on the west side of the house, and they were hustled inside and down a long hallway to a heavy, polished door.

Count Dravor was a thin, vague-looking man with deep pouches under his eyes, and he sprawled in a chair in the center of a richly furnished room. He looked up with a pleasant, almost dreamy smile on his face as they entered. His mantle was a pale rose color with silver trim at the hem and around the sleeves to indicate his rank. It was badly wrinkled and none too clean. "And who are these guests?" he asked, his voice slurred and barely audible.

"The prisoners, my Lord," the three-fingered soldier explained. "The ones you ordered arrested."

"Did I order someone arrested?" the count asked, his voice still slurred. "What a remarkable thing for me to do. I hope I haven't inconvenienced you, my friends."

"We were a bit surprised, that's all," Silk said carefully.

"I wonder why I did that." The count pondered. "I must have had a reason—I never do anything without a reason. What have you done wrong?"

"We haven't done anything wrong, my Lord," Silk assured him.

"Then why would I have you arrested? There must be some sort of mistake."

"That's what we thought, my Lord," Silk said.

"Well, I'm glad that's all cleared up," the count said happily. "May I offer you some dinner, perhaps?"

"We've already eaten, my Lord."

"Oh." The count's face fell with disappointment. "I have so few visitors."

"Perhaps your steward Y'diss may remember the reason these people were detained, my Lord," the three-fingered soldier suggested.

"Of course," the count said. "Why didn't I think of that? Y'diss remembers everything. Please send for him at once."

"Yes, my Lord." The soldier bowed and jerked his head curtly at one of his men.

Count Dravor dreamily began playing with one of the folds of his mantle, humming tunelessly as they waited.

After a few moments a door at the end of the room opened, and a man in an iridescent and intricately embroidered robe entered. His face was grossly sensual, and his head was shaved. "You sent for me, my Lord?" His rasping voice was almost a hiss.

"Ah, Y'diss," Count Dravor said happily, "how good of you to join us."

"It's my pleasure to serve you, my Lord," the steward said with a sinuous bow.

"I was wondering why I asked these friends to stop by," the count said. "I seem to have forgotten. Do you by any chance recall?"

"It's just a small matter, my Lord," Y'diss answered. "I can easily handle it for you. You need your rest. You mustn't overtire yourself, you know."

The count passed a hand across his face. "Now that you mention it, I do feel a bit fatigued, Y'diss. Perhaps you could entertain our guests while I rest a bit."

"Of course, my Lord," Y'diss said with another bow.

The count shifted around in his chair and almost immediately fell asleep.

"The count is in delicate health," Y'diss said with an oily smile. "He seldom leaves that chair these days. Let's move away a bit so that we don't disturb him."

"I'm only a Drasnian merchant, your Eminence," Silk said, "and these are my servants—except for my sister there. We're baffled by all of this."

Y'diss laughed. "Why do you persist in this absurd fiction, Prince Kheldar? I know who you are. I know you all, and I know your mission."

"What's your interest in us, Nyissan?" Mister Wolf asked bluntly.

"I serve my mistress, Eternal Salmissra," Y'diss said.

"Has the Snake Woman become the pawn of the Grolims, then," Aunt Pol asked, "or does she bow to the will of Zedar?"

"My queen bows to no man, Polgara," Y'diss said scornfully.

"Really?" She raised one eyebrow. "It's curious to find her servant dancing to a Grolim tune, then."

"I have no dealings with the Grolims," Y'diss said. "They're scouring all Tolnedra for you, but I'm the one who found you."

"Finding isn't keeping, Y'diss," Mister Wolf stated quietly. "Suppose you tell us what this is all about."

"I'll tell you only what I feel like telling you, Belgarath."

"I think that's about enough, father," Aunt Pol said. "We really don't have time for Nyissan riddle games, do we?"

"Don't do it, Polgara," Y'diss warned. "I know all about your power. My soldiers will kill your friends if you so much as raise your hand."

Garion felt himself roughly grabbed from behind, and a sword blade was pressed firmly against his throat.

Aunt Pol's eyes blazed suddenly. "You're walking on dangerous ground!"

"I don't think we need to exchange threats," Mister Wolf said. "I gather, then, that you don't intend to turn us over to the Grolims?"

"I'm not interested in the Grolims," Y'diss said. "My queen has instructed me to deliver you to her in Sthiss Tor."

"What's Salmissra's interest in this matter?" Wolf asked. "It doesn't concern her."

"I'll let her explain that to you when you get to Sthiss Tor. In the meantime, there are a few things I'll require you to tell me."

"I think thou wilt have scant success in that," Mandorallen said stiffly. "It is not our practice to discuss private matters with unwholesome strangers."

"And I think you're wrong, my dear Baron," Y'diss replied with a cold smile. "The cellars of this house are deep, and what happens there can be most unpleasant. I have servants highly skilled in applying certain exquisitely persuasive torments."

"I do not fear thy torments, Nyissan," Mandorallen said contemptuously.

"No. I don't imagine you do. Fear requires imagination, and you Arends aren't bright enough to be imaginative. The torments, however, will wear down your will—and provide entertainment for my servants. Good torturers are hard to find, and they grow sullen if they aren't allowed to practice—I'm sure you understand. Later, after you've all had the chance to visit with them a time or two, we'll try something else. Nyissa abounds with roots and leaves and curious little berries with strange properties. Oddly enough, most men prefer the rack or the wheel to my little concoctions." Y'diss laughed then, a brutal sound with no mirth in it. "We'll discuss all this further after I have the count settled in for the night. For right now, the guards will take you downstairs to the places I've prepared for you all."

Count Dravor roused himself and looked around dreamily. "Are our friends departing so soon?" he asked.

"Yes, my Lord," Y'diss told him.

"Well then," the count said with a vague smile, "farewell, dear people. I hope you'll return someday so that we can continue our delightful conversation."

The cell to which Garion was taken was dank and clammy, and it smelled of sewage and rotting food. Worst of all was the darkness. He huddled beside the iron door with the blackness pressing in on him palpably. From one corner of the cell came little scratchings and skittering sounds. He thought of rats and tried to stay as near to the door as possible. Water trickled somewhere, and his throat began to burn with thirst.

It was dark, but it was not silent. Chains clinked in a nearby cell, and someone was moaning. Farther off, there was insane laughter, a meaningless cackle repeated over and over again without pause, endlessly rattling in the dark. Someone screamed, a piercing, shocking sound, and then again. Garion cringed back against the slimy stones of the wall, his imagination immediately manufacturing tortures to account for the agony in those screams.

Time in such a place was nonexistent, and so there was no way to know how long he had huddled in his cell, alone and afraid, before he began to hear a faint metallic scraping and clicking that seemed to come from the door itself. He scrambled away, stumbling across the uneven floor of his cell to the far wall. "Go away!" he cried.

"Keep your voice down!" Silk whispered from the far side of the door.

"Is that you, Silk?" Garion almost sobbed with relief.

"Who were you expecting?"

"How did you get loose?"

"Don't talk so much," Silk said from between clenched teeth. "Accursed rust!" he swore. Then he grunted, and there was a grating click from the door. "There!" The cell door creaked open, and the dim light from torches somewhere filtered in. "Come along," Silk whispered. "We have to hurry."

Garion almost ran from the cell. Aunt Pol was waiting a few steps down the gloomy stone corridor. Without a word, Garion went to her. She looked at him gravely for a moment and then put her arms about him. They did not speak.

Silk was working on another door, his face gleaming with perspiration. The lock clicked, and the door creaked open. Hettar stepped out. "What took you so long?" he asked Silk.

"Rust!" Silk snapped in a low voice. "I'd like to flog all the jailers in this place for letting the locks get into this condition."

"Do you suppose we could hurry a bit?" Barak suggested over his shoulder from where he stood guard.

"Do you want to do this?" Silk demanded.

"Just move along as quickly as you can," Aunt Pol said. "We don't have the time for bickering just now." She primly folded her blue cloak over one arm.

Silk grunted sourly and moved on to the next door.

"Is all this oratory actually necessary?" Mister Wolf, the last to be released, asked crisply as he stepped out of his cell. "You've all been babbling like a flock of geese out here."

"Prince Kheldar felt need to make observations about the condition of the locks," Mandorallen said lightly.

Silk scowled at him and led the way toward the end of the corridor where the torches fumed greasily onto the blackened ceiling.

"Have a care," Mandorallen whispered urgently. "There's a guard." A bearded man in a dirty leather jerkin sat on the floor with his back against the wall of the corridor, snoring.

"Can we get past without waking him up?" Durnik breathed.

"He isn't going to wake up for several hours," Barak said grimly. The large purple swelling on the side of the guard's face immediately explained.

"Dost think there might be others?" Mandorallen asked, flexing his hands.

"There were a few," Barak said. "They're sleeping too."

"Let's get out of here, then," Wolf suggested.

"We'll take Y'diss with us, won't we?" Aunt Pol asked.

"What for?"

"I'd like to talk with him." she said. "At great length."

"It would be a waste of time," Wolf said. "Salmissra's involved herself in this affair. That's all we really need to know. Her motives don't really interest me all that much. Let's just get out of here as quietly as we can."

They crept past the snoring guard, turned a corner and moved softly down another corridor.

"Did he die?" a voice, shockingly loud, asked from behind a barred door that emitted a smoky red light.

"No," another voice said, "only fainted. You pulled too hard on the lever. You have to keep the pressure steady. Otherwise they faint, and you have to start over."

"This is a lot harder than I thought," the first voice complained.

"You're doing fine," the second voice said. "The rack's always tricky. Just remember to keep a steady pressure and not to jerk the lever. They usually die if you pull their arms out of the sockets."

Aunt Pol's face went rigid, and her eyes blazed briefly. She made a small gesture and whispered something. A brief, hushed sound murmured in Garion's mind.

"You know," the first voice said rather faintly, "suddenly I don't feel so good."

"Now that you mention it, I don't either," the second voice agreed. "Did that meat we had for supper taste all right to you?"

"It *seemed* all right." There was a long pause. "I *really* don't feel good at all."

They tiptoed past the barred door, and Garion carefully avoided looking in. At the end of the corridor was a stout oak door bound with iron. Silk ran his fingers around the handle. "It's locked from the outside," he said.

"Someone's coming," Hettar warned.

There was the tramp of heavy feet on the stone stairs beyond the door, the murmur of voices and a harsh laugh.

Wolf turned quickly to the door of a nearby cell. He touched his fingers to the rusty iron lock, and it clicked smoothly. "In here," he whispered. They all crowded into the cell, and Wolf pulled the door shut behind them.

"When we've got some leisure, I'll want to talk to you about that," Silk said.

"You were having such a good time with the locks that I didn't want to interfere." Wolf smiled blandly. "Now listen. We're going to have to deal with these men before they find out that our cells are empty and rouse the whole house."

"We can do that," Barak said confidently.

They waited.

"They're opening the door," Durnik whispered.

"How many are there?" Mandorallen asked.

"I can't tell."

"Eight," Aunt Pol said firmly.

"All right," Barak decided. "We'll let them pass and then jump on them from behind. A scream or two won't matter much in a place like this, but let's put them down quickly."

They waited tensely in the darkness of the cell.

"Y'diss says it doesn't matter if some of them die under the questioning," one of the men outside said. "The only ones we have to keep alive are the old man, the woman, and the boy."

"Let's kill the big one with the red whiskers, then," another suggested. "He looks like he might be troublesome, and he's probably too stupid to know anything useful."

"I *want* that one," Barak whispered.

The men in the corridor passed their cell.

"Let's go," Barak said.

It was a short, ugly fight. They swarmed over the startled jailers in a savage rush. Three were down before the others fully realized what was happening. One made a startled outcry, dodged past the fight and ran back toward the stairs. Without thinking, Garion dove in front of the running man. Then he rolled, tangling the man's feet, tripping him up. The guard fell, started to rise, then sagged back down in a limp heap as Silk neatly kicked him just below the ear.

"Are you all right?" Silk asked.

Garion squirmed out from under the unconscious jailer and scrambled to his feet, but the fight was nearly over. Durnik was pounding a stout man's head against the wall, and Barak was driving his fist into another's face. Mandorallen was strangling a third, and Hettar stalked a fourth, his hands out. The wide-eyed man cried out once just as Hettar's hands closed on him. The tall Algar straightened, spun about and slammed the man into the stone wall with terrific force. There was the grating sound of bones breaking, and the man went limp.

"Nice little fight," Barak said, rubbing his knuckles.

"Entertaining," Hettar agreed, letting the limp body slide to the floor.

"Are you about through?" Silk demanded hoarsely from the door by the stairs.

"Almost," Barak said. "Need any help, Durnik?"

Durnik lifted the stout man's chin and examined the vacant eyes critically. Then he prudently banged the jailer's head against the wall once more and let him fall.

"Shall we go?" Hettar suggested.

"Might as well," Barak agreed, surveying the littered corridor.

"The door's unlocked at the top of the stairs," Silk said as they joined him, "and the hallway's empty beyond it. The house seems to be asleep, but let's be quiet."

They followed him silently up the stairs. He paused briefly at the door. "Wait here a moment," he whispered. Then he disappeared, his feet making absolutely no sound. After what seemed a long time, he returned with the weapons the soldiers had taken from them. "I thought we might need these."

Garion felt much better after he had belted on his sword.

"Let's go," Silk said and led them to the end of the hall and around a corner.

"I think I'd like some of the green, Y'diss," Count Dravor's voice came from behind a partially open door.

"Certainly, my Lord," Y'diss said in his sibilant, rasping voice.

"The green tastes bad," Count Dravor said drowsily, "but it gives me such lovely dreams. The red tastes better, but the dreams aren't so nice."

"Soon you'll be ready for the blue, my Lord," Y'diss promised. There was a faint clink and the sound of liquid being poured into a glass. "Then the yellow, and finally the black. The black's best of all."

Silk led them on tiptoe past the half-open door. The lock on the outside door yielded quickly to his skill, and they all slipped out into the cool, moonlit night. The stars twinkled overhead, and the air was sweet. "I'll get the horses," Hettar said.

"Go with him, Mandorallen," Wolf said. "We'll wait over there." He pointed at the shadowy garden. The two men disappeared around the corner, and the rest of them followed Mister Wolf into the looming shadow of the hedge which surrounded Count Dravor's garden.

They waited. The night was chilly, and Garion found himself shivering. Then there was a click of a hoof touching a stone, and Hettar and Mandorallen came back, leading the horses.

"We'd better hurry," Wolf said. "As soon as Dravor drops off to sleep, Y'diss is going to go down to his dungeon and find out that we've left. Lead the horses. Let's get away from the house before we start making any noise."

They went down through the moonlit garden with the horses trailing along after them until they emerged on the open lawn beyond. They mounted carefully.

"We'd better hurry," Aunt Pol suggested, glancing back at the house.

"I bought us a little time before I left," Silk said with a short laugh.

"How'd you manage that?" Barak asked.

"When I went to get our weapons, I also set fire to the kitchen." Silk smirked. "That'll keep their attention for a bit."

A tendril of smoke rose from the back of the house.

"Very clever," Aunt Pol said with a certain grudging admiration.

"Why thank you, my Lady." Silk made a mocking little bow.

Mister Wolf chuckled and led them away at an easy trot.

The tendril of smoke at the back of the house became thicker as they rode away, rising black and oily toward the uncaring stars.

CHAPTER FIFTEEN

They rode hard for the next several days, stopping only long enough to rest the horses and catch a few hours' sleep at infrequent intervals. Garion found that he could doze in his saddle whenever they walked the horses. He found, indeed, that if he were tired enough, he could sleep almost anyplace. One afternoon as they rested from the driving pace Wolf set, he heard Silk talking to the old man and Aunt Pol. Curiosity finally won out over exhaustion, and he roused himself enough to listen.

"I'd still like to know more about Salmissra's involvement in this," the little man was saying.

"She's an opportunist," Wolf said. "Anytime there's turmoil, she tries to turn it to her own advantage."

"That means we'll have to dodge Nyissans as well as Murgos."

Garion opened his eyes. "Why do they call her Eternal Salmissra?" he asked Aunt Pol. "Is she very old?"

"No," Aunt Pol answered. "The Queens of Nyissa are always named Salmissra, that's all."

"Do you know this particular one?"

"I don't have to," she told him. "They're always exactly the same. They all look alike and act alike. If you know one, you know them all."

"She's going to be terribly disappointed with Y'diss," Silk observed, grinning.

"I imagine that Y'diss has taken some quiet, painless way out by now," Wolf said. "Salmissra grows a bit excessive when she's irritated."

"Is she so cruel then?" Garion asked.

"Not cruel exactly," Wolf explained. "Nyissans admire serpents. If you annoy a snake, he'll bite you. He's a simple creature, but very logical. Once he bites you, he doesn't hold any further grudges."

"Do we have to talk about snakes?" Silk asked in a pained voice.

"I think the horses are rested now," Hettar said from behind them. "We can go now."

They pushed the horses back into a gallop and pounded south toward the broad valley of the Nedrane River and Tol Honeth. The sun turned warm, and the trees along the way were budding in the first days of spring.

The gleaming Imperial City was situated on an island in the middle of the river, and all roads led there. It was clearly visible in the distance as they crested the last ridge and looked down into the fertile valley, and it seemed to grow larger with each passing mile as they approached it. It was built entirely of white marble and it dazzled the eye in the midmorning sun. The walls were high and thick, and towers soared above them within the city.

A bridge arched gracefully across the rippled face of Nedrane to the bronze expanse of the north gate where a glittering detachment of legion-naires marched perpetual guard.

Silk pulled on his conservative cloak and cap and drew himself up, his face assuming that sober, businesslike expression that meant that he was undergoing a private internal transition that seemed to make him almost believe himself that he was the Drasnian merchant whose identity he assumed.

"Your business in Tol Honeth?" one of the legionnaires asked politely.

"I am Radek of Boktor," Silk said with the preoccupied air of a man whose mind was on business. "I have Sendarian woolens of the finest quality."

"You'll probably want to talk with the Steward of the Central Market, then," the legionnaire suggested.

"Thank you." Silk nodded and led them through the gate into the broad and crowded streets beyond.

"I think I'd better stop by the palace and have a talk with Ran Borune," Mister Wolf said. "The Borunes aren't the easiest emperors to deal with, but they're the most intelligent. I shouldn't have too much trouble convincing him that the situation's serious."

"How are you going to get to see him?" Aunt Pol asked him. "It could take weeks to get an appointment. You know how they are."

Mister Wolf made a sour face. "I suppose I could make a ceremonial visit of it," he said as they pushed their horses through the crowd.

"And announce your presence to the whole city?"

"Do I have any choice? I have to nail down the Tolnedrans. We can't afford to have them neutral."

"Could I make a suggestion?" Barak asked.

"I'll listen to anything at this point."

"Why don't we go see Grinneg?" Barak said. "He's the Cherek Ambassador here in Tol Honeth. He could get us into the palace to see the Emperor without all that much fuss."

"That's not a bad idea, Belgarath," Silk agreed. "Grinneg's got enough connections in the palace to get us inside quickly, and Ran Borune respects him."

"That only leaves the problem of getting in to see the ambassador," Durnik said as they stopped to let a heavy wagon pass into a side street.

"He's my cousin," Barak said. "He and Anheg and I used to play together when we were children." The big man looked around. "He's supposed to have a house near the garrison of the Third Imperial Legion. I suppose we could ask somebody the way."

"That won't be necessary," Silk said. "I know where it is."

"I should have known." Barak grinned.

"We can go through the north marketplace," Silk said. "The garrison's located near the main wharves on the downstream end of the island."

"Lead the way," Wolf told him. "I don't want to waste too much time here."

The streets of Tol Honeth teemed with people from all over the world. Drasnians and Rivans rubbed elbows with Nyissans and Thulls. There was a sprinkling of Nadraks in the crowd and, to Garion's eye, a disproportionate number of Murgos. Aunt Pol rode close beside Hettar, talking quietly to him and frequently laying her hand lightly on his sword arm. The lean Algar's eyes burned, and his nostrils flared dangerously each time he saw a scarred Murgo face.

The houses along the wide streets were imposing, with white marble façades and heavy doors, quite often guarded by private mercenary soldiers, who glared belligerently at passersby.

"The Imperial city seems awash with suspicion," Mandorallen observed. "Do they fear their neighbors so?"

"Troubled times," Silk explained. "And the merchant princes of Tol Honeth keep a great deal of the world's wealth in their counting rooms. There are men along this street who could buy most of Arendia if they wanted to."

"Arendia is not for sale," Mandorallen said stiffly.

"In Tol Honeth, my dear Baron, everything's for sale," Silk told him. "Honor, virtue, friendship, love. It's a wicked city full of wicked people, and money's the only thing that matters."

"I expect you fit right in, then," Barak said.

Silk laughed. "I like Tol Honeth," he admitted. "The people here have no illusions. They're refreshingly corrupt."

"You're a bad man, Silk," Barak stated bluntly.

"So you've said before," the rat-faced little Drasnian said with a mocking grin.

The banner of Cherek, the outline of a white war-boat on an azure background, fluttered from a pole surmounting the gate of the ambassador's house. Barak dismounted a bit stiffly and strode to the iron grille which blocked the gate. "Tell Grinneg that his cousin Barak is here to see him," he announced to the bearded guards inside.

"How do we know you're his cousin?" one of the guards demanded roughly.

Barak reached through the grille almost casually and took hold of the front of the guard's mail shirt. He pulled the man up firmly against the bars. "Would you like to rephrase that question," he asked, "while you still have your health?"

"Excuse me, Lord Barak," the man apologized quickly. "Now that I'm closer, I do seem to recognize your face."

"I was almost sure you would," Barak said.

"Let me unlock the gate for you," the guard suggested.

"Excellent idea," Barak said, letting go of the man's shirt. The guard opened the gate quickly, and the party rode into a spacious courtyard.

Grinneg, the ambassador of King Anheg to the Imperial Court at Tol Honeth, was a burly man almost as big as Barak. His beard was trimmed very short, and he wore a Tolnedran-style blue mantle. He came down the stairs two at a time and caught Barak in a vast bear hug. "You pirate!" he roared. "What are you doing in Tol Honeth?"

"Anheg's decided to invade the place," Barak joked. "As soon as we've rounded up all the gold and young women, we're going to let you burn the city."

Grinneg's eyes glittered with a momentary hunger. "Wouldn't that infuriate them?" he said with a vicious grin.

"What happened to your beard?" Barak asked.

Grinneg coughed and looked embarrassed. "It's not important," he said quickly.

"We've never had any secrets," Barak accused.

Grinneg spoke quietly to his cousin for a moment, looking very ashamed of himself, and Barak burst out with a great roar of laughter. "Why did you let her do that?" he demanded.

"I was drunk," Grinneg said. "Let's go inside. I've got a keg of good ale in my cellar."

The rest of them followed the two big men into the house, and they went down a broad hallway to a room with Cherek furnishings—heavy chairs and benches covered with skins, a rush-strewn floor and a huge fireplace where the butt end of a large log smoldered. Several pitch-smeared torches smoked in iron rings on the stone wall. "I feel more at home here," Grinneg said.

A servant brought tankards of dark brown ale for them all and then quietly left the room. Garion quickly lifted his tankard and took a large swallow of the bitter drink before Aunt Pol could suggest something more bland. She watched him without comment, her eyes expressionless.

Grinneg sprawled in a large, hand-hewn chair with a bearskin tossed over it. "Why are you really in Tol Honeth, Barak?" he asked.

"Grinneg," Barak said seriously, "this is Belgarath. I'm sure you've heard of him."

The ambassador's eyes widened, and he inclined his head. "My house is yours," he said respectfully.

"Can you get me in to see Ran Borune?" Mister Wolf asked, sitting on a rough bench near the fireplace.

"Without any difficulty."

"Good," Wolf said. "I have to talk to him, and I don't want to stir up any fuss in the process."

Barak introduced the others, and his cousin nodded politely to each of them.

"You've come to Tol Honeth during a turbulent period," he said after the amenities were over. "The nobility of Tolnedra are gathering in the city like ravens on a dead cow."

"We picked up a hint or two of that on our way south," Silk told him. "Is it as bad as we heard?"

"Probably worse," Grinneg said, scratching one ear. "Dynastic succession only happens a few times in each eon. The Borunes have been in power now for over six hundred years, and the other houses are anticipating the changeover with a great deal of enthusiasm."

"Who's the most likely to succeed Ran Borune?" Mister Wolf asked.

"Right at the moment the best bet would probably be the Grand Duke Kador of Tol Vordue," Grinneg answered. "He seems to have more money than the rest. The Honeths are richer, of course, but they've got seven candidates, and their wealth is spread out a little too thin. The other families aren't really in the running. The Borunes don't have anyone suitable, and no one takes the Ranites seriously."

Garion carefully set his tankard on the floor beside the stool he sat on. The bitter ale didn't really taste that good, and he felt vaguely cheated somehow. The half-tankard he had drunk made his ears quite warm, though, and the end of his nose seemed a little numb.

"A Vorduvian we met said that the Horbites are using poison," Silk said.

"They all are." Grinneg wore a slightly disgusted look. "The Horbites are just a little more obvious about it, that's all. If Ran Borune dies tomorrow, though, Kador will be the next Emperor."

Mister Wolf frowned. "I've never had much success dealing with the Vorduvians. They don't really have imperial stature."

"The old Emperor's still in pretty fair health," Grinneg said. "If he hangs on for another year or two, the Honeths will probably fall into line behind one candidate—whichever one survives—and then they'll be able to bring all their money to bear on the situation. These things take time, though. The candidates themselves are staying out of town for the most part, and they're all being extremely careful, so the assassins are having a great deal of difficulty reaching them." He laughed, taking a long drink of ale. "They're a funny people."

"Could we go to the palace now?" Mister Wolf asked.

"We'll want to change clothes first," Aunt Pol said firmly.

"Again, Polgara?" Wolf gave her a long-suffering look.

"Just do it, father," she said. "I won't let you embarrass us by wearing rags to the palace."

"I'm not going to wear that robe again." The old man's voice was stubborn.

"No," she said. "It wouldn't be suitable. I'm sure the ambassador can lend you a mantle. You won't be quite so obvious that way."

"Whatever you say, Pol." Wolf sighed, giving up.

After they had changed, Grinneg formed up his honor-guard, a grim-looking group of Cherek warriors, and they were escorted along the broad avenues of Tol Honeth toward the palace. Garion, all bemused by the opulence of the city and feeling just a trifle giddy from the effects of the half-tankard of ale he had drunk, rode quietly beside Silk, trying not to gawk at the huge buildings or the richly dressed Tolnedrans strolling with grave decorum in the noonday sun.

CHAPTER SIXTEEN

The Imperial Palace sat on a high hill in the center of Tol Honeth. It consisted not of one building, but rather was a complex of many, large and small, all built of marble and surrounded by gardens and lawns where cypress trees cast a pleasing shade. The entire compound was enclosed by a high wall, surmounted by statues spaced at intervals along its top. The legionnaires at the palace gate recognized the Cherek ambassador and sent immediately for one of the Emperor's chamberlains, a gray-haired official in a brown mantle.

"I need to see Ran Borune, Lord Morin," Grinneg told him as they all dismounted in a marble courtyard just inside the palace gate. "It's a matter of urgency."

"Of course, Lord Grinneg," the gray-haired man assented. "His Imperial Majesty is always delighted to speak with the personal envoy of King Anheg. Unfortunately, his Majesty is resting just now. I should be able to get you in to see him sometime this afternoon—tomorrow morning at the latest."

"This won't wait, Morin," Grinneg said. "We have to see the Emperor immediately. You'd better go wake him up."

Lord Morin looked surprised. "It can't be *that* urgent," he suggested chidingly.

"I'm afraid so," Grinneg said.

Morin pursed his lips thoughtfully as he looked at each member of the party.

"You know me well enough to realize that I wouldn't ask this lightly, Morin," Grinneg said.

Morin sighed. "I'm trusting you a great deal, Grinneg. All right. Come along. Ask your soldiers to wait."

Grinneg made a curt gesture to his guards, and the party followed Lord Morin through a broad courtyard to a columned gallery that ran along one of the buildings.

"How's he been?" Grinneg asked as they walked along the shady gallery.

"His health is still good," Morin answered, "but his temper's been deteriorating lately. The Borunes have been resigning their posts in flocks and returning to Tol Borune."

"That seems prudent under the circumstances," Grinneg said. "I suspect that a certain number of fatalities are likely to accompany the succession."

"Probably so," Morin agreed, "but his Majesty finds it a bit distressing to be abandoned by members of his own family." He stopped by an arched marble gate where two legionnaires in gold-embellished breastplates stood stiffly. "Please leave your weapons here. His Majesty is sensitive about such things—I'm sure you can understand."

"Of course," Grinneg said, pulling a heavy sword out from under his mantle and leaning it against the wall.

They all followed his example, and Lord Morin's eyes flickered slightly with surprise when Silk removed three different daggers from various places beneath his garments.—*Formidable equipment*— the chamberlain's hands flickered in the gestures of the secret language.

—*Troubled times*— Silk's fingers explained deprecatingly.

Lord Morin smiled faintly and led them through the gate into the garden beyond. The lawn in the garden was neatly manicured. There were softly splashing fountains, and the rosebushes were all well-pruned. Fruit trees that seemed to be very old were budding, almost ready to burst into bloom in the warm sun. Sparrows bickered over nesting sites on the twisted limbs. Grinneg and the others followed Morin along a curving marble walk toward the center of the garden.

Ran Borune XXIII, Emperor of Tolnedra, was a small, elderly man, quite bald and dressed in a gold-colored mantle. He lounged in a heavy chair beneath a budding grape arbor, feeding small seeds to a bright canary perched on the arm of his chair. The Emperor had a little, beaklike nose and bright, inquisitive eyes. "I said I wanted to be left alone, Morin," he said in a testy voice, looking up from the canary.

"A million apologies, your Majesty," Lord Morin explained, bowing deeply. "Lord Grinneg, the ambassador of Cherek, wishes to present you a matter of gravest urgency. He convinced me that it simply could not wait."

The Emperor looked sharply at Grinneg. His eyes grew sly, almost malicious. "I see that your beard's beginning to grow back, Grinneg."

Grinneg's face flushed slowly. "I should have known that your Majesty would have heard of my little misfortune."

"I know everything that happens in Tol Honeth, Lord Grinneg," the Emperor snapped. "Even if all my cousins and nephews are running like rats out of a burning house, I still have a *few* faithful people around me. Whatever possessed you to take up with that Nadrak woman? I thought you Alorns despised Angaraks."

Grinneg coughed awkwardly and glanced quickly at Aunt Pol. "It was a kind of joke, your Majesty," he said. "I thought it might embarrass the Nadrak ambassador—and his wife is, after all, a handsome-looking woman. I didn't know she kept a pair of scissors under her bed."

"She keeps your beard in a little gold box, you know." The Emperor smirked. "And she shows it to all her friends."

"She's an evil woman," Grinneg said mournfully.

"Who are these?" the Emperor asked, waving one finger at the members of the party standing on the grass somewhat behind Ambassador Grinneg.

"My cousin Barak and some friends," Grinneg said. "They're the ones who need to talk to you."

"The Earl of Trellheim?" the Emperor asked. "What are you doing in Tol Honeth, my Lord?"

"Passing through, your Majesty," Barak replied, bowing.

Ran Borune looked sharply at each of the rest in turn as if actually seeing them for the first time. "And this would be Prince Kheldar of Drasnia," he said, "who left Tol Honeth in a hurry last time he was here—posing as an acrobat in a traveling circus, I believe, and about one jump ahead of the police."

Silk also bowed politely.

"And Hettar of Algaria," the Emperor continued, "the man who's trying to depopulate Cthol Murgos single-handedly."

Hettar inclined his head.

"Morin," the Emperor demanded sharply, "why have you surrounded me with Alorns? I don't like Alorns."

"It's this matter of urgency, your Majesty," Morin replied apologetically.

"And an Arend?" the Emperor said, looking at Mandorallen. "A Mimbrate, I should say." His eyes narrowed. "From the descriptions I've heard, he could only be the Baron of Vo Mandor."

Mandorallen's bow was gracefully elaborate. "Thine eye is most keen, your Majesty, to have read us each in turn without prompting."

"Not all of you precisely," the Emperor said. "I don't recognize the Sendar or the Rivan lad."

Garion's mind jumped. Barak had once told him that he resembled a Rivan more than anything else, but that thought had been lost in the welter of events which had followed the chance remark. Now the Emperor of Tolnedra, whose eye seemed to have an uncanny ability to penetrate to the true nature of things, had also identified him as a Rivan. He glanced quickly at Aunt Pol, but she seemed absorbed in examining the buds on a rosebush.

"The Sendar is Durnik," Mister Wolf said, "a smith. In Sendaria that useful trade is considered somewhat akin to nobility. The lad's my grandson, Garion."

The Emperor looked at the old man. "It seems that I should know who you are. There's something about you—" He paused thoughtfully.

The canary, which had been perched on the arm of the Emperor's chair, suddenly burst into song. He launched himself into the air and fluttered directly to Aunt Pol. She held out her finger, and the bright bird landed there, tipped back his head and sang ecstatically as if his tiny heart were breaking with adoration. She listened gravely to his song. She wore a dark blue dress, elaborately laced at the bodice, and a short sable cape.

"What are you doing with my canary?" the Emperor demanded.

"Listening," she said.

"How did you get him to sing? I've been trying to coax him into song for months."

"You didn't take him seriously enough."

"Who is this woman?" the Emperor asked.

"My daughter Polgara," Mister Wolf said. "She has a particularly keen understanding of birds."

The Emperor laughed suddenly, a harshly skeptical laugh. "Oh, come now. You really don't expect me to accept that, do you?"

Wolf looked at him gravely. "Are you really sure you don't know me, Ran Borune?" he asked mildly. The pale green mantle Grinneg had lent him made him look almost like a Tolnedran—almost, but not quite.

"It's a clever ruse," the Emperor said. "You look the part, and so does she, but I'm not a child. I gave up fairy tales a long time ago."

"That's a pity. I'd guess that your life's been a little empty since then." Wolf looked around at the manicured garden with the servants and fountains and the members of the Emperor's personal guard posted unobtrusively here and there among the flowerbeds. "Even with all this, Ran Borune, a life without any wonder left in it is flat and stale." His voice was a little sad. "I think that perhaps you gave up too much."

"Morin," Ran Borune demanded peremptorily, "send for Zereel. We'll settle this immediately."

"At once, your Majesty," Morin said and beckoned to one of the servants.

"May I have my canary back?" the Emperor asked Aunt Pol rather plaintively.

"Of course." She moved across the grass toward the chair, stepping slowly to avoid startling the trilling little bird.

"Sometimes I wonder what they're saying when they sing," Ran Borune said.

"Right now he's telling me about the day he learned to fly," Aunt Pol said. "That's a very important day for a bird." She reached out her hand, and the canary hopped onto the Emperor's finger, still singing and with its bright eye cocked toward Ran Borune's face.

"That's an amusing conceit, I suppose." The little old man smiled, staring out at the sunlight sparkling on the water in one of the fountains. "But I'm afraid I don't have time for that kind of thing. Right now the whole nation is holding its breath in anticipation of my death. They all seem to think that the greatest thing I can do for Tolnedra is to die immediately. Some of them have even gone to the trouble of trying to help me along. We caught four assassins inside the palace grounds just last week. The Borunes, my own family, are deserting me to the point that I scarcely have enough people left to run the palace, much less the Empire. Ah, here comes Zereel."

A lean, bushy-browed man in a red mantle covered with mystic symbols scurried across the lawn and bowed deeply to the Emperor. "You sent for me, your Majesty?"

"I am informed that this woman is Polgara the Sorceress," the Emperor said, "and that the old man there is Belgarath. Be a good fellow, Zereel, and have a look into their credentials."

"Belgarath and Polgara?" the bushy-browed man scoffed. "Surely your Majesty isn't serious. The names are mythological. No such people exist."

"You see," the Emperor said to Aunt Pol. "You don't exist. I have it on the very best authority. Zereel's a wizard himself, you know."

"Really?"

"One of the very best," he assured her. "Of course most of his tricks are just sleight of hand, since sorcery's only a sham, but he amuses me—and he takes himself very seriously. You may proceed, Zereel, but try not to raise an awful stink, the way you usually do."

"That won't be necessary, your Majesty," Zereel said flatly. "If they were wizards of any kind, I'd have recognized them immediately. We have special ways of communicating, you know."

Aunt Pol looked at the wizard with one eyebrow slightly raised. "I think that you should look a bit closer, Zereel," she suggested. "Sometimes we miss things." She made an almost imperceptible gesture, and Garion seemed to hear a faint rush of sound.

The wizard stared, his eyes fixed on open air directly in front of him. His eyes began to bulge, and his face turned deathly pale. As if his legs had been cut from under him, he fell onto his face. "Forgive me, Lady Polgara," he croaked, groveling.

"That's supposed to impress me, I assume," the Emperor said. "I've seen men's minds overwhelmed before, however, and Zereel's mind isn't all that strong to begin with."

"This is getting tiresome, Ran Borune," she said tartly.

"You really ought to believe her, you know." The canary spoke in a tiny, piping voice. "I knew who she was immediately—of course, we're much more perceptive than you things that creep around on the ground—why do you do that? If you'd just try, I'm sure you'd be able to fly. And I wish you'd stop eating so much garlic—it makes you smell awful."

"Hush, now," Aunt Pol said gently to the bird. "You can tell him all about it later."

The Emperor was trembling violently, and he stared at the bird as if it were a snake.

"Why don't we all just behave as if we believed that Polgara and I are who we say we are?" Mister Wolf suggested. "We could spend the rest of the day trying to convince you, and we really don't have that much time. There are some things I have to tell you, and they're important—no matter who I am."

"I think I can accept that," Ran Borune said, still trembling and staring at the now-silent canary.

Mister Wolf clasped his hands behind his back and stared up at a cluster of bickering sparrows on the limb of a nearby tree. "Early last fall," he began, "Zedar the Apostate crept into the throne room at Riva and stole the Orb of Aldur."

"He did *what?*" Ran Borune demanded, sitting up quickly. "How?"

"We don't know," Wolf answered. "When I catch up with him, maybe I'll ask him. I'm sure, however, that you can see the importance of the event."

"Obviously," the Emperor said.

"The Alorns and the Sendars are quietly preparing for war," Wolf told him.

"War?" Ran Borune asked in a shocked voice. "With whom?"

"The Angaraks, of course."

"What's Zedar got to do with the Angaraks? He could be acting on his own, couldn't he?"

"Surely you're not *that* simple," Aunt Pol remarked.

"You forget yourself, Lady," Ran Borune said stiffly. "Where's Zedar now?"

"He went through Tol Honeth about two weeks ago," Wolf replied. "If he can get across the border into one of the Angarak kingdoms before I can stop him, the Alorns will march."

"And Arendia with them," Mandorallen said firmly. "King Korodullin hath also been advised."

"You'll tear the world apart," the Emperor protested.

"Perhaps," Wolf admitted, "but we can't let Zedar get to Torak with the Orb."

"I'll send emissaries at once," Ran Borune said. "This has to be headed off before it gets out of hand."

"It's a little late for that," Barak said grimly. "Anheg and the others aren't in any mood for Tolnedran diplomacy right now."

"Your people have a bad reputation in the north, your Majesty," Silk pointed out. "They always seem to have a few trade agreements up their sleeves. Every time Tolnedra mediates a dispute, it seems to cost a great deal. I don't think we can afford your good offices anymore."

A cloud passed in front of the sun, and the garden seemed suddenly chilly in its shadow.

"This is being blown all out of proportion," the Emperor protested. "The Alorns and the Angaraks have been squabbling over that worthless stone for thousands of years. You've been waiting for the chance to fall on each other, and now you've got an excuse. Well, enjoy yourselves. Tolnedra's not going to get involved as long as I'm her Emperor."

"You're not going to be able to sit to one side in this, Ran Borune," Aunt Pol said.

"Why not? The Orb doesn't concern me one way or the other. Go ahead and destroy each other if you want. Tolnedra will still be here when it's all over."

"I doubt it," Wolf told him. "Your Empire's crawling with Murgos. They could overrun you in a week."

"They're honest merchants—here on honest business."

"Murgos don't have honest business," Aunt Pol told him. "Every Murgo in Tolnedra is here because he was sent by the Grolim High Priest."

"That's an exaggeration," Ran Borune said stubbornly. "The whole world knows that you and your father have an obsessive hatred of all Angaraks, but times have changed."

"Cthol Murgos is still ruled from Rak Cthol," Wolf said, "and Ctuchik is master there. Ctuchik hasn't changed, even if the world has. The merchants from Rak Goska might seem civilized to you, but they all jump when Ctuchik whistles, and Ctuchik's the disciple of Torak."

"Torak's dead."

"Really?" Aunt Pol said. "Have you seen his grave? Have you opened the grave and seen his bones?"

"My Empire's very expensive to run," the Emperor said, "and I need the revenue the Murgos bring me. I've got agents in Rak Goska and all along the South Caravan Route, so I'd know if the Murgos were getting ready for any kind of move against me. I'm just a little suspicious that all this might be the result of some internal contention within the Brotherhood of Sorcerers. You people have your own motives, and I'm not going to let you use my Empire as a pawn in your power struggles."

"And if the Angaraks win?" Aunt Pol said. "How do you plan to deal with Torak?"

"I'm not afraid of Torak."

"Have you ever met him?" Wolf asked.

"Obviously not. Listen, Belgarath, you and your daughter have never been friendly to Tolnedra. You treated us like a defeated enemy after Vo Mimbre. Your information's interesting, and I'll consider it in its proper perspective, but Tolnedran policy is not dominated by Alorn preconceptions. Our economy relies heavily on trade along the South Caravan Route. I'm not going to disrupt my Empire simply because you happen to dislike Murgos."

"You're a fool, then," Wolf said bluntly.

"You'd be surprised at how many people think so," the Emperor replied. "Maybe you'll have better luck with my successor. If he's a Vorduvian or a Honeth, you might even be able to bribe him, but Borunes don't take bribes."

"Or advice," Aunt Pol added.

"Only when it suits us, Lady Polgara," Ran Borune said.

"I think we've done everything we can here," Wolf decided.

A bronze door at the back of the garden slammed open, and a tiny girl with flaming hair stormed through, her eyes ablaze. At first Garion thought she was a child, but as she came closer, he realized that she was somewhat older than that. Although she was very small, the short, sleeveless green tunic she wore displayed limbs that were much closer to maturity. He felt a peculiar kind of shock when he saw her—almost, but not quite, like recognition. Her hair was a tumbled mass with long, elaborate curls cascading down over her neck and shoulders, and it was a color that Garion had never seen before, a deep, burnished red that seemed somehow to glow from within. Her skin was a golden color that seemed, as she swept through the shadows of the trees near the gate, to have an almost greenish cast to it. She was in a state verging on sheer rage. "Why am I being kept prisoner here?" she demanded of the Emperor.

"What are you talking about?" Ran Borune asked.

"The legionnaires won't let me leave the palace grounds!"

"Oh," the Emperor said, "that."

"Exactly. *That*."

"They're acting on my orders, Ce'Nedra," the Emperor told her.

"So they said. Tell them to stop it."

"No."

"*No?*" Her tone was incredulous. "*No?*" Her voice climbed several octaves. "What do you mean, no?"

"It's too dangerous for you to be out in the city just now," the Emperor said placatingly.

"Nonsense," she snapped. "I don't intend to sit around in this stuffy palace just because you're afraid of your own shadow. I need some things from the market."

"Send someone."

"I don't *want* to send anyone!" she shouted at him. "I want to go myself."

"Well, you can't," he said flatly. "Spend your time on your studies instead."

"I don't *want* to study," she cried. "Jeebers is a stuffy idiot, and he bores me. I don't want to sit around talking about history or politics or any of the rest of it. I just want an afternoon to myself."

"I'm sorry."

"Please, father," she begged, her tone dropping into a wheedling note. She took hold of one of the folds of his gold mantle and twisted it around one of her tiny fingers. "Please." The look she directed at the Emperor through her lashes would have melted stone.

"Absolutely not," he said, refusing to look at her. "My order stands. You will *not* leave the palace grounds."

"I *hate* you!" she cried. Then she ran from the garden in tears.

"My daughter," the Emperor explained almost apologetically. "You can't imagine what it's like having a child like that."

"Oh, I can imagine, all right," Mister Wolf said, glancing at Aunt Pol.

She looked back at him, her eyes challenging. "Go ahead and say it, father," she told him. "I'm sure you won't be happy until you do."

Wolf shrugged. "Forget it."

Ran Borune looked thoughtfully at the two of them. "It occurs to me that we might be able to negotiate a bit here," he said, his eyes narrowing.

"What did you have in mind?" Wolf asked.

"You have a certain authority among the Alorns," the Emperor suggested.

"Some," Wolf admitted carefully.

"If you were to ask them, I'm sure they'd be willing to overlook one of the more absurd provisions of the Accords of Vo Mimbre."

"Which one is that?"

"There's really no necessity for Ce'Nedra to journey to Riva, is there? I'm the last emperor of the Borune Dynasty, and when I die, she won't be an Imperial Princess anymore. Under the circumstances, I'd say that the requirement doesn't really apply to her. It's nonsense anyway. The line of the Rivan King became extinct thirteen hundred years ago, so there isn't going to be any bridegroom waiting for her in the Hall of the Rivan King. As you've seen, Tolnedra's a very dangerous place just now. Ce'Nedra's sixteenth birthday's only a year or so off, and the date's well known. If I have to send her to Riva, half the assassins in the Empire are going to be lurking outside the palace gates, waiting for her to come out. I'd rather not take that kind of risk. If you could see your way clear to speak to the Alorns, I might be able to make a few concessions regarding the Murgos—restrictions on their numbers, closed areas, that sort of thing."

"No, Ran Borune," Aunt Pol said flatly. "Ce'Nedra *will* go to Riva. You've failed to understand that the Accords are only a formality. If your daughter's the one destined to become the bride of the Rivan King, no force on earth can prevent her from being in the throne room at Riva on the appointed day. My father's recommendations about the Murgos are only suggestions—for your own good. What you choose to do about the matter is your affair."

"I think we've just about exhausted the possibilities of this conversation," the Emperor stated coldly.

Two important-looking officials came into the garden and spoke briefly to Lord Morin.

"Your Majesty," the gray-haired chamberlain said deferentially, "the Minister of Trade wanted to inform you that he's reached an excellent agreement with the trade deputation from Rak Goska. The gentlemen from Cthol Murgos were most accommodating."

"I'm delighted to hear it," Ran Borune said, throwing a meaningful look at Mister Wolf.

"The contingent from Rak Goska would like to pay their respects before they leave," Morin added.

"By all means," the Emperor said. "I'll be delighted to receive them here."

Morin turned and nodded shortly to the two officials near the gate. The officials turned and spoke to someone outside, and the gate swung open.

Five Murgos strode into the garden. Their coarse black robes were hooded, but the hoods were thrown back. The front of their robes were unclasped, and the chain mail shirts they all wore gleamed in the sunlight. The Murgo in front was a bit taller than the others, and his bearing indicated that he was the leader of the deputation. A welter of images and partial memories flooded Garion's mind as he looked at the scar-faced enemy he had known all his life. The strange pull of the silent, hidden linkage between them touched him. It was Asharak.

Something brushed Garion's mind, tentative only—not the powerful force the Murgo had directed at him in the dim hallway in Anheg's palace at Val Alorn. The amulet under his tunic became very cold and yet seemed to burn at the same time.

"Your Imperial Majesty," Asharak said, striding forward with a cold smile, "we are honored to be admitted into your august presence." He bowed, his mail shirt clinking.

Barak was holding Hettar's right arm firmly, and Mandorallen moved and took the other.

"I'm overjoyed to see you again, worthy Asharak," the Emperor said. "I'm told that an agreement has been reached."

"Beneficial to both sides, your Majesty."

"The best kind of agreement," Ran Borune approved.

"Taur Urgas, King of the Murgos, sends greetings," Asharak said. "His Majesty feels most keenly the desirability of cementing relations between Cthol Murgos and Tolnedra. He hopes that one day he may call your Imperial Majesty brother."

"We respect the peaceful intentions and legendary wisdom of Taur Urgas." The Emperor smiled with a certain smugness.

Asharak looked around, his black eyes flat. "Well, Ambar," he said to Silk, "your fortunes seem to have improved since we met last in Mingan's counting room in Darine."

Silk spread his hands in an innocent-looking gesture. "The Gods have been kind—most of them, anyway."

Asharak smiled briefly.

"You know each other?" the Emperor asked, a bit surprised.

"We've met, your Majesty," Silk admitted.

"In another kingdom," Asharak added. He looked directly then at Mister Wolf. "Belgarath," he said politely with a brief nod.

"Chamdar," the old man replied.

"You're looking well."

"Thank you."

"It seems that I'm the only stranger here," the Emperor said.

"Chamdar and I have known each other for a very long time," Mister Wolf told him. He glanced at the Murgo with a faintly malicious twinkle in his eyes. "I see that you've managed to recover from your recent indisposition."

Asharak's face flickered with annoyance, and he looked quickly at his shadow on the grass as if for reassurance.

Garion remembered what Wolf had said atop the tor after the attack of the Algroths—something about a shadow returning by an "indirect route." For some reason the information that Asharak the Murgo and Chamdar the Grolim were the same man did not particularly surprise him. Like a complex melody that had been faintly out of tune, the sudden merging of the two seemed right somehow. The knowledge clicked in his mind like a key in a lock.

"Someday you'll have to show me how you did that," Asharak was saying. "I found the experience interesting. My horse had hysterics, however."

"My apologies to your horse."

"Why is it that I feel as if I'm missing about half of this conversation?" Ran Borune asked.

"Forgive us, your Majesty," Asharak said. "Ancient Belgarath and I are renewing an old enmity. We've seldom had the opportunity to speak to each other with any degree of civility." He turned and bowed politely to Aunt Pol. "My Lady Polgara. You're as beautiful as ever." He eyed her with a deliberately suggestive stare.

"You haven't changed much either, Chamdar." Her tone was mild, even bland, but Garion, who knew her so well, recognized immediately the deadly insult she had just delivered to the Grolim.

"Charming," Asharak said with a faint smile.

"This is better than a play," the Emperor cried delightedly. "You people are actually dripping with malice. I wish I'd had the opportunity to see the first act."

"The first act was *very* long, your Majesty," Asharak said, "and quite often tedious. As you may have noticed, Belgarath sometimes gets carried away with his own cleverness."

"I'm certain I'll be able to make up for that," Mister Wolf told him with a slight smile. "I promise you that the last act will be extremely short, Chamdar."

"Threats, old man?" Asharak asked. "I thought we'd agreed to be civilized."

"I can't recall when we ever agreed on anything," Wolf said. He turned to the Emperor. "I think we'll leave now, Ran Borune," he said. "With your permission, of course."

"Of course," the Emperor replied. "I'm pleased to have met you—though I still don't believe in you, naturally. My skepticism, however, is theological, not personal."

"I'm glad of that," Wolf said, and quite suddenly he grinned impishly at the Emperor.

Ran Borune laughed.

"I look forward to our next meeting, Belgarath," Asharak said.

"I wouldn't if I were you," Wolf advised him, then turned and led the way out of the Emperor's garden.

CHAPTER SEVENTEEN

It was midafternoon when they emerged from the palace gate. The broad lawns were green in the warm spring sunlight, and the cypress trees stirred in a faint breeze.

"I don't think we want to stay in Tol Honeth too much longer," Wolf said.

"Do we leave now, then?" Mandorallen asked.

"There's something I have to do first," Wolf replied, squinting into the sunlight. "Barak and his cousin will come along with me. The rest of you go on back to Grinneg's house and wait there."

"We'll stop by the central market on our way," Aunt Pol told him. "There are a few things I need."

"This isn't a shopping expedition, Pol."

"The Grolims already know we're here, father," she said, "so there's no point in creeping about like sneak thieves, is there?"

He sighed. "All right, Pol."

"I knew you'd see it my way," she said.

Mister Wolf shook his head helplessly and rode off with Barak and Grinneg. The rest of them rode down the hill from the palace toward the gleaming city below. The streets at the foot of the hill were broad and lined on either side by magnificent houses—each almost a palace in itself.

"The rich and the noble," Silk said. "In Tol Honeth, the closer you live to the palace, the more important you are."

" 'Tis oft times thus, Prince Kheldar," Mandorallen observed. "Wealth and position sometimes need the reassurance of proximity to the seat of power. By ostentation and propinquity to the throne, small men are able to avoid facing their own inadequacy."

"I couldn't have said it better myself," Silk said.

The central marketplace of Tol Honeth was a vast square filled with bright-colored booths and stalls where a significant portion of the goods of the world were on display. Aunt Pol dismounted, left her horse with one of the Cherek guards, and moved busily from booth to booth, buying, it appeared, almost everything in sight. Silk's face blanched often at her purchases, since he was paying for them. "Can't you talk to her?" the small man pleaded with Garion. "She's destroying me."

"What makes you think she'd listen to me?" Garion asked.

"You could at least *try*," Silk said desperately.

Three richly mantled men stood near the center of the market, arguing heatedly.

"You're mad, Haldor," one of them, a thin man with a snub nose, said agitatedly. "The Honeths would strip the Empire for their own profit." His face was flushed, and his eyes bulged dangerously.

"Would Kador of the Vorduvians be any better?" the stout man named Haldor demanded. "You're the one who's mad, Radan. If we put Kador on the throne, he'll grind us all underfoot. There's such a thing as being *too* imperial."

"How dare you?" Radan almost screamed, his perspiring face growing darker. "Grand Duke Kador is the only possible choice. I'd vote for him even if he hadn't paid me." He flung his arms about wildly as he talked, and his tongue seemed to stumble over his words.

"Kador's a pig," Haldor said flatly, carefully watching Radan as if gauging the impact of his words. "An arrogant, brutal pig with no more right to the throne than a mongrel dog. His great-grandfather bought his way into the House of Vordue, and I'd sooner open a vein than bow to the offspring of a sneak thief from the docks of Tol Vordue."

Radan's eyes almost started from his head at Haldor's calculated insults.

He opened his mouth several times as if trying to speak, but his tongue seemed frozen with fury. His face turned purple, and he clawed at the air in front of him. Then his body stiffened and began to arch backward.

Haldor watched him with an almost clinical detachment.

With a strangled cry, Radan toppled back onto the cobblestones, his arms and legs thrashing violently. His eyes rolled back in his head, and he began to foam at the mouth as his convulsions became more violent. He began to bang his head on the stones, and his twitching fingers clutched at his throat.

"Amazing potency," the third mantled man said to Haldor. "Where did you find it?"

"A friend of mine recently made a voyage to Sthiss Tor," Haldor said, watching Radan's convulsions with interest. "The beautiful part of it is that it's completely harmless unless one gets excited. Radan wouldn't drink the wine until I tasted it first to prove that it was safe."

"You've got the same poison in your own stomach?" the other man asked with astonishment.

"I'm quite safe," Haldor said. "My emotions never get the best of me."

Radan's convulsions had grown weaker. His heels beat at the stones with a rapid pattering sound; then he stiffened, gave a long, gurgling sigh, and died.

"I don't suppose you've got any of the drug left, do you?" Haldor's friend asked thoughtfully. "I'd be willing to pay quite a bit for something like that."

Haldor laughed. "Why don't we go to my house, and we'll talk about it? Over a cup of wine, perhaps?"

The other man threw him a startled glance; then he laughed too, although a bit nervously. The two of them turned and walked away, leaving the dead man sprawled on the stones.

Garion stared in horror at them and then at the black-faced corpse lying so grotesquely twisted in the center of the marketplace. The Tolnedrans near the body seemed to ignore its existence. "Why doesn't somebody do something?" he demanded.

"They're afraid," Silk said. "If they show any concern, they might be mistaken for partisans. Politics here in Tol Honeth are taken very seriously."

"Shouldn't someone notify the authorities?" Durnik suggested, his face pale and his voice shaking.

"I'm sure it's already been taken care of," Silk said. "Let's not stand around staring. I don't think we want to get involved in this sort of thing."

Aunt Pol came back to where they were standing. The two Cherek warriors from Grinneg's house who had been accompanying her were loaded down with bundles and both of them looked a little sheepish about it.

"What are you doing?" she asked Silk.

"We were just watching a bit of Tolnedran politics in action," Silk said, pointing at the dead man in the center of the square.

"Poison?" she asked, noting Radan's contorted limbs.

Silk nodded. "A strange one. It doesn't seem to work unless the victim gets excited."

"Athsat," she said with a grim nod.

"You've heard of it before?" Silk seemed surprised.

She nodded. "It's quite rare, and very expensive. I didn't think the Nyissans would be willing to sell any of it."

"I think we should move away from here," Hettar suggested. "There's a squad of legionnaires coming, and they might want to question any witnesses."

"Good idea," Silk said and led them toward the far side of the marketplace.

Near the row of houses that marked the edge of the square, eight burly men carried a heavily veiled litter. As the litter approached, a slender, jeweled hand reached languidly out from behind the veil and touched one of the porters on the shoulder. The eight men stopped immediately and set the litter down.

"Silk," a woman's voice called from within the litter, "what are you doing back in Tol Honeth?"

"Bethra?" Silk said. "Is that you?"

The veil was drawn back, revealing a lushly endowed woman lounging on crimson satin cushions inside the litter. Her dark hair was elaborately curled with strings of pearls woven into her tresses. Her pink silken gown clung to her body, and golden rings and bracelets clasped her arms and fingers. Her face was breathtakingly beautiful, and her long-lashed eyes were wicked. There was about her a kind of overripeness and an almost overpowering sense of self-indulgent corruption. For some reason Garion felt himself blushing furiously.

"I thought you'd still be running," she said archly to Silk. "The men I sent after you were very professional."

Silk bowed with an ironic little flourish. "They *were* quite good, Bethra," he agreed with a wry grin. "Not quite good enough, but very good, actually. I hope you didn't need them anymore."

"I always wondered why they didn't come back." She laughed. "I should have known, of course. I hope you didn't take it personally."

"Certainly not, Bethra. It's just part of the profession, after all."

"I knew you'd understand," she said. "I had to get rid of you. You were disrupting my entire plan."

Silk grinned wickedly. "I know," he gloated. "And after all you had to go through to set it up—and with the Thullish ambassador, no less."

She made a disgusted face.

"Whatever happened to him?" Silk asked.

"He went swimming in the Nedrane."

"I didn't know that Thulls swam all that well."

"They don't—particularly not with large rocks tied to their feet. After you'd destroyed the whole thing, I didn't really need him anymore, and there were some things I didn't want him mentioning in certain quarters."

"You always were prudent, Bethra."

"What are you up to now?" she asked curiously.

Silk shrugged. "A little of this; a little of that."

"The succession?"

"Oh, no." He laughed. "I know better than to get involved in that. Which side are you on?"

"Wouldn't you like to know?"

Silk looked around, his eyes narrowing. "I could use some information, Bethra—if you're free to talk about it, of course."

"About what, Silk?"

"The city seems to be awash with Murgos," Silk said. "If you're not presently involved with them, I'd appreciate anything you could tell me."

She smiled at him archly. "And what would you be willing to pay?" she asked.

"Couldn't we just call it professional courtesy?"

She smiled wickedly at him; then she laughed. "Why not? I like you, Silk, and I think I'll like you even more if you owe me a favor."

"I'll be your slave," he promised.

"Liar." She thought for a moment. "The Murgos have never really shown all that much interest in trade," she said. "But a few years ago they began arriving in twos and threes; and then late last summer, whole caravans started coming in from Rak Goska."

"You think they want to influence the succession?" Silk asked.

"That would be my guess," she said. "There's a great deal of red gold in Tol Honeth suddenly. My coin chests are full of it."

Silk grinned. "It all spends."

"It does indeed."

"Have they picked any one candidate?"

"Not that I've been able to determine. They seem to be divided into two different factions, and there's quite a bit of antagonism between them."

"That could be a ruse, of course."

"I don't think so. I think the antagonism has to do with the quarrel between Zedar and Ctuchik. Each side wants to get control of the next Emperor. They're spending money like water."

"Do you know the one called Asharak?"

"Ah, *that* one," she replied. "The other Murgos are all afraid of him. At the moment he *seems* to be working for Ctuchik, but I think he's playing some game of his own. He owns the Grand Duke Kador outright, and Kador's closest to the throne right now. That puts Asharak in a very powerful position. That's about all I really know."

"Thank you, Bethra," Silk said respectfully.

"Are you planning to stay in Tol Honeth for long?" she asked.

"Unfortunately no."

"Pity. I was hoping you might be able to come by for a visit. We could talk over old times. I don't have many close friends anymore—or dear enemies, like you."

Silk laughed dryly. "I wonder why," he said. "I don't imagine I could swim much better than the Thullish ambassador did. You're a dangerous woman, Bethra."

"In more ways than one," she admitted, stretching languidly. "But your life's not really in any danger from me, Silk—not anymore."

"It wasn't my life I was worried about." Silk grinned.

"That's another matter, of course," she admitted. "Don't forget that you owe me a favor."

"I hunger for the opportunity to repay my debt," he said impudently.

"You're impossible." She laughed, then gestured to her porters, and they lifted her litter to their shoulders. "Good-bye, Silk," she said.

"Good-bye, Bethra," he replied with a deep bow.

"Absolutely disgusting," Durnik said in a voice strangled with outrage as the porters marched away with the litter. "Why is a woman like that even permitted to stay in the city?"

"Bethra?" Silk asked in surprise. "She's the most brilliant and fascinating woman in Tol Honeth. Men come from all over the world just for an hour or two with her."

"For a price, of course," Durnik said.

"Don't misunderstand her, Durnik," Silk told him. "Her conversation's probably more valuable than—" He coughed slightly with a quick glance at Aunt Pol.

"Really?" Durnik questioned in a voice heavy with sarcasm.

Silk laughed. "Durnik," he said, "I love you like a brother, but you're a terrible prude, do you know that?"

"Leave him alone, Silk," Aunt Pol said firmly. "I like him exactly the way he is."

"I'm only trying to improve him, Lady Polgara," Silk explained innocently.

"Barak's right about you, Prince Kheldar," she said. "You're a very bad man."

"It's all in the line of duty. I sacrifice my more delicate feelings for the sake of my country."

"Of course!"

"Surely you don't imagine that I *enjoy* that sort of thing?"

"Why don't we just let it drop?" she suggested.

Grinneg, Barak, and Mister Wolf returned to Grinneg's house not long after the others had arrived.

"Well?" Aunt Pol asked Wolf as the old man came into the room where they had been waiting.

"He went south," Wolf said.

"South? He didn't turn east toward Cthol Murgos?"

"No," Wolf said. "He's probably trying to avoid a meeting with Ctuchik's people. He'll look for a quiet place to slip across the border. Either that or he's headed for Nyissa. Perhaps he's made some arrangement with Salmissra. We'll have to follow him to find out."

"I met an old friend in the marketplace," Silk said from the chair in which he lounged. "She tells me that Asharak's been involved in the politics of succession. It appears that he's managed to buy the Grand Duke of Vordue. If the Vorduvians get the throne, Asharak's going to have Tolnedra in the palm of his hand."

Mister Wolf scratched thoughtfully at his beard. "We're going to have to do something about him sooner or later. He's beginning to make me just a little tired."

"We could stop over for a day or so," Aunt Pol suggested. "Attend to it once and for all."

"No," Wolf decided. "It's probably best not to do that sort of thing here in the city. The business is likely to be a bit noisy, and Tolnedrans get excited about things they can't understand. I'm sure he'll give us an opportunity later—in some less-populated place."

"Do we leave now, then?" Silk asked.

"Let's wait until early morning," Wolf told him. "We'll probably be followed, but if the streets are empty, it'll make things a little more difficult for them."

"I'll talk to my cook, then," Grinneg said. "The least I can do is send you on your way with a good meal to help you face the road. Then, of course, there's still that barrel of ale to be dealt with."

Mister Wolf smiled broadly at that, then caught Aunt Pol's reproving frown. "It would only go flat, Pol," he explained. "Once it's broached, you have to drink it up fairly quickly. It'd be a shame to waste it, wouldn't it?"

CHAPTER EIGHTEEN

They left Grinneg's house before dawn the next morning, dressed once more in their traveling clothes. They slipped quietly out a back gate and proceeded through those narrow alleys and back streets Silk always seemed able to find. The sky to the east was beginning to lighten when they reached the massive bronze gate on the south end of the island.

"How long until the gate opens?" Mister Wolf asked one of the legionnaires.

"Not much longer," the legionnaire told him. "Just as soon as we can see the far bank clearly."

Wolf grunted. He had grown quite mellow the evening before and he was obviously troubled by a headache this morning. He dismounted, went to one of the packhorses, and drank from a leather waterskin.

"That isn't going to help, you know," Aunt Pol told him a bit smugly. He chose not to answer.

"I think it's going to be a lovely day today," she said brightly, looking first at the sky and then at the men around her who slumped in their saddles in attitudes of miserable dejection.

"You're a cruel woman, Polgara," Barak said sadly.

"Did you talk to Grinneg about that ship?" Mister Wolf asked.

"I think so," Barak replied. "I seem to remember saying something about it."

"It's fairly important," Wolf said.

"What's this?" Aunt Pol asked.

"I thought it might not be a bad idea to have a ship waiting off the mouth of the River of the Woods," Wolf said. "If we have to go to Sthiss Tor, it would probably be better to sail there rather than wade through the swamps in northern Nyissa."

"That's a very good idea, actually," she approved. "I'm surprised it occurred to you—considering your condition last night."

"Do you suppose we could talk about something else?" he asked somewhat plaintively.

It grew imperceptibly lighter, and the command to open the gate came from the watchtower on the wall above. The legionnaires slipped the iron bar and swung the ponderous gate open. With Mandorallen at his side, Silk led them out through the thick portal and across the bridge that spanned the dark waters of the Nedrane.

By noon they were eight leagues south of Tol Honeth, and Mister Wolf had somewhat regained his composure, though his eyes still seemed a bit sensitive to the bright spring sunlight, and he winced now and then when a bird sang a bit too near.

"Riders coming up behind," Hettar said.

"How many?" Barak asked.

"Two."

"Ordinary travelers, perhaps," Aunt Pol said.

The two figures on horseback appeared from around a bend behind them and stopped. They spoke together for a moment or two and then came on, their bearing somewhat cautious. They were a peculiar pair. The man wore a green Tolnedran mantle, a garment not really suited for riding. His forehead was quite high, and his hair was carefully combed to conceal his encroaching baldness. He was very skinny, and his ears stuck out from the side of his head like flaps. His companion appeared to be a child dressed in a hooded traveling cloak and with a kerchief across her face to keep out the dust.

"Good day to you," the skinny man greeted them politely as the pair drew alongside.

"Hello," Silk returned.

"Warm for so early in the year, isn't it?" the Tolnedran said.

"We noticed that," Silk agreed.

"I wonder," the skinny man asked, "do you have a bit of water you could spare?"

"Of course," Silk said. He looked at Garion and gestured toward the pack animals. Garion dropped back and unhooked a leather waterskin from one of the packs. The stranger removed the wooden stopper and carefully wiped the mouth of the skin. He offered the bag to his companion. She removed her kerchief and looked at the skin with an expression of perplexity.

"Like this, your—uh—my Lady," the man explained, taking the skin back, raising it in both hands and drinking.

"I see," the girl said.

Garion looked at her more closely. The voice was familiar for some reason, and there was something about her face. She was not a child, though she was very small, and there was a kind of self-indulged petulance about her tiny face. Garion was almost certain he had seen her somewhere before.

The Tolnedran handed the waterskin back to her, and she drank, making a small face at the resinous taste. Her hair was a purplish black, and there were faint dark smears on the collar of her traveling cloak that indicated that the color was not natural.

"Thank you, Jeebers," she said after she had drunk. "And thank you, sir," she said to Silk.

Garion's eyes narrowed as a dreadful suspicion began to grow in his mind.

"Are you going far?" the skinny man asked Silk.

"Quite a ways," Silk answered. "I'm Radek of Boktor, a Drasnian merchant, and I'm bound to the south with Sendarian woolens. This break in the weather destroyed the market in Tol Honeth, so I thought I'd try Tol Rane. It's in the mountains, and it's probably still cold there."

"You're taking the wrong road, then," the stranger said. "The road to Tol Rane lies off to the east."

"I've had trouble on that road," Silk said glibly. "Robbers, you know. I thought it'd be safer to go through Tol Borune."

"What a coincidence," the skinny man told him. "My pupil and I are bound for Tol Borune ourselves."

"Yes," Silk admitted. "Quite a coincidence."

"Perhaps we could ride along together."

Silk looked doubtful.

"I don't see any reason why not," Aunt Pol decided before he could refuse.

"You're most kind, gracious lady," the stranger said. "I am Master Jeebers, Fellow of the Imperial Society, a tutor by profession. Perhaps you've heard of me."

"I can't really say so," Silk told him, "although that's not too remarkable, since we're strangers here in Tolnedra."

Jeebers looked a bit disappointed. "I suppose that's true," he said. "This is my pupil, Lady Sharell. Her father's a grand master merchant, the Baron Reldon. I'm accompanying her to Tol Borune where she's to visit relatives."

Garion knew that was not true. The tutor's name had confirmed his suspicions.

They rode several miles farther, with Jeebers babbling animatedly at Silk.

He spoke endlessly about his learning and continually prefaced his remarks with references to important people who seemed to rely on his judgment. Although he was tiresome, he appeared to be quite harmless. His pupil rode beside Aunt Pol, saying very little.

"I think it's time we stopped for a bite to eat," Aunt Pol announced. "Would you and your pupil care to join us, Master Jeebers? We have plenty."

"I'm quite overcome by your generosity," the tutor said. "We'd be delighted."

They stopped the horses near a small bridge that crossed a brook and led them into the shade of a thick clump of willows not far from the road. Durnik built a fire, and Aunt Pol began to unload her pots and kettles.

Master Jeebers' pupil sat in her saddle until the tutor quickly stepped over to help her down. She looked at the slightly marshy ground near the brook unenthusiastically. Then she glanced imperiously at Garion. "You— boy," she called, "fetch me a cup of fresh water."

"The brook's right there," he told her, pointing.

She stared at him in amazement. "But the ground's all muddy," she objected.

"It does seem that way, doesn't it?" he admitted and then quite deliberately turned his back on her and went over to help his aunt.

"Aunt Pol," he said after several moments of debating with himself.

"Yes, dear?"

"I don't think the Lady Sharell's who she says she is."

"Oh?"

"I'm not completely positive, but I think she's the Princess Ce'Nedra— the one who came into the garden when we were at the palace."

"Yes, dear. I know."

"You know?"

"Of course. Would you hand me the salt, please?"

"Isn't it dangerous to have her with us?"

"Not really," she said. "I think we can manage it."

"Won't she be a lot of bother?"

"An Imperial Princess is supposed to be a lot of bother, dear."

After they had eaten a savory stew which seemed to Garion quite good but which their little guest appeared to find distasteful, Jeebers began to approach a subject which had obviously been on his mind since they had first met. "Despite the best efforts of the legions, the roads are never entirely safe," the fussy man said. "It's imprudent to travel alone, and the Lady Sharell's been entrusted to my care. Since I'm responsible for her safety, I was wondering if we might travel along with you. We wouldn't be any bother, and I'd be more than happy to pay for whatever food we eat."

Silk glanced quickly at Aunt Pol.

"Of course," she said.

Silk looked surprised.

"There's no reason we can't travel together," she went on. "We're all going to the same place, after all."

Silk shrugged. "Anything you say."

Garion knew the idea was a mistake so serious that it bordered on disaster. Jeebers would not be a good traveling companion, and his pupil showed every sign of quickly becoming intolerable. She was obviously accustomed to extensive personal service, and her demands were probably made without thought. They were still demands, however, and Garion knew immediately who was most likely to be expected to attend to them. He got up and walked around to the far side of the clump of willows.

The fields beyond the trees were pale green in the spring sunshine, and small white clouds drifted lazily across the sky. Garion leaned against a tree and gazed out at the fields without actually seeing them. He would *not* become a servant—no matter who their little guest might be. He wished there were some way he could get that firmly established right at the outset—before things got out of hand.

"Have you lost your senses, Pol?" he heard Mister Wolf say somewhere behind him among the trees. "Ran Borune's probably got every legion in Tolnedra looking for her by now."

"This is my province, Old Wolf," Aunt Pol told him. "Don't interfere. I can manage things so that we won't be bothered by the legions."

"We don't have the time to coddle her," the old man said. "I'm sorry, Pol, but the child's going to be an absolute little monster. You saw the way she acted toward her father."

"It's no great chore to break bad habits," she said, unconcerned.

"Wouldn't it be simpler just to arrange to have her taken back to Tol Honeth?"

"She's already run away once," Aunt Pol answered. "If we· send her back, she'll just run away again. I'll feel much more comfortable having her Imperial little Highness where I can put my hands on her when I need her. When the proper time comes, I don't want to have to take the world apart looking for her."

Wolf sighed. "Have it your way, Pol."

"Naturally."

"Just keep the brat away from me," he said. "She sets my teeth on edge. Do any of the others know who she is?"

"Garion does."

"Garion? That's surprising."

"Not really," Aunt Pol said. "He's brighter than he looks."

A new emotion began to grow in Garion's already confused mind. Aunt Pol's obvious interest in Ce'Nedra sent a sharp pang through him. With a certain amount of shame, he realized that he was jealous of the attention the girl was receiving.

In the days that followed, Garion's fears quickly proved to be well-founded. An inadvertent remark about Faldor's farm had revealed quite early to the princess his former status as a scullery boy, and she used the knowledge heartlessly to browbeat him into a hundred stupid little errands every day. To make it all worse, each time he tried to resist, Aunt Pol would firmly remind him to pay more attention to his manners. Inevitably, he became quite surly about the whole business.

The princess developed a story about the reason for her departure from Tol Honeth as they rode south. The story changed daily, growing more wildly implausible with every passing league. At first she seemed content to be on a simple excursion to visit relatives; then she dropped dark hints about flight from a marriage to an ugly old merchant. Next, there were even darker hints about a plot to capture her and hold her for ransom. Finally, in a crowning effort, she confided to them that the proposed kidnapping was politically motivated—a part of some vast scheme to gain power in Tolnedra.

"She's an awful liar, isn't she?" Garion asked Aunt Pol when they were alone one evening.

"Yes, dear," Aunt Pol agreed. "Lying is an art. A good lie shouldn't be embellished so much. She'll need a lot more practice if she plans to make a career of it."

Finally, about ten days after they had left Tol Honeth, the city of Tol Borune came into sight in the afternoon sun. "It looks like this is where we part company," Silk said to Jeebers with a certain amount of relief.

"Aren't you going into the city?" Jeebers asked.

"I don't think so," Silk answered. "We don't really have any business to take care of there, and the usual explanations and searches just waste time— not to mention the expense of the bribes. We'll go around Tol Borune and pick up the road to Tol Rane on the other side."

"We can ride a bit farther with you then," Ce'Nedra said quickly. "My relatives live on an estate to the south of the city."

Jeebers stared at her in amazement.

Aunt Pol drew in her horse and looked at the small girl with a raised eyebrow. "This seems like as good a place as any for us to have a little talk," she said.

Silk looked quickly at her and then nodded.

"I believe, little lady," Aunt Pol told the girl when they had all dismounted, "that the time has come for you to tell us the truth."

"But I have," Ce'Nedra protested.

"Oh, come now, child," Aunt Pol said. "Those stories of yours have been very entertaining, but you don't actually think anyone believed them, do you? Some of us already know who you are, but I really think we should get it out in the open."

"You know?" Ce'Nedra faltered.

"Of course, dear," Aunt Pol said. "Would you like to tell them, or shall I?"

Ce'Nedra's little shoulders drooped. "Tell them who I am, Master Jeebers," she ordered quietly.

"Do you really think that's wise, your Ladyship?" Jeebers asked nervously.

"They already know anyway," she said. "If they were going to do anything to us, they'd have done it a long time ago. We can trust them."

Jeebers drew in a deep breath and then spoke rather formally. "I have the honor to introduce her Imperial Highness, the Princess Ce'Nedra, daughter to his Imperial Majesty, Ran Borune XXIII, and the jewel of the House of Borune."

Silk whistled, and his eyes widened momentarily. The others showed similar signs of amazement.

"The political situation in Tol Honeth had become far too volatile, too menacing, for her Highness to remain safely in the capital," Jeebers went on. "The Emperor commissioned me to convey his daughter secretly here to Tol Borune where the members of the Borune family can protect her from the plots and machinations of the Vordues, the Honeths, and the Horbites. I'm proud to say that I've managed to execute my commission rather brilliantly—with your help, of course. I'll mention your assistance in my report—a footnote, perhaps, or maybe even an appendix."

Barak pulled at his beard, his eyes thoughtful. "An Imperial Princess travels across half of Tolnedra with only a schoolmaster for protection?" he questioned. "At a time when they're knifing and poisoning each other in the streets?"

"It does seem a trifle risky, doesn't it?" Hettar agreed.

"Did thine Emperor charge thee with this task in person?" Mandorallen asked Jeebers.

"It wasn't necessary," Jeebers said stiffly. "His Majesty has a great deal of respect for my judgment and discretion. He knew that I'd be able to devise a safe disguise and a secure mode of travel. The princess assured me of his absolute confidence in me. It all had to be done in utmost secrecy, of course. That's why she came to my chambers in the middle of the night to advise me of his instructions and why we left the palace without telling anyone what we were—" His voice trailed off, and he stared at Ce'Nedra in horror.

"You might as well tell him the truth, dear," Aunt Pol advised the little princess. "I think he's guessed already."

Ce'Nedra's chin lifted arrogantly. "The orders came from me, Jeebers," she told him. "My father had nothing to do with it."

Jeebers went deathly pale and he nearly collapsed.

"What idiocy made you decide to run away from your father's palace?" Barak demanded of the tiny girl. "All Tolnedra's probably looking for you, and we're caught right in the middle."

"Gently," Wolf said to the hulking Cherek. "She may be a princess, but she's still a little girl. Don't frighten her."

"The question's to the point, though," Hettar observed. "If we're caught with an Imperial Princess in our company, we'll all see the inside of a Tolnedran dungeon." He turned to Ce'Nedra. "Do you have an answer, or were you just playing games?"

She drew herself up haughtily. "I'm not accustomed to explaining my actions to servants."

"We're going to have to clear up a few misconceptions before long, I see," Wolf said.

"Just answer the question, dear," Aunt Pol told the girl. "Never mind who asked it."

"My father had imprisoned me in the palace," Ce'Nedra said in a rather offhand way, as if that explained everything. "It was intolerable, so I left. There's another matter, too, but that's a matter of politics. You wouldn't understand."

"You'd probably be surprised at what we'd understand, Ce'Nedra," Mister Wolf told her.

"I'm accustomed to being addressed as my Lady," she said tartly, "or as your Highness."

"And I'm accustomed to being told the truth."

"I thought you were in charge," Ce'Nedra said to Silk.

"Appearances are deceiving," Silk observed blandly. "I'd answer the question."

"It's an old treaty," she said. "I didn't sign it, so I don't see why I should be bound by it. I'm supposed to present myself in the throne room at Riva on my sixteenth birthday."

"We know that," Barak said impatiently. "What's the problem?"

"I'm not going, that's all," Ce'Nedra announced. "I won't go to Riva, and no one can make me go. The queen in the Wood of the Dryads is my kins-woman and she'll give me sanctuary."

Jeebers had partially recovered. "What have you done?" he demanded, aghast. "I undertook this with the clear understanding that I'd be rewarded—even promoted. You've put my head on the block, you little idiot!"

"Jeebers!" she cried, shocked at his words.

"Let's get off the road a ways," Silk suggested. "We've obviously got quite a bit to discuss, and we're likely to be interrupted here on the main highway."

"Probably a good idea," Wolf agreed. "Let's find some quiet place and set up for the night. We'll decide what we're going to do and then we can start out fresh in the morning."

They remounted and rode across the rolling fields toward a line of trees that marked the course of a winding country lane about a mile away.

"How about there?" Durnik suggested, pointing at a broad oak which stood beside the lane, its branches beginning to leaf out in the late afternoon sunlight.

"That should do," Wolf said.

It was pleasant in the dappled shade beneath the spreading limbs of the oak. The lane was lined with low stone walls, mossy and cool. A stile stepped up over one of the walls just there, and a path meandered across the field from it toward a nearby pond, sparkling in the sun.

"We can put the fire down behind one of the walls," Durnik said. "It won't be seen from the main road that way."

"I'll get some wood," Garion volunteered, looking at the dead limbs lit-tering the grass beneath the tree.

They had by now established a sort of routine in the setting up of a night's encampment. The tents were erected, the horses watered and pick-eted, and the fire was started all within the space of an hour. Then Durnik, who had noticed a few telltale circles on the surface of the pond, heated an iron pin in the fire and carefully hammered it into a hook.

"What's that for?" Garion asked him.

"I thought some fish might be good for supper," the smith said, wiping the hook on the skirt of his leather tunic. He laid it aside then and lifted a second pin out of the fire with a pair of tongs. "Would you like to try your luck too?"

Garion grinned at him.

Barak, who sat nearby combing the snarls out of his beard, looked up rather wistfully. "I don't suppose you'd have time to make another hook, would you?" he asked.

Durnik chuckled. "It only takes a couple minutes."

"We'll need bait," Barak said, getting up quickly. "Where's your spade?"

Not long afterward, the three of them crossed the field to the pond, cut some saplings for poles and settled down to serious fishing.

The fish, it appeared, were ravenous and attacked the worm-baited hooks in schools. Within the space of an hour nearly two dozen respectable-sized trout lay in a gleaming row on the grassy bank of the pond.

Aunt Pol inspected their catch gravely when they returned as the sky turned rosy overhead with the setting of the sun. "Very nice," she told them, "but you forgot to clean them."

"Oh," Barak said. He looked slightly pained. "We thought that—well, what I mean is—as long as *we* caught them—" He left it hanging.

"Go on," she said with a level gaze.

Barak sighed. "I guess we'd better clean them," he regretfully told Durnik and Garion.

"You're probably right," Durnik agreed.

The sky had turned purple with evening, and the stars had begun to come out when they sat down to eat. Aunt Pol had fried the trout to a crisp, golden brown, and even the sulky little princess found nothing to complain about as she ate.

After they had finished, they set aside their plates and took up the problem of Ce'Nedra and her flight from Tol Honeth. Jeebers had sunk into such abject melancholy that he could offer little to the discussion, and Ce'Nedra adamantly announced that even if they were to turn her over to the Borunes in the city, she would run away again. In the end, they reached no conclusion.

"We're in trouble no matter what we do," Silk summed it all up ruefully. "Even if we try to deliver her to her family, there are bound to be some embarrassing questions, and I'm sure she can be counted on to invent a colorful story that will put us in the worst possible light."

"We can talk about it some more in the morning," Aunt Pol said. Her placid tone indicated that she had already made up her mind about something, but she did not elaborate.

Shortly before midnight, Jeebers made his escape. They were all awakened by the thudding of his horse's hooves as the panic-stricken tutor fled at a gallop toward the walls of Tol Borune.

Silk stood in the flickering light of the dying fire, his face angry. "Why didn't you stop him?" he asked Hettar, who had been standing watch.

"I was told not to," the leather-clad Algar said with a glance at Aunt Pol.

"It solves the only real problem we had," Aunt Pol explained. "The schoolmaster would only have been excess baggage."

"You knew he was going to run away?" Silk asked.

"Naturally. I helped him to arrive at the decision. He'll go straight to the Borunes and try to save his own skin by informing them that the princess ran away from the palace on her own and that we have her now."

"You have to stop him, then," Ce'Nedra said in a ringing voice. "Go after him! Bring him back!"

"After all the trouble I went to persuading him to leave?" Aunt Pol asked. "Don't be foolish."

"How *dare* you speak to me like that?" Ce'Nedra demanded. "You seem to forget who I am."

"Young lady," Silk said urbanely, "I think you'd be amazed at how little Polgara's concerned about who you are."

"Polgara?" Ce'Nedra faltered. "*The* Polgara? I thought you said that she was your sister."

"I lied," Silk confessed. "It's a vice I have."

"You're not an ordinary merchant," the girl accused him.

"He's Prince Kheldar of Drasnia," Aunt Pol said. "The others have a similar eminence. I'm sure you can see how little your title impresses us. We have our own titles, so we know how empty they are."

"If you're Polgara, then he must be—" The princess turned to stare at Mister Wolf, who had seated himself on the lowest step of the stile to pull on his shoes.

"Yes," Aunt Pol said. "He doesn't really look the part, does he?"

"What are you doing in Tolnedra?" Ce'Nedra asked in a stunned voice. "Are you going to use magic of some kind to control the outcome of the succession?"

"Why should we?" Mister Wolf said, getting to his feet. "Tolnedrans always seem to think that their politics shake the whole world, but the rest of the world's really not all that concerned about who gains the throne in Tol Honeth. We're here on a matter of much greater urgency." He looked off into the darkness in the direction of Tol Borune. "It'll take Jeebers a certain amount of time to convince the people in the city that he's not a lunatic," he said, "but it would probably be a good idea if we left the area. I imagine we'd better stay away from the main highway."

"That's no problem," Silk assured him.

"What about me?" Ce'Nedra asked.

"You wanted to go to the Wood of the Dryads," Aunt Pol told her. "We're going in that direction anyway, so you'll stay with us. We'll see what Queen Xantha says when we get you there."

"Am I to consider myself a prisoner, then?" the princess asked stiffly.

"You can if it makes you feel better, dear," Aunt Pol said. She looked at the tiny girl critically in the flickering firelight. "I'm going to have to do something about your hair, though. What did you use for dye? It looks awful."

CHAPTER NINETEEN

They moved rapidly south for the next few days, traveling frequently at night to avoid the mounted patrols of legionnaires who were beating the countryside in their efforts to locate Ce'Nedra.

"Maybe we should have hung on to Jeebers," Barak muttered sourly after one near-brush with the soldiers. "He's roused every garrison from here to the border. It might have been better to have dropped him off in some isolated place or something."

"That 'or something' has a certain ring of finality to it, old friend," Silk said with a sharp little grin.

Barak shrugged. "It's a solution to a problem."

Silk laughed. "You really should try not to let your knife do all your thinking for you. That's the one quality we find least attractive in our Cherek cousins."

"And we find this compulsion to make clever remarks which seems to overwhelm our Drasnian brothers now and then almost equally unattractive," Barak told him coolly.

"Nicely put," Silk said with mock admiration.

They rode on, watchful, always ready to hide or to run. During those days they relied heavily on Hettar's curious ability. Since the patrols searching for them were inevitably mounted, the tall, hawk-faced Algar swept their surroundings with his mind, searching for horses. The warnings he could thus provide usually gave them sufficient notice of the approach of the patrols.

"What's it like?" Garion asked him one cloudy midmorning as they rode along a seldom-used and weed-grown track to which Silk had led them. "I mean being able to hear a horse's thoughts?"

"I don't think I can describe it exactly," Hettar answered. "I've always been able to do it, so I can't imagine what it's like not doing it. There's a kind of reaching-out in a horse's mind—a sort of inclusiveness. A horse seems to think 'we' instead of 'I.' I suppose it's because in their natural condition they're members of a herd. After they get to know you, they think of you as a herd mate. Sometimes they even forget that you're not a horse." He broke off suddenly. "Belgarath," he announced sharply, "there's another patrol coming—just beyond that hill over there. Twenty or thirty of them."

Mister Wolf looked about quickly. "Have we got time to reach those trees?" He pointed at a thick stand of scrub maple about a half mile ahead.

"If we hurry."

"Then run!" Wolf ordered, and they all kicked their horses into a sudden burst of speed. They reached the trees just as the first few raindrops of the spring shower that had been threatening all morning pattered on the broad leaves. They dismounted and pushed in among the springy saplings, worming their way back out of sight, leading their horses.

The Tolnedran patrol came over the hilltop and swept down into the shallow valley. The captain in charge of the legionnaires pulled in his horse not far from the stand of maples and dispersed his men with a series of sharp commands. They moved out in small groups, scouting the weedy road in both directions and surveying the surrounding countryside from the top of the next rise. The officer and a civilian in a gray riding cloak remained behind, sitting their horses beside the track.

The captain squinted distastefully up into the sprinkling rain. "It's going to be a wet day," he said, dismounting and pulling his crimson cloak tighter around him.

His companion also swung down and turned so that the party hiding among the maples was able to see his face. Garion felt Hettar tense suddenly. The man in the cloak was a Murgo.

"Over here, Captain," the Murgo said, leading his horse into the shelter provided by the outspreading limbs of the saplings at the edge of the stand.

The Tolnedran nodded and followed the man in the riding cloak.

"Have you had the chance to think over my offer?" the Murgo asked.

"I thought it was only speculation," the captain replied. "We don't even know that these foreigners are in this quadrant."

"My information is that they're going south, Captain," the Murgo told him. "I think you can be quite certain that they're somewhere in your quadrant."

"There's no guarantee that we'll find them, though," the captain said. "And even if we do, it'd be very difficult to do what you propose."

"Captain," the Murgo explained patiently, "it's for the safety of the princess, after all. If she's returned to Tol Honeth, the Vorduvians are going to kill her. You've read those documents I brought you."

"She'll be safe with the Borunes," the captain said. "The Vorduvians aren't going to come into Southern Tolnedra after her."

"The Borunes are only going to turn her over to her father. You're a Borune yourself. Would *you* defy an Emperor of your own house?"

The captain's face was troubled.

"Her only hope of safety is with the Horbites," the Murgo pressed.

"What guarantees do I have that she'll be safe with them?"

"The best guarantee of all—politics. The Horbites are doing everything in their power to block the Grand Duke Kador on his march to the throne. Since he wants the princess dead, the Horbites naturally want to keep her alive. It's the only way really to ensure her safety—and you become a wealthy man in the process." He jingled a heavy purse suggestively.

The captain still looked doubtful.

"Suppose we double the amount," the Murgo said in a voice that almost purred.

The captain swallowed hard. "It *is* for her safety, isn't it?"

"Of course it is."

"It's not as if I were betraying the House of Borune."

"You're a patriot, Captain," the Murgo assured the officer with a cold smile.

Aunt Pol was holding Ce'Nedra's arm quite firmly as they crouched together among the trees. The tiny girl's face was outraged, and her eyes were blazing.

Later, after the legionnaires and their Murgo friend had departed, the princess exploded. "How *dare* they?" she raged. "And for money!"

"That's Tolnedran politics for you," Silk said as they led their horses out of the stand of saplings into the drizzly morning.

"But he's a Borune," she protested, "a member of my own family."

"A Tolnedran's first loyalty is to his purse," Silk told her. "I'm surprised you haven't discovered that by now, your Highness."

A few days later they topped a hill and saw the Wood of the Dryads spreading like a green smudge on the horizon. The showers had blown off, and the sun was very bright.

"We'll be safe once we reach the Wood," the princess told them. "The legions won't follow us there."

"What's to stop them?" Garion asked her.

"The treaty with the Dryads," she said. "Don't you know anything?"

Garion resented that.

"There's no one about," Hettar reported to Mister Wolf. "We can go slow or wait for dark."

"Let's make a run for it," Wolf said. "I'm getting tired of dodging patrols." They started down the hill at a gallop toward the forest lying ahead of them.

There seemed to be none of the usual brushy margin which usually marked the transition from fields to woodlands. The trees simply began. When Wolf led them beneath those trees, the change was as abrupt as if they had suddenly gone inside a house. The Wood itself was a forest of incredible antiquity. The great oaks spread so broadly that the sky was almost never visible. The forest floor was mossy and cool, and there was very little undergrowth. It seemed to Garion that they were all quite tiny under the vast trees, and there was a strange, hushed quality about the wood. The air was very still, and there was a hum of insects and, from far overhead, a chorus of birdsong.

"Strange," Durnik said, looking around, "I don't see any sign of woodcutters."

"Woodcutters?" Ce'Nedra gasped. "In here? They wouldn't dare come into this wood."

"The Wood is inviolate, Durnik," Mister Wolf explained. "The Borune family has a treaty with the Dryads. No one has touched a tree here for over three thousand years."

"This is a curious place," Mandorallen said, looking around a bit uncomfortably. "Methinks I feel a presence here—a presence not altogether friendly."

"The Wood is alive," Ce'Nedra told him. "It doesn't really like strangers—but don't worry, Mandorallen, you're safe as long as you're with me." She sounded quite smug about it.

"Are you sure the patrols won't follow us?" Durnik asked Mister Wolf. "Jeebers knew we were coming here, after all, and I'm sure he told the Borunes."

"The Borunes won't violate their treaty with the Dryads," Wolf assured him. "Not for any reason."

"I've never known of a treaty a Tolnedran wouldn't step around if it was to his advantage." Silk spoke skeptically.

"This one is a bit different," Wolf said. "The Dryads gave one of their princesses to a young noble of the House of Borune. She became the mother of the Emperor of the First Borune Dynasty. The fortunes of the Borunes are very intimately tied up with the treaty. They're not going to gamble with that—not for any reason."

"What exactly is a Dryad?" Garion asked. The strange sense of a presence, an awareness in the Wood, made him want to talk to cover the oppressive, watchful silence.

"A small group," Mister Wolf said. "Quite gentle. I've always rather liked them. They aren't human, of course, but that's not all that important."

"I'm a Dryad," Ce'Nedra said rather proudly.

Garion stared at her.

"Technically she's right," Wolf said. "The Dryad line seems to breed true on the female side of the House of Borune. That's one of the things that keeps the family honest about the treaty—all those wives and mothers who'd pack up and leave if it were ever broken."

"She *looks* human," Garion objected, still staring at the princess.

"The Dryads are so closely related to humans that the differences are hardly significant," Wolf said. "That probably explains why they didn't go mad like the other monsters did when Torak cracked the world."

"*Monsters!*" Ce'Nedra protested loudly.

"Your pardon, Princess," Wolf apologized. "It's an Ulgo term used to describe the non-humans who supported Gorim at Prolgu when he met with the God UL."

"Do I look like a monster to you?" she demanded, tossing her head angrily.

"A poor choice of words, perhaps," Wolf murmured. "Forgive me."

"Monsters indeed!" Ce'Nedra fumed.

Wolf shrugged. "There's a stream not far ahead, if I remember right. We'll stop there and wait until word of our arrival reaches Queen Xantha. It's not a good idea to go into the territory of the Dryads without the queen's permission. They can get quite nasty if they're provoked."

"I thought you said they were gentle," Durnik said.

"Within reason," Wolf told him. "But it's not a good idea to irritate people who communicate with trees when you're in the middle of the forest. Unpleasant things have a way of happening." He frowned. "That reminds me.
You'd better stow your axe away out of sight. Dryads have strong feelings
about axes—and fires. They're most unreasonable about fire. We'll have to
keep our fires small and only for cooking."

They rode in under a colossal oak beside a sparkling stream purling over
mossy rocks, dismounted and set up their dun-colored tents. After they had
eaten, Garion wandered around feeling bored. Mister Wolf was napping, and
Silk had lured the others into a dice game. Aunt Pol had seated the princess
on a log and was stripping the purple dye from her hair.

"If you don't have anything else to do, Garion," she said, "why don't you
go bathe?"

"Bathe?" he asked. "Where?"

"I'm sure you'll find a pool somewhere along the stream," she said, carefully lathering Ce'Nedra's hair.

"You want me to bathe in that water? Aren't you afraid I'll catch cold?"

"You're a healthy boy, dear," she told him, "but a very dirty one. Now go
wash."

Garion gave her a dark look and went to one of the packs for clean
clothing, soap, and a towel. Then he stamped off upstream, grumbling at every step.

Once he was alone under the trees, he felt even more strongly that peculiar sense of being watched. It was not anything definable. There seemed
to be nothing specific about it, but rather it felt as if the oaks themselves
were aware of him and were passing information about his movements among
themselves with a kind of vegetative communication he could not begin to
understand. There seemed to be no menace in it—merely a kind of
watchfulness.

Some distance from the tents he found a fairly large pool where the
stream dropped in a waterfall from the rocks above. The water in the pool
was very clear, and he could see the bright pebbles on the bottom and several
large trout that eyed him warily. He tested the water with his hand and shuddered. He considered subterfuge—a quick splashing of water on his body and
a bit of soap on the more obvious smudges—but on reflection, he gave up the
notion. Aunt Pol would settle for nothing less than a complete bath. He
sighed bitterly and began to take off his clothing.

The first shock was awful, but after a few minutes he found that he could
bear it. In a short time it even became exhilarating. The waterfall provided
a convenient means for rinsing off the soap, and before long he found that
he was actually enjoying himself.

"You're making an awful lot of noise," Ce'Nedra said, standing on the
bank and appraising him quite calmly.

Garion immediately dove to the bottom of the pool.

Unless one is a fish, however, one can hardly remain underwater indefinitely. After about a minute, he struggled to the surface and popped his head out of the water, gasping and sputtering.

"Whatever are you doing?" Ce'Nedra asked. She was wearing a short white tunic, sleeveless and belted at the waist, and open sandals with laces that crisscrossed her slender ankles and calves and tied just below her knees. She carried a towel in one hand.

"Go away," Garion spluttered.

"Don't be so silly," she said, sitting down on a large stone and beginning to unlace her sandals. Her coppery hair was still damp and tumbled in a heavy mass about her shoulders.

"What are you doing?"

"I want to bathe," she said. "Are you going to be much longer?"

"Go someplace else," Garion cried, starting to shiver, but remaining determinedly crouched over in the water with only his head sticking out.

"This place looks just fine," she said. "How's the water?"

"Cold," he chattered, "but I'm not coming out until you go away."

"Don't be such a ninny," she told him.

He shook his head stubbornly, his face flaming.

She sighed with exasperation. "Oh, very well," she said. "I won't look, but I think you're being very silly. At the baths in Tol Honeth, no one thinks anything at all about such things."

"This isn't Tol Honeth," he told her pointedly.

"I'll turn my back, if that'll make you feel better," she said, getting up and standing with her back to the pool.

Not entirely trusting her, Garion crept from the pool and, still dripping, jerked on his drawers and hose. "All right," he called, "you can have the pool now." He mopped at his streaming face and hair with his towel. "I'm going back to the tents."

"The Lady Polgara says that you're to stay with me," she said, calmly untying the cord about her waist.

"Aunt Pol said *what?*" he demanded, terribly shocked.

"You're supposed to stay with me to protect me," she told him. She took hold of the hem of her tunic, obviously preparing to take it off.

Garion spun about and stared determinedly at the trees. His ears flamed, and his hands trembled uncontrollably.

She laughed a small, silvery laugh, and he could hear splashing as she entered the pool. She squealed from the shock of the cold water, and then there was more splashing.

"Bring me the soap," she commanded.

Without thinking, he bent to pick up the soap and caught one brief glimpse of her standing waist-deep in the water before he shut his eyes tightly. He backed toward the pool, his eyes closed and the hand holding the soap thrust out awkwardly behind him.

She laughed again and took the soap from his hand.

After what seemed an eternity, the princess completed her bath, emerged from the pool, dried herself and put her clothes back on. Garion kept his eyes firmly shut the entire time.

"You Sendars have such curious notions," she said as they sat together in the sun-warmed glade beside the pool. She was combing her deep red hair, her head inclined to one side and the comb pulling down through the thick, damp tangles. "The baths in Tol Honeth are open to all, and athletic contests are always conducted without clothing. Just last summer I myself ran against a dozen other girls in the Imperial Stadium. The spectators were most appreciative."

"I can imagine," Garion said dryly.

"What's that?" she asked, pointing at the amulet resting against his bare chest.

"My grandfather gave it to me last Erastide," Garion answered.

"Let me see." She held out her hand.

He leaned forward.

"Take it off so I can see it," she ordered.

"I'm not supposed to take it off," he told her. "Mister Wolf and Aunt Pol say I'm never supposed to take it off for any reason. I think there's a spell of some kind on it."

"What a strange idea," she remarked as she bent to examine the amulet. "They aren't really sorcerers, are they?"

"Mister Wolf is seven thousand years old," Garion said. "He knew the God Aldur. I've seen him make a tree grow from a small twig in a matter of minutes and set rocks on fire. Aunt Pol cured a blind woman with a single word, and she can turn herself into an owl."

"I don't believe in such things," Ce'Nedra told him. "I'm sure there's another explanation."

Garion shrugged and pulled on his linen shirt and brown tunic. He shook his head and raked his fingers through his still-damp hair.

"You're making an awful mess of it," she observed critically. "Here." She stood up and stepped behind him. "Let me do it." She put the comb to his hair and began pulling it through carefully. "You have nice hair for a man," she said.

"It's just hair," he said indifferently.

She combed in silence for a moment or two, then took his chin in her hand, turned his head and looked at him critically. She touched his hair at the sides a time or two until it was arranged to her satisfaction. "That's better," she decided.

"Thank you." He was a bit confused by the change in her.

She sat down again on the grass, clasped her arms around one knee and gazed at the sparkling pool. "Garion," she said finally.

"Yes?"

"What's it like to grow up as an ordinary person?"

He shrugged. "I've never been anything but an ordinary person," he told her, "so I wouldn't know what to compare it to."

"You know what I mean. Tell me about where you grew up—and what you did and all."

So he told her about Faldor's farm, about the kitchen and Durnik's smithy and Doroon and Rundorig and Zubrette.

"You're in love with Zubrette, aren't you?" She asked it almost accusingly.

"I thought I was, but so much has happened since we left the farm that sometimes I can't even remember what she looks like. I think I could do without being in love anyway. From what I've seen of it, it's pretty painful most of the time."

"You're impossible," she said, and then she smiled at him, her little face framed in the blazing mass of her suntouched hair.

"Probably," he admitted. "All right, now you tell me what it's like to grow up as a very special person."

"I'm not that special."

"You're an Imperial Princess," he reminded her. "I'd call that pretty special."

"Oh, that," she said, and then giggled. "You know, sometimes since I joined you people, I almost forget that I'm an Imperial Princess."

"Almost," he said with a smile, "but not quite."

"No," she agreed, "not quite." She looked out across the pool again. "Most of the time being a princess is very boring. It's all ceremonies and formalities. You have to stand around most of the time listening to speeches or receiving state visitors. There are guards around all the time, but sometimes I sneak away so I can be by myself. It makes them furious." She giggled again, and then her gaze turned pensive. "Let me tell your fortune," she said, taking his hand.

"Can you tell fortunes?" Garion asked.

"It's only make-believe," she admitted. "My maids and I play at it sometimes. We all promise each other high-born husbands and many children." She turned his hand over and looked at it. The silvery mark on his palm was very plain now that the skin was clean. "Whatever is that?" she asked.

"I don't know."

"It's not a disease, is it?"

"No," he said. "It's always been there. I think it's got something to do with my family. Aunt Pol doesn't like to have people see it for some reason, so she tries to keep it hidden."

"How could you hide something like that?"

"She finds things for me to do that keep my hands dirty most of the time."

"How strange," she said. "I have a birthmark too—right over my heart. Would you like to see it?" She took hold of the neck of her tunic.

"I'll take your word for it," Garion told her, blushing furiously.

She laughed a silvery, tinkling little laugh. "You're a strange boy, Garion. You're not at all like the other boys I've met."

"They were Tolnedrans probably," Garion pointed out. "I'm a Sendar—or at least that's the way I was raised—so there are bound to be differences."

"You sound as if you're not sure what you are."

"Silk says I'm not a Sendar," Garion said. "He says he isn't sure exactly what I am, and that's very odd. Silk can recognize anybody for what he is immediately. Your father thought I was a Rivan."

"Since the Lady Polgara's your Aunt and Belgarath's your Grandfather, you're probably a sorcerer," Ce'Nedra observed.

Garion laughed. "Me? That's silly. Besides, the sorcerers aren't a race—not like Chereks or Tolnedrans or Rivans. It's more like a profession, I think—sort of like being a lawyer or a merchant—only there aren't any new ones. The sorcerers are all thousands of years old. Mister Wolf says that maybe people have changed in some way so that they can't become sorcerers anymore."

Ce'Nedra had leaned back and was resting on her elbows, looking up at him. "Garion?"

"Yes?"

"Would you like to kiss me?"

Garion's heart started to pound.

Then Durnik's voice called to them from not far away, and for one flaming instant Garion hated his old friend.

CHAPTER TWENTY

"Mistress Pol says that it's time for you to come back to the tents," Durnik told them when he reached the glade. There was a faint hint of amusement on his plain, dependable face, and he looked knowingly at the two of them.

Garion blushed and then grew angry with himself for blushing. Ce'Nedra, however, showed no concern at all.

"Have the Dryads come yet?" she asked, getting to her feet and brushing the grass from the back of her tunic.

"Not yet," Durnik answered. "Wolf says that they should find us soon. There seems to be some kind of storm building up to the south, and Mistress Pol thought the two of you ought to come back."

Garion glanced at the sky and saw a layer of inky clouds moving up from the south, staining the bright blue sky as they rolled ponderously northward. He frowned. "I've never seen clouds like that, have you, Durnik?"

Durnik looked up. "Strange," he agreed.

Garion rolled up the two wet towels, and they started back down the stream. The clouds blotted out the sun, and the woods became suddenly very dark. The sense of watchfulness was still there, that wary awareness they had all felt since they had entered the Wood, but now there was something else as well. The great trees stirred uneasily, and a million tiny messages seemed to pass among the rustling leaves.

"They're afraid," Ce'Nedra whispered. "Something's frightening them."

"What?" Durnik asked.

"The trees—they're afraid of something. Can't you feel it?"

He stared at her in perplexity.

Far above them the birds suddenly fell silent, and a chill breeze began to blow, carrying with it a foul reek of stagnant water and rotting vegetation.

"What's that smell?" Garion asked, looking about nervously.

"Nyissa is south of here," Ce'Nedra said. "It's mostly swamps."

"Is it that close?" Garion asked.

"Not really," she said with a small frown. "It must be sixty leagues or more."

"Would a smell carry that far?"

"It's not likely," Durnik said. "At least it wouldn't be in Sendaria."

"How far is it to the tents?" Ce'Nedra asked.

"About a half-mile," Durnik answered.

"Maybe we should run," she suggested.

Durnik shook his head. "The ground's uneven," he said, "and running in bad light's dangerous. We can walk a bit faster, though."

They hurried on through the gathering gloom. The wind began to blow harder, and the trees trembled and bent with its force. The strange fear that seemed to permeate the Wood grew stronger.

"There's something moving over there," Garion whispered urgently and pointed at the dark trees on the other side of the stream.

"I don't see anything," Ce'Nedra said.

"There, just beyond the tree with the large white limb. Is it a Dryad?"

A vague shape slid from one tree to another in the half-light. There was something chillingly wrong with the figure. Ce'Nedra stared at it with revulsion. "It's not a Dryad," she said. "It's something alien."

Durnik picked up a fallen limb and gripped it like a cudgel with both hands. Garion looked quickly around and saw another limb. He too armed himself.

Another figure shambled between two trees, a bit closer this time.

"We'll have to chance it," Durnik said grimly. "Be careful, but run. Get the others. Now go!"

Garion took Ce'Nedra's hand, and they started to run along the streambank, stumbling often. Durnik lagged farther and farther behind, his two-handed club swinging warningly about him.

The figures were now all around them, and Garion felt the first surges of panic.

Then Ce'Nedra screamed. One of the figures had risen from behind a low bush directly in front of them. It was large and ill-shaped, and there was no face on the front of its head. Two eye-holes stared vacantly as it shambled forward with its half-formed hands reaching out for them. The entire figure was a dark gray mud color, and it was covered with rotting, stinking moss that adhered to its oozing body.

Without thinking, Garion thrust Ce'Nedra behind him and leaped to the attack. The first blow of his club struck the creature solidly in the side, and the club merely sank into the body with no visible effect. One of the outstretched hands touched his face, and he recoiled from that slimy touch with revulsion. Desperately he swung again and struck the thing solidly on the forearm. With horror he saw the arm break off at the elbow. The creature paused to pick up the still-moving arm.

Ce'Nedra screamed again, and Garion spun about. Another of the mudmen had come up behind her and had grasped her about the waist with both arms. It was starting to turn, lifting the struggling princess from the ground when Garion swung his club with all his might. The blow was not aimed at head or back, but rather at the ankles.

The mud-man toppled backward with both of its feet broken off. Its grip about Ce'Nedra's waist, however, did not loosen as it fell.

Garion jumped forward, discarding his club and drawing his dagger. The substance of the thing was surprisingly tough. Vines and dead twigs were encased in the clay which gave it its shape. Feverishly, Garion cut away one of the arms and then tried to pull the screaming princess free. The other arm still clung to her. Almost sobbing with the need to hurry, Garion started hacking at the remaining arm.

"Look out!" Ce'Nedra shrieked. "Behind you!"

Garion looked quickly over his shoulder. The first mud-man was reaching for him. He felt a cold grip about his ankle. The arm he had just severed had inched its way across the ground and grasped him.

"Garion!" Barak's voice roared from a short distance.

"Over here!" Garion shouted. "Hurry!"

There was a crashing in the bushes, and the great, red-bearded Cherek appeared, sword in hand, with Hettar and Mandorallen close behind. With a mighty swing, Barak cut off the head of the first mud-man. It sailed through the air and landed with a sickening thump several yards away. The headless creature turned and groped blindly, trying to put its hands on its attacker. Barak paled visibly and then chopped away both outstretched arms. Still the thing shambled forward.

"The legs," Garion said quickly. He bent and hacked at the clay hand about his ankle.

Barak lopped off the mud-man's legs, and the thing fell. The dismembered pieces crawled toward him.

Other mud-men had appeared, and Hettar and Mandorallen were laying about them with their swords, filling the air with chunks and pieces of living clay.

Barak bent and ripped away the remaining arm which held Ce'Nedra. Then he jerked the girl to her feet and thrust her at Garion. "Get her back to the tents!" he ordered. "Where's Durnik?"

"He stayed behind to hold them off," Garion said.

"We'll go help him," Barak said. "Run!"

Ce'Nedra was hysterical, and Garion had to drag her to the tents.

"What is it?" Aunt Pol demanded.

"Monsters out there in the woods," Garion said, pushing Ce'Nedra at her. "They're made out of mud, and you can't kill them. They've got Durnik." He dove into one of the tents and emerged a second later with his sword in his hand and fire in his brain.

"Garion!" Aunt Pol shouted, trying to disentangle herself from the sobbing princess. "What are you doing?"

"I've got to help Durnik," he said.

"You stay where you are."

"No!" he shouted. "Durnik's my friend." He dashed back toward the fight, brandishing his sword.

"Garion! Come back here!"

He ignored her and ran through the dark woods.

The fray was raging about a hundred yards from the tents. Barak, Hettar and Mandorallen were systematically chopping the slime-covered mud-men into chunks, and Silk darted in and out of the mêlée, his short sword leaving great gaping holes in the thick, moss-covered monsters. Garion plunged into the fight, his ears ringing and a kind of desperate exultation surging through him.

And then Mister Wolf and Aunt Pol were there with Ce'Nedra hovering ashen-faced and trembling behind them. Wolf's eyes blazed, and he seemed to tower over them all as he gathered his will. He thrust one hand forward, palm up. "Fire!" he commanded, and a sizzling bolt of lightning shot upward from his hand into the whirling clouds overhead. The earth trembled with the violence of the shattering thunderclap. Garion reeled at the force of the roaring in his mind.

Aunt Pol raised her hand. "Water!" she said in a powerful voice.

The clouds burst open, and rain fell so heavily that it seemed that the air itself had turned to water.

The mud-men, still mindlessly stumbling forward, began to ooze and dissolve in the thundering downpour. With a kind of sick fascination, Garion watched them disintegrate into sodden lumps of slime and rotten vegetation, surging and heaving as the pounding rain destroyed them.

Barak reached forward with his dripping sword and tentatively poked at the shapeless lump of clay that had been the head of one of their attackers. The lump broke apart, and a coiled snake unwound from its center. It raised itself as if to strike, and Barak chopped it in two.

Other snakes began to appear as the mud which had encased them dissolved in the roaring deluge. "That one," Aunt Pol said, pointing at a dull green reptile struggling to free itself from the clay. "Fetch it for me, Garion."

"Me?" Garion gasped, his flesh crawling.

"I'll do it," Silk said. He picked up a forked stick and pinned the snake's head down with it. Then he carefully took hold of the wet skin at the back of the serpent's neck and lifted the twisting reptile.

"Bring it here," Aunt Pol ordered, wiping the water from her face.

Silk carried the snake to her and held it out. The forked tongue flickered nervously, and the dead eyes fixed on her.

"What does this mean?" she demanded of the snake.

The serpent hissed at her. Then in a voice that was a sibilant whisper it replied, "That, Polgara, is the affair of my mistress."

Silk's face blanched as the dripping snake spoke, and he tightened his grip.

"I see," Aunt Pol said.

"Abandon this search," the snake hissed. "My mistress will allow you to go no further."

Aunt Pol laughed scornfully. "Allow?" she said. "Your mistress hasn't the power to allow me anything."

"My mistress is the queen of Nyissa," the snake said in its whispering hiss. "Her power there is absolute. The ways of the serpent are not the ways of men, and my mistress is queen of the serpents. You will enter Nyissa at your own peril. We are patient and not afraid. We will await you where you least expect us. Our sting is a small injury, scarce noted, but it is death."

"What's Salmissra's interest in this matter?" Aunt Pol asked.

The serpent's flickering tongue darted at her. "She has not chosen to reveal that to me, and it is not in my nature to be curious. I have delivered my message and already received my reward. Now do with me as you wish."

"Very well," Aunt Pol said. She looked coldly at the snake, her face streaming in the heavy rain.

"Shall I kill it?" Silk asked, his face set and his fingers white-knuckled from the strain of holding the thick-coiling reptile.

"No," she said quietly. "There's no point in destroying so excellent a messenger." She fixed the snake with a flinty look. "Return with these others to Salmissra," she said. "Tell her that if she interferes again, I'll come after her, and the deepest slime-pit in all Nyissa won't hide her from my fury."

"And my reward?" the snake asked.

"You have your life as a reward," she said.

"That's true," the serpent hissed. "I will deliver your message, Polgara."

"Put it down," Aunt Pol told Silk.

The small man bent and lowered his arm to the ground. The snake uncoiled from about his arm, and Silk released it and jumped back. The snake glanced once at him, then slithered away.

"I think that's enough rain, Pol," Wolf said, mopping at his face.

Aunt Pol waved her hand almost negligently, and the rain stopped as if a bucket had emptied itself.

"We have to find Durnik," Barak reminded them.

"He was behind us." Garion pointed back up the now-overflowing stream. His chest felt constricted with a cold fear at what they might find, but he steeled himself and led the way back into the trees.

"The smith is a good companion," Mandorallen said. "I should not care to lose him." There was a strange, subdued quality in the knight's voice, and his face seemed abnormally pale in the dim light. The hand holding his great broadsword, however, was rock-steady. Only his eyes betrayed a kind of doubt Garion had never seen there before.

Water dripped around them as they walked through the sodden woods. "It was about here," Garion said, looking around. "I don't see any sign of him."

"I'm up here." Durnik's voice came from above them. He was a goodly distance up a large oak tree and was peering down. "Are they gone?" He carefully began climbing down the slippery tree trunk. "The rain came just in time," he said, jumping down the last few feet. "I was starting to have a little trouble keeping them out of the tree."

Quickly, without a word, Aunt Pol embraced the good man, and then, as if embarrassed by that sudden gesture, she began to scold him.

Durnik endured her words patiently, and there was a strange expression on his face.

CHAPTER TWENTY-ONE

Garion's sleep that night was troubled. He awoke frequently, shuddering at the remembered touch of the mud-men. But in time the night, as all nights must, came to an end, and the morning dawned clear and bright. He drowsed for a while, rolled in his blankets, until Ce'Nedra came to get him up.

"Garion," she said softly, touching his shoulder, "are you awake?"

He opened his eyes and looked up at her. "Good morning."

"Lady Polgara says that you're supposed to get up," she told him.

Garion yawned, stretched and sat up. He glanced out the tent flap and saw that the sun was shining.

"She's teaching me how to cook," Ce'Nedra said rather proudly.

"That's nice," Garion told her, pushing his hair out of his eyes.

She looked at him for a long moment, her small face serious and her green eyes intent. "Garion."

"Yes?"

"You were very brave yesterday."

He shrugged slightly. "I'll probably get a scolding for it today."

"What for?"

"Aunt Pol and my grandfather don't like it when I try to be brave," he explained. "They think I'm still a child, and they don't want me to get hurt."

"Garion!" Aunt Pol called from the small fire where she was cooking. "I need more firewood."

Garion sighed and rolled out of his blankets. He pulled on his half-boots, belted on his sword and went off into the woods.

It was still damp under the huge oaks from the downpour Aunt Pol had called down the day before, and dry wood was hard to find. He wandered about, pulling limbs out from under fallen trees and from beneath overhanging rocks. The silent trees watched him, but they seemed somehow less unfriendly this morning.

"What are you doing?" a light voice came from above him.

He looked up quickly, his hand going to his sword.

A girl was standing on a broad limb just over his head. She wore a belted tunic and sandals. Her hair was a tawny color, her gray eyes were curious, and her pale skin had that faint greenish hue to it that identified her as a Dryad. In her left hand she held a bow, and her right held an arrow against the taut string. The arrow was pointed directly at Garion.

He carefully took his hand away from his sword. "I'm gathering wood," he said.

"What for?"

"My aunt needs it for the fire," he explained.

"*Fire?*" The girl's face hardened, and she half-drew her bow.

"A small one," he said quickly, "for cooking."

"Fire isn't permitted here," the girl said sternly.

"You'll have to explain that to Aunt Pol," Garion told her. "I just do what I'm told."

The girl whistled, and another girl came from behind a nearby tree. She also carried a bow. Her hair was almost as red as Ce'Nedra's, and her skin was also touched with the color of leaves.

"It says it's gathering wood," the first girl reported, "for a fire. Do you think I should kill it?"

"Xantha says we're supposed to find out who they are," the red-haired one said thoughtfully. "If it turns out that they don't have any business here, then you can kill it."

"Oh, very well," the tawny-haired girl agreed, with obvious disappointment. "But don't forget that I found this one. When the time comes, I get to kill it."

Garion felt the hair beginning to rise on the back of his neck.

The red-haired one whistled, and a half-dozen other armed Dryads drifted out of the trees. They were all quite small, and their hair was various shades of reds and golds, not unlike the color of autumn leaves. They gathered about Garion, giggling and chattering as they examined him.

"That one is mine," the tawny-haired Dryad said, climbing down from the tree. "I found it, and Xera says that I get to kill it."

"It looks healthy," one of the others observed, "and quite tame. Maybe we should keep it. Is it a male?"

Another one giggled. "Let's check and find out."

"I'm a male," Garion said quickly, blushing in spite of himself.

"It seems a shame to waste it," one remarked. "Maybe we could keep it for a while and then kill it."

"It's mine," the tawny-haired Dryad stated stubbornly, "and if I want to kill it, I will." She took hold of Garion's arm possessively.

"Let's go look at the others," the one called Xera suggested. "They're building fires, and we'll want to stop that."

"*Fires?*" several of the others gasped, and they all glared at Garion accusingly.

"Only a small one," Garion said quickly.

"Bring it along," Xera ordered and started off through the Wood toward the tents. Far overhead the trees murmured to each other.

Aunt Pol was waiting calmly when they reached the clearing where the tents were. She looked at the Dryads clustered around Garion without changing expression. "Welcome, ladies," she said.

The Dryads began whispering to each other.

"Ce'Nedra!" the one called Xera exclaimed.

"Cousin Xera," Ce'Nedra replied, and the two ran to embrace each other. The other Dryads came out a little farther into the clearing, looking nervously at the fire.

Ce'Nedra spoke quickly with Xera, explaining to her cousin who they were, and Xera motioned for the others to come closer. "It seems that these are friends," she said. "We'll take them to my mother, Queen Xantha."

"Does that mean that I won't get to kill this one?" The tawny-haired Dryad demanded petulantly, pointing a small finger at Garion.

"I'm afraid not," Xera answered.

The tawny one stamped away, pouting.

Garion breathed a sigh of relief.

Then Mister Wolf came out of one of the tents and looked at the cluster of Dryads with a broad smile.

"It's Belgarath!" one of the Dryads squealed and ran to him happily. She threw her arms around his neck, pulled his head down and kissed him soundly. "Did you bring us any sweets?" she demanded.

The old man put on a sober expression and began rummaging through his many pockets. Bits of sweetmeats began to appear, and just as quickly disappeared as the Dryads gathered about him, snatching them as fast as he took them from his pockets.

"Have you got any new stories for us?" one of the Dryads asked.

"Many stories," Wolf told her, touching one finger to the side of his nose slyly. "But we ought to wait so your sisters can hear them too, shouldn't we?"

"We want one just for ourselves," the Dryad said.

"And what would you give me for this special story?"

"Kisses," the Dryad offered promptly. "Five kisses from each of us."

"I've got a very good story," Wolf bargained. "It's worth more than five. Let's say ten."

"Eight," the little Dryad countered.

"All right," Wolf agreed. "Eight sounds about right."

"I see you've been here before, Old Wolf," Aunt Pol remarked dryly.

"I visit from time to time," he admitted with a bland expression.

"Those sweets aren't good for them, you know," she chided.

"A little bit won't hurt them, Pol," he said, "and they like them very much. A Dryad will do almost anything for sweets."

"You're disgusting," she told him.

The Dryads were all clustered around Mister Wolf, looking almost like a garden of spring flowers—all, that is, except for the tawny one who'd captured Garion. She stood a bit apart, sulking and fingering the point of her arrow. She finally came over to Garion. "You're not thinking about running away, are you?" she asked hopefully.

"No," Garion denied emphatically.

She sighed with disappointment. "I don't suppose you'd consider it, would you—as a special favor to me?"

"I'm sorry," he said.

She sighed again, bitterly this time. "I never get to have any fun," she complained and went to join the others.

Silk emerged from a tent, moving slowly and carefully; and after the Dryads had become accustomed to him, Durnik appeared.

"They're just children, aren't they?" Garion commented to Aunt Pol.

"They seem to be," she said, "but they're much older than they look. A Dryad lives as long as her tree does, and oak trees live for a long time."

"Where are the boy Dryads?" he asked. "All I see are girls."

"There aren't any boy Dryads, dear," she explained, returning to her cooking.

"Then how—? I mean—" He faltered and felt his ears growing hot.

"They catch human males for that," she said. "Travelers and the like."

"Oh." He delicately let the subject drop.

After they had eaten breakfast and carefully quenched their fire with water from the stream, they saddled their horses and started off through the Wood. Mister Wolf walked ahead with the tiny Dryads still gathered around him, laughing and chattering like happy children. The murmuring of the trees about them was no longer unfriendly, and they moved through a kind of welcoming rustle from a million leaves.

It was late afternoon by the time they reached a large clearing in the center of the Wood. Standing alone in the middle of the clearing was an oak so large that Garion could hardly accept the idea that anything so enormous could be alive. Here and there in its mossy trunk were openings almost like caverns, and its lower limbs were as broad as highways and they spread out to shade nearly the entire clearing. There was about the tree a sense of vast age and a patient wisdom. Tentatively Garion felt a faint touch on his mind, almost like the soft brush of a leaf against his face. The touch was unlike anything he had ever felt before, but it also seemed to welcome him.

The tree was literally alive with Dryads, clustering randomly on the limbs like blossoms. Their laughter and girlish chatter filled the air like birdsongs.

"I'll tell my mother you've arrived," the one called Xera said and went toward the tree.

Garion and the others dismounted and stood uncertainly near their horses. From overhead Dryads peered curiously down at them, whispering among themselves and giggling often.

For some reason the frank, mirthful stares of the Dryads made Garion feel very self-conscious. He moved closer to Aunt Pol and noticed that the others were also clustering around her as if unconsciously seeking her protection.

"Where's the princess?" she asked.

"She's just over there, Mistress Pol," Durnik answered, "visiting with that group of Dryads."

"Keep your eye on her," Aunt Pol said. "And where's my vagrant father?"

"Near the tree," Garion replied. "The Dryads seem very fond of him."

"The old fool," Aunt Pol said darkly.

Then, from a hollow in the tree some distance above the first broad limbs, another Dryad appeared. Instead of the short tunic the others wore, this one was garbed in a flowing green gown, and her golden hair was caught in with a circlet of what appeared to be mistletoe. Gracefully she descended to the ground.

Aunt Pol went forward to meet her, and the others trailed behind at a respectful distance.

"Dear Polgara," the Dryad said warmly, "it's been so long."

"We all have our duties, Xantha," Aunt Pol explained.

The two embraced fondly.

"Have you brought us these as gifts?" Queen Xantha asked, looking admiringly at the men standing behind Aunt Pol.

Aunt Pol laughed. "I'm afraid not, Xantha. I'd be happy to give them to you, but I think I may need them later."

"Ah well," the queen said with a mock sigh. "Welcome all," she greeted them. "You'll sup with us, of course."

"We'd be delighted," Aunt Pol said. Then she took the queen's arm. "Can we talk for a moment first, Xantha?" The two moved apart from the others and spoke quietly together as the Dryads carried bundles and sacks down from the hollows in the tree and began to lay a feast on the grass beneath the broad limbs.

The meal which was spread out looked peculiar. The common food of the Dryads seemed to consist entirely of fruits, nuts, and mushrooms, all prepared without any cooking. Barak sat down and looked sourly at what was offered. "No meat," he grumbled.

"It heats up your blood anyway," Silk told him.

Barak sipped suspiciously at his cup. "Water," he said with distaste.

"You might find it a novelty to go to bed sober for a change," Aunt Pol observed as she rejoined them.

"I'm sure it's unhealthy," Barak said.

Ce'Nedra seated herself near Queen Xantha. She obviously wanted to talk to her, but since there was no opportunity for privacy, she finally spoke out in front of them all. "I have a favor to ask, your Majesty."

"You may ask, child," the queen said, smiling.

"It's only a small thing," Ce'Nedra explained. "I'll need sanctuary for a few years. My father's growing unreasonable in his old age. I'll have to stay away from him until he comes to his senses."

"In what way is Ran Borune growing unreasonable?" Xantha asked.

"He won't let me go out of the palace, and he insists that I go to Riva on my sixteenth birthday," Ce'Nedra said in an outraged tone. "Have you ever heard of such a thing?"

"And why does he want you to go to Riva?"

"Some foolish treaty. No one even remembers the reason for it."

"If it's a treaty, it must be honored, dear," the queen said gently.

"I won't go to Riva," Ce'Nedra announced. "I'll stay here until after my sixteenth birthday's passed, and that'll be the end of it."

"No, dear," the queen said firmly, "you won't."

"*What?*" Ce'Nedra was stunned.

"We have a treaty too," Xantha explained. "Our agreement with the House of Borune is most explicit. Our Wood remains inviolate only for so long as the female descendants of the Princess Xoria stay with the Borunes. It's your duty to remain with your father and to obey him."

"But I'm a Dryad," Ce'Nedra wailed. "I belong here."

"You're also human," the queen said, "and you belong with your father."

"I don't want to go to Riva," Ce'Nedra protested. "It's degrading."

Xantha looked at her sternly. "Don't be a foolish child," she said. "Your duties are clear. You have a duty as a Dryad, as a Borune, and as an Imperial Princess. Your silly little whims are quite beside the point. If you have an obligation to go to Riva, then you must go."

Ce'Nedra appeared shaken by the finality of the queen's tone, and she sulked in silence after that.

Then the queen turned to Mister Wolf. "There are many rumors abroad," she said, "and some of them have even reached us here. I think something momentous is happening out there in the world of the humans, and it may even touch our lives in this Wood. I think I should know what this thing is."

Wolf nodded gravely. "I expect you should," he agreed. "The Orb of Aldur has been stolen from the throne in the Hall of the Rivan King by Zedar the Apostate."

Xantha caught her breath. "How?" she demanded.

Wolf spread his hands. "We don't know. Zedar's trying to reach the kingdoms of the Angaraks with the Orb. Once he's there, he'll try to use its powers to awaken Torak."

"That must never happen," the queen said. "What's being done?"

"The Alorns and the Sendars are getting ready for war," Wolf replied. "The Arends have promised aid, and Ran Borune has been advised, though he didn't make any promises. The Borunes can be difficult at times." He glanced at the pouting Ce'Nedra.

"Then it means war?" the queen asked sadly.

"I'm afraid so, Xantha," he said. "I'm pursuing Zedar with these others, and I hope we can catch him and get the Orb back before he can reach Torak with it. If we're successful, I think the Angaraks will attack the West anyway out of desperation. Certain ancient prophecies are getting close to their fulfillment. There are signs everywhere, and even the twisted perceptions of the Grolims can read them."

The queen sighed. "I've seen some of the signs myself, Belgarath," she said. "I'd hoped I was wrong. What does this Zedar look like?"

"A great deal like me," Wolf told her. "We served the same Master for a very long time, and that puts a certain mark on people."

"Someone like that passed through the upper reaches of our Wood last week and crossed over into Nyissa," Xantha said. "If I'd known, we might have been able to detain him."

"We're closer than I thought, then. Was he alone?"

"No," Xantha reported. "He had two of the servants of Torak with him and a small boy."

Wolf looked startled. "A boy?"

"Yes—about six years old or so."

The old man frowned, and then his eyes opened very wide. "So *that's* how he did it," he exclaimed. "I never thought of that."

"We can show you where he crossed the river into Nyissa," the queen offered. "I should warn you though that it's going to be dangerous for so large a party to go there. Salmissra has eyes everywhere in those swamps."

"I've already made plans for that," Mister Wolf assured her. He turned to Barak. "Are you sure that ship's going to be waiting at the mouth of the River of the Woods?" he asked.

"She'll be there," Barak rumbled. "Her captain's a dependable man."

"Good," Wolf said. "Silk and I'll pick up Zedar's trail then, and the rest of you can follow the river to the sea. Take the ship down the coast and then up the River of the Serpent to Sthiss Tor. We'll meet you there."

"Dost thou think it wise to separate our party in so perilous a place as Nyissa?" Mandorallen asked.

"It's necessary," Wolf said. "The snake people are at home in their jungles, and they don't like outsiders. Silk and I can move swiftly and with greater stealth if we're alone."

"Where do you want us to meet you?" Barak asked.

"There's a Drasnian trade enclave near the wharves in Sthiss Tor," Silk said. "Several of the merchants there are my friends. Just ask for Radek of Boktor. If we can't meet you there, we'll leave word of our whereabouts with the merchants."

"What about me?" Ce'Nedra asked.

"I think you'll have to stay with us," Aunt Pol answered.

"There's no reason for me to go to Nyissa," Ce'Nedra said.

"You'll go because I tell you to go," Aunt Pol told the tiny girl. "I'm not your father, Ce'Nedra. Your pouting doesn't wring my heart, and your fluttering eyelashes don't really impress me."

"I'll run away," Ce'Nedra threatened.

"That would be very foolish," Aunt Pol said coldly. "I'd just have to bring you back again, and you'd find that unpleasant. Affairs in the world just now are much too serious to allow the whims of one spoiled little girl to have very much importance. You'll stay with me, and you *will* stand in the Hall of the Rivan King on your sixteenth birthday—even if I have to take you there in chains. We're all much too busy to pamper you any further."

Ce'Nedra stared at her, and then she suddenly burst into tears.

CHAPTER TWENTY-TWO

The next morning before the sun rose and while filmy mist still hovered beneath the limbs of the great oaks, Silk and Mister Wolf made preparations to leave for Nyissa. Garion sat on a log, somberly watching the old man bundle up some food.

"Why so glum?" Wolf asked him.

"I wish we didn't have to separate this way," Garion said.

"It's only for a couple of weeks."

"I know, but I still wish—" Garion shrugged.

"Keep an eye on your aunt for me while I'm gone," Wolf said, tying up his bundle.

"All right."

"And keep your amulet on. Nyissa's a dangerous place."

"I'll remember," Garion promised. "You'll be careful, won't you, grandfather?"

The old man looked at him gravely, his white beard glistening in the misty light. "I'm always careful, Garion," he said.

"It's getting late, Belgarath," Silk called, leading two horses up to where the two of them were talking.

Wolf nodded. "We'll see you in two weeks in Sthiss Tor," he said to Garion.

Garion embraced the old man quickly and then turned away so that he wouldn't have to watch the two of them leave. He crossed the clearing to where Mandorallen stood pensively looking out into the mist.

"Parting is a melancholy business," the knight said moodily. He sighed.

"It's more than that though, isn't it, Mandorallen?" Garion asked.

"Thou art a perceptive lad."

"What's been troubling you? You've been acting strangely for the last two days."

"I have discovered a strange feeling within myself, Garion, and I like it not."

"Oh? What is it?"

"Fear," Mandorallen said shortly.

"Fear? Of what?"

"The clay men. I know not why, but their very existence struck a chill into my soul."

"They frightened us all, Mandorallen," Garion told him.

"I have never been afraid before," Mandorallen said quietly.

"Never?"

"Not even as a child. The clay men made my very flesh creep, and I wanted most desperately to run away."

"But you didn't," Garion pointed out. "You stayed and fought."

"That time yes," Mandorallen admitted. "But what of next time? Now that fear has found its way into my spirit, who can say when it might return? In some desperate hour when the outcome of our quest hangs in the balance, might not vile fear lay its cold hand upon my heart and unman me? It is that possibility which doth gnaw upon my soul. I am sorely ashamed of my weakness and my fault."

"Ashamed? For being human? You're too hard on yourself, Mandorallen."

"Thou art kind thus to excuse me, lad, but my failing is too grievous for such simple forgiveness. I have striven for perfection and struck, I think, not too far off the mark; but now that perfection, which was the marvel of the world, is flawed. It is a bitter thing to accept." He turned, and Garion was startled to see tears standing in his eyes. "Wilt thou assist me into mine armor?" he asked.

"Of course."

"I feel profoundly the need to be encased in steel. 'Twill perchance strengthen my cowardly heart."

"You're not a coward," Garion insisted.

Mandorallen sighed sadly. "Only time can reveal that."

When it was time to leave, Queen Xantha spoke briefly to them. "I wish you all well," she said. "I'd help you in your search if possible, but a Dryad's bound to her tree by ties which can't be broken. My tree here is very old, and I must care for him." She looked fondly up at the vast oak rising into the morning mist. "We're in bondage to each other, but it's a bondage of love."

Once again Garion felt that same faint touch on his mind that he had experienced the day before when he had first seen the huge tree. There was a sense of farewell in that touch, and what seemed to be a warning.

Queen Xantha exchanged a startled glance with Aunt Pol and then looked at Garion rather closely. "Some of my younger daughters will guide you to the river that marks the southern border of our Wood," she continued. "From there your way to the sea is clear." Her voice showed no sign of any change, but her eyes seemed thoughtful.

"Thank you, Xantha," Aunt Pol said warmly, embracing the Dryad queen. "If you can send word to the Borunes that Ce'Nedra's safe and with me, it might relieve the Emperor's mind somewhat."

"I will, Polgara," Xantha promised.

They mounted then and followed the half-dozen or so Dryads who flitted ahead of them like butterflies, guiding them southward into the forest. For some reason Garion felt profoundly depressed, and he paid little attention to his surroundings as he rode beside Durnik along the winding forest trail.

About midmorning it began to grow darker under the trees, and they rode in silence through the now-somber Wood. The warning Garion had seemed to hear in Queen Xantha's clearing echoed somehow in the creak of limbs and the rustling of leaves.

"The weather must be changing," Durnik said, looking up. "I wish I could see the sky."

Garion nodded and tried to shake off the sense of impending danger.

Mandorallen in his armor and Barak in his mail shirt rode at the head of the party, and Hettar in his horsehide jacket with steel plates riveted to it rode at the rear. The ominous sense of foreboding seemed to have reached them all, and they rode warily with their hands near their weapons and their eyes searching for trouble.

Then quite suddenly Tolnedran legionnaires were all around them, rising from the bushes or stepping out from behind trees. They made no attempt to attack, but stood in their brightly polished breastplates with their short spears at the ready.

Barak swore, and Mandorallen reined in his charger sharply. "Stand aside!" he ordered the soldiers, lowering his lance.

"Easy," Barak cautioned.

The Dryads, after one startled look at the soldiers, melted into the gloomy woods.

"What thinkest thou, Lord Barak?" Mandorallen asked blithely. "They cannot be over an hundred. Shall we attack them?"

"One of these days you and I are going to have to have a long talk about a few things," Barak said. He glanced back over his shoulder and saw that Hettar was edging closer, then he sighed. "Well, I suppose we might as well get on with it." He tightened the straps on his shield and loosened his sword in his sheath. "What do you think Mandorallen? Should we give them a chance to run away?"

"A charitable suggestion, Lord Barak," Mandorallen agreed.

Then, some distance up the trail, a body of horsemen rode out from under the shadowy trees. Their leader was a large man wearing a blue cloak trimmed with silver. His breastplate and helmet were inlaid with gold, and he rode a prancing chestnut stallion whose hooves churned the damp leaves lying on the ground. "Splendid," he said as he rode up. "Absolutely splendid."

Aunt Pol fixed the newcomer with a cold eye. "Don't the legions have anything better to do than to waylay travelers?" she demanded.

"This is my legion, Madam," the man in the blue cloak said arrogantly, "and it does what I tell it to. I see that you have the Princess Ce'Nedra with you."

"Where I go and with whom is my concern, your Grace," Ce'Nedra said loftily. "It's of no concern to the Grand Duke Kador of the House of Vordue."

"Your father is most concerned, Princess," Kador said. "All Tolnedra's searching for you. Who are these people?"

Garion tried with a dark scowl and a shake of his head to warn her, but it was too late.

"The two knights who lead our party are Sir Mandorallen, Baron of Vo Mandor, and Lord Barak, Earl of Trellheim," she announced. "The Algar warrior who guards our rear is Hettar, son of Cho-Hag, Chief of the Clan-Chiefs of Algaria. The lady—"

"I can speak for myself, dear," Aunt Pol said smoothly. "I'm curious to know what brings the Grand Duke of Vordue so far into southern Tolnedra."

"I have interests here, Madam," Kador said.

"Evidently," Aunt Pol replied.

"All the legions of the Empire are searching for the princess, but it's I who have found her."

"I'm amazed to find a Vorduvian so willing to aid in the search for a Borune princess," Aunt Pol observed. "Especially considering the centuries of enmity between your two houses."

"Shall we cease this idle banter?" Kador suggested icily. "My motives are my own affair."

"And unsavory, no doubt," she added.

"I think you forget yourself, Madam," Kador said. "I am, after all, who I am—and more to the point, who I will become."

"And who will you become, your Grace?" she inquired.

"I will be Ran Vordue, Emperor of Tolnedra," Kador announced.

"Oh? And just what's the future Emperor of Tolnedra doing in the Wood of the Dryads?"

"I'm doing what's necessary to protect my interests," Kador said stiffly. "For the moment, it's essential that the Princess Ce'Nedra be in my custody."

"My father may have something to say about that, Duke Kador," Ce'Nedra said, "and about this ambition of yours."

"What Ran Borune says is of no concern to me, your Highness," Kador told her. "Tolnedra needs me, and no Borune trick is going to deny me the Imperial Crown. It's obvious that the old man plans to marry you to a Honeth or a Horbite to raise some spurious claim to the throne. That could complicate matters, but I intend to keep things simple."

"By marrying me yourself?" Ce'Nedra asked scornfully. "You'll never live that long."

"No," Kador said. "I wouldn't be interested in a Dryad wife. Unlike the

Borunes, the House of Vordue believes in keeping its line pure and uncontaminated."

"So you're going to hold me prisoner?" Ce'Nedra asked.

"That'd be impossible, I'm afraid," Duke Kador told her. "The Emperor has ears everywhere. It's really a shame you ran away just when you did, your Highness. I'd gone to a great expense to get one of my agents into the Imperial kitchen and to obtain a quantity of a rare Nyissan poison. I'd even taken the trouble to compose a letter of sympathy to your father."

"How considerate of you," Ce'Nedra said, her face turning pale.

"Unfortunately, I'll have to be more direct now," Kador went on. "A sharp knife and a few feet of dirt should end your unfortunate involvement in Tolnedran politics. I'm very sorry, Princess. There's nothing personal in it, you understand, but I have to protect my interests."

"Thy plan, Duke Kador, hath one small flaw," Mandorallen said, carefully leaning his lance against a tree.

"I fail to see it, Baron," Kador said smugly.

"Thine error lay in rashly coming within reach of my sword," Mandorallen told him. "Thy head is forfeit now, and a man with no head has little need of a crown."

Garion knew that a part of Mandorallen's brashness arose from his desperate need to prove to himself that he was no longer afraid.

Kador looked at the knight apprehensively. "You wouldn't do that," he said without much certainty. "You're too badly outnumbered."

"Thou art imprudent to think so," Mandorallen said. "I am the hardiest knight on life and fully armed. Thy soldiers will be as blades of grass before me. Thou art doomed, Kador." And with that he drew his great sword.

"It was bound to happen," Barak said wryly to Hettar and drew his own sword.

"I don't think we'll do that," a new voice announced harshly. A familiar black-robed man rode out from behind a nearby tree on a sable-colored horse. He muttered a few quick words and gestured sharply with his right hand. Garion felt a dark rush and a strange roaring in his mind. Mandorallen's sword spun from his grip.

"My thanks, Asharak," Kador said in a relieved tone. "I hadn't anticipated that."

Mandorallen pulled off his mailed gauntlet and nursed his hand as if he had been struck a heavy blow. Hettar's eyes narrowed, and then went strangely blank. The Murgo's black mount glanced curiously at him once and then looked away almost contemptuously.

"Well, Sha-dar," Asharak gloated with an ugly smirk on his scarred face, "would you like to try that again?"

Hettar's face had a sick look of revulsion on it. "It's not a horse," he said. "It looks like a horse, but it's something else."

"Yes," Asharak agreed. "Quite different, really. You can sink yourself into its mind if you want, but I don't think you'll like what you find there." He swung down from his saddle and walked toward them, his eyes burning. He stopped in front of Aunt Pol and made an ironic bow. "And so we meet again, Polgara."

"You've been busy, Chamdar," she replied.

Kador, in the act of dismounting, seemed startled. "You know this woman, Asharak?"

"His name is Chamdar, Duke Kador," Aunt Pol said, "and he's a Grolim priest. You thought he was only buying your honor, but you'll soon find that he's bought much more than that." She straightened in her saddle, the white lock at her brow suddenly incandescently bright. "You've been an interesting opponent, Chamdar. I'll almost miss you."

"Don't do it, Polgara," the Grolim said quickly. "I've got my hand around the boy's heart. The instant you start to gather your Will, he'll die. I know who he is and how much you value him."

Her eyes narrowed. "An easy thing to say, Chamdar."

"Would you like to test it?" he mocked.

"Get down off your horses," Kador ordered sharply, and the legionnaires all took a threatening step forward.

"Do as he says," Aunt Pol ordered quietly.

"It's been a long chase, Polgara," Chamdar said. "Where's Belgarath?"

"Not far," she told him. "Perhaps if you start running now, you can get away before he comes back."

"No, Polgara." He laughed. "I'd know if he were that close." He turned and looked intently at Garion. "You've grown, boy. We haven't had a chance to talk for quite some time, have we?"

Garion stared back at the scarred face of his enemy, alert, but strangely not afraid. The contest between them for which he had been waiting all his life was about to begin, and something deep within his mind told him that he was ready.

Chamdar looked into his eyes, probing. "He doesn't know, does he?" he asked Aunt Pol. And then he laughed. "How like a woman you are, Polgara. You've kept the secret from him simply for the sake of the secret itself. I should have taken him away from you years ago."

"Leave him alone, Chamdar," she ordered.

He ignored that. "What's his real name, Polgara? Have you told him yet?"

"That doesn't concern you," she said flatly.

"But it does, Polgara. I've watched over him almost as carefully as you have." He laughed again. "You've been his mother, but I've been his father. Between us we've raised a fine son—but I still want to know his real name."

She straightened. "I think this has gone far enough, Chamdar," she said coldly. "What are your terms?"

"No terms, Polgara," the Grolim answered. "You and the boy and I are going to the place where Lord Torak awaits the moment of his awakening. My hand will be about the boy's heart the entire time, so you'll be suitably docile. Zedar and Ctuchik are going to destroy each other fighting over the Orb—unless Belgarath finds them first and destroys them himself—but the

Orb doesn't really interest me. It's been you and the boy I've been after from the very beginning."

"You weren't really trying to stop us, then?" she asked.

Chamdar laughed. "Stop you? I've been trying to help you. Ctuchik and Zedar both have underlings here in the West. I've delayed and deceived them at every turn just so you could get through. I knew that sooner or later Belgarath would find it necessary to pursue the Orb alone, and when that happened, I could take you and the boy."

"For what purpose?"

"You still don't see?" he asked. "The first two things Lord Torak sees when he awakens will be his bride and his mortal enemy, kneeling in chains before him. I'll be exalted above all for so royal a gift."

"Let the others go, then," she said.

"The others don't concern me," Chamdar said. "I'll leave them with the noble Kador. I don't imagine he'll find it convenient to keep them alive, but that's up to him. I've got what I want."

"You swine!" Aunt Pol raged helplessly. "You filthy swine!"

With a bland smile Chamdar slapped her sharply across the face. "You really must learn to control your tongue, Polgara," he said.

Garion's brain seemed to explode. Dimly he saw Durnik and the others being restrained by the legionnaires, but no soldier seemed to consider him a danger. He started toward his enemy without thinking, reaching for his dagger.

"*Not that way!*" It was that dry voice in his mind that had always been there, but the voice was no longer passive, disinterested.

"*I'll kill him!*" Garion said silently in the vaults of his brain.

"*Not that way!*" the voice warned again. "*They won't let you—not with your knife.*"

"How, then?"

"*Remember what Belgarath said—the Will and the Word.*"

"*I don't know how. I can't do that.*"

"*You are who you are. I'll show you. Look!*" Unbidden and so clearly that it was almost as if he were watching it happen, the image of the God Torak writhing in the fire of Aldur's Orb rose before his eyes. He saw Torak's face melting and his fingers aflame. Then the face shifted and altered until it was the face of the dark watcher whose mind had been linked with his for as long as he could remember. He felt a terrible force building in him as the image of Chamdar wrapped in seething flame stood before him.

"*Now!*" the voice commanded him. "*Do it!*"

It required a blow. His rage would be satisfied with nothing less. He leaped at the smirking Grolim so quickly that none of the legionnaires could stop him. He swung his right arm, and at the instant his palm struck Chamdar's scarred left cheek, he felt all the force that had built in him surge out from the silvery mark on his palm. "Burn!" he commanded, willing it to happen.

Taken off guard, Chamdar jerked back. A momentary anger began to appear on his face, and then his eyes widened with an awful realization. For an instant he stared at Garion in absolute horror, and then his face contorted with agony. "No!" he cried out hoarsely, and then his cheek began to smoke and seethe where the mark on Garion's hand had touched it. Wisps of smoke drifted from his black robe as if it had suddenly been laid on a red-hot stove. Then he shrieked and clutched at his face. His fingers burst into flame. He shrieked again and fell writhing to the damp earth.

"*Stand still!*" It was Aunt Pol's voice this time, sounding sharply inside Garion's head.

Chamdar's entire face was engulfed in flames now, and his shrieks echoed in the dim wood. The legionnaires recoiled from the burning man, and Garion suddenly felt sick. He started to turn away.

"*Don't weaken!*" Aunt Pol's voice told him. "*Keep your Will on him!*"

Garion stood over the blazing Grolim. The wet leaves on the ground smoked and smoldered where Chamdar thrashed and struggled with the fire that was consuming him. Flames were spurting from his chest, and his shrieks grew weaker. With an enormous effort, he struggled to his feet and held out his flaming hands imploringly to Garion. His face was gone, and greasy black smoke rolled off his body, drifting low to the ground. "Master," he croaked, "have mercy!"

Garion's heart wrenched with pity. All the years of that secret closeness between them pulled at him.

"*No!*" Aunt Pol's stern voice commanded. "*He'll kill you if you release him!*"

"I can't do it," Garion said. "I'm going to stop it." As once before, he began to gather his Will, feeling it build in him like some vast tide of pity and compassion. He half-reached toward Chamdar, focusing his thought on healing.

"*Garion!*" Aunt Pol's voice rang. "*It was Chamdar who killed your parents!*"

The thought forming in his mind froze.

"*Chamdar killed Geran and Ildera. He burned them alive—just as he's burning now. Avenge them, Garion! Keep the fire on him!*"

All the rage and fury he had carried within him since Wolf had told him of the deaths of his parents flamed in his brain. The fire, which a moment before he had almost extinguished, was suddenly not enough. The hand he had begun to reach out in compassion stiffened. In terrible anger he raised it, palm out. A strange sensation tingled in that palm, and then his own hand burst into flames. There was no pain, not even a feeling of heat, as a bright blue fire burst from the mark on his hand and wreathed up through his fingers. The blue fire became brighter—so bright that he could not even look at it.

Even in the extremity of his mortal agony, Chamdar the Grolim recoiled from that blazing hand. With a hoarse, despairing cry he tried to cover his blackened face, staggered back a few steps, and then, like a burning house, he collapsed in upon himself and sank back to earth.

"*It is done!*" Aunt Pol's voice came again. "*They are avenged!*" And then her voice rang in the vaults of his mind with a soaring exultation. "*Belgarion!*" she sang. "*My Belgarion!*"

Ashen-faced Kador, trembling in every limb, backed in horror from the still-burning heap that had been Chamdar the Grolim. "Sorcery!" he gasped.

"Indeed," Aunt Pol said coolly. "I don't think you're ready for this kind of game yet, Kador."

The frightened legionnaires were also backing away, their eyes bulging at what they had just seen.

"I think the Emperor's going to take this whole affair rather seriously," Aunt Pol told them. "When he hears that you were going to kill his daughter, he'll probably take it personally."

"It wasn't us," one of the soldiers said quickly. "It was Kador. We were just following orders."

"He *might* accept that as an excuse," she said doubtfully. "If it were me, though, I'd take him some kind of gift to prove my loyalty—something appropriate to the circumstances." She looked significantly at Kador.

Several of the legionnaires took her meaning, drew their swords and moved into position around the Grand Duke.

"What are you doing?" Kador demanded of them.

"I think you've lost more than a throne today, Kador," Aunt Pol said.

"You can't do this," Kador told the legionnaires.

One of the soldiers put the point of his sword against the Grand Duke's throat. "We're loyal to the Emperor, my Lord," he said grimly. "We're placing you under arrest for high treason, and if you give us any trouble, we'll settle for just delivering your head to Tol Honeth—if you take my meaning."

One of the legion officers knelt respectfully before Ce'Nedra. "Your Imperial Highness," he said to her, "how may we serve you?"

The princess, still pale and trembling, drew herself up. "Deliver this traitor to my father," she said in a ringing voice, "and tell him what happened here. Inform him that you have arrested the Grand Duke Kador at my command."

"At once, your Highness," the officer said, springing to his feet. "Chain the prisoner!" he ordered sharply, then turned back to Ce'Nedra. "May we provide you an escort to your destination, your Highness?"

"That won't be necessary, Captain," she told him. "Just remove this traitor from my sight."

"As your Highness wishes," the captain said with a deep bow. He gestured sharply, and the soldiers led Kador away.

Garion was staring at the mark on his palm. There was no sign of the fire that had burned there.

Durnik, released now from the grip of the soldiers, looked at Garion, his eyes wide. "I thought I knew you," he whispered. "Who are you, Garion, and how did you do this?"

"Dear Durnik," Aunt Pol said fondly, touching his arm. "Still willing to believe only what you can see. Garion's the same boy he's always been."

"You mean it was you?" Durnik looked at Chamdar's body and pulled his eyes quickly away.

"Of course," she said. "You know Garion. He's the most ordinary boy in the world."

But Garion knew differently. The Will had been his, and the Word had come from him.

"*Keep still!*" her voice warned inside his head. "*No one must know.*"

"*Why did you call me Belgarion?*" he demanded silently.

"*Because it's your name,*" her voice replied. "*Now try to act natural and don't bother me with questions. We'll talk about it later.*" And then her voice was gone.

The others stood around awkwardly until the legionnaires left with Kador. Then, when the soldiers were out of sight and the need for imperial self-possession was gone, Ce'Nedra began to cry. Aunt Pol took the tiny girl in her arms and began to comfort her.

"I guess we'd better bury this," Barak said, nudging what was left of Chamdar with his foot. "The Dryads might be offended if we went off and left it still smoking."

"I'll fetch my spade," Durnik said.

Garion turned away and brushed past Mandorallen and Hettar. His hands were trembling violently, and he was so exhausted that his legs barely held him.

She had called him Belgarion, and the name had rung in his mind as if he had always known that it was his—as if for all his brief years he had been incomplete until in that instant the name itself had completed him. But Belgarion was a being who with Will and Word and the touch of his hand could turn flesh into living fire.

"*You did it!*" he accused the dry awareness in one corner of his mind.

"*No,*" the voice replied. "*I only showed you how. The Will and the Word and the touch were all yours.*"

Garion knew that it was true. With horror he remembered his enemy's final supplication and the flaming, incandescent hand with which he had spurned that agonized appeal for mercy. The revenge he had wanted so desperately for the past several months was dreadfully complete, but the taste of it was bitter, bitter.

Then his knees buckled, and he sank to the earth and wept like a broken-hearted child.

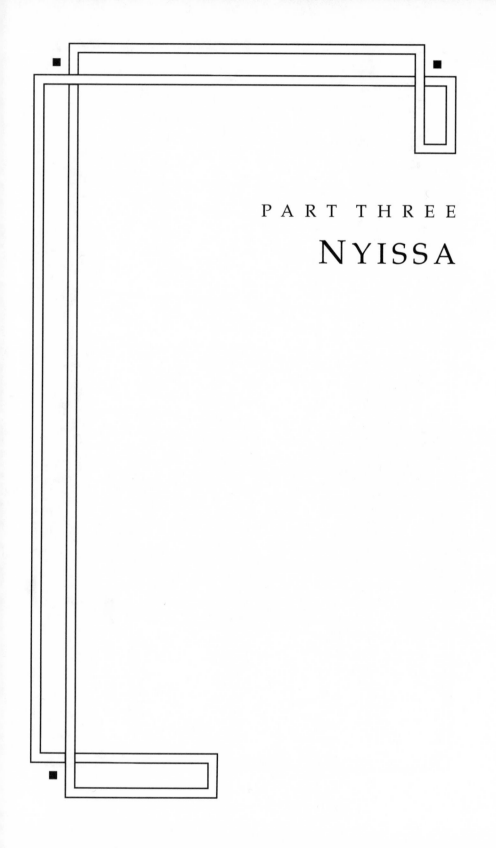

PART THREE

NYISSA

The earth was still the same. The trees had not changed, nor had the sky. It was still spring, for the seasons had not altered their stately march. But for Garion nothing would ever again be the way that it had been.

They rode down through the Wood of the Dryads to the banks of the River of the Woods which marked the southern boundary of Tolnedra, and from time to time as they rode he caught strange glances from his friends. The looks were speculative, thoughtful, and Durnik—good, solid Durnik—behaved as if he were almost afraid. Only Aunt Pol seemed unchanged, unconcerned. *"Don't worry about it, Belgarion,"* her voice murmured in his mind.

"Don't call me that," he replied with an irritated thought.

"It's your name," the silent voice said. *"You might as well get used to it."*

"Leave me alone."

And then the sense of her presence in his mind was gone.

It took them several days to reach the sea. The weather remained intermittently cloudy, though it did not rain. A stiff onshore breeze was blowing when they rode out onto the wide beach at the mouth of the river. The surf boomed against the sand, and whitecaps flecked the tops of the waves.

Out beyond the surf, a lean, black Cherek war-boat swung at anchor, the air above her alive with screeching gulls. Barak pulled his horse in and shaded his eyes. "She looks familiar," he rumbled, peering intently at the narrow ship.

Hettar shrugged. "They all look the same to me."

"There's all the difference in the world," Barak said, sounding a bit injured. "How would you feel if I said that all horses looked the same?"

"I'd think you were going blind."

Barak grinned at him. "It's exactly the same thing," he said.

"How do we let them know we're here?" Durnik asked.

"They know already," Barak said, "unless they're drunk. Sailors always watch an unfriendly shore very carefully."

"Unfriendly?" Durnik asked.

"Every shore is unfriendly when a Cherek war-boat comes in sight," Barak answered. "It's some kind of superstition, I think."

The ship came about and her anchor was raised. Her oars came out like long, spidery legs, and she seemed to walk through the froth-topped combers toward the mouth of the river. Barak led the way toward the riverbank, then rode along the broad flow until he found a spot deep enough so that the ship could be moored next to the shore.

The fur-clad sailors who threw Barak a mooring line looked familiar, and the first one who leaped across to the riverbank was Greldik, Barak's old friend.

"You're a long ways south," Barak said as if they had only just parted.

Greldik shrugged. "I heard you needed a ship. I wasn't doing anything, so I thought I'd come down and see what you were up to."

"Did you talk to my cousin?"

"Grinneg? No. We made a run down from Kotu to the harbor at Tol Horb for some Drasnian merchants. I ran into Elteg—you remember him—black beard, only one eye?"

Barak nodded.

"He told me that Grinneg was paying him to meet you here. I remembered that you and Elteg didn't get along very well, so I offered to come down instead."

"And he agreed?"

"No," Greldik replied, pulling at his beard. "As a matter of fact, he told me to mind my own business."

"I'm not surprised," Barak said. "Elteg always was greedy, and Grinneg probably offered him a lot of money."

"More than likely." Greldik grinned. "Elteg didn't say how much, though."

"How did you persuade him to change his mind?"

"He had some trouble with his ship," Greldik said with a straight face.

"What kind of trouble?"

"It seems that one night after he and his crew were all drunk, some scoundrel slipped aboard and chopped down his mast."

"What's the world coming to?" Barak asked, shaking his head.

"My thought exactly," Greldik agreed.

"How did he take it?"

"Not very well, I'm afraid," Greldik said sadly. "When we rowed out of the harbor, he sounded as if he was inventing profanities on the spot. You could hear him for quite some distance."

"He should learn to control his temper. That's the kind of behavior that gives Chereks a bad name in the ports of the world."

Greldik nodded soberly and turned to Aunt Pol. "My Lady," he said with a polite bow, "my ship is at your disposal."

"Captain," she asked, acknowledging his bow. "How long will it take you to get us to Sthiss Tor?"

"Depends on the weather," he answered, squinting at the sky. "Probably ten days at the most. We picked up fodder for your horses on the way here, but we'll have to stop for water from time to time."

"We'd better get started, then," she said.

It took a bit of persuading to get the horses aboard the ship, but Hettar managed it without too much difficulty. Then they pushed away from the bank, crossed the bar at the mouth of the river and reached the open sea. The crew raised the sails, and they quartered the wind down along the gray-green coastline of Nyissa.

Garion went forward to his customary place in the bow of the ship and sat there, staring bleakly out at the tossing sea. The image of the burning man back in the forest filled his mind.

There was a firm step behind him and a faint, familiar fragrance. "Do you want to talk about it?" Aunt Pol asked.

"What's there to talk about?"

"Many things," she told him.

"You knew I could do that kind of thing, didn't you?"

"I suspected it," she said, sitting down beside him. "There were several hints. One can never be sure, though, until it's used for the first time; I've known any number of people who had the capability and just never used it."

"I wish I never had," Garion said.

"I don't see that you really had much choice. Chamdar was your enemy."

"But did it have to be that way?" he demanded. "Did it have to be fire?"

"The choice was yours," she answered. "If fire bothers you so much, don't do it that way next time."

"There isn't going to be a next time," he stated flatly. "Not ever."

"Belgarion," her voice snapped within his mind, *"stop this foolishness at once. Stop feeling sorry for yourself."*

"Quit that," he said aloud. "Stay out of my mind—and don't call me Belgarion."

"You *are* Belgarion," she insisted. "Like it or not, you will use the power again. Once it's been released, you can never cage it up. You'll get angry or frightened or excited, and you'll use it without even thinking. You can no more choose not to use it than you can choose not to use one of your hands. The important thing now is to teach you how to control it. We can't have you blundering through the world uprooting trees and flattening hills with random thoughts. You must learn to control it and yourself. I didn't raise you to let you become a monster."

"It's too late," he said. "I'm already a monster. Didn't you see what I did back there?"

"All this self-pity is very tedious, Belgarion," her voice told him. *"I don't think we're getting anywhere."* She stood up. "Do try to grow up a little, dear," she said aloud. "It's very hard to instruct someone who's so self-absorbed that he won't listen."

"I'll never do it again," he told her defiantly.

"Oh, yes, you will, Belgarion. You'll learn and you'll practice and you'll develop the discipline this requires. If you don't want to do it willingly, then we'll have to do it the other way. Think about it, dear, and make up your mind—but don't take too long. It's too important to be put off." She reached out and gently touched his cheek; then she turned and walked away.

"She's right, you know," the voice in his mind told him.

"You stay out of this," Garion said.

In the days that followed, he avoided Aunt Pol as much as possible, but he could not avoid her eyes. Wherever he went on the narrow ship, he knew that she was watching him, her eyes calm, speculative.

Then, at breakfast on the third day out, she looked at his face rather closely as if noticing something for the first time. "Garion," she said, "you're starting to look shaggy. Why don't you shave?"

Garion blushed furiously and put his fingers to his chin. There were definitely whiskers there—downy, soft, more like fuzz than bristles, but whiskers all the same.

"Thou art truly approaching manhood, young Garion," Mandorallen assured him rather approvingly.

"The decision doesn't have to be made immediately, Polgara," Barak said, stroking his own luxuriant red beard. "Let the whiskers grow for a while. If they don't turn out well, he can always shave them off later."

"I think your neutrality in the matter is suspect, Barak," Hettar remarked. "Don't most Chereks wear beards?"

"No razor's ever touched my face," Barak admitted. "But I just don't think it's the sort of thing to rush into. It's very hard to stick whiskers back on if you decide later that you wanted to keep them after all."

"I think they're kind of funny," Ce'Nedra said. Before Garion could stop her, she reached out two tiny fingers and tugged the soft down on his chin. He winced and blushed again.

"They come off," Aunt Pol ordered firmly.

Wordlessly, Durnik went below decks. When he came back, he carried a basin, a chunk of brown-colored soap, a towel, and a fragment of mirror. "It isn't really hard, Garion," he said, putting the things on the table in front of the young man. Then he took a neatly folded razor out of a case at his belt. "You just have to be careful not to cut yourself, that's all. The whole secret is not to rush."

"Pay close attention when you're near your nose," Hettar advised. "A man looks very strange without a nose."

The shaving proceeded with a great deal of advice, and on the whole it did not turn out too badly. Most of the bleeding stopped after a few minutes, and, aside from the fact that his face felt as if it had been peeled, Garion was quite satisfied with the results.

"Much better," Aunt Pol said.

"He'll catch cold in his face now," Barak predicted.

"Will you stop that?" she told him.

The coast of Nyissa slid by on their left, a blank wall of tangled vegetation, festooned with creepers and long tatters of moss. Occasional eddies in the breeze brought the foul reek of the swamps out to the ship. Garion and Ce'Nedra stood together in the prow of the ship, looking toward the jungle.

"What are those?" Garion asked, pointing at some large things with legs slithering around on a mud bank along a stream that emptied into the sea.

"Crocodiles," Ce'Nedra answered.

"What's a crocodile?"

"A big lizard," she said.

"Are they dangerous?"

"Very dangerous. They eat people. Haven't you ever read about them?"

"I can't read," Garion admitted without thinking.

"What?"

"I can't read," Garion repeated. "Nobody ever taught me how."

"That's ridiculous!"

"It's not my fault," he said defensively.

She looked at him thoughtfully. She had seemed almost half-afraid of him since the meeting with Chamdar, and her insecurity had probably been increased by the fact that, on the whole, she had not treated him very well. Her first assumption that he was only a servant boy had gotten their whole relationship off on the wrong foot, but she was far too proud to admit that initial mistake. Garion could almost hear the little wheels clicking around in her head. "Would you like to have me teach you how?" she offered. It was probably the closest thing he'd ever get to an apology from her.

"Would it take very long?"

"That depends on how clever you are."

"When do you think we could start?"

She frowned. "I've got a couple of books, but we'll need something to write on."

"I don't know that I need to learn how to write," he said. "Reading ought to be enough for right now."

She laughed. "They're the same thing, you goose."

"I didn't know that," Garion said, flushing slightly. "I thought—" He floundered with the whole idea. "I guess I never really thought about it," he concluded lamely. "What sort of thing do we need to write on?"

"Parchment's the best," she said, "and a charcoal stick to write with—so we can rub it off and write on the parchment again."

"I'll go talk to Durnik," he decided. "He'll be able to think of something."

Durnik suggested sailcloth and a charred stick. Within an hour Garion and Ce'Nedra were sitting in a sheltered spot in the bow of the ship, their heads close together over a square of canvas nailed to a plank. Garion glanced up once and saw Aunt Pol not far away. She was watching the two of them with an indecipherable expression. Then he lowered his eyes again to the strangely compelling symbols on the canvas.

His instruction went on for the next several days. Since his fingers were naturally nimble, he quickly picked up the trick of forming the letters.

"No, no," Ce'Nedra said one afternoon, "you've spelled it wrong—used the wrong letters. Your name's Garion, not Belgarion."

He felt a sudden chill and looked down at the canvas square. The name was spelled out quite clearly—"Belgarion."

He looked up quickly. Aunt Pol was standing where she usually stood, her eyes on him as always.

"*Stay out of my mind!*" He snapped the thought at her.

"*Study hard, dear,*" her voice urged him silently. "*Learning of any kind is useful, and you have a great deal to learn. The sooner you get the habit, the better.*" Then she smiled, turned and walked away.

The next day, Greldik's ship reached the mouths of the River of the Serpent in central Nyissa, and his men struck the sail and set their oars into the locks along the sides of the ship in preparation for the long pull upriver to Sthiss Tor.

CHAPTER TWENTY-FOUR

There was no air. It seemed as if the world had suddenly been turned into a vast, reeking pool of stagnant water. The River of the Serpent had a hundred mouths, each creeping sluggishly through the jellied muck of the delta as if reluctant to join the boisterous waves of the sea. The reeds which grew in that vast swamp reached a height of twenty feet and were as thick as woven fabric. There was a tantalizing sound of a breeze brushing the tops of the reeds, but down among them, all thought or memory of breeze was lost. There was no air. The delta steamed and stank beneath a sun that did not burn so much as boil. Each breath seemed to be half water. Insects rose in clouds from the reeds and settled in mindless gluttony on every inch of exposed skin, biting, feeding on blood.

They were a day and a half among the reeds before they reached the first trees, low, scarcely more than bushes. The main river channel began to take shape as they moved slowly on into the Nyissan heartland. The sailors sweated and swore at their oars, and the ship moved slowly against the current, almost as if she struggled against a tide of thick oil that clung to her like some loathsome glue.

The trees grew taller, then immense. Great, gnarled roots twisted up out of the ooze along the banks like grotesquely misshapen legs, and trunks vast as castles reached up into the steaming sky. Ropey vines undulated down from the limbs overhead, moving, seeming to writhe with a kind of vegetable will of their own in the breathless air. Shaggy tatters of grayish moss descended in hundred-foot-long streamers from the trees, and the river wound spitefully in great coils that made their journey ten times as long as it needed to be.

"Unpleasant sort of place," Hettar grumbled, dispiritedly looking out over the bow at the weedy surface of the river ahead. He had removed his horsehide jacket and linen undertunic, and his lean torso gleamed with sweat. Like most of them, he was covered with the angry welts of insect bites.

"My very thought," Mandorallen agreed.

One of the sailors shouted and jumped up, kicking at his oar-handle.

Something long, slimy, and boneless had crawled unseen up his oar, seeking his flesh with an eyeless voracity.

"Leech," Durnik said with a shudder as the hideous thing dropped with a wet plop back into the stinking river. "I've never seen one so big. It must be a foot long or more."

"Probably not a good place for swimming," Hettar observed.

"I wasn't considering it," Durnik said.

"Good."

Aunt Pol, wearing a light linen dress, came out of the cabin beneath the high stern where Greldik and Barak were taking turns at the tiller. She had been caring for Ce'Nedra, who had drooped and wilted like a flower in the brutal climate of the river.

"Can't you do something?" Garion demanded of her silently.

"About what?"

"All of this." He looked around helplessly.

"What do you want me to do?"

"Drive off the bugs, if nothing else."

"Why don't you do it yourself, Belgarion?"

He set his jaw. *"No!"* It was almost a silent shout.

"It isn't really very hard."

"No!"

She shrugged and turned away, leaving him seething with frustration.

It took them three more days to reach Sthiss Tor. The city was embraced in a wide coil of the river and was built of black stone. The houses and buildings were low and for the most part were windowless. In the center of the city a vast pile of a building rose with strangely shaped spires and domes and terraces, oddly alien-looking. Wharves and jetties poked out into the turbid river, and Greldik guided his ship toward one which was much larger than the rest. "We have to stop at customs," he explained.

"Inevitably," Durnik said.

The exchange at customs was brief. Captain Greldik announced that he was delivering the goods of Radek of Boktor to the Drasnian trade enclave. Then he handed a jingling purse to the shaven-headed customs official, and the ship was allowed to proceed without inspection.

"You owe me for that, Barak," Greldik said. "The trip here was out of friendship, but the money's something else again."

"Write it down someplace," Barak told him. "I'll take care of it when I get back to Val Alorn."

"If you ever get back to Val Alorn," Greldik said sourly.

"I'm sure you'll remember me in your prayers, then," Barak said. "I know you pray for me all the time anyway, but now you've got a bit more incentive."

"Is every official in the whole world corrupt?" Durnik demanded irritably. "Doesn't anyone do his job the way it's supposed to be done without taking bribes?"

"The world would come to an end if one of them did," Hettar replied.

"You and I are too simple and honest for these affairs, Durnik. We're better off leaving this kind of thing to others."

"It's disgusting, that's all."

"That may be true," Hettar agreed, "but I'm just as happy that the customs man didn't look below decks. We might have had some trouble explaining the horses."

The sailors had backed the ship into the river again and rowed toward a series of substantial wharves. They pulled up beside the outer wharf, shipped their oars and looped the hawsers around the tar-blackened pilings of a mooring spot.

"You can't moor here," a sweaty guard told them from the wharf. "This is for Drasnian ships."

"I'll moor anyplace it suits me," Greldik said shortly.

"I'll call out the soldiers," the guard threatened. He took hold of one of their hawsers and pulled out a long knife.

"If you cut that rope, friend, I'll come down there and tear off your ears," Greldik warned.

"Go ahead and tell him," Barak suggested. "It's too hot for fighting."

"My ship's carrying Drasnian goods," Greldik told the guard on the wharf, "belonging to a man named Radek—from Boktor, I think."

"Oh," the guard said, putting away his knife, "why didn't you say so in the first place?"

"Because I didn't like your attitude," Greldik replied bluntly. "Where do I find the man in charge?"

"Droblek? His house is just up that street past the shops. It's the one with the Drasnian emblem on the door."

"I've got to talk with him," Greldik said. "Do I need a pass to go off the wharf? I've heard some strange things about Sthiss Tor."

"You can move around inside the enclave," the guard informed him. "You only need a pass if you want to go into the city."

Greldik grunted and went below. A moment later he came back with several packets of folded parchment. "Do you want to talk to this official?" he asked Aunt Pol. "Or do you want me to take care of it?"

"We'd better come along," she decided. "The girl's asleep. Tell your men not to disturb her."

Greldik nodded and spoke briefly to his first mate. The sailors ran a plank across to the wharf, and Greldik led the way ashore. Thick clouds were rolling in overhead, darkening the sun.

The street which ran down to the wharf was lined on both sides with the shops of Drasnian merchants, and Nyissans moved torpidly from shop to shop, stopping now and then to haggle with the sweating shopkeepers. The Nyissan men all wore loose-fitting robes of a light, iridescent fabric, and their heads were all shaved completely bald. As he walked along behind Aunt Pol, Garion noticed with a certain distaste that the Nyissans wore elaborate makeup on their eyes, and that their lips and cheeks were rouged. Their speech was rasping and sibilant, and they all seemed to affect a lisp.

The heavy clouds had by now completely obscured the sky, and the street seemed suddenly dark. A dozen wretched, near-naked men were repairing a section of cobblestones. Their unkempt hair and shaggy beards indicated that they were not Nyissan, and there were shackles and chains attached to their ankles. A brutal-looking Nyissan stood over them with a whip, and the fresh welts and cuts on their bodies spoke mutely of the freedom with which he used it. One of the miserable slaves accidentally dropped an armload of crudely squared-off stones on his foot and opened his mouth with an animal-like howl of pain. With horror, Garion saw that the slave's tongue had been cut out.

"They reduce men to the level of beasts," Mandorallen growled, his eyes burning with a terrible anger. "Why has this cesspool not been cleansed?"

"It was once," Barak said grimly. "Just after the Nyissans assassinated the Rivan King, the Alorns came down here and killed every Nyissan they could find."

"Their numbers appear undiminished," Mandorallen said, looking around.

Barak shrugged. "It was thirteen hundred years ago. Even a single pair of rats could reestablish their species in that length of time."

Durnik, who was walking beside Garion, gasped suddenly and averted his eyes, blushing furiously.

A Nyissan lady had just stepped from a litter carried by eight slaves. The fabric of her pale green gown was so flimsy that it was nearly transparent and left very little to the imagination. "Don't look at her, Garion," Durnik whispered hoarsely, still blushing. "She's a wicked woman."

"I'd forgotten about that," Aunt Pol said with a thoughtful frown. "Maybe we should have left Durnik and Garion on the ship."

"Why's she dressed like that?" Garion asked, watching the nearly nude woman.

"Undressed, you mean." Durnik's voice was strangled with outrage.

"It's the custom," Aunt Pol explained. "It has to do with the climate. There are some other reasons, of course, but we don't need to go into those just now. All Nyissan women dress that way."

Barak and Greldik were watching the woman also, their broad grins appreciative.

"Never mind," Aunt Pol told them firmly.

Not far away a shaven-headed Nyissan stood leaning against a wall, staring at his hand and giggling senselessly. "I can see right through my fingers," he announced in a hissing lisp. "Right through them."

"Drunk?" Hettar asked.

"Not exactly," Aunt Pol answered. "Nyissans have peculiar amusements—leaves, berries, certain roots. Their perceptions get modified. It's a bit more serious than the common drunkenness one finds among Alorns."

Another Nyissan shambled by, his gait curiously jerky and his expression blank.

"Doth this condition prevail widely?" Mandorallen asked.

"I've never met a Nyissan yet who wasn't at least partially drugged," Aunt Pol said. "It makes them difficult to talk to. Isn't that the house we're looking for?" She pointed at a solid building across the street.

There was an ominous rumble of thunder off to the south as they crossed to the large house. A Drasnian servant in a linen tunic answered their knock, let them into a dimly lighted antechamber, and told them to wait.

"An evil city," Hettar said quietly. "I can't see why any Alorn in his right mind would come here willingly."

"Money," Captain Greldik replied shortly. "The Nyissan trade is very profitable."

"There are more important things than money," Hettar muttered.

An enormously fat man came into the dim room. "More light," he snapped at his servant. "You didn't have to leave them here in the dark."

"You said that the lamps just made it hotter," the servant protested in a surly tone. "I wish you'd make up your mind."

"Never mind what I said; just do as I say."

"The climate's making you incoherent, Droblek," the servant noted acidly. He lit several lamps and left the room muttering to himself.

"Drasnians make the world's worst servants," Droblek grumbled. "Shall we get down to business?" He lowered his vast bulk into a chair. The sweat rolled continually down his face and into the damp collar of his brown silk robe.

"My name's Greldik," the bearded seaman said. "I've just arrived at your wharves with a shipload of goods belonging to the merchant, Radek of Boktor." He presented the folded packets of parchment.

Droblek's eyes narrowed. "I didn't know that Radek was interested in the southern trade. I thought he dealt mostly in Sendaria and Arendia."

Greldik shrugged indifferently. "I didn't ask him. He pays me to carry his goods in my ship, not to ask questions about his business."

Droblek looked at them all, his sweating face expressionless. Then his fingers moved slightly. —*Is everything here what it seems to be?*— The Drasnian secret language made his fat fingers suddenly nimble.

—*Can we speak openly here?*— Aunt Pol's fingers asked him. Her gestures were stately, somehow archaic. There was a kind of formality to her movements that Garion had not seen in the signs made by others.

—*As openly as anyplace in this pest-hole*— Droblek replied. —*You have a strange accent, lady. There's something about it that it seems I should remember*—

—*I learned the language a very long time ago*— she replied. —*You know who Radek of Boktor really is, of course*—

"Naturally," Droblek said aloud. "Everyone knows that. Sometimes he calls himself Ambar of Kotu—when he wants to have dealings that are not, strictly speaking, legitimate."

"Shall we stop fencing with each other, Droblek?" Aunt Pol asked quietly. "I'm quite certain you've received instructions from King Rhodar by now. All this dancing about is tiresome."

Droblek's face darkened. "I'm sorry," he said stiffly. "I'll need a bit more in the way of verification."

"Don't be an idiot, Droblek," Barak rumbled at the fat man. "Use your eyes. You're an Alorn; you know who the lady is."

Droblek looked suddenly at Aunt Pol, his eyes going very wide. "It's not possible," he gasped.

"Would you like to have her prove it to you?" Hettar suggested. The house shook with a sudden crash of thunder.

"No, no," Droblek refused hastily, still staring at Aunt Pol. "It just never occurred to me—I mean, I just never—" He floundered with it.

"Have you heard from Prince Kheldar or my father?" Aunt Pol asked crisply.

"Your father? You mean—? Is *he* involved in this too?"

"Really, Droblek," she said tartly, "don't you *believe* the communications King Rhodar sends you?"

Droblek shook his head like a man trying to clear his mind. "I'm sorry, Lady Polgara," he said. "You surprised me, that's all. It takes a moment to get used to. We didn't think you'd be coming this far south."

"It's obvious then that you haven't received any word from Kheldar or the old man."

"No, my Lady," Droblek said. "Nothing. Are they supposed to be here?"

"So they said. They were either going to meet us here or send word."

"It's very hard to get messages any place in Nyissa," Droblek explained. "The people here aren't very reliable. The prince and your father could be upcountry, and their messenger could very well have gone astray. I sent a message to a place not ten leagues from the city once, and it took six months to arrive. The Nyissan who was carrying it found a certain berry patch along the way. We found him sitting in the middle of the patch, smiling." Droblek made a sour face. "There was moss growing on him," he added.

"Dead?" Durnik asked.

Droblek shrugged. "No, just very happy. He enjoyed the berries very much. I dismissed him at once, but he didn't seem to mind. For all I know, he's still sitting there."

"How extensive is your network here in Sthiss Tor?" Aunt Pol asked.

Droblek spread his pudgy hands modestly. "I manage to pick up a bit of information here and there. I've got a few people in the palace and a minor official at the Tolnedran embassy. The Tolnedrans are very thorough." He grinned impishly. "It's cheaper to let them do all the work and then buy the information after they've gathered it."

"If you can believe what they tell you," Hettar suggested.

"I never take what they say at face value," Droblek said. "The Tolnedran ambassador knows that I've bought his man. He tries to trip me up with false leads now and then."

"Does the ambassador know that you know?" Hettar asked.

"Of course he does." The fat man laughed. "But he doesn't think that I'm aware of the fact that he knows that I know." He laughed again. "It's all terribly complicated, isn't it?"

"Most Drasnian games usually are," Barak observed.

"Does the name Zedar mean anything to you?" Aunt Pol asked.

"I've heard it, naturally," Droblek said.

"Has he been in touch with Salmissra?"

Droblek frowned. "I couldn't say for sure. I haven't heard that he has, but that doesn't mean that he hasn't. Nyissa's a murky sort of place, and Salmissra's palace is the murkiest spot in the whole country. You wouldn't believe some of the things that go on there."

"I'd believe them," Aunt Pol said, "and probably things you haven't even begun to guess." She turned back to the others. "I think we're at a standstill. We can't make any kind of move until we hear from Silk and the Old Wolf."

"Could I offer you my house?" Droblek asked.

"I think we'll stay on board Captain Greldik's ship," she told him. "As you say, Nyissa's a murky place, and I'm sure that the Tolnedran ambassadors bought a few people in *your* establishment."

"Naturally," Droblek agreed. "But I know who they are."

"We'd better not chance it," she told him. "There are several reasons for our avoiding Tolnedrans just now. We'll stay aboard the ship and keep out of sight. Let us know as soon as Prince Kheldar gets in touch with you."

"Of course," Droblek said. "You'll have to wait until the rain lets up, though. Listen to it." There was the thundering sound of a downpour on the roof overhead.

"Will it last long?" Durnik asked.

Droblek shrugged. "An hour or so usually. It rains every afternoon during this season."

"I imagine it helps to cool the air," the smith said.

"Not significantly," the Drasnian told him. "Usually it just makes things worse." He mopped the sweat from his fat face.

"How can you live here?" Durnik asked.

Droblek smiled blandly. "Fat men don't move around all that much. I'm making a great deal of money, and the game I'm playing with the Tolnedran ambassador keeps my mind occupied. It's not all that bad, once you get used to it. It helps if I keep telling myself that."

They sat quietly then, listening to the pounding rain.

■ | CHAPTER TWENTY-FIVE | ■

For the next several days they all remained aboard Greldik's ship, waiting for word from Silk and Mister Wolf. Ce'Nedra recovered from her indisposition and appeared on deck wearing a pale-colored Dryad tunic which seemed to Garion to be only slightly less revealing than the gowns worn by Nyissan women. When he rather stiffly suggested that she ought to put on a few more clothes, however, she merely laughed at him. With a single-mindedness that made him want to grind his teeth, she returned to the task of teaching him to read and write. They sat together in an out-of-the-way spot on deck, pouring over a tedious book on Tolnedran diplomacy. The whole business seemed to Garion to be taking forever, though in fact his mind was very quick, and he was learning surprisingly fast. Ce'Nedra was too thoughtless to compliment him, though she seemed to await his next mistake almost breathlessly, delighting it seemed in each opportunity to ridicule him. Her proximity and her light, spicy perfume distracted him as they sat close beside each other, and he perspired as much from their occasional touch of hand or arm or hip as he did from the climate. Because they were both young, she was intolerant and he was stubborn. The sticky, humid heat made them both short-tempered and irritable, so the lessons erupted into bickering more often than not.

When they arose one morning, a black, square-rigged Nyissan ship rocked in the river current at a nearby wharf. A foul, evil kind of reek carried to them from her on the fitful morning breeze.

"What's that smell?" Garion asked one of the sailors.

"Slaver," the sailor answered grimly, pointing at the Nyissan ship. "You can smell them twenty miles away when you're at sea."

Garion looked at the ugly black ship and shuddered.

Barak and Mandorallen drifted across the deck and joined Garion at the rail. "Looks like a scow," Barak said of the Nyissan ship, his voice heavy with contempt. He was stripped to the waist, and his hairy torso ran with sweat.

"It's a slave ship," Garion told him.

"It smells like an open sewer," Barak complained. "A good fire would improve it tremendously."

"A sorry trade, my Lord Barak," Mandorallen said. "Nyissa hath dealt in human misery for untold centuries."

"Is that a Drasnian wharf?" Barak asked with narrowed eyes.

"No," Garion answered. "The sailors say that everything on that side's Nyissan."

"That's a shame," Barak growled.

A group of mail-shirted men in black cloaks walked out onto the wharf where the slave ship was moored and stopped near the vessel's stern.

"Oh-oh," Barak said. "Where's Hettar?"

"He's still below," Garion replied. "What's the matter?"

"Keep an eye out for him. Those are Murgos."

The shaven-head Nyissan sailors pulled open a hatch on their ship and barked a few rough orders down into the hold. Slowly, a line of dispirited-looking men came up. Each man wore an iron collar, and a long chain fastened them together.

Mandorallen stiffened and began to swear.

"What's wrong?" Barak asked.

"Arendishmen!" the knight exclaimed. "I had heard of this, but I did not believe it."

"Heard of what?"

"An ugly rumor hath persisted in Arendia for some years," Mandorallen answered, his face white with rage. "We are told that some of our nobles have upon occasion enriched themselves by selling their serfs to the Nyissans."

"Looks like it's more than a rumor," Barak said.

"There," Mandorallen growled. "See that crest upon the tunic of that one there? It's the crest of Vo Toral. I know the Baron of Vo Toral for a notorious spendthrift, but had not thought him dishonorable. Upon my return to Arendia, I will denounce him publicly."

"What good's that going to do?" Barak asked.

"He will be forced to challenge me," Mandorallen said grimly. "I will prove his villainy upon his body."

Barak shrugged. "Serf or slave—what's the difference?"

"Those men have rights, my Lord," Mandorallen stated. "Their Lord is required to protect them and care for them. The oath of knighthood demands it of us. This vile transaction hath stained the honor of every true Arendish knight. I shall not rest until I have bereft that foul baron of his miserable life."

"Interesting idea," Barak said. "Maybe I'll go with you."

Hettar came up on deck, and Barak moved immediately to his side and began talking quietly to him, holding one of his arms firmly.

"Make them jump around a bit," one of the Murgos ordered harshly. "I want to see how many are lame."

A heavy-shouldered Nyissan uncoiled a long whip and began to flick it deftly at the legs of the chained men. The slaves began to dance feverishly on the wharf beside the slave ship.

"Dog's blood!" Mandorallen swore, and his knuckles turned white as he gripped the railing.

"Easy," Garion warned. "Aunt Pol says we're supposed to stay pretty much out of sight."

"It cannot be borne!" Mandorallen cried.

The chain that bound the slaves together was old and pitted with rust. When one slave tripped and fell, a link snapped, and the man found himself suddenly free. With an agility born of desperation, he rolled quickly to his feet, took two quick steps and plunged off the wharf into the murky waters of the river.

"This way, man!" Mandorallen called to the swimming slave.

The burly Nyissan with the whip laughed harshly and pointed at the escaping slave. "Watch," he told the Murgos.

"Stop him, you idiot," one of the Murgos snapped. "I paid good gold for him."

"It's too late." The Nyissan looked on with an ugly grin. "Watch."

The swimming man suddenly shrieked and sank out of sight. When he came up again, his face and arms were covered with the slimy, foot-long leeches that infested the river. Screaming, the struggling man tore at the writhing leeches, ripping out chunks of his own flesh in his efforts to pull them off.

The Murgos began to laugh.

Garion's mind exploded. He gathered himself with an awful concentration, pointed one hand at the wharf just beyond their own ship and said, "Be there!" He felt an enormous surge as if some vast tide were rushing out of him, and he reeled almost senseless against Mandorallen. The sound inside his head was deafening.

The slave, still writhing and covered with the oozing leeches, was suddenly lying on the wharf. A wave of exhaustion swept over Garion; if Mandorallen had not caught him, he would have fallen.

"Where did he go?" Barak demanded, still staring at the turbulent spot on the surface of the river where the slave had been an instant before. "Did he go under?"

Wordlessly and with a shaking head, Mandorallen pointed at the slave, who lay still weakly struggling on the Drasnian wharf about twenty yards in front of the bow of their ship.

Barak looked at the slave, then back at the river. The big man blinked with surprise.

A small boat with four Nyissans at the oars put out from the other wharf and moved deliberately toward Greldik's ship. A tall Murgo stood in the bow, his scarred face angry.

"You have my property," he shouted across the intervening water. "Return the slave to me at once."

"Why don't you come and claim him, Murgo?" Barak called back. He released Hettar's arm. The Algar moved to the side of the ship, stopping only to pick up a long boathook.

"Will I be unmolested?" the Murgo asked a bit doubtfully.

"Why don't you come alongside, and we'll discuss it?" Barak suggested pleasantly.

"You're denying me my rights to my own property," the Murgo complained.

"Not at all," Barak told him. "Of course there might be a fine point of law involved here. This wharf is Drasnian territory, and slavery isn't legal in Drasnia. Since that's the case, the man's not a slave anymore."

"I'll get my men," the Murgo said. "We'll take the slave by force if we have to."

"I think we'd have to look on that as an invasion of Alorn territory," Barak warned with a great show of regret. "In the absence of our Drasnian cousins, we'd almost be compelled to take steps to defend their wharf for them. What do you think, Mandorallen?"

"Thy perceptions are most acute, my Lord," Mandorallen replied. "By common usage, honorable men are morally obliged to defend the territory of kinsmen in their absence."

"There," Barak said to the Murgo. "You see how it is. My friend here is an Arend, so he's totally neutral in this matter. I think we'd have to accept his interpretation of the affair."

Greldik's sailors had begun to climb the rigging by now, and they clung to the ropes like great, evil-looking apes, fingering their weapons and grinning at the Murgo.

"There is yet another way," the Murgo said ominously.

Garion could feel a force beginning to build, and a faint sound seemed to echo inside his head. He drew himself up, putting his hands on the wooden rail in front of him. He felt a terrible weakness, but he steeled himself and tried to gather his strength.

"That's enough of that," Aunt Pol said crisply, coming up on deck with Durnik and Ce'Nedra behind her.

"We were merely having a little legal discussion," Barak said innocently.

"I know what you were doing," she snapped. Her eyes were angry. She looked coldly across the intervening stretch of river at the Murgo. "You'd better leave," she told him.

"I have something to retrieve first," the man in the boat called back.

"I'd forget about it!"

"We'll see," he said. He straightened and began muttering as if to himself, his hands moving rapidly in a series of intricate gestures. Garion felt something pushing at him almost like a wind, though the air was completely still.

"Be sure you get it right," Aunt Pol advised quietly. "If you forget even the tiniest part of it, it'll explode in your face."

The man in the boat froze, and a faintly worried frown crossed his face. The secret wind that had been pushing at Garion stopped. The man began again, his fingers weaving in the air and his face fixed with concentration.

"You do it like this, Grolim," Aunt Pol said. She moved her hand slightly, and Garion felt a sudden rush as if the wind pushing at him had turned and begun to blow the other way. The Grolim threw his hands up and reeled back, stumbling and falling into the bottom of his boat. As if he had been given a heavy push, the boat surged backward several yards.

The Grolim half-raised, his eyes wide and his face deathly pale.

"Return to your master, dog," Aunt Pol said scathingly. "Tell him to beat you for not learning your lessons properly."

The Grolim spoke quickly to the Nyissans at the oars, and they immediately turned the boat and rowed back toward the slave ship.

"We had a nice little fight brewing there, Polgara," Barak complained. "Why did you have to spoil it?"

"Grow up," she ordered bluntly. Then she turned on Garion, her eyes blazing and the white lock at her brow like a streak of fire. "You idiot! You refuse any kind of instruction, and then you burst out like a raging bull. Have you the slightest conception of what an uproar translocation causes? You've alerted every Grolim in Sthiss Tor to the fact that we're here."

"He was dying," Garion protested, gesturing helplessly at the slave lying on the wharf. "I had to do something."

"He was dead as soon as he hit the water," she said flatly. "Look at him."

The slave had stiffened into an arched posture of mortal agony, his head twisted back and his mouth agape. He was obviously dead. "What happened to him?" Garion asked, feeling suddenly sick.

"The leeches are poisonous. Their bites paralyze their victims so that they can feed on them undisturbed. The bites stopped his heart. You exposed us to the Grolims for the sake of a dead man."

"He wasn't dead when I did it!" Garion shouted at her. "He was screaming for help." He was angrier than he had ever been in his life.

"He was beyond help." Her voice was cold, even brutal.

"What kind of monster are you?" he asked from between clenched teeth. "Don't you have any feelings? You'd have just let him die, wouldn't you?"

"I don't think this is the time or place to discuss it."

"No! This *is* the time—right now, Aunt Pol. You're not even human, did you know that? You left being human behind so long ago that you can't even remember where you lost it. You're three thousand years old. Our whole lives go by while you blink your eyes. We're just an entertainment for you—an hour's diversion. You manipulate us like puppets for your own amusement. Well, I'm tired of being manipulated. You and I are finished!"

It probably went further than he'd intended, but his anger had finally run away with him, and the words seemed to rush out before he could stop them.

She looked at him, her face as pale as if he had suddenly struck her. Then she drew herself up. "You stupid boy," she said in a voice that was all the more terrible because it was so quiet. "Finished? You and I? How can you even begin to understand what I've had to do to bring you to this world? You've been my only care for over a thousand years. I've endured anguish and loss and pain beyond your ability to understand what the words mean—all for you. I've lived in poverty and squalor for hundreds of years at a time— all for you. I gave up a sister I loved more than my life itself—all for you. I've gone through fire and despair worse than fire a dozen times over—all for you. And you think this has all been an entertainment for me?—some idle amusement? You think the kind of care I've devoted to you for a thousand years and more comes cheaply? You and I will *never* be finished, Belgarion. *Never!* We will go on together until the end of days if necessary. We will never be finished. You owe me too much for that!"

There was a dreadful silence. The others, shocked by the intensity of Aunt Pol's words, stood staring first at her and then at Garion.

Without speaking further, she turned and went below decks again.

Garion looked around helplessly, suddenly terribly ashamed and terribly alone.

"I *had* to do it, didn't I?" he asked of no one in particular and not entirely sure exactly what it was that he meant.

They all looked at him, but no one answered his question.

CHAPTER TWENTY-SIX

By midafternoon the clouds had rolled in again, and the thunder began to rumble off in the distance as the rain swept in to drown the steaming city once more. The afternoon thunderstorm seemed to come at the same time each day, and they had even grown accustomed to it. They all moved below deck and sat sweltering as the rain roared down on the deck above them.

Garion sat stiffly, his back planted against a rough-hewn oak rib of the ship and watched Aunt Pol, his face set stubbornly and his eyes unforgiving.

She ignored him and sat talking quietly with Ce'Nedra.

Captain Greldik came through the narrow companionway door, his face and beard streaming water. "The Drasnian—Droblek—is here," he told them. "He says he's got word for you."

"Send him in," Barak said.

Droblek squeezed his vast bulk through the narrow door. He was totally drenched from the rain and stood dripping on the floor. He wiped his face. "It's wet out there," he commented.

"We noticed," Hettar said.

"I've received a message," Droblek told Aunt Pol. "It's from Prince Kheldar."

"Finally," she said.

"He and Belgarath are coming downriver," Droblek reported. "As closely as I can make out, they should be here in a few days—a week at the most. The messenger isn't very coherent."

Aunt Pol looked at him inquiringly.

"Fever," Droblek explained. "The man's a Drasnian, so he's reliable—one of my agents at an upcountry trading post—but he's picked up one of the diseases that infest this stinking swamp. He's a little delirious just now. We hope we can break the fever in a day or so and get some sense out of him. I came as soon as I got the general idea of his message. I thought you'd want to know immediately."

"We appreciate your concern," Aunt Pol said.

"I'd have sent a servant," Droblek explained, "but messages sometimes go astray in Sthiss Tor, and servants sometimes get things twisted around." He grinned suddenly. "That's not the real reason, of course."

Aunt Pol smiled. "Of course not."

"A fat man tends to stay in one place and let others do his walking around for him. From the tone of King Rhodar's message, I gather that this business might be the most important thing happening in the world just now. I wanted to take part in it." He made a wry face. "We all lapse into childishness from time to time, I suppose."

"How serious is the condition of the messenger?" Aunt Pol asked.

Droblek shrugged. "Who can say? Half of these pestilential fevers in Nyissa don't even have names, and we can't really tell one from another. Sometimes people die very quickly from them; sometimes they linger for weeks. Now and then someone even recovers. About all we can do is make them comfortable and wait to see what happens."

"I'll come at once," Aunt Pol said, rising. "Durnik, would you get me the green bag from our packs? I'll need the herbs I have in it."

"It's not always a good idea to expose oneself to some of these fevers, my Lady," Droblek cautioned.

"I won't be in any danger," she said. "I want to question your messenger closely, and the only way I'll be able to get any answers from him is to rid him of his fever."

"Durnik and I'll come along," Barak offered.

She looked at him.

"It doesn't hurt to be on the safe side," the big man said, belting on his sword.

"If you wish." She put on her cloak and turned up the hood. "This may take most of the night," she told Greldik. "There are Grolims about, so have your sailors stay alert. Put a few of the more sober ones on watch."

"Sober, my Lady?" Greldik asked innocently.

"I've heard the singing coming from the crew's quarters, Captain," she said a bit primly. "Chereks don't sing unless they're drunk. Keep the lid on your ale-barrel tonight. Shall we go, Droblek?"

"At once, my Lady," the fat man assented with a sly look at Greldik.

Garion felt a certain relief after they had gone. The strain of maintaining his rancor in Aunt Pol's presence had begun to wear on him. He found himself in a difficult position. The horror and self-loathing which had gnawed at him since he had unleashed the dreadful fire upon Chamdar in the Wood of the Dryads had grown until he could scarcely bear it. He looked forward to each night with dread, for his dreams were always the same. Over and over again he saw Chamdar, his face burned away, pleading, "Master, have mercy." And over and over again he saw the awful blue flame that had come from his own hand in answer to that agony. The hatred he had carried since Val Alorn had died in that flame. His revenge had been so absolute that there was no possible way he could evade or shift the responsibility for it. His outburst that morning had been directed almost more at himself than at Aunt Pol. He had called her a monster, but it was the monster within himself he hated. The dreadful catalogue of what she had suffered over uncounted years for him and the passion with which she had spoken—evidence of the pain his words had caused her—twisted searingly in his mind. He was ashamed, so ashamed that he could not even bear to look into the faces of his friends. He sat alone and vacant-eyed with Aunt Pol's words thundering over and over in his mind.

The rain slackened on the deck above them as the storm passed. Swirling little eddies of raindrops ran across the muddy surface of the river in the fitful wind. The sky began to clear, and the sun sank into the roiling clouds, staining them an angry red. Garion went up on deck to wrestle alone with his troubled conscience.

After a while he heard a light step behind him. "I suppose you're proud of yourself?" Ce'Nedra asked acidly.

"Leave me alone."

"I don't think so. I think I want to tell you just exactly how we all felt about your little speech this morning."

"I don't want to hear about it."

"That's too bad. I'm going to tell you anyway."

"I won't listen."

"Oh yes, you will." She took him by the arm and turned him around. Her eyes were blazing and her tiny face filled with a huge anger. "What you did was absolutely inexcusable," she said. "Your aunt raised you from a baby. She's been a mother to you."

"My mother's dead."

"The Lady Polgara's the only mother you ever knew, and what did you give her for thanks? You called her a monster. You accused her of not caring."

"I'm not listening to you," Garion cried. Knowing that it was childish—even infantile—he put his hands over his ears. The Princess Ce'Nedra always seemed to bring out the worst in him.

"Move your hands!" she commanded in a ringing voice. "You're going to hear me even if I have to scream."

Garion, afraid that she meant it, took his hands away.

"She carried you when you were a baby," Ce'Nedra went on, seeming to know exactly where the sorest spot on Garion's wounded conscience lay. "She watched your very first steps. She fed you; she watched over you; she held you when you were afraid or hurt. Does that sound like a monster? She watches you all the time, did you know that? If you even so much as stumble, she almost reaches out to catch you. I've seen her cover you when you're asleep. Does that sound like someone who doesn't care?"

"You're talking about something you don't understand," Garion told her. "Please, just leave me alone."

"Please?" she repeated mockingly. "What a strange time for you to re-member your manners. I didn't hear you saying please this morning. I didn't hear a single please. I didn't hear any thank you's either. Do you know what you are, Garion? You're a spoiled child, that's what you are."

That did it! To have this pampered, willful little princess call *him* a spoiled child was more than Garion could bear. Infuriated, he began to shout at her. Most of what he said was wildly incoherent, but the shouting made him feel better.

They started with accusations, but the argument soon degenerated into name-calling. Ce'Nedra was screeching like a Camaar fishwife, and Garion's voice cracked and warbled between a manly baritone and a boyish tenor. They shook their fingers in each other's faces and shouted. Ce'Nedra stamped her feet, and Garion waved his arms. All in all, it was a splendid little fight. Garion felt much better when it was over. Yelling insults at Ce'Nedra was an innocent diversion compared to some of the deadly things he'd said to Aunt Pol that morning, and it allowed him to vent his confusion and anger harmlessly.

In the end, of course, Ce'Nedra resorted to tears and fled, leaving him feeling more foolish than ashamed. He fumed a bit, muttering a few choice insults he hadn't had the opportunity to deliver, and then he sighed and leaned pensively on the rail to watch night settle in over the dank city.

Though he would not have cared to admit it, even to himself, he was grateful to the princess. Their descent into absurdity had cleared his head. Quite clearly now he saw that he owed Aunt Pol an apology. He had lashed out at her out of his own sense of deep-seated guilt, trying somehow to shift the blame to her. Quite obviously there was no way to evade his own responsibility. Having accepted that, he seemed for some reason to feel better.

It grew darker. The tropical night was heavy, and the smell of rotting vegetation and stagnant water rolled in out of the trackless swamps. A vicious little insect crawled down inside his tunic and began to bite him somewhere between his shoulders where he could not reach.

There was absolutely no warning—no sound or lurch of the ship or any hint of danger. His arms were seized from behind and a wet cloth was pressed firmly over his mouth and nose. He tried to struggle, but the hands holding him were very strong. He tried to twist his head to get his face clear enough to shout for help. The cloth smelled strange—cloying, sickeningly sweet, thick somehow. He began to feel dizzy, and his struggles grew weaker. He made one last effort before the dizziness overcame him and he sank down into unconsciousness.

CHAPTER TWENTY-SEVEN

They were in a long hallway of some sort. Garion could see the flagstone floor quite clearly. Three men were carrying him facedown, and his head bobbed and swung on his neck uncomfortably. His mouth was dry, and the thick, sweet smell that had impregnated the cloth they had crushed to his face lingered. He raised his head, trying to look around.

"He's awake," the man holding one of his arms said.

"Finally," one of the others muttered. "You held the cloth to his face too long, Issus."

"I know what I'm doing," the first one said. "Put him down."

"Can you stand?" Issus asked Garion. His shaved head was stubbled, and he had a long scar running from his forehead to his chin directly through the puckered vacancy of an empty eye-socket. His belted robe was stained and spotted.

"Get up," Issus ordered in a hissing kind of voice. He nudged Garion with his foot. Garion struggled to rise. His knees were shaky, and he put his hand on the wall to steady himself. The stones were damp and covered with a kind of mold.

"Bring him," Issus told the others. They took Garion's arms and half-dragged, half-carried him down the damp passageway behind the one-eyed man. When they came out of the corridor, they were in a vaulted area that seemed not so much like a room but rather a large roofed place. Huge pillars, covered with carvings, supported the soaring ceiling, and small oil lamps hung on long chains from above or sat on little stone shelves on the pillars. There was a confused sense of movement as groups of men in varicolored robes drifted from place to place in a kind of languorous stupor.

"You," Issus snapped at a plump young man with dreamy eyes, "tell Sadi, the chief eunuch, that we have the boy."

"Tell him yourself," the young man said in a piping voice. "I don't take orders from your kind, Issus."

Issus slapped the plump young man sharply across the face.

"You hit me!" the plump one wailed, putting his hand to his mouth. "You made my lip bleed—see?" He held out his hand to show the blood.

"If you don't do what I tell you to do, I'll cut your fat throat," Issus told him in a flat, unemotional voice.

"I'm going to tell Sadi what you did."

"Go ahead. And as long as you're there, tell him that we've got the boy the queen wanted."

The plump young man scurried away.

"Eunuchs!" One of the men holding Garion's arm spat.

"They have their uses," the other said with a coarse laugh.

"Bring the boy," Issus ordered. "Sadi doesn't like to be kept waiting."

They pulled Garion across the lighted area.

A group of wretched-looking men with unkempt hair and beards sat chained together on the floor. "Water," one of them croaked. "Please." He stretched out an imploring hand.

Issus stopped to stare at the slave in amazement. "Why does this one still have its tongue?" he demanded of the guard who stood over the slaves.

The guard shrugged. "We haven't had time to attend to that yet."

"Take time," Issus told him. "If one of the priests hears it talk, he'll have you questioned. You wouldn't like that."

"I'm not afraid of the priests," the guard said, but he looked nervously over his shoulder.

"Be afraid," Issus advised him. "And water these animals. They're no good to anybody dead." He started to lead the men holding Garion through a shadowy area between two pillars, then stopped again. "Get out of my way," he said to something lying in the shadows. Grudgingly, the thing began to move. With revulsion Garion realized that it was a large snake.

"Get over there with the others," Issus told the snake. He pointed toward a dimly lighted corner where a large mass seemed to be undulating, moving with a kind of sluggish seething. Faintly Garion could hear the dry hiss of scales rubbing together. The snake which had barred their way flicked a nervous tongue at Issus, then slithered toward the dim corner.

"Someday you're going to get bitten, Issus," one of the men warned. "They don't like being ordered around."

Issus shrugged indifferently and moved on.

"Sadi wants to talk to you," the plump young eunuch said spitefully to Issus as they approached a large polished door. "I told him that you hit me. Maas is with him."

"Good," Issus said. He pushed the door open. "Sadi," he called sharply, "tell your friend I'm coming in. I don't want him making any mistakes."

"He knows you, Issus," a voice on the other side of the door said. "He won't do anything by mistake."

Issus went in and closed the door behind him.

"You can leave now," one of the men holding Garion told the young eunuch.

The plump one sniffed. "I go when Sadi tells me to go."

"And come running when Sadi whistles, too."

"That's between Sadi and me, isn't it?"

"Bring him in," Issus ordered, opening the door again.

The two men pushed Garion into the room. "We'll wait out here," one of them said nervously.

Issus laughed harshly, pushed the door shut with his foot, and pulled Garion to the front of a table where a single oil lamp flickered with a tiny flame that barely held back the darkness. A thin man with dead-looking eyes sat at the table, lightly stroking his hairless head with the long fingers of one hand.

"Can you speak, boy?" he asked Garion. His voice had a strange contralto quality to it, and his silk robe was a solid crimson rather than varicolored.

"Could I have a drink of water?" Garion asked.

"In a minute."

"I'll take my money now, Sadi," Issus said.

"As soon as we're sure this is the right boy," Sadi replied.

"Ask it what its name is," a hissing whisper said from the darkness behind Garion.

"I will, Maas." Sadi looked faintly annoyed at the suggestion. "I've done this before."

"You're taking too long," the whisper said.

"Say your name, boy," Sadi told Garion.

"Doroon," Garion lied quickly. "I'm really very thirsty."

"Do you take me for a fool, Issus?" Sadi asked. "Did you think just any boy would satisfy me?"

"This is the boy you told me to fetch," Issus said. "I can't help it if your information was wrong."

"You say your name is Doroon?" Sadi asked.

"Yes," Garion said. "I'm the cabin boy on Captain Greldik's ship. Where are we?"

"I'll ask the questions, boy," Sadi said.

"It's lying," the sibilant whisper came from behind Garion.

"I know that, Maas," Sadi replied calmly. "They always do at first."

"We don't have time for all this," the hiss said. "Give it oret. I need the truth immediately."

"Whatever you say, Maas," Sadi agreed. He rose to his feet and disappeared momentarily into the shadows behind the table. Garion heard a clink and then the sound of water pouring. "Remember that this was your idea, Maas. If *she* becomes angry about it, I don't want to be the one she blames."

"She'll understand, Sadi."

"Here, boy," Sadi offered, coming back into the light and holding out a brown earthenware cup.

"Uh—no, thank you," Garion said. "I guess I'm not really thirsty after all."

"You might as well drink it, boy," Sadi told him. "If you don't, Issus will hold you, and I'll pour it down your throat. It isn't going to hurt you."

"Drink," the hissing voice commanded.

"Better do as they say," Issus advised.

Helplessly Garion took the cup. The water had a strangely bitter taste and seemed to burn his tongue.

"Much better," Sadi said, resuming his seat behind the table. "Now, you say your name is Doroon?"

"Yes."

"Where are you from, Doroon?"

"Sendaria."

"Where exactly in Sendaria?"

"Near Darine on the north coast."

"What are you doing on a Cherek ship?"

"Captain Greldik's a friend of my father," Garion said. For some reason he suddenly wanted to explain further. "My father wanted me to learn about ships. He says that being a sailor's better than being a farmer. Captain Greldik agreed to teach me what I'd need to know to be a sailor. He says I'll be good at it because I didn't even get seasick, and I'm not afraid to climb up the ropes that hold the sails in place, and I'm almost strong enough to pull an oar already, and—"

"What did you say your name was, boy?"

"Garion—I mean—uh—Doroon. Yes, Doroon, and—"

"How old are you, Garion?"

"Fifteen last Erastide. Aunt Pol says that people who are born on Erastide are very lucky, only I haven't noticed that I'm luckier than—"

"And who is Aunt Pol?"

"She's my aunt. We used to live on Faldor's farm, but Mister Wolf came and we—"

"Do people call her something besides Aunt Pol?"

"King Fulrach called her Polgara—that was when Captain Brendig took us all to the palace in Sendar. Then we went to King Anheg's palace in Val Alorn, and—"

"Who's Mister Wolf?"

"My grandfather. They call him Belgarath. I didn't used to believe it, but I guess it has to be true because one time he—"

"And why did you all leave Faldor's farm?"

"I didn't know why at first, but then I found out that it was because Zedar stole the Orb of Aldur off the pommel of the Sword of the Rivan King, and we've got to get it back before Zedar can take it to Torak and wake him up and—"

"This is the boy we want," the hissing voice whispered.

Garion turned around slowly. The room seemed brighter now, as if the tiny flame were putting out more light. In the corner, rearing out of its own coils and with a strangely flattened neck and glowing eyes, was a very large snake.

"We can take it to Salmissra now," the snake hissed. It lowered itself to the floor and crawled across to Garion. He felt its cold, dry nose touch his leg, and then, though a hidden part of his mind shrieked, he stood unresisting as the scaly body slowly mounted his leg and coiled upward until the snake's head reared beside his face and its flickering tongue touched his face. "Be very good, boy," the snake hissed in his ear, "very, *very* good." The reptile was heavy, and its coils thick and cold.

"This way, boy," Sadi told Garion, rising to his feet.

"I want my money," Issus demanded.

"Oh," Sadi said almost contemptuously, "that. It's in that pouch there on the table." Then he turned and led Garion from the room.

"*Garion.*" The dry voice that had always been in his mind spoke quietly to him. "*I want you to listen carefully. Don't say anything or let anything show on your face. Just listen to me.*"

"*W-who are you?*" Garion asked silently, struggling with the fog in his brain.

"*You know me,*" the dry voice told him. "*Now, listen. They've given you something that makes you do what they want you to do. Don't fight against it. Just relax and don't fight it.*"

"*But—I said things I shouldn't have. I—*"

"*That doesn't matter now. Just do as I say. If anything happens and it starts to get dangerous, don't fight. I'll take care of it—but I can't do it if you're struggling. You have to relax so that I can do what has to be done. If you suddenly find yourself doing things or saying things you don't understand, don't be afraid and don't try to fight. It won't be them; it will be me.*"

Comforted by this silent reassurance, Garion walked obediently beside Sadi the eunuch while the coils of the snake, Maas, lay heavily about his chest and shoulders and the bluntly pointed reptilian head rested, almost nuzzling, against his cheek.

They entered a large room where the walls were heavily draped and crystal oil lamps hung glittering on silver chains. An enormous stone statue, its upper third lost in the shadows high above, raised its mass titanically at one end of the room, and directly in front of the statue was a low stone platform, carpeted and strewn with cushions. Upon the platform stood a heavy divan that was not quite a chair and not quite a couch.

There was a woman on the divan. Her hair was raven-black, cascading in loose coils down her back and across her shoulders. About her head was an intricately wrought golden crown sparkling with jewels. Her gown was white and spun of the filmiest gauze. It did not in any way conceal her body, but rather seemed to be worn only to provide a material to which her jewels and adornments could be attached. Beneath the gauze, her skin was almost chalky white, and her face was extraordinarily beautiful. Her eyes were pale, even colorless. A large, gold-framed mirror stood on a pedestal at one side of the divan, and the woman lounged at ease, admiring herself in the glass.

Two dozen shaven-headed eunuchs in crimson robes knelt in a cluster to one side of the dais, resting on their haunches and gazing at the woman and the statue behind her with worshipful adoration.

Among the cushions at the side of the divan lolled an indolent, pampered-looking young man whose head was not shaved. His hair was elaborately curled, his cheeks were rouged, and his eyes were fantastically made up. He wore only the briefest of loincloths, and his expression was bored and sulky. The woman absently ran the fingers of one hand through his curls as she watched herself in the mirror.

"The queen has visitors," one of the kneeling eunuchs announced in a singsong voice.

"Ah," the others chanted in unison, "visitors."

"Hail, Eternal Salmissra," Sadi the eunuch said, prostrating himself before the dais and the pale-eyed woman.

"What is it, Sadi?" she demanded. Her voice was vibrant and had a strange, dark timbre.

"The boy, my Queen," Sadi announced, his face still pressed to the floor.

"On your knees before the Serpent Queen," the snake hissed in Garion's ear. The coils tightened about Garion's body, and he fell to his knees in their sudden crushing grip.

"Come here, Maas," Salmissra said to the snake.

"The queen summons the beloved serpent," the eunuch intoned.

"Ah."

The reptile uncoiled itself from about Garion's body and undulated up to the foot of the divan, reared half its length above the reclining woman and then lowered itself upon her body, its thick length curving, fitting itself to her. The blunt head reached up to her face, and she kissed it affectionately. The long, forked tongue flickered over her face, and Maas began to whisper sibilantly in her ear. She lay in the embrace of the serpent, listening to its hissing voice and looking at Garion with heavy-lidded eyes.

Then, pushing the reptile aside, the queen rose to her feet and stood over Garion. "Welcome to the land of the snake-people, Belgarion," she said in her purring voice.

The name, which he had heard only from Aunt Pol before, sent a strange shock through Garion, and he tried to shake the fog from his head.

"Not yet," the dry voice in his mind warned him.

Salmissra stepped down from the dais, her body moving with a sinuous grace beneath her transparent gown. She took one of Garion's arms and drew him gently to his feet; then she touched his face lingeringly. Her hand seemed very cold. "A pretty young man," she breathed, almost as if to herself. "So young. So warm." Her look seemed somehow hungry.

A strange confusion seemed to fill Garion's mind. The bitter drink Sadi had given him still lay on his consciousness like a blanket. Beneath it he felt at once afraid and yet strangely attracted to the queen. Her chalky skin and dead eyes were repellent, yet there was a kind of lush invitation about her, an overripe promise of unspeakable delights. Unconsciously he took a step backward.

"Don't be afraid, my Belgarion," she purred at him. "I won't hurt you— not unless you want me to. Your duties here will be very pleasant, and I can teach you things that Polgara hasn't even dreamed of."

"Come away from him, Salmissra," the young man on the dais ordered petulantly. "You know I don't like it when you pay attention to others."

A flicker of annoyance showed in the queen's eyes. She turned and looked rather coldly at the young man. "What you like or don't like doesn't really concern me anymore, Essia," she said.

"What?" Essia cried incredulously. "Do as I say at once!"

"No, Essia," she told him.

"I'll punish you," he threatened.

"No," she said, "you won't. That sort of thing doesn't amuse me anymore, and all your pouting and tantrums have begun to grow boring. Leave now."

"Leave?" Essia's eyes bulged with disbelief.

"You're dismissed, Essia."

"Dismissed? But you can't live without me. You said so yourself."

"We all say things we don't mean sometimes."

The arrogance went out of the young man like water poured from a bucket. He swallowed hard and began to tremble. "When do you want me to come back?" he whined.

"I don't, Essia."

"Never?" he gasped.

"Never," she told him. "Now go, and stop making a scene."

"What's to become of me?" Essia cried. He began to weep, the makeup around his eyes running in grotesque streaks down his face.

"Don't be tiresome, Essia," Salmissra said. "Pick up your belongings and leave—now! I have a new consort." She stepped back up on the dais.

"The queen has chosen a consort," the eunuch intoned.

"Ah," the others chanted. "Hail the consort of Eternal Salmissra, most fortunate of men."

The sobbing young man grabbed up a pink robe and an ornately carved jewel box. He stumbled down from the dais. "*You* did this," he accused Garion. "It's all your fault." Suddenly, out of the folds of the robe draped over his arm, he pulled a small dagger. "I'll fix you," he screamed, raising the dagger to strike.

There was no thought this time, no gathering of will. The surge of force came without warning, pushing Essia away, driving him back. He slashed futilely at the air with his little knife. Then the surge was gone.

Essia lunged forward again, his eyes insane and his dagger raised. The surge came again, stronger this time. The young man was spun away. He fell, and his dagger clattered across the floor.

Salmissra, her eyes ablaze, pointed at the prostrate Essia and snapped her fingers twice. So fast that it seemed almost like an arrow loosed from a bow, a small green snake shot from beneath the divan, its mouth agape and its hiss a kind of snarl. It struck once, hitting Essia on the leg, then slithered quickly to one side and watched with dead eyes.

Essia gasped and turned white with horror. He tried to rise, but his legs and arms suddenly sprawled out from under him on the polished stones. He gave one strangled cry and then the convulsions began. His heels pattered rapidly on the floor, and his arms flailed wildly. His eyes turned vacant and staring, and a green froth shot like a fountain from his mouth. His body arched back, every muscle writhing beneath his skin, and his head began to pound on the floor. He gave one thrashing, convulsive leap, his entire body bounding up from the floor. When he came down, he was dead.

Salmissra watched him die, her pale eyes expressionless, incurious, with no hint of anger or regret.

"Justice is done," the eunuch announced.

"Swift is the justice of the Queen of the Serpent People," the others replied.

CHAPTER TWENTY-EIGHT

There were other things they made him drink—some bitter, some sickeningly sweet—and his mind seemed to sink deeper with each cup he raised to his lips. His eyes began to play strange tricks on him. It seemed somehow that the world had suddenly been drowned and that all of this was taking place underwater. The walls wavered and the figures of the kneeling eunuchs seemed to sway and undulate like seaweed in the endless wash and eddy of tide and current. The lamps sparkled like jewels, casting out brilliant colors in slow-falling showers. Garion slumped, all bemused, on the dais near Salmissra's divan, his eyes filled with light and his head washed clean of all thought. There was no sense of time, no desire, no will. He briefly and rather vaguely remembered his friends, but the knowledge that he would never see them again brought only a brief, passing regret, a temporary melancholy that was rather pleasant. He even shed one crystal tear over his loss, but the tear landed on his wrist and sparkled with such an unearthly beauty that he lost himself utterly in contemplating it.

"How did he do it?" the queen's voice said somewhere behind him. Her voice was so beautifully musical that the sound of it pierced Garion's very soul.

"It has power," Maas replied, his serpent voice thrilling Garion's nerves, vibrating them like the strings of a lute. "Its power is untried, undirected, but it is very strong. Beware of this one, beloved Salmissra. It can destroy quite by accident."

"I will control him," she said.

"Perhaps," the snake replied.

"Sorcery requires will," Salmissra pointed out. "I will take his will away from him. Your blood is cold, Maas, and you've never felt the fire that fills the veins with the taste of oret or athal or kaldiss. Your passions are also cold, and you can't know how much the body can be used to enslave the will. I'll put his mind to sleep and then smother his will with love."

"Love, Salmissra?" the snake asked, sounding faintly amused.

"The term serves as well as any other," she replied. "Call it appetite, if you wish."

"That I can understand," Maas agreed. "But don't underestimate this one—or overestimate your own power. It does not have an ordinary mind. There's something strange about it that I can't quite penetrate."

"We'll see," she said. "Sadi," she called the eunuch.

"Yes, my Queen?"

"Take the boy. Have him bathed and perfumed. He smells of boats and tar and salt water. I don't like such Alorn smells."

"At once, Eternal Salmissra."

Garion was led away to a place where there was warm water. His clothes were taken from him, and he was immersed and soaped and immersed again. Fragrant oils were rubbed into his skin, and a brief loincloth was tied about his waist. Then he was taken quite firmly by the chin and rouge was applied to his cheeks. It was during this process that he realized that the person painting his face was a woman. Slowly, almost incuriously, he let his eyes move around the bath chamber. He realized then that except for Sadi, everyone there was female. It seemed that something about that should bother him—something having to do with appearing naked in the presence of women—but he could not exactly remember what it was.

When the woman had finished painting his face, Sadi the eunuch took his arm and led him again through the dim, endless corridors back to the room where Salmissra half-lay on her divan beneath the statue, admiring herself in the pedestaled mirror beside her.

"Much better," she said, looking Garion up and down with a certain appreciation. "He's much more muscular than I thought. Bring him here."

Sadi led Garion to the side of the queen's divan and gently pressed him down onto the cushions where Essia had lounged.

Salmissra reached out with a lingeringly slow hand and brushed her cold fingertips across his face and chest. Her pale eyes seemed to burn, and her lips parted slightly. Garion's eyes fixed themselves on her pale arm. There was no trace of hair on that white skin.

"Smooth," he said vaguely, struggling to focus on that peculiarity.

"Of course, my Belgarion," she murmured. "Serpents are hairless, and I am the queen of the serpents."

Slowly, puzzled, he raised his eyes to the lustrous black tresses tumbling down across one of her white shoulders.

"Only this," she said, touching the curls with a sensuous kind of vanity.

"How?" he asked.

"It's a secret." She laughed. "Someday perhaps I'll show you. Would you like that?"

"I suppose so."

"Tell me, Belgarion," she said, "do you think I'm beautiful?"

"I think so."

"How old would you say I am?" She spread her arms so that he could see her body through the filmy gauze of her gown.

"I don't know," Garion said. "Older than I am, but not too old."

A brief flicker of annoyance crossed her face. "Guess," she ordered somewhat harshly.

"Thirty perhaps," he decided, confused.

"*Thirty?*" Her voice was stricken. Swiftly she turned to her mirror and examined her face minutely. "You're blind, you idiot!" she snapped, still staring at herself in the glass. "That's not the face of a woman of thirty. Twenty-three—twenty-five at the most."

"Whatever you say," he agreed.

"Twenty-three," she stated firmly. "Not a single day over twenty-three."

"Of course," he said mildly.

"Would you believe that I'm nearly sixty?" she demanded, her eyes suddenly flint-hard.

"No," Garion denied. "I couldn't believe that—not sixty."

"What a charming boy you are, Belgarion," she breathed at him, her glance melting. Her fingers returned to his face, touching, stroking, caressing. Slowly, beneath the pale skin of her naked shoulder and throat, curious patches of color began to appear, a faint mottling of green and purple that seemed to shift and pulsate, growing first quite visible and then fading. Her lips parted again, and her breathing grew faster. The mottling spread down her torso beneath her transparent gown, the colors seeming to writhe beneath her skin.

Maas crept nearer, his dead eyes suddenly coming awake with a strange adoration. The vivid pattern of his own scaly skin so nearly matched the colors that began to emerge upon the body of the Serpent Queen that when he draped a caressing coil across one of her shoulders it became impossible to say exactly where lay the boundary between the snake and the woman.

Had Garion not been in a half-stupor, he would have recoiled from the queen. Her colorless eyes and mottled skin seemed reptilian, and her openly lustful expression spoke of some dreadful hunger. Yet there was a curious attraction about her. Helplessly he felt drawn by her blatant sensuality.

"Come closer, my Belgarion," she ordered softly. "I'm not going to hurt you." Her eyes gloated over her possession of him.

Not far from the dais, Sadi the eunuch cleared his throat. "Divine Queen," he announced, "the emissary of Taur Urgas requests a word with you."

"Of Ctuchik, you mean," Salmissra said, looking faintly annoyed. Then a thought seemed to cross her mind, and she smiled maliciously. The mottling of her skin faded. "Bring the Grolim in," she instructed Sadi.

Sadi bowed and withdrew to return a moment later with a scar-faced man in the garb of a Murgo.

"Give welcome to the emissary of Taur Urgas," the eunuch chanted.

"Welcome," the chorus replied.

"*Carefully now,*" the dry voice in his mind said to Garion. "*That's the one we saw at the harbor.*"

Garion looked more carefully at the Murgo and realized that it was true.

"Hail, Eternal Salmissra," the Grolim said perfunctorily, bowing first to the queen and then to the statue behind her. "Taur Urgas, King of Cthol Murgos, sends greetings to the Spirit of Issa and to his handmaiden."

"And are there no greetings from Ctuchik, High Priest of the Grolims?" she asked, her eyes bright.

"Of course," the Grolim said, "but those are customarily given in private."

"Is your errand here on behalf of Taur Urgas or of Ctuchik?" she inquired, turning to examine her reflection in the mirror.

"May we speak in private, your Majesty?" the Grolim asked.

"We *are* in private," she said.

"But—" He looked around at the kneeling eunuchs in the room.

"My body servants," she said. "A Nyissan queen is never left alone. You should know that by now."

"And that one?" The Grolim pointed at Garion.

"He is also a servant—but of a slightly different kind."

The Grolim shrugged. "Whatever you wish. I salute you in the name of Ctuchik, High Priest of the Grolims and Disciple of Torak."

"The Handmaiden of Issa salutes Ctuchik of Rak Cthol," she responded formally. "What does the Grolim High Priest want of me?"

"The boy, your Majesty," the Grolim said bluntly.

"Which boy is that?"

"The boy you stole from Polgara and who now sits at your feet."

She laughed scornfully. "Convey my regrets to Ctuchik," she said, "but that would be impossible."

"It's unwise to deny the wishes of Ctuchik," the Grolim warned.

"It's even more unwise to make demands of Salmissra in her own palace," she said. "What is Ctuchik prepared to offer for this boy?"

"His eternal friendship."

"What need has the Serpent Queen of friends?"

"Gold, then," the Grolim offered with annoyance.

"I know the secret of the red gold of Angarak," she told him. "I don't wish to become a slave to it. Keep your gold, Grolim."

"Might I say that the game you play is very dangerous, your Majesty?" the Grolim said coolly. "You've already made Polgara your enemy. Can you afford the enmity of Ctuchik as well?"

"I'm not afraid of Polgara," she answered. "Nor of Ctuchik."

"The queen's bravery is remarkable," he said dryly.

"This is beginning to get tiresome. My terms are very simple. Tell Ctuchik that I have Torak's enemy, and I will keep him—unless—" She paused.

"Unless what, your Highness?"

"If Ctuchik will speak to Torak for me, an agreement might be reached."

"What sort of agreement?"

"I will give the boy to Torak as a wedding gift."

The Grolim blinked.

"If Torak will make me his bride and give me immortality, I will deliver Belgarion up to him."

"All the world knows that the Dragon God of Angarak is bound in slumber," the Grolim objected.

"But he will not sleep forever," Salmissra said flatly. "The priests of Angarak and the sorcerers of Aloria always seem to forget that Eternal Salmissra can read the signs in the heavens as clearly as they. The day of Torak's awakening is at hand. Tell Ctuchik that upon the day that I am wed to Torak, Belgarion will be in his hands. Until that day, the boy is mine."

"I shall deliver your message to Ctuchik," the Grolim said with a stiff, icy bow.

"Leave, then," she told him with an airy wave of her hand.

"So that's it," the voice in Garion's mind said as the Grolim left. "I should have known, I suppose."

Maas the serpent suddenly raised his head, his great neck flaring and his eyes burning. "Beware!" he hissed.

"Of the Grolim?" Salmissra laughed. "I have nothing to fear from him."

"Not the Grolim," Maas said. "That one." He flickered his tongue at Garion. "Its mind is awake."

"That's impossible," she objected.

"Nevertheless, its mind is awake. It has to do, I think, with that metal thing around its neck."

"Remove the ornament, then," she told the snake.

Maas lowered his length to the floor and slid around the divan toward Garion.

"*Remain very still,*" Garion's inner voice told him. "*Don't try to fight.*"

Numbly, Garion watched the blunt head draw closer.

Maas raised his head, his hood flaring. His nervous tongue darted. Slowly he leaned forward. His nose touched the silver amulet hanging about Garion's neck.

There was a bright blue spark as the reptile's head came in contact with the amulet. Garion felt the familiar surge, but tightly controlled now, focused down to a single point. Maas recoiled, and the spark from the amulet leaped out, sizzling through the air, linking the silver disc to the reptile's nose. The snake's eyes began to shrivel and steam poured from his nostrils and his gaping mouth.

Then the spark was gone, and the body of the dead snake writhed and twisted convulsively on the polished stone floor of the chamber.

"Maas!" Salmissra shrieked.

The eunuchs scrambled out of the way of the wildly thrashing body of the snake.

"My Queen!" a shaved-headed functionary gibbered from the door, "the world is ending!"

"What?" Salmissra tore her eyes from the convulsions of the snake.

"The sun has gone out! Noon is as dark as midnight! The city is gone mad with terror!"

CHAPTER TWENTY-NINE

In the tumult which followed that announcement, Garion sat quietly on the cushions beside Salmissra's throne. The quiet voice in his mind, however, was speaking to him rapidly. "*Stay very still,*" the voice told him. "*Don't say anything, and don't do anything.*"

"Get my astronomers here immediately!" Salmissra ordered. "I want to know why I wasn't warned about this eclipse."

"It's not an eclipse, my Queen," the bald functionary wailed, groveling on the polished floor not far from the still-writhing Maas. "The dark came like a great curtain. It was like a moving wall—no wind, no rain, no thunder. It swallowed the sun without a sound." He began to sob brokenly. "We shall never see the sun again."

"Stop that, you idiot," Salmissra snapped. "Get on your feet. Sadi, take this babbling fool out of here and go look at the sky. Then come back to me here. I have to know what's going on."

Sadi shook himself almost like a dog coming out of the water and pulled his fascinated eyes off the dead, fixed grin on the face of Maas. He pulled the blubbering functionary to his feet and led him out of the chamber.

Salmissra turned then on Garion. "How did you do that?" she demanded, pointing at the twitching form of Maas.

"I don't know," he said. His mind was still sunk in fog. Only the quiet corner where the voice lived was alert.

"Take off that amulet," she commanded.

Obediently, Garion reached his hands toward the medallion. Suddenly his hands froze. They would not move. He let them fall. "I can't," he said.

"Take it from him," she ordered one of the eunuchs. The man glanced once at the dead snake, then stared at Garion. He shook his head and backed away in fright.

"Do as I say!" the Snake Queen ordered sharply.

From somewhere in the palace came a hollow, reverberating crash. There was the sound of nails screeching out of heavy wood and the avalanche noise of a wall collapsing. Then, a long way down one of the dim corridors, some-one screamed in agony.

The dry consciousness in his mind reached out, probing. "At last," it said with obvious relief.

"What's going on out there?" Salmissra blazed.

"Come with me," the voice in Garion's mind said. "I need your help."

Garion put his hands under him and started to push himself up.

"No. This way." A strange image of separation rose in Garion's mind. Unthinking, he willed the separation and felt himself rising and yet not mov-ing. Suddenly he had no sense of his body—no arms or legs—yet he seemed to move. He saw himself—his own body—sitting stupidly on the cushions at Salmissra's feet.

"Hurry," the voice said to him. It was no longer inside his mind but seemed to be somewhere beside him. A dim shape was there, formless but somehow very familiar.

The fog that had clouded Garion's wits was gone, and he felt very alert. "Who are you?" he demanded of the shape beside him.

"There isn't time to explain. Quickly, we have to lead them back before Salmissra has time to do anything."

"Lead who?"

"Polgara and Barak."

"Aunt Pol? Where is she?"

"Come," the voice said urgently. Together Garion and the strange pres-ence at his side seemed to waft toward the closed door. They passed through it as if it were no more than insubstantial mist and emerged in the corridor outside.

Then they were flying, soaring down the corridor with no sense of air rushing past or even of movement. A moment later they came out into that vast open hall where Issus had first brought Garion when they had entered the palace. There they stopped, hovering in the air.

Aunt Pol, her splendid eyes ablaze and a fiery nimbus about her, strode through the hall. Beside her hulked the great shaggy bear Garion had seen before. Barak's face seemed vaguely within that bestial head, but there was no humanity in it. The beast's eyes were afire with raging madness, and its mouth gaped horribly.

Desperate guards tried to push the bear back with long pikes, but the beast swiped the pikes away and fell upon the guards. Its vast embrace crushed them, and its flailing claws ripped them open. The trail behind Aunt Pol and the bear was littered with maimed bodies and quivering chunks of flesh.

The snakes which had lain in the corners were seething across the floor, but as they came into contact with the flaming light which surrounded Aunt Pol, they died even as Maas had died.

Methodically, Aunt Pol was blasting down doors with word and gesture. A thick wall barred her way, and she brushed it into rubble as if it had been made of cobwebs.

Barak raged through the dim hall, roaring insanely, destroying everything in his path. A shrieking eunuch tried desperately to climb one of the pillars. The great beast reared up and hooked his claws into the man's back and pulled him down. The shrieks ended abruptly in a spurt of brains and blood when the massive jaws closed with a sickening crunch on the eunuch's head.

"Polgara!" the presence beside Garion shouted soundlessly. "This way!"

Aunt Pol turned quickly.

"Follow us," the presence said. "Hurry!"

Then Garion and that other part of himself were flying back down the corridor toward Salmissra and the semiconscious body they had recently vacated. Behind them came Aunt Pol and the ravening Barak.

Garion and his strange companion passed again through the heavy, closed door.

Salmissra, her naked body mottled now with rage rather than lust beneath her transparent gown, stood over the vacant-eyed form on the cushions. "Answer me!" she was shouting. "Answer me!"

"When we get back," the shapeless presence said, "let me handle things. We have to buy some time."

And then they were back. Garion felt his body shudder briefly, and he was looking out through his own eyes again. The fog which had benumbed him before came rushing back. "What?" his lips said, though he had not consciously formed the word.

"I said, is this your doing?" Salmissra demanded.

"Is what my doing?" The voice coming from his lips sounded like his, but there was a subtle difference.

"All of it," she said. "The darkness. The attack on my palace."

"I don't think so. How could I? I'm only a boy."

"Don't lie to me, Belgarion," she demanded. "I know who you are. I know what you are. It has to be you. Belgarath himself could not blot out the sun. I warn you, Belgarion, what you have drunk today is death. Even now the poison in your veins is killing you."

"Why did you do that to me?"

"To keep you. You must have more or you will die. You must drink what only I can give you, and you must drink every day of your life. You're mine, Belgarion, *mine!*"

Despairing shrieks came from just outside the door.

The Serpent Queen looked up, startled, then she turned to the huge statue behind her, bowed down in a strange ceremonial way and began to weave her hands through the air in a series of intricate gestures. She started to pronounce an involved formula in a language Garion had never heard before, a language filled with guttural hissings and strange cadences.

The heavy door exploded inward, blasted into splinters, and Aunt Pol stood in the shattered doorway, her white lock ablaze and her eyes dreadful. The great bear at her side roared, his teeth dripping blood and with tatters of flesh still hanging from his claws.

"I've warned you, Salmissra." Aunt Pol spoke in a deadly voice.

"Stop where you are, Polgara," the queen ordered. She did not turn around, and her fingers continued their sinuous weaving in the air. "The boy is dying," she said. "Nothing can save him if you attack me."

Aunt Pol stopped. "What have you done?" she demanded.

"Look at him," Salmissra said. "He has drunk athal and kaldiss. Even now their fire is in his veins. He will need more very soon." Her hands still moved in the air, and her face was fixed in extreme concentration. Her lips began moving again in that guttural hissing.

"*Is it true?*" Aunt Pol's voice echoed in Garion's mind.

"*It seems to be,*" the dry voice replied. "*They made him drink things, and he seems different now.*"

Aunt Pol's eyes widened. "*Who are you?*"

"*I've always been here, Polgara. Didn't you know that?*"

"*Did Garion know?*"

"*He knows that I'm here. He doesn't know what it means.*"

"*We can talk about that later,*" she decided. "*Watch very closely. This is what you have to do.*" A confused blur of images welled up in Garion's mind. "*Do you understand?*"

"*Of course. I'll show him how.*"

"*Can't you do it?*"

"*No, Polgara,*" the dry voice said. "*The power is his, not mine. Don't worry. He and I understand each other.*"

Garion felt strangely alone as the two voices spoke together in his mind.

"*Garion.*" The dry voice spoke quietly. "*I want you to think about your blood.*"

"*My blood?*"

"*We're going to change it for a moment.*"

"*Why?*"

"*To burn away the poison they gave you. Now concentrate on your blood.*"

Garion did.

"*You want it to be like this.*" An image of yellow came into Garion's mind. "*Do you understand?*"

"*Yes.*"

"Do it, then. Now."

Garion put his fingertips to his chest and willed his blood to change. He suddenly felt as if he were on fire. His heart began to pound, and a heavy sweat burst out all over his body.

"A *moment longer*," the voice said.

Garion was dying. His altered blood seared through his veins, and he began to tremble violently. His heart hammered in his chest like a tripping sledge. His eyes went dark, and he began to topple slowly forward.

"*Now!*" the voice demanded sharply. "*Change it back.*"

Then it was over. Garion's heart stuttered and then faltered back to its normal pace. He was exhausted, but the fog in his brain was gone.

"It's done, Polgara," the other Garion said. "*You can do what needs doing now.*"

Aunt Pol had watched anxiously, but now her face became dreadfully stern. She walked across the polished floor toward the dais. "Salmissra," she said, "turn around and look at me."

The queen's hands were raised above her head now, and the hissing words tumbled from her lips, rising finally to a hoarse shout.

Then, far above them in the shadows near the ceiling, the eyes of the huge statue opened and began to glow a deep emerald fire. A polished jewel on Salmissra's crown began also to burn with the same glow.

The statue moved. The sound it made was a kind of ponderous creaking, deafeningly loud. The solid rock from which the huge shape had been hewn bent and flexed as the statue took a step forward and then another.

"Why—did—you—summon—me?" An enormous voice demanded through stiff, stony lips. The voice reverberated hollowly up from the massive chest.

"Defend thy handmaiden, Great Issa," Salmissra cried, turning to look triumphantly at Aunt Pol. "This evil sorceress hath invaded thy domain to slay me. Her wicked power is so great that none may withstand her. I am thy promised bride, and I place myself under thy protection."

"Who is this who defiles my temple?" the statue demanded in a vast roar. "Who dares to raise her hand against my chosen and beloved?" The emerald eyes flashed in dreadful wrath.

Aunt Pol stood alone in the center of the polished floor with the vast statue looming above her. Her face was unafraid. "You go too far, Salmissra," she said. "This is forbidden."

The Serpent Queen laughed scornfully. "Forbidden? What does your forbidding mean to me? Flee now, or face the wrath of Divine Issa. Contend if you will with a God!"

"If I must," Aunt Pol said. She straightened then and spoke a single word. The roaring in Garion's mind at that word was overwhelming. Then, suddenly, she began to grow. Foot by foot she towered up, rising like a tree, expanding, growing gigantic before Garion's stunned eyes. Within a moment she faced the great stone God as an equal.

"Polgara?" The God's voice sounded puzzled. "Why have you done this?"

"I come in fulfillment of the Prophecy, Lord Issa," she said. "Thy hand-maiden hath betrayed thee and thy brothers."

"It cannot be so," Issa said. "She is my chosen one. Her face is the face of my beloved."

"The face is the same," Aunt Pol said, "but this is not the Salmissra beloved of Issa. A hundred Salmissras have served thee in this temple since thy beloved died."

"Died?" the God said incredulously.

"She lies!" Salmissra shrieked. "I am thy beloved, O my Lord. Let not her lies turn thee from me. Kill her."

"The Prophecy approaches its day," Aunt Pol said. "The boy at Salmissra's feet is its fruit. He must be returned to me, or the Prophecy will fail."

"Is the day of the Prophecy come so soon?" the God asked.

"It is not soon, Lord Issa," Aunt Pol said. "It is late. Thy slumber hath encompassed eons."

"Lies! All lies!" Salmissra cried desperately, clinging to the ankle of the huge stone God.

"I must test out the truth of this," the God said slowly. "I have slept long and deeply, and now the world comes upon me unaware."

"Destroy her, O my Lord!" Salmissra demanded. "Her lies are an abomination and a desecration of thy holy presence."

"I will find the truth, Salmissra," Issa said.

Garion felt a brief, enormous touch upon his mind. Something had brushed him—something so vast that his imagination shuddered back from its immensity. Then the touch moved on.

"Ahhh—" the sigh came from the floor. The dead snake Maas stirred. "Ahhh— Let me sleep," it hissed.

"In but a moment," Issa said. "What was your name?"

"I was called Maas," the snake said. "I was counsellor and companion to Eternal Salmissra. Send me back, Lord. I cannot bear to live again."

"Is this my beloved Salmissra?" the God asked.

"Her successor." Maas sighed. "Thy beloved priestess died thousands of years ago. Each new Salmissra is chosen because of her resemblance to thy beloved."

"Ah," Issa said with pain in his huge voice. "And what was this woman's purpose in removing Belgarion from Polgara's care?"

"She sought alliance with Torak," Maas said. "She thought to trade Belgarion to the Accursed One in exchange for the immortality his embrace would bestow upon her."

"His embrace? My priestess would submit to the foul embrace of my mad brother?"

"Willingly, Lord," Maas said. "It is her nature to seek the embrace of any man or God or beast who passes."

A look of repugnance flickered across Issa's stony face. "Has it always been so?" he asked.

"Always, Lord," Maas said. "The potion which maintains her youth and semblance to thy beloved sets her veins afire with lust. That fire remains unquenched until she dies. Let me go, Lord. The pain!"

"Sleep, Maas," Issa granted sorrowfully. "Take my thanks with you down into silent death."

"Ahhh—" Maas sighed and sank down again.

"I too will return to slumber," Issa said. "I must not remain, lest my presence rouse Torak to that war which would unmake the world." The great statue stepped back to the spot where it had stood for thousands of years. The deafening creak and groan of flexing rock again filled the huge chamber. "Deal with this woman as it pleases thee, Polgara," the stone God said. "Only spare her life out of remembrance of my beloved."

"I will, Lord Issa," Aunt Pol said, bowing to the statue.

"And carry my love to my brother, Aldur," the hollow voice said, fading even as it spoke.

"Sleep, Lord," Aunt Pol said. "May thy slumber wash away thy grief."

"No!" Salmissra wailed, but the green fire had already died in the statue's eyes, and the jewel on her crown flickered and went dark.

"It's time, Salmissra," Aunt Pol, vast and terrible, announced.

"Don't kill me, Polgara," the queen begged, falling to her knees. "Please don't kill me."

"I'm not going to kill you, Salmissra," Aunt Pol told her. "I promised Lord Issa that I would spare your life."

"I didn't make any such promise," Barak said from the doorway. Garion looked sharply at his huge friend, dwarfed now by Aunt Pol's immensity. The bear was gone, and in its place the big Cherek stood, sword in hand.

"No, Barak. I'm going to solve the problem of Salmissra once and for all." Aunt Pol turned back to the groveling queen. "You will live, Salmissra. You'll live for a very long time—eternally, perhaps."

An impossible hope dawned in Salmissra's eyes. Slowly she rose to her feet and looked up at the huge figure rising above. her. "Eternally, Polgara?" she asked.

"But I must change you," Aunt Pol said. "The poison you've drunk to keep you young and beautiful is slowly killing you. Even now its traces are beginning to show on your face."

The queen's hands flew to her cheeks, and she turned quickly to look into her mirror.

"You're decaying, Salmissra," Aunt Pol said. "Soon you'll be ugly and old. The lust which fills you will burn itself out, and you'll die. Your blood's too warm; that's the whole problem."

"But how—" Salmissra faltered.

"A little change," Aunt Pol assured her. "Just a small one, and you'll live forever." Garion could feel the force of her will gathering itself. "I will make you eternal, Salmissra." She raised her hand and spoke a single word. The terrible force of that word shook Garion like a leaf in the wind.

At first nothing seemed to happen. Salmissra stood fixed with her pale nakedness gleaming through her gown. Then the strange mottling grew more pronounced, and her thighs pressed tightly together. Her face began to shift, to grow more pointed. Her lips disappeared as her mouth spread, and its corners slid up into a fixed reptilian grin.

Garion watched in horror, unable to take his eyes off the queen. Her gown slid away as her shoulders disappeared and her arms adhered to her sides. Her body began to elongate, and her legs, grown completely together now, began to loop into coils. Her lustrous hair disappeared, and the last vestiges of humanity faded from her face. Her golden crown, however, remained firmly upon her head. Her tongue flickered as she sank down into the mass of her loops and coils. The hood upon her neck spread as she looked with flat, dead eyes at Aunt Pol, who had somehow during the queen's transformation resumed her normal size.

"Ascend your throne, Salmissra," Aunt Pol said.

The queen's head remained immobile, but her coils looped and mounted the cushioned divan, and the sound of coil against coil was a dry, dusty rasp.

Aunt Pol turned to Sadi the eunuch. "Behold the Handmaiden of Issa, the queen of the snake-people, whose dominion shall endure until the end of days, for she *is* immortal now and will reign in Nyissa forever."

Sadi's face was ghastly pale, and his eyes bulged wildly. He swallowed hard and nodded.

"I'll leave you with your queen, then," she told him. "I'd prefer to go peacefully, but one way or another, the boy and I are leaving."

"I'll send word ahead," Sadi agreed quickly. "No one will try to bar your way."

"Wise decision," Barak said dryly.

"All hail the Serpent Queen of Nyissa," one of the crimson-robed eunuchs pronounced in a shaking voice, sinking to his knees before the dais.

"Praise her," the others responded ritualistically, also kneeling.

"Her glory is revealed to us."

"Worship her."

Garion glanced back once as he followed Aunt Pol toward the shattered door. Salmissra lay upon her throne with her mottled coils redundantly piled and her hooded head turned toward the mirror. The golden crown sat atop her head, and her flat, serpent eyes regarded her reflection in the glass. There was no expression on her reptile face, so it was impossible to know what she was thinking.

CHAPTER THIRTY

The corridors and vaulted halls of the palace were empty as Aunt Pol led them from the throne room where the eunuchs knelt, chanting their praises to the Serpent Queen. Sword in hand, Barak stalked grimly through the awful carnage that marked the trail he had left when he had entered. The big man's face was pale, and he frequently averted his eyes from some of the more savagely mutilated corpses that littered their way.

When they emerged, they found the streets of Sthiss Tor darker than night and filled with hysterical crowds wailing in terror. Barak, with a torch he had taken from the palace wall in one hand and his huge sword in the other, led them into the street. Even in their panic the Nyissans made way for him.

"What is this, Polgara?" he growled over his shoulder, waving the torch slightly as if to brush the darkness away. "Is it some kind of sorcery?"

"No," she answered. "It's not sorcery."

Tiny flecks of gray were falling through the torchlight.

"Snow?" Barak asked incredulously.

"No," she said. "Ashes."

"What's burning?"

"A mountain," she replied. "Let's go back to the ship as quickly as we can. There's more danger from this crowd than from any of this." She threw her light cloak about Garion's shoulders and pointed down a street where a few torches bobbed here and there. "Let's go that way."

The ash began to fall more heavily. It was almost like dirty gray flour sifting down through the sodden air, and there was a dreadful, sulfurous stink to it.

By the time they reached the wharves, the absolute darkness had begun to pale. The ash continued to drift down, seeping into the cracks between the cobblestones and gathering in little windrows along the edges of the buildings. Though it was growing lighter, the falling ash, like fog, blotted out everything more than ten feet away.

The wharves were total chaos. Crowds of Nyissans, shrieking and wailing, were trying to climb into boats to flee from the choking ash that sifted with deadly silence down through the damp air. Mad with terror, many even leaped into the deadly water of the river.

"We're not going to be able to get through that mob, Polgara," Barak said. "Stay here a moment." He sheathed his sword, jumped up and caught the edge of a low roof. He pulled himself up and stood outlined dimly above them. "Ho, Greldik!" he roared in a huge voice that carried even over the noise of the crowd.

"Barak!" Greldik's voice came back. "Where are you?"

"At the foot of the pier," Barak shouted. "We can't get through the crowd."

"Stay there," Greldik yelled back. "We'll come and get you."

After a few moments there was the tramp of heavy feet on the wharf and the occasional sound of blows. A few cries of pain mingled with the sounds of panic from the crowd. Then Greldik, Mandorallen and a half-dozen burly sailors armed with clubs strode out of the ashfall, clearing a path with brutal efficiency.

"Did you get lost?" Greldik yelled up to Barak.

Barak jumped down from the roof. "We had to stop by the palace," he answered shortly.

"We were growing concerned for thy safety, my Lady," Mandorallen told Aunt Pol, pushing a gibbering Nyissan out of his way. "Good Durnik re-turned some hours ago."

"We were delayed," she said. "Captain, can you get us on board your ship?"

Greldik gave her an evil grin.

"Let's go, then," she urged. "As soon as we get on board, it might be a good idea to anchor out in the river a little way. This ash will settle after a while, but these people are going to be hysterical until it does. Has there been any word from Silk or my father yet?"

"Nothing, my Lady," Greldik said.

"What *is* he doing?" she demanded irritably of no one in particular.

Mandorallen drew his broadsword and marched directly into the face of the crowd, neither slowing nor altering his course. The Nyissans melted out of his path.

The crowd pressing at the edge of the wharf beside Greldik's ship was even thicker, and Durnik, Hettar and the rest of the sailors lined the rail with long boat-hooks, pushing the terror-stricken people away.

"Run out the plank," Greldik shouted as they reached the edge of the wharf.

"Noble captain," a bald Nyissan blubbered, clinging to Greldik's fur vest. "I'll give you a hundred gold pieces if you'll let me aboard your ship."

Disgusted, Greldik pushed him away.

"A thousand gold pieces," the Nyissan promised, clutching Greldik's arm and waving a purse.

"Get this baboon off me," Greldik ordered.

One of the sailors rather casually clubbed the Nyissan into insensibility, then bent and yanked the purse from his grip. He opened the purse and poured the coins out into one hand. "Three pieces of silver," he said with dis-gust. "All the rest is copper." He turned back and kicked the unconscious man in the stomach.

They crossed to the ship one by one while Barak and Mandorallen held the crowd back with the threat of massive violence.

"Cut the hawsers," Greldik shouted when they were all aboard.

The sailors chopped the thick hawsers loose to a great cry of dismay from the Nyissans crowding the edge of the wharf. The sluggish current pulled the ship slowly away, and wails and despairing moans followed them as they drifted.

"Garion," Aunt Pol said, "why don't you go below and put on some decent clothes? And wash that disgusting rouge off your face. Then come back up here. I want to talk to you."

Garion had forgotten how scantily he was dressed and he flushed slightly and went quickly below decks.

It had grown noticeably lighter when he came back up, dressed again in tunic and hose, but the gray ash still sifted down through the motionless air, making the world around them hazy and coating everything with a heavy layer of fine grit. They had drifted some distance out into the river, and Greldik's sailors had dropped the anchor. The ship swung slowly in the sluggish current.

"Over here, Garion," Aunt Pol called. She was standing near the prow, looking out into the dusty haze. Garion went to her a little hesitantly, the memory of what had happened at the palace still strong in his mind.

"Sit down, dear," she suggested. "There's something I have to talk to you about."

"Yes, ma'am," he said, sitting on the bench there.

"Garion." She turned to look at him. "Did anything happen while you were in Salmissra's palace?"

"What do you mean?"

"You know what I mean," she said rather crisply. "You're not going to embarrass us both by making me ask certain questions, are you?"

"Oh." Garion blushed. "That! No, nothing like that happened." He remembered the lush overripeness of the queen with a certain regret.

"Good. That was the one thing I was afraid of. You can't afford to get involved in any of that sort of thing just yet. It has some peculiar effects on one in your rather special circumstances."

"I'm not sure I understand," he said.

"You have certain abilities," she told him. "And if you start experimenting with that other thing before they're fully matured, the results can sometimes be a bit unpredictable. It's better not to confuse things at this point."

"Maybe it'd be better if something *had* happened, then," Garion blurted. "Maybe it would have fixed it so I couldn't hurt people anymore."

"I doubt it," she said. "Your power's too great to be neutralized so easily. Do you remember what we talked about that day when we left Tolnedra— about instruction?"

"I don't need any instruction," he protested, his tone growing sullen.

"Yes, you do," she said, "and you need it now. Your power is enormous— more power than I've ever seen before, and some of it so complex that I can't even begin to understand it. You *must* begin your instruction before something disastrous happens. You're totally out of control, Garion. If you're really serious about not wanting to hurt people, you should be more than willing to start learning how to keep any accidents from happening."

"I don't *want* to be a sorcerer," he objected. "All I want to do is get rid of it. Can't you help me do that?"

She shook her head. "No. And I wouldn't even if I could. You can't renounce it, my Garion. It's part of you."

"Then I'm going to be a monster?" Garion demanded bitterly. "I'm going to go around burning people alive or turning them into toads or snakes? And maybe after a while I'll get so used to it that it won't even bother me anymore. I'll live forever—like you and grandfather—but I won't be human anymore. Aunt Pol, I think I'd rather be dead."

"*Can't you reason with him?*" Her voice inside his head spoke directly to that other awareness.

"*Not at the moment, Polgara,*" the dry voice replied. "*He's too busy wallowing in self-pity.*"

"*He must learn to control the power he has,*" she said.

"*I'll keep him out of mischief,*" the voice promised. "*I don't think there's much else we can do until Belgarath gets back. He's going through a moral crisis, and we can't really tamper with him until he works out his own solutions to it.*"

"*I don't like to see him suffering this way.*"

"*You're too tender-hearted, Polgara. He's a sturdy boy, and a bit of suffering won't damage him.*"

"Will the two of you stop treating me as if I'm not even here?" Garion demanded angrily.

"Mistress Pol," Durnik said, coming across the deck to them, "I think you'd better come quickly. Barak's going to kill himself."

"He's *what?*" she asked.

"It's something about some curse," Durnik explained. "He says he's going to fall on his sword."

"That idiot! Where is he?"

"He's back by the stern," Durnik said. "He's got his sword out, and he won't let anybody near him."

"Come with me." She started toward the stern with Garion and Durnik behind her.

"We have all experienced battle madness, my Lord," Mandorallen was saying, trying to reason with the big Cherek. "It is not a thing of which to be proud, but neither is it a cause for such bleak despair."

Barak did not answer, but stood at the very stern of the ship, his eyes blank with horror and his huge sword weaving in a slow, menacing arc, holding everyone at bay.

Aunt Pol walked through the crowd of sailors and directly up to him.

"Don't try to stop me, Polgara," he warned.

She reached out quite calmly and touched the point of his sword with one finger. "It's a little dull," she said thoughtfully. "Why don't we have

Durnik sharpen it? That way it'll slip more smoothly between your ribs when you fall on it."

Barak looked a bit startled.

"Have you made all the necessary arrangements?" she asked.

"What arrangements?"

"For the disposal of your body," she told him. "Really, Barak, I thought you had better manners. A decent man doesn't burden his friends with that kind of chore." She thought a moment. "Burning is customary, I suppose, but the wood here in Nyissa's very soggy. You'd probably smolder for a week or more. I imagine we'll have to settle for just dumping you in the river. The leeches and crayfish should have you stripped to the bone in a day or so."

Barak's expression grew hurt.

"Did you want us to take your sword and shield back to your son?" she asked.

"I don't have a son," he answered sullenly. He was obviously not prepared for her brutal practicality.

"Oh, didn't I tell you? How forgetful of me."

"What are you talking about?"

"Never mind," she said. "It's not important now. Were you just going to fall on your sword, or would you prefer to run up against the mast with the hilt? Either way works rather well." She turned to the sailors. "Would you clear a path so the Earl of Trellheim can get a good run at the mast?"

The sailors stared at her.

"What did you mean about a son?" Barak asked, lowering his sword.

"It would only unsettle your mind, Barak," she answered. "You'd probably make a mess of killing yourself if I told you about it. We'd really rather not have you lying around groaning for weeks on end. That sort of thing is so depressing, you know."

"I want to know what you're talking about!"

"Oh, very well," she said with a great sigh. "Your wife Merel is with child—the result of certain courtesies you exchanged when we visited Val Alorn, I imagine. She looks like a rising moon at the moment, and your lusty brat is making her life miserable with his kicking."

"A son?" Barak said, his eyes suddenly very wide.

"Really, Barak," she protested. "You must learn to pay attention. You'll never make anything of yourself if you keep blundering around with your ears closed like this."

"A son?" he repeated, his sword sliding out of his fingers.

"Now you've dropped it," she chided him. "Pick it up immediately, and let's get on with this. It's very inconsiderate to take all day to kill yourself like this."

"I'm not going to kill myself," he told her indignantly.

"You're not?"

"Of course not," he sputtered, and then he saw the faint flicker of a smile playing about the corners of her mouth. He hung his head sheepishly.

"You great fool," she said. Then she took hold of his beard with both hands, pulled his head down and kissed his ash-dusted face soundly.

Greldik began to chortle, and Mandorallen stepped forward and caught Barak in a rough embrace. "I rejoice with thee, my friend," he said. "My heart soars for thee."

"Bring up a cask," Greldik told the sailors, pounding on his friend's back. "We'll salute Trellheim's heir with the bright brown ale of timeless Cherek."

"I expect this will get rowdy now," Aunt Pol said quietly to Garion. "Come with me." She led the way back toward the ship's prow.

"Will she ever change back?" Garion asked when they were alone again.

"What?"

"The queen," Garion explained. "Will she ever change back again?"

"In time she won't even want to," Aunt Pol answered. "The shapes we assume begin to dominate our thinking after a while. As the years go by, she'll become more and more a snake and less and less a woman."

Garion shuddered. "It would have been kinder to have killed her."

"I promised Lord Issa that I wouldn't," she said.

"Was that really the God?"

"His spirit," she replied, looking out into the hazy ashfall. "Salmissra infused the statue with Issa's spirit. For a time at least the statue was the God. It's all very complicated." She seemed a bit preoccupied. "Where *is* he?" She seemed suddenly irritated.

"Who?"

"Father. He should have been here days ago."

They stood together looking out at the muddy river.

Finally she turned from the railing and brushed at the shoulders of her cloak with distaste. The ash puffed from under her fingers in tiny clouds. "I'm going below," she told him, making a face. "It's just too dirty up here."

"I thought you wanted to talk to me," he said.

"I don't think you're ready to listen. It'll wait." She stepped away, then stopped. "Oh, Garion."

"Yes?"

"I wouldn't drink any of that ale the sailors are swilling. After what they made you drink at the palace, it would probably make you sick."

"Oh," he agreed a trifle regretfully. "All right."

"It's up to you, of course," she said, "but I thought you ought to know." Then she turned again and went to the hatch and disappeared down the stairs.

Garion's emotions were turbulent. The entire day had been vastly eventful, and his mind was filled with a welter of confusing images.

"*Be quiet,*" the voice in his mind said.

"What?"

"*I'm trying to hear something. Listen.*"

"Listen to what?"

"*There. Can't you hear it?*"

Faintly, as if from a very long way off, Garion seemed to hear a muffled thudding.

"What is it?"

The voice did not answer, but the amulet about his neck began to throb in time with the distant thudding.

Behind him he heard a rush of tiny feet.

"Garion!" He turned just in time to be caught in Ce'Nedra's embrace. "I was so worried about you. Where did you go?"

"Some men came on board and grabbed me," he said, trying to untangle himself from her arms. "They took me to the palace."

"How awful!" she said. "Did you meet the queen?"

Garion nodded and then shuddered, remembering the hooded snake lying on the divan looking at itself in the mirror.

"What's wrong?" the girl asked.

"A lot of things happened," he answered. "Some of them weren't very pleasant." Somewhere at the back of his awareness, the thudding continued.

"Do you mean they tortured you?" Ce'Nedra asked, her eyes growing very wide.

"No, nothing like that."

"Well, what happened?" she demanded. "Tell me."

He knew that she would not leave him alone until he did, so he described what had happened as best he could. The throbbing sound seemed to grow louder while he talked, and his right palm began to tingle. He rubbed at it absently.

"How absolutely dreadful," Ce'Nedra said after he had finished. "Weren't you terrified?"

"Not really," he told her, still scratching at his palm. "Most of the time the things they made me drink made my head so foggy I couldn't feel anything."

"Did you really kill Maas?" she asked, "just like that?" She snapped her fingers.

"It wasn't exactly just like that," he tried to explain. "There was a little more to it."

"I *knew* you were a sorcerer," she said. "I told you that you were that day at the pool, remember?"

"I don't want to be," he protested. "I didn't ask to be."

"I didn't ask to be a princess either."

"It's not the same. Being a king or a princess is what one *is*. Being a sorcerer has to do with what one *does*."

"I really don't see that much difference," she objected stubbornly.

"I can make things happen," he told her. "Awful things, usually."

"So?" she said maddeningly. "I can make awful things happen too—or at least I could back in Tol Honeth. One word from me could have sent a servant to the whipping-post—or to the headsman's block. I didn't do it of course, but I could have. Power is power, Garion. The results are the same. You don't have to hurt people if you don't want to."

"It just happens sometimes. It's not that I want to do it." The throbbing had become a nagging thing, almost like a dull headache.

"Then you have to learn to control it."

"Now you sound like Aunt Pol."

"She's trying to help you," the princess said. "She keeps trying to get you to do what you're going to have to do eventually anyway. How many more people are you going to have to burn up before you finally accept what she says?"

"You didn't have to say that." Garion was stung deeply by her words.

"Yes," she told him, "I think I did. You're lucky *I'm* not your aunt. I wouldn't put up with your foolishness the way Lady Polgara does."

"You don't understand," Garion muttered sullenly.

"I understand much better than you think, Garion. You know what your problem is? You don't want to grow up. You want to keep on being a boy forever. You can't, though; nobody can. No matter how much power you have—whether you're an emperor or a sorcerer—you can't stop the years from going by. I realized that a long time ago, but then I'm probably much smarter than you are." Then without any word of explanation, she raised up on her toes and kissed him lightly full on the lips.

Garion blushed and lowered his head in embarrassment.

"Tell me," Ce'Nedra said, toying with the sleeve of his tunic, "was Queen Salmissra as beautiful as they say?"

"She was the most beautiful woman I've ever seen in my life," Garion answered without thinking.

The princess caught her breath sharply. "I *hate* you," she cried from between clenched teeth. Then she turned and ran sobbing in search of Aunt Pol.

Garion stared after her in perplexity. He turned then to stare moodily out at the river and the drifting ash. The tingling in his palm was becoming intolerable, and he scratched at it, digging in with his fingernails.

"You'll just make it sore," the voice in his mind said.

"It itches. I can't stand it."

"Stop being a baby."

"What's causing it?"

"Do you mean to say you really don't know? You've got further to go than I thought. Put your right hand on the amulet."

"Why?"

"Just do it, Garion."

Garion reached inside his tunic and put his burning palm on his medallion. As a key fitting into the lock for which it was made, the contact between his hand and the throbbing amulet seemed somehow enormously right. The tingling became that now-familiar surge, and the throbbing began to echo hollowly in his ears.

"Not too much," the voice warned him. *"You're not trying to dry up the river, you know."*

"What's happening? What is all this?"

"*Belgarath's trying to find us.*"

"Grandfather? Where?"

"*Be patient.*"

The throbbing seemed to grow louder until Garion's entire body quivered with each thudding beat. He stared out over the rail, trying to see through the haze. The settling ash, so light that it coated the muddy surface of the river, made everything more than twenty paces away indistinct. It was impossible to see the city, and the wails and cries from the hidden streets seemed somehow muffled. Only the slow wash of the current against the hull seemed clear.

Then a long way out on the river, something moved. It was not very large and seemed to be little more than a dark shadow ghosting silently with the current.

The throbbing grew even louder.

The shadow drew closer, and Garion could just begin to make out the shape of a small boat. An oar caught the surface of the water with a small splash. The man at the oars turned to look over his shoulder. It was Silk. His face was covered with gray ash, and tiny rivulets of sweat streaked his cheeks.

Mister Wolf sat in the stern of the little boat, muffled in his cloak and with his hood turned up.

"*Welcome back, Belgarath,*" the dry voice said.

"*Who's that?*" Wolf's voice in Garion's mind sounded startled. "*Is that you, Belgarion?*"

"*Not quite,*" the voice replied. "*Not yet anyway, but we're getting closer.*"

"*I wondered who was making all the noise.*"

"*He overdoes things sometimes. He'll learn eventually.*"

A shout came from one of the sailors clustered around Barak at the stern, and they all turned to watch the small boat drifting toward them.

Aunt Pol came up from below and stepped to the rail. "You're late," she called.

"Something came up," the old man answered across the narrowing gap. He pushed back his hood and shook the floury ash out of his cloak. Then Garion saw that the old man's left arm was bound up in a dirty sling across the front of his body.

"What happened to your arm?" Aunt Pol asked.

"I'd rather not talk about it." There was an ugly scratch running down one of Wolf's cheeks into his short, white beard, and his eyes seemed to glitter with some huge irritation.

The grin on Silk's ash-coated face was malicious as he dipped his oars once, deftly pulling the little boat in beside Greldik's ship with a slight thump.

"I don't imagine you can be persuaded to keep your mouth shut," Wolf said irritably to the small man.

"Would I say anything, mighty sorcerer?" Silk asked mockingly, his ferret eyes wide with feigned innocence.

"Just help me aboard," Wolf told him, his voice testy. His entire bearing was that of a man who had been mortally insulted.

"Whatever you say, ancient Belgarath," Silk said, obviously trying to keep from laughing. He steadied Wolf as the old man awkwardly climbed over the ship's rail.

"Let's get out of here," Mister Wolf curtly told Captain Greldik, who had just joined them.

"Which way, Ancient One?" Greldik asked carefully, clearly not wanting to aggravate the old man further.

Wolf stared hard at him.

"Upstream or down?" Greldik explained mollifyingly.

"Upstream, of course," Wolf snapped.

"How was I supposed to know?" Greldik appealed to Aunt Pol. Then he turned and crossly began barking orders to his sailors.

Aunt Pol's expression was a peculiar mixture of relief and curiosity. "I'm sure your story's going to be absolutely fascinating, father," she said as the sailors began raising the heavy anchors. "I simply can't wait to hear it."

"I can do without the sarcasm, Pol," Wolf told her. "I've had a very bad day. Try not to make it any worse."

That last was finally too much for Silk. The little man, in the act of climbing across the rail, suddenly collapsed in helpless glee. He tumbled forward to the deck, howling with laughter.

Mister Wolf glared at his laughing companion with a profoundly affronted expression as Greldik's sailors ran out their oars and began turning the ship in the sluggish current.

"What happened to your arm, father?" Aunt Pol's gaze was penetrating, and her tone said quite clearly that she did not intend to be put off any longer.

"I broke it," Wolf told her flatly.

"How did you manage that?"

"It was just a stupid accident, Pol. Those things happen sometimes."

"Let me see it."

"In a minute." He scowled at Silk, who was still laughing. "Will you stop that? Go tell the sailors where we're going."

"Where *are* we going, father?" Aunt Pol asked him. "Did you find Zedar's trail?"

"He crossed into Cthol Murgos. Ctuchik was waiting for him."

"And the Orb?"

"Ctuchik's got it now."

"Are we going to be able to cut him off before he gets to Rak Cthol with it?"

"I doubt it. Anyway, we have to go to the Vale first."

"The Vale? Father, you're not making any sense."

"Our Master's summoned us, Pol. He wants us at the Vale, so that's where we're going."

"What about the Orb?"

"Ctuchik's got it, and I know where to find Ctuchik. He isn't going anyplace. For right now, we're going to the Vale."

"All right, father," she concurred placatingly. "Don't excite yourself." She looked at him closely. "Have you been fighting, father?" she asked dangerously.

"No, I haven't been fighting." He sounded disgusted.

"What happened, then?"

"A tree fell on me."

"What?"

"You heard me."

Silk exploded into fresh howls of mirth at the old man's grudging confession. From the stern of the ship where Greldik and Barak stood at the tiller, the slow beat of the drum began, and the sailors dug in with their oars. The ship slid through the oily water, moving upstream against the current, with Silk's laughter trailing behind in the ash-laden air.

MAGICIAN'S
GAMBIT

For Dorothy,
who has the enduring grace to put up with Eddings men,
and for Wayne,
for reasons we both understand but could never put into words.

PROLOGUE

Being an Account of how Gorim sought a God for his People and of how he found UL upon the sacred Mountain of Prolgu.

—BASED UPON THE BOOK OF ULGO
AND OTHER FRAGMENTS

At the Beginning of Days, the world was spun out of darkness by the seven Gods, and they also created beasts and fowls, serpents and fishes, and lastly Man.

Now there dwelt in the heavens a spirit known as UL who did not join in this creation. And because he withheld his power and wisdom, much that was made was marred and imperfect. Many creatures were unseemly and strange. These the younger Gods sought to unmake, so that all upon the world might be fair.

But UL stretched forth his hand and prevented them, saying: "What you have wrought you may not unmake. You have torn asunder the fabric and peace of the heavens to bring forth this world as a plaything and an entertainment. Know, however, that whatsoever you make, be it ever so monstrous, shall abide as a rebuke for your folly. In the day that one thing which you have made is unmade, *all* shall be unmade."

The younger Gods were angered. To each monstrous or unseemly thing they had made they said: "Go thou unto UL and let *him* be thy God." Then from the races of men, each God chose that people which pleased him. And when there were yet peoples who had no God, the younger Gods drove them forth and said: "Go unto UL, and *he* shall be your God." And UL did not speak.

For long and bitter generations, the Godless Ones wandered and cried out unheard in the wastelands and wilderness of the West.

Then there appeared among their numbers a just and righteous man named Gorim. He gathered the multitudes before him and spoke to them: "We wither and fall as the leaves from the rigors of our wanderings. Our children and our old men die. Better it is that only one shall die. Therefore, stay here and rest upon this plain. I will search for the God named UL so that we may worship him and have a place in this world."

For twenty years, Gorim sought UL, but in vain. Yet the years passed, his hair turned gray, and he wearied of his search. In despair, he went up onto a high mountain and cried in a great voice to the sky: "No more! I will search no longer. The Gods are a mockery and deception, and the world is a barren void. There is no UL, and I am sick of the curse and affliction of my life."

The Spirit of UL heard and replied: "Why art thou wroth with me, Gorim? Thy making and thy casting out were none of my doing."

Gorim was afraid and fell upon his face. And UL spoke again, saying: "Rise, Gorim, for I am not thy God."

Gorim did not arise. "O my God," he cried, "hide not thy face from thy people who are sorely afflicted because they are outcast and have no God to protect them."

"Rise, Gorim," UL repeated, "and quit this place. Cease thy drasty complaining. Seek thou a God elsewhere and leave me in peace."

Still Gorim did not rise. "O my God," he said, "I will still abide. Thy people hunger and thirst. They seek thy blessing and a place where they may dwell."

"Thy speech wearies me," UL said and he departed.

Gorim remained on the mountain, and the beasts of the field and fowls of the air brought him sustenance. For more than a year he remained. Then the monstrous and unseemly things which the Gods had made came and sat at his feet, watching him.

The Spirit of UL was troubled. At last he appeared to Gorim. "Abidest thou still?"

Gorim fell on his face and said: "O my God, thy people cry unto thee in their affliction."

The Spirit of UL fled. But Gorim abode there for another year. Dragons brought him meat, and unicorns gave him water. And again UL came to him, asking: "Abidest thou still?"

Gorim fell on his face. "O my God," he cried, "thy people perish in the absence of thy care." And UL fled from the righteous man.

Another year passed while nameless, unseen things brought him food and drink. And the Spirit of UL came to the high mountain and ordered: "Rise, Gorim."

From his prostrate position, Gorim pleaded: "O my God, have mercy."

"Rise, Gorim," UL replied. He reached down and lifted Gorim up with his hands. "I am UL—thy God. I command thee to rise and stand before me."

"Then wilt thou be my God?" Gorim asked. "And God unto my people?"

"I am thy God and the God of thy people also," UL said.

Gorim looked down from his high place and beheld the unseemly creatures which had cared for him in his travail. "What of these, O my God? Wilt thou be God unto the basilisk and the minotaur, the Dragon and the chimera, the unicorn and the thing unnamed, the winged serpent and the thing unseen? For these are also outcast. Yet there is beauty in each. Turn not thy face from them, O my God, for in them is great worthiness. They were sent to thee by the younger Gods. Who will be their God if you refuse them?"

"It was done in my despite," UL said. "These creatures were sent unto me to bring shame upon me that I had rebuked the younger Gods. I will in no wise be God unto monsters."

The creatures at Gorim's feet moaned. Gorim seated himself on the earth and said: "Yet will I abide, O my God."

"Abide if it please thee," UL said and departed.

It was even as before. Gorim abode, the creatures sustained him, and UL was troubled. And before the holiness of Gorim, the Great God repented and came again. "Rise, Gorim, and serve thy God." UL reached down and lifted Gorim. "Bring unto me the creatures who sit before thee and I will consider them. If each hath beauty and worthiness, as thou sayest, then I will consent to be their God also."

Then Gorim brought the creatures before UL. The creatures prostrated themselves before the God and moaned to beseech his blessing. UL marveled that he had not seen the beauty of each creature before. He raised up his hands and blessed them, saying: "I am UL and I find beauty and worthiness in each of you. I will be your God, and you shall prosper, and peace shall be among you."

Gorim was glad of heart and he named the high place where all had come to pass *Prolgu*, which means "Holy Place." Then he departed and returned to the plain to bring his people unto their God. But they did not know him, for the hands of UL had touched him, and all color had fled, leaving his body and hair as white as new snow. The people feared him and drove him away with stones.

Gorim cried unto UL: "O my God, thy touch has changed me, and my people know me not."

UL raised his hand, and the people were made colorless like Gorim. The Spirit of UL spoke to them in a great voice: "Hearken unto the words of your God. This is he whom you call Gorim, and he has prevailed upon me to accept you as my people, to watch over you, provide for you, and be God over you. Henceforth shall you be called UL-Go in remembrance of me and in token of his holiness. You shall do as he commands and go where he leads. Any who fail to obey him or follow him will I cut off to wither and perish and be no more."

Gorim commanded the people to take up their goods and their cattle and follow him to the mountains. But the elders of the people did not believe him, nor that the voice had been the voice of UL. They spoke to Gorim in despite, saying: "If you are the servant of the God UL, perform a wonder in proof of it."

Gorim answered: "Behold your skin and hair. Is that not wonder enough for you?"

They were troubled and went away. But they came to him again, saying: "The mark upon us is because of a pestilence which you brought from some unclean place and no proof of the favor of UL."

Gorim raised his hands, and the creatures which had sustained him came to him like lambs to a shepherd. The elders were afraid and went away for a time. But soon they came again, saying: "The creatures are monstrous and unseemly. You are a demon sent to lure the people to destruction, not a servant of the Great God UL. We have still seen no proof of the favor of UL."

Now Gorim grew weary of them. He cried in a great voice: "I say to the people that they have heard the voice of UL. I have suffered much in your behalf. Now I return to Prolgu, the holy place. Let him who would follow me do so; let him who would not remain." He turned and went toward the mountains.

Some few people went with him, but the greater part of the people remained, and they reviled Gorim and those who followed him: "Where is this wonder which proves the favor of UL? We do not follow or obey Gorim, yet neither do we wither and perish."

Then Gorim looked upon them in great sadness and spoke to them for the last time: "You have besought a wonder from me. Then behold this wonder. Even as the voice of UL said, you are withered like the limb of a tree that is cut off. Truly, this day you have perished." And he led the few who followed him into the mountains and to Prolgu.

The multitude of the people mocked him and returned to their tents to laugh at the folly of those who followed him. For a year they laughed and mocked. Then they laughed no more, for their women were barren and bore no children. The people withered and in time they perished and were no more.

The people who followed Gorim came with him to Prolgu. There they built a city. The Spirit of UL was with them, and they dwelt in peace with the creatures which had sustained Gorim. Gorim lived for many lifetimes; and after him, each High Priest of UL was named Gorim and lived to a great age. For two thousand years, the peace of UL was with them, and they believed it would last forever.

But the evil God Torak stole the Orb that was made by the God Aldur, and the war of men and Gods began. Torak used the Orb to break the earth asunder and let in the sea, and the Orb burned him horribly. And he fled into Mallorea.

The earth was maddened by her wounding, and the creatures which had dwelt in peace with the people of Ulgo were also maddened by that wounding. They rose against the fellowship of UL and cast down the cities and slew the people, until few remained.

Those who escaped fled to Prolgu, where the creatures dared not follow for fear of the wrath of UL. Loud were the cries and lamentations of the people. UL was troubled and he revealed to them the caves that lay under Prolgu. The people went down into the sacred caves of UL and dwelt there.

In time, Belgarath the Sorcerer led the king of the Alorns and his sons into Mallorea to steal back the Orb. When Torak sought to pursue, the wrath of the Orb drove him back. Belgarath gave the Orb to the first Rivan King, saying that so long as one of his descendants held the Orb, the West would be safe.

Now the Alorns scattered and pushed southward into new lands. And the peoples of other Gods were troubled by the war of Gods and men and fled to seize other lands which they called by strange names. But the people of UL held to the caverns of Prolgu and had no dealings with them. UL protected them and hid them, and the strangers did not know that the people were there. For century after century, the people of UL took no note of the outer world, even when that world was rocked by the assassination of the last Rivan King and his family.

But when Torak came ravening into the West, leading a mighty army through the lands of the children of UL, the Spirit of UL spoke with the Gorim. And the Gorim led forth his people in stealth by night. They fell upon the sleeping army and wreaked mighty havoc. Thus the army of Torak was weakened and fell in defeat before the armies of the West at a place called Vo Mimbre.

Then the Gorim girded himself and went forth to hold council with the victors. And he brought back word that Torak had been gravely wounded. Though the evil God's body was stolen away and hidden by his disciple Belzedar, it was said that Torak would lie bound in a sleep like death itself until a descendant of the Rivan line should again sit upon the throne at Riva—which meant never, since it was known that no descendants of that line lived.

Shocking as the visit of the Gorim to the outer world had been, no harm seemed to come of it. The children of UL still prospered under the care of their God, and life went on almost as before. It was noticed that the Gorim seemed to spend less time studying *The Book of Ulgo* and more searching through moldy old scrolls of prophecy. But a certain oddity might be expected of one who had gone forth from the caverns of UL into the world of other peoples.

Then a strange old man appeared before the entrance to the caverns, demanding to speak with the Gorim. And such was the power of his voice that the Gorim was summoned. Then, for the first time since the people had sought safety in the caverns, one who was not of the people of UL was admitted. The Gorim took the stranger into his chambers and remained closeted with him for days. And thereafter, the strange man with the white beard and tattered clothing appeared at long intervals and was welcomed by the Gorim.

It was even reported once by a young boy that there was a great gray wolf with the Gorim. But that was probably only some dream brought on by sickness, though the boy refused to recant.

The people adjusted and accepted the strangeness of their Gorim. And the years passed, and the people gave thanks to their God, knowing that they were the chosen people of the Great God UL.

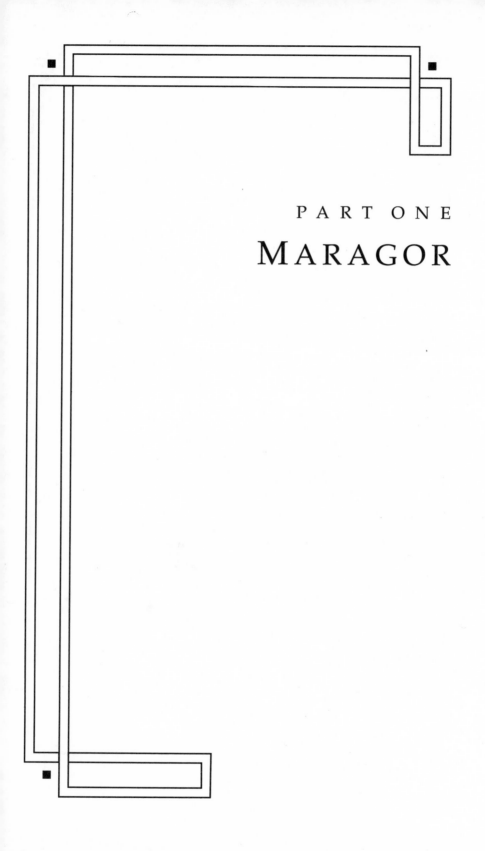

PART ONE

MARAGOR

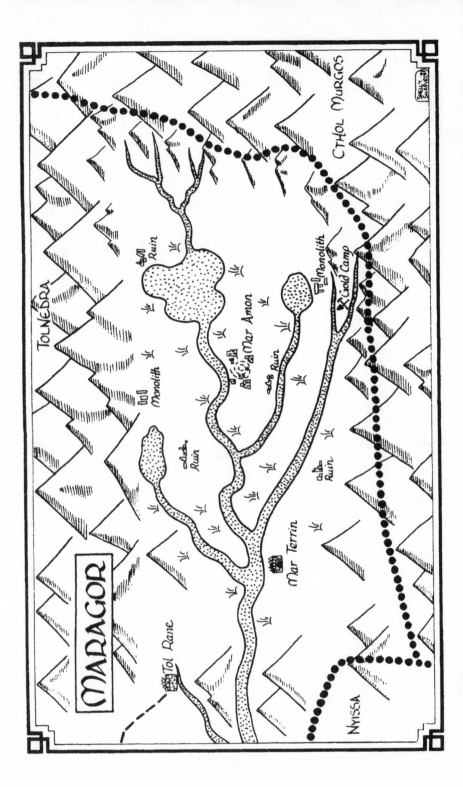

CHAPTER ONE

H er Imperial Highness, Princess Ce'Nedra, jewel of the House
of Borune and the loveliest flower of the Tolnedran Empire,
sat cross-legged on a sea chest in the oak-beamed cabin beneath the stern of
Captain Greldik's ship, nibbling thoughtfully on the end of a tendril of her
coppery hair as she watched the Lady Polgara attend to the broken arm of
Belgarath the Sorcerer. The princess wore a short, pale-green Dryad tunic,
and there was a smudge of ash on one of her cheeks. On the deck above she
could hear the measured beat of the drum that paced the oar strokes of Greldik's sailors as they rowed upstream from the ash-choked city of Sthiss Tor.

It was all absolutely dreadful, she decided. What had begun as merely another move in the interminable game of authority and rebellion against it
that she had been playing with her father, the Emperor, for as long as she
could remember had suddenly turned deadly serious. She had never really intended for things to go this far when she and Master Jeebers had crept from
the Imperial Palace in Tol Honeth that night so many weeks ago. Jeebers had
soon deserted her—he had been no more than a temporary convenience,
anyway—and now she was caught up with this strange group of grim-faced
people from the north in a quest she could not even understand. The Lady
Polgara, whose very name sent a chill through the princess, had rather
bluntly informed her in the Wood of the Dryads that the game was over and
that no evasion, wheedling, or coaxing would alter the fact that she, Princess
Ce'Nedra, *would* stand in the Hall of the Rivan King on her sixteenth
birthday—in chains if necessary. Ce'Nedra knew with absolute certainty that
Lady Polgara had meant exactly that, and she had a momentary vision of being dragged, clanking and rattling in her chains, to stand in total humiliation
in that grim hall while hundreds of bearded Alorns laughed at her. That had
to be avoided at any cost. And so it had been that she had accompanied
them—not willingly, perhaps—but never openly rebellious. The hint of steel
in Lady Polgara's eyes always seemed to carry with it the suggestion of man-
acles and clinking chains, and that suggestion cowed the princess into obedience far more than all the Imperial power her father possessed had ever
been able to do.

Ce'Nedra had only the faintest idea of what these people were doing.
They seemed to be following someone or something, and the trail had led
them here into the snake-infested swamps of Nyissa. Murgos seemed to be
somehow involved, throwing frightful obstacles in their path, and Queen

Salmissra also seemed to take an interest, even going so far as to have young Garion abducted.

Ce'Nedra interrupted her musing to look across the cabin at the boy. Why would the queen of Nyissa want him? He was so *ordinary*. He was a peasant, a scullion, a nobody. He was a nice enough boy, certainly, with rather plain, sandy hair that kept tumbling down across his forehead, making her fingers itch to push it back. He had a nice enough face—in a plain sort of way—and he was somebody she could talk to when she was lonely or frightened, and somebody she could fight with when she felt peevish, since he was only slightly older than she was. But he completely refused to treat her with the respect due her—he probably didn't even know how. Why all this excruciating interest in him? She pondered that, looking thoughtfully at him.

She was doing it again. Angrily she jerked her eyes from his face. Why was she always watching him? Each time her thoughts wandered, her eyes automatically sought out his face, and it wasn't really that exciting a face to look at. She had even caught herself making up excuses to put herself into places where she could watch him. It was stupid!

Ce'Nedra nibbled at her hair and thought and nibbled some more, until once again her eyes went back to their minute study of Garion's features.

"Is he going to be all right?" Barak, the Earl of Trellheim, rumbled, tugging absently at his great red beard as he watched the Lady Polgara put the finishing touches on Belgarath's sling.

"It's a simple break," she replied professionally, putting away her bandages. "And the old fool heals fast."

Belgarath winced as he shifted his newly splinted arm. "You didn't have to be so rough, Pol." His rust-colored old tunic showed several dark mud smears and a new rip, evidence of his encounter with a tree.

"It had to be set, father," she told him. "You didn't want it to heal crooked, did you?"

"I think you actually enjoyed it," he accused.

"Next time you can set it yourself," she suggested coolly, smoothing her gray dress.

"I need a drink," Belgarath grumbled to the hulking Barak.

The Earl of Trellheim went to the narrow door. "Would you have a tankard of ale brought for Belgarath?" he asked the sailor outside.

"How is he?" the sailor inquired.

"Bad-tempered," Barak replied. "And he'll probably get worse if he doesn't get a drink pretty soon."

"I'll go at once," the sailor said.

"Wise decision."

This was yet another confusing thing for Ce'Nedra. The noblemen in their party all treated this shabby-looking old man with enormous respect; but so far as she could tell, he didn't even have a title. She could determine with exquisite precision the exact difference between a baron and a general of the Imperial Legions, between a grand duke of Tolnedra and a crown prince of Arendia, between the Rivan Warder and the king of the Chereks; but she had not the faintest idea where sorcerers fit in. The materially oriented mind of Tolnedra refused even to admit that sorcerers existed. While it was quite true that Lady Polgara, with titles from half the kingdoms of the West, was the most respected woman in the world, Belgarath was a vagabond, a vagrant—quite frequently a public nuisance. And Garion, she reminded herself, was his grandson.

"I think it's time you told us what happened, father," Lady Polgara was saying to her patient.

"I'd really rather not talk about it," he replied shortly.

She turned to Prince Kheldar, the peculiar little Drasnian nobleman with the sharp face and sardonic wit, who lounged on a bench with an impudent expression on his face. "Well, Silk?" she asked him.

"I'm sure you can see my position, old friend," the prince apologized to Belgarath with a great show of regret. "If I try to keep secrets, she'll only force things out of me—unpleasantly, I imagine."

Belgarath looked at him with a stony face, then snorted with disgust.

"It's not that I *want* to say anything, you realize."

Belgarath turned away.

"I knew you'd understand."

"The story, Silk!" Barak insisted impatiently.

"It's really very simple," Kheldar told him.

"But you're going to complicate it, right?"

"Just tell us what happened, Silk," Polgara said.

The Drasnian sat up on his bench. "It's not really much of a story," he began. "We located Zedar's trail and followed it down into Nyissa about three weeks ago. We had a few encounters with some Nyissan border guards— nothing very serious. Anyway, the trail of the Orb turned east almost as soon as it crossed the border. That was a surprise. Zedar had been headed for Nyissa with so much single-mindedness that we'd both assumed that he'd made some kind of arrangement with Salmissra. Maybe that's what he wanted everybody to think. He's very clever, and Salmissra's notorious for involving herself in things that don't really concern her."

"I've attended to that," Lady Polgara said somewhat grimly.

"What happened?" Belgarath asked her.

"I'll tell you about it later, father. Go on, Silk."

Silk shrugged. "There isn't a great deal more to it. We followed Zedar's trail into one of those ruined cities up near the old Marag border. Belgarath had a visitor there—at least he said he did. *I* didn't see anybody. At any rate, he told me that something had happened to change our plans and that we were going to have to turn around and come on downriver to Sthiss Tor to rejoin all of you. He didn't have time to explain much more, because the jungles were suddenly alive with Murgos—either looking for us or for Zedar, we never found out which. Since then we've been dodging Murgos and Nyissans both—traveling at night, hiding—that sort of thing. We sent a messenger once. Did he ever get through?"

"The day before yesterday," Polgara replied. "He had a fever, though, and it took a while to get your message from him."

Kheldar nodded. "Anyway, there were Grolims with the Murgos, and they were trying to find us with their minds. Belgarath was doing something to keep them from locating us that way. Whatever it was must have taken a great deal of concentration, because he wasn't paying too much attention to where he was going. Early this morning we were leading the horses through a patch of swamp. Belgarath was sort of stumbling along with his mind on other things, and that was when the tree fell on him."

"I might have guessed," Polgara said. "Did someone make it fall?"

"I don't think so," Silk answered. "It might have been an old deadfall, but I rather doubt it. It was rotten at the center. I tried to warn him, but he walked right under it."

"All right," Belgarath said.

"I *did* try to warn you."

"Don't belabor it, Silk."

"I wouldn't want them to think I didn't try to warn you," Silk protested.

Polgara shook her head and spoke with a profound note of disappointment in her voice. *"Father!"*

"Just let it lie, Polgara," Belgarath told her.

"I dug him out from under the tree and patched him up as best I could," Silk went on. "Then I stole that little boat and we started downriver. We were doing fine until all this dust started falling."

"What did you do with the horses?" Hettar asked. Ce'Nedra was a little afraid of this tall, silent Algar lord with his shaved head, his black leather clothing, and his flowing black scalp lock. He never seemed to smile, and the expression on his hawklike face at even the mention of the word "Murgo" was as bleak as stone. The only thing that even slightly humanized him was his overwhelming concern for horses.

"They're all right," Silk assured him. "I left them picketed where the Nyissans won't find them. They'll be fine where they are until we pick them up."

"You said when you came aboard that Ctuchik has the Orb now," Polgara said to Belgarath. "How did that happen?"

The old man shrugged. "Beltira didn't go into any of the details. All he told me was that Ctuchik was waiting when Zedar crossed the border into Cthol Murgos. Zedar managed to escape, but he had to leave the Orb behind."

"Did you speak with Beltira?"

"With his mind," Belgarath answered.

"Did he say why the Master wants us to go to the Vale?"

"No. It probably never occurred to him to ask. You know how Beltira is."

"It's going to take months, father," Polgara objected with a worried frown. "It's two hundred and fifty leagues to the Vale."

"Aldur wants us to go there," he answered. "I'm not going to start disobeying him after all these years."

"And in the meantime, Ctuchik's got the Orb at Rak Cthol."

"It's not going to do him any good, Pol. Torak himself couldn't make the Orb submit to him, and he tried for over two thousand years. I know where Rak Cthol is; Ctuchik can't hide it from me. He'll be there with the Orb when I decide to go take it away from him. I know how to deal with *that* magician." He said the word "magician" with a note of profound contempt in his voice.

"What's Zedar going to be doing all that time?"

"Zedar's got problems of his own. Beltira says that he's moved Torak from the place where he had him hidden. I think we can depend on him to keep Torak's body as far away from Rak Cthol as he possibly can. Actually, things have worked out rather well. I was getting a little tired of chasing Zedar anyway."

Ce'Nedra found all this a bit confusing. Why were they all so caught up in the movements of a strangely named pair of Angarak sorcerers and this mysterious jewel which everyone seemed to covet? To her, one jewel was much the same as another. Her childhood had been surrounded by such opulence that she had long since ceased to attach much importance to ornaments. At the moment, her only adornment consisted of a pair of tiny gold earrings shaped like little acorns, and her fondness for them arose not so much from the fact that they were gold but rather from the tinkling sound the cunningly contrived clappers inside them made when she moved her head.

All of this sounded like one of the Alorn myths she'd heard from a storyteller in her father's court years before. There had been a magic jewel in that, she remembered. It was stolen by the God of the Angaraks, Torak, and rescued by a sorcerer and some Alorn kings who put it on the pommel of a sword kept in the throne room at Riva. It was somehow supposed to protect the West from some terrible disaster that would happen if it were lost. Curious—the name of the sorcerer in the legend was Belgarath, the same as that of this old man.

But that would make him thousands of years old, which was ridiculous! He must have been named after the ancient mythic hero—unless he'd assumed the name to impress people.

Once again her eyes wandered to Garion's face. The boy sat quietly in one corner of the cabin, his eyes grave and his expression serious. She thought perhaps that it was his seriousness that so piqued her curiosity and kept drawing her eyes to him. Other boys she had known—nobles and the sons of nobles—had tried to be charming and witty, but Garion never tried to joke or to say clever things to try to amuse her. She was not entirely certain how to take that. Was he such a lump that he didn't know how he was supposed to behave? Or perhaps he knew but didn't care enough to make the effort. He might at least *try*—even if only occasionally. How could she possibly deal with him if he was going to refuse flatly to make a fool of himself for her benefit?

She reminded herself sharply that she was angry with him. He had said that Queen Salmissra had been the most beautiful woman he had ever seen, and it was far, far too early to forgive him for such an outrageous statement. She was definitely going to have to make him suffer extensively for *that* insulting lapse. Her fingers toyed absently with one of the curls cascading down the side of her face, her eyes boring into Garion's face.

The following morning the ashfall that was the result of a massive volcanic eruption somewhere in Cthol Murgos had diminished sufficiently to make the deck of the ship habitable again. The jungle along the riverbank was still partially obscured in the dusty haze, but the air was clear enough to breathe, and Ce'Nedra escaped from the sweltering cabin below deck with relief.

Garion was sitting in the sheltered spot near the bow of the ship where he usually sat and he was deep in conversation with Belgarath. Ce'Nedra noted with a certain detachment that he had neglected to comb his hair that morning. She resisted her immediate impulse to go fetch comb and brush to rectify the situation. She drifted instead with artful dissimulation to a place along the rail where, without seeming to, she could conveniently eavesdrop.

"—It's always been there," Garion was saying to his grandfather. "It used to just talk to me—tell me when I was being childish or stupid—that sort of thing. It seemed to be off in one corner of my mind all by itself."

Belgarath nodded, scratching absently at his beard with his good hand. "It seems to be completely separate from you," he observed. "Has this voice in your head ever actually done anything? Besides talk to you, I mean?"

Garion's face grew thoughtful. "I don't think so. It tells me how to do things, but I think that I'm the one who has to do them. When we were at Salmissra's palace, I think it took me out of my body to go look for Aunt Pol." He frowned. "No," he corrected. "When I stop and think about it, it told me how to do it, but I was the one who actually did it. Once we were out, I could feel it beside me—it's the first time we've ever been separate. I couldn't actually see it, though. It *did* take over for a few minutes, I think. It talked to Salmissra to smooth things over and to hide what we'd been doing."

"You've been busy since Silk and I left, haven't you?"

Garion nodded glumly. "Most of it was pretty awful. I burned Asharak. Did you know that?"

"Your Aunt told me about it."

"He slapped her in the face," Garion told him. "I was going to go after him with my knife for that, but the voice told me to do it a different way. I hit him with my hand and said 'burn.' That's all—just 'burn'—and he caught on fire. I was going to put it out until Aunt Pol told me he was the one who killed my mother and father. Then I made the fire hotter. He begged me to put it out, but I didn't do it." He shuddered.

"I tried to warn you about that," Belgarath reminded him gently. "I told you that you weren't going to like it very much after it was over."

Garion sighed. "I should have listened. Aunt Pol says that once you've used this—" He floundered, looking for a word.

"Power?" Belgarath suggested.

"All right," Garion assented. "She says that once you've used it, you never forget how, and you'll keep doing it again and again. I wish I *had* used my knife instead. Then this thing in me never would have gotten loose."

"You're wrong, you know," Belgarath told him quite calmly. "You've been bursting at the seams with it for several months now. You've used it without knowing it at least a half dozen times that I know about."

Garion stared at him incredulously.

"Remember that crazy monk just after we crossed into Tolnedra? When you touched him, you made so much noise that I thought for a moment you'd killed him."

"You said Aunt Pol did that."

"I lied," the old man admitted casually. "I do that fairly often. The whole point, though, is that you've always had this ability. It was bound to come out sooner or later. I wouldn't feel too unhappy about what you did to Chamdar. It was a little exotic perhaps—not exactly the way I might have done it—but there was a certain justice to it, after all."

"It's always going to be there, then?"

"Always. That's the way it is, I'm afraid."

The Princess Ce'Nedra felt rather smug about that. Belgarath had just confirmed something she herself had told Garion. If the boy would just stop being so stubborn, his Aunt and his grandfather and of course she herself— all of whom knew much better than he what was right and proper and good for him—could shape his life to their satisfaction with little or no difficulty.

"Let's get back to this other voice of yours," Belgarath suggested. "I need to know more about it. I don't want you carrying an enemy around in your mind."

"It's not an enemy," Garion insisted. "It's on our side."

"It might seem that way," Belgarath observed, "but things aren't always what they seem. I'd be a lot more comfortable if I knew just exactly what it is. I don't like surprises."

The Princess Ce'Nedra, however, was already lost in thought. Dimly, at the back of her devious and complex little mind, an idea was beginning to take shape—an idea with very interesting possibilities.

CHAPTER TWO

The trip up to the rapids of the River of the Serpent took the better part of a week. Although it was still swelteringly hot, they had all by now grown at least partially accustomed to the climate. Princess Ce'Nedra spent most of her time sitting on deck with Polgara, pointedly ignoring

Garion. She did, however, glance frequently his way to see if she could detect any signs of suffering.

Since her life was entirely in the hands of these people, Ce'Nedra felt keenly the necessity for winning them over. Belgarath would be no problem. A few winsome little-girl smiles, a bit of eyelash fluttering, and a spontaneous-seeming kiss or two would wrap him neatly around one of her fingers. That particular campaign could be conducted at any time she felt it convenient, but Polgara was a different matter. For one thing, Ce'Nedra was awed by the lady's spectacular beauty. Polgara was flawless. Even the white lock in the midnight of her hair was not so much a defect as it was a sort of accent— a personal trademark. Most disconcerting to the princess were Polgara's eyes. Depending on her mood, they ranged in color from gray to a deep, deep blue and they saw through everything. No dissimulation was possible in the face of that calm, steady gaze. Each time the princess looked into those eyes, she seemed to hear the clink of chains. She definitely had to get on Polgara's good side.

"Lady Polgara?" the princess said one morning as they sat together on deck, while the steaming, gray-green jungle slid by on either bank and the sweating sailors labored at their oars.

"Yes, dear?" Polgara looked up from the button she was sewing on one of Garion's tunics. She wore a pale blue dress, open at the throat in the heat.

"What *is* sorcery? I was always told that such things didn't exist." It seemed like a good place to start the discussion.

Polgara smiled at her. "Tolnedran education tends to be a bit one-sided."

"Is it a trick of some kind?" Ce'Nedra persisted. "I mean, is it like showing people something with one hand while you're taking something away with the other?" She toyed with the laces on her sandals.

"No, dear. It's nothing at all like that."

"Exactly how much can one do with it?"

"We've never explored that particular boundary," Polgara replied, her needle still busy. "When something has to be done, we do it. We don't bother worrying about whether we can or not. Different people are better at different things, though. It's somewhat on the order of some men being better at carpentry while others specialize in stonemasonry."

"Garion's a sorcerer, isn't he? How much can he do?" Now why had she asked *that*?

"I was wondering where this was leading," Polgara said, giving the tiny girl a penetrating look.

Ce'Nedra blushed slightly.

"Don't chew on your hair, dear," Polgara told her. "You'll split the ends." Ce'Nedra quickly removed the curl from between her teeth.

"We're not sure what Garion can do yet," Polgara continued. "It's probably much too early to tell. He seems to have talent. He certainly makes enough noise whenever he does something, and that's a fair indication of his potential."

"He'll probably be a very powerful sorcerer, then."

A faint smile touched Polgara's lips. "Probably so," she replied. "Always assuming that he learns to control himself."

"Well," Ce'Nedra declared, "we'll just have to teach him to control himself, then, won't we?"

Polgara looked at her for a moment, and then she began to laugh.

Ce'Nedra felt a bit sheepish, but she also laughed.

Garion, who was standing not far away, turned to look at them. "What's so funny?" he asked.

"Nothing you'd understand, dear," Polgara told him.

He looked offended and moved away, his back stiff and his face set.

Ce'Nedra and Polgara laughed again.

When Captain Greldik's ship finally reached the point where rocks and swiftly tumbling water made it impossible to go any farther, they moored her to a large tree on the north bank, and the party prepared to go ashore. Barak stood sweating in his mail shirt beside his friend Greldik, watching Hettar oversee the unloading of the horses. "If you happen to see my wife, give her my greetings," the red-bearded man said.

Greldik nodded. "I'll probably be near Trellheim sometime during the coming winter."

"I don't know that you need to tell her that I know about her pregnancy. She'll probably want to surprise me with my son when I get home. I wouldn't want to spoil that for her."

Greldik looked a little surprised. "I thought you enjoyed spoiling things for her, Barak."

"Maybe it's time that Merel and I made peace with each other. This little war of ours was amusing when we were younger, but it might not be a bad idea to put it aside now—for the sake of the children, if nothing else."

Belgarath came up on deck and joined the two bearded Chereks. "Go to Val Alorn," he told Captain Greldik. "Tell Anheg where we are and what we're doing. Have him get word to the others. Tell them that I absolutely forbid their going to war with the Angaraks just now. Ctuchik has the Orb at Rak Cthol, and if there's a war, Taur Urgas will seal the borders of Cthol Murgos. Things are going to be difficult enough for us without that to contend with."

"I'll tell him," Greldik replied doubtfully. "I don't think he'll like it much, though."

"He doesn't have to like it," Belgarath said bluntly. "He just has to do it."

Ce'Nedra, standing not far away, felt a little startled when she heard the shabby-looking old man issuing his peremptory commands. How could he speak so to sovereign kings? And what if Garion, as a sorcerer, should someday have a similar authority? She turned and gazed at the young man who was helping Durnik the smith calm an excited horse. He didn't *look* authoritative. She pursed her lips. A robe of some kind might help, she thought, and maybe some sort of book of magic in his hands—and perhaps just the hint of a beard. She narrowed her eyes, imagining him so robed, booked and bearded.

Garion, obviously feeling her eyes on him, looked quickly in her direction, his expression questioning. He was so *ordinary*. The image of this plain, unassuming boy in the finery she had concocted for him in her mind was suddenly ludicrous. Without meaning to, she laughed. Garion flushed and stiffly turned his back on her.

Since the rapids of the River of the Serpent effectively blocked all further navigation upriver, the trail leading up into the hills was quite broad, indicating that most travelers struck out overland at that point. As they rode up out of the valley in the midmorning sunlight, they passed rather quickly out of the tangled jungle growth lining the river and moved into a hardwood forest that was much more to Ce'Nedra's liking. At the crest of the first rise, they even encountered a breeze that seemed to brush away the sweltering heat and stink of Nyissa's festering swamps. Ce'Nedra's spirits lifted immediately. She considered the company of Prince Kheldar, but he was dozing in his saddle, and Ce'Nedra was just a bit afraid of the sharp-nosed Drasnian. She recognized immediately that the cynical, wise little man could probably read her like a book, and she didn't really care for that idea. Instead she rode forward along the column to ride with Baron Mandorallen, who led the way, as was his custom. Her move was prompted in part by the desire to get as far away from the steaming river as possible, but there was more to it than that. It occurred to her that this might be an excellent opportunity to question this Arendish nobleman about a matter that interested her.

"Your Highness," the armored knight said respectfully as she pulled her horse in beside his huge charger, "dost think it prudent to place thyself in the vanguard thus?"

"Who would be so foolish as to attack the bravest knight in the world?" she asked with artful innocence.

The baron's expression grew melancholy, and he sighed.

"And why so great a sigh, Sir Knight?" she bantered.

"It is of no moment, your Highness," he replied.

They rode along in silence through the dappled shade where insects hummed and darted and small, scurrying things skittered and rustled in the bushes at the side of the trail. "Tell me," the princess said finally, "have you known Belgarath for long?"

"All my life, your Highness."

"Is he highly regarded in Arendia?"

"Highly regarded? Holy Belgarath is the paramount man in the world! Surely thou knowest that, Princess."

"I'm Tolnedran, Baron Mandorallen," she pointed out. "Our familiarity with sorcerers is limited. Would an Arend describe Belgarath as a man of noble birth?"

Mandorallen laughed. "Your Highness, holy Belgarath's birth is so far lost in the dim reaches of antiquity that thy question hath no meaning."

Ce'Nedra frowned. She did not particularly like being laughed at. "Is he or is he not a nobleman?" she pressed.

"He is Belgarath," Mandorallen replied, as if that explained everything.

"There are hundreds of barons, earls by the score, and lords without number, but there is only one Belgarath. All men give way to him."

She beamed at him. "And what about Lady Polgara?"

Mandorallen blinked, and Ce'Nedra saw that she was going too fast for him. "The Lady Polgara is revered above all women," he said in puzzled response. "Highness, could I but know the direction of thine inquiry, I might provide thee with more satisfactory response."

She laughed. "My dear Baron, it's nothing important or serious—just curiosity, and a way to pass the time as we ride."

Durnik the smith came forward at a trot just then, his sorrel horse's hoofbeats thudding on the packed earth of the trail. "Mistress Pol wants you to wait for a bit," he told them.

"Is anything wrong?" Ce'Nedra asked.

"No. It's just that there's a bush not far from the trail that she recognized. She wants to harvest the leaves—I think they have certain medicinal uses. She says it's very rare and only found in this part of Nyissa." The smith's plain, honest face was respectful as it always was when he spoke of Polgara. Ce'Nedra had certain private suspicions about Durnik's feelings, but she kept them to herself. "Oh," he went on, "she said to warn you about the bush. There might be others around. It's about a foot tall and has very shiny green leaves and a little purple flower. It's deadly poisonous—even to touch."

"We will not stray from the trail, Goodman," Mandorallen assured him, "but will abide here against the lady's permission to proceed."

Durnik nodded and rode on back down the trail.

Ce'Nedra and Mandorallen pulled their horses into the shade of a broad tree and sat waiting. "How do the Arends regard Garion?" Ce'Nedra asked suddenly.

"Garion is a good lad," Mandorallen replied, somewhat confused.

"But hardly noble," she prompted him.

"Highness," Mandorallen told her delicately, "thine education, I fear, hath led thee astray. Garion is of the line of Belgarath and Polgara. Though he hath no rank such as thou and I both have, his blood is the noblest in the world. I would give precedence to him without question should he ask it of me—which he would not, being a modest lad. During our sojourn at the court of King Korodullin at Vo Mimbre, a young countess pursued him most fervently, thinking to gain status and prestige by marriage to him."

"Really?" Ce'Nedra asked with a hard little edge coming into her voice.

"She sought betrothal and trapped him often with blatant invitation to dalliance and sweet conversation."

"A *beautiful* countess?"

"One of the great beauties of the kingdom."

"I see." Ce'Nedra's voice was like ice.

"Have I given offense, Highness?"

"It's not important."

Mandorallen sighed again.

"What is it now?" she snapped.

"I perceive that my faults are many."

"I thought you were supposed to be the perfect man." She regretted that instantly.

"Nay, Highness. I am marred beyond thy conception."

"A bit undiplomatic, perhaps, but that's no great flaw—in an Arend."

"Cowardice is, your Highness."

She laughed at the notion. "Cowardice? You?"

"I have found that fault in myself," he admitted.

"Don't be ridiculous," she scoffed. "If anything, your fault lies in the other direction."

"It is difficult to believe, I know," he replied. "But I assure thee with great shame that I have felt the grip of fear upon my heart."

Ce'Nedra was baffled by the knight's mournful confession. She was struggling to find some proper reply when a great crashing rush burst out of the undergrowth a few yards away. With a sudden start of panic, her horse wheeled and bolted. She caught only the briefest glimpse of something large and tawny leaping out of the bushes at her—large, tawny, and with a great gaping mouth. She tried desperately to cling to her saddle with one hand and to control her terrified horse with the other, but its frantic flight took him under a low branch, and she was swept off its back to land unceremoniously in the middle of the trail. She rolled to her hands and knees and then froze as she faced the beast that had so clumsily burst forth from concealment.

She saw at once that the lion was not very old. She noted that, though his body was fully developed, he had only a half-grown mane. Clearly, he was an adolescent, unskilled at hunting. He roared with frustration as he watched the fleeing horse disappear back down the trail, and his tail lashed. The princess felt a momentary touch of amusement—he was so young, so awkward. Then her amusement was replaced by irritation with this clumsy young beast who had caused her humiliating unhorsing. She rose to her feet, brushed off her knees, and looked at him sternly. "Shoo!" she said with an insistent flip of her hand. She was, after all, a princess, and he was only a lion—a very young and foolish lion.

The yellow eyes fell on her then and narrowed slightly. The lashing tail grew suddenly quite still. The young lion's eyes widened with a sort of dreadful intensity, and he crouched, his belly going low to the ground. His upper lip lifted to reveal his very long, white teeth. He took one slow step toward her, his great paw touching down softly.

"Don't you dare," she told him indignantly.

"Remain quite still, Highness," Mandorallen warned her in a deathly quiet voice. From the corner of her eye she saw him slide out of his saddle. The lion's eyes flickered toward him with annoyance.

Carefully, one step at a time, Mandorallen crossed the intervening space until he had placed his armored body between the lion and the princess. The lion watched him warily, not seeming to realize what he was doing until it was too late. Then, cheated of another meal, the cat's eyes went flat with rage. Mandorallen drew his sword very carefully; then, to Ce'Nedra's amazement, he passed it back hilt-first to her. "So that thou shalt have means of defending thyself, should I fail to withstand him," the knight explained.

Doubtfully, Ce'Nedra took hold of the huge hilt with both hands. When Mandorallen released his grip on the blade, however, the point dropped immediately to the ground. Try though she might, Ce'Nedra could not even lift the huge sword.

Snarling, the lion crouched even lower. His tail lashed furiously for a moment, then stiffened out behind him. "Mandorallen, look out!" Ce'Nedra screamed, still struggling with the sword.

The lion leaped.

Mandorallen flung his steel-cased arms wide and stepped forward to meet the cat's charge. They came together with a resounding crash, and Mandorallen locked his arms around the beast's body. The lion wrapped his huge paws around Mandorallen's shoulders and his claws screeched deafeningly as they raked the steel of the knight's armor. His teeth grated and ground as he gnawed and bit at Mandorallen's helmeted head. Mandorallen tightened his deadly embrace.

Ce'Nedra scrambled out of the way, dragging the sword behind her, and stared wide-eyed with fright at the dreadful struggle.

The lion's clawing became more desperate, and great, deep scratches appeared on Mandorallen's armor as the Mimbrate's arms tightened inexorably. The roars became yowls of pain, and the lion struggled now not to fight or kill, but to escape. He wriggled and thrashed and tried to bite. His hind paws came up to rake furiously on Mandorallen's armored trunk. His yowls grew more shrill, more filled with panic.

With a superhuman effort, Mandorallen jerked his arms together. Ce'Nedra heard the cracking of bones with a sickening clarity, and an enormous fountain of blood erupted from the cat's mouth. The young lion's body quivered, and his head dropped. Mandorallen unclenched his locked hands, and the dead beast slid limply from his grasp to the ground at his feet.

Stunned, the princess stared at the stupendous man in blood-smeared and clawed armor standing before her. She had just witnessed the impossible. Mandorallen had killed a lion with no weapon but his mighty arms—and all for her! Without knowing why, she found herself crowing with delight. "Mandorallen!" She sang his name. "You are *my* knight!"

Still panting from his efforts, Mandorallen pushed up his visor. His blue eyes were wide, as if her words had struck him with a stunning impact. Then he sank to his knees before her. "Your Highness," he said in a choked voice, "I pledge to thee here upon the body of this beast to be thy true and faithful knight for so long as I have breath."

Deep inside her, Ce'Nedra felt a profound sort of click—the sound of two things, fated from time's beginning to come together, finally meeting. Something—she did not know exactly what—but something very important had happened there in that sun-dappled glade.

And then Barak, huge and imposing, came galloping up the trail with Hettar at his side and the others not far behind. "What happened?" the big Cherek demanded, swinging down from his horse.

Ce'Nedra waited until they had all reined in to make her announcement. "The lion there attacked me," she said, trying to make it sound like an everyday occurrence. "Mandorallen killed him with his bare hands."

"I was in fact wearing these, Highness," the still-kneeling knight reminded her, holding up his gauntleted fists.

"It was the bravest thing I've ever seen in my life," Ce'Nedra swept on.

"Why are you down on your knees?" Barak asked Mandorallen. "Are you hurt?"

"I have just made Sir Mandorallen my very own knight," Ce'Nedra declared, "and as is quite proper, he knelt to receive that honor from my hands." From the corner of her eye she saw Garion in the act of sliding down from his horse. He was scowling like a thundercloud. Silently, Ce'Nedra exulted. Leaning forward then, she placed a sisterly kiss on Mandorallen's brow. "Rise, Sir Knight," she commanded, and Mandorallen creaked to his feet.

Ce'Nedra was enormously pleased with herself.

The remainder of the day passed without incident. They crossed a low range of hills and came down into a little valley as the sun settled slowly into a cloudbank off to the west. The valley was watered by a small stream, sparkling and cold, and they stopped there to set up their night's encampment. Mandorallen, in his new role as knight-protector, was suitably attentive, and Ce'Nedra accepted his service graciously, casting occasional covert glances at Garion to be certain that he was noticing everything.

Somewhat later, when Mandorallen had gone to see to his horse and Garion had stomped off to sulk, she sat demurely on a moss-covered log congratulating herself on the day's accomplishments.

"You're playing a cruel game, Princess," Durnik told her bluntly from the spot a few feet away where he was building a fire.

Ce'Nedra was startled. So far as she could remember, Durnik had never spoken directly to her since she had joined the party. The smith was obviously uncomfortable in the presence of royalty and, indeed, seemed actually to avoid her. Now, however, he looked straight into her face, and his tone was reproving.

"I don't know what you're talking about," she declared.

"I think you do." His plain, honest face was serious, and his gaze was steady.

Ce'Nedra lowered her eyes and flushed slowly.

"I've seen village girls play this same game," he continued. "Nothing good ever comes of it."

"I'm not trying to hurt anybody, Durnik. There isn't really anything of that sort between Mandorallen and me—we both know that."

"Garion doesn't."

Ce'Nedra was amazed. "Garion?"

"Isn't that what it's all about?"

"Of course not!" she objected indignantly.

Durnik's look was profoundly skeptical.

"Such a thing never entered my mind," Ce'Nedra rushed on. "It's absolutely absurd."

"Really?"

Ce'Nedra's bold front collapsed. "He's so stubborn," she complained. "He just won't do anything the way he's supposed to."

"He's an honest boy. Whatever else he is or might become, he's still the plain, simple boy he was at Faldor's farm. He doesn't know the rules of the gentry. He won't lie to you or flatter you or say things he doesn't really feel. I think something very important is going to happen to him before very long—I don't know what—but I do know it's going to take all his strength and courage. Don't weaken him with all this childishness."

"Oh, Durnik," she said with a great sigh. "What am I going to do?"

"Be honest. Say only what's in your heart. Don't say one thing and mean another. That won't work with him."

"I know. That's what makes it all so difficult. He was raised one way, and I was raised another. We're never going to get along." She sighed again.

Durnik smiled, a gentle, almost whimsical smile. "It's not all that bad, Princess," he told her. "You'll fight a great deal at first. You're almost as stubborn as he is, you know. You were born in different parts of the world, but you're not really all that different inside. You'll shout at each other and shake your fingers in each other's faces; but in time that will pass, and you won't even remember what you were shouting about. Some of the best marriages I know of started that way."

"*Marriage!*"

"That's what you've got in mind, isn't it?"

She stared at him incredulously. Then she suddenly laughed. "Dear, dear Durnik," she said. "You don't understand at all, do you?"

"I understand what I see," he replied. "And what I see is a young girl doing everything she possibly can to catch a young man."

Ce'Nedra sighed. "That's completely out of the question, you know— even if I felt that way—which of course I don't."

"Naturally not." He looked slightly amused.

"Dear Durnik," she said again, "I can't even allow myself such thoughts. You forget who I am."

"That isn't very likely," he told her. "You're usually very careful to keep the fact firmly in front of everybody."

"Don't you know what it means?"

He looked a bit perplexed. "I don't quite follow."

"I'm an Imperial Princess, the jewel of the Empire, and I *belong* to the Empire. I'll have absolutely no voice in the decision about whom I'm going to marry. That decision will be made by my father and the Council of Advisers. My husband will be rich and powerful—probably much older than I am—and my marriage to him will be to the advantage of the Empire and the House of Borune. I probably won't even be consulted in the matter."

Durnik looked stunned. "That's outrageous!" he objected.

"Not really," she told him. "My family has the right to protect its interests, and I'm an extremely valuable asset to the Borunes." She sighed again, a forlorn little sigh. "It might be nice, though—to be able to choose for myself, I mean. If I could, I might even look at Garion the way you seem to think I have been looking—even though he's absolutely impossible. The way things are, though, all he can ever be is a friend."

"I didn't know," he apologized, his plain, practical face melancholy.

"Don't take it so seriously, Durnik," she said lightly. "I've always known that this was the way things have to be."

A large, glistening tear, however, welled into the corner of her eye, and Durnik awkwardly put his work-worn hand on her arm to comfort her. Without knowing why, she threw her arms around his neck, buried her face in his chest, and sobbed.

"There, there," he said, clumsily patting her shaking shoulder. "There, there."

CHAPTER THREE

Garion did not sleep well that night. Although he was young and inexperienced, he was not stupid, and Princess Ce'Nedra had been fairly obvious. Over the months since she had joined them, he had seen her attitude toward him change until they had shared a rather specialized kind of friendship. He liked her; she liked him. Everything had been fine up to that point. Why couldn't she just leave it alone? Garion surmised that it probably had something to do with the inner workings of the female mind. As soon as a friendship passed a certain point—some obscure and secret boundary—a woman quite automatically became overwhelmed by a raging compulsion to complicate things.

He was almost certain that her transparent little game with Mandorallen had been aimed at *him*, and he wondered if it might not be a good idea to warn the knight to spare him more heartbreak in the future. Ce'Nedra's toying with the great man's affections was little more than the senseless cruelty of a spoiled child. Mandorallen must be warned. His Arendish thick-headedness might easily cause him to overlook the obvious.

And yet, Mandorallen *had* killed the lion for her. Such stupendous bravery could quite easily have overwhelmed the flighty little princess. What if her admiration and gratitude had pushed her over the line into infatuation?

That possibility, coming to Garion as it did in those darkest hours just before dawn, banished all possibility of further sleep. He arose the next morning sandy-eyed and surly and with a terrible worry gnawing at him.

As they rode out through the blue-tinged shadows of early morning with the slanting rays of the newly risen sun gleaming on the treetops above them, Garion fell in beside his grandfather, seeking the comfort of the old man's companionship. It was not only that, however. Ce'Nedra was riding demurely with Aunt Pol just ahead, and Garion felt very strongly that he should keep an eye on her.

Mister Wolf rode in silence, looking cross and irritable, and he frequently dug his fingers under the splint on his left arm.

"Leave it alone, father," Aunt Pol told him without turning around. .

"It itches."

"That's because it's healing. Just leave it alone."

He grumbled about that under his breath.

"Which route are you planning to take to the Vale?" she asked him.

"We'll go around by way of Tol Rane," he replied.

"The season's moving on, father," she reminded him. "If we take too long, we'll run into bad weather in the mountains."

"I know that, Pol. Would you rather cut straight across Maragor?"

"Don't be absurd."

"Is Maragor really all that dangerous?" Garion asked.

Princess Ce'Nedra turned in her saddle and gave him a withering look. "Don't you know *anything?*" she asked him with towering superiority.

Garion drew himself up, a dozen suitable responses to that coming to mind almost at once.

Mister Wolf shook his head warningly. "Just let it pass," the old man told him. "It's much too early to start in on that just now."

Garion clenched his teeth together.

They rode for an hour or more through the cool morning, and Garion gradually felt his temper improving. Then Hettar rode up to speak with Mister Wolf. "There are some riders coming," he reported.

"How many?" Wolf asked quickly.

"A dozen or more—coming in from the west."

"They could be Tolnedrans."

"I'll see," Aunt Pol murmured. She lifted her face and closed her eyes for a moment. "No," she said. "Not Tolnedrans. Murgos."

Hettar's eyes went flat. "Do we fight?" he asked with a dreadful kind of eagerness, his hand going to his sabre.

"No," Wolf replied curtly. "We hide."

"There aren't really that many of them."

"Never mind, Hettar," Wolf told him. "Silk," he called ahead, "there are some Murgos coming toward us from the west. Warn the others and find us all a place to hide."

Silk nodded curtly and galloped forward.

"Are there any Grolims with them?" the old man asked Aunt Pol.

"I don't think so," she answered with a small frown. "One of them has a strange mind, but he doesn't seem to be a Grolim."

Silk rode back quickly. "There's a thicket off to the right," he told them. "It's big enough to hide in."

"Let's go, then," Wolf said.

The thicket was fifty yards back among the larger trees. It appeared to be a patch of dense brush surrounding a small hollow. The ground in the hollow was marshy, and there was a spring at its center.

Silk had swung down from his horse and was hacking a thick bush off close to the ground with his short sword. "Take cover in here," he told them. "I'll go back and brush out our tracks." He picked up the bush and wormed his way out of the thicket.

"Be sure the horses don't make any noise," Wolf told Hettar.

Hettar nodded, but his eyes showed his disappointment.

Garion dropped to his knees and wormed his way through the thick brush until he reached the edge of the thicket; then he sank down on the leaves covering the ground to peer out between the gnarled and stumpy trunks.

Silk, walking backward and swinging his bush, was sweeping leaves and twigs from the forest floor over the tracks they had made from the trail to the thicket. He was moving quickly, but was careful to obliterate their trail completely.

From behind him, Garion heard a faint snap and rustle in the leaves, and Ce'Nedra crawled up and sank to the ground at his side. "You shouldn't be this close to the edge of the brush," he told her in a low voice.

"Neither should you," she retorted.

He let that pass. The princess had a warm, flowerlike smell; for some reason, that made Garion very nervous.

"How far away do you think they are?" she whispered.

"How would I know?"

"You're a sorcerer, aren't you?"

"I'm not that good at it."

Silk finished brushing away the tracks and stood for a moment studying the ground as he looked for any trace of their passage he might have missed. Then he burrowed his way into the thicket and crouched down a few yards from Garion and Ce'Nedra.

"Lord Hettar wanted to fight them," Ce'Nedra whispered to Garion.

"Hettar always wants to fight when he sees Murgos."

"Why?"

"The Murgos killed his parents when he was very young. He had to watch while they did it."

She gasped. "How awful!"

"If you children don't mind," Silk said sarcastically, "I'm trying to listen for horses."

Somewhere beyond the trail they had just left, Garion heard the thudding sound of horses' hooves moving at a trot. He sank down deeper into the leaves and watched, scarcely breathing.

When the Murgos appeared, there were about fifteen of them, mail-shirted and with the scarred cheeks of their race. Their leader, however, was a man in a patched and dirty tunic and with coarse black hair. He was unshaven, and one of his eyes was out of line with its fellow. Garion knew him.

Silk drew in a sharp breath with an audible hiss. "Brill," he muttered.

"Who's Brill?" Ce'Nedra whispered to Garion.

"I'll tell you later," he whispered back. "Shush!"

"Don't shush me!" she flared.

A stern look from Silk silenced them.

Brill was talking sharply to the Murgos, gesturing with short, jerky movements. Then he raised his hands with his fingers widespread and stabbed them forward to emphasize what he was saying. The Murgos all nodded, their faces expressionless, and spread out along the trail, facing the woods and the thicket where Garion and the others were hiding. Brill moved farther up the trail. "Keep your eyes open," he shouted to them. "Let's go."

The Murgos started to move forward at a walk, their eyes searching. Two of them rode past the thicket so close that Garion could smell the sweat on their horses' flanks.

"I'm getting tired of that man," one of them remarked to the other.

"I wouldn't let it show," the second one advised.

"I can take orders as well as any man," the first one said, "but that one's beginning to irritate me. I think he'd look better with a knife between his shoulder blades."

"I don't think he'd like that much, and it might be a little hard to manage."

"I could wait until he was asleep."

"I've never seen him sleep."

"Everybody sleeps—sooner or later."

"It's up to you," the second replied with a shrug, "but I wouldn't try anything rash—unless you've given up the idea of ever seeing Rak Hagga again."

The two of them moved on out of earshot.

Silk crouched, gnawing nervously at a fingernail. His eyes had narrowed to slits, and his sharp little face was intent. Then he began to swear under his breath.

"What's wrong, Silk?" Garion whispered to him.

"I've made a mistake," Silk answered irritably. "Let's go back to the others." He turned and crawled through the bushes toward the spring at the center of the thicket.

Mister Wolf was seated on a log, scratching absently at his splinted arm. "Well?" he asked, looking up.

"Fifteen Murgos," Silk replied shortly. "And an old friend."

"It was Brill," Garion reported. "He seemed to be in charge."

"Brill?" The old man's eyes widened with surprise.

"He was giving orders and the Murgos were following them," Silk said.

"They didn't like it much, but they were doing what he told them to do. They seemed to be afraid of him. I think Brill's something more than an ordinary hireling."

"Where's Rak Hagga?" Ce'Nedra asked.

Wolf looked at her sharply.

"We heard two of them talking," she explained. "They said they were from Rak Hagga. I thought I knew the names of all the cities in Cthol Murgos, but I've never heard of that one."

"You're sure they said Rak Hagga?" Wolf asked her, his eyes intent.

"I heard them too," Garion told him. "That was the name they used—Rak Hagga."

Mister Wolf stood up, his face suddenly grim. "We're going to have to hurry, then. Taur Urgas is preparing for war."

"How do you know that?" Barak asked him.

"Rak Hagga's a thousand leagues south of Rak Goska, and the southern Murgos are never brought up into this part of the world unless the Murgo king is on the verge of going to war with someone."

"Let them come," Barak said with a bleak smile.

"If it's all the same to you, I'd like to get our business attended to first. I've got to go to Rak Cthol, and I'd prefer not to have to wade through whole armies of Murgos to get there." The old man shook his head angrily. "What *is* Taur Urgas thinking of?" he burst out. "It's not time yet."

Barak shrugged. "One time's as good as another."

"Not for *this* war. Too many things have to happen first. Can't Ctuchik keep a leash on that maniac?"

"Unpredictability is part of Taur Urgas' unique charm," Silk observed sardonically. "He doesn't know himself what he's going to do from one day to the next."

"Knowest thou the king of the Murgos?" Mandorallen inquired.

"We've met," Silk replied. "We're not fond of each other."

"Brill and his Murgos should be gone by now," Mister Wolf said. "Let's move on. We've got a long way to go, and time's starting to catch up with us." He moved quickly toward his horse.

Shortly before sundown they went through a high pass lying in a notch between two mountains and stopped for the night in a little glen a few miles down on the far side.

"Keep the fire down as much as you can, Durnik," Mister Wolf warned the smith. "Southern Murgos have sharp eyes and they can see the light from a fire from miles away. I'd rather not have company in the middle of the night."

Durnik nodded soberly and dug his firepit somewhat deeper than usual.

Mandorallen was attentive to the Princess Ce'Nedra as they set up for the night, and Garion watched sourly. Though he had violently objected each time Aunt Pol had insisted that he serve as Ce'Nedra's personal attendant, now that the tiny girl had her knight to fetch and carry for her, Garion felt somehow that his rightful position had in some way been usurped.

"We're going to have to pick up our pace," Wolf told them after they had finished a meal of bacon, bread, and cheese. "We've got to get through the mountains before the first storms hit, and we're going to have to try to stay ahead of Brill and his Murgos." He scraped a space clear on the ground in front of him with one foot, picked up a stick, and began sketching a map in the dirt. "We're here." He pointed. "Maragor's directly ahead of us. We'll circle to the west, go through Tol Rane, and then strike northeast toward the Vale."

"Might it not be shorter to cross Maragor?" Mandorallen suggested, pointing at the crude map.

"Perhaps," the old man replied, "but we won't do that unless we have to. Maragor's haunted, and it's best to avoid it if possible."

"We are not children to be frightened of insubstantial shades," Mandorallen declared somewhat stiffly.

"No one's doubting your courage, Mandorallen," Aunt Pol told him, "but the spirit of Mara wails in Maragor. It's better not to offend him."

"How far is it to the Vale of Aldur?" Durnik asked.

"Two hundred and fifty leagues," Wolf answered. "We'll be a month or more in the mountains, even under the best conditions. Now we'd better all get some sleep. Tomorrow's likely to be a hard day."

CHAPTER FOUR

When they rose the next morning as the first pale hint of light was appearing on the eastern horizon, there was a touch of silvery frost on the ground and a thin scum of ice around the edges of the spring at the bottom of the glen. Ce'Nedra, who had gone to the spring to wash her face, lifted a leaf-thin shard from the water and stared at it.

"It's much colder up in the mountains," Garion told her as he belted on his sword.

"I'm aware of that," she replied loftily.

"Forget it," he said shortly and stamped away, muttering.

They rode down out of the mountains in the bright morning sunlight, moving at a steady trot. As they rounded a shoulder of outcropping rock, they saw the broad basin that had once been Maragor, the District of the Marags, stretching out below them. The meadows were a dusty autumn green, and the streams and lakes sparkled in the sun. A tumbled ruin, looking tiny in the distance, gleamed far out on the plain.

Princess Ce'Nedra, Garion noticed, kept her eyes averted, refusing even to look.

Not far down the slope below them, a cluster of crude huts and lopsided tents lay in a steep gully where a frothy creek had cut down through the rocks and gravel. Dirt streets and paths wandered crookedly up and down the sides of the gully, and a dozen or so ragged-looking men were hacking somewhat dispiritedly at the creek bank with picks and mattocks, turning the water below the shabby settlement a muddy yellow brown.

"A town?" Durnik questioned. "Out here?"

"Not exactly a town," Wolf replied. "The men in those settlements sift gravel and dig up the streambanks, looking for gold."

"Is there gold here?" Silk asked quickly, his eyes bright.

"A little," Wolf said. "Probably not enough to make it worth anyone's time to look for it."

"Why do they bother, then?"

Wolf shrugged. "Who knows?"

Mandorallen and Barak took the lead, and they moved down the rocky trail toward the settlement. As they approached, two men came out of one of the huts with rusty swords in their hands. One, a thin, unshaven man with a high forehead, wore a greasy Tolnedran jerkin. The other, much taller and bulkier, was dressed in the ragged tunic of an Arendish serf.

"That's far enough," the Tolnedran shouted. "We don't let armed men come in here until we know what their business is."

"You're blocking the trail, friend," Barak advised him. "You might find that unhealthy."

"One shout from me will bring fifty armed men," the Tolnedran warned.

"Don't be an idiot, Reldo," the big Arend told him. "That one with all the steel on him is a Mimbrate knight. There aren't enough men on the whole mountain to stop him, if he decides to go through here." He looked warily at Mandorallen. "What're your intentions, Sir Knight?" he asked respectfully.

"We are but following the trail," Mandorallen replied. "We have no interest in thy community."

The Arend grunted. "That's good enough for me. Let them pass, Reldo." He slid his sword back under his rope belt.

"What if he's lying?" Reldo retorted. "What if they're here to steal our gold?"

"What gold, you jackass?" the Arend demanded with contempt. "There isn't enough gold in the whole camp to fill a thimble—and Mimbrate knights don't lie. If you want to fight with him, go ahead. After it's over, we'll scoop up what's left of you and dump you in a hole someplace."

"You've got a bad mouth, Berig," Reldo observed darkly.

"And what do you plan to do about it?"

The Tolnedran glared at the larger man and then turned and walked away, muttering curses.

Berig laughed harshly, then turned back to Mandorallen. "Come ahead, Sir Knight," he invited. "Reldo's all mouth. You don't have to worry about him."

Mandorallen moved forward at a walk. "Thou art a long way from home, my friend."

Berig shrugged. "There wasn't anything in Arendia to keep me, and I had a misunderstanding with my lord over a pig. When he started talking about hanging, I thought I'd like to try my luck in a different country."

"Seems like a sensible decision." Barak laughed.

Berig winked at him. "The trail goes right on down to the creek," he told them, "then up the other side behind those shacks. The men over there are Nadraks, but the only one who might give you any trouble is Tarlek. He got drunk last night, though, so he's probably still sleeping it off."

A vacant-eyed man in Sendarian clothing shambled out of one of the tents. Suddenly he lifted his face and howled like a dog. Berig picked up a rock and shied it at him. The Sendar dodged the rock and ran yelping behind one of the shacks. "One of these days I'm going to do him a favor and stick a knife in him," Berig remarked sourly. "He bays at the moon all night long."

"What's his problem?" Barak asked.

Berig shrugged. "Crazy. He thought he could make a dash into Maragor and pick up some gold before the ghosts caught him. He was wrong."

"What did they do to him?" Durnik asked, his eyes wide.

"Nobody knows," Berig replied. "Every so often somebody gets drunk or greedy and thinks he can get away with it. It wouldn't do any good, even if the ghosts didn't catch you. Anybody coming out is stripped immediately by his friends. Nobody gets to keep any gold he brings out, so why bother?"

"You've got a charming society here," Silk observed wryly.

Berig laughed. "It suits me. It's better than decorating a tree in my lord's apple orchard back in Arendia." He scratched absently at one armpit. "I guess I'd better go do some digging," he sighed. "Good luck." He turned and started toward one of the tents.

"Let's move along," Wolf said quietly. "These places tend to get rowdy as the day wears on."

"You seem to know quite a bit about them, father," Aunt Pol noticed.

"They're good places to hide," he replied. "Nobody asks any questions. I've needed to hide a time or two in my life."

"I wonder why?"

They started along the dusty street between the slapped-together shacks and patched tents, moving down toward the roiling creek.

"Wait!" someone called from behind. A scruffy-looking Drasnian was running after them, waving a small leather pouch. He caught up with them, puffing. "Why didn't you wait?" he demanded.

"What do you want?" Silk asked him.

"I'll give you fifty pennyweight of fine gold for the girl," the Drasnian panted, waving his leather sack again.

Mandorallen's face went bleak, and his hand moved toward his sword hilt.

"Why don't you let me deal with this, Mandorallen?" Silk suggested mildly, swinging down from his saddle.

Ce'Nedra's expression had first registered shock, then outrage. She appeared almost on the verge of explosion before Garion reached her and put his hand on her arm. "Watch," he told her softly.

"How dare—"

"Hush. Just watch. Silk's going to take care of it."

"That's a pretty paltry offer," Silk said, his fingers flicking idly.

"She's still young," the other Drasnian pointed out. "She obviously hasn't had much training yet. Which one of you owns her?"

"We'll get to that in a moment," Silk replied. "Surely you can make a better offer than that."

"It's all I've got," the scruffy man answered plaintively, waving his fingers, "and I don't want to go into partnership with any of the brigands in this place. I'd never get to see any of the profits."

Silk shook his head. "I'm sorry," he refused. "It's out of the question. I'm sure you can see our position."

Ce'Nedra was making strangled noises.

"Be quiet," Garion snapped. "This isn't what it seems to be."

"What about the older one?" the scruffy man suggested, sounding desperate. "Surely fifty pennyweight's a good price for her."

Without warning Silk's fist lashed out, and the scruffy Drasnian reeled back from the apparent blow. His hand flew to his mouth, and he began to spew curses.

"Run him off, Mandorallen," Silk said quite casually.

The grim-faced knight drew his broadsword and moved his warhorse deliberately at the swearing Drasnian. After one startled yelp, the man turned and fled.

"What did he say?" Wolf asked Silk. "You were standing in front of him, so I couldn't see."

"The whole region's alive with Murgos," Silk replied, climbing back on his horse. "Kheran says that a dozen parties of them have been through here in the last week."

"You *knew* that animal?" Ce'Nedra demanded.

"Kheran? Of course. We went to school together."

"Drasnians like to keep an eye on things, Princess," Wolf told her. "King Rhodar has agents everywhere."

"That awful man is an agent of King Rhodar?" Ce'Nedra asked incredulously.

Silk nodded. "Actually Kheran's a Margrave," he said. "He has exquisite manners under normal circumstances. He asked me to convey his compliments."

Ce'Nedra looked baffled.

"Drasnians talk to each other with their fingers," Garion explained. "I thought everybody knew that."

Ce'Nedra's eyes narrowed at him.

"What Kheran actually said was, 'Tell the red-haired wench that I apologize for the insult,' " Garion informed her smugly. "He needed to talk to Silk, and he had to have an excuse."

"*Wench?*"

"His word, not mine," Garion replied quickly.

"*You* know this sign language?"

"Naturally."

"That'll do, Garion," Aunt Pol said firmly.

"Kheran recommends that we get out of here immediately," Silk told Mister Wolf. "He says that the Murgos are looking for somebody—us, probably."

From the far side of the camp there were sudden angry voices. Several dozen Nadraks boiled out of their shanties to confront a group of Murgo horsemen who had just ridden up out of a deep gully. At the forefront of the Nadraks hulked a huge, fat man who looked more animal than human. In his right hand he carried a brutal-looking steel mace. "Kordoch!" he bellowed. "I told you I'd kill you next time you came here."

The man who stepped out from among the Murgo horses to face the hulking Nadrak was Brill. "You've told me a lot of things, Tarlek," he shouted back.

"This time you get what's coming to you, Kordoch," Tarlek roared, striding forward and swinging his mace.

"Stay back," Brill warned, stepping away from the horses. "I don't have time for this right now."

"You don't have any time left at all, Kordoch—for anything."

Barak was grinning broadly. "Would anyone like to take this opportunity to say good-bye to our friend over there?" he said. "I think he's about to leave on a very long journey."

But Brill's right hand had dipped suddenly inside his tunic. With a flickering movement, he whipped out a peculiar-looking triangular steel object about six inches across. Then, in the same movement, he flipped it, spinning and whistling, directly at Tarlek. The flat steel triangle sailed, flashing in the sun as it spun, and disappeared with a sickening sound of shearing bone into the hulking Nadrak's chest. Silk hissed with amazement.

Tarlek stared stupidly at Brill, his mouth agape and his left hand going to the spurting hole in his chest. Then his mace slid out of his right hand, his knees buckled, and he fell heavily forward.

"Let's get out of here!" Mister Wolf barked. "Down the creek! Go!"

They plowed into the rocky streambed at a plunging gallop, and the muddy water sprayed out from under their horses' hooves. After several hundred yards they turned sharply to scramble up a steep gravel bank.

"That way!" Barak shouted, pointing toward more level ground. Garion did not have time to think, only to cling to his horse and try to keep up with the others. Faintly, far behind, he could hear shouts.

They rode behind a low hill and reined in for a moment at Wolf's signal. "Hettar," the old man said, "see if they're coming."

Hettar wheeled his horse and loped up to a stand of trees on the brow of the hill.

Silk was muttering curses, his face livid.

"What's your problem now?" Barak demanded.

Silk kept on swearing.

"What's got him so worked up?" Barak asked Mister Wolf.

"Our friend's just had a nasty shock," the old man answered. "He misjudged somebody—so did I, as a matter of fact. That weapon Brill used on the big Nadrak is called an adder-sting."

Barak shrugged. "It looked like just an odd-shaped throwing knife to me."

"There's a bit more to it than that," Wolf told him. "It's as sharp as a razor on all three sides, and the points are usually dipped in poison. It's the special weapon of the Dagashi. That's what has got Silk so upset."

"I should have known," Silk berated himself. "Brill's been a little too good all along to be just an ordinary Sendarian footpad."

"Do you know what they're talking about, Polgara?" Barak asked.

"The Dagashi are a secret society in Cthol Murgos," she told him. "Trained killers—assassins. They answer only to Ctuchik and their own elders. Ctuchik's been using them for centuries to eliminate people who get in his way. They're very efficient."

"I've never been that curious about the peculiarities of Murgo culture," Barak replied. "If they want to creep around and kill each other, so much the better." He glanced up the hill quickly to find out if Hettar had seen anything behind them. "That thing Brill used might be an interesting toy, but it's no match for armor and a good sword."

"Don't be so provincial, Barak," Silk said, beginning to regain his composure. "A well-thrown adder-sting can cut right through a mail shirt; if you know how, you can even sail it around corners. Not only that, a Dagashi could kill you with his hands and feet, whether you're wearing armor or not." He frowned. "You know, Belgarath," he mused, "we might have been making a mistake all along. We assumed that Asharak was using Brill, but it might have been the other way around. Brill has to be good, or Ctuchik wouldn't have sent him into the West to keep an eye on us." He smiled then, a chillingly bleak little smile. "I wonder just how good he is." He flexed his fingers. "I've met a few Dagashi, but never one of their best. That might be very interesting."

"Let's not get sidetracked," Wolf told him. The old man's face was grim. He looked at Aunt Pol, and something seemed to pass between them.

"You're not serious," she said.

"I don't think we've got much choice, Pol. There are Murgos all around us—too many and too close. I don't have any room to move—they've got us pinned right up against the southern edge of Maragor. Sooner or later, we're going to get pushed out onto the plain anyway. At least if we make the decision ourselves, we'll be able to take some precautions."

"I don't like it, father," she stated bluntly.

"I don't care much for it myself," he admitted, "but we've got to shake off all these Murgos or we'll never make it to the Vale before winter sets in."

Hettar rode back down the hill. "They're coming," he reported quietly. "And there's another group of them circling in from the west to cut us off."

Wolf drew in a deep breath. "I think that pretty well decides it, Pol," he said. "Let's go."

As they passed into the belt of trees dotting the last low line of hills bordering the plain, Garion glanced back once. A half dozen dust clouds spotted the face of the miles-wide slope above them. Murgos were converging on them from all over the mountains.

They galloped on into the trees and thundered through a shallow draw. Barak, riding in the lead, suddenly held up his hand. "Men ahead of us," he warned.

"Murgos?" Hettar asked, his hand going to his sabre.

"I don't think so," Barak replied. "The one I saw looked more like some of those we saw back at the settlement."

Silk, his eyes very bright, pushed his way to the front. "I've got an idea," he said. "Let me talk to them." He pushed his horse into a dead run, plunging directly into what seemed to be an ambush. "Comrades!" he shouted. "Get ready! They're coming—and they've got the gold!"

Several shabby-looking men with rusty swords and axes rose from the bushes or stepped out from behind trees to surround the little man. Silk was talking very fast, gesticulating, waving his arms and pointing back toward the slope looming behind them.

"What's he doing?" Barak asked.

"Something devious, I imagine," Wolf replied.

The men surrounding Silk looked dubious at first, but their expressions gradually changed as he continued to talk excitedly. Finally he turned in his saddle to look back. He jerked his arm in a broad, overhead sweep. "Let's go!" he shouted. "They're with us!" He spun his horse to scramble up the graveled side of the gully.

"Don't get separated," Barak warned, shifting his shoulders under his mail shirt. "I'm not sure what he's up to, but these schemes of his sometimes fall apart."

They pounded down through the grim-looking brigands and up the side of the gully on Silk's heels. "What did you say to them?" Barak shouted as they rode.

"I told them that fifteen Murgos had made a dash into Maragor and come out with three heavy packs of gold." The little man laughed. "Then I said that the men at the settlement had turned them back and that they were trying to double around this way with the gold. I told them that we'd cover this next gully if they'd cover that one back there."

"Those scoundrels will swarm all over Brill and his Murgos when they try to come through," Barak suggested.

"I know." Silk laughed. "Terrible, isn't it?"

They rode on at a gallop. After about a half mile, Mister Wolf raised his arm, and they all reined in. "This should be far enough," he told them. "Now listen very carefully, all of you. These hills are alive with Murgos, so we're going to have to go into Maragor."

Princess Ce'Nedra gasped, and her face turned deathly pale.

"It'll be all right, dear," Aunt Pol soothed her.

Wolf's face was grimly serious. "As soon as we ride out onto the plain, you're going to start hearing certain things," he continued. "Don't pay any attention. Just keep riding. I'm going to be in the lead and I want you all to watch me very closely. As soon as I raise my hand, I want you to stop and get down off your horses immediately. Keep your eyes on the ground and don't look up, no matter what you hear. There are things out there that you don't want to see. Polgara and I are going to put you all into a kind of sleep. Don't try to fight us. Just relax and do exactly what we tell you to do."

"Sleep?" Mandorallen protested. "What if we are attacked? How may we defend ourselves if we are asleep?"

"There isn't anything alive out there to attack you, Mandorallen," Wolf told him. "And it isn't your body that needs to be protected; it's your mind."

"What about the horses?" Hettar asked.

"The horses will be all right. They won't even see the ghosts."

"I can't do it," Ce'Nedra declared, her voice hovering on the edge of hysteria. "I *can't* go into Maragor."

"Yes, you can, dear," Aunt Pol told her in that same calm, soothing voice. "Stay close to me. I won't let anything happen to you."

Garion felt a sudden profound sympathy for the frightened little girl, and he drew his horse over beside hers. "I'll be here, too," he told her.

She looked at him gratefully, but her lower lip still trembled, and her face was very pale.

Mister Wolf took a deep breath and glanced once at the long slope behind them. The dust clouds raised by the converging Murgos were much closer now. "All right," he said, "let's go." He turned his horse and began to ride at an easy trot down toward the mouth of the gully and the plain stretching out before them.

The sound at first seemed faint and very far away, almost like the murmur of wind among the branches of a forest or the soft babble of water over stones. Then, as they rode farther out onto the plain, it grew louder and more distinct. Garion glanced back once, almost longingly, at the hills behind them. Then he pulled his horse close in beside Ce'Nedra's and locked his eyes on Mister Wolf's back, trying to close his ears.

The sound was now a chorus of moaning cries punctuated by occasional shrieks. Behind it all, and seeming to carry and sustain all the other sounds, was a dreadful wailing—a single voice surely, but so vast and all-encompassing that it seemed to reverberate inside Garion's head, erasing all thought.

Mister Wolf suddenly raised his hand, and Garion slid out of his saddle, his eyes fixed almost desperately on the ground. Something flickered at the edge of his vision, but he refused to look.

Then Aunt Pol was speaking to them, her voice calm, reassuring. "I want you to form a circle," she told them, "and take each other's hands. Nothing will be able to enter the circle, so you'll all be safe."

Trembling in spite of himself, Garion stretched out his hands. Someone took his left, he didn't know who; but he instantly knew that the tiny hand that clung so desperately to his right was Ce'Nedra's.

Aunt Pol stood in the center of their circle, and Garion could feel the force of her presence there washing over all of them. Somewhere outside the circle, he could feel Wolf. The old man was doing something that swirled faint surges through Garion's veins and set off staccato bursts of the familiar roaring sound.

The wailing of the dreadful, single voice grew louder, more intense, and Garion felt the first touches of panic. It was not going to work. They were all going to go mad.

"Hush, now," Aunt Pol's voice came to him, and he knew that she spoke inside his mind. His panic faded, and he felt a strange, peaceful lassitude. His eyes grew heavy, and the sound of the wailing grew fainter. Then, enfolded in a comforting warmth, he fell almost at once into a profound slumber.

CHAPTER FIVE

Garion was not exactly sure when it was that his mind shook off Aunt Pol's soft compulsion to sink deeper and deeper into protective unawareness. It could not have been long. Falteringly, like someone rising slowly from the depths, he swam back up out of sleep to find himself moving stiffly, even woodenly, toward the horses with the others. When he glanced at them, he saw that their faces were blank, uncomprehending. He seemed to hear Aunt Pol's whispered command to "sleep, sleep, sleep," but it somehow lacked the power necessary to compel him to obey.

There was to his consciousness, however, a subtle difference. Although his mind was awake, his emotions seemed not to be. He found himself looking at things with a calm, lucid detachment, uncluttered by those feelings which so often churned his thoughts into turmoil. He knew that in all probability he should tell Aunt Pol that he was not asleep, but for some obscure reason he chose not to. Patiently, he began to sort through the notions and ideas surrounding that decision, trying to isolate the single thought which he knew must lie behind the choice not to speak. In his search, he touched that quiet corner where the other mind stayed. He could almost sense its sardonic amusement.

"Well?" he said silently to it.

"I see that you're finally awake," the other mind said to him.

"No," Garion corrected rather meticulously, "actually a part of me is asleep, I think."

"That was the part that kept getting in the way. We can talk now. We have some things to discuss."

"Who are you?" Garion asked, absently following Aunt Pol's instructions to get back on his horse.

"I don't actually have a name."

"You're separate from me, though, aren't you? I mean, you're not just another part of me, are you?"

"No," the voice replied, "we're quite separate."

The horses were moving at a walk now, following Aunt Pol and Mister Wolf across the meadow.

"What do you want?" Garion asked.

"I need to make things come out the way they're supposed to. I've been doing that for a very long time now."

Garion considered that. Around him the wailing grew louder, and the chorus of moans and shrieks became more distinct. Filmy, half-formed tatters of shape began to appear, floating across the grass toward the horses. "I'm going to go mad, aren't I?" he asked somewhat regretfully. "I'm not asleep like the others are, and the ghosts will drive me mad, won't they?"

"I doubt it," the voice answered. "You'll see some things you'd probably rather not see, but I don't think it'll destroy your mind. You might even learn some things about yourself that'll be useful later on."

"You're very old, aren't you?" Garion asked as the thought occurred to him.

"That term doesn't have any meaning in my case."

"Older than my grandfather?" Garion persisted.

"I knew him when he was a child. It might make you feel better to know that he was even more stubborn than you are. It took me a very long time to get him started in the direction he was supposed to go."

"Did you do it from inside his mind?"

"Naturally."

Garion noted that his horse was walking obliviously through one of the filmy images that was taking shape in front of him. "Then he knows you, doesn't he—if you were in his mind, I mean?"

"He didn't know I was there."

"I've always known you were there."

"You're different. That's what we need to talk about."

Rather suddenly, a woman's head appeared in the air directly in front of Garion's face. The eyes were bulging, and the mouth was agape in a soundless scream. The ragged, hacked-off stump of its neck streamed blood that seemed to dribble off into nowhere. "Kiss me," it croaked at him. Garion closed his eyes as his face passed through the head.

"You see," the voice pointed out conversationally. "It's not as bad as you thought it was going to be."

"In what way am I different?" Garion wanted to know.

"Something needs to be done, and you're the one who's going to do it. All the others have just been in preparation for you."

"What is it exactly that I have to do?"

"You'll know when the time comes. If you find out too soon, it might frighten you." The voice took on a somewhat wry note. "You're difficult enough to manage without additional complications."

"Why are we talking about it, then?"

"You need to know *why* you have to do it. That might help you when the time comes."

"All right," Garion agreed.

"A very long time ago, something happened that wasn't supposed to happen," the voice in his mind began. "The universe came into existence for a reason, and it was moving toward that purpose smoothly. Everything was happening the way it was supposed to happen, but then something went wrong. It wasn't really a very big thing, but it just happened to be in the right place at the right time—or perhaps in the wrong place at the wrong time might be a better way to put it. Anyway, it changed the direction of events. Can you understand that?"

"I think so," Garion replied, frowning with the effort. "Is it like when you throw a rock at something but it bounces off something else instead and goes where you don't want it to go—like the time Doroon threw that rock at the crow and it hit a tree limb and bounced off and broke Faldor's window instead?"

"That's exactly it," the voice congratulated him. "Up to that point there had always been only one possibility—the original one. Now there were suddenly two. Let's take it one step further. If Doroon—or you—had thrown another rock very quickly and hit the first rock before it got to Faldor's window, it's possible that the first rock might have been knocked back to hit the crow instead of the window."

"Maybe," Garion conceded doubtfully. "Doroon wasn't really that good at throwing rocks."

"I'm much better at it than Doroon," the voice told him. "That's the whole reason I came into existence in the first place. In a very special way, you're the rock that I've thrown. If you hit the other rock just right, you'll turn it and make it go where it was originally intended to go."

"And if I don't?"

"Faldor's window gets broken."

The figure of a naked woman with her arms chopped off and a sword thrust through her body was suddenly in front of Garion. She shrieked and moaned at him, and the stumps of her arms spurted blood directly into his face. Garion reached up to wipe off the blood, but his face was dry. Unconcerned, his horse walked through the gibbering ghost.

"We have to get things back on the right course," the voice went on. "This certain thing you have to do is the key to the whole business. For a long time, what was supposed to happen and what was actually happening went off in different directions. Now they're starting to converge again. The point where they meet is the point where you'll have to act. If you succeed, things will be all right again; if you don't, everything will keep going wrong, and the purpose for which the universe came into existence will fail."

"How long ago was it when this started?"

"Before the world was made. Even before the Gods."

"Will I succeed?" Garion asked.

"I don't know," the voice replied. "I know what's supposed to happen—not what will. There's something else you need to know, too. When this mistake occurred, it set off two separate lines of possibility, and a line of possibility has a kind of purpose. To have a purpose, there has to be awareness of that purpose. To put it rather simply, that's what I am—the awareness of the original purpose of the universe."

"Only now there's another one, too, isn't there?" Garion suggested. "Another awareness, I mean—one connected with the other set of possibilities."

"You're even brighter than I thought."

"And wouldn't it want things to keep going wrong?"

"I'm afraid so. Now we come to the important part. The spot in time where all this is going to be decided one way or another is getting very close, and you've got to be ready."

"Why me?" Garion asked, brushing away a disconnected hand that appeared to be trying to clutch at his throat. "Can't somebody else do it?"

"No," the voice told him. "That's not the way it works. The universe has been waiting for you for more millions of years than you could even imagine. You've been hurtling toward this event since before the beginning of time. It's yours alone. You're the only one who can do what needs to be done, and it's the most important thing that'll ever happen—not just in this world but in all the worlds in all the universe. There are whole races of men on worlds so far away that the light from their suns will never reach this world, and they'll cease to exist if you fail. They'll never know you or thank you, but their entire existence depends on you. The other line of possibility leads to absolute chaos and the ultimate destruction of the universe, but you and I lead to something else."

"What?"

"If you're successful, you'll live to see it happen."

"All right," Garion said. "What do I have to do—now, I mean?"

"You have enormous power. It's been given to you so that you can do what you have to do, but you've got to learn how to use it. Belgarath and Polgara are trying to help you learn, so stop fighting with them about it. You've got to be ready when the time comes, and the time is much closer than you might think."

A decapitated figure stood in the trail, holding its head by the hair with its right hand. As Garion approached, the figure raised the head. The twisted mouth shrieked curses at him.

After he had ridden through the ghost, Garion tried to speak to the mind within his mind again, but it seemed to be gone for the moment.

They rode slowly past the tumbled stones of a ruined farmstead. Ghosts clustered thickly on the stones, beckoning and calling seductively.

"A disproportionate number seem to be women," Aunt Pol observed calmly to Mister Wolf.

"It was a peculiarity of the race," Wolf replied. "Eight out of nine births were female. It made certain adjustments necessary in the customary relationships between men and women."

"I imagine you found that entertaining," she said dryly.

"The Marags didn't look at things precisely the way other races do. Marriage never gained much status among them. They were quite liberal about certain things."

"Oh? Is that the term for it?"

"Try not to be so narrow-minded, Pol. The society functioned; that's what counts."

"There's a bit more to it than that, father," she said. "What about their cannibalism?"

"That was a mistake. Somebody misinterpreted a passage in one of their sacred texts, that's all. They did it out of a sense of religious obligation, not out of appetite. On the whole, I rather liked the Marags. They were generous, friendly, and very honest with each other. They enjoyed life. If it hadn't been for the gold here, they'd probably have worked out their little aberration."

Garion had forgotten about the gold. As they crossed a small stream, he looked down into the sparkling water and saw the butter-yellow flecks glittering among the pebbles on the bottom.

A naked ghost suddenly appeared before him. "Don't you think I'm beautiful?" she leered. Then she took hold of the sides of the great slash that ran up her abdomen, pulled it open and spilled out her entrails in a pile on the bank of the stream.

Garion gagged and clenched his teeth together.

"Don't think about the gold!" the voice in his mind said sharply. "The ghosts come at you through your greed. If you think about gold, you'll go mad."

They rode on, and Garion tried to push the thought of gold out of his mind.

Mister Wolf, however, continued to talk about it. "That's always been the problem with gold. It seems to attract the worst kind of people—the Tolnedrans in this case."

"They were trying to stamp out cannibalism, father," Aunt Pol replied. "That's a custom most people find repugnant."

"I wonder how serious they'd have been about it if all that gold hadn't been lying on the bed of every stream in Maragor."

Aunt Pol averted her eyes from the ghost of a child impaled on a Tolnedran spear. "And now no one has the gold," she said. "Mara saw to that."

"Yes," Wolf agreed, lifting his face to listen to the dreadful wail that seemed to come from everywhere. He winced at a particularly shrill note in the wailing. "I wish he wouldn't scream so loud."

They passed the ruins of what appeared to have been a temple. The white stones were tumbled, and grass grew up among them. A broad tree standing nearby was festooned with hanging bodies, twisting and swinging on their ropes. "Let us down," the bodies murmured. "Let us down."

"Father!" Aunt Pol said sharply, pointing at the meadow beyond the fallen temple. "Over there! Those people are real."

A procession of robed and hooded figures moved slowly through the meadow, chanting in unison to the sound of a mournfully tolling bell supported on a heavy pole they carried on their shoulders.

"The monks of Mar Terrin," Wolf said. "Tolnedra's conscience. They aren't anything to worry about."

One of the hooded figures looked up and saw them. "Go back!" he shouted. He broke away from the others and ran toward them, recoiling often from things Garion could not see. "Go back!" he cried again. "Save yourselves! You approach the very center of the horror. Mar Amon lies just beyond that hill. Mara himself rages through its haunted streets!"

CHAPTER SIX

The procession of monks moved on, the sound of their chanting and slowly tolling bell growing fainter as they crossed the meadow. Mister Wolf seemed deep in thought, the fingers of his good hand stroking his beard. Finally he sighed rather wryly. "I suppose we might as well deal with him here and now, Pol. He'll just follow us if we don't."

"You're wasting your time, father," Aunt Pol replied. "There's no way to reason with him. We've tried before."

"You're probably right," he agreed, "but we should try at least. Aldur would be disappointed if we didn't. Maybe when he finds out what's happening, he'll come around to the point where we can at least talk to him."

A piercing wail echoed across the sunny meadow, and Mister Wolf made a sour face. "You'd think that he'd have shrieked himself out by now. All right, let's go to Mar Amon." He turned his horse toward the hill the wild-eyed monk had pointed out to them. A maimed ghost gibbered at him from the air in front of his face. "Oh, stop that!" he said irritably. With a startled flicker, the ghost disappeared.

There had perhaps been a road leading over the hill at some time in the past. The faint track of it was dimly visible through the grass, but the thirty-two centuries which had passed since the last living foot had touched its surface had all but erased it. They wound to the top of the hill and looked down into the ruins of Mar Amon. Garion, still detached and unmoved, perceived and deduced things about the city he would not have otherwise noted. Though the destruction had been nearly total, the shape of the city was clearly evident. The street—for there was only one—was laid out in a spiral, winding in toward a broad, circular plaza in the precise center of the ruins. With a peculiar flash of insight, Garion became immediately convinced that the city had been designed by a woman. Men's minds ran to straight lines, but women thought more in terms of circles.

With Aunt Pol and Mister Wolf in the lead and the rest following in wooden-faced unconsciousness, they started down the hill to the city. Garion rode at the rear, trying to ignore the ghosts rising from the earth to confront him with their nudity and their hideous maiming. The wailing sound which they had heard from the moment they had entered Maragor grew louder, more distinct. The wail had sometimes seemed to be a chorus, confused and distorted by echoes, but now Garion realized that it was one single, mighty voice, filled with a grief so vast that it reverberated through all the kingdom.

As they approached the city, a terrible wind seemed to come up, deadly chill and filled with an overpowering charnel-house stench. As Garion reached automatically to draw his cloak tighter about him, he saw that the cloak did not in any way react to that wind, and that the tall grass through which they rode did not bend before it. He considered it, turning it over in his mind as he tried to close his nostrils to the putrid stench of decay and corruption carried on that ghostly wind. If the wind did not move the grass, it could not be a real wind. Furthermore, if the horses could not hear the wails, they could not be real wails either. He grew colder and he shivered, even as he told himself that the chill—like the wind and the grief-laden howling—was spiritual rather than real.

Although Mar Amon, when he had first glimpsed it from the top of the hill, had appeared to be in total ruin, when they entered the city Garion was startled to see the substantial walls of houses and public buildings surrounding him; and somewhere not far away he seemed to hear the sound of laughing children. There was also the sound of singing off in the distance.

"Why does he keep doing this?" Aunt Pol asked sadly. "It doesn't do any good."

"It's all he has, Pol," Mister Wolf replied.

"It always ends the same way, though."

"I know, but for a little while it helps him forget."

"There are things we'd all like to forget, father. This isn't the way to do it."

Wolf looked admiringly at the substantial-seeming houses around them. "It's very good, you know."

"Naturally," she said. "He's a God, after all—but it's still not good for him."

It was not until Barak's horse inadvertently stepped directly through one of the walls—disappearing through the solid-looking stone and then reemerging several yards farther down the street—that Garion understood what his aunt and grandfather were talking about. The walls, the buildings, the whole city was an illusion—a memory. The chill wind with its stink of corruption seemed to grow stronger and carried with it now the added reek of smoke. Though Garion could still see the sunlight shining brightly on the grass, it seemed for some reason that it was growing noticeably darker. The laughter of children and the distant singing faded; instead, Garion heard screams.

A Tolnedran legionnaire in burnished breastplate and plumed helmet, as solid-looking as the walls around them, came running down the long curve of the street. His sword dripped blood, his face was fixed in a hideous grin, and his eyes were wild.

Hacked and mutilated bodies sprawled in the street now, and there was blood everywhere. The wailing climbed into a piercing shriek as the illusion moved on toward its dreadful climax.

The spiral street opened at last into the broad circular plaza at the center of Mar Amon. The icy wind seemed to howl through the burning city, and the dreadful sound of swords chopping through flesh and bone seemed to fill Garion's entire mind. The air grew even darker.

The stones of the plaza were thick with the illusory memory of un-counted scores of Marag dead lying beneath rolling clouds of dense smoke. But what stood in the center of the plaza was not an illusion, nor even a ghost. The figure towered and seemed to shimmer with a terrible presence, a reality that was in no way dependent upon the mind of the observer for its existence. In its arms it held the body of a slaughtered child that seemed somehow to be the sum and total of all the dead of haunted Maragor; and its face, lifted in anguish above the body of that dead child, was ravaged by an expression of inhuman grief. The figure wailed; and Garion, even in the half-somnolent state that protected his sanity, felt the hair on the back of his neck trying to rise in horror.

Mister Wolf grimaced and climbed down from his saddle. Carefully step-ping over the illusions of bodies littering the plaza, he approached the enor-mous presence. "Lord Mara," he said, respectfully bowing to the figure.

Mara howled.

"Lord Mara," Wolf said again. "I would not lightly intrude myself upon thy grief, but I must speak with thee."

The dreadful face contorted, and great tears streamed down the God's cheeks. Wordlessly, Mara held out the body of the child and lifted his face and wailed.

"Lord Mara!" Wolf tried once again, more insistent this time.

Mara closed his eyes and bowed his head, sobbing over the body of the child.

"It's useless, father," Aunt Pol told the old man. "When he's like this, you can't reach him."

"Leave me, Belgarath," Mara said, still weeping. His huge voice rolled and throbbed in Garion's mind. "Leave me to my grief."

"Lord Mara, the day of the fulfillment of the prophecy is at hand," Wolf told him.

"What is that to me?" Mara sobbed, clutching the body of the child closer. "Will the prophecy restore my slaughtered children to me? I am beyond its reach. Leave me alone."

"The fate of the world hinges upon the outcome of events which will happen very soon, Lord Mara," Mister Wolf insisted. "The kingdoms of East and West are girding for the last war, and Torak One-Eye, thine accursed brother, stirs in his slumber and will soon awaken."

"Let him awaken," Mara replied and bowed down over the body in his arms as a storm of fresh weeping swept him.

"Wilt thou then submit to his dominion, Lord Mara?" Aunt Pol asked him.

"I am beyond his dominion, Polgara," Mara answered. "I will not leave this land of my murdered children, and no man or God will intrude upon me here. Let Torak have the world if he wants it."

"We might as well leave, father," Aunt Pol said. "Nothing's going to move him."

"Lord Mara," Mister Wolf said to the weeping God, "we have brought before thee the instruments of prophecy. Wilt thou bless them before we go?"

"I have no blessings, Belgarath," Mara replied. "Only curses for the savage children of Nedra. Take these strangers and go."

"Lord Mara," Aunt Pol said firmly, "a part is reserved for thee in the working-out of the prophecy. The iron destiny which compels us all compels thee as well. Each must play that part laid out for him from the beginning of days, for in the day that the prophecy is turned aside from its terrible course, the world will be unmade."

"Let it be unmade," Mara groaned. "It holds no more joy for me, so let it perish. My grief is eternal, and I will not abandon it, though the cost be the unmaking of all that has been made. Take these children of the prophecy and depart."

Mister Wolf bowed with resignation, turned, and came back toward the rest of them. His expression registered a certain hopeless disgust.

"Wait!" Mara roared suddenly. The images of the city and its dead wavered and shimmered away. "What is this?" the God demanded.

Mister Wolf turned quickly.

"What hast thou done, Belgarath?" Mara accused, suddenly towering into immensity. "And thou, Polgara. Is my grief now an amusement for thee? Wilt thou cast my sorrow into my teeth?"

"My Lord?" Aunt Pol seemed taken aback by the God's sudden fury.

"Monstrous!" Mara roared. "Monstrous!" His huge face convulsed with rage. In terrible anger, he strode toward them and then stopped directly in front of the horse of Princess Ce'Nedra. "I will rend thy flesh!" he shrieked at her. "I will fill thy brain with the worms of madness, daughter of Nedra. I will sink thee in torment and horror for all the days of thy life."

"Leave her alone!" Aunt Pol said sharply.

"Nay, Polgara," he raged. "Upon her will fall the brunt of my wrath." His dreadful, clutching fingers reached out toward the uncomprehending princess, but she stared blankly through him, unflinching and unaware.

The God hissed with frustration and whirled to confront Mister Wolf. "Tricked!" he howled. "Her mind is asleep."

"They're all asleep, Lord Mara," Wolf replied. "Threats and horrors don't mean anything to them. Shriek and howl until the sky falls down; she cannot hear thee."

"I will punish thee for this, Belgarath," Mara snarled, "and Polgara as well. You will all taste pain and terror for this arrogant despite of me. I will wring the sleep from the minds of these intruders, and they will know the agony and madness I will visit upon them all." He swelled suddenly into vastness.

"That's enough! Mara! Stop!" The voice was Garion's, but Garion knew that it was not he who spoke.

The Spirit of Mara turned on him, raising his vast arm to strike, but Garion felt himself slide from his horse to approach the vast threatening figure. "Your vengeance stops here, Mara," the voice coming from Garion's mouth said. "The girl is bound to *my* purpose. You will not touch her." Garion realized with a certain alarm that he had been placed between the raging God and the sleeping princess.

"Move out of my way, boy, lest I slay thee," Mara threatened.

"Use your mind, Mara," the voice told him, "if you haven't howled it empty by now. You know who I am."

"I *will* have her!" Mara howled. "I will give her a multitude of lives and tear each one from her quivering flesh."

"No," the voice replied, "you *won't*."

The God Mara drew himself up again, raising his dreadful arms; but at the same time, his eyes were probing—and more than his eyes. Garion once again felt a vast touch on his mind as he had in Queen Salmissra's throne room when the Spirit of Issa had touched him. A dreadful recognition began to dawn in Mara's weeping eyes. His raised arms fell. "Give her to me," he pleaded. "Take the others and go, but give the Tolnedran to me. I beg it of thee."

"No."

What happened then was not sorcery—Garion knew it instantly. The noise was not there nor that strange, rushing surge that always accompanied sorcery. Instead, there seemed to be a terrible pressure as the full force of Mara's mind was directed crushingly at him. Then the mind within his mind responded. The power was so vast that the world itself was not large enough to contain it. It did not strike back at Mara, for that dreadful collision would have shattered the world, but it stood rather, calmly unmoved and immovable against the raging torrent of Mara's fury. For a fleeting moment, Garion shared the awareness of the mind within his mind, and he shuddered back from its immensity. In that instant, he saw the birth of uncounted suns swirling in vast spirals against the velvet blackness of the void, their birth and gathering into galaxies and ponderously turning nebulae encompassing but a moment. And beyond that, he looked full in the face of time itself— seeing its beginning and its ending in one awful glimpse.

Mara fell back. "I must submit," he said hoarsely, and then he bowed to

Garion, his ravaged face strangely humble. He turned away and buried his face in his hands, weeping uncontrollably.

"Your grief will end, Mara," the voice said gently. "One day you will find joy again."

"Never," the God sobbed. "My grief will last forever."

"Forever is a very long time, Mara," the voice replied, "and only I can see to the end of it."

The weeping God did not answer, but moved away from them, and the sound of his wailing echoed again through the ruins of Mar Amon.

Mister Wolf and Aunt Pol were both staring at Garion with stunned faces. When the old man spoke, his voice was awed. "Is it possible?"

"Aren't you the one who keeps saying that anything is possible, Belgarath?"

"We didn't know you could intervene directly," Aunt Pol said.

"I nudge things a bit from time to time—make a few suggestions. If you think back carefully, you might even remember some of them."

"Is the boy aware of any of this?" she asked.

"Of course. We had a little talk about it."

"How much did you tell him?"

"As much as he could understand. Don't worry, Polgara, I'm not going to hurt him. He realizes how important all this is now. He knows that he needs to prepare himself and that he doesn't have a great deal of time for it. I think you'd better leave here now. The Tolnedran girl's presence is causing Mara a great deal of pain."

Aunt Pol looked as if she wanted to say more, but she glanced once at the shadowy figure of the God weeping not far away and nodded. She turned to her horse and led the way out of the ruins.

Mister Wolf fell in beside Garion after they had remounted to follow her. "Perhaps we could talk as we ride along," he suggested. "I have a great many questions."

"He's gone, Grandfather," Garion told him.

"Oh," Wolf answered with obvious disappointment.

It was nearing sundown by then, and they stopped for the night in a grove about a mile away from Mar Amon. Since they had left the ruins, they had seen no more of the maimed ghosts. After the others had been fed and sent to their blankets, Aunt Pol, Garion, and Mister Wolf sat around their small fire. Since the presence in his mind had left him, following the meeting with Mara, Garion had felt himself sinking deeper toward sleep. All emotion was totally gone now, and he seemed no longer able to think independently.

"Can we talk to the—other one?" Mister Wolf asked hopefully.

"He isn't there right now," Garion replied.

"Then he isn't always with you?"

"Not always. Sometimes he goes away for months—sometimes even longer. He's been there for quite a long while this time—ever since Asharak burned up."

"Where exactly is he when he's with you?" the old man asked curiously.

"In here." Garion tapped his head.

"Have you been awake ever since we entered Maragor?" Aunt Pol asked.

"Not exactly awake," Garion answered. "Part of me was asleep."

"You could see the ghosts?"

"Yes."

"But they didn't frighten you?"

"No. Some of them surprised me, and one of them made me sick."

Wolf looked up quickly. "It wouldn't make you sick now though, would it?"

"No. I don't think so. Right at first I could still feel things like that a little bit. Now I can't."

Wolf looked thoughtfully at the fire as if looking for a way to phrase his next question. "What did the other one in your head say to you when you talked together?"

"He told me that something had happened a long time ago that wasn't supposed to happen and that I was supposed to fix it."

Wolf laughed shortly. "That's a succinct way of putting it," he observed. "Did he say anything about how it was going to turn out?"

"He doesn't know."

Wolf sighed. "I'd hoped that maybe we'd picked up an advantage somewhere, but I guess not. It looks like both prophecies are still equally valid."

Aunt Pol was looking steadily at Garion. "Do you think you'll be able to remember any of this when you wake up again?" she asked.

"I think so."

"All right, then, listen carefully. There are two prophecies, both leading toward the same event. The Grolims and the rest of the Angaraks are following one; we're following the other. The event turns out differently at the end of each prophecy."

"I see."

"Nothing in either prophecy excludes anything that will happen in the other *until* they meet in that event," she continued. "The course of everything that follows will be decided by how that event turns out. One prophecy will succeed; the other will fail. Everything that *has* happened and *will* happen comes together at that point and becomes one. The mistake will be erased, and the universe will go in one direction or the other, as if that were the direction it had been going from its very beginning. The only real difference is that something that's very important will never happen if we fail."

Garion nodded, feeling suddenly very tired.

"Beldin calls it the theory of convergent destinies," Mister Wolf said. "Two equally possible possibilities. Beldin can be very pompous sometimes."

"It's not an uncommon failing, father," Aunt Pol told him.

"I think I'd like to sleep now," Garion said.

Wolf and Aunt Pol exchanged a quick glance. "All right," Aunt Pol said. She rose and took him by the arm and led him to his blankets.

After she had covered him, drawing the blankets up snugly, she laid one cool hand on his forehead. "Sleep, my Belgarion," she murmured.

And he did that.

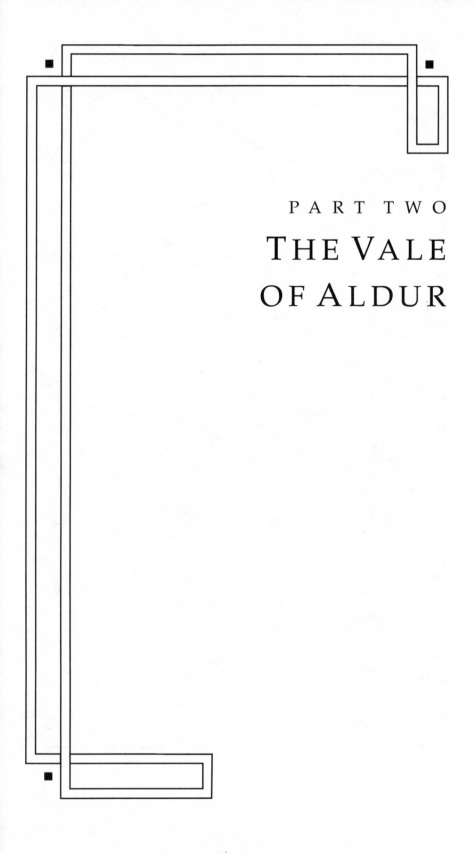

PART TWO

THE VALE
OF ALDUR

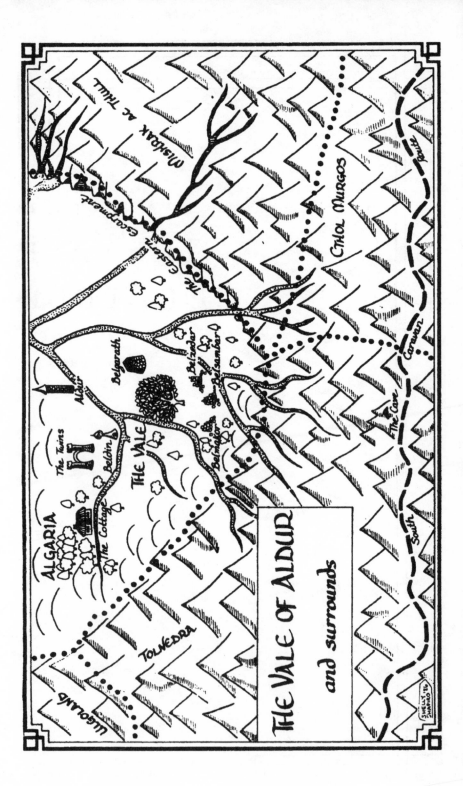

THE VALE OF ALDUR
and surrounds

They were all standing in a circle with their hands joined when they awoke. Ce'Nedra was holding Garion's left hand, and Durnik was on his right. Garion's awareness came flooding back as sleep left him. The breeze was fresh and cool, and the morning sun was very bright. Yellow-brown foothills rose directly in front of them and the haunted plain of Maragor lay behind.

Silk looked around sharply as he awoke, his eyes wary. "Where are we?" he asked quickly.

"On the northern edge of Maragor," Wolf told him, "about eighty leagues east of Tol Rane."

"How long were we asleep?"

"A week or so."

Silk kept looking around, adjusting his mind to the passage of time and distance. "I guess it was necessary," he conceded finally.

Hettar went immediately to check the horses, and Barak began massaging the back of his neck with both hands. "I feel as if I've been sleeping on a pile of rocks," he complained.

"Walk around a bit," Aunt Pol advised. "That'll work the stiffness out."

Ce'Nedra had not removed her hand from Garion's, and he wondered if he should mention it to her. Her hand felt very warm and small in his and, on the whole, it was not unpleasant. He decided not to say anything about it.

Hettar was frowning when he came back. "One of the pack mares is with foal, Belgarath," he said.

"How long has she got to go?" Wolf asked, looking quickly at him.

"It's hard to say for sure—no more than a month. It's her first."

"We can break down her pack and distribute the weight among the other horses," Durnik suggested. "She'll be all right if she doesn't have to carry anything."

"Maybe." Hettar sounded dubious.

Mandorallen had been studying the yellowed foothills directly ahead. "We are being watched, Belgarath," he said somberly, pointing at several wispy columns of smoke rising toward the blue morning sky.

Mister Wolf squinted at the smoke and made a sour face. "Gold-hunters, probably. They hover around the borders of Maragor like vultures over a sick cow. Take a look, Pol."

But Aunt Pol's eyes already had that distant look in them as she scanned the foothills ahead. "Arends," she said, "Sendars, Tolnedrans, a couple of Drasnians. They aren't very bright."

"Any Murgos?"

"No."

"Common rabble, then," Mandorallen observed. "Such scavengers will not impede us significantly."

"I'd like to avoid a fight if possible," Wolf told him. "These incidental skirmishes are dangerous and don't really accomplish anything." He shook his head with disgust. "We'll never be able to convince them that we're not carrying gold out of Maragor, though, so I guess there's no help for it."

"If gold's all they want, why don't we just give them some?" Silk suggested.

"I didn't bring all that much with me, Silk," the old man replied.

"It doesn't have to be real," Silk said, his eyes bright. He went to one of the packhorses, came back with several large pieces of canvas, and quickly cut them into foot-wide squares. Then he took one of the squares and laid a double handful of gravel in its center. He pulled up the corners and wrapped a stout piece of cord around them, forming a heavy-looking pouch. He hefted it a few times. "Looks about like a sackful of gold, wouldn't you say?"

"He's going to do something clever again," Barak said.

Silk smirked at him and quickly made up several more pouches. "I'll take the lead," he said, hanging the pouches on their saddles. "Just follow me and let me do the talking. How many of them are up there, Polgara?"

"About twenty," she replied.

"That'll work out just fine," he stated confidently. "Shall we go?"

They mounted their horses and started across the ground toward the broad mouth of a dry wash that opened out onto the plain. Silk rode at the front, his eyes everywhere. As they entered the mouth of the wash, Garion heard a shrill whistle and saw several furtive movements ahead of them. He was very conscious of the steep banks of the wash on either side of them.

"I'm going to need a bit of open ground to work with," Silk told them. "There." He pointed with his chin at a spot where the slope of the bank was a bit more gradual. When they reached the spot, he turned his horse sharply. "Now!" he barked. "Ride!"

They followed him, scrambling up the bank and kicking up a great deal of gravel; a thick cloud of choking yellow dust rose in the air as they clawed their way up out of the wash.

Shouts of dismay came from the scrubby thornbushes at the upper end of the wash, and a group of rough-looking men broke out into the open, running hard up through the knee-high brown grass to head them off. A black-bearded man, closer and more desperate than the rest, jumped out in front of them, brandishing a rust-pitted sword. Without hesitation, Mandorallen rode him down. The black-bearded man howled as he rolled and tumbled beneath the churning hooves of the huge warhorse.

When they reached the hilltop above the wash, they gathered in a tight group. "This'll do," Silk said, looking around at the rounded terrain. "All I need is for the mob to have enough room to think about casualties. I definitely want them to be thinking about casualties."

An arrow buzzed toward them, and Mandorallen brushed it almost contemptuously out of the air with his shield.

"Stop!" one of the brigands shouted. He was a lean, pockmarked Sendar with a crude bandage wrapped around one leg, wearing a dirty green tunic.

"Who says so?" Silk yelled back insolently.

"I'm Kroldor," the bandaged man announced importantly. "Kroldor the robber. You've probably heard of me."

"Can't say that I have," Silk replied pleasantly.

"Leave your gold—and your women," Kroldor ordered. "Maybe I'll let you live."

"If you get out of our way, maybe we'll let *you* live."

"I've got fifty men," Kroldor threatened, "all desperate, like me."

"You've got twenty," Silk corrected. "Runaway serfs, cowardly peasants, and sneak thieves. My men are trained warriors. Not only that, we're mounted, and you're on foot."

"Leave your gold," the self-proclaimed robber insisted.

"Why don't you come and take it?"

"Let's go!" Kroldor barked at his men. He lunged forward. A couple of his outlaws rather hesitantly followed him through the brown grass, but the rest hung back, eyeing Mandorallen, Barak, and Hettar apprehensively. After a few paces, Kroldor realized that his men were not with him. He stopped and spun around. "You cowards!" he raged. "If we don't hurry, the others will get here. We won't get any of the gold."

"I'll tell you what, Kroldor," Silk said. "We're in kind of a hurry, and we've got more gold than we can conveniently carry." He unslung one of his bags of gravel from his saddle and shook it suggestively. "Here." Negligently he tossed the bag into the grass off to one side. Then he took another bag and tossed it over beside the first. At his quick gesture the others all threw their bags on the growing heap. "There you are, Kroldor," Silk continued. "Ten bags of good yellow gold that you can have without a fight. If you want more, you'll have to bleed for it."

The rough-looking men behind Kroldor looked at each other and began moving to either side, their eyes fixed greedily on the heap of bags lying in the tall grass.

"Your men are having thoughts about mortality, Kroldor," Silk said dryly. "There's enough gold there to make them all rich, and rich men don't take unnecessary risks."

Kroldor glared at him. "I won't forget this," he growled.

"I'm sure you won't," Silk replied. "We're coming through now. I suggest that you get out of our way."

Barak and Hettar moved up to flank Mandorallen, and the three of them started deliberately forward at a slow, menacing walk.

Kroldor the robber stood his ground until the last moment, then turned and scurried out of their path, spouting curses.

"Let's go," Silk snapped.

They thumped their heels to their horses' flanks and charged through at a gallop. Behind them, the outlaws circled and then broke and ran toward the heap of canvas bags. Several ugly little fights broke out almost immediately, and three men were down before anyone thought to open one of the bags. The howls of rage could be heard quite clearly for some distance.

Barak was laughing when they finally reined in their horses after a couple of miles of hard riding. "Poor Kroldor." He chortled. "You're an evil man, Silk."

"I've made a study of the baser side of man's nature," Silk replied innocently. "I can usually find a way to make it work for me."

"Kroldor's men are going to blame him for the way things turned out," Hettar observed.

"I know. But then, that's one of the hazards of leadership."

"They might even kill him."

"I certainly hope so. I'd be terribly disappointed in them if they didn't."

They pushed on through the yellow foothills for the rest of the day and camped that night in a well-concealed little canyon where the light from their fire would not betray their location to the brigands who infested the region. The next morning they started out early, and by noon they were in the mountains. They rode on up among the rocky crags, moving through a thick forest of dark green firs and spruces where the air was cool and spicy. Although it was still summer in the lowlands, the first signs of autumn had begun to appear at the higher elevations. The leaves on the underbrush had begun to turn, the air had a faint, smoky haze, and there was frost on the ground each morning when they awoke. The weather held fair, however, and they made good time.

Then, late one afternoon after they had been in the mountains for a week or more, a heavy bank of clouds moved in from the west, bringing with it a damp chill. Garion untied his cloak from the back of his saddle and pulled it around his shoulders as he rode, shivering as the afternoon grew colder.

Durnik lifted his face and sniffed at the air. "We'll have snow before morning," he predicted.

Garion could also smell the chill, dusty odor of snow in the air. He nodded glumly.

Mister Wolf grunted. "I knew this was too good to last." Then he shrugged. "Oh, well," he added, "we've all lived through winters before."

When Garion poked his head out of the tent the next morning, an inch of snow lay on the ground beneath the dark firs. Soft flakes were drifting down, settling soundlessly and concealing everything more than a hundred yards away in a filmy haze. The air was cold and gray, and the horses, looking very dark under a dusting of snow, stamped their feet and flicked their ears at the fairy touch of the snowflakes settling on them. Their breath steamed in the damp cold.

Ce'Nedra emerged from the tent she shared with Aunt Pol with a squeal of delight. Snow, Garion realized, was probably a rarity in Tol Honeth, and the tiny girl romped through the soft drifting flakes with childish abandon. He smiled tolerantly until a well-aimed snowball caught him on the side of the head. Then he chased her, pelting her with snowballs, while she dodged in and out among the trees, laughing and squealing. When he finally caught her, he was determined to wash her face with snow, but she exuberantly threw her arms around his neck and kissed him, her cold little nose rubbing against his cheek and her eyelashes thick with snowflakes. He didn't realize the full extent of her deceitfulness until she had already poured a handful of snow down the back of his neck. Then she broke free and ran toward the tents, hooting with laughter, while he tried to shake the snow out of the back of his tunic before it all melted.

By midday, however, the snow on the ground had turned to slush, and the drifting flakes had become a steady, unpleasant drizzle. They rode up a narrow ravine under dripping firs while a torrentlike stream roared over boulders beside them.

Mister Wolf finally called a halt. "We're getting close to the western border of Cthol Murgos," he told them. "I think it's time we started to take a few precautions."

"I'll ride out in front," Hettar offered quickly.

"I don't think that's a very good idea," Wolf replied. "You tend to get distracted when you see Murgos."

"I'll do it," Silk said. He had pulled his hood up, but water still dripped from the end of his long, pointed nose. "I'll stay about half a mile ahead and keep my eyes open."

Wolf nodded. "Whistle if you see anything."

"Right." Silk started off up the ravine at a trot.

Late that afternoon, the rain began to freeze as it hit, coating the rocks and trees with gray ice. They rounded a large outcropping of rock and found Silk waiting for them. The stream had turned to a trickle, and the walls of the ravine had opened out onto the steep side of a mountain. "We've got about an hour of daylight left," the little man said. "What do you think? Should we go on, or do you want to drop back down the ravine a bit and set up for the night?"

Mister Wolf squinted at the sky and then at the mountainside ahead. The steep slope was covered with stunted trees, and the timberline lay not far above them. "We have to go around this and then down the other side. It's only a couple of miles. Let's go ahead."

Silk nodded and led out again.

They rounded the shoulder of the mountain and looked down into a deep gorge that separated them from the peak they had crossed two days before. The rain had slackened with the approach of evening, and Garion could see the other side of the gorge clearly. It was no more than half a mile away, and his eyes caught a movement near the rim. "What's that?" He pointed.

Mister Wolf brushed the ice out of his beard. "I was afraid of that."

"What?"

"It's an Algroth."

With a shudder of revulsion, Garion remembered the scaly, goat-faced apes that had attacked them in Arendia. "Hadn't we better run?" he asked.

"It can't get to us," Wolf replied. "The gorge is at least a mile deep. The Grolims have turned their beasts loose, though. It's something we're going to have to watch out for." He motioned for them to continue.

Faintly, distorted by the wind that blew perpetually down the yawning gorge, Garion could hear the barking yelps of the Algroth on the far side as it communicated with the rest of its pack. Soon a dozen of the loathsome creatures were scampering along the rocky rim of the gorge, barking to one another and keeping pace with the party as they rode around the steep mountain face toward a shallow draw on the far side. The draw led away from the gorge; after a mile, they stopped for the night in the shelter of a grove of scrubby spruces.

It was colder the next morning and still cloudy, but the rain had stopped. They rode on back down to the mouth of the draw and continued following the rim of the gorge. The face on the other side fell away in a sheer, dizzying drop for thousands of feet to the tiny-looking ribbon of the river at the bottom. The Algroths still kept pace with them, barking and yelping and looking across with a dreadful hunger. There were other things as well, dimly seen back among the trees on the other side. One of them, huge and shaggy, seemed even to have a human body, but its head was the head of a beast. A herd of swift-moving animals galloped along the far rim, manes and tails tossing.

"Look," Ce'Nedra exclaimed, pointing. "Wild horses."

"They're not horses," Hettar said grimly.

"They look like horses."

"They may look like it, but they aren't."

"Hrulgin," Mister Wolf said shortly.

"What's that?"

"A Hrulga is a four-legged animal—like a horse—but it has fangs instead of teeth, and clawed feet instead of hooves."

"But that would mean—" The princess broke off, her eyes wide.

"Yes. They're meat-eaters."

She shuddered. "How dreadful."

"That gorge is getting narrower, Belgarath," Barak growled. "I'd rather not have any of those things on the same side with us."

"We'll be all right. As I remember, it narrows down to about a hundred yards and then widens out again. They won't be able to get across."

"I hope your memory hasn't failed you."

The sky above looked ragged, tattered by a gusty wind. Vultures soared and circled over the gorge, and ravens flapped from tree to tree, croaking and squawking to one another. Aunt Pol watched the birds with a look of stern disapproval, but said nothing.

They rode on. The gorge grew narrower, and soon they could see the brutish faces of the Algroths on the other side clearly. When the Hrulgin, manes tossing in the wind, opened their mouths to whinny to each other, their long, pointed teeth were plainly visible.

Then, at the narrowest point of the gorge, a party of mail-shirted Murgos rode out onto the opposite precipice. Their horses were lathered from hard riding, and the Murgos themselves were gaunt-faced and travel-stained. They stopped and waited until Garion and his friends were opposite them. At the very edge, staring first across the gorge and then down at the river far below, stood Brill.

"What kept you?" Silk called in a bantering tone that had a hard edge just below the surface. "We thought perhaps you'd gotten lost."

"Not very likely, Kheldar," Brill replied. "How did you get across to that side?"

"You go back that way about four days' ride," Silk shouted, pointing back the way they had come. "If you look very carefully, you'll find the canyon that leads up here. It shouldn't take you more than a day or two to find it."

One of the Murgos pulled a short bow out from beneath his left leg and set an arrow to it. He pointed the arrow at Silk, drew back the string and released. Silk watched the arrow calmly as it fell down into the gorge, spinning in a long, slow-looking spiral. "Nice shot," he called.

"Don't be an idiot," Brill snapped at the Murgo with the bow. He looked back at Silk. "I've heard a great deal about you, Kheldar," he said.

"One has developed a certain reputation," Silk replied modestly.

"One of these days I'll have to find out if you're as good as they say."

"That particular curiosity could be the first symptom of a fatal disease."

"For one of us, at least."

"I look forward to our next meeting, then," Silk told him. "I hope you'll excuse us, my dear fellow—pressing business, you know."

"Keep an eye out behind you, Kheldar," Brill threatened. "One day I'll be there."

"I always keep an eye out behind me, Kordoch," Silk called back, "so don't be too surprised if I'm waiting for you. It's been wonderful chatting with you. We'll have to do it again—soon."

The Murgo with the bow shot another arrow. It followed his first into the gorge.

Silk laughed and led the party away from the brink of the precipice. "What a splendid fellow," he said as they rode away. He looked up at the murky sky overhead. "And what an absolutely beautiful day."

The clouds thickened and grew black as the day wore on. The wind picked up until it howled among the trees. Mister Wolf led them away from the gorge which separated them from Brill and his Murgos, moving steadily toward the northeast.

They set up for the night in a rock-strewn basin just below the timberline. Aunt Pol prepared a meal of thick stew; as soon as they had finished eating, they let the fire go out. "There's no point in lighting beacons for them," Wolf observed.

"They can't get across the gorge, can they?" Durnik asked.

"It's better not to take chances," Wolf replied. He walked away from the last few embers of the dying fire and looked out into the darkness. On an impulse, Garion followed him.

"How much farther is it to the Vale, Grandfather?" he asked.

"About seventy leagues," the old man told him. "We can't make very good time up here in the mountains."

"The weather's getting worse, too."

"I noticed that."

"What happens if we get a real snowstorm?"

"We take shelter until it blows over."

"What if—"

"Garion, I know it's only natural, but sometimes you sound a great deal like your Aunt. She's been saying 'what if' to me since she was about seventeen. I've gotten terribly tired of it over the years."

"I'm sorry."

"Don't be sorry. Just don't do it anymore."

Overhead in the pitch-blackness of the blustery sky, there was a sudden, ponderous flap as of enormous wings.

"What's that?" Garion asked, startled.

"Be still!" Wolf stood with his face turned upward. There was another great flap. "Oh, that's sad."

"What?"

"I thought the poor old brute had been dead for centuries. Why don't they leave her alone?"

"What is it?"

"It doesn't have a name. It's big and stupid and ugly. The Gods only made three of them, and the two males killed each other during the first mating season. She's been alone for as long as I can remember."

"It sounds huge," Garion said, listening to the enormous wings beat overhead and peering up into the darkness. "What does it look like?"

"She's as big as a house, and you really wouldn't want to see her."

"Is she dangerous?"

"Very dangerous, but she can't see too well at night." Wolf sighed. "The Grolims must have chased her out of her cave and put her to hunting for us. Sometimes they go too far."

"Should we tell the others about her?"

"It would only worry them. Sometimes it's better not to say anything."

The great wings flapped again, and there was a long, despairing cry from the darkness, a cry filled with such aching loneliness that Garion felt a great surge of pity welling up in him.

Wolf sighed again. "There's nothing we can do," he said. "Let's go back to the tents."

CHAPTER EIGHT

The weather continued raw and unsettled as they rode for the next two days up the long, sloping rise toward the snow-covered summits of the mountains. The trees became sparser and more stunted as they climbed and finally disappeared entirely. The ridgeline flattened out against the side of one of the mountains, and they rode up onto a steep slope of tumbled rock and ice where the wind scoured continually.

Mister Wolf paused to get his bearings, looking around in the pale afternoon light. "That way," he said finally, pointing. A saddleback stretched between two peaks, and the sky beyond roiled in the wind. They rode up the slope, their cloaks pulled tightly about them.

Hettar came forward with a worried frown on his hawk face. "That pregnant mare's in trouble," he told Wolf. "I think her time's getting close."

Without a word Aunt Pol dropped back to look at the mare, and her face was grave when she returned. "She's no more than a few hours away, father," she reported.

Wolf looked around. "There's no shelter on this side."

"Maybe there'll be something on the other side of the pass," Barak suggested, his beard whipping in the wind.

Wolf shook his head. "I think it's the same as this side. We're going to have to hurry. We don't want to spend the night up here."

As they rode higher, occasional spits of stinging sleet pelted them, and the wind gusted even stronger, howling among the rocks. As they crested the slope and started through the saddle, the full force of the gale struck them, driving a tattered sleet squall before it.

"It's even worse on this side, Belgarath," Barak shouted over the wind. "How far is it down to the trees?"

"Miles," Wolf replied, trying to keep his flying cloak pulled around him.

"The mare will never make it," Hettar said. "We've got to find shelter."

"There isn't any," Wolf stated. "Not until we get to the trees. It's all bare rock and ice up here."

Without knowing why he said it—not even aware of it until he spoke— Garion made a shouted suggestion. "What about the cave?"

Mister Wolf turned and looked sharply at him. "What cave? Where?"

"The one in the side of the mountain. It isn't far." Garion knew the cave was there, but he did not know how he knew.

"Are you sure?"

"Of course. It's this way." Garion turned his horse and rode up the slope of the saddle toward the vast, craggy peak on their left. The wind tore at them as they rode, and the driving sleet half-blinded them. Garion moved confidently, however. For some reason every rock about them seemed absolutely familiar, though he could not have said why. He rode just fast enough to stay in front of the others. He knew they would ask questions, and he didn't have any answers. They rounded a shoulder of the peak and rode out onto a broad rock ledge. The ledge curved along the mountainside, disappearing in the swirling sleet ahead.

"Where art thou taking us, lad?" Mandorallen shouted to him.

"It's not much farther," Garion yelled back over his shoulder.

The ledge narrowed as it curved around the looming granite face of the mountain. Where it bent around a jutting cornice, it was hardly more than a footpath. Garion dismounted and led his horse around the cornice. The wind blasted directly into his face as he stepped around the granite outcrop, and he had to put his hand in front of his face to keep the sleet from blinding him. Walking that way, he did not see the door until it was almost within reach of his hands.

The door in the face of the rock was made of iron, black and pitted with rust and age. It was broader than the gate at Faldor's farm, and the upper edge of it was lost in the swirling sleet.

Barak, following close behind him, reached out and touched the iron door. Then he banged on it with his huge fist. The door echoed hollowly. "There *is* a cave," he said back over his shoulder to the others. "I thought that the wind had blown out the boy's senses."

"How do we get inside?" Hettar shouted, the wind snatching away his words.

"The door's as solid as the mountain itself," Barak said, hammering with his fist again.

"We've got to get out of this wind," Aunt Pol declared, one of her arms protectively above Ce'Nedra's shoulders.

"Well, Garion?" Mister Wolf asked.

"It's easy," Garion replied. "I just have to find the right spot." He ran his fingers over the icy iron, not knowing just what he was looking for. He found a spot that felt a little different. "Here it is." He put his right hand on the spot and pushed lightly. With a vast, grating groan, the door began to move. A line that had not even been visible before suddenly appeared like a razor-cut down the precise center of the pitted iron surface, and flakes of rust showered from the crack, to be whipped away by the wind.

Garion felt a peculiar warmth in the silvery mark on the palm of his right hand where it touched the door. Curious, he stopped pushing, but the door continued to move, swinging open, it seemed, almost in response to the presence of the mark on his palm. It continued to move even after he was no longer touching it. He closed his hand, and the door stopped moving.

He opened his hand, and the door, grating against stone, swung open even wider.

"Don't play with it, dear," Aunt Pol told him. "Just open it."

It was dark in the cave beyond the huge door, but it seemed not to have the musty smell it should have had. They entered cautiously, feeling at the floor carefully with their feet.

"Just a moment," Durnik murmured in a strangely hushed voice. They heard him unbuckling one of his saddlebags and then heard the rasp of his flint against steel. There were a few sparks, then a faint glow as the smith blew on his tinder. The tinder flamed, and he set it to the torch he had pulled from his saddlebag. The torch sputtered briefly, then caught. Durnik raised it, and they all looked around at the cave.

It was immediately evident that the cave was not natural. The walls and floor were absolutely smooth, almost polished, and the light of Durnik's torch reflected back from the gleaming surfaces. The chamber was perfectly round and about a hundred feet in diameter. The walls curved inward as they rose, and the ceiling high overhead seemed also to be round. In the precise center of the floor stood a round stone table, twenty feet across, with its top higher than Barak's head. A stone bench encircled the table. In the wall directly opposite the door was a circular arch of a fireplace. The cave was cool, but it did not seem to have the bitter chill it should have had.

"Is it all right to bring in the horses?" Hettar asked quietly.

Mister Wolf nodded. His expression seemed bemused in the flickering torchlight, and his eyes were lost in thought.

The horses' hooves clattered sharply on the smooth stone floor as they were led inside, and they looked around, their eyes wide and their ears twitching nervously.

"There's a fire laid in here," Durnik said from the arched fireplace. "Shall I light it?"

Wolf looked up. "What? Oh—yes. Go ahead."

Durnik reached into the fireplace with his torch, and the wood caught immediately. The fire swelled up very quickly, and the flames seemed inordinately bright.

Ce'Nedra gasped. "The walls! Look at the walls!" The light from the fire was somehow being refracted through the crystalline structure of the rock itself, and the entire dome began to glow with a myriad of shifting colors, filling the chamber with a soft, multihued radiance.

Hettar had moved around the circle of the wall and was peering into another arched opening. "A spring," he told them. "This is a good place to ride out a storm."

Durnik put out his torch and pulled off his cloak. The chamber had become warm almost as soon as he had lighted the fire. He looked at Mister Wolf. "You know about this place, don't you?" he asked.

"None of us has ever been able to find it before," the old man replied, his eyes still thoughtful. "We weren't even sure it still existed."

"What is this strange cave, Belgarath?" Mandorallen asked.

Mister Wolf took a deep breath. "When the Gods were making the world, it was necessary for them to meet from time to time to discuss what each of them had done and was going to do so that everything would fit together and work in harmony—the mountains, the winds, the seasons and so on." He looked around. "This is the place where they met."

Silk, his nose twitching with curiosity, had climbed up onto the bench surrounding the huge table. "There are bowls up here," he said. "Seven of

them—and seven cups. There seems to be some kind of fruit in the bowls."
He began to reach out with one hand.

"Silk!" Mister Wolf told him sharply. "Don't touch anything."

Silk's hand froze, and he looked back over his shoulder at the old man,
his face startled.

"You'd better come down from there," Wolf said gravely.

"The door!" Ce'Nedra exclaimed.

They all turned in time to see the massive iron door gently swinging
closed. With an oath, Barak leaped toward it, but he was too late. Booming
hollowly, it clanged shut just before his hands reached it. The big man
turned, his eyes filled with dismay.

"It's all right, Barak," Garion told him. "I can open it again."

Wolf turned then and looked at Garion, his eyes questioning. "How did
you know about the cave?" he asked.

Garion floundered helplessly. "I don't know. I just did. I think I've
known we were getting close to it for the last day or so."

"Does it have anything to do with the voice that spoke to Mara?"

"I don't think so. He doesn't seem to be there just now, and my knowing
about the cave seemed to be different somehow. I think it came from me, not
him, but I'm not sure how. For some reason, it seems that I've always known
this place was here—only I didn't think about it until we started to get near
it. It's awfully hard to explain it exactly."

Aunt Pol and Mister Wolf exchanged a long glance. Wolf looked as if
he were about to ask another question, but just then there was a groan at the
far end of the chamber.

"Somebody help me," Hettar called urgently. One of the horses, her sides
distended and her breath coming in short, heaving gasps, stood swaying as if
her legs were about to give out from under her. Hettar stood at her side, trying to support her. "She's about to foal," he said.

They all turned then and went quickly to the laboring mare. Aunt Pol
immediately took charge of the situation, giving orders crisply. They eased
the mare to the floor, and Hettar and Durnik began to work with her, even
as Aunt Pol filled a small pot with water and set it carefully in the fire. "I'll
need some room," she told the rest of them pointedly as she opened the bag
which contained her jars of herbs.

"Why don't we all get out of your way?" Barak suggested, looking uneasily at the gasping horse.

"Splendid idea," she agreed. "Ce'Nedra, you stay here. I'll need your
help."

Garion, Barak, and Mandorallen moved a few yards away and sat down,
leaning back against the glowing wall, while Silk and Mister Wolf went off
to explore the rest of the chamber. As he watched Durnik and Hettar with
the mare and Aunt Pol and Ce'Nedra by the fire, Garion felt strangely abstracted. The cave had drawn him, there was no question of that, and even
now it was exerting some peculiar force on him. Though the situation with
the mare was immediate, he seemed unable to focus on it. He had a strange

certainty that finding the cave was only the first part of whatever it was that was happening. There was something else he had to do, and his abstraction was in some way a preparation for it.

"It is not an easy thing to confess," Mandorallen was saying somberly. Garion glanced at him. "In view of the desperate nature of our quest, however," the knight continued, "I must openly acknowledge my great failing. It may come to pass that this flaw of mine shall in some hour of great peril cause me to turn and flee like the coward I am, leaving all your lives in mortal danger."

"You're making too much of it," Barak told him.

"Nay, my Lord. I urge that you consider the matter closely to determine if I am fit to continue in our enterprise." He started to creak to his feet.

"Where are you going?" Barak asked.

"I thought to go apart so that you may freely discuss this matter."

"Oh, sit down, Mandorallen," Barak said irritably. "I'm not going to say anything behind your back I wouldn't say to your face."

The mare, lying close to the fire with her head cradled in Hettar's lap, groaned again. "Is that medicine almost ready, Polgara?" the Algar asked in a worried voice.

"Not quite," she replied. She turned back to Ce'Nedra, who was carefully grinding up some dried leaves in a small cup with the back of a spoon. "Break them up a little finer, dear," she instructed.

Durnik was standing astride the mare, his hands on her distended belly. "We may have to turn the foal," he said gravely. "I think it's trying to come the wrong way."

"Don't start on that until this has a chance to work," Aunt Pol told him, slowly tapping a grayish powder from an earthen jar into her bubbling pot. She took the cup of leaves from Ce'Nedra and added that as well, stirring as she poured.

"I think, my Lord Barak," Mandorallen urged, "that thou hast not fully considered the import of what I have told thee."

"I heard you. You said you were afraid once. It's nothing to worry about. It happens to everybody now and then."

"I cannot live with it. I live in constant apprehension, never knowing when it will return to unman me."

Durnik looked up from the mare. "You're afraid of being afraid?" he asked in a puzzled voice.

"You cannot know what it was like, good friend," Mandorallen replied.

"Your stomach tightened up," Durnik told him. "Your mouth was dry, and your heart felt as if someone had his fist clamped around it?"

Mandorallen blinked.

"It's happened to me so often that I know exactly how it feels."

"Thou? Thou art among the bravest men I have ever known."

Durnik smiled wryly. "I'm an ordinary man, Mandorallen," he said. "Ordinary men live in fear all the time. Didn't you know that? We're afraid of the weather, we're afraid of powerful men, we're afraid of the night and the monsters that lurk in the dark, we're afraid of growing old and of dying. Sometimes we're even afraid of living. Ordinary men are afraid almost every minute of their lives."

"How canst thou bear it?"

"Do we have any choice? Fear's a part of life, Mandorallen, and it's the only life we have. You'll get used to it. After you've put it on every morning like an old tunic, you won't even notice it anymore. Sometimes laughing at it helps—a little."

"Laughing?"

"It shows the fear that you know it's there, but that you're going to go ahead and do what you have to do anyway." Durnik looked down at his hands, carefully kneading the mare's belly. "Some men curse and swear and bluster," he continued. "That does the same thing, I suppose. Every man has to come up with his own technique for dealing with it. Personally, I prefer laughing. It seems more appropriate somehow."

Mandorallen's face became gravely thoughtful as Durnik's words slowly sank in. "I will consider this," he said. "It may be, good friend, that I will owe thee more than my life for thy gentle instruction."

Once more the mare groaned, a deep, tearing sound, and Durnik straightened and began rolling up his sleeves. "The foal's going to have to be turned, Mistress Pol," he said decisively. "And soon, or we'll lose the foal and the mare both."

"Let me get some of this into her first," she replied, quenching her boiling pot with some cold water. "Hold her head," she told Hettar. Hettar nodded and firmly wrapped his arms around the laboring mare's head. "Garion," Aunt Pol said, as she spooned the liquid between the mare's teeth, "why don't you and Ce'Nedra go over there where Silk and your grandfather are?"

"Have you ever turned a foal before, Durnik?" Hettar asked anxiously.

"Not a foal, but calves many times. A horse isn't that much different from a cow, really."

Barak stood up quickly. His face had a slight greenish cast to it. "I'll go with Garion and the princess," he rumbled. "I don't imagine I'd be much help here."

"And I will join thee," Mandorallen declared. His face was also visibly pale. "It were best, I think, to leave our friends ample room for their midwifery."

Aunt Pol looked at the two warriors with a slight smile on her face, but said nothing.

Garion and the others moved rather quickly away.

Silk and Mister Wolf were standing beyond the huge stone table, peering into another of the circular openings in the shimmering wall. "I've never seen fruits exactly like those," the little man was saying.

"I'd be surprised if you had," Wolf replied.

"They look as fresh as if they'd just been picked." Silk's hand moved almost involuntarily toward the tempting fruit.

"I wouldn't," Wolf warned.

"I wonder what they taste like."

"Wondering won't hurt you. Tasting might."

"I *hate* an unsatisfied curiosity."

"You'll get over it." Wolf turned to Garion and the others. "How's the horse?"

"Durnik says he's going to have to turn the foal," Barak told him. "We thought it might be better if we all got out of the way."

Wolf nodded. "Silk!" he admonished sharply, not turning around.

"Sorry." Silk snatched his hand back.

"Why don't you just get away from there? You're only going to get yourself in trouble."

Silk shrugged. "I do that all the time anyway."

"Just do it, Silk," Wolf told him firmly. "I can't watch over you every minute." He slipped his fingers up under the dirty and rather ragged bandage on his arm, scratching irritably. "That's enough of that," he declared. "Garion, take this thing off me." He held out his arm.

Garion backed away. "Not me," he refused. "Do you know what Aunt Pol would say to me if I did that without her permission?"

"Don't be silly. Silk, you do it."

"First you say to stay out of trouble, and then you tell me to cross Polgara? You're inconsistent, Belgarath."

"Oh, here," Ce'Nedra said. She took hold of the old man's arm and began picking at the knotted bandage with her tiny fingers. "Just remember that this was your idea. Garion, give me your knife."

Somewhat reluctantly, Garion handed over his dagger. The princess sawed through the bandage and began to unwrap it. The splints fell clattering to the stone floor.

"What a dear child you are." Mister Wolf beamed at her and began to scratch at his arm with obvious relief.

"Just remember that you owe me a favor," she told him.

"She's a Tolnedran, all right," Silk observed.

It was about an hour later when Aunt Pol came around the table to them, her eyes somber.

"How's the mare?" Ce'Nedra asked quickly.

"Very weak, but I think she'll be all right."

"What about the baby horse?"

Aunt Pol sighed. "We were too late. We tried everything, but we just couldn't get him to start breathing."

Ce'Nedra gasped, her little face suddenly a deathly white. "You're not going to just give up, are you?" She said it almost accusingly.

"There's nothing more we can do, dear," Aunt Pol told her sadly. "It took too long. He just didn't have enough strength left."

Ce'Nedra stared at her, unbelieving. "*Do* something!" she demanded. "You're a sorceress. Do something!"

"I'm sorry, Ce'Nedra, that's beyond our power. We can't reach beyond that barrier."

The little princess wailed then and began to cry bitterly. Aunt Pol put her arms comfortingly about her and held her as she sobbed.

But Garion was already moving. With absolute clarity he now knew what it was that the cave expected of him, and he responded without thinking, not running or even hurrying. He walked quietly around the stone table toward the fire.

Hettar sat cross-legged on the floor with the unmoving colt in his lap, his head bowed with sorrow and his manelike scalp lock falling across the spindle-shanked little animal's silent face.

"Give him to me, Hettar," Garion said.

"Garion! No!" Aunt Pol's voice, coming from behind him, was alarmed.

Hettar looked up, his hawk face filled with deep sadness.

"Let me have him, Hettar," Garion repeated very quietly.

Wordlessly Hettar raised the limp little body, still wet and glistening in the firelight, and handed it to Garion. Garion knelt and laid the foal on the floor in front of the shimmering fire. He put his hands on the tiny rib cage and pushed gently. "Breathe," he almost whispered.

"We tried that, Garion," Hettar told him sadly. "We tried everything."

Garion began to gather his will.

"Don't do that, Garion," Aunt Pol told him firmly. "It isn't possible, and you'll hurt yourself if you try."

Garion was not listening to her. The cave itself was speaking to him too loudly for him to hear anything else. He focused his every thought on the wet, lifeless body of the foal. Then he stretched out his right hand and laid his palm on the unblemished, walnut-colored shoulder of the dead animal. Before him there seemed to be a blank wall—black and higher than anything else in the world, impenetrable and silent beyond his comprehension. Tentatively he pushed at it, but it would not move. He drew in a deep breath and hurled himself entirely into the struggle.

"Live," he said.

"Garion, stop."

"Live," he said again, throwing himself deeper into his effort against that blackness.

"It's too late now, Pol," he heard Mister Wolf say from somewhere. "He's already committed himself."

"Live," Garion repeated, and the surge he felt welling up out of him was so vast that it drained him utterly. The glowing walls flickered and then suddenly rang as if a bell had been struck somewhere deep inside the mountain. The sound shimmered, filling the air inside the domed chamber with a vibrant ringing. The light in the walls suddenly flared with a searing brightness, and the chamber was as bright as noon.

The little body under Garion's hand quivered, and the colt drew in a deep, shuddering breath. Garion heard the others gasp as the sticklike little legs began to twitch. The colt inhaled again, and his eyes opened.

"A miracle," Mandorallen said in a choked voice.

"Perhaps even more than that," Mister Wolf replied, his eyes searching Garion's face.

The colt struggled, his head wobbling weakly on his neck. He pulled his legs under him and began to struggle to his feet. Instinctively, he turned to his mother and tottered toward her to nurse. His coat, which had been a deep, solid brown before Garion had touched him, was now marked on the shoulder with a single incandescently white patch exactly the size of the mark on Garion's palm.

Garion lurched to his feet and stumbled away, pushing past the others. He staggered to the icy spring bubbling in the opening in the wall and splashed water over his head and neck. He knelt before the spring, shaking and breathing hard for a very long time. Then he felt a tentative, almost shy touch on his elbow. When he warily raised his head, he saw the now steadier colt standing at his side and gazing at him with adoration in its liquid eyes.

CHAPTER NINE

The storm blew itself out the next morning, but they stayed in the cave for another day after the wind had died down to allow the mare to recover and the newborn colt to gain a bit more strength. Garion found the attention of the little animal disturbing. It seemed that no matter where he went in the cave, those soft eyes followed him, and the colt was continually nuzzling at him. The other horses also watched him with a kind of mute respect. All in all it was a bit embarrassing.

On the morning of their departure, they carefully removed all traces of their stay from the cave. The cleaning was spontaneous, neither the result of some suggestion nor of any discussion, but rather was something in which they all joined without comment.

"The fire's still burning," Durnik fretted, looking back into the glowing dome from the doorway as they prepared to leave.

"It'll go out by itself after we leave," Wolf told him. "I don't think you could put it out anyway—no matter how hard you tried."

Durnik nodded soberly. "You're probably right," he agreed.

"Close the door, Garion," Aunt Pol said after they had led their horses out onto the ledge outside the cave.

Somewhat self-consciously, Garion took hold of the edge of the huge iron door and pulled it. Although Barak with all his great strength had tried without success to budge the door, it moved easily as soon as Garion's hand touched it. A single tug was enough to set it swinging gently closed. The two solid edges came together with a great, hollow boom, leaving only a thin, nearly invisible line where they met.

Mister Wolf put his hand lightly on the pitted iron, his eyes far away. Then he sighed once, turned, and led them back along the ledge the way they had come two days before.

Once they had rounded the shoulder of the mountain, they remounted and rode on down through the tumbled boulders and patches of rotten ice to the first low bushes and stunted trees a few miles below the pass. Although the wind was still brisk, the sky overhead was blue, and only a few fleecy clouds raced by, appearing strangely close.

Garion rode up to Mister Wolf and fell in beside him. His mind was filled with confusion by what had happened in the cave, and he desperately needed to get things straightened out. "Grandfather," he said.

"Yes, Garion?" the old man answered, rousing himself from his half-doze.

"Why did Aunt Pol try to stop me? With the colt, I mean?"

"Because it was dangerous," the old man replied. "Very dangerous."

"Why dangerous?"

"When you try to do something that's impossible, you can pour too much energy into it; and if you keep trying, it can be fatal."

"Fatal?"

Wolf nodded. "You drain yourself out completely, and you don't have enough strength left to keep your own heart beating."

"I didn't know that." Garion was shocked.

Wolf ducked as he rode under a low branch. "Obviously."

"Don't you keep saying that *nothing* is impossible?"

"Within reason, Garion. Within reason."

They rode on quietly for a few minutes, the sound of their horses' hooves muffled by the thick moss covering the ground under the trees.

"Maybe I'd better find out more about all this," Garion said finally.

"That's not a bad idea. What was it you wanted to know?"

"Everything, I guess."

Mister Wolf laughed. "That would take a very long time, I'm afraid."

Garion's heart sank. "Is it that complicated?"

"No. Actually it's very simple, but simple things are always the hardest to explain."

"That doesn't make any sense," Garion retorted, a bit irritably.

"Oh?" Wolf looked at him with amusement. "Let me ask you a simple question, then. What's two and two?"

"Four," Garion replied promptly.

"Why?"

Garion floundered for a moment. "It just is," he answered lamely.

"But why?"

"There isn't any why to it. It just is."

"There's a why to everything, Garion."

"All right, why is two and two four, then?"

"I don't know," Wolf admitted. "I thought maybe you might."

They passed a dead snag standing twisted and starkly white against the deep blue sky.

"Are we getting anywhere?" Garion asked, even more confused now.

"Actually, I think we've come a very long way," Wolf replied. "Precisely what was it you wanted to know?"

Garion put it as directly as he knew how. "What is sorcery?"

"I told you that once already. The Will and the Word."

"That doesn't really mean anything, you know."

"All right, try it this way. Sorcery is doing things with your mind instead of your hands. Most people don't use it because at first it's much easier to do things the other way."

Garion frowned. "It doesn't seem hard."

"That's because the things you've been doing have come out of impulse. You've never sat down and thought your way through something—you just do it."

"Isn't it easier that way? What I mean is, why not just do it and not think about it?"

"Because spontaneous sorcery is just third-rate magic—completely uncontrolled. Anything can happen if you simply turn the power of your mind loose. It has no morality of its own. The good or the bad of it comes out of *you*, not out of the sorcery."

"You mean that when I burned Asharak, it was me and not the sorcery?" Garion asked, feeling a bit sick at the thought.

Mister Wolf nodded gravely. "It might help if you remember that you were also the one who gave life to the colt. The two things sort of balance out."

Garion glanced back over his shoulder at the colt, who was frisking along behind him like a puppy. "What you're saying is that it can be either good or bad."

"No," Wolf corrected. "By itself it has nothing to do with good or bad. And it won't help you in any way to make up your mind how to use it. You can do anything you want to with it—almost anything, that is. You can bite the tops off all the mountains or stick the trees in the ground upside down or turn all the clouds green, if you feel like it. What you have to decide is whether you *should* do something, not whether you *can* do it."

"You said *almost* anything," Garion noted quickly.

"I'm getting to that," Wolf said. He looked thoughtfully at a low-flying cloud—an ordinary-looking old man in a rusty tunic and gray hood looking at the sky. "There's one thing that's absolutely forbidden. You can never destroy anything—not ever."

Garion was baffled by that. "I destroyed Asharak, didn't I?"

"No. You killed him. There's a difference. You set fire to him, and he burned to death. To destroy something is to try to uncreate it. That's what's forbidden."

"What would happen if I *did* try?"

"Your power would turn inward on you, and you'd be obliterated in an instant."

Garion blinked and then suddenly went cold at the thought of how close he had come to crossing that forbidden line in his encounter with Asharak.

"How do I tell the difference?" he asked in a hushed voice. "I mean, how do I go about explaining that I only meant to kill somebody and not destroy him?"

"It's not a good area for experimentation," Wolf told him. "If you really want to kill somebody, stick your sword in him. Hopefully you won't have occasion to do that sort of thing too often."

They stopped at a small brook trickling out of some mossy stones to allow their horses to drink.

"You see, Garion," Wolf explained, "the ultimate purpose of the universe is to create things. It won't permit you to come along behind it uncreating all the things it went to so much trouble to create in the first place. When you kill somebody, all you've really done is alter him a bit. You've changed him from being alive to being dead. He's still there. To uncreate him, you have to will him out of existence entirely. When you feel yourself on the verge of telling something to 'vanish' or 'go away' or 'be not,' you're getting very close to the point of self-destruction. That's the main reason we have to keep our emotions under control all the time."

"I didn't know that," Garion admitted.

"You do now. Don't even try to unmake a single pebble."

"A pebble?"

"The universe doesn't make any distinction between a pebble and a man." The old man looked at him somewhat sternly. "Your Aunt's been trying to explain the necessity for keeping yourself under control for several months now, and you've been fighting her every step of the way."

Garion hung his head. "I didn't know what she was getting at," he apologized.

"That's because you weren't listening. That's a great failing of yours, Garion."

Garion flushed. "What happened the first time *you* found out you could—well—do things?" he asked quickly, wanting to change the subject.

"It was something silly," Wolf replied. "It usually is, the first time."

"What was it?"

Wolf shrugged. "I wanted to move a big rock. My arms and back weren't strong enough, but my mind was. After that I didn't have any choice but to learn to live with it because, once you unlock it, it's unlocked forever. That's the point where your life changes and you have to start learning to control yourself."

"It always gets back to that, doesn't it?"

"Always," Wolf said. "It's not as difficult as it sounds, really. Look at Mandorallen." He pointed at the knight, who was riding with Durnik. The two of them were in a deep discussion. "Now, Mandorallen's a nice enough fellow—honest, sincere, toweringly noble—but let's be honest. His mind has never been violated by an original thought—until now. He's learning to control fear, and learning to control it is forcing him to think—probably for the first time in his whole life. It's painful for him, but he's doing it. If Mandorallen can learn to control fear with that limited brain of his, surely *you* can learn the same kind of control over the other emotions. After all, you're quite a bit brighter than he is."

Silk, who had been scouting ahead, came riding back to join them. "Belgarath," he said, "there's something about a mile in front of us that I think you'd better take a look at."

"All right," Wolf replied. "Think about what I've been saying, Garion. We'll talk more about it later." Then he and Silk moved off through the trees at a gallop.

Garion pondered what the old man had told him. The one thing that bothered him the most was the crushing responsibility his unwanted talent placed upon him.

The colt frisked along beside him, galloping off into the trees from time to time and then rushing back, his little hooves pattering on the damp ground. Frequently he would stop and stare at Garion, his eyes full of love and trust.

"Oh, stop that," Garion told him.

The colt scampered away again.

Princess Ce'Nedra moved her horse up until she was beside Garion. "What were you and Belgarath talking about?" she asked.

Garion shrugged. "A lot of things."

There was immediately a hard little tightening around her eyes. In the months that they had known each other, Garion had learned to catch those minute danger signals. Something warned him that the princess was spoiling for an argument, and with an insight that surprised him he reasoned out the source of her unspoken belligerence. What had happened in the cave had shaken her badly, and Ce'Nedra did not like to be shaken. To make matters even worse, the princess had made a few coaxing overtures to the colt, obviously wanting to turn the little animal into her personal pet. The colt, however, ignored her completely, fixing all his attention on Garion, even to the point of ignoring his own mother unless he was hungry. Ce'Nedra disliked being ignored even more than she disliked being shaken. Glumly, Garion realized how small were his chances of avoiding a squabble with her.

"I certainly wouldn't want to pry into a private conversation," she said tartly.

"It wasn't private. We were talking about sorcery and how to keep accidents from happening. I don't want to make any more mistakes."

She turned that over in her mind, looking for something offensive in it. His mild answer seemed to irritate her all the more. "I don't believe in sorcery," she said flatly. In the light of all that had recently happened, her declaration was patently absurd, and she seemed to realize that as soon as she said it. Her eyes hardened even more.

Garion sighed. "All right," he said with resignation, "was there anything in particular you wanted to fight about, or did you just want to start yowling and sort of make it up as we go along?"

"Yowling?" Her voice went up several octaves. *"Yowling?"*

"Screeching, maybe," he suggested as insultingly as possible. As long as the fight was inevitable anyway, he determined to get in a few digs at her before her voice rose to the point where she could no longer hear him.

"SCREECHING?" she screeched.

The fight lasted for about a quarter of an hour before Barak and Aunt Pol moved forward to separate them. On the whole, it was not very satisfactory. Garion was a bit too preoccupied to put his heart into the insults he flung at the tiny girl, and Ce'Nedra's irritation robbed her retorts of their usual fine edge. Toward the end, the whole thing had degenerated into a tedious repetition of "spoiled brat" and "stupid peasant" echoing endlessly back from the surrounding mountains.

Mister Wolf and Silk rode back to join them. "What was all the yelling?" Wolf asked.

"The children were playing," Aunt Pol replied with a withering look at Garion.

"Where's Hettar?" Silk asked.

"Right behind us," Barak said. He turned to look back toward the packhorses, but the tall Algar was nowhere to be seen. Barak frowned. "He was just there. Maybe he stopped for a moment to rest his horse or something."

"Without saying anything?" Silk objected. "That's not like him. And it's not like him to leave the packhorses unattended."

"He must have some good reason," Durnik said.

"I'll go back and look for him," Barak offered.

"No," Mister Wolf told him. "Wait a few minutes. Let's not get scattered all over these mountains. If anybody goes back, we'll all go back."

They waited. The wind stirred the branches of the pines around them, making a mournful, sighing sound. After several moments, Aunt Pol let out her breath almost explosively. "He's coming." There was a steely note in her voice. "He's been entertaining himself."

From far back up the trail, Hettar appeared in his black leather clothing, riding easily at a loping canter with his long scalp lock flowing in the wind. He was leading two saddled but riderless horses. As he drew nearer, they could hear him whistling rather tunelessly to himself.

"What have you been doing?" Barak demanded.

"There were a couple of Murgos following us," Hettar replied as if that explained everything.

"You might have asked me to go along," Barak said, sounding a little injured.

Hettar shrugged. "There were only two. They were riding Algar horses, so I took it rather personally."

"It seems that you always find some reason to take it personally where Murgos are concerned," Aunt Pol said crisply.

"It does seem to work out that way, doesn't it?"

"Didn't it occur to you to let us know you were going?" she asked.

"There were only two," Hettar said again. "I didn't expect to be gone for very long."

She drew in a deep breath, her eyes flashing dangerously.

"Let it go, Pol," Mister Wolf told her.

"But—"

"You're not going to change him, so why excite yourself about it? Besides, it's just as well to discourage pursuit." The old man turned to Hettar, ignoring the dangerous look Aunt Pol leveled at him. "Were the Murgos some of those who were with Brill?" he asked.

Hettar shook his head. "No. Brill's Murgos were from the south and they were riding Murgo horses. These two were northern Murgos."

"Is there a visible difference?" Mandorallen asked curiously.

"The armor is slightly different, and the southerners have flatter faces and they're not quite so tall."

"Where did they get Algar horses?" Garion asked.

"They're herd raiders," Hettar answered bleakly. "Algar horses are valuable in Cthol Murgos, and certain Murgos make a practice of creeping down into Algaria on horse-stealing expeditions. We try to discourage that as much as possible."

"These horses aren't in very good shape," Durnik observed, looking at the two weary-looking animals Hettar was leading. "They've been ridden hard, and there are whip cuts on them."

Hettar nodded grimly. "That's another reason to hate Murgos."

"Did you bury them?" Barak asked.

"No. I left them where any other Murgos who might be following could find them. I thought it might help to educate any who come along later."

"There are some signs that others have been through here, too," Silk said. "I found the tracks of a dozen or so up ahead."

"It was to be expected, I suppose," Mister Wolf commented, scratching at his beard. "Ctuchik's got his Grolims out in force, and Taur Urgas is probably having the region patrolled. I'm sure they'd like to stop us if they could. I think we should move on down into the Vale as fast as possible. Once we're there, we won't be bothered anymore."

"Won't they follow us into the Vale?" Durnik asked, looking around nervously.

"No. Murgos won't go into the Vale—not for any reason. Aldur's Spirit is there, and the Murgos are desperately afraid of him."

"How many days to the Vale?" Silk asked.

"Four or five, if we ride hard," Wolf replied.

"We'd better get started, then."

CHAPTER TEN

The weather, which had seemed on the brink of winter in the higher mountains, softened back into autumn as they rode down from the peaks and ridges. The forests in the hills above Maragor had been thick with fir and spruce and heavy undergrowth. On this side, however, the dominant tree was the pine, and the undergrowth was sparse. The air seemed drier, and the hillsides were covered with high, yellow grass.

They passed through an area where the leaves on the scattered bushes were bright red; then, as they moved lower, the foliage turned first yellow, then green again. Garion found this reversal of the seasons strange. It seemed to violate all his perceptions of the natural order of things. By the time they reached the foothills above the Vale of Aldur, it was late summer again, golden and slightly dusty. Although they frequently saw evidences of the Murgo patrols which were crisscrossing the region, they had no further encounters. After they crossed a certain undefined line, there were no more tracks of Murgo horses.

They rode down beside a turbulent stream which plunged over smooth, round rocks, frothing and roaring. The stream was one of several forming the headwaters of the Aldur River, a broad flow running through the vast Algarian plain to empty into the Gulf of Cherek, eight hundred leagues to the northwest.

The Vale of Aldur was a valley lying in the embrace of the two mountain ranges which formed the central spine of the continent. It was lush and green, covered with high grass and dotted here and there with huge, solitary trees. Deer and wild horses grazed there, as tame as cattle. Skylarks wheeled and dove, filling the air with their song. As the party rode out into the valley, Garion noticed that the birds seemed to gather wherever Aunt Pol moved, and many of the braver ones even settled on her shoulders, warbling and trilling to her in welcome and adoration.

"I'd forgotten about that," Mister Wolf said to Garion. "It's going to be difficult to get her attention for the next few days."

"Oh?"

"Every bird in the Vale is going to stop by to visit her. It happens every time we come here. The birds go wild at the sight of her."

Out of the welter of confused bird sound it seemed to Garion that faintly, almost like a murmuring whisper, he could hear a chorus of chirping voices repeating, "Polgara. Polgara. Polgara."

"Is it my imagination, or are they actually talking?" he asked.

"I'm surprised you haven't heard them before," Wolf replied. "Every bird we've passed for the last ten leagues has been babbling her name."

"Look at me, Polgara, look at me," a swallow seemed to say, hurling himself into a wild series of swooping dives around her head. She smiled gently at him, and he redoubled his efforts.

"I've never heard them talk before," Garion marveled.

"They talk to her all the time," Wolf said. "Sometimes they go on for hours. That's why she seems a little abstracted sometimes. She's listening to the birds. Your Aunt moves through a world filled with conversation."

"I didn't know that."

"Not many people do."

The colt, who had been trotting rather sedately along behind Garion as they had come down out of the foothills, went wild with delight when he reached the lush grass of the Vale. With an amazing burst of speed, he ran out over the meadows. He rolled in the grass, his thin legs flailing. He galloped in long, curving sweeps over the low, rolling hills. He deliberately ran at herds of grazing deer, startling them into flight and then plunging along after them. "Come back here!" Garion shouted at him.

"He won't hear you," Hettar said, smiling at the little horse's antics. "At least, he'll pretend that he doesn't. He's having too much fun."

Get back here right now! Garion projected the thought a bit more firmly than he'd intended. The colt's forelegs stiffened, and he slid to a stop. Then he turned and trotted obediently back to Garion, his eyes apologetic. "Bad horse!" Garion chided.

The colt hung his head.

"Don't scold him," Wolf said. "You were very young once yourself."

Garion immediately regretted what he had said and reached down to pat the little animal's shoulder. "It's all right," he apologized. The colt looked at him gratefully and began to frisk through the grass again, although staying close.

Princess Ce'Nedra had been watching him. She always seemed to be watching him for some reason. She would look at him, her eyes speculative and a tendril of her coppery hair coiled about one finger and raised absently to her teeth. It seemed to Garion that every time he turned around she was watching and nibbling. For some reason he could not quite put his finger on, it made him very nervous. "If he were mine, *I* wouldn't be so cruel to him," she accused, taking the tip of the curl from between her teeth.

Garion chose not to answer that.

As they rode down the valley, they passed three ruined towers, standing some distance apart and all showing signs of great antiquity. Each of them appeared to have originally been about sixty feet high, though weather and the passage of years had eroded them down considerably. The last of the three looked as if it had been blackened by some intensely hot fire.

"Was there some kind of war here, Grandfather?" Garion asked.

"No," Wolf replied rather sadly. "The towers belonged to my brothers. That one over there was Belsambar's, and the one near it was Belmakor's. They died a long time ago."

"I didn't think sorcerers ever died."

"They grew tired—or maybe they lost hope. They caused themselves no longer to exist."

"They killed themselves?"

"In a manner of speaking. It was a little more complex than that, though."

Garion didn't press it, since the old man appeared to prefer not to go into details. "What about the other one—the one that's been burned? Whose tower was that?"

"Belzedar's."

"Did you and the other sorcerers burn it after he went over to Torak?"

"No. He burned it himself. I suppose he thought that was a way to show us that he was no longer a member of our brotherhood. Belzedar always liked dramatic gestures."

"Where's *your* tower?"

"Farther on down the Vale."

"Will you show it to me?"

"If you like."

"Does Aunt Pol have her own tower?"

"No. She stayed with me while she was growing up, and then we went out into the world. We never got around to building her one of her own."

They rode until late afternoon and stopped for the day beneath an enormous tree which stood alone in the center of a broad meadow. The tree quite literally shaded whole acres. Ce'Nedra sprang out of her saddle and ran toward the tree, her deep red hair flying behind her. "He's beautiful!" she exclaimed, placing her hands with reverent affection on the rough bark.

Mister Wolf shook his head. "Dryads. They grow giddy at the sight of trees."

"I don't recognize it," Durnik said with a slight frown. "It's not an oak."

"Maybe it's some southern species," Barak suggested. "I've never seen one exactly like it myself."

"He's very old," Ce'Nedra said, putting her cheek fondly against the tree trunk, "and he speaks strangely—but he likes me."

"What kind of tree is it?" Durnik asked. He was still frowning, his need to classify and categorize frustrated by the huge tree.

"It's the only one of its kind in the world," Mister Wolf told him. "I don't think we ever named it. It was always just 'the tree.' We used to meet here sometimes."

"It doesn't seem to drop any berries or fruit or seeds of any kind," Durnik observed, examining the ground beneath the spreading branches.

"It doesn't need them," Wolf replied. "As I told you, it's the only one of its kind. It's always been here—and always will be. It feels no urge to propagate itself."

Durnik seemed worried about it. "I've never heard of a tree with no seeds."

"It's a rather special tree, Durnik," Aunt Pol said. "It sprouted on the day the world was made, and it will probably stand here for as long as the world exists. It has a purpose other than reproducing itself."

"What purpose is that?"

"We don't know," Wolf answered. "We only know that it's the oldest living thing in the world. Maybe that's its purpose. Maybe it's here to demonstrate the continuity of life."

Ce'Nedra had removed her shoes and was climbing up into the thick branches, making little sounds of affection and delight.

"Is there by any chance a tradition linking Dryads with squirrels?" Silk asked.

Mister Wolf smiled. "If the rest of you can manage without us, Garion and I have something to attend to."

Aunt Pol looked questioningly at him.

"It's time for a little instruction, Pol," he explained.

"We can manage, father," she said. "Will you be back in time for supper?"

"Keep it warm for us. Coming, Garion?"

The two of them rode in silence through the green meadows with the golden afternoon sunlight making the entire Vale warm and lovely. Garion was baffled by Mister Wolf's curious change of mood. Always before, there had been a sort of impromptu quality about the old man. He seemed frequently to be making up his life as he went along, relying on chance, his wits, and his power, when necessary, to see him through. Here in the Vale, he seemed serene, undisturbed by the chaotic events taking place in the world outside.

About two miles from the tree stood another tower. It was rather squat and round and was built of rough stone. Arched windows near the top faced out in the directions of the four winds, but there seemed to be no door.

"You said you'd like to visit my tower," Wolf said, dismounting. "This is it."

"It isn't ruined like the others."

"I take care of it from time to time. Shall we go up?"

Garion slid down from his horse. "Where's the door?" he asked.

"Right there." Wolf pointed at a large stone in the rounded wall.

Garion looked skeptical.

Mister Wolf stepped in front of the stone. "It's me," he said. "Open."

The surge Garion felt at the old man's word seemed commonplace—ordinary—a household kind of surge that spoke of something that had been done so often that it was no longer a wonder. The rock turned obediently, revealing a sort of narrow, irregular doorway. Motioning for Garion to follow, Wolf squeezed through into the dim chamber beyond the door.

The tower, Garion saw, was not a hollow shell as he had expected, but rather was a solid pedestal, pierced only by a stairway winding upward.

"Come along," Wolf told him, starting up the worn stone steps. "Watch that one," he said about halfway up, pointing at one of the steps. "The stone is loose."

"Why don't you fix it?" Garion asked, stepping up over the loose stone.

"I've been meaning to, but I just haven't gotten around to it. It's been that way for a long time. I'm so used to it now that I never seem to think of fixing it when I'm here."

The chamber at the top of the tower was round and very cluttered. A thick coat of dust lay over everything. There were several tables in various parts of the room, covered with rolls and scraps of parchment, strange-looking implements and models, bits and pieces of rock and glass, and a couple of birds' nests; on one, a curious stick was so wound and twisted and coiled that Garion's eye could not exactly follow its convolutions. He picked it up and turned it over in his hands, trying to trace it out. "What's this, Grandfather?" he asked.

"One of Polgara's toys," the old man said absently, staring around at the dusty chamber.

"What's it supposed to do?"

"It kept her quiet when she was a baby. It's only got one end. She spent five years trying to figure it out."

Garion pulled his eyes off the fascinatingly compelling piece of wood. "That's a cruel sort of thing to do to a child."

"I had to do something," Wolf answered. "She had a penetrating voice as a child. Beldaran was a quiet, happy little girl, but your Aunt never seemed satisfied."

"Beldaran?"

"Your Aunt's twin sister." The old man's voice trailed off, and he looked sadly out of one of the windows for a few moments. Finally he sighed and turned back to the round room. "I suppose I ought to clean this up a bit," he said, looking around at the dust and litter.

"Let me help," Garion offered.

"Just be careful not to break anything," the old man warned. "Some of those things took me centuries to make." He began moving around the chamber, picking things up and setting them down again, blowing now and then on them to clear away a bit of the dust. His efforts didn't really seem to be getting anywhere.

Finally he stopped, staring at a low, rough-looking chair with the rail along its back, scarred and gashed as if it had been continually grasped by strong claws. He sighed again.

"What's wrong?" Garion asked.

"Poledra's chair," Wolf said. "—My wife. She used to perch there and watch me—sometimes for years on end."

"Perch?"

"She was fond of the shape of the owl."

"Oh." Garion had somehow never thought of the old man as ever having been married, although he obviously had to have been at some time, since Aunt Pol and her twin sister were his daughters. The shadowy wife's affinity for owls, however, explained Aunt Pol's own preference for that shape. The two women, Poledra and Beldaran, were involved rather intimately in his own background, he realized, but quite irrationally he resented them. They had shared a part of the lives of his aunt and his grandfather that he would never—could never know.

The old man moved a parchment and picked up a peculiar-looking device with a sighting glass in one end of it. "I thought I'd lost you," he told the device, touching it with a familiar fondness. "You've been under that parchment all this time."

"What is it?" Garion asked him.

"A thing I made when I was trying to discover the reason for mountains."

"The reason?"

"Everything has a reason." Wolf raised the instrument. "You see, what you do is—" He broke off and laid the device back on the table. "It's much too complicated to explain. I'm not even sure if I remember exactly how to use it myself. I haven't touched it since before Belzedar came to the Vale. When he arrived, I had to lay my studies aside to train him." He looked around at the dust and clutter. "This is useless," he said. "The dust will just come back anyway."

"Were you alone here before Belzedar came?"

"My Master was here. That's his tower over there." Wolf pointed through the north window at a tall, slender stone structure about a mile away.

"Was he really here?" Garion asked. "I mean, not just his spirit?"

"No. He was really here. That was before the Gods departed."

"Did you live here always?"

"No. I came like a thief, looking for something to steal—well, that's not actually true, I suppose. I was about your age when I came here, and I was dying at the time."

"Dying?" Garion was startled.

"Freezing to death. I'd left the village I was born in the year before—after my mother died—and spent my first winter in the camp of the Godless Ones. They were very old by then."

"Godless Ones?"

"Ulgos—or rather the ones who decided not to follow Gorim to Prolgu. They stopped having children after that, so they were happy to take me in. I couldn't understand their language at the time, and all their pampering got on my nerves, so I ran away in the spring. I was on my way back the next fall, but I got caught in an early snowstorm not far from here. I lay down against the side of my Master's tower to die—I didn't know it was a tower at first. With all the snow swirling around, it just looked like a pile of rock. As I recall, I was feeling rather sorry for myself at the time."

"I can imagine." Garion shivered at the thought of being alone and dying.

"I was sniveling a bit, and the sound disturbed my Master. He let me in—probably more to quiet me than for any other reason. As soon as I got inside, I started looking for things to steal."

"But he made you a sorcerer instead."

"No. He made me a servant—a slave. I worked for him for five years before I even found out who he was. Sometimes I think I hated him, but I had
to do what he told me to—I didn't really know why. The last straw came
when he told me to move a big rock out of his way. I tried with all my
strength, but I couldn't budge it. Finally I got angry enough to move it with
my mind instead of my back. That's what he'd been waiting for, of course.
After that we got along better. He changed my name from Garath to
Belgarath, and he made me his pupil."

"And his disciple?"

"That took a little longer. I had a lot to learn. I was examining the reason that certain stars fell at the time he first called me his disciple—and he
was working on a round, gray stone he'd picked up by the riverbank."

"Did you ever discover the reason—that stars fall, I mean?"

"Yes. It's not all that complicated. It has to do with balance. The world
needs a certain weight to keep it turning. When it starts to slow down, a few
nearby stars fall. Their weight makes up the difference."

"I never thought of that."

"Neither did I—not for quite some time."

"The stone you mentioned. Was it—"

"The Orb," Wolf confirmed. "Just an ordinary rock until my Master
touched it. Anyway, I learned the secret of the Will and the Word—which
isn't really that much of a secret, after all. It's there in all of us—or did I say
that before?"

"I think so."

"Probably so. I tend to repeat myself." The old man picked up a roll of
parchment and glanced at it, then laid it aside again. "So much that I started
and haven't finished." He sighed.

"Grandfather?"

"Yes, Garion?"

"This—thing of ours—how much can you actually do with it?"

"That depends on your mind, Garion. The complexity of it lies in the
complexity of the mind that puts it to use. Quite obviously, it can't do something that can't be imagined by the mind that focuses it. That was the purpose of our studies—to expand our minds so that we could use the power
more fully."

"Everybody's mind is different, though." Garion was struggling toward
an idea.

"Yes."

"Wouldn't that mean that—this thing—" He shied away from the word
"power." "What I mean is, is it different? Sometimes you do things, and other
times you have Aunt Pol do them."

Wolf nodded. "It's different in each one of us. There are certain things
we can all do. We can all move things, for example."

"Aunt Pol called it trans—" Garion hesitated, not remembering the word.

"Translocation," Wolf supplied. "Moving something from one place to another. It's the simplest thing you can do—usually the thing you do first—and it makes the most noise."

"That's what she told me." Garion remembered the slave he had jerked from the river at Sthiss Tor—the slave who had died.

"Polgara can do things that I can't," Wolf continued. "Not because she's any stronger than I am, but because she thinks differently than I do. We're not sure how much you can do yet, because we don't know exactly how your mind works. You seem to be able to do certain things quite easily that I wouldn't even attempt. Maybe it's because you don't realize how difficult they are."

"I don't quite understand what you mean."

The old man looked at him. "Perhaps you don't, at that. Remember the crazy monk who tried to attack you in that village in northern Tolnedra just after we left Arendia?"

Garion nodded.

"You cured his madness. That doesn't sound like much until you realize that in the instant you cured him, you had to understand fully the nature of his insanity. That's an extremely difficult thing, and you did it without even thinking about it. And then, of course, there was the colt."

Garion glanced down through the window at the little horse friskily running through the field surrounding the tower.

"The colt was dead, but you made him start to breathe. In order for you to do that, you had to be able to understand death."

"It was just a wall," Garion explained. "All I did was reach through it."

"There's more to it than that, I think. What you seem to be able to do is to visualize extremely difficult ideas in very simple terms. That's a rare gift, but there are some dangers involved in it that you should be aware of."

"Dangers? Such as what?"

"Don't *oversimplify*. If a man's dead, for example, he's usually dead for a very good reason—like a sword through the heart. If you bring him back, he'll only die immediately again anyway. As I said before, just because you *can* do something doesn't necessarily mean that you *should*."

Garion sighed. "I'm afraid this is going to take a very long time, Grandfather," he said. "I have to learn how to keep myself under control; I have to learn what I can't do, so I don't kill myself trying to do something impossible; I have to learn what I can do and what I should do. I wish this had never happened to me."

"We all do sometimes," the old man told him. "The decision wasn't ours to make, though. I haven't always liked some of the things I've had to do, and neither has your Aunt; but what we're doing is more important than we are, so we do what's expected of us—like it or not."

"What if I just said, 'No. I won't do it'?"

"You *could* do that, I suppose, but you won't, will you?"

Garion sighed again. "No," he said, "I guess not."

The old sorcerer put his arm around the boy's shoulders. "I thought you might see things that way, Belgarion. You're bound to this the same way we all are."

The strange thrill he always felt at the sound of his other, secret name ran through Garion. "Why do you all insist on calling me that?" he asked.

"Belgarion?" Wolf said mildly. "Think, boy. Think what it means. I haven't been talking to you and telling you stories all these years just because I like the sound of my own voice."

Garion turned it over carefully in his mind. "You were Garath," he mused thoughtfully, "but the God Aldur changed your name to Belgarath. Zedar was Zedar first and then Belzedar—and then he went back to being Zedar again."

"And in my old tribe, Polgara would have just been Gara. Pol is like Bel. The only difference is that she's a woman. Her name comes from mine—because she's my daughter. Your name comes from mine, too."

"Garion—Garath," the boy said. "Belgarath—Belgarion. It all fits together, doesn't it?"

"Naturally," the old man replied. "I'm glad you noticed it."

Garion grinned at him. Then a thought occurred. "But I'm not really Belgarion yet, am I?"

"Not entirely. You still have a way to go."

"I suppose I'd better get started, then." Garion said it with a certain ruefulness. "Since I don't really have any choice."

"Somehow I knew that eventually you'd come around," Mister Wolf said.

"Don't you sometimes wish that I was just Garion again, and you were the old storyteller coming to visit Faldor's farm—with Aunt Pol making supper in the kitchen as she did in the old days—and we were hiding under a haystack with a bottle I'd stolen for you?" Garion felt homesickness welling up in him.

"Sometimes, Garion, sometimes," Wolf admitted, his eyes far away.

"We won't ever be able to go back there again, will we?"

"Not the same way, no."

"I'll be Belgarion, and you'll be Belgarath. We won't even be the same people anymore."

"Everything changes, Garion," Belgarath told him.

"Show me the rock," Garion said suddenly.

"Which rock?"

"The one Aldur made you move—the day you first discovered the power."

"Oh," Belgarath said, "*that* rock. It's right over there—the white one. The one the colt's sharpening his hooves on."

"It's a very big rock."

"I'm glad you appreciate that," Belgarath replied modestly. "I thought so myself."

"Do you suppose *I* could move it?"

"You never know until you try, Garion," Belgarath told him.

CHAPTER ELEVEN

The next morning when Garion awoke, he knew immediately that he was not alone.

"*Where have you been?*" he asked silently.

"*I've been watching,*" the other consciousness in his mind said. "*I see that you've finally come around.*"

"*What choice did I have?*"

"*None. You'd better get up. Aldur's coming.*"

Garion quickly rolled out of his blankets. "*Here? Are you sure?*"

The voice in his mind didn't answer.

Garion put on a clean tunic and hose and wiped off his half-boots with a certain amount of care. Then he went out of the tent he shared with Silk and Durnik.

The sun was just coming up over the high mountains to the east, and the line between sunlight and shadow moved with a stately ponderousness across the dewy grass of the Vale. Aunt Pol and Belgarath stood near the small fire where a pot was just beginning to bubble. They were talking quietly, and Garion joined them.

"You're up early," Aunt Pol said. She reached out and smoothed his hair.

"I was awake," he replied. He looked around, wondering from which direction Aldur would come.

"Your grandfather tells me that the two of you had a long talk yesterday."

Garion nodded. "I understand a few things a little better now. I'm sorry I've been so difficult."

She drew him to her and put her arms around him. "It's all right, dear. You had some hard decisions to make."

"You're not angry with me, then?"

"Of course not, dear."

The others had begun to get up, coming out of their tents, yawning and stretching and rumpled-looking.

"What do we do today?" Silk asked, coming to the fire and rubbing the sleep from his eyes.

"We wait," Belgarath told him. "My Master said he'd meet us here."

"I'm curious to see him. I've never met a God before."

"Thy curiosity, methinks, will soon be satisfied, Prince Kheldar," Mandorallen said. "Look there."

Coming across the meadow not far from the great tree beneath which they had pitched their tents, a figure in a blue robe was approaching. A soft nimbus of blue light surrounded the figure, and the immediate sense of presence made it instantly clear that what approached was not a man. Garion was not prepared for the impact of that presence. His meeting with the Spirit of Issa in Queen Salmissra's throne room had been clouded by the narcotic effects of the things the Serpent Queen had forced him to drink. Similarly, half his mind had slept during the confrontation with Mara in the ruins of Mar Amon. But now, fully awake in the first light of morning, he found himself in the presence of a God.

Aldur's face was kindly and enormously wise. His long hair and beard were white—from conscious choice, Garion felt, rather than from any result of age. The face was very familiar to him somehow. It bore a startling resemblance to Belgarath's, but Garion perceived immediately, with a sudden curious inversion of his original notion, that it was Belgarath who resembled Aldur—as if their centuries of association had stamped Aldur's features upon the face of the old man. There were differences, of course. That certain mischievous roguishness was not present on the calm face of Aldur. That quality was Belgarath's own, the last remnant, perhaps, of the face of the thieving boy Aldur had taken into his tower on a snowy day some seven thousand years ago.

"Master," Belgarath said, bowing respectfully as Aldur approached.

"Belgarath," the God acknowledged. His voice was very quiet. "I have not seen thee in some time. The years have not been unkind to thee."

Belgarath shrugged wryly. "Some days I feel them more than others, Master. I carry a great number of years with me."

Aldur smiled and turned to Aunt Pol. "My beloved daughter," he said fondly, reaching out to touch the white lock at her brow. "Thou art as lovely as ever."

"And thou as kind, Master," she replied, smiling and inclining her head.

There passed among the three of them a kind of intensely personal linkage, a joining of minds that marked their reunion. Garion could feel the edges of it with his own mind, and he was somewhat wistful at being excluded—though he realized at once that there was no intent to exclude him. They were merely reestablishing an eons-old companionship—shared experiences that stretched back into antiquity.

Aldur then turned to look at the others. "And so you have come together at last, as it hath been foretold from the beginning of days you should. You are the instruments of destiny, and my blessing goes with each as you move toward that awful day when the universe will become one again."

The faces of Garion's companions were awed and puzzled by Aldur's enigmatic blessing. Each, however, bowed with profound respect and humility.

And then Ce'Nedra emerged from the tent she shared with Aunt Pol. The tiny girl stretched luxuriantly and ran her fingers through the tumbled mass of her flaming hair. She was dressed in a Dryad tunic and sandals.

"Ce'Nedra," Aunt Pol called her, "come here."

"Yes, Lady Polgara," the little princess replied obediently. She crossed to the fire, her feet seeming barely to touch the ground. Then she saw Aldur standing with the others and stopped, her eyes wide.

"This is our Master, Ce'Nedra," Aunt Pol told her. "He wanted to meet you."

The princess stared at the glowing presence in confusion. Nothing in her life had prepared her for such a meeting. She lowered her eyelashes and then looked up shyly, her tiny face artfully and automatically assuming its most appealing expression.

Aldur smiled gently. "She's like a flower that charms without knowing it." His eyes looked deeply into those of the princess. "There is steel in this one, however. She is fit for her task. My blessings upon thee, my child."

Ce'Nedra responded with an instinctively graceful curtsy. It was the first time Garion had ever seen her bow to anyone.

Aldur turned then to look full at Garion. A brief, unspoken acknowledgment passed between the God and the consciousness that shared Garion's thoughts. There was in that momentary meeting a sense of mutual respect and of shared responsibility. And then Garion felt the massive touch of Aldur's mind upon his own and knew that the God had instantly seen and understood his every thought and feeling.

"Hail, Belgarion," Aldur said gravely.

"Master," Garion replied. He dropped to one knee, not really knowing why.

"We have awaited thy coming since time's beginning. Thou art the vessel of all our hopes." Aldur raised his hand. "My blessing, Belgarion. I am well pleased with thee."

Garion's entire being was suffused with love and gratitude as the warmth of Aldur's benediction filled him.

"Dear Polgara," Aldur said to Aunt Pol, "thy gift to us is beyond value. Belgarion has come at last, and the world trembles at his coming."

Aunt Pol bowed again.

"Let us now go apart," Aldur said to Belgarath and Aunt Pol. "Your task is well begun, and I must now provide you with that instruction I promised when first I set your steps upon this path. That which was once clouded becomes clearer, and we now can see what lies before us. Let us look toward that day we have all awaited and make our preparations."

The three of them moved away from the fire, and it seemed to Garion that, as they went, the glowing nimbus which had surrounded Aldur now enclosed Aunt Pol and his grandfather as well. Some movement or sound distracted his eye for a moment, and when he looked back, the three had vanished.

Barak let out his breath explosively. "Belar! That was something to see!"

"We have been favored, I think, beyond all men," Mandorallen said.

They all stood staring at each other, caught up in the wonder of what they had just witnessed. Ce'Nedra, however, broke the mood. "All right," she ordered peremptorily, "don't just stand there gaping. Move away from the fire."

"What are you going to do?" Garion asked her.

"The Lady Polgara's going to be busy," the little girl said loftily, "so I'm going to make breakfast." She moved toward the fire with a businesslike bustling.

The bacon was not too badly burned, but Ce'Nedra's attempt to toast slices of bread before the open fire turned out disastrously, and her porridge had lumps in it as solid as clods in a sun-baked field. Garion and the others, however, ate what she offered without comment, prudently avoiding the direct gaze she leveled at them, as if daring them to speak so much as one word of criticism.

"I wonder how long they're going to be," Silk said after breakfast.

"Gods, I think, have little notion of time," Barak replied sagely, stroking at his beard. "I don't expect them back until sometime this afternoon at the earliest."

"It's a good time to check over the horses," Hettar decided. "Some of them have picked up a few burrs along the way, and I'd like to have a look at their hooves—just to be on the safe side."

"I'll help you," Durnik offered, getting up.

Hettar nodded, and the two went off to the place where the horses were picketed.

"And I've got a nick or two in my sword edge," Barak remembered, fishing a piece of polishing stone out of his belt and laying his heavy blade across his lap.

Mandorallen went to his tent and brought out his armor. He laid it out on the ground and began a minute inspection for dents and spots of rust.

Silk rattled a pair of dice hopefully in one hand, looking inquiringly at Barak.

"If it's all the same to you, I think I'd like to enjoy the company of my money for a while longer," the big man told him.

"This whole place absolutely *reeks* of domesticity," Silk complained. Then he sighed, put away his dice, and went to fetch a needle and thread and a tunic he'd torn on a bush up in the mountains.

Ce'Nedra had returned to her communion with the vast tree and was scampering among the branches, taking what Garion felt to be inordinate risks as she jumped from limb to limb with a catlike unconcern. After watching her for a few moments, he fell into a kind of reverie, thinking back to the awesome meeting that morning. He had met the Gods Issa and Mara already, but there was something special about Aldur. The affinity Belgarath and Aunt Pol showed so obviously for this God who had always remained aloof from men spoke loudly to Garion. The devotional activities of Sendaria, where he had been raised, were inclusive rather than exclusive. A good Sendar prayed impartially, and honored all the Gods—even Torak. Garion now, however, felt a special closeness and reverence for Aldur, and the adjustment in his theological thinking required a certain amount of thought.

A twig dropped out of the tree onto his head, and he glanced up with annoyance.

Ce'Nedra, grinning impishly, was directly over his head. "Boy," she said in her most superior and insulting tone, "the breakfast dishes are getting cold. The grease is going to be difficult to wash off if you let it harden."

"I'm not your scullion," he told her.

"Wash the dishes, Garion," she ordered him, nibbling at the tip of a lock of hair.

"Wash them yourself."

She glared down at him, biting rather savagely at the unoffending lock.

"Why do you keep chewing on your hair like that?" he asked irritably.

"What are you talking about?" she demanded, removing the lock from between her teeth.

"Every time I look at you, you've got your hair stuck in your mouth."

"I do *not*," she retorted indignantly. "Are you going to wash the dishes?"

"No." He squinted up at her. The short Dryad tunic she was wearing seemed to expose an unseemly amount of leg. "Why don't you go put on some clothes?" he suggested. "Some of us don't appreciate the way you run around half-naked all the time."

The fight got under way almost immediately after that.

Finally Garion gave up his efforts to get in the last word and stamped away in disgust.

"Garion!" she screamed after him. "Don't you *dare* go off and leave me with all these dirty dishes!"

He ignored her and kept walking.

After a short distance, he felt a familiar nuzzling at his elbow and he rather absently scratched the colt's ears. The small animal quivered with delight and rubbed against him affectionately. Then, unable to restrain himself anymore, the colt galloped off into the meadow to pester a family of docilely feeding rabbits. Garion found himself smiling. The morning was just too beautiful to allow the squabble with the princess to spoil it.

There was, it seemed, something rather special about the Vale. The world around grew cold with the approach of winter and was buffeted by storms and dangers, but here it seemed as if the hand of Aldur stretched protectively above them, filling this special place with warmth and peace and a kind of eternal and magical serenity. Garion, at this trying point in his life, needed all the warmth and peace he could get. There were things that had to be worked out, and he needed a time, however brief, without storms and dangers to deal with them.

He was halfway to Belgarath's tower before he realized that it had been there that he had been going all along. The tall grass was wet with dew, and his boots were soon soaked, but even that did not spoil the day.

He walked around the tower several times, gazing up at it. Although he found the stone that marked the door quite easily, he decided not to open it. It would not be proper to go uninvited into the old man's tower; and beyond that, he was not entirely certain that the door would respond to any voice but Belgarath's.

He stopped quite suddenly at that last thought and started searching back, trying to find the exact instant when he had ceased to think of his grandfather as Mister Wolf and had finally accepted the fact that he was Belgarath. The changeover seemed significant—a kind of turning point.

Still lost in thought, he turned then and walked across the meadow toward the large, white rock the old man had pointed out to him from the tower window. Absently he put one hand on it and pushed. The rock didn't budge.

Garion set both hands on it and pushed again, but the rock remained motionless. He stepped back and considered it. It wasn't really a vast boulder. It was rounded and white and not quite as high as his waist—heavy, certainly, but it should not be so inflexibly solid. He bent over to look at the bottom, and then he understood. The underside of the rock was flat. It would never roll. The only way to move it would be to lift one side and tip it over. He walked around the rock, looking at it from every angle. He judged that it was marginally movable. If he exerted every ounce of his strength, he might be able to lift it. He sat down and looked at it, thinking hard. As he sometimes did, he talked to himself, trying to lay out the problem.

"The first thing to do is to *try* to move it," he concluded. "It doesn't really look totally impossible. Then, if that doesn't work, we'll try it the other way."

He stood up, stepped purposefully to the rock, wormed his fingers under the edge of it and heaved. Nothing happened.

"Have to try a little harder," he told himself. He spread his feet and set himself. He began to lift again, straining, the cords standing out in his neck. For the space of about ten heartbeats he tried as hard as he could to lift the stubborn rock—not to roll it over; he'd given that up after the first instant—but simply to make it budge, to acknowledge his existence. Though the ground was not particularly soft there, his feet actually sank a fraction of an inch or so as he strained against the rock's weight.

His head was swimming, and little dots seemed to swirl in front of his eyes as he released the rock and collapsed, gasping, against it. He lay against the cold, gritty surface for several minutes, recovering.

"All right," he said finally, "now we know that *that* won't work." He stepped back and sat down.

Each time he'd done something with his mind before, it had been on impulse, a response to some crisis. He had never sat down and deliberately worked himself up to it. He discovered almost at once that the entire set of circumstances was completely different. The whole world seemed suddenly filled with distractions. Birds sang. A breeze brushed his face. An ant crawled across his hand. Each time he began to bring his will to bear, something pulled his attention away.

There was a certain feeling to it, he knew that, a tightness in the back of his head and a sort of pushing out with his forehead. He closed his eyes, and that seemed to help. It was coming. It was slow, but he felt the Will begin to build in him. Remembering something, he reached inside his tunic and put the mark on his palm against the amulet. The force within him, amplified by that touch, built to a great roaring crescendo. He kept his eyes closed and stood up. Then he opened his eyes and looked hard at the stubborn white rock. "You *will* move," he muttered. He kept his right hand on the amulet and held out his left hand, palm up.

"Now!" he said sharply and slowly began to raise his left hand in a lifting motion. The force within him surged, and the roaring sound inside his head became deafening.

Slowly the edge of the rock came up out of the grass. Worms and burrowing grubs who had lived out their lives in the safe, comfortable darkness under the rock flinched as the morning sunlight hit them. Ponderously, the rock raised, obeying Garion's inexorably lifting hand. It teetered for a second on its edge, then toppled slowly over.

The exhaustion he had felt after trying to lift the rock with his back was nothing compared to the bone-deep weariness that swept over him after he let the clenching of his Will relax. He folded his arms on the grass and let his head sink down on them.

After a moment or two, that peculiar fact began to dawn on him. He was still standing, but his arms were folded comfortably in front of him on the grass. He jerked his head up and looked around in confusion. He had moved the rock, certainly. That much was obvious, since the rock now lay on its rounded top with its damp underside turned up. Something else had also happened, however. Though he had not touched the rock, its weight had nonetheless been upon him as he had lifted it, and the force he had directed at it had not all gone at the rock.

With dismay, Garion realized that he had sunk up to his armpits in the firm soil of the meadow.

"Now what do I do?" he asked himself helplessly. He shuddered away from the idea of once again mustering his Will to pull himself out of the ground. He was too exhausted even to consider it. He tried to wriggle, thinking that he might be able to loosen the earth around him and work his way up an inch at a time, but he could not so much as budge.

"Look what you've done," he accused the rock.

The rock ignored him.

A thought occurred to him. "Are *you* in there?" he asked that awareness that seemed always to have been with him.

The silence in his mind was profound.

"Help!" he shouted.

A bird, attracted by the exposed worms and bugs that had been under the rock, cocked one eye at him and then went back to its breakfast.

Garion heard a light step behind him and craned around, trying to see. The colt was staring at him in amazement. Hesitantly, the small horse thrust out his nose and nuzzled Garion's face.

"Good horse," Garion said, relieved not to be alone, at least. An idea came to him. "You're going to have to go get Hettar," he told the colt.

The colt pranced about and nuzzled his face again.

"Stop that," Garion commanded. "This is serious." Cautiously, he tried to push his mind into the colt's thoughts. He tried a dozen different ways until he finally struck the right combination by sheer accident. The colt's mind flitted from here to there without purpose or pattern. It was a baby's mind, vacant of thought, receiving only sense impressions. Garion caught flickering images of green grass and running and clouds in the sky and warm milk. He also felt the sense of wonder in the little mind, and the abiding love the colt had for him.

Slowly, painfully, Garion began constructing a picture of Hettar in the colt's wandering thoughts. It seemed to take forever.

"Hettar," Garion said over and over. "Go get Hettar. Tell him that I'm in trouble."

The colt scampered around and came back to stick his soft nose in Garion's ear.

"Please pay attention," Garion cried. *"Please!"*

Finally, after what seemed hours, the colt seemed to understand. He went several paces away, then came back to nuzzle Garion again.

"Go—get—Hettar," Garion ordered, stressing each word.

The colt pawed at the ground, then turned and galloped away—going in the wrong direction. Garion started to swear. For almost a year now he had been exposed to some of the more colorful parts of Barak's vocabulary. After he had repeated all the phrases he remembered six or eight times, he began to extemporize.

A flickering thought came back to him from the now-vanished colt. The little beast was chasing butterflies. Garion pounded the ground with his fists, wanting to howl with frustration.

The sun rose higher, and it started to get hot.

It was early afternoon when Hettar and Silk, following the prancing little colt, found him.

"How in the world did you manage to do that?" Silk asked curiously.

"I don't want to talk about it," Garion muttered, somewhere between relief and total embarrassment.

"He probably can do many things that we can't," Hettar observed, climbing down from his horse and untying Durnik's shovel from his saddle. "The thing I can't understand, though, is *why* he'd want to do it."

"I'm positive he had a good reason for it," Silk assured him.

"Do you think we should ask him?"

"It's probably very complicated," Silk replied. "I'm sure simple men like you and me wouldn't be able to understand it."

"Do you suppose he's finished with whatever it is he's doing?"

"We could ask him, I suppose."

"I wouldn't want to disturb him," Hettar said. "It could be very important."

"It almost has to be," Silk agreed.

"Will you *please* get me out of here?" Garion begged.

"Are you sure you're finished?" Silk asked politely. "We can wait if you're not done yet."

"Please," Garion asked, almost in tears.

CHAPTER TWELVE

"Why did you try to *lift* it?" Belgarath asked Garion the next morning after he and Aunt Pol had returned and Silk and Hettar had solemnly informed them of the predicament in which they had found the young man the afternoon before.

"It seemed like the best way to tip it over," Garion answered. "You know, kind of get hold of it from underneath and then roll it—sort of."

"Why didn't you just push against it—close to the top? It would have rolled over if you'd done it that way."

"I didn't think of it."

"Don't you realize that soft earth won't accept that kind of pressure?" Aunt Pol asked.

"I do now," Garion replied. "But wouldn't pushing on it have just moved me backward?"

"You have to brace yourself," Belgarath explained. "That's part of the whole trick. As much of your Will goes to holding yourself immobile as it does to pushing against the object you're trying to move. Otherwise all you do is just shove yourself away."

"I didn't know that," Garion admitted. "It's the first time I've ever tried to do anything unless it was an emergency ... Will you *stop* that?" he demanded crossly of Ce'Nedra, who had collapsed into gales of laughter as soon as Silk had finished telling them about Garion's blunder.

She laughed even harder.

"I think you're going to have to explain a few things to him, father," Aunt Pol said. "He doesn't seem to have even the most rudimentary idea about the way forces react against each other." She looked at Garion critically. "It's lucky you didn't decide to throw it," she told him. "You might have flung yourself halfway back to Maragor."

"I really don't think it's all that funny," Garion told his friends, who were all grinning openly at him. "This isn't as easy as it looks, you know." He realized that he had just made a fool of himself and he was not sure if he was more embarrassed or hurt by their amusement.

"Come with me, boy," Belgarath said firmly. "It looks as if we're going to have to start at the very beginning."

"It's not my fault I didn't know," Garion protested. "You should have told me."

"I didn't know you were planning to start experimenting so soon," the old man replied. "Most of us have sense enough to wait for guidance before we start rearranging local geography."

"Well, at least I *did* manage to move it," Garion said defensively as he followed the old man across the meadow toward the tower.

"Splendid. Did you put it back the way you found it?"

"Why? What difference does it make?"

"We don't move things here in the Vale. Everything that's here is here for a reason, and they're all supposed to be exactly where they are."

"I didn't know," Garion apologized.

"You do now. Let's go put it back where it belongs."

They trudged along in silence.

"Grandfather?" Garion said finally.

"Yes?"

"When I moved the rock, it seemed that I was getting the strength to do it from all around me. It seemed just to flow in from everyplace. Does that mean anything?"

"That's the way it works," Belgarath explained. "When we do something, we take the power to do it from our surroundings. When you burned Chamdar, for example, you drew the heat from all around you—from the air, from the ground, and from everyone who was in the area. You drew a little heat from everything to build the fire. When you tipped the rock over, you took the force to do it from everything nearby."

"I thought it all came from inside."

"Only when you create things," the old man replied. "That force has to come from within us. For anything else, we borrow. We gather up a little power from here and there and put it all together and then turn it loose all at one spot. Nobody's big enough to carry around the kind of force it would take to do even the simplest sort of thing."

"Then that's what happens when somebody tries to unmake something," Garion said intuitively. "He pulls in all the force, but then he can't let it go, and it just—" He spread his hands and jerked them suddenly apart.

Belgarath looked narrowly at him. "You've got a strange sort of mind, boy. You understand the difficult things quite easily, but you can't seem to get hold of the simple ones. There's the rock." He shook his head. "That'll never do. Put it back where it belongs, and try not to make so much noise this time. That racket you raised yesterday echoed all over the Vale."

"What do I do?" Garion asked.

"Gather in the force," Belgarath told him. "Take it from everything around."

Garion tried that.

"Not from *me*!" the old man exclaimed sharply.

Garion excluded his grandfather from his field of reaching out and pulling in. After a moment or two, he felt as if he were tingling all over and that his hair was standing on end. "Now what?" he asked, clenching his teeth to hold it in.

"Push out behind you and push at the rock at the same time."

"What do I push at behind me?"

"Everything—and at the rock as well. It has to be simultaneous."

"Won't I get—sort of squeezed in between?"

"Tense yourself up."

"We'd better hurry, Grandfather," Garion said. "I feel like I'm going to fly apart."

"Hold it in. Now put your Will on the rock, and say the Word."

Garion put his hands out in front of him and straightened his arms. "Push," he commanded. He felt the surge and the roaring.

With a resounding thud, the rock teetered and then rolled back smoothly to where it had been the morning before. Garion suddenly felt bruised all over, and he sank to his knees in exhaustion.

"Push?" Belgarath said incredulously.

"You said to say push."

"I said to push. I didn't say to *say* push."

"It went over. What difference does it make what Word I used?"

"It's a question of style," the old man said with a pained look. "Push sounds so—so babyish."

Weakly, Garion began to laugh.

"After all, Garion, we do have a certain dignity to maintain," the old man said loftily. "If we go around saying 'push' or 'flop' or things like that, no one's ever going to take us seriously."

Garion wanted to stop laughing, but he simply couldn't.

Belgarath stalked away indignantly, muttering to himself.

When they returned to the others, they found that the tents had been struck and the packhorses loaded.

"There's no point in staying here," Aunt Pol told them, "and the others are waiting for us. Did you manage to make him understand anything, father?"

Belgarath grunted, his face set in an expression of profound disapproval.

"Things didn't go well, I take it."

"I'll explain later," he said shortly.

During Garion's absence, Ce'Nedra, with much coaxing and a lapful of apples from their stores, had seduced the little colt into a kind of ecstatic subservience. He followed her about shamelessly, and the rather distant look he gave Garion showed not the slightest trace of guilt.

"You're going to make him sick," Garion accused her.

"Apples are good for horses," she replied airily.

"Tell her, Hettar," Garion said.

"They won't hurt him," the hook-nosed man answered. "It's a customary way to gain the trust of a young horse."

Garion tried to think of another suitable objection, but without success. For some reason the sight of the little animal nuzzling at Ce'Nedra offended him, though he couldn't exactly put his finger on why.

"Who are these others, Belgarath?" Silk asked as they rode. "The ones Polgara mentioned."

"My brothers," the old sorcerer replied. "Our Master's advised them that we're coming."

"I've heard stories about the Brotherhood of Sorcerers all my life. Are they as remarkable as everyone says?"

"I think you're in for a bit of a disappointment," Aunt Pol told him rather primly. "For the most part, sorcerers tend to be crotchety old men with a wide assortment of bad habits. I grew up amongst them, so I know them all rather well." She turned her face to the thrush perched on her shoulder, singing adoringly. "Yes," she said to the bird, "I know."

Garion pulled closer to his Aunt and began to listen very hard to the birdsong. At first it was merely noise—pretty, but without sense. Then, gradually, he began to pick up scraps of meaning—a bit here, a bit there. The bird was singing of nests and small, speckled eggs and sunrises and the overwhelming joy of flying. Then, as if his ears had suddenly opened, Garion began to understand. Larks sang of flying and singing. Sparrows chirped of hidden little pockets of seeds. A hawk, soaring overhead, screamed its lonely song of riding the wind alone and the fierce joy of the kill. Garion was awed as the air around him suddenly came alive with words.

Aunt Pol looked at him gravely. "It's a beginning," she said without bothering to explain.

Garion was so caught up in the world that had just opened to him that he did not see the two silvery-haired men at first. They stood together beneath a tall tree, waiting as the party rode nearer. They wore identical blue robes, and their white hair was quite long, though they were clean-shaven. When Garion looked at them for the first time, he thought for a moment that his eyes were playing tricks. The two were so absolutely identical that it was impossible to tell them apart.

"Belgarath, our brother," one of them said, "it's been such—"

"—a terribly long time," the other finished.

"Beltira," Belgarath said. "Belkira." He dismounted and embraced the twins.

"Dearest little Polgara," one of them said then.

"The Vale has been—" the other started.

"—empty without you," the second completed. He turned to his brother. "That was very poetic," he said admiringly.

"Thank you," the first replied modestly.

"These are my brothers, Beltira and Belkira," Belgarath informed the members of the party who had begun to dismount. "Don't bother to try to keep them separate. Nobody can tell them apart anyway."

"We can," the two said in unison.

"I'm not even sure of that," Belgarath responded with a gentle smile. "Your minds are so close together that your thoughts start with one and finish with the other."

"You always complicate it so much, father," Aunt Pol said. "This is Beltira." She kissed one of the sweet-faced old men. "And this is Belkira." She kissed the other. "I've been able to tell them apart since I was a child."

"Polgara knows—"

"—all our secrets." The twins smiled. "And who are—"

"—your companions?"

"I think you'll recognize them," Belgarath answered. "Mandorallen, Baron of Vo Mandor."

"The Knight Protector," the twins said in unison, bowing.

"Prince Kheldar of Drasnia."

"The Guide," they said.

"Barak, Earl of Trellheim."

"The Dreadful Bear." They looked at the big Cherek apprehensively. Barak's face darkened, but he said nothing.

"Hettar, son of Cho-Hag of Algaria."

"The Horse Lord."

"And Durnik of Sendaria."

"The One with Two Lives," they murmured with profound respect.

Durnik looked baffled at that.

"Ce'Nedra, Imperial Princess of Tolnedra."

"The Queen of the World," they replied with another deep bow.

Ce'Nedra laughed nervously.

"And this—"

"—can only be Belgarion," they said, their faces alive with joy, "the Chosen One." The twins reached out in unison and laid their right hands on Garion's head. Their voices sounded within his mind. *"Hail, Belgarion, Overlord and Champion, hope of the world."*

Garion was too surprised at this strange benediction to do more than awkwardly nod his head.

"If this gets any more cloying, I think I'll vomit," a new voice, harsh and rasping, announced. The speaker, who had just stepped out from behind the tree, was a squat, misshapen old man, dirty and profoundly ugly. His legs were bowed and gnarled like oak trunks. His shoulders were huge, and his hands dangled below his knees. There was a large hump in the middle of his back, and his face was twisted into a grotesque caricature of a human countenance. His straggly, iron-gray hair and beard were matted, and twigs and bits of leaves were caught in the tangles. His hideous face wore an expression of perpetual contempt and anger.

"Beldin," Belgarath said mildly, "we weren't sure you would come."

"I shouldn't have, you bungler," the ugly man snapped. "You've made a mess of things as usual, Belgarath." He turned to the twins. "Get me something to eat," he told them peremptorily.

"Yes, Beldin," they said quickly and started away.

"And don't be all day," he shouted after them.

"You seem to be in a good humor today, Beldin," Belgarath said with no trace of sarcasm. "What's made you so cheerful?"

The ugly dwarf scowled at him, then laughed, a short, barking sound. "I saw Belzedar. He looked like an unmade bed. Something had gone terribly wrong for him, and I enjoy that sort of thing."

"Dear Uncle Beldin," Aunt Pol said fondly, putting her arms around the filthy little man. "I've missed you so much."

"Don't try to charm me, Polgara," he told her, though his eyes seemed to soften slightly. "This is as much your fault as it is your father's. I thought you were going to keep an eye on him. How did Belzedar get his hands on our Master's Orb?"

"We think he used a child," Belgarath answered seriously. "The Orb won't strike an innocent."

The dwarf snorted. "There's no such thing as an innocent. All men are born corrupt." He turned his eyes back to Aunt Pol and looked appraisingly at her. "You're getting fat," he said bluntly. "Your hips are as wide as an ox cart."

Durnik immediately clenched his fists and went for the hideous little man.

The dwarf laughed, and one of his big hands caught the front of the smith's tunic. Without any seeming effort, he lifted the surprised Durnik and threw him several yards away. "You can start your second life right now if you want," he growled threateningly.

"Let me handle this, Durnik," Aunt Pol told the smith. "Beldin," she said coolly, "how long has it been since you've had a bath?"

The dwarf shrugged. "It rained on me a couple months ago."

"Not hard enough, though. You smell like an uncleaned pigsty."

Beldin grinned at her. "That's my girl." He chortled. "I was afraid the years had taken off your edge."

The two of them then began to trade the most hair-raising insults Garion had ever heard in his life. Graphic, ugly words passed back and forth between them, almost sizzling in the air. Barak's eyes widened in astonishment, and Mandorallen's face blanched often. Ce'Nedra, her face flaming, bolted out of earshot.

The worse the insults, however, the more the hideous Beldin smiled. Finally Aunt Pol delivered an epithet so vile that Garion actually cringed, and the ugly little man collapsed on the ground, roaring with laughter and hammering at the dirt with his great fists. "By the Gods, I've missed you, Pol!" he gasped. "Come here and give us a kiss."

She smiled, kissing his dirty face affectionately. "Mangy dog."

"Big cow." He grinned, catching her in a crushing embrace.

"I'll need my ribs more or less in one piece, uncle," she told him.

"I haven't cracked any of your ribs in years, my girl."

"I'd like to keep it that way."

The twins hurried across to the dwarf Beldin, carrying a large plate of steaming stew and a huge tankard. The ugly man looked curiously at the plate, then casually dumped the stew on the ground and tossed the plate away. "Doesn't smell too bad." He squatted and began to stuff the food into his mouth with both hands, pausing only now and then to spit out some of the larger pebbles that clung to the chunks of meat. When he had finished, he swilled down the contents of the tankard, belched thunderously, and sat back, scratching at his matted hair with gravy-smeared fingers. "Let's get down to business," he said.

"Where have you been?" Belgarath asked him.

"Central Cthol Murgos. I've been sitting on a hilltop since the Battle of Vo Mimbre, watching the cave where Belzedar took Torak."

"Five hundred years?" Silk gasped.

Beldin shrugged. "More or less," he replied indifferently. "Somebody had to keep an eye on Burnt-Face, and I wasn't doing anything that couldn't be interrupted."

"You said you saw Belzedar," Aunt Pol said.

"About a month ago. He came to the cave as if he had a demon on his tail and pulled Torak out. Then he changed himself into a vulture and flew off with the body."

"That must have been right after Ctuchik caught him at the Nyissan border and took the Orb away from him," Belgarath mused.

"I wouldn't know about that. That was part of your responsibility, not mine. All I was supposed to do was keep watch over Torak. Did any of the ashes fall on you?"

"Which ashes?" one of the twins asked.

"When Belzedar took Torak out of the cave, the mountain exploded—blew its guts out. I imagine it had something to do with the force surrounding One-Eye's body. It was still blowing when I left."

"We wondered what had caused the eruption," Aunt Pol commented. "It put ash down an inch deep all over Nyissa."

"Good. Too bad it wasn't deeper."

"Did you see any signs—"

"—of Torak stirring?" the twins asked.

"Can't you two ever talk straight?" Beldin demanded.

"We're sorry—"

"—it's our nature."

The ugly little man shook his head with disgust. "Never mind. No. Torak didn't move once in the whole five hundred years. There was mold on him when Belzedar dragged him out of the cave."

"Did you follow Belzedar?" Belgarath asked.

"Naturally."

"Where did he take Torak?"

"Now where do you think, idiot? To the ruins of Cthol Mishrak in Mallorea, of course. There are only a few places on earth that'll bear Torak's weight, and that's one of them. Belzedar has to keep Ctuchik and the Orb away from Torak, and that's the only place he *could* go. The Mallorean Grolims refuse to accept Ctuchik's authority, so Belzedar will be safe there. It'll cost him a great deal to pay for their aid, but they'll keep Ctuchik out of Mallorea—unless he raises an army of Murgos and invades."

"That's something we could hope for," Barak said.

"You're supposed to be a bear, not a donkey," Beldin told him. "Don't base your hopes on the impossible. Neither Ctuchik nor Belzedar would start that sort of war at this particular time—not with Belgarion here stalking through the world like an earthquake." He scowled at Aunt Pol. "Can't you teach him to be a little quieter? Or are your wits getting as flabby as your behind?"

"Be civil, uncle," she replied. "The boy's just coming into his strength. We were all a bit clumsy at first."

"He doesn't have time to be a baby, Pol. The stars are dropping into southern Cthol Murgos like poisoned roaches, and dead Grolims are moaning in their tombs from Rak Cthol to Rak Hagga. The time's on us, and he has to be ready."

"He'll be ready, uncle."

"Maybe," the filthy man said sourly.

"Are you going back to Cthol Mishrak?" Belgarath asked.

"No. Our Master told me to stay here. The twins and I have work to do and we don't have much time."

"He spoke to—"

"—us, too."

"Stop that!" Beldin snapped. He turned back to Belgarath. "Are you going to Rak Cthol now?"

"Not yet. We've got to go to Prolgu first. I have to talk to the Gorim, and we've got to pick up another member of the party."

"I noticed that your group wasn't complete yet. What about the last one?"

Belgarath spread his hands. "That's the one that worries me. I haven't been able to find any trace of her—and I've been looking for three thousand years."

"You spent too much time looking in alehouses."

"I noticed the same thing, uncle," Aunt Pol said with a sweet little smile.

"Where do we go after Prolgu?" Barak asked.

"I think that then we'll go to Rak Cthol," Belgarath replied rather grimly. "We've got to get the Orb back from Ctuchik, and I've been meaning to have a rather pointed discussion with the magician of the Murgos for a long, long time, now."

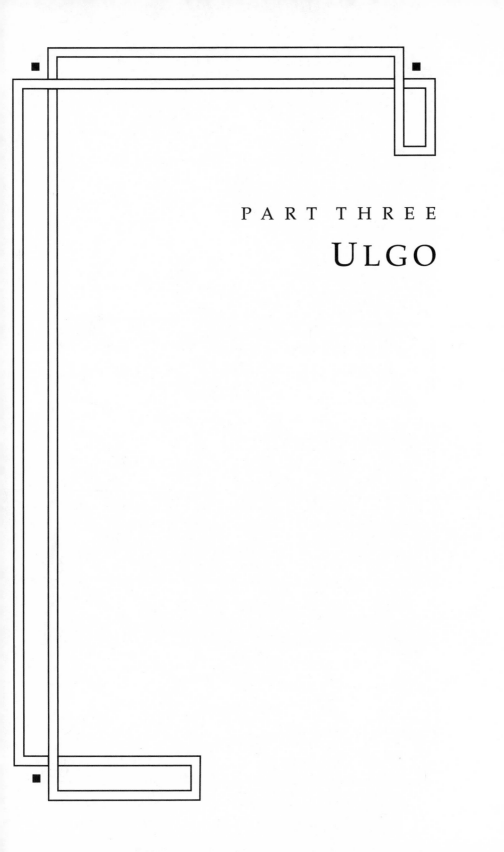

PART THREE

ULGO

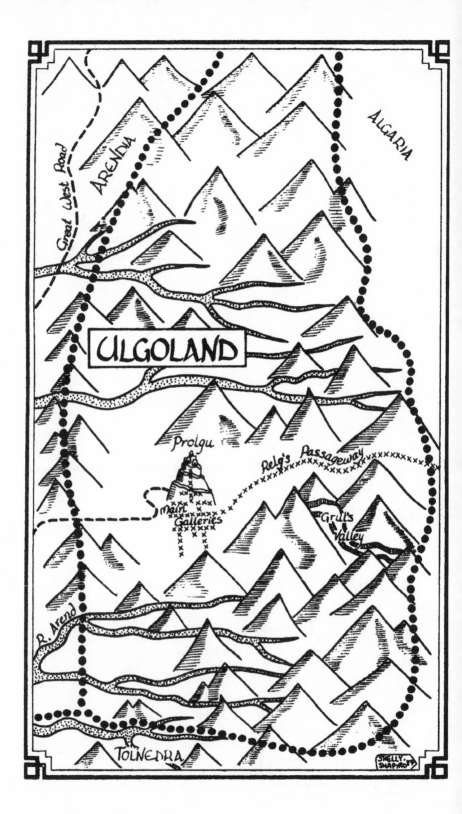

The following morning they turned northwest and rode toward the stark, white peaks of the mountains of Ulgo, glittering in the morning sun above the lush meadows of the Vale.

"Snow up there," Barak observed. "It could be a difficult trip."

"It always is," Hettar told him.

"Have you been to Prolgu before?" Durnik asked.

"A few times. We keep communications open with the Ulgos. Our visits are mostly ceremonial."

Princess Ce'Nedra had been riding beside Aunt Pol, her tiny face troubled. "How can you *stand* him, Lady Polgara?" she burst out finally. "He's so *ugly*."

"Who's that, dear?"

"That awful dwarf."

"Uncle Beldin?" Aunt Pol looked mildly surprised. "He's always been like that. You have to get to know him, that's all."

"But he says such terrible things to you."

"It's the way he hides his real feelings," Aunt Pol explained. "He's a very gentle person, really, but people don't expect that—coming from him. When he was a child, his people drove him out because he was so deformed and hideous. When he finally came to the Vale, our Master saw past the ugliness to the beauty in his mind."

"But does he have to be so *dirty?*"

Aunt Pol shrugged slightly. "He hates his deformed body, so he ignores it." She looked at the princess, her eyes calm. "It's the easiest thing in the world to judge things by appearances, Ce'Nedra," she said, "and it's usually wrong. Uncle Beldin and I are very fond of each other. That's why we take the trouble to invent such elaborate insults. Compliments would be hypocrisy—he *is*, after all, very ugly."

"I just don't understand." Ce'Nedra sounded baffled.

"Love can show itself in many strange ways," Aunt Pol told her. Her tone was offhand, but the look she directed at the tiny princess was penetrating.

Ce'Nedra flickered one quick look at Garion, and then averted her eyes, blushing slightly.

Garion considered the exchange between his Aunt Pol and the princess as he rode. It was quite obvious that Aunt Pol had been telling the little girl something important, but whatever it was escaped him.

They rode for several days across the Vale and then moved up into the foothills which clustered along the flanks of the ragged peaks that formed the land of the Ulgos. Once again the seasons changed as they rode. It was early autumn as they crested the first low range, and the valleys beyond were aflame with crimson leaves. At the top of a second, higher range, the trees had been swept bare, and the wind had the first bite of winter in it as it whistled down from the peaks. The sky grew overcast, and tendrils of cloud seeped down the rocky gorges above them. Spits of intermittent snow and rain pelted them as they climbed higher up the rocky slopes.

"I suppose we'd better start keeping an eye out for Brill," Silk said hopefully one snowy afternoon. "It's about time for him to show up again."

"Not very likely," Belgarath replied. "Murgos avoid Ulgoland even more than they avoid the Vale. Ulgos dislike Angaraks intensely."

"So do Alorns."

"Ulgos can see in the dark, though," the old man told him. "Murgos who come into these mountains tend not to wake up from their first night's sleep up here. I don't think we need to worry about Brill."

"Pity," Silk murmured with a certain disappointment.

"It won't hurt to keep our eyes open, though. There are worse things than Murgos in the mountains of Ulgo."

Silk scoffed. "Aren't those stories exaggerated?"

"No. Not really."

"The region abounds with monsters, Prince Kheldar," Mandorallen assured the little man. "Some years back, a dozen foolish young knights of my acquaintance rode into these mountains to test their bravery and prowess against the unseemly beasts. Not one returned."

When they crested the next ridge, the full force of a winter gale struck them. Snow, which had grown steadily heavier as they climbed, drove horizontally in the howling wind.

"We'll have to take cover until this blows over, Belgarath," Barak shouted above the wind, fighting to keep his flapping bearskin cape around him.

"Let's drop down into this next valley," Belgarath replied, also struggling with his cloak. "The trees down there should break the wind."

They crossed the ridge and angled down toward the pines clustered at the bottom of the basin ahead. Garion pulled his cloak tighter and bowed his head into the shrieking wind.

The thick stand of sapling pine in the basin blocked the force of the gale, but the snow swirled about them as they reined in.

"We're not going to get much farther today, Belgarath," Barak declared, trying to brush the snow out of his beard. "We might as well hole up here and wait for morning."

"What's that?" Durnik asked sharply, cocking his head to one side.

"The wind," Barak shrugged.

"No. Listen."

Above the howling of the wind, a shrill whinnying sound came to them.
"Look there." Hettar pointed.

Dimly they saw a dozen horselike animals crossing the ridge behind
them. Their shapes were blurred by the thickly falling snow, and their line
as they moved seemed almost ghostly. On a rise just above them stood a huge
stallion, his mane and tail tossing in the wind. His neigh was almost a shrill
scream.

"Hrulgin!" Belgarath said sharply.

"Can we outrun them?" Silk asked hopefully.

"I doubt it," Belgarath replied. "Besides, they've got our scent now.
They'll dog our trail from here to Prolgu if we try to run."

"Then we must teach them to fear our trail and avoid it," Mandorallen
declared, tightening the straps on his shield. His eyes were very bright.

"You're falling back into your old habits, Mandorallen," Barak observed
in a grumpy voice.

Hettar's face had assumed that curiously blank expression it usually did
when he was communicating with his horses. He shuddered finally, and his
eyes went sick with revulsion.

"Well?" Aunt Pol asked him.

"They aren't horses," he began.

"We know that, Hettar," she replied. "Can you do anything with them?
Frighten them off perhaps?"

He shook his head. "They're hungry, Polgara," he told her, "and they
have our scent. The herd stallion seems to have much more control over
them than he would if they were horses. I might be able to frighten one or
two of the weaker ones—if it weren't for him."

"Then we'll have to fight them all," Barak said grimly, buckling on his
shield.

"I don't think so," Hettar replied, his eyes narrowing. "The key seems to
be the stallion. He dominates the whole herd. I think that if we kill him, the
rest will turn and run."

"All right," Barak said, "we try for the stallion, then."

"We might want to make some kind of noise," Hettar suggested. "Something that sounds like a challenge. That might make him come out to the
front to answer it. Otherwise, we'll have to go through the whole herd to get
to him."

"Mayhap this will provoke him," Mandorallen said. He lifted his horn to
his lips and blew a brassy note of ringing defiance that was whipped away by
the gale.

The stallion's shrill scream answered immediately.

"It sounds like it's working," Barak observed. "Blow it again,
Mandorallen."

Mandorallen sounded his horn again, and again the stallion shrilled his
reply. Then the great beast plunged down from the ridgetop and charged fu-

riously through the herd toward them. When he reached the forefront, he shrieked again and reared up on his hind legs, his front claws flashing in the snowy air.

"That did it," Barak barked. "Let's go!" He jammed his spurs home, and his big gray leaped forward, spraying snow behind him. Hettar and Mandorallen swept out to flank him, and the three plunged forward through the thickly falling snow toward the screaming Hrulga stallion. Mandorallen set his lance as he charged, and a strange sound drifted back on the wind as he thundered toward the advancing Hrulgin. Mandorallen was laughing.

Garion drew his sword and pulled his horse in front of Aunt Pol and Ce'Nedra. He realized that it was probably a futile gesture, but he did it anyway.

Two of the Hrulgin, perhaps at the herd stallion's unspoken command, bounded forward to cut off Barak and Mandorallen while the stallion himself moved to meet Hettar as if recognizing the Algar as the greatest potential danger to the herd. As the first Hrulga reared, his fangs bared in a catlike snarl and his clawed feet widespread, Mandorallen lowered his lance and drove it through the snarling monster's chest. Bloody froth burst from the Hrulga's mouth, and he toppled over backward, clawing the broken shaft of Mandorallen's lance into splinters as he fell.

Barak caught a clawed swipe on his shield and split open the head of the second Hrulga with a vast overhand swing of his heavy sword. The beast collapsed, his convulsions churning the snow.

Hettar and the herd stallion stalked each other in the swirling snow. They moved warily, circling, their eyes locked on each other with a deadly intensity. Suddenly the stallion reared and lunged all in one motion, his great forelegs wide and his claws outspread. But Hettar's horse, his mind linked with his rider's, danced clear of the furious charge. The Hrulga spun and charged again, and once again Hettar's horse jumped to one side. The infuriated stallion screamed his frustration and lunged in, his claws flailing. Hettar's horse sidestepped the enraged beast, then darted in, and Hettar launched himself from his saddle and landed on the stallion's back. His long, powerful legs locked about the Hrulga's ribs and his right hand gathered a great fistful of the animal's mane.

The stallion went mad as he felt for the first time in the entire history of his species the weight of a rider on his back. He plunged and reared and shrieked, trying to shake Hettar off. The rest of the herd, which had been moving to the attack, faltered and stared in uncomprehending horror at the stallion's wild attempts to dislodge his rider. Mandorallen and Barak reined in, dumbfounded, as Hettar rode the raging stallion in circles through the blizzard. Then, grimly, Hettar slid his left hand down his leg and drew a long, broad dagger from his boot. He knew horses, and he knew where to strike.

His first thrust was lethal. The churned snow turned red. The stallion reared one last time, screaming and with blood pouring out of his mouth, and then he dropped back to stand on shuddering legs. Slowly his knees buckled and he toppled to one side. Hettar jumped clear.

The herd of Hrulgin turned and fled, squealing, back into the blizzard.

Hettar grimly cleaned his dagger in the snow and resheathed it in his boot. Briefly he laid one hand on the dead stallion's neck, then turned to look through the trampled snow for the sabre he had discarded in his wild leap onto the stallion's back.

When the three warriors returned to the shelter of the trees, Mandorallen and Barak were staring at Hettar with a look of profound respect.

"It's a shame they're mad," the Algar said with a distant look on his face. "There was a moment—just a moment—when I almost got through to him, and we moved together. Then the madness came back, and I had to kill him. If they could be tamed—" He broke off and shook his head. "Oh, well." He shrugged regretfully.

"You wouldn't actually ride something like that?" Durnik's voice was shocked.

"I've never had an animal like that under me," Hettar said quietly. "I don't think I'll ever forget what it was like." The tall man turned and walked some distance away and stood staring out into the swirling snow.

They set up for the night in the shelter of the pines. The next morning the wind had abated, although it was still snowing heavily when they set out again. The snow was already knee-deep, and the horses struggled as they climbed.

They crossed yet another ridge and started down into the next valley. Silk looked dubiously around at the thickly-falling snow settling through the silent air. "If it gets much deeper, we're going to bog down, Belgarath," he said glumly. "Particularly if we have to keep climbing like this."

"We'll be all right now," the old man assured him. "We follow a series of valleys from here. They lead right up to Prolgu, so we can avoid the peaks."

"Belgarath," Barak said back over his shoulder from his place in the lead, "there are some fresh tracks up here." He pointed ahead at a line of footprints plowed through the new snow across their path.

The old man moved ahead and stopped to examine the tracks. "Algroth," he said shortly. "We'd better keep our eyes open."

They rode warily down into the valley where Mandorallen paused long enough to cut himself a fresh lance.

"I'd be a little dubious about a weapon that keeps breaking," Barak observed as the knight remounted.

Mandorallen shrugged, his armor creaking. "There are always trees about, my Lord," he replied.

Back among the pines that carpeted the valley floor, Garion heard a familiar barking. "Grandfather," he warned.

"I hear them," Belgarath answered.

"How many, do you think?" Silk asked.

"Perhaps a dozen," Belgarath said.

"Eight," Aunt Pol corrected firmly.

"If they are but eight, will they dare attack?" Mandorallen asked. "Those we met in Arendia seemed to seek courage in numbers."

"Their lair's in this valley, I think," the old man replied. "Any animal tries to defend its lair. They're almost certain to attack."

"We must seek them out, then," the knight declared confidently. "Better to destroy them now on ground of our own choosing than to be surprised in some ambush."

"He's definitely backsliding," Barak observed sourly to Hettar.

"He's probably right this time, though," Hettar replied.

"Have you been drinking, Hettar?" Barak asked suspiciously.

"Come, my Lords," Mandorallen said gaily. "Let us rout the brutes so that we may continue our journey unmolested." He plowed off through the snow in search of the barking Algroths.

"Coming, Barak?" Hettar invited as he drew his sabre.

Barak sighed. "I guess I'd better," he answered mournfully. He turned to Belgarath. "This shouldn't take long. I'll try to keep our bloodthirsty friends out of trouble."

Hettar laughed.

"You're getting to be as bad as he is," Barak accused as the two of them moved into a gallop in Mandorallen's wake.

Garion and the others sat waiting tensely in the sifting snowfall. Then the barking sounds off in the woods suddenly turned into yelps of surprise. The sound of blows began to ring through the trees, and there were shrieks of pain and shouts as the three warriors called to each other. After perhaps a quarter of an hour, they came galloping back with the deep snow spraying out from their horses' hooves.

"Two of them got away," Hettar reported regretfully.

"What a shame," Silk replied.

"Mandorallen," Barak said with a pained look, "you've picked up a bad habit somewhere. Fighting's a serious business, and all this giggling and laughing of yours smacks of frivolity."

"Doth it offend thee, my Lord?"

"It's not so much that it offends me, Mandorallen. It's more a distraction. It breaks my concentration."

"I shall strive to moderate my laughter in future, then."

"I'd appreciate it."

"How did it go?" Silk asked.

"It wasn't much of a fight," Barak replied. "We caught them completely by surprise. I hate to admit it, but our chortling friend there was right for once."

Garion thought about Mandorallen's changed behavior as they rode on down the valley. Back at the cave where the colt had been born, Durnik had told Mandorallen that fear could be conquered by laughing at it, and, though Durnik had probably not meant it in precisely that way, Mandorallen had taken his words quite literally. The laughter which so irritated Barak was not directed at the foe he met, but rather at the enemy within him. Mandorallen was laughing at his own fear as he rode to each attack.

"It's unnatural," Barak was muttering to Silk. "That's what bothers me so much. Not only that, it's a breach of etiquette. If we ever get into a serious fight, it's going to be terribly embarrassing to have him giggling and carrying on like that. What will people think?"

"You're making too much of it, Barak," Silk told him. "Actually, I think it's rather refreshing."

"You think it's *what*?"

"Refreshing. An Arend with a sense of humor is a novelty, after all—sort of like a talking dog."

Barak shook his head in disgust. "There's absolutely no point in ever trying to discuss anything seriously with you, Silk, do you know that? This compulsion of yours to make clever remarks turns everything into a joke."

"We all have our little shortcomings," Silk admitted blandly.

CHAPTER FOURTEEN

The snow gradually slackened throughout the rest of the day and by evening only a few solitary flakes drifted down through the darkening air as they set up for the night in a grove of dense spruces. During the night, however, the temperature fell, and the air was bitterly cold when they arose the next morning.

"How much farther to Prolgu?" Silk asked, standing close to the fire with his shivering hands stretched out to its warmth.

"Two more days," Belgarath replied.

"I don't suppose you'd consider doing something about the weather?" the little man asked hopefully.

"I prefer not to do that unless I absolutely have to," the old man told him. "It disrupts things over a very wide area. Besides, the Gorim doesn't like us to tamper with things in his mountains. The Ulgos have reservations about that sort of thing."

"I was afraid you might look at it that way."

Their route that morning twisted and turned so often that by noon Garion was completely turned around. Despite the biting cold, the sky was overcast, a solid lead-gray. It seemed somehow as if the cold had frozen all color from the world. The sky was gray; the snow was a flat, dead white; and the tree trunks were starkly black. Even the rushing water in the streams they followed flowed black between snow-mounded banks. Belgarath moved confidently, pointing their direction as each succeeding valley intersected with another.

"Are you sure?" the shivering Silk asked him at one point. "We've been going upstream all day, now you say we go down."

"We'll hit another valley in a few miles. Trust me, Silk. I've been here before."

Silk pulled his heavy cloak tighter. "It's just that I get nervous on unfamiliar ground," he objected, looking at the dark water of the river they followed.

From far upstream came a strange sound, a kind of mindless hooting that was almost like laughter. Aunt Pol and Belgarath exchanged a quick look.

"What is it?" Garion asked.

"Rock-wolf," Belgarath answered shortly.

"It doesn't sound like a wolf."

"It isn't." The old man looked around warily. "They're scavengers for the most part and, if it's just a wild pack, they probably won't attack. It's too early in the winter for them to be that desperate. If it's one of the packs that has been raised by the Eldrakyn, though, we're in for trouble." He stood up in his stirrups to look ahead. "Let's pick up the pace a bit," he called to Mandorallen, "and keep your eyes open."

Mandorallen, his armor glittering with frost, glanced back, nodded, and moved out at a trot, following the seething black water of the mountain river.

Behind them the shrill, yelping laughter grew louder.

"They're following us, father," Aunt Pol said.

"I can hear that." The old man began searching the sides of the valley with his eyes, his face creased with a worried frown. "You'd better have a look, Pol. I don't want any surprises."

Aunt Pol's eyes grew distant as she probed the thickly forested sides of the valley with her mind. After a moment, she gasped and then shuddered. "There's an Eldrak out there, father. He's watching us. His mind is a sewer."

"They always are," the old man replied. "Could you pick up his name?"

"Grul."

"That's what I was afraid of. I knew we were getting close to his range." He put his fingers to his lips and whistled sharply.

Barak and Mandorallen halted to wait while the rest caught up with them. "We've got trouble," Belgarath told them all seriously. "There's an Eldrak out there with a pack of rock-wolves. He's watching us right now. It's only a question of time until he attacks."

"What's an Eldrak?" Silk asked.

"The Eldrakyn are related to Algroths and Trolls, but they're more intelligent—and much bigger."

"But only one?" Mandorallen asked.

"One's enough. I've met this one. His name is Grul. He's big, quick, and as cruel as a hook-pointed knife. He'll eat anything that moves, and he doesn't really care if it's dead or not before he starts to eat."

The hooting laughter of the rock-wolves drew closer.

"Let's find an open place and build a fire," the old man said. "The rock-wolves are afraid of fire, and there's no point in fighting with them *and* Grul if we don't have to."

"There?" Durnik suggested, pointing to a broad, snow-covered bar protruding out into the dark water of the river. The bar was joined to the near bank by a narrow neck of gravel and sand.

"It's defensible, Belgarath," Barak approved, squinting at the bar. "The river will keep them off our backs, and they can only come at us across that one narrow place."

"It'll do," Belgarath agreed shortly. "Let's go."

They rode out onto the snow-covered bar and quickly scraped an area clear with their feet while Durnik worked to build a fire under a large, gray driftwood snag that half-blocked the narrow neck of the bar. Within a few moments, orange flames began to lick up around the snag. Durnik fed the fire with sticks until the snag was fully ablaze. "Give me a hand," the smith said, starting to pile larger pieces of wood on the fire. Barak and Mandorallen went to the jumbled mass of driftwood piled against the upstream edge of the gravel and began hauling limbs and chunks of log to the fire. At the end of a quarter of an hour they had built a roaring bonfire that stretched across the narrow neck of sand, cutting them off completely from the dark trees on the riverbank.

"It's the first time I've been warm all day." Silk grinned, backing up to the fire.

"They're coming," Garion warned. Back among the dark tree trunks, he had caught a few glimpses of furtive movements.

Barak peered through the flames. "Big brutes, aren't they?" he observed grimly.

"About the size of a donkey," Belgarath confirmed.

"Are you sure they're afraid of fire?" Silk asked nervously.

"Most of the time."

"*Most* of the time?"

"Once in a while they get desperate—or Grul could drive them toward us. They'd be more afraid of him than of the fire."

"Belgarath," the weasel-faced little man objected, "sometimes you've got a nasty habit of keeping things to yourself."

One of the rock-wolves came out onto the riverbank just upstream from the bar and stood sniffing the air and looking nervously at the fire. Its forelegs were noticeably longer than its hind ones, giving it a peculiar, half-erect stance, and there was a large, muscular hump across its shoulders. Its muzzle was short, and it seemed snub-faced, almost like a cat. Its coat was a splotchy black and white, marked with a pattern hovering somewhere between spots and stripes. It paced nervously back and forth, staring at them with a dreadful intensity and yelping its high-pitched, hooting laugh. Soon another came out to join it, and then another. They spread out along the bank, pacing and hooting, but staying well back from the fire.

"They don't look like dogs exactly," Durnik said.

"They're not," Belgarath replied. "Wolves and dogs are related, but rock-wolves belong to a different family."

By now ten of the ugly creatures lined the bank, and their hooting rose in a mindless chorus.

Then Ce'Nedra screamed, her face deathly pale and her eyes wide with horror.

The Eldrak shambled out of the trees and stood in the middle of the yelping pack. It was about eight feet tall and covered with shaggy black fur. It wore an armored shirt that had been made of large scraps of chainmail tied together with thongs; over the mail, also held in place with thongs, was a rusty breastplate that appeared to have been hammered out with rocks until it was big enough to fit around the creature's massive chest. A conical steel helmet, split up the back to make it fit, covered the brute's head. In its hand the Eldrak held a huge, steel-wrapped club, studded with spikes. It was the face, however, that had brought the scream to Ce'Nedra's lips. The Eldrak had virtually no nose, and its lower jaw jutted, showing two massive, protruding tusks. Its eyes were sunk in deep sockets beneath a heavy ridge of bone across its brow, and they burned with a hideous hunger.

"That's far enough, Grul," Belgarath warned the thing in a cold, deadly voice.

"'Grat come back to Grul's mountains?" the monster growled. Its voice was deep and hollow, chilling.

"It talks?" Silk gasped incredulously.

"Why are you following us, Grul?" Belgarath demanded.

The creature stared at them, its eyes like fire. "Hungry, 'Grat," it growled.

"Go hunt something else," the old man told the monster.

"Why? Horses here—men. Plenty to eat."

"But not easy food, Grul," Belgarath replied.

A hideous grin spread across Grul's face. "Fight first," he said, "then eat. Come, 'Grat. Fight again."

"Grat?" Silk asked.

"He means me. He can't pronounce my name—it has to do with the shape of his jaw."

"You *fought* that thing?" Barak sounded stunned.

Belgarath shrugged. "I had a knife up my sleeve. When he grabbed me, I sliced him open. It wasn't much of a fight."

"Fight!" Grul roared. He hammered on his breastplate with his huge fist. "Iron," he said. "Come, 'Grat. Try to cut Grul's belly again. Now Grul wear iron—like men wear." He began to pound on the frozen ground with his steel-shod club. "Fight!" he bellowed. "Come, 'Grat. Fight!"

"Maybe if we all go after him at once, one of us might get in a lucky thrust," Barak said, eyeing the monster speculatively.

"Thy plan is flawed, my Lord," Mandorallen told him. "We must lose several companions should we come within range of that club."

Barak looked at him in astonishment. "Prudence, Mandorallen? Prudence from you?"

"It were best, I think, should I undertake this alone," the knight stated gravely. "My lance is the only weapon that can seek out the monster's life with safety."

"There's something to what he says," Hettar agreed.

"Come fight!" Grul roared, still beating on the ground with his club.

"All right," Barak agreed dubiously. "We'll distract him, then—come at him from two sides to get his attention. Then Mandorallen can make his charge."

"What about the rock-wolves?" Garion asked.

"Let me try something," Durnik said. He took up a burning stick and threw it, spinning and flaring, at the nervous pack surrounding the monster. The rock-wolves yelped and shied quickly away from the tumbling brand. "They're afraid of the fire, all right," the smith said. "I think that if we all throw at once and keep throwing, their nerve will break and they'll run."

They all moved to the fire.

"Now!" Durnik shouted sharply. They began throwing the blazing sticks as fast as they could. The rock-wolves yelped and dodged, and several of them screamed in pain as the tumbling firebrands singed them.

Grul roared in fury as the pack dodged and scurried around his feet, trying to escape the sudden deluge of fire. One of the singed beasts, maddened by pain and fright, tried to leap at him. The Eldrak jumped out of its way with astonishing agility and smashed the rock-wolf to the ground with his great club.

"He's quicker than I thought," Barak said. "We'll have to be careful."

"They're running!" Durnik shouted, throwing another fiery stick.

The pack had broken under the rain of burning brands and turned to flee howling back into the woods, leaving the infuriated Grul standing alone on the riverbank, hammering at the snow-covered ground with his spiked club. "Come fight!" he roared again. "Come fight!" He advanced one huge step and smashed his club at the snow again.

"We'd better do whatever we're going to do now," Silk said tensely. "He's getting himself worked up. We'll have him out here on the bar with us in another minute or two."

Mandorallen nodded grimly and turned to mount his charger.

"Let the rest of us distract him first," Barak said. He drew his heavy sword. "Let's go!" he shouted and leaped over the fire. The others followed him, spreading out in a half-circle in front of the towering Grul.

Garion reached for his sword.

"Not you," Aunt Pol snapped. "You stay here."

"But—"

"Do as I say."

One of Silk's daggers, skillfully thrown from several yards away, sank into Grul's shoulder while the creature was advancing on Barak and Durnik. Grul howled and turned to charge Silk and Hettar, swinging his vast club. Hettar dodged, and Silk danced back out of reach. Durnik began pelting the monster with fist-sized rocks from the riverbank. Grul turned back, raging now, with flecks of foam dripping from his pointed tusks.

"Now, Mandorallen!" Barak shouted.

Mandorallen couched his lance and spurred his warhorse. The huge armored animal leaped forward, its hooves churning gravel, jumped the fire, and bore down on the astonished Grul. For a moment it looked as if their plan might work. The deadly, steel-pointed lance was leveled at Grul's chest, and it seemed that nothing could stop it from plunging through his huge body. But the monster's quickness again astonished them all. He leaped to one side and smashed his spiked club down on Mandorallen's lance, shattering the stout wood.

The force of Mandorallen's charge, however, could not be stopped. Horse and man crashed into the great brute with a deafening impact. Grul reeled back, dropping his club, tripping, falling with Mandorallen and his warhorse on top of him.

"Get him!" Barak roared, and they all dashed forward to attack the fallen Grul with swords and axes. The monster, however, levered his legs under Mandorallen's thrashing horse and thrust the big animal off. A great, flailing fist caught Mandorallen in the side, throwing him for several yards. Durnik spun and dropped, felled by a glancing blow to the head even as Barak, Hettar, and Silk swarmed over the fallen Grul.

"Father!" Aunt Pol cried in a ringing voice.

There was suddenly a new sound directly behind Garion—first a deep, rumbling snarl followed instantly by a hair-raising howl. Garion turned quickly and saw the huge wolf he had seen once before in the forests of northern Arendia. The old gray wolf bounded across the fire and entered the fight, his great teeth flashing and tearing.

"Garion, I need you!" Aunt Pol was shaking off the panic-stricken princess and pulling her amulet out of her bodice. "Take out your medallion—quickly!"

He did not understand, but he drew his amulet out from under his tunic. Aunt Pol reached out, took his right hand, and placed the mark on his palm against the figure of the owl on her own talisman; at the same time, she took his medallion in her other hand. "Focus your will," she commanded.

"On what?"

"On the amulets. Quickly!"

Garion brought his will to bear, feeling the power building in him tremendously, amplified somehow by his contact with Aunt Pol and the two amulets. Polgara closed her eyes and raised her face to the leaden sky. "*Mother!*" she cried in a voice so loud that the echo rang like a trumpet note in the narrow valley.

The power surged out of Garion in so vast a rush that he collapsed to his knees, unable to stand. Aunt Pol sank down beside him.

Ce'Nedra gasped.

As Garion weakly raised his head, he saw that there were *two* wolves attacking the raging Grul—the gray old wolf he knew to be his grandfather, and another, slightly smaller wolf that seemed surrounded by a strange, flickering blue light.

Grul had struggled to his feet and was laying about him with his huge fists as the men attacking him chopped futilely at his armored body. Barak was flung out of the fight and fell to his hands and knees, shaking his head groggily. Grul brushed Hettar aside, his eyes alight with dreadful glee as he lunged toward Barak with both huge arms raised. But the blue wolf leaped snarling at his face. Grul swung his fist and gaped with astonishment as it passed directly through the flickering body. Then he shrieked with pain and began to topple backward as Belgarath, darting in from behind to employ the wolf's ancient tactic, neatly hamstrung him with great, ripping teeth. The towering Grul, howling, fell and struck the earth like some vast tree.

"Keep him down!" Barak roared, stumbling to his feet and staggering forward.

The wolves were ripping at Grul's face, and he flailed his arms, trying to beat them away. Again and again his hands passed through the body of the strange, flickering blue wolf. Mandorallen, his feet spread wide apart and holding the hilt of his broadsword with both hands, chopped steadily at the monster's body, his great blade shearing long rents in Grul's breastplate. Barak swung huge blows at Grul's head, his sword striking sparks from the rusty steel helmet. Hettar crouched at one side, eyes intent, sabre ready, waiting. Grul raised his arm to ward off Barak's blows, and Hettar lunged, thrusting his sabre through the exposed armpit and into the huge chest. A bloody froth spouted from Grul's mouth as the sabre ripped through his lungs. He struggled to a half-sitting position.

Then Silk, who had lurked just at the edge of the fight, darted in, set the point of his dagger against the back of Grul's neck and smashed a large rock against the dagger's pommel. With a sickening crunch, the dagger drove through bone, angling up into the monster's brain. Grul shuddered convulsively. Then he collapsed.

In the moment of silence that followed, the two wolves looked at each other across the monster's dead face. The blue wolf seemed to wink once; in a voice which Garion could hear quite clearly—a woman's voice— she said, "How remarkable." With a seeming smile and one last flicker, she vanished.

The old gray wolf raised his muzzle and howled, a sound of such piercing anguish and loss that Garion's heart wrenched within him. Then the old wolf seemed to shimmer, and Belgarath knelt in his place. He rose slowly to his feet and walked back toward the fire, tears streaming openly down his grizzled cheeks.

CHAPTER FIFTEEN

"Is he going to be all right?" Barak asked anxiously, hovering over the still-unconscious Durnik as Aunt Pol examined the large purple contusion on the side of the smith's face.

"It's nothing serious," she replied in a voice seeming to droop with a great weariness.

Garion sat nearby with his head in his hands. He felt as if all the strength had been wrenched out of his body.

Beyond the heaped coals of the rapidly dying bonfire, Silk and Hettar were struggling to remove Mandorallen's dented breastplate. A deep crease running diagonally from shoulder to hip gave mute evidence of the force of Grul's blow and placed so much stress on the straps beneath the shoulder plates that they were almost impossible to unfasten.

"I think we're going to have to cut them," Silk said.

"I pray thee, Prince Kheldar, avoid that if possible," Mandorallen answered, wincing as they wrenched at the fastenings. "Those straps are crucial to the fit of the armor, and are most difficult to replace properly."

"This one's coming now," Hettar grunted, prying at a buckle with a short iron rod. The buckle released suddenly and the taut breastplate rang like a softly struck bell.

"Now I can get it," Silk said, quickly loosening the other shoulder buckle.

Mandorallen sighed with relief as they pulled off the dented breastplate. He took a deep breath and winced again.

"Tender right here?" Silk asked, putting his fingers lightly to the right side of the knight's chest. Mandorallen grunted with pain, and his face paled visibly. "I think you've got some cracked ribs, my splendid friend," Silk told him. "You'd better have Polgara take a look."

"In a moment," Mandorallen said. "My horse?"

"He'll be all right," Hettar replied. "A strained tendon in his right foreleg is all."

Mandorallen let out a sigh of relief. "I had feared for him."

"I feared for us all there for a while," Silk said. "Our oversized playmate there was almost more than we could handle."

"Good fight, though," Hettar remarked.

Silk gave him a disgusted look, then glanced up at the scudding gray clouds overhead. He jumped across the glowing coals of their fire and went over to where Belgarath sat staring into the icy river. "We're going to have to get off this bar, Belgarath," he urged. "The weather's going bad on us again, and we'll all freeze to death if we stay out here in the middle of the river tonight."

"Leave me alone," Belgarath muttered shortly, still staring at the river.

"Polgara?" Silk turned to her.

"Just stay away from him for a while," she told him. "Go find a sheltered place for us to stay for a few days."

"I'll go with you," Barak offered, hobbling toward his horse.

"You'll stay here," Aunt Pol declared firmly. "You creak like a wagon with a broken axle. I want to have a look at you before you get a chance to damage yourself permanently."

"I know a place," Ce'Nedra said, rising and pulling her cloak about her shoulders. "I saw it when we were coming down the river. I'll show you."

Silk looked inquiringly at Aunt Pol.

"Go ahead," she told him. "It's safe enough now. Nothing else would live in the same valley with an Eldrak."

Silk laughed. "I wonder why? Coming, Princess?" The two of them mounted and rode off through the snow.

"Shouldn't Durnik be coming around?" Garion asked his Aunt.

"Let him sleep," she replied wearily. "He'll have a blinding headache when he wakes up."

"Aunt Pol?"

"Yes?"

"Who was the other wolf?"

"My mother, Poledra."

"But isn't she—"

"Yes. It was her spirit."

"You can do *that?*" Garion was stunned by the enormity of it.

"Not alone," she said. "You had to help me."

"Is that why I feel so—" It was an effort even to talk.

"It took everything we could both raise to do it. Don't ask so many questions just now, Garion. I'm very tired and I still have many things to do."

"Is Grandfather all right?"

"He'll come around. Mandorallen, come here."

The knight stepped over the coals at the neck of the bar and walked slowly toward her, his hand pressed lightly against his chest.

"You'll have to take off your shirt," she told him. "And please sit down."

About a half-hour later Silk and the princess returned. "It's a good spot," Silk reported. "A thicket in a little ravine. Water, shelter—everything we need. Is anybody seriously hurt?"

"Nothing permanent." Aunt Pol was applying a salve to Barak's hairy leg.

"Do you suppose you could hurry, Polgara?" Barak asked. "It's a little chilly for standing around half-dressed."

"Stop being such a baby," she said heartlessly.

The ravine to which Silk and Ce'Nedra led them was a short way back upriver. A small mountain brook trickled from its mouth, and a dense thicket of spindly pines filled it seemingly from wall to wall. They followed the brook for a few hundred yards until they came to a small clearing in the center of the thicket. The pines around the inner edge of the clearing, pressed by the limbs of the others in the thicket, leaned inward, almost touching above the center of the open area.

"Good spot." Hettar looked around approvingly. "How did you find it?"

"She did." Silk nodded to Ce'Nedra.

"The trees told me it was here," she said. "Young pine trees babble a lot." She looked at the clearing thoughtfully. "We'll build our fire there," she decided, pointing at a spot near the brook at the upper end of the clearing, "and set up our tents along the edge of the trees just back from it. You'll need to pile rocks around the fire and clear away all the twigs from the ground near it. The trees are very nervous about the fire. They promised to keep the wind off us, but only if we keep our fire strictly under control. I gave them my word."

A faint smile flickered across Hettar's hawklike face.

"I'm serious," she said, stamping her little foot.

"Of course, your Highness," he replied, bowing.

Because of the incapacity of the others, the work of setting up the tents and building the firepit fell largely upon Silk and Hettar. Ce'Nedra commanded them like a little general, snapping out her orders in a clear, firm voice. She seemed to be enjoying herself immensely.

Garion was sure that it was some trick of the fading light, but the trees almost seemed to draw back when the fire first flared up, though after a while they seemed to lean back in again to arch protectively over the little clearing. Wearily he got to his feet and began to gather sticks and dead limbs for firewood.

"Now," Ce'Nedra said, bustling about the fire in a thoroughly business-like way, "what would you all like for supper?"

They stayed in their protected little clearing for three days while their battered warriors and Mandorallen's horse recuperated from the encounter with the Eldrak. The exhaustion which had fallen upon Garion when Aunt Pol had summoned all his strength to help call the spirit of Poledra was largely gone after one night's sleep, though he tired easily during the next day. He found Ce'Nedra's officiousness in her domain near the fire almost unbearable, so he passed some time helping Durnik hammer the deep crease out of Mandorallen's breastplate; after that, he spent as much time as possible with the horses. He began teaching the little colt a few simple tricks, though he had never attempted training animals before. The colt seemed to enjoy it, although his attention wandered frequently.

The incapacity of Durnik, Barak, and Mandorallen was easy to understand, but Belgarath's deep silence and seeming indifference to all around him worried Garion. The old man appeared to be sunk in a melancholy reverie that he could not or would not shake off.

"Aunt Pol," Garion said finally on the afternoon of the third day, "you'd better do something. We'll be ready to leave soon, and Grandfather has to be able to show us the way. Right now I don't think he even cares where he is."

Aunt Pol looked across at the old sorcerer, who sat on a rock, staring into the fire. "Possibly you're right. Come with me." She led the way around the fire and stopped directly in front of the old man. "All right, father," she said crisply, "I think that's about enough."

"Go away, Polgara," he told her.

"No, father," she replied. "It's time for you to put it away and come back to the real world."

"That was a cruel thing to do, Pol," he said reproachfully.

"To mother? She didn't mind."

"How do you know that? You never knew her. She died when you were born."

"What's that got to do with it?" She looked at him directly. "Father," she declared pointedly, "you of all people should know that mother was extremely strong-minded. She's always been with me, and we know each other very well."

He looked dubious.

"She has her part to play in this just the same as the rest of us do. If you'd been paying attention all these years, you'd have realized that she's never really been gone."

The old man looked around a little guiltily.

"Precisely," Aunt Pol said with just the hint of a barb in her voice. "You really should have behaved yourself, you know. Mother's very tolerant for the most part, but there were times when she was quite vexed with you."

Belgarath coughed uncomfortably.

"Now it's time for you to pull yourself out of this and stop feeling sorry for yourself," she continued crisply.

His eyes narrowed. "That's not entirely fair, Polgara," he replied.

"I don't have time to be fair, father."

"Why did you choose that particular form?" he asked with a hint of bitterness.

"I didn't, father. She did. It's her natural form, after all."

"I'd almost forgotten that," he mused.

"She didn't."

The old man straightened and drew back his shoulders. "Is there any food around?" he asked suddenly.

"The princess has been doing the cooking," Garion warned him. "You might want to think it over before you decide to eat anything she's had a hand in."

The next morning under a still-threatening sky, they struck their tents, packed their gear again, and rode down along the narrow bed of the brook back into the river valley.

"Did you thank the trees, dear?" Aunt Pol asked the princess.

"Yes, Lady Polgara," Ce'Nedra replied. "Just before we left."

"That's nice," Aunt Pol said.

The weather continued to threaten for the next two days, and finally the blizzard broke in full fury as they approached a strangely pyramidal peak. The sloping walls of the peak were steep, rising sharply up into the swirling snow, and they seemed to have none of the random irregularities of the surrounding mountains. Though he rejected the idea immediately, Garion could not quite overcome the notion that the curiously angular peak had somehow been constructed—that its shape was the result of a conscious design.

"Prolgu," Belgarath said, pointing at the peak with one hand while he clung to his wind-whipped cloak with the other.

"How do we get up there?" Silk asked, staring at the steep walls dimly visible in the driving snow.

"There's a road," the old man replied. "It starts over there." He pointed to a vast pile of jumbled rock to one side of the peak.

"We'd better hurry, then, Belgarath," Barak said. "This storm isn't going to improve much."

The old man nodded and moved his horse into the lead. "When we get up there," he shouted back to them over the sound of the shrieking wind, "we'll find the city. It's abandoned, but you may see a few things lying about—broken pots, some other things. Don't touch any of them. The Ulgos have some peculiar beliefs about Prolgu. It's a very holy place to them, and everything there is supposed to stay just where it is."

"How do we get down into the caves?" Barak asked.

"The Ulgos will let us in," Belgarath assured him. "They already know we're here."

The road that led to the mountaintop was a narrow ledge, inclining steeply up and around the sides of the peak. They dismounted before they started up and led their horses. The wind tugged at them as they climbed, and the driving snow, more pellets than flakes, stung their faces.

It took them two hours to wind their way to the top, and Garion was numb with cold by the time they got there. The wind seemed to batter at him, trying to pluck him off the ledge, and he made a special point of staying as far from the edge as possible.

Though the wind had been brutal on the sides of the peak, once they reached the top it howled at them with unbroken force. They passed through a broad, arched gate into the deserted city of Prolgu with snow swirling about them and the wind shrieking insanely in their ears.

There were columns lining the empty streets, tall, thick columns reaching up into the dancing snow. The buildings, all unroofed by time and the endless progression of the seasons, had a strange, alien quality about them. Accustomed to the rigid rectangularity of the structures in the other cities he had seen, Garion was unprepared for the sloped corners of Ulgo architecture. Nothing seemed exactly square. The complexity of the angles teased at his mind, suggesting a subtle sophistication that somehow just eluded him. There was a massiveness about the construction that seemed to defy time, and the weathered stones sat solidly, one atop the other, precisely as they had been placed thousands of years before.

Durnik seemed also to have noticed the peculiar nature of the structures, and his expression was one of disapproval. As they all moved behind a building to get out of the wind and to rest for a moment from the exertions of the climb, he ran his hand up one of the slanted corners. "Hadn't they ever heard of a plumb line?" he muttered critically.

"Where do we go to find the Ulgos?" Barak asked, pulling his bearskin cloak even tighter about him.

"It isn't far," Belgarath answered.

They led their horses back out into the blizzard-swept streets, past the strange, pyramidal buildings.

"An eerie place," Mandorallen said, looking around him. "How long hath it been abandoned thus?"

"Since Torak cracked the world," Belgarath replied. "About five thousand years."

They trudged across a broad street through the deepening snow to a building somewhat larger than the ones about it and passed inside through a wide doorway surmounted by a huge stone lintel. Inside, the air hung still and calm. A few flakes of snow drifted down through the silent air, sifting through the narrow opening at the top where the roof had been and lightly dusting the stone floor.

Belgarath moved purposefully to a large black stone in the precise center of the floor. The stone was cut in such a way as to duplicate the truncated pyramid shape of the buildings in the city, angling up to a flat surface about four feet above the floor. "Don't touch it," he warned them, carefully stepping around the stone.

"Is it dangerous?" Barak asked.

"No," Belgarath said. "It's holy. The Ulgos don't want it profaned. They believe that UL himself placed it here." He studied the floor intently, scraping away the thin dusting of snow with his foot in several places. "Let's see." He frowned slightly. Then he uncovered a single flagstone that seemed a slightly different color from those surrounding it. "Here we are," he grunted. "I always have to look for it. Give me your sword, Barak."

Wordlessly the big man drew his sword and handed it to the old sorcerer.

Belgarath knelt beside the flagstone he'd uncovered and rapped sharply on it three times with the pommel of Barak's heavy sword. The sound seemed to echo hollowly from underneath.

The old man waited for a moment, then repeated his signal.

Nothing happened.

A third time Belgarath hammered his three measured strokes on the echoing flagstone. A slow grinding sound started in one corner of the large chamber.

"What's that?" Silk demanded nervously.

"The Ulgos," Belgarath replied, rising to his feet and dusting off his knees. "They're opening the portal to the caves."

The grinding continued and a line of faint light appeared suddenly about twenty feet out from the east wall of the chamber. The line became a crack and then slowly yawned wider as a huge stone in the floor tilted up, rising with a ponderous slowness. The light from below seemed very dim.

"Belgarath," a deep voice echoed from beneath the slowly tilting stone, "Yad ho, groja UL."

"Yad ho, groja UL. Vad mar ishum," Belgarath responded formally.

"Veed mo, Belgarath. Mar ishum Ulgo," the unseen speaker said.

"What was that?" Garion asked in perplexity.

"He invited us into the caves," the old man said. "Shall we go down now?"

CHAPTER SIXTEEN

It took all of Hettar's force of persuasion to start the horses moving down the steeply inclined passageway that led into the dimness of the caves of Ulgo. Their eyes rolled nervously as they took step after braced step down the slanting corridor, and they all flinched noticeably as the grinding stone boomed shut behind them. The colt walked so close to Garion that they frequently bumped against each other, and Garion could feel the little animal's trembling with every step.

At the end of the corridor two figures stood, each with his face veiled in a kind of filmy cloth. They were short men, shorter even than Silk, but their shoulders seemed bulky beneath their dark robes. Just beyond them an irregularly shaped chamber opened out, faintly lighted by a dim, reddish glow.

Belgarath moved toward the two, and they bowed respectfully to him as he approached. He spoke with them briefly, and they bowed again, pointing toward another corridor opening on the far side of the chamber. Garion nervously looked around for the source of the faint red light, but it seemed lost in the strange, pointed rocks hanging from the ceiling.

"We go this way," Belgarath quietly told them, crossing the chamber toward the corridor the two veiled men had indicated to him.

"Why are their faces covered?" Durnik whispered.

"To protect their eyes from the light when they opened the portal."

"But it was almost dark inside that building up there," Durnik objected.

"Not to an Ulgo," the old man replied.

"Don't any of them speak our language?"

"A few—not very many. They don't have much contact with outsiders. We'd better hurry. The Gorim is waiting for us."

The corridor they entered ran for a short distance and then opened abruptly into a cavern so vast that Garion could not even see the other side of it in the faint light that seemed to pervade the caves.

"How extensive are these caverns, Belgarath?" Mandorallen asked, somewhat awed by the immensity of the place.

"No one knows for sure. The Ulgos have been exploring the caves since they came down here, and they're still finding new ones."

The passageway they had followed from the portal chamber had emerged high up in the wall of the cavern near the vaulted roof, and a broad ledge sloped downward from the opening, running along the sheer wall. Garion glanced once over the edge. The cavern floor was lost in the gloom far below. He shuddered and stayed close to the wall after that.

As they descended, they found that the huge cavern was not silent. From what seemed infinitely far away there was the cadenced sound of chanting by a chorus of deep male voices, the words blurred and confused by the echoes reverberating from the stone walls and seeming to die off, endlessly repeated.

Then, as the last echoes of the chant faded, the chorus began to sing, their song strangely disharmonic and in a mournful, minor key. In a peculiar fashion, the disharmony of the first phrases echoing back joined the succeeding phrases and merged with them, moving inexorably toward a final harmonic resolution so profound that Garion felt his entire being moved by it. The echoes merged as the chorus ended its song, and the caves of Ulgo sang on alone, repeating that final chord over and over.

"I've never heard anything like that," Ce'Nedra whispered softly to Aunt Pol.

"Few people have," Polgara replied, "though the sound lingers in some of these galleries for days."

"What were they singing?"

"A hymn to UL. It's repeated every hour, and the echoes keep it alive. These caves have been singing that same hymn for five thousand years now."

There were other sounds as well, the scrape of metal against metal, snatches of conversation in the guttural language of the Ulgos, and an endless chipping sound, coming, it seemed, from a dozen places.

"There must be a lot of them down there," Barak observed, peering over the edge.

"Not necessarily," Belgarath told him. "Sound lingers in these caves, and the echoes keep coming back over and over again."

"Where does the light come from?" Durnik asked, looking puzzled. "I don't see any torches."

"The Ulgos grind two different kinds of rock to powder," Belgarath replied. "When you mix them, they give off a glow."

"It's pretty dim light," Durnik observed, looking down toward the floor of the cavern.

"Ulgos don't need all that much light."

It took them almost half an hour to reach the cavern floor. The walls around the bottom were pierced at regular intervals with the openings of corridors and galleries radiating out into the solid rock of the mountain. As they passed, Garion glanced down one of the galleries. It was very long and dimly lighted with openings along its walls and a few Ulgos moving from place to place far down toward the other end.

In the center of the cavern lay a large, silent lake, and they skirted the edge of it as Belgarath moved confidently, seeming to know precisely where he was going. Somewhere from far out on the dim lake, Garion heard a faint splash, a fish perhaps or the sound of a dislodged pebble from far above falling into the water. The echo of the singing they had heard when they entered the cavern still lingered, curiously loud in some places and very faint in others.

Two Ulgos waited for them near the entrance to one of the galleries. They bowed and spoke briefly to Belgarath. Like the men who had met them in the portal chamber, both were short and heavy-shouldered. Their hair was very pale and their eyes large and almost black.

"We'll leave the horses here," Belgarath said. "We have to go down some stairs. These men will care for them."

The colt, still trembling, had to be told several times to stay with his mother, but he finally seemed to understand. Then Garion hurried to catch up to the others, who had already entered the mouth of one of the galleries.

There were doors in the walls of the gallery they followed, doors opening into small cubicles, some of them obviously workshops of one kind or another and others just as obviously arranged for domestic use. The Ulgos inside the cubicles continued at their tasks, paying no attention to the party passing in the gallery. Some of the pale-haired people were working with metal, some with stone, a few with wood or cloth. An Ulgo woman was nursing a small baby.

Behind them in the cavern they had first entered, the sound of the chanting began again. They passed a cubicle where seven Ulgos, seated in a circle, were reciting something in unison.

"They spend a great deal of time in religious observances," Belgarath remarked as they passed the cubicle. "Religion's the central fact of Ulgo life."

"Sounds dull," Barak grunted.

At the end of the gallery a flight of steep, worn stairs descended sharply, and they went down, their hands on the wall to steady themselves.

"It'd be easy to get turned around down here," Silk observed. "I've lost track of which direction we're going."

"Down," Hettar told him.

"Thanks," Silk replied dryly.

At the bottom of the stairs they entered another cavern, once again high up in the wall, but this time the cavern was spanned by a slender bridge, arching across to the other side. "We cross that," Belgarath told them and led them out onto the bridge that arched through the half light to the other side.

Garion glanced down once and saw a myriad of gleaming openings dotting the cavern walls far below. The openings did not appear to have any systematic arrangement, but rather seemed scattered randomly. "There must be a lot of people living here," he said to his grandfather.

The old man nodded. "It's the home cave of one of the major Ulgo tribes," he replied.

The first disharmonic phrases of the ancient hymn to UL drifted up to them as they neared the other end of the bridge. "I wish they'd find another tune," Barak muttered sourly. "That one's starting to get on my nerves."

"I'll mention that to the first Ulgo I meet," Silk told him lightly. "I'm sure they'll be only too glad to change songs for you."

"Very funny," Barak said.

"It probably hasn't occurred to them that their song isn't universally admired."

"Do you mind?" Barak asked acidly.

"They've only been singing it for five thousand years now."

"That'll do, Silk," Aunt Pol told the little man.

"Anything you say, great lady," Silk answered mockingly.

They entered another gallery on the far side of the cavern and followed it until it branched. Belgarath firmly led them to the left.

"Are you sure?" Silk asked. "I could be wrong, but it seems like we're going in a circle."

"We are."

"I don't suppose you'd care to explain that."

"There's a cavern we wanted to avoid, so we had to go around it."

"Why did we have to avoid it?"

"It's unstable. The slightest sound there might bring the roof down."

"Oh."

"That's one of the dangers down here."

"You don't really need to go into detail, old friend," Silk said, looking nervously at the roof above. The little man seemed to be talking more than usual, and Garion's own sense of oppression at the thought of all the rock surrounding him gave him a quick insight into Silk's mind. The sense of being closed in was unbearable to some men, and Silk, it appeared, was one of them. Garion glanced up also, and seemed to feel the weight of the mountain above pressing down firmly on him. Silk, he decided, might not be the only one disturbed by the thought of all that dreadful mass above them.

The gallery they followed opened out into a small cavern with a glass-clear lake in its center. The lake was very shallow and it had a white gravel bottom. An island rose from the center of the lake, and on the island stood a building constructed in the same curiously pyramidal shape as the buildings in the ruined city of Prolgu far above. The building was surrounded by a ring of columns, and here and there benches were carved from white stone. Glowing crystal globes were suspended on long chains from the ceiling of the cavern about thirty feet overhead, and their light, while still faint, was noticeably brighter than that in the galleries through which they had passed. A white marble causeway crossed to the island, and a very old man stood at its end, peering across the still water toward them as they entered the cavern.

"*Yad ho*, Belgarath," the old man called. "*Groja UL.*"

"Gorim," Belgarath replied with a formal bow. "*Yad ho, groja UL.*"

He led them across the marble causeway to the island in the center of the lake and warmly clasped the old man's hand, speaking to him in the guttural Ulgo language.

The Gorim of Ulgo appeared to be very old. He had long, silvery hair and beard, and his robe was snowy white. There was a kind of saintly serenity about him that Garion felt immediately, and the boy knew, without knowing how he knew, that he was approaching a holy man—perhaps the holiest on earth.

The Gorim extended his arms fondly to Aunt Pol, and she embraced him affectionately as they exchanged the ritual greeting, "*Yad ho, groja UL.*"

"Our companions don't speak your language, old friend," Belgarath said to the Gorim. "Would it offend you if we conversed in the language of the outside?"

"Not at all, Belgarath," the Gorim replied. "UL tells us that it's important for men to understand one another. Come inside, all of you. I've had food and drink prepared for you." As the old man looked at each of them, Garion noticed that his eyes, unlike those of the other Ulgos he had seen, were a deep, almost violet blue. Then the Gorim turned and led them along a path to the doorway of the pyramid-shaped building.

"Has the child come yet?" Belgarath asked the Gorim as they passed through the massive stone doorway.

The Gorim sighed. "No, Belgarath, not yet, and I am very weary. There's hope at each birth. But after a few days, the eyes of the child darken. It appears that UL is not finished with me yet."

"Don't give up hope, Gorim," Belgarath told his friend. "The child will come—in UL's own time."

"So we are told." The Gorim sighed again. "The tribes are growing restless, though, and there's bickering—and worse—in some of the farther galleries. The zealots grow bolder in their denunciations, and strange aberrations and cults have begun to appear. Ulgo needs a new Gorim. I've outlived my time by three hundred years."

"UL still has work for you," Belgarath replied. "His ways are not ours, Gorim, and he sees time in a different way."

The room they entered was square but had, nonetheless, the slightly sloping walls characteristic of Ulgo architecture. A stone table with low benches on either side sat in the center of the room, and there were a number of bowls containing fruit sitting upon it. Among the bowls sat several tall flasks and round crystal cups. "I'm told that winter has come early to our mountains," the Gorim said to them. "The drink should help to warm you."

"It's chilly outside," Belgarath admitted.

They sat down on the benches and began to eat. The fruit was tangy and wild-tasting, and the clear liquid in the flasks was fiery and brought an immediate warm glow that radiated out from the stomach.

"Forgive us our customs, which may seem strange to you," the Gorim said, noting that Barak and Hettar in particular approached the meal of fruit with a distinct lack of enthusiasm. "We are a people much tied to ceremony. We begin our meals with fruit in remembrance of the years we spent wandering in search of UL. The meat will come in due time."

"Where do you obtain such food in these caves, Holy One?" Silk asked politely.

"Our gatherers go out of the caves at night," the Gorim replied. "They tell us that the fruits and grains they bring back with them grow wild in the mountains, but I suspect that they have long since taken up the cultivation of certain fertile valleys. They also maintain that the meat they carry down to us is the flesh of wild cattle, taken in the hunt, but I have my doubts about that as well." He smiled gently. "I permit them their little deceptions."

Perhaps emboldened by the Gorim's geniality, Durnik raised a question that had obviously been bothering him since he had entered the city on the mountaintop above. "Forgive me, your Honor," he began, "but why do your builders make everything crooked? What I mean is, nothing seems to be square. It all leans over."

"It has to do with weight and support, I understand," the Gorim replied. "Each wall is actually falling down; but since they're all falling against each other, none of them can move so much as a finger's width—and, of course, their shape reminds us of the tents we lived in during our wanderings."

Durnik frowned thoughtfully, struggling with the alien idea.

"And have you as yet recovered Aldur's Orb, Belgarath?" the Gorim inquired then, his face growing serious.

"Not yet," Belgarath replied. "We chased Zedar as far as Nyissa, but when he crossed over into Cthol Murgos, Ctuchik was waiting and took the Orb away from him. Ctuchik has it now—at Rak Cthol."

"And Zedar?"

"He escaped Ctuchik's ambush and carried Torak off to Cthol Mishrak in Mallorea to keep Ctuchik from raising him with the Orb."

"Then you'll have to go to Rak Cthol."

Belgarath nodded as an Ulgo servingman brought in a huge, steaming roast, set it on the table, and left with a respectful bow.

"Has anyone found out how Zedar was able to take the Orb without being struck down?" the Gorim asked.

"He used a child," Aunt Pol told him. "An innocent."

"Ah." The Gorim stroked his beard thoughtfully. "Doesn't the prophecy say, 'And the child shall deliver up the birthright unto the Chosen One'?"

"Yes," Belgarath replied.

"Where's the child now?"

"So far as we know, Ctuchik has him at Rak Cthol."

"Will you assault Rak Cthol, then?"

"I'd need an army, and it could take years to reduce that fortress. There's another way, I think. A certain passage in the Darine Codex speaks of caves under Rak Cthol."

"I know that passage, Belgarath. It's very obscure. It *could* mean that, I suppose, but what if it doesn't?"

"It's confirmed by the Mrin Codex," Belgarath said a little defensively.

"The Mrin Codex is even worse, old friend. It's obscure to the point of being gibberish."

"I somehow have the feeling that when we look back at it—after all this is over—we're going to find that the Mrin Codex is the most accurate version of all. I do have certain other verification, however. Back during the time when the Murgos were constructing Rak Cthol, a Sendarian slave escaped and made his way back to the West. He was delirious when he was found, but he kept talking of caves under the mountain before he died. Not only that, Anheg of Cherek found a copy of *The Book of Torak* that contains a fragment of a very old Grolim prophecy—'Guard well the temple, above and beneath, for Cthrag Yaska will summon foes down from the air or up from the earth to bear it away again.' "

"That's even more obscure," the Gorim objected.

"Grolim prophecies usually are, but it's all I've got to work with. If I reject the notion of caves under Rak Cthol, I'll have to lay siege to the place. It would take all the armies of the West to do that, and then Ctuchik would summon the Angarak armies to defend the city. Everything points to some final battle, but I'd prefer to pick the time and place—and the Wasteland of Murgos is definitely *not* one of the places I'd choose."

"You're leading someplace with this, aren't you?"

Belgarath nodded. "I need a diviner to help me find the caves beneath Rak Cthol and to lead me up through them to the city."

The Gorim shook his head. "You're asking the impossible, Belgarath. The diviners are all zealots—mystics. You'll never persuade one of them to leave the holy caverns here beneath Prolgu—particularly not now. All of Ulgo is waiting for the coming of the child, and every zealot is firmly convinced that he will be the one to discover the child and reveal him to the tribes. I couldn't even order one of them to accompany you. The diviners are regarded as holy men, and I have no authority over them."

"It may not be as hard as you think, Gorim." Belgarath pushed back his plate and reached for his cup. "The diviner I need is one named Relg."

"Relg? He's the worst of the lot. He's gathered a following and he preaches to them by the hour in some of the far galleries. He believes that he's the most important man in Ulgo just now. You'll never persuade him to leave these caves."

"I don't think I'll have to, Gorim. I'm not the one who selected Relg. That decision was made for me long before I was born. Just send for him."

"I'll send for him if you want," the Gorim said doubtfully. "I don't think he'll come, though."

"He'll come," Aunt Pol told him confidently. "He won't know why, but he'll come. And he *will* go with us, Gorim. The same power that brought us all together will bring him as well. He doesn't have any more choice in the matter than we do."

CHAPTER SEVENTEEN

It all seemed so tedious. The snow and cold they had endured on the journey to Prolgu had numbed Ce'Nedra, and the warmth here in the caverns made her drowsy. The endless, obscure talk of Belgarath and the strange, frail old Gorim seemed to pull her toward sleep. The peculiar singing began again somewhere, echoing endlessly through the caves, and that too lulled her. Only a lifetime of training in the involved etiquette of court behavior kept her awake.

The journey had been ghastly for Ce'Nedra. Tol Honeth was a warm city, and she was not accustomed to cold weather. It seemed that her feet would never be warm again. She had also discovered a world filled with shocks, terrors, and unpleasant surprises. At the Imperial Palace in Tol Honeth, the enormous power of her father, the Emperor, had shielded her from danger of any kind, but now she felt vulnerable. In a rare moment of absolute truth with herself, she admitted that much of her spiteful behavior toward Garion had grown out of her dreadful new sense of insecurity. Her safe, pampered little world had been snatched away from her, and she felt exposed, unprotected, and afraid.

Poor Garion, she thought. He was such a nice boy. She felt a little ashamed that he had been the one who'd had to suffer from her bad temper. She promised herself that soon—very soon—she would sit down with him and explain it all. He was a sensible boy, and he'd be sure to understand. That, of course, would immediately patch up the rift which had grown between them.

Feeling her eyes on him, he glanced once at her and then looked away with apparent indifference. Ce'Nedra's eyes hardened like agates. How *dared* he? She made a mental note of it and added it to her list of his many imperfections.

The frail-looking old Gorim had sent one of the strange, silent Ulgos to fetch the man he and Belgarath and Lady Polgara had been discussing, and then they turned to more general topics. "Were you able to pass through the mountains unmolested?" the Gorim asked.

"We had a few encounters," Barak, the big, red-bearded Earl of Trellheim, replied with what seemed to Ce'Nedra gross understatement.

"But thanks to UL you're all safe," the Gorim declared piously. "Which of the monsters are still abroad at this season? I haven't been out of the caves in years, but as I recall most of them seek their lairs when the snow begins."

"We encountered Hrulgin, Holy One," Baron Mandorallen informed him, "and some Algroths. And there was an Eldrak."

"The Eldrak was troublesome," Silk said dryly.

"Understandably. Fortunately there aren't very many Eldrakyn. They're fearsome monsters."

"We noticed that," Silk said.

"Which one was it?"

"Grul," Belgarath replied. "He and I had met before, and he seemed to hold a grudge. I'm sorry, Gorim, but we had to kill him. There wasn't any other way."

"Ah," the Gorim said with a slight note of pain in his voice. "Poor Grul."

"I personally don't miss him very much," Barak said. "I'm not trying to be forward, Holy One, but don't you think it might be a good idea to exterminate some of the more troublesome beasts in these mountains?"

"They're the children of UL, even as we," the Gorim explained.

"But if they weren't out there, you could return to the world above," Barak pointed out.

The Gorim smiled at that. "No," he said gently. "Ulgo will never leave the caves now. We've dwelt here for five millennia and, over the years, we've changed. Our eyes could not bear the sunlight now. The monsters above cannot reach us here, and their presence in the mountains keeps strangers out of Ulgo. We're not at ease with strangers, really, so it's probably for the best."

The Gorim was sitting directly across the narrow stone table from Ce'Nedra. The subject of the monsters obviously pained him, and he looked at her for a moment, then gently reached out his frail old hand and cupped her little chin in it, lifting her face to the dim light of the hanging globe suspended above the table. "All of the alien creatures are not monsters," he said, his large, violet eyes calm and very wise. "Consider the beauty of this Dryad."

Ce'Nedra was a little startled—not by his touch, certainly, for older people had responded to her flowerlike face with that same gesture for as long as she could remember—but rather by the ancient man's immediate recognition of the fact that she was not entirely human.

"Tell me, child," the Gorim asked, "do the Dryads still honor UL?"

She was completely unprepared for the question. "I—I'm sorry, Holy One," she floundered. "Until quite recently, I'd not even heard of the God UL. For some reason, my tutors have very little information about your people or your God."

"The princess was raised as a Tolnedran," Lady Polgara explained. "She's a Borune—I'm sure you've heard of the link between that house and the Dryads. As a Tolnedran, her religious affiliation is to Nedra."

"A serviceable God," the Gorim said. "Perhaps a bit stuffy for my taste, but certainly adequate. The Dryads themselves, though—do they still know their God?"

Belgarath coughed a bit apologetically. "I'm afraid not, Gorim. They've drifted away, and the eons have erased what they knew of UL. They're flighty creatures anyway, not much given to religious observances."

The Gorim's face was sad. "What God do they honor now?"

"None, actually," Belgarath admitted. "They have a few sacred groves—a rough idol or two fashioned from the root of a particularly venerated tree. That's about it. They don't really have any clearly formulated theology."

Ce'Nedra found the whole discussion a trifle offensive. Rising to the occasion, she drew herself up slightly and smiled winsomely at the old Gorim. She knew exactly how to charm an elderly man. She'd practiced for years on her father. "I feel the shortcomings of my education most keenly, Holy One," she lied. "Since mysterious UL is the hereditary God of the Dryads, I should know him. I hope that someday soon I may receive instruction concerning him. It may be that I—unworthy though I am—can be the instrument of renewing the allegiance of my sisters to their rightful God."

It was an artful little speech, and on the whole Ce'Nedra was rather proud of it. To her surprise, however, the Gorim was not satisfied to accept a vague expression of interest and let it go at that. "Tell your sisters that the core of our faith is to be found in *The Book of Ulgo*," he told her seriously.

"*The Book of Ulgo*," she repeated. "I must remember that. As soon as I return to Tol Honeth, I'll obtain a copy and deliver it to the Wood of the Dryads personally." That, she thought, should satisfy him.

"I'm afraid that such copies as you'd find in Tol Honeth would be much corrupted," the Gorim told her. "The tongue of my people is not easily understood by strangers, and translations are difficult." Ce'Nedra definitely felt that the dear old man was becoming just a bit tiresome about the whole thing. "As is so often the case with scriptures," he was saying, "our Holy Book is bound up in our history. The wisdom of the Gods is such that their instruction is concealed within stories. Our minds delight in the stories, and the messages of the Gods are implanted thus. All unaware, we are instructed even as we are entertained."

Ce'Nedra was familiar with the theory. Master Jeebers, her tutor, had lectured her tediously concerning it. She cast about rather desperately, trying to find some graceful way to change the subject.

"Our story is very old," the Gorim continued inexorably. "Would you like to hear it?"

Caught by her own cleverness, Ce'Nedra could only nod helplessly.

And so the Gorim began: "At the Beginning of Days when the World was spun out of darkness by the wayward Gods, there dwelt in the silences of the heavens a spirit known only as UL."

In utter dismay, Ce'Nedra realized that he fully intended to recite the *entire* book to her. After a few moments of chagrin, however, she began to feel the strangely compelling quality of his story. More than she would have cared to admit, she was moved by the first Gorim's appeal to the indifferent spirit that appeared to him at Prolgu. What manner of man would thus dare to accuse a God?

As she listened, a faint flicker seemed to tug at the corner of her eye. She glanced toward it and saw a soft glow somewhere deep within the massive rocks that formed one of the walls of the chamber. The glow was peculiarly different from the dim light of the hanging crystal globes.

"Then the heart of Gorim was made glad," the old man continued his recitation, "and he called the name of the high place where all this had come to pass Prolgu, which is Holy Place. And he departed from Prolgu and returned unto—"

"*Ya! Garach tek*, Gorim!" The words were spat out in the snarling Ulgo language, and the harsh voice that spoke them was filled with outrage.

Ce'Nedra jerked her head around to look at the intruder. Like all Ulgos, he was short, but his arms and shoulders were so massively developed that he seemed almost deformed. His colorless hair was tangled and unkempt. He wore a hooded leather smock, stained and smeared with some kind of mud, and his large black eyes burned with fanaticism. Crowded behind him were a dozen or more other Ulgos, their faces set in expressions of shock and righteous indignation. The fanatic in the leather smock continued his stream of crackling vituperation.

The Gorim's face set, but he endured the abuse from the wild-eyed man at the door patiently. Finally, when the fanatic paused for breath, the frail old man turned to Belgarath. "This is Relg," he said a bit apologetically. "You see what I mean about him? Trying to convince him of anything is impossible."

"What use would he be to us?" Barak demanded, obviously irritated by the newcomer's attitude. "He can't even speak a civilized tongue."

Relg glared at him. "I speak your language, foreigner," he said with towering contempt, "but I choose not to defile the holy caverns with its unsanctified mouthings." He turned back to Gorim. "Who gave you the right to speak the words of the Holy Book to unbelieving foreigners?" he demanded.

The gentle old Gorim's eyes hardened slightly. "I think that's about enough, Relg," he said firmly. "Whatever idiocies you babble in out-of-the-way galleries to those gullible enough to listen is your concern, but what you say to me in my house is mine. I am still Gorim in Ulgo, whatever you may think, and I am not required to answer to you." He looked past Relg at the shocked faces of the zealot's followers. "This is not a general audience," he informed Relg. "You were summoned here; they were not. Send them away."

"They came to be sure you intended me no harm," Relg replied stiffly. "I have spoken the truth about you, and powerful men fear the truth."

"Relg," the Gorim said in an icy voice, "I don't think you could even begin to realize how indifferent I am to anything you might have said about me. Now send them away—or would you rather have me do it?"

"They won't obey you," Relg sneered. "I am their leader."

The Gorim's eyes narrowed, and he rose to his feet. Then he spoke in the Ulgo tongue directly to Relg's adherents. Ce'Nedra could not understand his words, but she did not really need to. She recognized the tone of authority instantly, and she was a bit startled at how absolutely the saintly old Gorim used it. Not even her father would have dared speak in that tone.

The men crowded behind Relg looked nervously at each other and began to back away, their faces frightened. The Gorim barked one final command, and Relg's followers turned and fled.

Relg scowled after them and seemed for a moment on the verge of raising his voice to call them back, but apparently thought better of it. "You go too far, Gorim," he accused. "*That* authority is not meant to be used in worldly matters."

"That authority is *mine*, Relg," the Gorim replied, "and it's up to me to decide when it's required. You've chosen to confront me on theological ground, therefore I needed to remind your followers—and you—just who I am."

"Why have you summoned me here?" Relg demanded. "The presence of these unsanctified ones is an affront to my purity."

"I require your service, Relg," the Gorim told him. "These strangers go to battle against our Ancient Foe, the one accursed above all others. The fate of the world hangs upon their quest, and your aid is needed."

"What do I care about the world?" Relg's voice was filled with contempt. "And what do I care about maimed Torak? I am safe within the hand of UL. He has need of me here, and I will not go from the holy caverns to risk defilement in the lewd company of unbelievers and monsters."

"The entire world will be defiled if Torak gains dominion over it," Belgarath pointed out, "and if we fail, Torak *will* become king of the world."

"He will not reign in Ulgo," Relg retorted.

"How little you know him," Polgara murmured.

"I will not leave the caves," Relg insisted. "The coming of the child is at hand, and I have been chosen to reveal him to Ulgo and to guide and instruct him until he is ready to become Gorim."

"How interesting," the Gorim observed dryly. "Just who was it who advised you of your election?"

"UL spoke to me," Relg declared.

"Odd. The caverns respond universally to the voice of UL. All Ulgo would have heard his voice."

"He spoke to me in my heart," Relg replied quickly.

"What a curious thing for him to do," the Gorim answered mildly.

"All of this is beside the point," Belgarath said brusquely. "I'd prefer to have you join us willingly, Relg; but willing or not, you *will* join us. A power greater than any of us commands it. You can argue and resist as much as you like, but when we leave here, you'll be going with us."

Relg spat. "Never! I will remain here in the service of UL and of the child who will become Gorim of Ulgo. And if you try to compel me, my followers will not permit it."

"Why do we need this blind mole, Belgarath?" Barak asked. "He's just going to be an aggravation to us. I've noticed that men who spend all their time congratulating themselves on their sanctity tend to be very poor companions, and what can this one do that I can't?"

Relg looked at the red-bearded giant with disdain. "Big men with big mouths seldom have big brains," he said. "Watch closely, hairy one." He walked over to the sloping wall of the chamber. "Can you do this?" he asked and slowly pushed his hand directly into the rock as if he were sinking it into water.

Silk whistled with amazement and moved quickly over to the wall beside the fanatic. As Relg pulled his hand out of the rock, Silk reached out to put his own hand on the precise spot. "How did you do that?" he demanded, shoving at the stones.

Relg laughed harshly and turned his back.

"That's the ability that makes him useful to us, Silk," Belgarath explained. "Relg's a diviner. He finds caves, and we need to locate the caves under Rak Cthol. If necessary, Relg can walk through solid rock to find them for us."

"How could anyone do that?" Silk asked, still staring at the spot where Relg had sunk his hand into the wall.

"It has to do with the nature of matter," the sorcerer replied. "What we see as solid isn't really all that impenetrable."

"Either something's solid or it's not," Silk insisted, his face baffled.

"Solidity's an illusion," Belgarath told him. "Relg can slip the bits and pieces that make up his substance through the spaces that exist between the bits and pieces that make up the substance of the rock."

"Can *you* do it?" Silk demanded skeptically.

Belgarath shrugged. "I don't know. I've never had occasion to try. Anyway, Relg can smell caves, and he goes straight to them. He probably doesn't know himself how he does it."

"I am led by my sanctity," Relg declared arrogantly.

"Perhaps that's it," the sorcerer agreed with a tolerant smile.

"The holiness of the caves draws me, since I am drawn to all holy things," Relg rasped on, "and for me to leave the caverns of Ulgo would be to turn my back on holiness and move toward defilement."

"We'll see," Belgarath told him.

The glow in the rock wall which Ce'Nedra had noticed before began to shimmer and pulsate, and the princess seemed to see a dim shape within the rocks. Then, as if the stones were only air, the shape became distinct and stepped out into the chamber. For just a moment, it seemed that the figure was an old man, bearded and robed like the Gorim, although much more robust. Then Ce'Nedra was struck by an overpowering sense of something more than human. With an awed shudder, she realized that she was in the presence of divinity.

Relg gaped at the bearded figure, and he began to tremble violently. With a strangled cry he prostrated himself.

The figure looked calmly at the groveling zealot. "Rise, Relg," it said in a soft voice that seemed to carry all the echoes of eternity in it, and the caverns outside rang with the sound of that voice. "Rise, Relg, and serve thy God."

CHAPTER EIGHTEEN

Ce'Nedra had received an exquisite education. She had been so thoroughly trained that she knew instinctively all the niceties of etiquette and all the proper forms to be observed upon coming into the presence of an emperor or a king, but the physical presence of a God still baffled and even frightened her. She felt awkward, even gauche, like some ignorant farm girl. She found herself trembling and, for one of the few times in her life, she hadn't the faintest idea what to do.

UL was still looking directly into Relg's awe-struck face. "Thy mind hath twisted what I told thee, my son," the God said gravely. "Thou hast turned my words to make them conform to thy desire, rather than to my will."

Relg flinched, and his eyes were stricken.

"I told thee that the child who will be Gorim will come to Ulgo through thee," UL continued, "and that thou must prepare thyself to nurture him and see to his rearing. Did I tell thee to exalt thyself by reason of this?"

Relg began to shake violently.

"Did I tell thee to preach sedition? Or to stir Ulgo against the Gorim whom I have chosen to guide them?"

Relg collapsed. "Forgive me, O my God," he begged, groveling again on the floor.

"Rise, Relg," UL told him sternly. "I am not pleased with thee, and thine obeisance offends me, for thine heart is filled with pride. I will bend thee to my will, Relg, or I will break thee. I will purge thee of this overweening esteem thou hast for thyself. Only then wilt thou be worthy of the task to which I have set thee."

Relg stumbled to his feet, his face filled with remorse. "O my God—" He choked.

"Hearken unto my words, Relg, and obey me utterly. It is my command that thou accompany Belgarath, Disciple of Aldur, and render unto him all aid within thy power. Thou wilt obey him even as if he were speaking in my voice. Dost thou understand this?"

"Yes, O my God," Relg replied humbly.

"And wilt thou obey?"

"I will do as thou hast commanded me, O my God—though it cost me my life."

"It shall not cost thee thy life, Relg, for I have need of thee. Thy reward for this shall be beyond thine imagining."

Relg bowed in mute acceptance.

The God then turned to the Gorim. "Abide yet awhile, my son," he said, "though the years press heavily upon thee. It shall not be long until thy burden shall be lifted. Know that I am pleased with thee."

The Gorim bowed in acceptance.

"Belgarath," UL greeted the sorcerer. "I have watched thee at thy task, and I share thy Master's pride in thee. The prophecy moves through thee and Polgara thy daughter toward that moment we have all awaited."

Belgarath also bowed. "It's been a long time, Most Holy," he replied, "and there were twists and turns to it that none of us could see at the beginning."

"Truly," UL agreed. "It hath surprised us all upon occasion. Hath Aldur's gift to the world come into his birthright as yet?"

"Not entirely, Most Holy," Polgara answered gravely. "He's touched the edges of it, however, and what he's shown us so far gives us hope for his success."

"Hail then, Belgarion," UL said to the startled young man. "Take my blessing with thee and know that I will join with Aldur to be with thee when thy great task begins."

Garion bowed—rather awkwardly, Ce'Nedra noticed. She decided that soon—very soon—she'd have to give him some schooling in such matters. He'd resist, naturally—he was impossibly stubborn—but she knew that if she nagged and badgered him enough, he'd eventually come around. And it was for his own good, after all.

UL seemed to be still looking at Garion, but there was a subtle difference in his expression. It seemed to Ce'Nedra that he was communicating word-lessly to some *other* presence—something that was a part of Garion and yet not a part of him. He nodded gravely then, and turned his gaze directly upon the princess herself.

"She seems but a child," he observed to Polgara.

"She's of a suitable age, Most Holy," Polgara replied. "She's a Dryad, and they're all quite small."

UL smiled gently at the princess, and she felt herself suddenly glowing in the warmth of that smile. "She is like a flower, is she not?" he said.

"She still has a few thorns, Most Holy," Belgarath replied wryly, "and a bit of bramble in her nature."

"We will value her all the more for that, Belgarath. The time will come when her fire and her brambles will serve our cause far more than her beauty." UL glanced once at Garion, and a strange, knowing smile crossed his face. For some reason, Ce'Nedra felt herself beginning to blush, then lifted her chin as if daring the blush to go any further.

"It is to speak with thee that I have come, my daughter," UL said di-rectly to her then, and his tone and face grew serious. "Thou must abide here when thy companions depart. Do not venture into the kingdom of the Murgos, for if it should come to pass that thou makest this journey unto Rak Cthol, thou shalt surely die, and without thee the struggle against the dark-ness must fail. Abide here in the safety of Ulgo until thy companions return."

This was the kind of thing Ce'Nedra completely understood. As a prin-cess, she knew the need for instant submission to authority. Though she had wheedled, coaxed, and teased her father all her life to get her own way, she had seldom directly rebelled. She bowed her head. "I will do as thou hast commanded, Most Holy," she replied without even thinking of the implica-tions of the God's words.

UL nodded with satisfaction. "Thus is the prophecy protected," he de-clared. "Each of ye hath his appointed tasks in this work of ours—and I have mine as well. I will delay ye no longer, my children. Fare ye all well in this. We will meet again." Then he vanished.

The sounds of his last words echoed in the caverns of Ulgo. After a mo-ment of stunned silence, the hymn of adoration burst forth again in a mighty chorus, as every Ulgo raised his voice in ecstasy at this divine visitation.

"Belar!" Barak breathed explosively. "Did you *feel* it?"

"UL has a commanding presence," Belgarath agreed. He turned to look at Relg, one eyebrow cocked rather whimsically. "I take it you've had a change of heart," he observed.

Relg's face had gone ashen, and he was still trembling violently. "I will obey my God," he vowed. "Where he has commanded me, I will go."

"I'm glad that's been settled," Belgarath told him. "At the moment he wants you to go to Rak Cthol. He may have other plans for you later, but right now Rak Cthol's enough to worry about."

"I will obey you without question," the fanatic declared, "even as my God has commanded me."

"Good," Belgarath replied, and then he went directly to the point. "Is there a way to avoid the weather and the difficulties above?"

"I know a way," Relg answered. "It's difficult and long, but it will lead us to the foothills above the land of the horse people."

"You see," Silk observed to Barak, "he's proving useful already."

Barak grunted, still not looking entirely convinced.

"May I know why we must go to Rak Cthol?" Relg asked, his entire manner changed by his meeting with his God.

"We have to reclaim the Orb of Aldur," Belgarath told him.

"I've heard of it," Relg admitted.

Silk was frowning. "Are you sure you'll be able to find the caves under Rak Cthol?" he asked Relg. "Those caves won't be the caverns of UL, you know, and in Cthol Murgos they're not likely to be holy—quite the opposite, most probably."

"I can find any cave—anywhere," Relg stated confidently.

"All right, then," Belgarath continued. "Assuming that all goes well, we'll go up through the caves and enter the city unobserved. We'll find Ctuchik and take the Orb away from him."

"Won't he try to fight?" Durnik asked.

"I certainly hope so," Belgarath replied fervently.

Barak laughed shortly. "You're starting to sound like an Alorn, Belgarath."

"That's not necessarily a virtue," Polgara pointed out.

"I'll deal with the magician of Rak Cthol when the time comes," the sorcerer said grimly. "At any rate, once we've recovered the Orb, we'll go back down through the caves and make a run for it."

"With all of Cthol Murgos hot on our heels," Silk added. "I've had dealings occasionally with Murgos. They're a persistent sort of people."

"That could be a problem," Belgarath admitted. "We don't want their pursuit gaining too much momentum. If an army of Murgos inadvertently follows us into the West, it'll be viewed as an invasion, and that'll start a war we aren't ready for yet. Any ideas?" He looked around.

"Turn them all into frogs," Barak suggested with a shrug.

Belgarath gave him a withering look.

"It was just a thought," Barak said defensively.

"Why not just stay in the caves under the city until they give up the search?" Durnik offered.

Polgara shook her head firmly. "No," she said. "There's a place we have to be at a certain time. We'll barely make it there as it is. We can't afford to lose a month or more hiding in some cave in Cthol Murgos."

"Where do we have to be, Aunt Pol?" Garion asked her.

"I'll explain later," she evaded, throwing a quick glance at Ce'Nedra. The princess perceived immediately that the appointment the Lady spoke of concerned *her*, and curiosity began to gnaw at her.

Mandorallen, his face thoughtful and his fingers lightly touching the ribs that had been cracked in his encounter with Grul, cleared his throat. "Does there perchance happen to be a map of the region we must enter somewhere nearby, Holy Gorim?" he asked politely.

The Gorim thought for a moment. "I believe I have one somewhere," he replied. He tapped his cup lightly on the table and an Ulgo servingman immediately entered the chamber. The Gorim spoke briefly to him, and the servingman went out. "The map I recall is very old," the Gorim told Mandorallen, "and I'm afraid it won't be very accurate. Our cartographers have difficulty comprehending the distances involved in the world above."

"The distances do not matter so much," Mandorallen assured him. "I wish but to refresh my memory concerning the contiguity of certain other realms upon the borders of Cthol Murgos. I was at best an indifferent student of geography as a schoolboy."

The servingman returned and handed a large roll of parchment to the Gorim. The Gorim in turn passed the roll to Mandorallen.

The knight carefully unrolled the chart and studied it for a moment. "It is as I recalled," he said. He turned to Belgarath. "Thou hast said, ancient friend, that no Murgo will enter the Vale of Aldur?"

"That's right," Belgarath replied.

Mandorallen pointed at the map. "The closest border from Rak Cthol is that which abuts Tolnedra," he showed them. "Logic would seem to dictate that our route of escape should lie in that direction—toward the nearest frontier."

"All right," Belgarath conceded.

"Let us then seem to make all haste toward Tolnedra, leaving behind us abundant evidence of our passage. Then, at some point where rocky ground would conceal signs of our change of direction, let us turn and strike out to the northwest toward the Vale. Might this not confound them? May we not confidently anticipate that they will continue to pursue our imagined course? In time, certainly, they will realize their error, but by then we will be many leagues ahead of them. Pursuing far to our rear, might not the further discouragement of the prohibited Vale cause them to abandon the chase entirely?"

They all looked at the map.

"I like it," Barak said, effusively slapping one huge hand on the knight's shoulder.

Mandorallen winced and put his hand to his injured ribs.

"Sorry, Mandorallen," Barak apologized quickly. "I forgot."

Silk was studying the map intently. "It's got a lot to recommend it, Belgarath," he urged, "and if we angle up to here—" He pointed. "—we'll come out on top of the eastern escarpment. We should have plenty of time to make the descent, but they'll definitely want to think twice before trying it. It's a good mile straight down at that point."

"We could send word to Cho-Hag," Hettar suggested. "If a few clans just happened to be gathered at the foot of the escarpment there, the Murgos would think more than twice before starting down."

Belgarath scratched at his beard. "All right," he decided after a moment, "we'll try it that way. As soon as Relg leads us out of Ulgo, you go pay your father a visit, Hettar. Tell him what we're going to do and invite him to bring a few thousand warriors down to the Vale to meet us."

The lean Algar nodded, his black scalp lock bobbing. His face, however, showed a certain disappointment.

"Forget it, Hettar," the old man told him bluntly. "I never had any intention of taking you into Cthol Murgos. There'd be too many opportunities there for you to get yourself in trouble."

Hettar sighed somewhat mournfully.

"Don't take it so hard, Hettar," Silk bantered. "Murgos are a fanatic race. You can be practically certain that a few of them at least will try the descent—no matter what's waiting for them at the bottom. You'd almost have to make an example of them, wouldn't you?"

Hettar's face brightened at that thought.

"Silk," Lady Polgara said reprovingly.

The little man turned an innocent face to her. "We have to discourage pursuit, Polgara," he protested.

"Of course," she replied sarcastically.

"It wouldn't do to have Murgos infesting the Vale, would it?"

"Do you mind?"

"I'm not really all that bloodthirsty, you know."

She turned her back on him.

Silk sighed piously. "She always thinks the worst of me."

By now Ce'Nedra had had sufficient time to consider the implications of the promise she had so unhesitatingly given to UL. The others would soon leave, and she must remain behind. Already she was beginning to feel isolated, cut off from them, as they made plans which did not include her. The more she thought about it, the worse it became. She felt her lower lip beginning to quiver.

The Gorim of the Ulgos had been watching her, his wise old face sympathetic. "It's difficult to be left behind," he said gently, almost as if his large eyes had seen directly into her thoughts, "and our caves are strange to you—dark and seemingly filled with gloom."

Wordlessly she nodded her agreement.

"In a day or so, however," he continued, "your eyes will become accustomed to the subdued light. There are beauties here which no one from the outside has ever seen. While it's true that we have no flowers, there are hidden caverns where gems bloom on the floors and walls like wild blossoms. No trees or foliage grow in our sunless world, but I know a cave wall where vines of pure gold twist in ropey coils down from the ceiling and spill out across the floor."

"Careful, Holy Gorim," Silk warned. "The Princess is Tolnedran. If you show her that kind of wealth, she may go into hysterics right before your eyes."

"I don't find that particularly amusing, Prince Kheldar," Ce'Nedra told him in a frosty tone.

"I'm overcome with remorse, your Imperial Highness," he apologized with towering hypocrisy and a florid bow.

In spite of herself, the princess laughed. The rat-faced little Drasnian was so absolutely outrageous that she found it impossible to remain angry with him.

"You'll be as my beloved granddaughter while you stay in Ulgo, Princess," the Gorim told her. "We can walk together beside our silent lakes and explore long-forgotten caves. And we can talk. The world outside knows little of Ulgo. It may well be that you will become the very first stranger to understand us."

Ce'Nedra impulsively reached out to take his frail old hand in hers. He was such a dear old man. "I'll be honored, Holy Gorim," she told him with complete sincerity.

They stayed that night in comfortable quarters in the Gorim's pyramid-shaped house—though the terms night and day had no meaning in this strange land beneath the earth. The following morning several Ulgos led the horses into the Gorim's cavern, traveling, the princess assumed, by some longer route than the one the party had followed, and her friends made their preparations to leave. Ce'Nedra sat to one side, feeling terribly alone already. Her eyes moved from face to face as she tried to fix each of them in her memory. When she came at last to Garion, her eyes brimmed.

Irrationally, she had already begun to worry about him. He was so impulsive. She knew that he'd do things that would put him in danger once he was out of her sight. To be sure, Polgara would be there to watch over him, but it wasn't the same. She felt quite suddenly angry with him for all the foolish things he was going to do and for the worry his careless behavior was going to cause her. She glared at him, wishing that he would do something for which she could scold him.

She had determined that she would not follow them out of the Gorim's house—that she would not stand forlornly at the edge of the water staring after them as they departed—but as they all filed out through the heavy-arched doorway, her resolution crumbled. Without thinking she ran after Garion and caught his arm.

He turned with surprise, and she stretched up on her tiptoes, took his face between her tiny hands and kissed him. "You *must* be careful," she commanded. Then she kissed him again, spun and ran sobbing back into the house, leaving him staring after her in baffled astonishment.

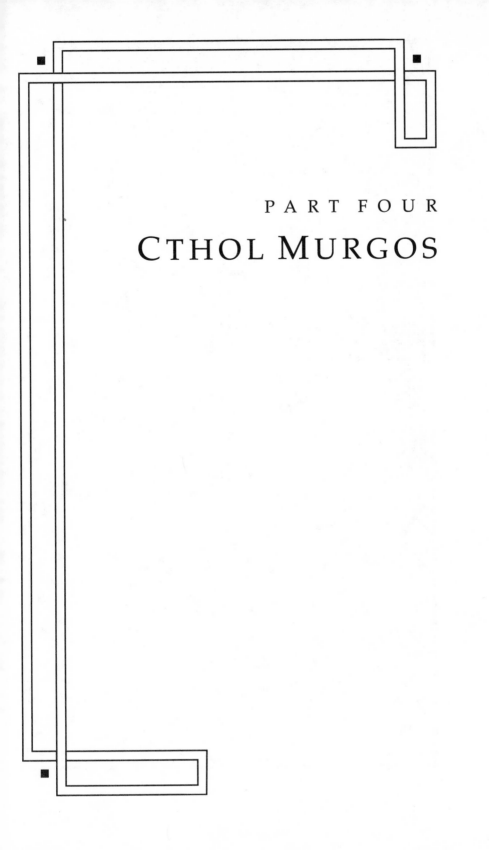

PART FOUR

CTHOL MURGOS

They had been in the darkness for days. The single dim light Relg carried could only provide a point of reference, something to follow. The darkness pressed against Garion's face, and he stumbled along the uneven floor with one hand thrust out in front of him to keep himself from banging his head onto unseen rocks. It was not only the musty-smelling darkness, however. He could sense the oppressive weight of the mountains above him and on all sides. The stone seemed to push in on him; he was closed in, sealed up in miles of solid rock. He fought continually with the faint, fluttering edges of panic and he often clenched his teeth to keep from screaming.

There seemed to be no purpose to the twisting, turning route Relg followed. At the branching of passageways, his choices seemed random, but always he moved with steady confidence through the dark, murmuring caves where the memory of sounds whispered in the dank air, voices out of the past echoing endlessly, whispering, whispering. Relg's air of confidence as he led them was the only thing that kept Garion from giving in to unreasoning panic.

At one point the zealot stopped.

"What's wrong?" Silk asked sharply, his voice carrying that same faint edge of panic that Garion felt gnawing at his own awareness.

"I have to cover my eyes here," Relg replied. He was wearing a peculiarly fashioned shirt of leaf-mail, a strange garment formed of overlapping metal scales, belted at the waist and with a snug-fitting hood that left only his face exposed. From his belt hung a heavy, hook-pointed knife, a weapon that made Garion cold just to look at it. He drew a piece of cloth out from under his mail shirt and carefully tied it over his face.

"Why are you doing that?" Durnik asked him.

"There's a vein of quartz in the cavern just ahead," Relg told him. "It reflects sunlight down from the outside. The light is very bright."

"How can you tell which way to go if you're blindfolded?" Silk protested.

"The cloth isn't that thick. I can see through it well enough. Let's go."

They rounded a corner in the gallery they were following, and Garion saw light ahead. He resisted an impulse to run toward it. They moved on, the hooves of the horses Hettar was leading clattering on the stone floor. The lighted cavern was huge, and it was filled with a glittering crystal light. A gleaming band of quartz angled across the ceiling, illuminating the cavern with a blazing radiance. Great points of stone hung like icicles from the ceiling, and other points rose from the floor to meet them. In the center of the cavern another underground lake stretched, its surface rippled by a tiny waterfall trickling down into its upper end with an endless tinkling sound that echoed in the cave like a little silver bell and joined harmoniously with the faint, remembered sigh of the singing of the Ulgos miles behind. Garion's eyes were dazzled by color that seemed to be everywhere. The prisms in the crystalline quartz twisted the light, breaking it into colored fragments and filling the cave with the multihued light of the rainbow. Garion found himself quite suddenly wishing that he could show the dazzling cave to Ce'Nedra, and the thought puzzled him.

"Hurry," Relg urged them, holding one hand across his brow as if to further shade his already veiled eyes.

"Why not stop here?" Barak suggested. "We need some rest, and this looks like a good place."

"It's the worst place in all the caves," Relg told him. "Hurry."

"Maybe *you* like the dark," Barak said, "but the rest of us aren't that fond of it." He looked around at the cave.

"Protect your eyes, you fool," Relg snapped.

"I don't care for your tone, friend."

"You'll be blind once we get past this place if you don't. It's taken your eyes two days to get used to the dark. You'll lose all of that if you stay here too long."

Barak stared hard at the Ulgo for a moment. Then he grunted and nodded shortly. "Sorry," he said. "I didn't understand." He reached out to put his hand on Relg's shoulder in apology.

"Don't touch me!" Relg cried, shrinking away from the big hand.

"What's the matter?"

"Just don't touch me—not ever." Relg hurried on ahead.

"What's the matter with him?" Barak demanded.

"He doesn't want you to defile him," Belgarath explained.

"Defile him? *Defile* him?"

"He's very concerned about his personal purity. The way he sees it, any kind of touch can soil him."

"Soil? He's as dirty as a pig in a wallow."

"It's a different kind of dirt. Let's move on."

Barak strode along behind the rest of them, grumbling and sputtering in outrage. They moved into another dark passageway, and Garion looked longingly back over his shoulder at the fading light from the glowing cavern behind. Then they rounded a corner and the light was gone.

There was no way to keep track of time in the murmuring darkness. They stumbled on, pausing now and then to eat or to rest, though Garion's sleep was filled with nightmares about mountains crushing in on him. He had almost given up all hope of ever seeing the sky again when the first faint cobweb touch of moving air brushed his cheek. It had been, as closely as he could judge, five days since they had left the last dimly lighted gallery of the Ulgos behind and plunged into this eternal night. At first he thought the faint hint of warmer air might only be his imagination, but then he caught the scent of trees and grass in the musty air of the cave, and he knew that somewhere ahead there lay an opening—a way out.

The touch of warmer outside air grew stronger, and the smell of grass began to fill the passageway along which they crept. The floor began to slope upward, and imperceptibly it grew less dark. It seemed somehow that they moved up out of endless night toward the light of the first morning in the history of the world. The horses, plodding along at the rear, had also caught the scent of fresh air, and their pace quickened. Relg, however, moved slower, and then slower still. Finally he stopped altogether. The faint metallic rustling of his leaf-mail shirt spoke loudly for him. Relg was trembling, bracing himself for what lay ahead. He bound his veil across his face again, mumbling something over and over in the snarling language of the Ulgos, fervent, almost pleading. Once his eyes were covered, he moved on again, reluctantly, his feet almost dragging.

Then there was golden light ahead. The mouth of the passageway was a jagged, irregular opening with a stiff tangle of limbs sharply outlined in front of it. With a sudden clatter of little hooves, the colt, ignoring Hettar's sharp command, bolted for the opening and plunged out into the light.

Belgarath scratched at his whiskers, squinting after the little animal. "Maybe you'd better take him and his mother with you when we separate," he said to Hettar. "He seems to have a little trouble taking things seriously, and Cthol Murgos is a very serious place."

Hettar nodded gravely.

"I can't," Relg blurted suddenly, turning his back to the light and pressing himself against the rock wall of the passageway. "I can't do it."

"Of course you can," Aunt Pol said comfortingly to him. "We'll go out slowly so you can get used to it a little at a time."

"Don't touch me," Relg replied almost absently.

"That's going to get very tiresome," Barak growled.

Garion and the rest of them pushed ahead eagerly, their hunger for light pulling at them. They shoved their way roughly through the tangle of bushes at the mouth of the cave and, blinking and shading their eyes, they emerged into the sunlight. The light at first stabbed Garion's eyes painfully; but after a few moments, he found that he could see again. The partially concealed entrance to the caves was near the midpoint of a rocky hillside. Behind them, the snow-covered mountains of Ulgo glittered in the morning sun, outlined against the deep blue sky, and a vast plain spread before them like a sea. The tall grass was golden with autumn, and the morning breeze touched it into long, undulating waves. The plain reached to the horizon, and Garion felt as if he had just awakened from a nightmare.

Just inside the mouth of the cave behind them, Relg knelt with his back to the light, praying and beating at his shoulders and chest with his fists.

"Now what's he doing?" Barak demanded.

"It's a kind of purification ritual," Belgarath explained. "He's trying to purge himself of all unholiness and draw the essence of the caves into his soul. He thinks it may help to sustain him while he's outside."

"How long's he going to be at it?"

"About an hour, I'd imagine. It's a fairly complicated ritual."

Relg stopped praying long enough to bind a second veil across his face on top of the first one.

"If he wraps any more cloth around his head, he's likely to smother," Silk observed.

"I'd better get started," Hettar said, tightening the straps on his saddle. "Is there anything else you wanted me to tell Cho-Hag?"

"Tell him to pass the word along to the others about what's happened so far," Belgarath answered. "Things are getting to the point where I'd like everybody to be more or less alert."

Hettar nodded.

"Do you know where you are?" Barak asked him.

"Of course." The tall man looked out at the seemingly featureless plain before him.

"It's probably going to take us at least a month to get to Rak Cthol and back," Belgarath advised. "If we get a chance, we'll light signal fires on top of the eastern escarpment before we start down. Tell Cho-Hag how important it is for him to be waiting for us. We don't want Murgos blundering into Algaria. I'm not ready for a war just yet."

"We'll be there," Hettar replied, swinging up into his saddle. "Be careful in Cthol Murgos." He turned his horse and started down the hill toward the plain with the mare and the colt tagging along behind him. The colt stopped once to look back at Garion, gave a forlorn little whinny, then turned to follow his mother.

Barak shook his head somberly. "I'm going to miss Hettar," he rumbled.

"Cthol Murgos wouldn't be a good place for Hettar," Silk pointed out. "We'd have to put a leash on him."

"I know that." Barak sighed. "But I'll miss him all the same."

"Which direction do we take?" Mandorallen asked, squinting out at the grassland.

Belgarath pointed to the southeast. "That way. We'll cross the upper end of the Vale to the escarpment and then go through the southern tip of Mishrak ac Thull. The Thulls don't put out patrols as regularly as the Murgos do."

"Thulls don't do much of anything unless they have to," Silk noted. "They're too preoccupied with trying to avoid Grolims."

"When do we start?" Durnik asked.

"As soon as Relg finishes his prayers," Belgarath replied.

"We'll have time for breakfast, then," Barak said dryly.

They rode all that day across the flat grassland of southern Algaria beneath the deep blue autumn sky. Relg, wearing an old hooded tunic of Durnik's over his mail shirt, rode badly, with his legs sticking out stiffly. He seemed to be concentrating more on keeping his face down than on watching where he was going.

Barak watched sourly, with disapproval written plainly on his face. "I'm not trying to tell you your business, Belgarath," he said after several hours, "but that one's going to be trouble before we're finished with this."

"The light hurts his eyes, Barak," Aunt Pol told the big man, "and he's not used to riding. Don't be so quick to criticize."

Barak clamped his mouth shut, his expression still disparaging.

"At least we'll be able to count on his staying sober," Aunt Pol observed primly. "Which is more than I can say about *some* members of this little group."

Barak coughed uncomfortably.

They set up for the night on the treeless bank of a meandering stream. Once the sun had gone down, Relg seemed less apprehensive, though he made an obvious point of not looking directly at the driftwood fire. Then he looked up and saw the first stars in the evening sky. He gaped up at them in horror, his unveiled face breaking out in a glistening sweat. He covered his head with his arms and collapsed face down on the earth with a strangled cry.

"Relg!" Garion exclaimed, jumping to the stricken man's side and putting his hands on him without thinking.

"Don't touch me," Relg gasped automatically.

"Don't be stupid. What's wrong? Are you sick?"

"The sky," Relg croaked in despair. "The sky! It terrifies me!"

"The sky?" Garion was baffled. "What's wrong with the sky?" He looked up at the familiar stars.

"There's no end to it," Relg groaned. "It goes up forever."

Quite suddenly Garion understood. In the caves *he* had been afraid—unreasoningly afraid—because he had been closed in. Out here under the open sky, Relg suffered from the same kind of blind terror. Garion realized with a kind of shock that quite probably Relg had never been outside the caves of Ulgo in his entire life. "It's all right," he assured him comfortingly. "The sky can't hurt you. It's just up there. Don't pay any attention to it."

"I can't bear it."

"Don't look at it."

"I still know it's there—all that emptiness."

Garion looked helplessly at Aunt Pol. She made a quick gesture that told him to keep talking. "It's not empty," he floundered. "It's full of things—all kinds of things—clouds, birds, sunlight, stars—"

"What?" Relg lifted his face up out of his hands. "What are those?"

"Clouds? Everyone knows what—" Garion stopped. Obviously Relg did *not* know what clouds were. He'd never seen a cloud in his life. Garion tried to rearrange his thoughts to take that into account. It was not going to be easy to explain. He took in a deep breath. "All right. Let's start with clouds, then."

It took a long time, and Garion was not really sure that Relg understood or if he was simply clinging to the words to avoid thinking about the sky. After clouds, birds were a bit easier, although feathers were very hard to explain.

"UL spoke to you," Relg interrupted Garion's description of wings. "He called you Belgarion. Is that your name?"

"Well—" Garion replied uncomfortably. "Not really. Actually my name is Garion, but I think the other name is supposed to be mine, too—sometime later, I believe—when I'm older."

"UL knows all things," Relg declared. "If he called you Belgarion, that's your true name. I will call you Belgarion."

"I really wish you wouldn't."

"My God rebuked me," Relg groaned, his voice sunk into a kind of sick self-loathing. "I have failed him."

Garion couldn't quite follow that. Somehow, even in the midst of his panic, Relg had been suffering the horrors of a theological crisis. He sat on the ground with his face turned away from the fire and his shoulders slumped in an attitude of absolute despair.

"I'm unworthy," he said, his voice on the verge of a sob. "When UL spoke in the silence of my heart, I felt that I had been exalted above all other men, but now I am lower than dirt." In his anguish he began to beat the sides of his head with his fists.

"Stop that!" Garion said sharply. "You'll hurt yourself. What's this all about?"

"UL told me that I was to reveal the child to Ulgo. I took his words to mean that I had found special grace in his eyes."

"What child are we talking about?"

"The child. The new Gorim. It's UL's way to guide and protect his people. When an old Gorim's work is done, UL places a special mark upon the eyes of the child who is to succeed him. When UL told me that I had been chosen to bring the child to Ulgo, I revealed his words to others, and they revered me and asked me to speak to them in the words of UL. I saw sin and corruption all around me and I denounced it, and the people listened to me—but the words were mine, not UL's. In my pride, I presumed to speak for UL. I ignored my own sins to accuse the sins of others." Relg's voice was harsh with fanatic self-accusation. "I am filth," he declared, "an abomination. UL should have raised his hand against me and destroyed me."

"That's forbidden," Garion told him without thinking.

"Who has the power to forbid anything to UL?"

"I don't know. All I know is that unmaking is forbidden—even to the Gods. It's the very first thing we learn."

Relg looked up sharply, and Garion knew instantly that he had made a dreadful mistake. "You know the secrets of the Gods?" the fanatic demanded incredulously.

"The fact that they're Gods doesn't have anything to do with it," Garion replied. "The rule applies to everybody."

Relg's eyes burned with a sudden hope. He drew himself up onto his knees and bowed forward until his face was in the dirt. "Forgive me my sins," he intoned.

"What?"

"I have exalted myself when I was unworthy."

"You made a mistake—that's all. Just don't do it anymore. Please get up, Relg."

"I'm wicked and impure."

"You?"

"I've had impure thoughts about women."

Garion flushed with embarrassment. "We all have those kinds of thoughts once in a while," he said with a nervous cough.

"My thoughts are wicked—wicked," Relg groaned with guilt. "I burn with them."

"I'm sure that UL understands. Please get up, Relg. You don't have to do this."

"I have prayed with my mouth when my mind and heart were not in my prayers."

"Relg—"

"I have sought out hidden caves for the joy of finding them rather than to consecrate them to UL. I have thus defiled the gift given me by my God."

"Please, Relg—"

Relg began to beat his head on the ground. "Once I found a cave where the echoes of UL's voice lingered. I did not reveal it to others, but kept the sound of UL's voice for myself."

Garion began to become alarmed. The fanatic Relg was working himself into a frenzy.

"Punish me, Belgarion," Relg pleaded. "Lay a hard penance on me for my iniquity."

Garion's mind was very clear as he answered. He knew exactly what he had to say. "I can't do that, Relg," he said gravely. "I can't punish you—any more than I can forgive you. If you've done things you shouldn't have, that's between you and UL. If you think you need to be punished, you'll have to do it yourself. I can't. I won't."

Relg lifted his stricken face out of the dirt and stared at Garion. Then with a strangled cry he lurched to his feet and fled wailing into the darkness.

"Garion!" Aunt Pol's voice rang with that familiar note.

"I didn't do anything," he protested almost automatically.

"What did you say to him?" Belgarath demanded.

"He said that he'd committed all kinds of sins," Garion explained. "He wanted me to punish him and forgive him."

"So?"

"I couldn't do that, Grandfather."

"What's so hard about it?"

Garion stared at him.

"All you had to do was lie to him a little. Is that so difficult?"

"Lie? About something like that?" Garion was horrified at the thought.

"I *need* him, Garion, and he can't function if he's incapacitated by some kind of religious hysteria. Use your head, boy."

"I can't do it, Grandfather," Garion repeated stubbornly. "It's too important to him for me to cheat him about it."

"You'd better go find him, father," Aunt Pol said.

Belgarath scowled at Garion. "You and I aren't finished with this yet, boy," he said, pointing an angry finger. Then, muttering irritably to himself, he went in search of Relg.

With a cold certainty Garion suddenly knew that the journey to Cthol Murgos was going to be very long and uncomfortable.

CHAPTER TWENTY

Though summer that year had lingered in the lowlands and on the plains of Algaria, autumn was brief. The blizzards and squalls they had encountered in the mountains above Maragor and again among the peaks of Ulgo had hinted that winter would be early and severe, and there was already a chill to the nights as they rode day after day across the open grassland toward the eastern escarpment.

Belgarath had recovered from his momentary fit of anger over Garion's failure to deal with Relg's attack of guilt, but then, with inescapable logic, he had placed an enormous burden squarely on Garion's shoulders. "For some reason he trusts you," the old man observed, "so I'm going to leave him entirely in your hands. I don't care what you have to do, but keep him from flying apart again."

At first, Relg refused to respond to Garion's efforts to draw him out; but after a while, one of the waves of panic caused by the thought of the open sky above swept over the zealot, and he began to talk—haltingly at first but then finally in a great rush. As Garion had feared, Relg's favorite topic was sin. Garion was amazed at the simple things that Relg considered sinful. Forgetting to pray before a meal, for example, was a major transgression. As the fanatic's gloomy catalogue of his faults expanded, Garion began to perceive that most of his sins were sins of thought rather than of action. The one matter that kept cropping up again and again was the question of lustful thoughts about women. To Garion's intense discomfort, Relg insisted on describing these lustful thoughts extensively.

"Women are not the same as we are, of course," the zealot confided one afternoon as they rode together. "Their minds and hearts are not drawn to holiness the way ours are, and they set out deliberately to tempt us with their bodies and draw us into sin."

"Why do you suppose that is?" Garion asked carefully.

"Their hearts are filled with lust," Relig declared adamantly. "They take particular delight in tempting the righteous. I tell you truly, Belgarion, you would not believe the subtlety of the creatures. I have seen the evidence of this wickedness in the soberest of matrons—the wives of some of my most devout followers. They're forever touching—brushing as if by accident—and they take great pains to allow the sleeves of their robes to slip up brazenly to expose their rounded arms—and the hems of their garments always seem to be hitching up to display their ankles."

"If it bothers you, don't look," Garion suggested.

Relg ignored that. "I have even considered banning them from my presence, but then I thought that it might be better if I kept my eyes on them so that I could protect my followers from their wickedness. I thought for a time that I should forbid marriage among my followers, but some of the older ones told me that I might lose the young if I did that. I still think it might not be a bad idea."

"Wouldn't that sort of eliminate your followers altogether?" Garion asked him. "I mean, if you kept it up long enough? No marriage, no children. You get my point?"

"That's the part I haven't worked out yet," Relg admitted.

"And what about the child—the new Gorim? If two people are supposed to get married so they can have a child—that particular, special child—and you persuade them not to, aren't you interfering with something that UL wants to happen?"

Relg drew in a sharp breath as if he had not considered that. Then he groaned. "You see? Even when I'm trying my very hardest, I always seem to stumble straight into sin. I'm cursed, Belgarion, cursed. Why did UL choose me to reveal the child when I am so corrupt?"

Garion quickly changed the subject to head off that line of thought.

For nine days they crossed the endless sea of grass toward the eastern escarpment, and for nine days the others, with a callousness that hurt Garion to the quick, left him trapped in the company of the ranting zealot. He grew sulky and frequently cast reproachful glances at them, but they ignored him.

Near the eastern edge of the plain, they crested a long hill and stared for the first time at the immense wall of the eastern escarpment, a sheer basalt cliff rising fully a mile above the rubble at its base and stretching off into the distance in either direction.

"Impossible," Barak stated flatly. "We'll never be able to climb that."

"We won't have to," Silk told him confidently. "I know a trail."

"A secret trail, I suppose?"

"Not exactly a secret," Silk replied. "I don't imagine too many people know about it, but it's right out in plain sight—if you know where to look. I had occasion to leave Mishrak ac Thull in a hurry once, and I stumbled across it."

"One gets the feeling that you've had occasion to leave just about every place in a hurry at one time or another."

Silk shrugged. "Knowing when it's time to run is one of the most important things people in my profession ever learn."

"Will the river ahead not prove a barrier?" Mandorallen asked, looking at the sparkling surface of the Aldur River lying between them and the grim, black cliff. He was running his fingertips lightly over his side, testing for tender spots.

"Mandorallen, stop that," Aunt Pol told him. "They'll never heal if you keep poking at them."

"Methinks, my Lady, that they are nearly whole again," the knight replied. "Only one still causes me any discomfort."

"Well, leave it alone."

"There's a ford a few miles upstream," Belgarath said in answer to the question. "The river's down at this time of year, so we won't have any difficulty crossing." He started out again, leading them down the gradual slope toward the Aldur. They forded late that afternoon and pitched their tents on the far side. The next morning they moved out to the foot of the escarpment.

"The trail's just a few miles south," Silk told them, leading the way along the looming black cliff.

"Do we have to go up along the face of it?" Garion asked apprehensively, craning his neck to look up the towering wall.

Silk shook his head. "The trail's a streambed. It cuts down through the cliff. It's a little steep and narrow, but it'll get us safely to the top."

Garion found that encouraging.

The trail appeared to be little more than a crack in the stupendous cliff, and a trickle of water ran out of the opening to disappear into the jumble of rocky debris along the base of the escarpment. "Are you sure it goes all the way to the top?" Barak asked, eyeing the narrow chimney suspiciously.

"Trust me," Silk assured him.

"Not if I can help it."

The trail was awful, steep and strewn with rock. At times it was so narrow that the packhorses had to be unloaded before they could make it through and they had to be literally manhandled up over basalt boulders that had fractured into squares, almost like huge steps. The trickle of water running down the cut made everything slick and muddy. To make matters even worse, thin, high clouds swept in from the west and a bitterly cold draft spilled down the narrow cut from the arid plains of Mishrak ac Thull, lying high above.

It took them two days, and by the time they reached the top, a mile or so back from the brink of the escarpment, they were all exhausted.

"I feel as if somebody's been beating me with a stick." Barak groaned, sinking to the ground in the brushy gully at the top of the cut. "A very big, dirty stick."

They all sat on the ground among the prickly thornbushes in the gully, recovering from the dreadful climb. "I'll have a look around," Silk said after only a few moments. The small man had the body of an acrobat—supple, strong, and quick to restore itself. He crept up to the rim of the gully, duck-

ing low under the thornbushes and worming his way the last few feet on his
stomach to peer carefully over the top. After several minutes, he gave a low
whistle, and they saw him motion sharply for them to join him.

Barak groaned again and stood up. Durnik, Mandorallen, and Garion
also got stiffly to their feet.

"See what he wants," Belgarath told them. "I'm not ready to start moving around just yet."

The four of them started up the slope through the loose gravel toward
the spot where Silk lay peering out from under a thornbush, crawling the last
few feet as he had done.

"What's the trouble?" Barak asked the little man as they came up beside him.

"Company," Silk replied shortly, pointing out over the rocky, arid plain
lying brown and dead under the flat gray sky.

A cloud of yellow dust, whipped low to the ground by the stiff, chill
wind, gave evidence of riders.

"A patrol?" Durnik asked in a hushed voice.

"I don't think so," Silk answered. "Thulls aren't comfortable on horses.
They usually patrol on foot."

Garion peered out across the arid waste. "Is that somebody out in front
of them?" he asked, pointing at a tiny, moving speck a half mile or so in
front of the riders.

"Ah," Silk said with a peculiar kind of sadness.

"What is it?" Barak asked. "Don't keep secrets, Silk. I'm not in the mood
for it."

"They're Grolims," Silk explained. "The one they're chasing is a Thull
trying to escape being sacrificed. It happens rather frequently."

"Should Belgarath be warned?" Mandorallen suggested.

"It's probably not necessary," Silk replied. "The Grolims around here are
mostly low-ranking. I doubt that any of them would have any skill at
sorcery."

"I'll go tell him anyway," Durnik said. He slid back away from the edge
of the gully, rose, and went back down to where the old man rested with
Aunt Pol and Relg.

"As long as we stay out of sight, we'll probably be all right," Silk told
them. "It looks as if there are only three of them, and they're concentrating
on the Thull."

The running man had moved closer. He ran with his head down and his
arms pumping at his sides.

"What happens if he tries to hide here in the gully?" Barak asked.

Silk shrugged. "The Grolims will follow him."

"We'd have to take steps at that point, wouldn't we?"

Silk nodded with a wicked little smirk.

"We could call him, I suppose," Barak suggested, loosening his sword in
its sheath.

"The same thought had just occurred to me."

Durnik came back up the slope, his feet crunching in the gravel. "Wolf says to keep an eye on them," he reported, "but he says not to do anything unless they actually start into the gully."

"What a shame!" Silk sighed regretfully.

The running Thull was clearly visible now. He was a thick-bodied man in a rough tunic, belted at the waist. His hair was shaggy and mud-colored, and his face was contorted into an expression of brutish panic. He passed the place where they hid, perhaps thirty paces out on the flats, and Garion could clearly hear his breath whistling in his throat as he pounded past. He was whimpering as he ran—an animal-like sound of absolute despair.

"They almost never try to hide," Silk said in a soft voice tinged with pity. "All they do is run." He shook his head.

"They'll overtake him soon," Mandorallen observed. The pursuing Grolims wore black, hooded robes and polished steel masks.

"We'd better get down," Barak advised.

They all ducked below the gully rim. A few moments later, the three horses galloped by, their hooves thudding on the hard earth.

"They'll catch him in a few more minutes," Garion said. "He's running right for the edge. He'll be trapped."

"I don't think so," Silk replied somberly.

A moment later they heard a long, despairing shriek, fading horribly into the gulf below.

"I more or less expected that," Silk said.

Garion's stomach wrenched at the thought of the dreadful height of the escarpment.

"They're coming back," Barak warned. "Get down."

The three Grolims rode back along the edge of the gully. One of them said something Garion could not quite hear, and the other two laughed.

"The world might be a brighter place with three less Grolims in it," Mandorallen suggested in a grim whisper.

"Attractive thought," Silk agreed, "but Belgarath would probably disapprove. I suppose it's better to let them go. We wouldn't want anybody looking for them."

Barak looked longingly after the three Grolims, then sighed with deep regret.

"Let's go back down," Silk said.

They all turned and crawled back down into the brushy gully.

Belgarath looked up as they returned. "Are they gone?"

"They're riding off," Silk told him.

"What was that cry?" Relg asked.

"Three Grolims chased a Thull off the edge of the escarpment," Silk replied.

"Why?"

"He'd been selected for a certain religious observance, and he didn't want to participate."

"He refused?" Relg sounded shocked. "He deserved his fate, then."

"I don't think you appreciate the nature of Grolim ceremonies, Relg," Silk said.

"One must submit to the will of one's God," Relg insisted. There was a sanctimonious note to his voice. "Religious obligations are absolute."

Silk's eyes glittered as he looked at the Ulgo fanatic. "How much do you know about the Angarak religion, Relg?" he asked.

"I concern myself only with the religion of Ulgo."

"A man ought to know what he's talking about before he makes judgments."

"Let it lie, Silk," Aunt Pol told him.

"I don't think so, Polgara. Not this time. A few facts might be good for our devout friend here. He seems to lack perspective." Silk turned back to Relg. "The core of the Angarak religion is a ritual most men find repugnant. Thulls devote their entire lives to avoiding it. That's the central reality of Thullish life."

"An abominable people." Relg's denunciation was harsh.

"No. Thulls are stupid—even brutish—but they're hardly abominable. You see, Relg, the ritual we're talking about involves human sacrifice."

Relg pulled the veil from his eyes to stare incredulously at the rat-faced little man.

"Each year two thousand Thulls are sacrificed to Torak," Silk went on, his eyes boring into Relg's stunned face. "The Grolims permit the substitution of slaves, so a Thull spends his whole life working in order to get enough money to buy a slave to take his place on the altar if he's unlucky enough to be chosen. But slaves die sometimes—or they escape. If a Thull without a slave is chosen, he usually tries to run. Then the Grolims chase him—they've had a lot of practice, so they're very good at it. I've never heard of a Thull actually getting away."

"It's their duty to submit," Relg maintained stubbornly, though he seemed a bit less sure of himself.

"How are they sacrificed?" Durnik asked in a subdued voice. The Thull's willingness to hurl himself off the escarpment had obviously shaken him.

"It's a simple procedure," Silk replied, watching Relg closely. "Two Grolims bend the Thull backward over the altar, and a third cuts his heart out. Then they burn the heart in a little fire. Torak isn't interested in the whole Thull. He only wants the heart."

Relg flinched at that.

"They sacrifice women, too," Silk pressed. "But women have a simpler means of escape. The Grolims won't sacrifice a pregnant woman—it confuses their count—so Thullish women try to stay pregnant constantly. That explains why there are so many Thulls and why Thullish women are notorious for their indiscriminate appetite."

"Monstrous." Relg gasped. "Death would be better than such vile corruption."

"Death lasts for a long time, Relg," Silk said with a cold little smile. "A little corruption can be forgotten rather quickly if you put your mind to it. That's particularly true if your life depends on it."

Relg's face was troubled as he struggled with the blunt description of the horror of Thullish life. "You're a wicked man," he accused Silk, though his voice lacked conviction.

"I know," Silk admitted.

Relg appealed to Belgarath. "Is what he says true?"

The sorcerer scratched thoughtfully at his beard. "He doesn't seem to have left out very much," he replied. "The word religion means different things to different people, Relg. It depends on the nature of one's God. You ought to try to get that sorted out in your mind. It might make some of the things you'll have to do a bit easier."

"I think we've just about exhausted the possibilities of this conversation, father," Aunt Pol suggested, "and we have a long way to go."

"Right," he agreed, getting to his feet.

They rode down through the arid jumble of rock and scrubby bushes that spread across the western frontier of the land of the Thulls. The continual wind that swept up across the escarpment was bitterly cold, though there were only a few patches of thin snow lying beneath the somber gray sky.

Relg's eyes adjusted to the subdued light, and the clouds appeared to quiet the panic the open sky had caused him. But this was obviously a difficult time for him. The world here aboveground was alien, and everything he encountered seemed to shatter his preconceptions. It was also a time of personal religious turmoil, and the crisis goaded him into peculiar fluctuations of speech and action. At one moment he would sanctimoniously denounce the sinful wickedness of others, his face set in a stern expression of righteousness; and in the next, he would be writhing in an agony of self-loathing, confessing his sin and guilt in an endless, repetitious litany to any who would listen. His pale face and huge, dark eyes, framed by the hood of his leaf-mail shirt, contorted in the tumult of his emotions. Once again the others—even patient, good-hearted Durnik—drew away from him, leaving him entirely to Garion. Relg stopped often for prayers and obscure little rituals that always seemed to involve a great deal of groveling in the dirt.

"It's going to take us all year to get to Rak Cthol at this rate," Barak rumbled sourly on one such occasion, glaring with open dislike at the ranting fanatic kneeling in the sand beside the trail.

"We need him," Belgarath replied calmly, "and he needs this. We can live with it if we have to."

"We're getting close to the northern edge of Cthol Murgos," Silk said, pointing ahead at a low range of hills. "We won't be able to stop like this once we cross the border. We'll have to ride as hard as we can until we get to the South Caravan Route. The Murgos patrol extensively, and they disapprove of side trips. Once we get to the track, we'll be all right, but we don't want to be stopped before we get there."

"Will we not be questioned even on the caravan route, Prince Kheldar?" Mandorallen asked. "Our company is oddly assorted, and Murgos are suspicious."

"They'll watch us," Silk admitted, "but they won't interfere as long as we don't stray from the track. The treaty between Taur Urgas and Ran Borune guarantees freedom of travel along the caravan route, and no Murgo alive would be foolish enough to embarrass his king by violating it. Taur Urgas is very severe with people who embarrass him."

They crossed into Cthol Murgos shortly after noon on a cold, murky day and immediately pushed into a gallop. After about a league or so, Relg began to pull in his horse.

"Not now, Relg," Belgarath told him sharply. "Later."

"But—"

"UL's a patient God. He'll wait. Keep going."

They galloped on across the high, barren plain toward the caravan route, their cloaks streaming behind them in the biting wind. It was midafternoon when they reached the track and reined in. The South Caravan Route was not precisely a road, but centuries of travel had clearly marked its course. Silk looked around with satisfaction. "Made it," he said. "Now we become honest merchants again, and no Murgo in the world is going to interfere with us." He turned his horse eastward then and led the way with a great show of confidence. He squared his shoulders, seeming to puff himself up with a kind of busy self-importance, and Garion knew that he was making mental preparations involved in assuming a new role. When they encountered the well-guarded packtrain of a Tolnedran merchant moving west, Silk had made his transition and he greeted the merchant with the easy camaraderie of a man of trade.

"Good day, Grand High Merchant," he said to the Tolnedran, noting the other's marks of rank. "If you can spare a moment, I thought we might exchange information about the trail. You've come from the east, and I've just come over the route to the west of here. An exchange might prove mutually beneficial."

"Excellent idea," the Tolnedran agreed. The Grand High Merchant was a stocky man with a high forehead and wore a fur-lined cloak pulled tightly about him to ward off the icy wind.

"My name is Ambar," Silk said. "From Kotu."

The Tolnedran nodded in polite acknowledgment. "Kalvor," he introduced himself, "of Tol Horb. You've picked a hard season for the journey east, Ambar."

"Necessity," Silk said. "My funds are limited, and the cost of winter lodgings in Tol Honeth would have devoured what little I have."

"The Honeths are rapacious," Kalvor concurred. "Is Ran Borune still alive?"

"He was when I left."

Kalvor made a face. "And the squabble over the succession goes on?"

Silk laughed. "Oh, yes."

"Is that swine Kador from Tol Vordue still dominant?"

"Kador fell upon hard times, I understand. I heard that he made an attempt on the life of Princess Ce'Nedra. I imagine that the Emperor's going to take steps to remove him from the race."

"What splendid news," Kalvor said, his face brightening.

"How's the trail to the east?" Silk asked.

"There's not much snow," Kalvor told him. "Of course, there never is in Cthol Murgos. It's a very dry kingdom. It's cold, though. It's bitter in the passes. What about the mountains in eastern Tolnedra?"

"It was snowing when we came through."

"I was afraid of that," Kalvor said with a gloomy look.

"You probably should have waited until spring, Kalvor. The worst part of the trip's still ahead of you."

"I had to get out of Rak Goska." Kalvor looked around almost as if expecting to see someone listening. "You're headed toward trouble, Ambar," he said seriously.

"Oh?"

"This is not the time to go to Rak Goska. The Murgos have gone insane there."

"Insane?" Silk said with alarm.

"There's no other explanation. They're arresting honest merchants on the flimsiest charges you ever heard of, and everyone from the West is followed constantly. It's certainly not the time to take a lady to that place."

"My sister," Silk replied, glancing at Aunt Pol. "She's invested in my venture, but she doesn't trust me. She insisted on coming along to make sure I don't cheat her."

"I'd stay out of Rak Goska," Kalvor advised.

"I'm committed now," Silk said helplessly. "I don't have any other choice, do I?"

"I'll tell you quite honestly, Ambar, it's as much as a man's life is worth to go to Rak Goska just now. A good merchant I know was actually accused of violating the women's quarters in a Murgo household."

"Well, I suppose that happens sometimes. Murgo women are reputed to be very handsome."

"Ambar," Kalvor said with a pained expression, "the man was seventy-three years old."

"His sons can be proud of his vitality, then." Silk laughed. "What happened to him?"

"He was condemned and impaled," Kalvor said with a shudder. "The soldiers rounded us all up and made us watch. It was ghastly."

Silk frowned. "There's no chance that the charges were true?"

"Seventy-three years old, Ambar," Kalvor repeated. "The charges were obviously false. If I didn't know better, I'd guess that Taur Urgas is trying to drive all western merchants out of Cthol Murgos. Rak Goska simply isn't safe for us anymore."

Silk grimaced. "Who can ever say what Taur Urgas is thinking?"

"He profits from every transaction in Rak Goska. He'd have to be insane to drive us out deliberately."

"I've met Taur Urgas," Silk said grimly. "Sanity's not one of his major failings." He looked around with a kind of desperation on his face. "Kalvor, I've invested everything I own and everything I can borrow in this venture. If I turn back now, I'll be ruined."

"You could turn north after you get through the mountains," Kalvor suggested. "Cross the river into Mishrak ac Thull and go to Thull Mardu."

Silk made a face. "I hate dealing with Thulls."

"There's another possibility," the Tolnedran said. "You know where the halfway point between Tol Honeth and Rak Goska is?"

Silk nodded.

"There's always been a Murgo resupply station there—food, spare horses, other necessities. Anyway, since the troubles in Rak Goska, a few enterprising Murgos have come out there and are buying whole caravan loads—horses and all. Their prices aren't as attractive as the prices in Rak Goska, but it's a chance for *some* profit, and you don't have to put yourself in danger to make it."

"But that way you have no goods for the return journey," Silk objected. "Half the profit's lost if you come back with nothing to sell in Tol Honeth."

"You'd have your life, Ambar," Kalvor said pointedly. He looked around again nervously, as if expecting to be arrested. "I'm not coming back to Cthol Murgos," he declared in a firm voice. "I'm as willing as any man to take risks for a good profit, but all the gold in the world isn't worth another trip to Rak Goska."

"How far is it to the halfway point?" Silk asked, seemingly troubled.

"I've ridden for three days since I left there," Kalvor replied. "Good luck, Ambar—whatever you decide." He gathered up his reins. "I want to put a few more leagues behind me before I stop for the night. There may be snow in the Tolnedran mountains, but at least I'll be out of Cthol Murgos and out from under the fist of Taur Urgas." He nodded briefly and moved off to the west at a fast trot, with his guards and his packtrain following after him.

CHAPTER TWENTY-ONE

The South Caravan Route wound through a series of high, arid valleys that ran in a generally east-west direction. The surrounding peaks were high—higher probably than the mountains to the west, but their upper slopes were only faintly touched with snow. The clouds overhead turned the sky a dirty slate-gray, but what moisture they held did not fall on this desiccated wilderness of sand, rock, and scrubby thorn. Though it did not snow, it was nonetheless bitterly cold. The wind blew continually, and its edge was like a knife.

They rode east, making good time.

"Belgarath," Barak said back over his shoulder, "there's a Murgo on that ridgeline ahead—just to the south of the track."

"I see him."

"What's he doing?"

"Watching us. He won't do anything as long as we stay on the caravan route."

"They always watch like that," Silk stated. "The Murgos like to keep a close watch on everybody in their kingdom."

"That Tolnedran—Kalvor," Barak said. "Do you think he was exaggerating?"

"No," Belgarath replied. "I'd guess that Taur Urgas is looking for an ex-cuse to close the caravan route and expel all the westerners from Cthol Murgos."

"Why?" Durnik asked.

Belgarath shrugged. "The war is coming. Taur Urgas knows that a good number of the merchants who take this route to Rak Goska are spies. He'll be bringing armies up from the south soon, and he'd like to keep their num-bers and movements a secret."

"What manner of army could be gathered from so bleak and uninhabited a realm?" Mandorallen asked.

Belgarath looked around at the high, bleak desert. "This is only the little piece of Cthol Murgos we're permitted to see. It stretches a thousand leagues or more to the south, and there are cities down there that no westerner has ever seen—we don't even know their names. Here in the north, the Murgos play a very elaborate game to conceal the real Cthol Murgos."

"Is it thy thought then that the war will come soon?"

"Next summer perhaps," Belgarath replied. "Possibly the summer following."

"Are we going to be ready?" Barak asked.

"We're going to try to be."

Aunt Pol made a brief sound of disgust.

"What's wrong?" Garion asked her quickly.

"Vultures," she said. "Filthy brutes."

A dozen heavy-bodied birds were flapping and squawking over something on the ground to one side of the caravan track.

"What are they feeding on?" Durnik asked. "I haven't seen any animals of any kind since we left the top of the escarpment."

"A horse, probably—or a man," Silk said. "There's nothing else up here."

"Would a man be left unburied?" the smith asked.

"Only partially," Silk told him. "Sometimes certain brigands decide that the pickings along the caravan route might be easy. The Murgos give them plenty of time to realize how wrong they were."

Durnik looked at him questioningly.

"The Murgos catch them," Silk explained, "and then they bury them up to the neck and leave them. The vultures have learned that a man in that situation is helpless. Often they get impatient and don't bother to wait for the man to finish dying before they start to eat."

"That's one way to deal with bandits," Barak said, almost approvingly. "Even a Murgo can have a good idea once in a while."

"Unfortunately, Murgos automatically assume that anybody who isn't on the track itself is a bandit."

The vultures brazenly continued to feed, refusing to leave their dreadful feast as the party passed no more than twenty yards from their flapping congregation. Their wings and bodies concealed whatever it was they were feeding on, a fact for which Garion was profoundly grateful. Whatever it was, however, was not very large.

"We should stay quite close to the track when we stop for the night, then," Durnik said, averting his eyes with a shudder.

"That's a very good idea, Durnik," Silk agreed.

The information the Tolnedran merchant had given them about the makeshift fair at the halfway point proved to be accurate. On the afternoon of the third day, they came over a rise and saw a cluster of tents surrounding a solid stone building set to one side of the caravan track. The tents looked small in the distance and they billowed and flapped in the endless wind that swept down the valley.

"What do you think?" Silk asked Belgarath.

"It's late," the old man replied. "We're going to have to stop for the night soon anyway, and it'd look peculiar if we didn't stop."

Silk nodded.

"We're going to have to try to keep Relg out of sight, though," Belgarath continued. "Nobody's going to believe we're ordinary merchants if they see an Ulgo with us."

Silk thought a moment. "We'll wrap him in a blanket," he suggested, "and tell anybody who asks that he's sick. People stay away from sick men."

Belgarath nodded. "Can you act sick?" he asked Relg.

"I *am* sick," the Ulgo said without any attempt at humor. "Is it always this cold up here?" He sneezed.

Aunt Pol pulled her horse over beside his and reached out to put her hand on his forehead.

"Don't touch me." Relg cringed away from her hand.

"Stop that," she told him. She briefly touched his face and looked at him closely. "He's coming down with a cold, father," she announced. "As soon as we get settled, I'll give him something for it. Why didn't you tell me?" she asked the fanatic.

"I will endure what UL chooses to send me," Relg declared. "It's his punishment for my sins."

"No," she told him flatly. "It has nothing to do with sin or punishment. It's a cold—nothing more."

"Am I going to die?" Relg asked calmly.

"Of course not. Haven't you ever had a cold before?"

"No. I've never been sick in my life."

"You won't be able to say that again," Silk said lightly, pulling a blanket out of one of the packs and handing it to him. "Wrap this around your shoulders and pull it up over your head. Try to look like you're suffering."

"I am," Relg said, starting to cough.

"But you have to *look* like it," Silk told him. "Think about sin—that ought to make you look miserable."

"I think about sin all the time," Relg replied, still coughing.

"I know," Silk said, "but try to think about it a little harder."

They rode down the hill toward the collection of tents with the dry, icy wind whipping at them as they rode. Very few of the assembled merchants were outside their tents, and those who were moved quickly about their tasks in the biting chill.

"We should stop by the resupply station first, I suppose," Silk suggested, gesturing toward the square stone building squatting among the tents. "That would look more natural. Let me handle things."

"Silk, you mangy Drasnian thief!" a coarse voice roared from a nearby tent.

Silk's eyes widened slightly, and then he grinned. "I seem to recognize the squeals of a certain Nadrak hog," he said, loud enough to be heard by the man in the tent.

A rangy Nadrak in a belted, ankle-length, black felt overcoat and a snug-fitting fur cap strode out of the tent. He had coarse, black hair and a thin, scraggly beard. His eyes had the peculiar angularity to them that was a characteristic of all Angaraks; but unlike the dead eyes of the Murgos, this Nadrak's eyes were alive with a kind of wary friendship. "Haven't they caught you yet, Silk?" he demanded raucously. "I was sure that by now someone would have peeled off your hide."

"Drunk as usual, I see." Silk grinned viciously. "How many days has it been this time, Yarblek?"

"Who counts?" The Nadrak laughed, swaying slightly on his feet. "What are you doing in Cthol Murgos, Silk? I thought your fat king needed you in Gar og Nadrak."

"I was getting to be a little too well-known on the streets of Yar Nadrak," Silk replied. "It was getting to the point that people were avoiding me."

"Now I wonder just why that could be," Yarblek retorted with heavy sarcasm. "You cheat at trade, you switch dice, you make free with other men's wives, and you're a spy. That shouldn't be any reason for men not to admire your good points—whatever they are."

"Your sense of humor's as overpowering as ever, Yarblek."

"It's my only failing," the slightly tipsy Nadrak admitted. "Get down off that horse, Silk. Come inside my tent and we'll get drunk together. Bring your friends." He lurched back inside the tent.

"An old acquaintance," Silk explained quickly, sliding out of his saddle.

"Can he be trusted?" Barak asked suspiciously.

"Not entirely, but he's all right. He's not a bad fellow, really—for a Nadrak. He'll know everything that's going on, and if he's drunk enough, we might be able to get some useful information out of him."

"Get in here, Silk," Yarblek roared from inside his gray felt tent.

"Let's see what he has to say," Belgarath said.

They all dismounted, tied up their horses to a picket line at the side of the Nadrak's tent, and trooped inside. The tent was large, and the floor and walls were covered with thick crimson carpets. An oil lamp hung from the ridgepole, and an iron brazier shimmered out waves of heat.

Yarblek was sitting cross-legged on the carpeting at the back of the tent, with a large black keg conveniently beside him. "Come in. Come in," he said brusquely. "Close the flap. You're letting out all the heat."

"This is Yarblek," Silk said by way of introduction, "an adequate merchant and a notorious drunkard. We've known each other for a long time now."

"My tent is yours." Yarblek hiccuped indifferently. "It's not much of a tent, but it's yours anyway. There are cups over there in that pile of things by my saddle—some of them are even clean. Let's all have a drink."

"This is Mistress Pol, Yarblek," Silk introduced her.

"Good-looking woman," Yarblek observed, looking at her boldly. "Forgive me for not getting up, Mistress, but I feel a bit giddy at the moment— probably something I ate."

"Of course," she agreed with a dry little smile. "A man should always be careful about what he puts in his stomach."

"I've made that exact point myself a thousand times." He squinted at her as she pulled back her hood and unfastened her cape. "That's a remarkably handsome woman, Silk," he declared. "I don't suppose you'd care to sell her."

"You couldn't afford me, Yarblek," she told him without seeming to take the slightest offense.

Yarblek stared at her and then roared with laughter. "By One-Eye's nose, I'd bet that I couldn't, at that—and you've probably got a dagger somewhere under your clothes, too. You'd slice open my belly if I tried to steal you, wouldn't you?"

"Naturally."

"What a woman!" Yarblek chortled. "Can you dance, too?"

"Like you've never seen before, Yarblek," she replied. "I could turn your bones to water."

Yarblek's eyes burned. "After we all get drunk, maybe you'll dance for us."

"We'll see," she said with a hint of promise. Garion was stunned at this uncharacteristic boldness. It was obviously the way Yarblek expected a woman to behave, but Garion wondered just when Aunt Pol had learned the customs of the Nadraks so well that she could respond without the slightest hint of embarrassment.

"This is Mister Wolf," Silk said, indicating Belgarath.

"Never mind names." Yarblek waved his hand. "I'd just forget them anyway." He did, however, look rather shrewdly at each of them. "As a matter of fact," he continued, sounding suddenly not nearly as drunk as he appeared, "it might be just as well if I didn't know your names. What a man doesn't know, he can't reveal, and you're too well-mixed a group to be in stinking Cthol Murgos on honest business. Fetch yourselves cups. This keg is almost full, and I've got another chilling out back of the tent."

At Silk's gesture, they each took a cup from the heap of cookware piled beside a well-worn saddle and joined Yarblek on the carpet near the keg.

"I'd pour for you like a proper host," Yarblek told them, "but I spill too much that way. Dip out your own."

Yarblek's ale was a very dark brown and had a rich, almost fruity flavor.

"Interesting taste," Barak said politely.

"My brewer chops dried apples into his vats," the Nadrak replied. "It smooths out some of the bite." He turned to Silk. "I thought you didn't like Murgos."

"I don't."

"What are you doing in Cthol Murgos, then?"

Silk shrugged. "Business."

"Whose? Yours or Rhodar's?"

Silk winked at him.

"I thought as much. I wish you luck, then. I'd even offer to help, but I'd probably better keep my nose out of it. Murgos distrust us even more than they distrust you Alorns—not that I can really blame them. Any Nadrak worth the name would go ten leagues out of his way for the chance to cut a Murgo's throat."

"Your affection for your cousins touches my heart." Silk grinned.

Yarblek scowled. "Cousins!" he spat. "If it weren't for the Grolims, we'd have exterminated the whole cold-blooded race generations ago." He dipped out another cup of ale, lifted it and said, "Confusion to the Murgos."

"I think we've found something we can drink to together," Barak said with a broad smile. "Confusion to the Murgos."

"And may Taur Urgas grow boils on his behind," Yarblek added. He drank deeply, scooped another cupful of ale from the open keg and drank again. "I'm a little drunk," he admitted.

"We'd never have guessed," Aunt Pol told him.

"I like you, girl." Yarblek grinned at her. "I wish I could afford to buy you. I don't suppose you'd consider running away?"

She sighed a mocking little sigh. "No," she refused. "I'm afraid not. That gives a woman a bad reputation, you know."

"Very true," Yarblek agreed owlishly. He shook his head sadly. "As I was saying," he went on, "I'm a little drunk. I probably shouldn't say anything about this, but it's not a good time for westerners to be in Cthol Murgos— Alorns particularly. I've been hearing some strange things lately. Word's been filtering out of Rak Cthol that Murgoland is to be purged of outsiders. Taur Urgas wears the crown and plays king in Rak Goska, but the old Grolim at

Rak Cthol has his hand around Taur Urgas' heart. The king of the Murgos knows that one squeeze from Ctuchik will leave his throne empty."

"We met a Tolnedran a few leagues west of here who said the same sort of thing," Silk said seriously. "He told us that merchants from the West were being arrested all over Rak Goska on false charges."

Yarblek nodded. "That's only the first step. Murgos are always predictable—they have so little imagination. Taur Urgas isn't quite ready to offend Ran Borune openly by butchering every western merchant in the kingdom, but it's getting closer. Rak Goska's probably a closed city by now. Taur Urgas is free to turn his attention to the outlands. I'd imagine that's why he's coming here."

"He's *what?*" Silk's face paled visibly.

"I thought you knew," Yarblek told him. "Taur Urgas is marching toward the frontier with his army behind him. My guess is that he plans to close the border."

"How far away is he?" Silk demanded.

"I was told that he was seen this morning not five leagues from here," Yarblek said. "What's wrong?"

"Taur Urgas and I have had some serious fallings-out," Silk answered quickly, his face filled with consternation. "I can't be here when he arrives." He jumped to his feet.

"Where are you going?" Belgarath asked quickly.

"Someplace safe. I'll catch up with you later." He turned then and bolted out of the tent. A moment later they heard the pounding of his horse's hooves.

"Do you want me to go with him?" Barak asked Belgarath.

"You'd never catch him."

"I wonder what he did to Taur Urgas," Yarblek mused. He chuckled then. "It must have been something pretty awful, the way the little thief ran out of here."

"Is it safe for him to go away from the caravan track?" Garion asked, remembering the vultures at their grisly feast beside the trail.

"Don't worry about Silk," Yarblek replied confidently.

From a great distance away, a slow thudding sound began to intrude itself. Yarblek's eyes narrowed with hate. "It looks like Silk left just in time," he growled.

The thudding became louder and turned into a hollow, booming sound. Dimly, behind the booming, they could hear a kind of groaning chant of hundreds of voices in a deep, minor key.

"What's that?" Durnik asked.

"Taur Urgas," Yarblek answered and spat. "That's the war song of the king of the Murgos."

"War?" Mandorallen demanded sharply.

"Taur Urgas is always at war," Yarblek replied with heavy contempt. "Even when there isn't anybody to be at war with. He sleeps in his armor, even in his own palace. It makes him smelly, but all Murgos stink anyway, so it doesn't really make any difference. Maybe I'd better go see what he's up to." He got heavily to his feet. "Wait here," he told them. "This is a Nadrak tent, and there are certain courtesies expected between Angaraks. His soldiers won't come in here, so you'll be safe as long as you stay inside." He lurched toward the door of the tent, an expression of icy hatred on his face.

The chanting and the measured drumbeats grew louder. Shrill fifes picked up a discordant, almost jigging accompaniment, and then there was a sudden blaring of deep-throated horns.

"What do you think, Belgarath?" Barak rumbled. "This Yarblek seems like a good enough fellow, but he's still an Angarak. One word from him, and we'll have a hundred Murgos in here with us."

"He's right, father," Aunt Pol agreed. "I know Nadraks well enough to know that Yarblek wasn't nearly as drunk as he pretended to be."

Belgarath pursed his lips. "Maybe it isn't too good an idea to gamble all that much on the fact that Nadraks despise Murgos," he conceded. "We might be doing Yarblek an injustice, but perhaps it might be better just to slip away before Taur Urgas has time to put guards around the whole place anyway. There's no way of knowing how long he's going to stay here; and once he settles in, we might have trouble leaving."

Durnik pulled aside the red carpeting that hung along the back wall, reached down, and tugged out several tent pegs. He lifted the canvas. "I think we can crawl out here."

"Let's go, then," Belgarath decided.

One by one, they rolled out of the tent into the chill wind.

"Get the horses," Belgarath said quietly. He looked around, his eyes narrowing. "That gully over there." He pointed at a wash opening just beyond the last row of tents. "If we keep the tents between us and the main caravan track, we should be able to get into it without being seen. Most likely everybody here's going to be watching the arrival of Taur Urgas."

"Would the Murgo king know thee, Belgarath?" Mandorallen asked.

"He might. We've never met, but my description's been noised about in Cthol Murgos for a long time now. It's best not to take any chances."

They led their horses along the back of the tents and gained the cover of the gully without incident.

"This wash comes down off the back side of that hill there." Barak pointed. "If we follow it, we'll be out of sight all the way, and once we get the hill between us and the camp, we'll be able to ride away without being seen."

"It's almost evening." Belgarath looked up at the lowering sky. "Let's go up a ways and then wait until after dark."

They moved on up the gully until they were behind the shoulder of the hill.

"Better keep an eye on things," Belgarath said.

Barak and Garion scrambled up out of the gully and moved at a crouch to the top of the hill, where they lay down behind a scrubby bush. "Here they come," Barak muttered.

A steady stream of grim-faced Murgo soldiers marched eight abreast into the makeshift fair to the cadenced beat of great drums. In their midst, astride a black horse and under a flapping black banner, rode Taur Urgas. He was a tall man with heavy, sloping shoulders and an angular, merciless face. The thick links of his mail shirt had been dipped in molten red gold, making it almost appear as if he were covered with blood. A thick metal belt encircled his waist, and the scabbard of the sword he wore on his left hip was jewel-encrusted. A pointed steel helmet sat low over his black eyebrows, and the bloodred crown of Cthol Murgos was riveted to it. A kind of chain-mail hood covered the back and sides of the king's neck and spread out over his shoulders.

When he reached the open area directly in front of the square stone supply post, Taur Urgas reined in his horse. "Wine!" he commanded. His voice, carried by the icy wind, seemed startlingly close. Garion squirmed a bit lower under the bush.

The Murgo who ran the supply post scurried inside and came back out, carrying a flagon and a metal goblet. Taur Urgas took the goblet, drank, and then slowly closed his big fist around it, crushing it in his grip. Barak snorted with contempt.

"What was that about?" Garion whispered.

"Nobody drinks from a cup once Taur Urgas has used it," the red-bearded Cherek replied. "If Anheg behaved like that, his warriors would dunk him in the bay at Val Alorn."

"Have you the names of all foreigners here?" the king demanded of the Murgo storekeeper, his wind-carried voice distinct in Garion's ears.

"As you commanded, dread king," the storekeeper replied with an obsequious bow. He drew a roll of parchment out of one sleeve and handed it up to his ruler.

Taur Urgas unrolled the parchment and glanced at it. "Summon the Nadrak, Yarblek," he ordered.

"Let Yarblek of Gar og Nadrak approach," an officer at the king's side bellowed.

Yarblek, his felt overcoat flapping stiffly in the wind, stepped forward.

"Our cousin from the north," Taur Urgas greeted him coldly.

"Your Majesty," Yarblek replied with a slight bow.

"It would be well if you departed, Yarblek," the king told him. "My soldiers have certain orders, and some of them might fail to recognize a fellow Angarak in their eagerness to obey my commands. I cannot guarantee your safety if you remain, and I would be melancholy if something unpleasant befell you."

Yarblek bowed again. "My servants and I will leave at once, your Majesty."

"If they are Nadraks, they have our permission to go," the king said. "All foreigners, however, must remain. You're dismissed, Yarblek."

"I think we got out of that tent just in time," Barak muttered.

Then a man in a rusty mail shirt covered with a greasy brown vest stepped out of the supply post. He was unshaven, and the white of one of his eyes gleamed unwholesomely.

"Brill!" Garion exclaimed.

Barak's eyes went flat.

Brill bowed to Taur Urgas with an unexpected grace. "Hail, Mighty King," he said. His tone was neutral, carrying neither respect nor fear.

"What are you doing here, Kordoch?" Taur Urgas demanded coldly.

"I'm on my master's business, Dread King," Brill replied.

"What business would Ctuchik have in a place like this?"

"Something personal, Great King," Brill answered evasively.

"I like to keep track of you and the other Dagashi, Kordoch. When did you come back to Cthol Murgos?"

"A few months ago, Mighty Arm of Torak. If I'd known you were interested, I'd have sent word to you. The people my master wants me to deal with know I'm following them, so my movements aren't secret."

Taur Urgas laughed shortly, a sound without any warmth. "You must be getting old, Kordoch. Most Dagashi would have finished the business by now."

"These are rather special people." Brill shrugged. "It shouldn't take me much longer, however. The game is nearly over. Incidentally, Great King, I have a gift for you." He snapped his fingers sharply, and two of his henchmen came out of the building, dragging a third man between them. There was blood on the front of the captive's tunic, and his head hung down as if he were only semiconscious. Barak's breath hissed between his teeth.

"I thought you might like a bit of sport," Brill suggested.

"I'm the king of Cthol Murgos, Kordoch," Taur Urgas replied coldly. "I'm not amused by your attitude, and I'm not in the habit of doing chores for the Dagashi. If you want him dead, kill him yourself."

"This would hardly be a chore, your Majesty," Brill said with an evil grin. "The man's an old friend of yours." He reached out, roughly grasped the prisoner's hair, and jerked his head up for the king to see.

It was Silk. His face was pale, and a deep cut on one side of his forehead trickled blood down the side of his face.

"Behold the Drasnian spy Kheldar." Brill smirked. "I make a gift of him to your Majesty."

Taur Urgas began to smile then, his eyes lighting with a dreadful pleasure. "Splendid," he said. "You have the gratitude of your king, Kordoch. Your gift is beyond price." His smile grew broader. "Greetings, Prince Kheldar," he said, almost purring. "I've been waiting for the chance to see you again for a long time now. We have many old scores to settle, don't we?"

Silk seemed to stare back at the Murgo king, but Garion could not be sure if he were conscious enough even to comprehend what was happening to him.

"Abide here a bit, Prince of Drasnia," Taur Urgas gloated. "I'll want to give some special thought to your final entertainment, and I'll want to be sure you're fully awake to appreciate it. You deserve something exquisite, I think—probably lingering—and I certainly wouldn't want to disappoint you by rushing into it."

Barak and Garion slid back down into the gully with the gravel rattling down the steep bank around them.

"They've got Silk," Barak reported quietly. "Brill's there. It looks as if he and his men caught Silk while he was trying to leave. They turned him over to Taur Urgas."

Belgarath stood up slowly, a sick look on his face. "Is he—" He broke off.

"No," Barak answered. "He's still alive. It looks as if they roughed him up a little, but he seemed to be all right."

Belgarath let out a long, slow breath. "That's something, anyway."

"Taur Urgas seemed to know him," Barak continued. "It sounded as if Silk had done something that offended the king pretty seriously, and Taur Urgas looks like the kind of man who holds grudges."

"Are they holding him someplace where we can get to him?" Durnik asked.

"We couldn't tell," Garion answered. "They all talked for a while, and then several soldiers took him around behind that building down there. We couldn't see where they took him from there."

"The Murgo who runs the place said something about a pit," Barak added.

"We have to do something, father," Aunt Pol said.

"I know, Pol. We'll come up with something." He turned to Barak again. "How many soldiers did Taur Urgas bring with him?"

"A couple of regiments at least. They're all over the place down there."

"We can translocate him, father," Aunt Pol suggested.

"That's a long way to lift something, Pol," he objected. "Besides, we'd have to know exactly where he's being held."

"I'll find that out." She reached up to unfasten her cloak.

"Better wait until after dark," he told her. "There aren't many owls in Cthol Murgos, and you'd attract attention in the daylight. Did Taur Urgas have any Grolims with him?" he asked Garion.

"I think I saw a couple."

"That's going to complicate things. Translocation makes an awful noise. We'll have Taur Urgas right on our heels when we leave."

"Do you have any other ideas, father?" Aunt Pol asked.

"Let me work on it," he replied. "At any rate, we can't do anything until it gets dark."

A low whistle came from some distance down the gully.

"Who's that?" Barak's hand went to his sword.

"Ho, Alorns." It was a hoarse whisper.

"Methinks it is the Nadrak Yarblek," Mandorallen said.

"How did he know we're here?" Barak demanded.

There was the crunching sound of footsteps in the gravel, and Yarblek came around a bend in the gully. His fur cap was low over his face, and the collar of his felt overcoat was pulled up around his ears. "There you are," he said, sounding relieved.

"Are you alone?" Barak's voice was heavy with suspicion.

"Of course I'm alone," Yarblek snorted. "I told my servants to go on ahead. You certainly left in a hurry."

"We didn't feel like staying to greet Taur Urgas," Barak replied.

"It's probably just as well. I'd have had a great deal of trouble getting you out of that mess back there. The Murgo soldiers inspected every one of my people to be sure they were all Nadraks before they'd let me leave. Taur Urgas has Silk."

"We know," Barak said. "How did you find us?"

"You left the pegs pulled up at the back of my tent, and this hill's the closest cover on this side of the fair. I guessed which way you'd go, and you left a track here and there to confirm it." The Nadrak's coarse face was serious, and he showed no signs of his extended bout at the ale barrel. "We're going to have to get you out of here," he said. "Taur Urgas will be putting out patrols soon, and you're almost in his lap."

"We must rescue our companion first," Mandorallen told him.

"Silk? You'd better forget that. I'm afraid my old friend has switched his last pair of dice." He sighed. "I liked him, too."

"He's not dead, is he?" Durnik's voice was almost sick.

"Not yet," Yarblek replied, "but Taur Urgas plans to correct that when the sun comes up in the morning. I couldn't even get close enough to that pit to drop a dagger to him so he could open a vein. I'm afraid his last morning's going to be a bad one."

"Why are you trying to help us?" Barak asked bluntly.

"You'll have to excuse him, Yarblek," Aunt Pol said. "He's not familiar with Nadrak customs." She turned to Barak. "He invited you into his tent and offered you his ale. That makes you the same as his brother until sunrise tomorrow."

Yarblek smiled briefly at her. "You seem to know us quite well, girl," he observed. "I never got to see you dance, did I?"

"Perhaps another time," she replied.

"Perhaps so." He squatted and pulled a curved dagger from beneath his overcoat. He smoothed a patch of sand with his other hand and began sketching rapidly with his dagger point. "The Murgos are going to watch me," he said, "so I can't add half a dozen or so more people to my party without having them all over me. I think the best thing would be for you to wait here until dark. I'll move out to the east and stop a league or so on up the caravan track. As soon as it gets dark, you slip around and catch up with me. We'll work something out after that."

"Why did Taur Urgas tell you to leave?" Barak asked him.

Yarblek looked grim. "There's going to be a large accident tomorrow. Taur Urgas will immediately send an apology to Ran Borune—something about inexperienced troops chasing a band of brigands and mistaking honest merchants for bandits. He'll offer to pay reparation, and things will all be smoothed over. Pay is a magic word when you're dealing with Tolnedrans."

"He's going to massacre the whole camp?" Barak sounded stunned.

"That's his plan. He wants to clean all the westerners out of Cthol Murgos, and he seems to think that a few accidents will do the job for him."

Relg had been standing to one side, his large eyes lost in thought. Suddenly he stepped across the gully to where Yarblek's sketch was. He smoothed it out of the sand. "Can you show me exactly where this pit in which they're holding our friend is located?" he asked.

"It won't do you any good," Yarblek told him. "It's guarded by a dozen men. Silk's got quite a reputation, and Taur Urgas doesn't want him to get away."

"Just show me," Relg insisted.

Yarblek shrugged. "We're here on the north side." He roughed in the fair and the caravan route. "The supply station is here." He pointed with his dagger. "The pit's just beyond it at the base of that big hill on the south side."

"What kind of walls does it have?"

"Solid stone."

"Is it a natural fissure in the rock, or has it been dug out?"

"What difference does it make?"

"I need to know."

"I didn't see any tool marks," Yarblek replied, "and the opening at the top is irregular. It's probably just a natural hole."

Relg nodded. "And the hill behind it—is it rock or dirt?"

"Mostly rock. All of stinking Cthol Murgos is mostly rock."

Relg stood up. "Thank you," he said politely.

"You're not going to be able to tunnel through to him, if that's what you're thinking," Yarblek said, also standing and brushing the sand off the skirts of his overcoat. "You don't have time."

Belgarath's eyes were narrowed with thought. "Thanks, Yarblek," he said. "You've been a good friend."

"Anything to irritate the Murgos," the Nadrak said. "I wish I could do something for Silk."

"Don't give up on him yet."

"There isn't much hope, I'm afraid. I'd better be going. My people will wander off if I'm not there to watch them."

"Yarblek," Barak said, holding out his hand, "someday we'll have to get together and finish getting drunk."

Yarblek grinned at him and shook his hand. Then he turned and caught Aunt Pol in a rough embrace. "If you ever get bored with these Alorns, girl, my tent flap is always open to you."

"I'll keep that in mind, Yarblek," she replied demurely.

"Luck," Yarblek told them. "I'll wait for you until midnight." Then he turned and strode off down the gully.

"That's a good man there," Barak said. "I think I could actually get to like him."

"We must make plans for Prince Kheldar's rescue," Mandorallen declared, beginning to take his armor out of the packs strapped to one of the horses. "All else failing, we must of necessity resort to main force."

"You're backsliding again, Mandorallen," Barak said.

"That's already been taken care of," Belgarath told them.

Barak and Mandorallen stared at him.

"Put your armor away, Mandorallen," the old man instructed the knight. "You're not going to need it."

"Who's going to get Silk out of there?" Barak demanded.

"I am," Relg answered quietly. "How much longer is it going to be before it gets dark?"

"About an hour. Why?"

"I'll need some time to prepare myself."

"Have you got a plan?" Durnik asked.

Relg shrugged. "There isn't any need. We'll just circle around until we're behind that hill on the other side of the encampment. I'll go get our friend, and then we can leave."

"Just like that?" Barak asked.

"More or less. Please excuse me." Relg started to turn away.

"Wait a minute. Shouldn't Mandorallen and I go with you?"

"You wouldn't be able to follow me," Relg told him. He walked up the gully a short distance. After a moment, they could hear him muttering his prayers.

"Does he think he can pray him out of that pit?" Barak sounded disgusted.

"No," Belgarath replied. "He's going to go through the hill and carry Silk back out. That's why he was asking Yarblek all those questions."

"He's going to *what*?"

"You saw what he did at Prolgu—when he stuck his arm into the wall?"

"Well, yes, but—"

"It's quite easy for him, Barak."

"What about Silk? How's he going to pull *him* through the rock?"

"I don't really know. He seems quite sure he can do it, though."

"If it doesn't work, Taur Urgas is going to have Silk roasting over a slow fire first thing tomorrow morning. You know that, don't you?"

Belgarath nodded somberly.

Barak shook his head. "It's unnatural," he grumbled.

"Don't let it upset you so much," Belgarath advised.

The light began to fade, and Relg continued to pray, his voice rising and falling in formal cadences. When it was fully dark, he came back to where the others waited. "I'm ready," he said quietly. "We can leave now."

"We'll circle to the west," Belgarath told them. "We'll lead the horses and stay under cover as much as we can."

"It'll take us a couple hours," Durnik said.

"That's all right. It'll give the soldiers time to settle down. Pol, see what the Grolims Garion saw are up to."

She nodded, and Garion felt the gentle push of her probing mind. "It's all right, father," she stated after a few moments. "They're preoccupied. Taur Urgas has them conducting services for him."

"Let's go, then," the old man said.

They moved carefully down the gully, leading the horses. The night was murky, and the wind bit at them as they came out from between the protecting gravel banks. The plain to the east of the fair was dotted with a hundred fires whipping in the wind and marking the vast encampment of the army of Taur Urgas.

Relg grunted and covered his eyes with his hands.

"What's wrong?" Garion asked him.

"Their fires," Relg said. "They stab at my eyes."

"Try not to look at them."

"My God has laid a hard burden on me, Belgarion." Relg sniffed and wiped at his nose with his sleeve. "I'm not meant to be out in the open like this."

"You'd better have Aunt Pol give you something for that cold. It'll taste awful, but you'll feel better after you drink it."

"Perhaps," Relg said, still shielding his eyes from the dim flicker of the Murgo watch fires.

The hill on the south side of the fair was a low outcropping of granite. Although eons of constant wind had covered it for the most part with a thick layer of blown sand and dirt, the rock itself lay solid beneath its covering mantle. They stopped behind it, and Relg began carefully to brush the dirt from a sloping granite face.

"Wouldn't it be closer if you started over there?" Barak asked quietly.

"Too much dirt," Relg replied.

"Dirt or rock—what's the difference?"

"A great difference. You wouldn't understand." He leaned forward and put his tongue to the granite face, seeming actually to taste the rock. "This is going to take a while," he said. He drew himself up, began to pray, and slowly pushed himself directly into the rock.

Barak shuddered and quickly averted his eyes.

"What ails thee, my Lord?" Mandorallen asked.

"It makes me cold all over just watching that," Barak replied.

"Our new friend is perhaps not the best of companions," Mandorallen said, "but if this gift succeeds in freeing Prince Kheldar, I will embrace him gladly and call him brother."

"If it takes him very long, we're going to be awfully close to this spot when morning comes and Taur Urgas finds out that Silk's gone," Barak mentioned.

"We'll just have to wait and see what happens," Belgarath told him.

The night dragged by interminably. The wind moaned and whistled around the rocks on the flanks of the stony hill, and the sparse thornbushes rustled stiffly. They waited. A growing fear oppressed Garion as the hours passed. More and more, he became convinced that they had lost Relg as well as Silk. He felt that same sick emptiness he had felt when it had been necessary to leave the wounded Lelldorin behind back in Arendia. He realized, feeling a bit guilty about it, that he hadn't thought about Lelldorin in months. He began to wonder how well the young hothead had recovered from his wound—or even *if* he had recovered. His thoughts grew bleaker as the minutes crawled.

Then, with no warning—with not even a sound—Relg stepped out of the rock face he had entered hours before. Astride his broad back and clinging desperately to him was Silk. The rat-faced little man's eyes were wide with horror, and his hair seemed to be actually standing on end.

They all crowded around the two, trying to keep their jubilation quiet, conscious of the fact that they were virtually on top of an army of Murgos.

"I'm sorry it took so long," Relg said, jerking his shoulders uncomfortably until Silk finally slid off his back. "There's a different kind of rock in the middle of the hill. I had to make certain adjustments."

Silk stood, gasping and shuddering uncontrollably. Finally he turned on Relg. "Don't *ever* do that to me again," he blurted. "Not ever."

"What's the trouble?" Barak asked.

"I don't want to talk about it."

"I had feared we had lost thee, my friend," Mandorallen said, grasping Silk's hand.

"How did Brill catch you?" Barak asked.

"I was careless; I didn't expect him to be here. His men threw a net over me as I was galloping through a ravine. My horse fell and broke his neck."

"Hettar's not going to like that."

"I'll cut the price of the horse out of Brill's skin—someplace close to the bone, I think."

"Why does Taur Urgas hate you so much?" Barak asked curiously.

"I was in Rak Goska a few years ago. A Tolnedran agent made a few false charges against me—I never found out exactly why. Taur Urgas sent some soldiers out to arrest me. I didn't particularly feel like being arrested, so I argued with the soldiers a bit. Several of them died during the argument—those things happen once in a while. Unfortunately, one of the casualties was Taur Urgas' oldest son. The king of the Murgos took it personally. He's very narrow-minded sometimes."

Barak grinned. "He'll be terribly disappointed in the morning when he finds out that you've left."

"I know," Silk replied. "He'll probably take this part of Cthol Murgos apart stone by stone trying to find me."

"I think it's time we left," Belgarath agreed.

"I thought you'd never get around to that," Silk said.

CHAPTER TWENTY-THREE

They rode hard through the rest of the night and for most of the following day. By evening their horses were stumbling with exhaustion, and Garion was as numb with weariness as with the biting cold.

"We'll have to find shelter of some kind," Durnik said as they reined in to look for a place to spend the night. They had moved up out of the series of connecting valleys through which the South Caravan Route wound and had entered the ragged, barren wilderness of the mountains of central Cthol Murgos. It had grown steadily colder as they had climbed into that vast jumble of rock and sand, and the endless wind moaned among the treeless crags. Durnik's face was creased with fatigue, and the gritty dust that drove before the wind had settled into the creases, etching them deeper. "We can't spend the night in the open," he declared. "Not with this wind."

"Go that way," Relg said, pointing toward a rockfall on the steep slope they were climbing. His eyes were squinted almost shut, though the sky was still overcast and the fading daylight was pale. "There's shelter there—a cave."

They had all begun to look at Relg in a somewhat different light since his rescue of Silk. His demonstration that he could, when necessary, take decisive action made him seem less an encumbrance and more like a companion. Belgarath had finally convinced him that he could pray on horseback just as well as he could on his knees, and his frequent devotions no longer interrupted their journey. His praying thus had become less an inconvenience and more a personal idiosyncrasy—somewhat like Mandorallen's archaic speech or Silk's sardonic witticisms.

"You're sure there's a cave?" Barak asked him.

Relg nodded. "I can feel it."

They turned and rode toward the rockfall. As they drew closer, Relg's eagerness became more obvious. He pushed his horse into the lead and nudged the tired beast into a trot, then a canter. At the edge of the rockslide, he swung down from his horse, stepped behind a large boulder, and disappeared.

"It looks as if he knew what he was talking about," Durnik observed. "I'll be glad to get out of this wind."

The opening to the cave was narrow, and it took some pushing and dragging to persuade the horses to squeeze through; but once they were inside, the cave widened out into a large, low-ceilinged chamber.

Durnik looked around with approval. "Good place." He unfastened his axe from the back of his saddle. "We'll need firewood."

"I'll help you," Garion said.

"I'll go, too," Silk offered quickly. The little man was looking around at the stone walls and ceiling nervously, and he seemed obviously relieved as soon as the three of them were back outside.

"What's wrong?" Durnik asked him.

"After last night, closed-in places make me a little edgy," Silk replied.

"What was it like?" Garion asked him curiously. "Going through stone, I mean?"

Silk shuddered. "It was hideous. We actually seeped into the rock. I could feel it sliding through me."

"It got you out, though," Durnik reminded him.

"I think I'd almost rather have stayed." Silk shuddered again. "Do we have to talk about it?"

Firewood was difficult to find on that barren mountainside and even more difficult to cut. The tough, springy thornbushes resisted the blows of Durnik's axe tenaciously. After an hour, as darkness began to close in on them, they had gathered only three very scanty armloads.

"Did you see anybody?" Barak asked as they reentered the cave.

"No," Silk replied.

"Taur Urgas is probably looking for you."

"I'm sure of it." Silk looked around. "Where's Relg?"

"He went back into the cave to rest his eyes," Belgarath told him. "He found water—ice actually. We'll have to thaw it before we can water the horses."

Durnik's fire was tiny, and he fed it with twigs and small bits of wood, trying to conserve their meager fuel supply. It proved to be an uncomfortable night.

In the morning Aunt Pol looked critically at Relg. "You don't seem to be coughing anymore," she told him. "How do you feel?"

"I'm fine," he replied, being careful not to look directly at her. The fact that she was a woman seemed to make him terribly uncomfortable, and he tried to avoid her as much as possible.

"What happened to that cold you had?"

"I don't think it could go through the rock. It was gone when I brought him out of the hillside last night."

She looked at him gravely. "I'd never thought of that," she mused. "No one's ever been able to cure a cold before."

"A cold isn't really that serious a thing, Polgara," Silk told her with a pained look. "I'll guarantee you that sliding through rock is never going to be a popular cure."

It took them four days to cross the mountains to reach the vast basin Belgarath referred to as the Wasteland of Murgos and another half day to make their way down the steep basalt face to the black sand of the floor.

"What hath caused this huge depression?" Mandorallen asked, looking around at the barren expanse of scab-rock, black sand and dirty gray salt flats.

"There was an inland sea here once," Belgarath replied. "When Torak cracked the world, the upheaval broke away the eastern edge and all the water drained out."

"That must have been something to see," Barak said.

"We had other things on our minds just then."

"What's that?" Garion asked in alarm, pointing at something sticking out of the sand just ahead of them. The thing had a huge head with a long, sharp-toothed snout. Its eye sockets, as big as buckets, seemed to stare balefully at them.

"I don't think it has a name," Belgarath answered calmly. "They lived in the sea before the water escaped. They've all been dead now for thousands of years."

As they passed the dead sea monster, Garion could see that it was only a skeleton. Its ribs were as big as the rafters of a barn, and its vast, bleached skull larger than a horse. The vacant eye sockets watched them as they rode past.

Mandorallen, dressed once again in full armor, stared at the skull. "A fearsome beast," he murmured.

"Look at the size of the teeth," Barak said in an awed voice. "It could bite a man in two with one snap."

"That happened a few times," Belgarath told him, "until people learned to avoid this place."

They had moved only a few leagues out into the wasteland when the wind picked up, scouring along the black dunes under the slate-gray sky. The sand began to shift and move and then, as the wind grew even stronger, it began to whip off the tops of the dunes, stinging their faces.

"We'd better take shelter," Belgarath shouted over the shrieking wind. "This sandstorm's going to get worse as we move out farther from the mountains."

"Are there any caves around?" Durnik asked Relg.

Relg shook his head. "None that we can use. They're all filled with sand."

"Over there." Barak pointed at a pile of scab-rock rising from the edge of a salt flat. "If we go to the leeward side, it'll keep the wind off us."

"No," Belgarath shouted. "We have to stay to the windward. The sand will pile up at the back. We could be buried alive."

They reached the rock pile and dismounted. The wind tore at their clothing, and the sand billowed across the wasteland like a vast, black cloud.

"This is poor shelter, Belgarath," Barak roared, his beard whipping about his shoulders. "How long is this likely to last?"

"A day—two days—sometimes as long as a week."

Durnik had bent to pick up a piece of broken scab-rock. He looked at it carefully, turning it over in his hands. "It's fractured into square pieces," he said, holding it up. "It'll stack well. We can build a wall to shelter us."

"That'll take quite a while," Barak objected.

"Did you have something else to do?"

By evening they had the wall up to shoulder height, and by anchoring the tents to the top of it and higher up on the side of the rock-pile, they were able to get in out of the worst of the wind. It was crowded, since they had to shelter the horses as well, but at least it was out of the storm.

They huddled in their cramped shelter for two days with the wind shrieking insanely around them and the taut tent canvas drumming overhead. Then, when the wind finally blew itself out and the black sand began to settle slowly, the silence seemed almost oppressive.

As they emerged, Relg glanced up once, then covered his face and sank to his knees, praying desperately. The clearing sky overhead was a bright, chilly blue. Garion moved over to stand beside the praying fanatic. "It'll be all right, Relg," he told him. He reached out his hand without thinking.

"Don't touch me," Relg said and continued to pray.

Silk stood, beating the dust and sand out of his clothing. "Do these storms come up often?" he asked.

"It's the season for them," Belgarath replied.

"Delightful," Silk said sourly.

Then a deep rumbling sound seemed to come from deep in the earth beneath them, and the ground heaved. "Earthquake!" Belgarath warned sharply. "Get the horses out of there!"

Durnik and Barak dashed back inside the shelter and led the horses out from behind the trembling wall and onto the salt flat.

After several moments the heaving subsided. "Is Ctuchik doing that?" Silk demanded. "Is he going to fight us with earthquakes and sandstorms?"

Belgarath shook his head. "No. Nobody's strong enough to do that. That's what's causing it." He pointed to the south. Far across the wasteland they could make out a line of dark peaks. A thick plume was rising from one of them, towering into the air, boiling up in great black billows as it rose. "Volcano," the old man said. "Probably the same one that erupted last summer and dropped all the ash on Sthiss Tor."

"A fire-mountain?" Barak rumbled, staring at the great cloud that was growing up out of the mountaintop. "I've never seen one before."

"That's fifty leagues away, Belgarath," Silk stated. "Would it make the earth shake even here?"

The old man nodded. "The earth's all one piece, Silk. The force that's causing that eruption is enormous. It's bound to cause a few ripples. I think we'd better get moving. Taur Urgas' patrols will be out looking for us again, now that the sandstorm's blown over."

"Which way do we go?" Durnik asked, looking around, trying to get his bearings.

"That way." Belgarath pointed toward the smoking mountain.

"I was afraid you were going to say that," Barak grumbled.

They rode at a gallop for the rest of the day, pausing only to rest the horses. The dreary wasteland seemed to go on forever. The black sand had shifted and piled into new dunes during the sandstorm, and the thick-crusted salt flats had been scoured by the wind until they were nearly white. They passed a number of the huge, bleached skeletons of the sea monsters which had once inhabited this inland ocean. The bony shapes appeared almost to be swimming up out of the black sand, and the cold, empty eye sockets seemed somehow hungry as they galloped past.

They stopped for the night beside another shattered outcropping of scab-rock. Although the wind had died, it was still bitterly cold, and firewood was scanty.

The next morning as they set out again, Garion began to smell a strange, foul odor. "What's that stink?" he asked.

"The Tarn of Cthok," Belgarath replied. "It's all that's left of the sea that used to be here. It would have dried out centuries ago, but it's fed by underground springs."

"It smells like rotten eggs," Barak said.

"There's quite a bit of sulfur in the ground water around here. I wouldn't drink from the lake."

"I wasn't planning to." Barak wrinkled his nose.

The Tarn of Cthok was a vast, shallow pond filled with oily-looking water that reeked like all the dead fish in the world. Its surface steamed in the icy air, and the wisps of steam gagged them with the dreadful stink. When they reached the southern tip of the lake, Belgarath signaled for a halt. "This next stretch is dangerous," he told them soberly. "Don't let your horses wander. Be sure you stay on solid rock. Ground that looks firm quite often won't be, and there are some other things we'll need to watch out for. Keep your eyes on me and do what I do. When I stop, you stop. When I run, you run." He looked thoughtfully at Relg. The Ulgo had bound another cloth across his eyes, partially to keep out the light and partially to hide the expanse of the sky above him.

"I'll lead his horse, Grandfather," Garion offered.

Belgarath nodded. "It's the only way, I suppose."

"He's going to have to get over that eventually," Barak said.

"Maybe, but this isn't the time or place for it. Let's go." The old man moved forward at a careful walk.

The region ahead of them steamed and smoked as they approached it. They passed a large pool of gray mud that bubbled and fumed, and beyond it a sparkling spring of clear water, boiling merrily and cascading a scalding brook down into the mud. "At least it's warmer," Silk observed.

Mandorallen's face was streaming perspiration beneath his heavy helmet. "Much warmer," he agreed.

Belgarath had been riding slowly, his head turned slightly as he listened intently. "Stop!" he said sharply.

They all reined in.

Just ahead of them another pool suddenly erupted as a dirty gray geyser of liquid mud spurted thirty feet into the air. It continued to spout for several minutes, then gradually subsided.

"Now!" Belgarath barked. "Run!" He kicked his horse's flanks, and they galloped past the still-heaving surface of the pool, the hooves of their horses splashing in the hot mud that had splattered across their path. When they had passed, the old man slowed again and once more rode with his ear cocked toward the ground.

"What's he listening for?" Barak asked Polgara.

"The geysers make a certain noise just before they erupt," she answered.

"I didn't hear anything."

"You don't know what to listen for."

Behind them the mud geyser spouted again.

"Garion!" Aunt Pol snapped as he turned to look back at the mud plume rising from the pool. "Watch where you're going!"

He jerked his eyes back. The ground ahead of him looked quite ordinary.

"Back up," she told him. "Durnik, get the reins of Relg's horse."

Durnik took the reins, and Garion began to turn his mount.

"I said to back up," she repeated.

Garion's horse put one front hoof on the seemingly solid ground, and the hoof sank out of sight. The horse scrambled back and stood trembling as Garion held him in tightly. Then, carefully, step by step, Garion backed to the solid rock of the path they followed.

"Quicksand," Silk said with a sharp intake of his breath.

"It's all around us," Aunt Pol agreed. "Don't wander off the path—any of you."

Silk stared with revulsion at the hoofprint of Garion's horse, disappearing on the surface of the quicksand. "How deep is it?"

"Deep enough," Aunt Pol replied.

They moved on, carefully picking their way through the quagmires and quicksand, stopping often as more geysers—some of mud, some of frothy, boiling water—shot high into the air. By late afternoon, when they reached a low ridge of hard, solid rock beyond the steaming bog, they were all exhausted from the effort of the concentration it had taken to pass through the hideous region.

"Do we have to go through any more like that?" Garion asked.

"No," Belgarath replied. "It's just around the southern edges of the Tarn."

"Can one not go around it, then?" Mandorallen inquired.

"It's much longer if you do, and the bog helps to discourage pursuit."

"What's that?" Relg cried suddenly.

"What's what?" Barak asked him.

"I heard something just ahead—a kind of click, like two pebbles knocking together."

Garion felt a quick kind of wave against his face, almost like an unseen ripple in the air, and he knew that Aunt Pol was searching ahead of them with her mind.

"Murgos!" she said.

"How many?' Belgarath asked her.

"Six—and a Grolim. They're waiting for us just behind the ridge."

"Only six?" Mandorallen said, sounding a little disappointed.

Barak grinned tightly. "Light entertainment."

"You're getting to be as bad as he is," Silk told the big Cherek.

"Thinkest thou that we might need some plan, my Lord?" Mandorallen asked Barak.

"Not really," Barak replied. "Not for just six. Let's go spring their trap."

The two warriors moved into the lead, unobtrusively loosening their swords in their scabbards.

"Has the sun gone down yet?" Relg asked Garion.

"It's just setting."

Relg pulled the binding from around his eyes and tugged down the dark veil. He winced and squinted his large eyes almost shut.

"You're going to hurt them," Garion told him. "You ought to leave them covered until it gets dark."

"I might need them," Relg said as they rode up the ridge toward the waiting Murgo ambush.

The Murgos gave no warning. They rode out from behind a large pile of black rock and galloped directly at Mandorallen and Barak, their swords swinging. The two warriors, however, were waiting for them and reacted without that instant of frozen surprise which might have made the attack successful. Mandorallen swept his sword from its sheath even as he drove his warhorse directly into the mount of one of the charging Murgos. He rose in his stirrups and swung a mighty blow downward, splitting the Murgo's head with his heavy blade. The horse, knocked off his feet by the impact, fell heavily backward on top of his dying rider. Barak, also charging at the attackers, chopped another Murgo out of the saddle with three massive blows, spattering bright red blood on the sand and rock around them.

A third Murgo sidestepped Mandorallen's charge and struck at the knight's back, but his blade clanged harmlessly off the steel armor. The Murgo desperately raised his sword to strike again, but stiffened and slid from his saddle as Silk's skillfully thrown dagger sank into his neck, just below the ear.

A dark-robed Grolim in his polished steel mask had stepped out from behind the rocks. Garion could quite clearly feel the priest's exultation turning to dismay as Barak and Mandorallen systematically chopped his warriors to pieces. The Grolim drew himself up, and Garion sensed that he was gathering his Will to strike. But it was too late. Relg had already closed on him. The zealot's heavy shoulders surged as he grasped the front of the Grolim's robe with his knotted hands. Without apparent effort he lifted and pushed the man back against the flattened face of a house-sized boulder.

At first it appeared that Relg only intended to hold the Grolim pinned against the rock until the others could assist him with the struggling captive, but there was a subtle difference. The set of his shoulders indicated that he had not finished the action he had begun with lifting the man from his feet.

The Grolim hammered at Relg's head and shoulders with his fists, but Relg pushed at him inexorably. The rock against which the Grolim was pinned seemed to shimmer slightly around him.

"Relg! No!" Silk's cry was strangled.

The dark-robed Grolim began to sink into the stone face, his arms flailing wildly as Relg pushed him in with a dreadful slowness. As he went deeper into the rock, the surface closed smoothly over him. Relg continued to push, his arms sliding into the stone as he sank the Grolim deeper and deeper. The priest's two protruding hands continued to twitch and writhe, even after the rest of his body had been totally submerged. Then Relg drew his arms out of the stone, leaving the Grolim behind. The two hands sticking out of the rock opened once in mute supplication, then stiffened into dead claws.

Behind him, Garion could hear the muffled sound of Silk's retching.

Barak and Mandorallen had by now engaged two of the remaining Murgos, and the sound of clashing sword blades rang in the chill air. The last Murgo, his eyes wide with fright, wheeled his horse and bolted. Without a word, Durnik jerked his axe free of his saddle and galloped after him. Instead of striking the man down, however, Durnik cut across in front of his opponent's horse, turning him, driving him back. The panic-stricken Murgo flailed at his horse's flanks with the flat of his sword, turning away from the grim-faced smith, and plunged at a dead run back up over the ridge with Durnik close behind him.

The last two Murgos were down by then, and Barak and Mandorallen, both wild-eyed with the exultation of battle, were looking around for more enemies. "Where's that last one?" Barak demanded.

"Durnik's chasing him," Garion said.

"We can't let him get away. He'll bring others."

"Durnik's going to take care of it," Belgarath told him.

Barak fretted. "Durnik's a good man, but he's not really a warrior. Maybe I'd better go help him."

From beyond the ridge there was a sudden scream of horror, then another. The third cut off quite suddenly, and there was silence.

After several minutes, Durnik came riding back alone, his face somber. "What happened?" Barak asked. "He didn't get away, did he?"

Durnik shook his head. "I chased him into the bog, and he ran into some quicksand."

"Why didn't you cut him down with your axe?"

"I don't really like hitting people," Durnik replied.

Silk was staring at Durnik, his face still ashen. "So you just chased him into quicksand instead and then stood there and watched him go down? Durnik, that's monstrous!"

"Dead is dead," Durnik told him with uncharacteristic bluntness. "When it's over, it doesn't really matter how it happened, does it?" He looked a bit thoughtful. "I *am* sorry about the horse, though."

The next morning they followed the ridgeline that angled off toward the east. The wintry sky above them was an icy blue, and there was no warmth to the sun. Relg kept his eyes veiled against the light and muttered prayers as he rode to ward off his panic. Several times they saw dust clouds far out on the desolation of sand and salt flats to the south, but they were unable to determine whether the clouds were caused by Murgo patrols or vagrant winds.

About noon, the wind shifted and blew in steadily from the south. A ponderous cloud, black as ink, blotted out the jagged line of peaks lying along the southern horizon. It moved toward them with a kind of ominous inexorability, and flickers of lightning glimmered in its sooty underbelly.

"That's a bad storm coming, Belgarath," Barak rumbled, staring at the cloud.

Belgarath shook his head. "It's not a storm," he replied. "It's ashfall. That volcano out there is erupting again, and the wind's blowing the ash this way."

Barak made a face, then shrugged. "At least we won't have to worry about being seen, once it starts," he said.

"The Grolims won't be looking for us with their eyes, Barak," Aunt Pol reminded him.

Belgarath scratched at his beard. "We'll have to take steps to deal with that, I suppose."

"This is a large group to shield, father," Aunt Pol pointed out, "and that's not even counting the horses."

"I think you can manage it, Pol. You were always very good at it."

"I can hold up my side as long as you can hold up yours, Old Wolf."

"I'm afraid I'm not going to be able to help you, Pol. Ctuchik himself is looking for us. I've felt him several times already and I'm going to have to concentrate on him. If he decides to strike at us, he'll come very fast. I'll have to be ready for him, and I can't do that if I'm all tangled up in a shield."

"I can't do it alone, father," she protested. "Nobody can enclose this many men and horses without help."

"Garion can help you."

"Me?" Garion jerked his eyes off the looming cloud to stare at his grandfather.

"He's never done it before, father," Aunt Pol pointed out.

"He's going to have to learn sometime."

"This is hardly the time or place for experimentation."

"He'll do just fine. Walk him through it a time or two until he gets the hang of it."

"Exactly what is it I'm supposed to do?" Garion asked apprehensively.

Aunt Pol gave Belgarath a hard look and then turned to Garion. "I'll show you, dear," she said. "The first thing you have to do is stay calm. It really isn't all that difficult."

"But you just said—"

"Never mind what I said, dear. Just pay attention."

"What do you want me to do?" he asked doubtfully.

"The first thing is to relax," she replied, "and think about sand and rock."

"That's all?"

"Just do that first. Concentrate."

He thought about sand and rock.

"No, Garion, not *white* sand. *Black* sand—like the sand all around us."

"You didn't say that."

"I didn't think I had to."

Belgarath started to laugh.

"Do *you* want to do this, father?" she demanded crossly. Then she turned back to Garion. "Do it again, dear. Try to get it right this time."

He fixed it in his mind.

"That's better," she told him. "Now, as soon as you get sand and rock firmly in your mind, I want you to sort of push the idea out in a half-circle so that it covers your entire right side. I'll take care of the left."

He strained with it. It was the hardest thing he had ever done.

"Don't push quite so hard, Garion. You're wrinkling it, and it's very hard for me to make the seams match when you do that. Just keep it steady and smooth."

"I'm sorry." He smoothed it out.

"How does it look, father?" she asked the old man.

Garion felt a tentative push against the idea he was holding.

"Not bad, Pol," Belgarath replied. "Not bad at all. The boy's got talent."

"Just exactly what are we doing?" Garion asked. In spite of the chill, he felt sweat standing out on his forehead.

"You're making a shield," Belgarath told him. "You enclose yourself in the idea of sand and rock, and it merges with the real sand and rock all around us. When Grolims go looking for things with their minds, they're looking for men and horses. They'll sweep right past us, because all they'll see here is more sand and more rock."

"That's all there is to it?" Garion was quite pleased with how simple it was.

"There's a bit more, dear," Aunt Pol said. "We're going to extend it now so that it covers all of us. Go out slowly, a few feet at a time."

That was much less simple. He tore the fabric of the idea several times before he got it pushed out as far as Aunt Pol wanted it. He felt a strange merging of his mind with hers along the center of the idea where the two sides joined.

"I think we've got it now, father," Aunt Pol said.

"I told you he could do it, Pol."

The purple-black cloud was rolling ominously up the sky toward them, and faint rumbles of thunder growled along its leading edge.

"If that ash is anything like what it was in Nyissa, we're going to be wandering blind out here, Belgarath," Barak said.

"Don't worry about it," the sorcerer replied. "I've got a lock on Rak Cthol. The Grolims aren't the only ones who can locate things that way. Let's move out."

They started along the ridge again as the cloud blotted out the sky overhead. The thunder shocks were a continuous rumble, and lightning seethed in the boiling cloud. The lightning had an arid, crackling quality about it as the billions of tiny particles seethed and churned, building enormous static discharges. Then the first specks of drifting ash began to settle down through the icy air, as Belgarath led them down off the ridge and out onto the sand flats.

By the end of the first hour, Garion found that holding the image in his mind had grown easier. It was no longer necessary to concentrate all his attention on it as it had been at first. By the end of the second hour, it had become no more than tedious. To relieve the boredom of it as they rode through the thickening ashfall, he thought about one of the huge skeletons they had passed when they had first entered the wasteland. Painstakingly he constructed one of them and placed it in the image he was holding. On the whole he thought it looked rather good, and it gave him something to do.

"Garion," Aunt Pol said crisply, "please don't try to be creative."

"What?"

"Just stick to sand. The skeleton's very nice, but it looks a bit peculiar with only one side."

"One side?"

"There wasn't a skeleton on my side of the image—just yours. Keep it simple, Garion. Don't embellish."

They rode on, their faces muffled to keep the choking ash out of their mouths and noses. Garion felt a tentative push against the image he was holding. It seemed to flutter against his mind, feeling almost like the wriggling touch of the tadpoles he had once caught in the pond at Faldor's farm.

"Hold it steady, Garion," Aunt Pol warned. "That's a Grolim."

"Did he see us?"

"No. There—he's moving on now." And the fluttering touch was gone.

They spent the night in another of the piles of broken rock that dotted the wasteland. Durnik once again devised a kind of low, hollowed-out shelter of piled rock and anchored-down tent cloth. They took a cold supper of bread and dried meat and built no fire. Garion and Aunt Pol took turns holding the image of empty sand over them like an umbrella. He discovered that it was much easier when they weren't moving.

The ash was still falling the next morning, but the sky was no longer the inky black it had been the day before. "I think it's thinning out, Belgarath," Silk said as they saddled their horses. "If it blows over, we'll have to start dodging patrols again."

The old man nodded. "We'd better hurry," he agreed. "There's a place I know of where we can hide—about five miles north of the city. I'd like to

get there before this ashfall subsides. You can see for ten leagues in any direction from the walls of Rak Cthol."

"Are the walls so high, then?" Mandorallen asked.

"Higher than you can imagine."

"Higher even than the walls of Vo Mimbre?"

"Ten times higher—fifty times higher. You'll have to see it to
understand."

They rode hard that day. Garion and Aunt Pol held their shield of
thought in place, but the searching touches of the Grolims came more frequently now. Several times the push against Garion's mind was very strong
and came without warning.

"They know what we're doing, father," Aunt Pol told the old man.
"They're trying to penetrate the screen."

"Hold it firm," he replied. "You know what to do if one of them breaks
through."

She nodded, her face grim.

"Warn the boy."

She nodded again, then turned to Garion. "Listen to me carefully, dear,"
she said gravely. "The Grolims are trying to take us by surprise. The best
shield in the world can be penetrated if you hit it quickly enough and hard
enough. If one of them does manage to break through, I'm going to tell you
to stop. When I say stop, I want you to erase the image immediately and put
your mind completely away from it."

"I don't understand."

"You don't have to. Just do exactly as I say. If I tell you to stop, pull your
thought out of contact with mine instantly. I'll be doing something that's
very dangerous, and I don't want you getting hurt."

"Can't I help?"

"No, dear. Not this time."

They rode on. The ashfall grew even thinner, and the sky overhead
turned a hazy, yellowish blue. The ball of the sun, pale and round like a full
moon, appeared not far above the southwestern horizon.

"Garion, stop!"

What came was not a push but a sharp stab. Garion gasped and jerked
his mind away, throwing the image of sand from him. Aunt Pol stiffened, and
her eyes were blazing. Her hand flicked a short gesture, and she spoke a single
word. The surge Garion felt as her Will unleashed was overpowering. With
a momentary dismay, he realized that his mind was still linked to hers. The
merging that had held the image together was too strong, too complete to
break. He felt himself drawn with her as their still-joined minds lashed out
like a whip. They flashed back along the faint trail of thought that had
stabbed at the shield and they found its origin. They touched another mind,
a mind filled with the exultation of discovery. Then, sure of her target now,
Aunt Pol struck with the full force of her will. The mind they had touched
flinched back, trying to break off the contact, but it was too late for that now.
Garion could feel the other mind swelling, expanding unbearably. Then it

suddenly burst, exploding into gibbering insanity, shattering as horror upon horror overwhelmed it. There was flight then, blind shrieking flight across dark stones of some kind, a flight with the single thought of a dreadful, final escape. The stones were gone, and there was a terrible sense of falling from some incalculable height. Garion wrenched his mind away from it.

"I told you to get clear," Aunt Pol snapped at him.

"I couldn't help it. I couldn't get loose."

"What happened?" Silk's face was startled.

"A Grolim broke through," she replied.

"Did he see us?"

"For a moment. It doesn't matter. He's dead now."

"You killed him? How?"

"He forgot to defend himself. I followed his thought back."

"He went crazy," Garion said in a choked voice, still filled with the horror of the encounter. "He jumped off something very high. He wanted to jump. It was the only way he could escape from what was happening to him." Garion felt sick.

"It was awfully noisy, Pol," Belgarath said with a pained expression. "You haven't been that clumsy in years."

"I had this passenger." She gave Garion an icy look.

"It wasn't my fault," Garion protested. "You were holding on so tight I couldn't break loose. You had us all tied together."

"You do that sometimes, Pol," Belgarath told her. "The contact gets a little too personal, and you seem to want to take up permanent residence. It has to do with love, I imagine."

"Do you have any idea what they're talking about?" Barak asked Silk.

"I wouldn't even want to guess."

Aunt Pol was looking thoughtfully at Garion. "Perhaps it was my fault," she admitted finally.

"You're going to have to let go someday, Pol," Belgarath said gravely.

"Perhaps—but not just yet."

"You'd better put the screen back up," the old man suggested. "They know we're out here now, and there'll be others looking for us."

She nodded. "Think about sand again, Garion."

The ash continued to settle as they rode through the afternoon, obscuring less and less with each passing mile. They were able to make out the shapes of the jumbled piles of rock around them and a few rounded spires of basalt thrusting up out of the sand. As they approached another of the low rock ridges that cut across the wasteland at regular intervals, Garion saw something dark and enormously high looming in the haze ahead.

"We can hide here until dark," Belgarath said, dismounting behind the ridge.

"Are we there?" Durnik asked, looking around.

"That's Rak Cthol." The old man pointed at the ominous shadow.

Barak squinted at it. "I thought that was just a mountain."

"It is. Rak Cthol's built on top of it."

"It's almost like Prolgu, then, isn't it?"

"The locations are similar, but Ctuchik the magician lives here. That makes it quite different from Prolgu."

"I thought Ctuchik was a sorcerer," Garion said, puzzled. "Why do you keep calling him a magician?"

"It's a term of contempt," Belgarath replied. "It's considered a deadly insult in our particular society."

They picketed their horses among some large rocks on the back side of the ridge and climbed the forty or so feet to the top, where they took cover to watch and wait for nightfall.

As the settling ash thinned even more, the peak began to emerge from the haze. It was not so much a mountain as a rock pinnacle towering up out of the wasteland. Its base, surrounded by a mass of shattered rubble, was fully five miles around, and its sides were sheer and black as night.

"How high doth it reach?" Mandorallen asked, his voice dropping almost unconsciously into a half-whisper.

"Somewhat more than a mile," Belgarath replied.

A steep causeway rose sharply from the floor of the wasteland to encircle the upper thousand or so feet of the black tower. "'I imagine that took a while to build," Barak noted.

"About a thousand years," Belgarath answered. "While it was under construction, the Murgos bought every slave the Nyissans could put their hands on."

"A grim business," Mandorallen observed.

"It's a grim place," Belgarath agreed.

As the chill breeze blew off the last of the haze, the shape of the city perched atop the crag began to emerge. The walls were as black as the sides of the pinnacle, and black turrets jutted out from them, seemingly at random. Dark spires rose within the walls, stabbing up into the evening sky like spears. There was a foreboding, evil air about the black city of the Grolims. It perched, brooding, atop its peak, looking out over the savage wasteland of sand, rock, and sulfur-reeking bogs that encircled it. The sun, sinking into the banks of cloud and ash along the jagged western rim of the wasteland, bathed the grim fortress above them in a sooty crimson glow. The walls of Rak Cthol seemed to bleed. It was as if all the blood that had been spilled on all the altars of Torak since the world began had been gathered together to stain the dread city above them and that all the oceans of the world would not be enough to wash it clean again.

CHAPTER TWENTY-FIVE

As the last trace of light slid from the sky, they moved carefully down off the ridge and crossed the ash-covered sand toward the rock tower looming above them. When they reached the shattered scree at its base, they dismounted, left the horses with Durnik and climbed up the steeply sloped rubble to the rock face of the basalt pinnacle that blotted out the stars. Although Relg had been shuddering and hiding his eyes a moment before, he moved almost eagerly now. He stopped and then carefully placed his hands and forehead against the icy rock.

"Well?" Belgarath asked after a moment, his voice hushed but carrying a note of dreadful concern. "Was I right? Are there caves?"

"There are open spaces," Relg replied. "They're a long way inside."

"Can you get to them?"

"There's no point. They don't go anywhere. They're just closed-in hollows."

"Now what?" Silk asked.

"I don't know," Belgarath admitted, sounding terribly disappointed.

"Let's try a little farther around," Relg suggested. "I can feel some echoes here. There might be something off in that direction." He pointed.

"I want one thing clearly understood right here and now," Silk announced, planting his feet firmly. "I'm not going to go through any more rock. If there's going to be any of that, I'll stay behind."

"We'll come up with something," Barak told him.

Silk shook his head stubbornly. "No passing through rock," he declared adamantly.

Relg was already moving along the face, his fingers lightly touching the basalt. "It's getting stronger," he told them. "It's large and it goes up." He moved on another hundred yards or so, and they followed, watching him intently. "It's right through here," he said finally, patting the rock face with one hand. "It might be the one we want. Wait here." He put his hands against the rock and pushed them slowly into the basalt.

"I can't stand this," Silk said, turning his back quickly. "Let me know once he's inside."

With a kind of dreadful determination, Relg pushed his way into the rock.

"Is he gone yet?" Silk asked.

"He's going in," Barak replied clinically. "Only half of him's still sticking out."

"Please, Barak, don't tell me about it."

"Was it really *that* bad?" the big man asked.

"You have no idea. You have absolutely no idea." The rat-faced man was shivering uncontrollably.

They waited in the chill darkness for half an hour or more. Somewhere high above them there was a scream.

"What was that cry?" Mandorallen asked.

"The Grolims are busy," Belgarath answered grimly. "It's the season of the wounding—when the Orb burned Torak's hand and face. A large number of sacrifices are called for at this time of year—usually slaves. Torak doesn't seem to insist on Angarak blood. As long as it's human, it seems to satisfy him."

There was a faint sound of steps somewhere along the cliff, and a few moments later Relg rejoined them. "I found it," he told them. "The opening's about a half-mile farther along. It's partially blocked."

"Does it go all the way up?" Belgarath demanded.

Relg shrugged. "It goes up. I can't say how far. The only way to find out for sure is to follow it. The whole series of caves is fairly extensive, though."

"Do we really have any choice, father?" Aunt Pol asked.

"No. I suppose not."

"I'll go get Durnik," Silk said. He turned and disappeared into the darkness.

The rest of them followed Relg until they reached a small hole in the rock face just above the tumbled scree. "We'll have to move some of this rubble if we're going to get your animals inside," he told them.

Barak bent and lifted a large stone block. He staggered under its weight and dropped it to one side with a clatter.

"Quietly!" Belgarath told him.

"Sorry," Barak mumbled.

For the most part, the stones were not large, but there were a great many of them. When Silk and Durnik joined them, they all fell to clearing the rubble out of the cave mouth. It took them nearly an hour to remove enough rock to make it possible for the horses to squeeze through.

"I wish Hettar was here," Barak grunted, putting his shoulder against the rump of a balky packhorse.

"Talk to him, Barak," Silk suggested.

"I *am* talking."

"Try it without all the swear words."

"There's going to be some climbing involved," Relg told them after they had pushed the last horse inside and stood in the total blackness of the cave. "As nearly as I can tell, the galleries run vertically, so we'll have to climb from level to level."

Mandorallen leaned against one of the walls, and his armor clinked.

"That's not going to work," Belgarath told him. "You wouldn't be able to climb in armor anyway. Leave it here with the horses, Mandorallen."

The knight sighed and began removing his armor.

A faint glow appeared as Relg mixed powders in a wooden bowl from two leather pouches he carried inside his mail shirt.

"That's better," Barak approved, "but wouldn't a torch be brighter?"

"Much brighter," Relg agreed, "but then I wouldn't be able to see. This will give you enough light to see where you're going."

"Let's get started," Belgarath said.

Relg handed the glowing bowl to Barak and turned to lead them up a dark gallery.

After they had gone a few hundred yards, they came to a steep slope of rubble rising up into darkness. "I'll look," Relg said and scrambled up the slope out of sight. After a moment or so, they heard a peculiar popping sound, and tiny fragments of rock showered down onto the rubble from above. "Come up now," Relg's voice came to them.

Carefully they climbed the rubble until they reached a sheer wall. "To your right," Relg said, still above them. "You'll find some holes in the rock you can use to climb up."

They found the holes, quite round and about six inches deep. "How did you make these?" Durnik asked, examining one of the holes.

"It's a bit difficult to explain," Relg replied. "There's a ledge up here. It leads to another gallery."

One by one they climbed the rock face to join Relg on the ledge. As he had told them, the ledge led to a gallery that angled sharply upward. They followed it toward the center of the peak, passing several passageways opening to the sides.

"Shouldn't we see where they go?" Barak asked after they had passed the third or fourth passageway.

"They don't go anyplace," Relg told him.

"How can you be sure?"

"A gallery that goes someplace feels different. That one we just passed comes to a blank wall about a hundred feet in."

Barak grunted dubiously.

They came to another sheer face, and Relg stopped to peer up into the blackness.

"How high is it?" Durnik asked.

"Thirty feet or so. I'll make some holes so we can climb up." Relg knelt and slowly pushed one hand into the face of the rock. Then he tensed his shoulder and twisted his arm slightly. The rock popped with a sharp little detonation; when Relg pulled his hand out, a shower of fragments came with it. He brushed the rest of the debris out of the hole he had made, stood up and sank his other hand into the rock about two feet above the first hole.

"Clever," Silk admired.

"It's a very old trick," Relg told him.

They followed Relg up the face and squeezed through a narrow crack at the top. Barak muttered curses as he wriggled through, leaving a fair amount of skin behind.

"How far have we come?" Silk asked. His voice had a certain apprehension in it, and he looked about nervously at the rock which seemed to press in all around them.

"We're about eight hundred feet above the base of the pinnacle," Relg replied. "We go that way now." He pointed up another sloping passageway.

"Isn't that back in the direction we just came?" Durnik asked.

"The cave zigzags," Relg told him. "We have to keep following the galleries that lead upward."

"Do they go all the way to the top?"

"They open out somewhere. That's all I can tell for sure at this point."

"What's that?" Silk cried sharply.

From somewhere along one of the dark passageways, a voice floated out at them, singing. There seemed to be a deep sadness in the song, but the echoes made it impossible to pick out the words. About all they could be sure of was the fact that the singer was a woman.

After a moment, Belgarath gave a startled exclamation.

"What's wrong?" Aunt Pol asked him.

"Marag!" the old man said.

"That's impossible."

"I know the song, Pol. It's a Marag funeral song. Whoever she is, she's very close to dying."

The echoes in the twisting passageways made it very difficult to pinpoint the singer's exact location; but as they moved, the sound seemed to be getting closer.

"Down here," Silk said finally, stopping with his head cocked to one side in front of an opening.

The singing stopped abruptly. "No closer," the unseen woman warned sharply. "I have a knife."

"We're friends," Durnik called to her.

She laughed bitterly at that. "I have no friends. You're not going to take me back. My knife is long enough to reach my heart."

"She thinks we're Murgos," Silk whispered.

Belgarath raised his voice, speaking in a language Garion had never heard before. After a moment, the woman answered haltingly, as if trying to remember words she had not spoken for years.

"She thinks it's a trick," the old man told them quietly. "She says she's got a knife right against her heart, so we're going to have to be careful." He spoke again into the dark passageway, and the woman answered him. The language they were speaking was liquid, musical.

"She says she'll let one of us go to her," Belgarath said finally. "She still doesn't trust us."

"I'll go," Aunt Pol told him.

"Be careful, Pol. She might decide at the last minute to use her knife on you instead of herself."

"I can handle it, father." Aunt Pol took the light from Barak and moved slowly on down the passageway, speaking calmly as she went.

The rest of them stood in the darkness, listening intently to the murmur of voices coming from the passageway, as Aunt Pol talked quietly to the Marag woman. "You can come now," she called to them finally, and they went down the passageway toward her voice.

The woman was lying beside a small pool of water. She was dressed only in scanty rags, and she was very dirty. Her hair was a lustrous black, but badly tangled, and her face had a resigned, hopeless look on it. She had wide cheekbones, full lips, and huge, violet eyes framed with sooty black lashes. The few pitiful rags she wore exposed a great deal of her pale skin. Relg drew in a sharp breath and immediately turned his back.

"Her name is Taiba," Aunt Pol told them quietly. "She escaped from the slave pens under Rak Cthol several days ago."

Belgarath knelt beside the exhausted woman. "You're a Marag, aren't you?" he asked her intently.

"My mother told me I was," she confirmed. "She's the one who taught me the old language." Her dark hair fell across one of her pale cheeks in a shadowy tangle.

"Are there any other Marags in the slave pens?"

"A few, I think. It's hard to tell. Most of the other slaves have had their tongues cut out."

"She needs food," Aunt Pol said. "Did anyone think to bring anything?"

Durnik untied a pouch from his belt and handed it to her. "Some cheese," he said, "and a bit of dried meat."

Aunt Pol opened the pouch.

"Have you any idea how your people came to be here?" Belgarath asked the slave woman. "Think. It could be very important."

Taiba shrugged. "We've always been here." She took the food Aunt Pol offered her and began to eat ravenously.

"Not too fast," Aunt Pol warned.

"Have you ever heard anything about how Marags wound up in the slave pens of the Murgos?" Belgarath pressed.

"My mother told me once that thousands of years ago we lived in a country under the open sky and that we weren't slaves then," Taiba replied. "I didn't believe her, though. It's the sort of story you tell children."

"There are some old stories about the Tolnedran campaign in Maragor, Belgarath," Silk remarked. "Rumors have been floating around for years that some of the legion commanders sold their prisoners to the Nyissan slavers instead of killing them. It's the sort of thing a Tolnedran would do."

"It's a possibility, I suppose," Belgarath replied, frowning.

"Do we have to stay here?" Relg demanded harshly. His back was still turned, and there was a rigidity to it that spoke his outrage loudly.

"Why is he angry with me?" Taiba asked, her voice dropping wearily from her lips in scarcely more than a whisper.

"Cover your nakedness, woman," Relg told her. "You're an affront to decent eyes."

"Is that all?" She laughed, a rich, throaty sound. "These are all the clothes I have." She looked down at her lush figure. "Besides, there's nothing wrong with my body. It's not deformed or ugly. Why should I hide it?"

"Lewd woman!" Relg accused her.

"If it bothers you so much, don't look," she suggested.

"Relg has a certain religious problem," Silk told her dryly.

"Don't mention religion," she said with a shudder.

"You see," Relg snorted. "She's completely depraved."

"Not exactly," Belgarath told him. "In Rak Cthol the word religion means the altar and the knife."

"Garion," Aunt Pol said, "give me your cloak."

He unfastened his heavy wool cloak and handed it to her. She started to cover the exhausted slave woman with it, but stopped suddenly and looked closely at her. "Where are your children?" she asked.

"The Murgos took them," Taiba replied in a dead voice. "They were two baby girls—very beautiful—but they're gone now."

"We'll get them back for you," Garion promised impulsively.

She gave a bitter little laugh. "I don't think so. The Murgos gave them to the Grolims, and the Grolims sacrificed them on the altar of Torak. Ctuchik himself held the knife."

Garion felt his blood run cold.

"This cloak is warm," Taiba said gratefully, her hands smoothing the rough cloth. "I've been cold for such a long time." She sighed with a sort of weary contentment.

Belgarath and Aunt Pol were looking at each other across Taiba's body. "I must be doing something right," the old man remarked cryptically after a moment. "To stumble across her like this after all these years of searching!"

"Are you sure she's the right one, father?"

"She almost has to be. Everything fits together too well—right down to the last detail." He drew in a deep breath and then let it out explosively. "That's been worrying me for a thousand years." He suddenly looked enormously pleased with himself. "How did you escape from the slave pens, Taiba?" he asked gently.

"One of the Murgos forgot to lock a door," she replied, her voice drowsy. "After I slipped out, I found this knife. I was going to try to find Ctuchik and kill him with it, but I got lost. There are so many caves down here—so many. I wish I could kill him before I die, but I don't suppose there's much hope for that now." She sighed regretfully. "I think I'd like to sleep now. I'm so very tired."

"Will you be all right here?" Aunt Pol asked her. "We have to leave, but we'll be back. Do you need anything?"

"A little light, maybe." Taiba sighed. "I've lived in the dark all my life. I think I'd like it to be light when I die."

"Relg," Aunt Pol said, "make her some light."

"We might need it ourselves." His voice was still stiffly offended.

"She needs it more."

"Do it, Relg," Belgarath told the zealot in a firm voice.

Relg's face hardened, but he mixed some of the contents of his two pouches together on a flat stone and dribbled a bit of water on the mixture. The pasty substance began to glow.

"Thank you," Taiba said simply.

Relg refused to answer or even to look at her.

They went back up the passageway, leaving her beside the small pool with her dim little light. She began to sing again, quite softly this time and in a voice near the edge of sleep.

Relg led them through the dark galleries, twisting and changing course frequently, always climbing. Hours dragged by, though time had little meaning in the perpetual darkness. They climbed more of the sheer faces and followed passageways that wound higher and higher up into the vast rock pillar. Garion lost track of direction as they climbed, and found himself wondering if even Relg knew which way he was going. As they rounded another corner in another gallery, a faint breeze seemed to touch their faces. The breeze carried a dreadful odor with it.

"What's that stink?" Silk asked, wrinkling his sharp nose.

"The slave pens, most likely," Belgarath replied. "Murgos are lax about sanitation."

"The pens are under Rak Cthol, aren't they?" Barak asked.

Belgarath nodded.

"And they open up into the city itself?"

"As I remember it, they do."

"You've done it, Relg," Barak said, clapping the Ulgo on the shoulder.

"Don't touch me," Relg told him.

"Sorry, Relg."

"The slave pens are going to be guarded," Belgarath told them. "We'll want to be very quiet now."

They crept on up the passageway, being careful where they put their feet. Garion was not certain at what point the gallery began to show evidence of human construction. Finally they passed a partially open iron door. "Is there anybody in there?" he whispered to Silk.

The little man sidled up to the opening, his dagger held low and ready. He glanced in, his head making a quick, darting movement. "Just some bones," he reported somberly.

Belgarath signaled for a halt. "These lower galleries have probably been abandoned," he told them in a very quiet voice. "After the causeway was finished, the Murgos didn't need all those thousands of slaves. We'll go on up, but be quiet and keep your eyes open."

They padded silently up the gradual incline of the gallery, passing more of the rusting iron doors, all standing partially ajar. At the top of the slope, the gallery turned back sharply on itself, still angling upward. Some words were crudely lettered on the wall in a script Garion could not recognize. "Grandfather," he whispered, pointing at the words.

Belgarath glanced at the lettering and grunted. "Ninth level," he muttered. "We're still some distance below the city."

"How far do we go before we start running into Murgos?" Barak rumbled, looking around with his hand on his sword hilt.

Belgarath shrugged slightly. "It's hard to say. I'd guess that only the top two or three levels are occupied."

They followed the gallery upward until it turned sharply, and once again there were words written on the wall in the alien script. "Eighth level," Belgarath translated. "Keep going."

The smell of the slave pens grew stronger as they progressed upward through the succeeding levels.

"Light ahead," Durnik warned sharply, just before they turned the corner to enter the fourth level.

"Wait here," Silk breathed and melted around the corner, his dagger held close against his leg.

The light was dim and seemed to be bobbing slightly, growing gradually brighter as the moments dragged by. "Someone with a torch," Barak muttered.

The torchlight suddenly flickered, throwing gyrating shadows. Then it grew steady, no longer bobbing. After a few moments, Silk came back, carefully wiping his dagger. "A Murgo," he told them. "I think he was looking for something. The cells up there are still empty."

"What did you do with him?" Barak asked.

"I dragged him into one of the cells. They won't stumble over him unless they're looking for him."

Relg was carefully veiling his eyes.

"Even that little bit of light?" Durnik asked him.

"It's the color of it," Relg explained.

They rounded the corner into the fourth level and started up again. A hundred yards up the gallery a torch was stuck into a crack in the wall, burning steadily. As they approached it, they could see a long smear of fresh blood on the uneven, littered floor.

Belgarath stopped outside the cell door, scratching at his beard. "What was he wearing?" he asked Silk.

"One of those hooded robes," Silk replied. "Why?"

"Go get it."

Silk looked at him briefly, then nodded. He went back into the cell and came out a moment later carrying a black Murgo robe. He handed it to the old man.

Belgarath held up the robe, looking critically at the long cut running up the back. "Try not to put such big holes in the rest of them," he told the little man.

Silk grinned at him. "Sorry. I guess I got a bit overenthusiastic. I'll be more careful from now on." He glanced at Barak. "Care to join me?" he invited.

"Naturally. Coming, Mandorallen?"

The knight nodded gravely, loosening his sword in its sheath.

"We'll wait here, then," Belgarath told them. "Be careful, but don't take any longer than you have to."

The three men moved stealthily on up the gallery toward the third level.

"Can you guess at the time, father?" Aunt Pol asked quietly after they had disappeared.

"Several hours after midnight."

"Will we have enough time left before dawn?"

"If we hurry."

"Maybe we should wait out the day here and go up when it gets dark again."

He frowned. "I don't think so, Pol. Ctuchik's up to something. He knows I'm coming—I've felt that for the last week—but he hasn't made a move of his own yet. Let's not give him any more time than we have to."

"He's going to fight you, father."

"It's long overdue anyway," he replied. "Ctuchik and I have been stepping around each other for thousands of years because the time was never just exactly right. Now it's finally come down to this." He looked off into the darkness, his face bleak. "When it starts, I want you to stay out of it, Pol."

She looked at the grim-faced old man for a long moment, then nodded. "Whatever you say, father," she said.

CHAPTER TWENTY-SIX

The Murgo robe was made of coarse, black cloth and it had a strange emblem woven into the fabric just over Garion's heart. It smelled of smoke and of something else even more unpleasant. There was a small ragged hole in the robe just under the left armpit, and the cloth around the hole was wet and sticky. Garion's skin cringed away from that wetness.

They were moving rapidly up through the galleries of the last three levels of the slave pens with the deep-cowled hoods of the Murgo robes hiding their faces. Though the galleries were lighted by sooty torches, they encountered no guards, and the slaves locked behind the pitted iron doors made no sound as they passed. Garion could feel the dreadful fear behind those doors.

"How do we get up into the city?" Durnik whispered.

"There's a stairway at the upper end of the top gallery," Silk replied softly.

"Is it guarded?"

"Not anymore."

An iron-barred gate, chained and locked, blocked the top of the stairway, but Silk bent and drew a slim metal implement from one boot, probed inside the lock for a few seconds, then grunted with satisfaction as the lock clicked open in his hand. "I'll have a look," he whispered and slipped out.

Beyond the gate Garion could see the stars and, outlined against them, the looming buildings of Rak Cthol. A scream, agonized and despairing, echoed through the city, followed after a moment by the hollow sound of some unimaginably huge iron gong. Garion shuddered.

A few moments later, Silk slipped back through the gate. "There doesn't seem to be anybody about," he murmured softly. "Which way do we go?"

Belgarath pointed. "That way. We'll go along the wall to the Temple."

"The Temple?" Relg asked sharply.

"We have to go through it to get to Ctuchik," the old man replied. "We're going to have to hurry. Morning isn't far off."

Rak Cthol was not like other cities. The vast buildings had little of that separateness that they had in other places. It was as if the Murgos and Grolims who lived here had no sense of personal possession, so their structures lacked that insularity of individual property to be found among the houses in the cities of the West. There were no streets in the ordinary sense of the word, but rather interconnecting courtyards and corridors that passed between and quite often through the buildings.

The city seemed deserted as they crept silently through the dark courtyards and shadowy corridors, yet there was a kind of menacing watchfulness about the looming, silent black walls around them. Peculiar-looking turrets jutted from the walls in unexpected places, leaning out over the courtyards, brooding down at them as they passed. Narrow windows stared accusingly at them, and the arched doorways were filled with lurking shadows. An oppressive air of ancient evil lay heavily on Rak Cthol, and the stones themselves seemed almost to gloat as Garion and his friends moved deeper and deeper into the dark maze of the Grolim fortress.

"Are you sure you know where you're going?" Barak whispered nervously to Belgarath.

"I've been here before," the old man told him quietly. "I like to keep an eye on Ctuchik from time to time. We go up those stairs. They'll take us to the top of the city wall."

The stairway was narrow and steep, with massive walls on either side and a vaulted roof overhead. The stone steps were worn by centuries of use. They climbed silently. Another scream echoed through the city, and the huge gong sounded its iron note once more.

When they emerged from the stairway, they were atop the outer wall. It was as broad as a highway and encircled the entire city. A parapet ran along its outer edge, marking the brink of the dreadful precipice that dropped away to the floor of the rocky wasteland a mile or more below. Once they emerged from the shelter of the buildings, the chill air bit at them, and the black flagstones and rough-hewn blocks of the outer parapet glittered with frost in the icy starlight.

Belgarath looked at the open stretch lying along the top of the wall ahead of them and at the shadowy buildings looming several hundred yards ahead. "We'd better spread out," he whispered. "Too many people in one place attract attention in Rak Cthol. We'll go across here two at a time. Walk—don't run or crouch down. Try to look as if you belong here. Let's go." He started along the top of the wall with Barak at his side, the two of them walking purposefully, but not appearing to hurry. After a few moments, Aunt Pol and Mandorallen followed.

"Durnik," Silk whispered. "Garion and I'll go next. You and Relg follow in a minute or so." He peered at Relg's face, shadowed beneath the Murgo hood. "Are you all right?" He asked.

"As long as I don't look up at the sky," Relg answered tightly. His voice sounded as if it were coming from between clenched teeth.

"Come along, then, Garion," Silk murmured.

It required every ounce of Garion's self-control to walk at a normal pace across the frosty stones. It seemed somehow that eyes watched from every shadowy building and tower as he and the little Drasnian crossed the open section atop the wall. The air was dead calm and bitterly cold, and the stone blocks of the outer parapet were covered with a lacy filigree of rime frost.

There was another scream from the Temple lying somewhere ahead.

The corner of a large tower jutted out at the end of the open stretch of wall, obscuring the walkway beyond. "Wait here a moment," Silk whispered as they stepped gratefully into its shadow and he slipped around the jutting corner.

Garion stood in the icy dark, straining his ears for any sound. He glanced once toward the parapet. Far out on the desolate wasteland below, a small fire was burning. It twinkled in the dark like a small red star. He tried to imagine how far away it might be.

Then there was a slight scraping sound somewhere above him. He spun quickly, his hand going to his sword. A shadowy figure dropped from a ledge on the side of the tower several yards over his head and landed with catlike silence on the flagstones directly in front of him. Garion caught a familiar sour, acid reek of stale perspiration.

"It's been a long time, hasn't it, Garion?" Brill said quietly with an ugly chuckle.

"Stay back," Garion warned, holding his sword with its point low as Barak had taught him.

"I knew that I'd catch you alone someday," Brill said, ignoring the sword. He spread his hands wide and crouched slightly, his cast eye gleaming in the starlight.

Garion backed away, waving his sword threateningly. Brill bounded to one side, and Garion instinctively followed him with the sword point. Then, so fast that Garion could not follow, Brill dodged back and struck his hand down sharply on the boy's forearm. Garion's sword skittered away across the icy flagstones. Desperately, Garion reached for his dagger.

Then another shadow flickered in the darkness at the corner of the tower. Brill grunted as a foot caught him solidly in the side. He fell, but rolled quickly across the stones and came back up onto his feet, his stance wide and his hands moving slowly in the air in front of him.

Silk dropped his Murgo robe behind him, kicked it out of the way, and crouched, his hands also spread wide.

Brill grinned. "I should have known you were around somewhere, Kheldar."

"I suppose I should have expected you too, Kordoch," Silk replied. "You always seem to show up."

Brill flicked a quick hand toward Silk's face, but the little man easily avoided it. "How do you keep getting ahead of us?" he asked, almost conversationally. "That's a habit of yours that's starting to irritate Belgarath." He launched a quick kick at Brill's groin, but the cast-eyed man jumped back agilely.

Brill laughed shortly. "You people are too tender-hearted with horses," he said. "I've had to ride quite a few of them to death chasing you. How did you get out of that pit?" He sounded interested. "Taur Urgas was furious the next morning."

"What a shame."

"He had the guards flayed."

"I imagine a Murgo looks a bit peculiar without his skin."

Brill dove forward suddenly, both hands extended, but Silk sidestepped the lunge and smashed his hand sharply down in the middle of Brill's back. Brill grunted again, but rolled clear farther out on the stones atop the wall. "You might be just as good as they say," he admitted grudgingly.

"Try me, Kordoch," Silk invited, with a nasty grin. He moved out from the wall of the tower, his hands in constant motion. Garion watched the two circling each other with his heart in his mouth.

Brill jumped again, with both feet lashing out, but Silk dove under him. They both rolled to their feet again. Silk's left hand flashed out, even as he came to his feet, catching Brill high on the head. Brill reeled from the blow, but managed to kick Silk's knee as he spun away. "Your technique's defensive, Kheldar," he grated, shaking his head to clear the effects of Silk's blow. "That's a weakness."

"Just a difference of style, Kordoch," Silk replied.

Brill drove a gouging thumb at Silk's eye, but Silk blocked it and slammed a quick counterblow to the pit of his enemy's stomach. Brill scissored his legs as he fell, sweeping Silk's legs out from under him. Both men tumbled across the frosty stones and sprang to their feet again, their hands flickering blows faster than Garion's eyes could follow them.

The mistake was a simple one, so slight that Garion could not even be sure it *was* a mistake. Brill flicked a jab at Silk's face that was an ounce or two harder than it should have been and traveled no more than a fraction of an inch too far. Silk's hands flashed up and caught his opponent's wrist with a deadly grip and he rolled backward toward the parapet, his legs coiling, even as the two of them fell. Jerked off balance, Brill seemed almost to dive forward. Silk's legs straightened suddenly, launching the cast-eyed man up and forward with a tremendous heave. With a strangled exclamation Brill clutched desperately at one of the stone blocks of the parapet as he sailed over, but he was too high and his momentum was too great. He hurtled over the parapet, plunging out and down into the darkness below the wall. His scream faded horribly as he fell, lost in the sound of yet another shriek from the Temple of Torak.

Silk rose to his feet, glanced once over the edge, and then came back to where Garion stood trembling in the shadows by the tower wall.

"Silk!" Garion exclaimed, catching the little man's arm in relief.

"What was that?" Belgarath asked, coming back around the corner.

"Brill," Silk replied blandly, pulling his Murgo robe back on.

"*Again?*" Belgarath demanded with exasperation. "What was he doing this time?"

"Trying to fly, last time I saw him." Silk smirked.

The old man looked puzzled.

"He wasn't doing it very well," Silk added.

Belgarath shrugged. "Maybe it'll come to him in time."

"He doesn't really have all that much time." Silk glanced out over the edge.

From far below—terribly far below—there came a faint, muffled crash; then, after several seconds, another. "Does bouncing count?" Silk asked.

Belgarath made a wry face. "Not really."

"Then I'd say he didn't learn in time," Silk said blithely. He looked around with a broad smile. "What a beautiful night this is," he remarked to no one in particular.

"Let's move along," Belgarath suggested, throwing a quick, nervous glance at the eastern horizon. "It'll start to lighten up over there anytime now."

They joined the others in the deep shadows beside the high wall of the Temple some hundred yards down the wall and waited tensely for Relg and Durnik to catch up.

"What kept you?" Barak whispered as they waited.

"I met an old friend of ours," Silk replied quietly. His grin was a flash of white teeth in the shadows.

"It was Brill," Garion told the rest of them in a hoarse whisper. "He and Silk fought with each other, and Silk threw him over the edge." Mandorallen glanced toward the frosty parapet. " 'Tis a goodly way down," he observed.

"Isn't it, though?" Silk agreed.

Barak chuckled and put his big hand wordlessly on Silk's shoulder.

Then Durnik and Relg came along the top of the wall to join them in the shadows.

"We have to go through the Temple," Belgarath told them in a quiet voice. "Pull your hoods as far over your faces as you can and keep your heads down. Stay in single file and mutter to yourselves as if you were praying. If anybody speaks to us, let me do the talking; and each time the gong sounds, turn toward the altar and bow." He led them then to a thick door bound with weathered iron straps. He looked back once to be sure they were all in line, then put his hand to the latch and pushed the door open.

The inside of the temple glowed with smoky red light, and a dreadful, charnel-house reek filled it. The door through which they entered led onto a covered balcony that curved around the back of the dome of the Temple. A stone balustrade ran along the edge of the balcony, with thick pillars at evenly spaced intervals. The openings between the pillars were draped with the same coarse, heavy cloth from which the Murgo robes were woven. Along the back wall of the balcony were a number of doors, set deep in the stone. Garion surmised that the balcony was largely used by Temple function-aries going to and fro on various errands.

As soon as they started along the balcony, Belgarath crossed his hands on his chest and led them at a slow, measured pace, chanting in a deep, loud voice.

A scream echoed up from below, piercing, filled with terror and agony. Garion involuntarily glanced through the parted drapery toward the altar. For the rest of his life he wished he had not.

The circular walls of the Temple were constructed of polished black stone, and directly behind the altar was an enormous face forged of steel and buffed to mirror brightness—the face of Torak and the original of the steel masks of the Grolims. The face was beautiful—there was no question of that—yet there was a kind of brooding evil in it, a cruelty beyond human ability to comprehend the meaning of the word. The Temple floor facing the God's image was densely packed with Murgos and Grolim priests, kneeling and chanting an unintelligible rumble in a dozen dialects. The altar stood on a raised dais directly beneath the glittering face of Torak. A smoking brazier on an iron post stood at each front corner of the blood-smeared altar, and a square pit opened in the floor immediately in front of the dais. Ugly red flames licked up out of the pit, and black, oily smoke rolled from it toward the dome high above.

A half dozen Grolims in black robes and steel masks were gathered around the altar, holding the naked body of a slave. The victim was already dead, his chest gaping open like the chest of a butchered hog, and a single Grolim stood in front of the altar, facing the image of Torak with raised hands. In his right, he held a long, curved knife; in his left, a dripping human heart. "Behold our offering, Dragon God of Angarak!" he cried in a huge voice, then turned and deposited the heart in one of the smoking braziers. There was a burst of steam and smoke from the brazier and a hideous sizzle as the heart dropped into the burning coals. From somewhere beneath the Temple floor, the huge iron gong sounded, its vibration shimmering in the air. The assembled Murgos and their Grolim overseers groaned and pressed their faces to the floor.

Garion felt a hand nudge his shoulder. Silk, already turned, was bowing toward the bloody altar. Awkwardly, sickened by the horror below, Garion also bowed.

The six Grolims at the altar lifted the lifeless body of the slave almost contemptuously and cast it into the pit before the dais. Flames belched up and sparks rose in the thick smoke as the body fell into the fire below.

A dreadful anger welled up in Garion. Without even thinking, he began to draw in his Will, fully intent upon shattering that vile altar and the cruel image hovering above it into shards and fragments in a single, cataclysmic unleashing of naked force.

"*Belgarion!*" the voice within his mind said sharply. "*Don't interfere. This isn't the time.*"

"I can't stand it," Garion raged silently. "*I've got to do something.*"

"*You can't. Not now. You'll rouse the whole city. Unclench your Will, Belgarion.*"

"*Do as he says, Garion,*" Aunt Pol's voice sounded quietly in his mind. The unspoken recognition passed between Aunt Pol's mind and that strange other mind as Garion helplessly let the anger and Will drain out of him.

"*This abomination won't stand much longer, Belgarion,*" the voice assured him. "*Even now the earth gathers to rid itself of it.*" And then the voice was gone.

"What are you doing up here?" a harsh voice demanded. Garion jerked his eyes away from the hideous scene below. A masked and robed Grolim stood in front of Belgarath, blocking their way.

"We are the servants of Torak," the old man replied in an accent that perfectly matched the gutturals of Murgo speech.

"All in Rak Cthol are the servants of Torak," the Grolim said. "You aren't attending the ritual of sacrifice. Why?"

"We're pilgrims from Rak Hagga," Belgarath explained, "only just arrived in the dread city. We were commanded to present ourselves to the Hierarch of Rak Hagga in the instant of our arrival. That stern duty prevents our participation in the celebration."

The Grolim grunted suspiciously.

"Could the revered priest of the Dragon God direct us to the chambers of our Hierarch? We are unfamiliar with the dark Temple."

There was another shriek from below. As the iron gong boomed, the Grolim turned and bowed toward the altar. Belgarath gave a quick jerk of his head to the rest of them, turned and also bowed.

"Go to the last door but one," the Grolim instructed, apparently satisfied by their gestures of piety. "It will lead you down to the halls of the Hierarchs."

"We are endlessly grateful to the priest of the Dark God," Belgarath thanked him, bowing. They filed past the steel-masked Grolim, their heads down and their hands crossed on their breasts, muttering to themselves as if in prayer.

"Vile!" Relg was strangling. "Obscenity! Abomination!"

"Keep your head down!" Silk whispered. "There are Grolims all around us."

"As UL gives me strength, I won't rest until Rak Cthol is laid waste," Relg vowed in a fervent mutter.

Belgarath had reached an ornately carved door near the end of the balcony, and he swung it open cautiously. "Is the Grolim still watching us?" he whispered to Silk.

The little man glanced back at the priest standing some distance behind them. "Yes. Wait—there he goes. The balcony's clear now."

The sorcerer let the door swing shut and stepped instead to the last door on the balcony. He tugged the latch carefully, and the door opened smoothly. He frowned. "It's always been locked before," he muttered.

"Do you think it's a trap?" Barak rumbled, his hand dipping under the Murgo robe to find his sword hilt.

"It's possible, but we don't have much choice." Belgarath pulled the door open the rest of the way, and they all slipped through as another shriek came from the altar. The door slowly closed behind them as the gong shuddered the stones of the Temple. They started down the worn stone steps beyond the door. The stairway was narrow and poorly lighted, and it went down sharply, curving always to the right.

"We're right up against the outer wall, aren't we?" Silk asked, touching the black stones on his left.

Belgarath nodded. "The stairs lead down to Ctuchik's private place." They continued down until the walls on either side changed from blocks to solid stone.

"He lives below the city?" Silk asked, surprised.

"Yes," Belgarath replied. "He built himself a sort of hanging turret out from the rock of the peak itself."

"Strange idea," Durnik said.

"Ctuchik's a strange sort of person," Aunt Pol told him grimly.

Belgarath stopped them. "The stairs go down about another hundred feet," he whispered. "There'll be two guards just outside the door to the turret. Not even Ctuchik could change that—no matter what he's planning."

"Sorcerers?" Barak asked softly.

"No. The guards are ceremonial more than functional. They're just ordinary Grolims."

"We'll rush them, then."

"That won't be necessary. I can get you close enough to deal with them, but I want it quick and quiet." The old man reached inside his Murgo robe and drew out a roll of parchment bound with a strip of black ribbon. He started down again with Barak and Mandorallen close behind him.

The curve of the stairway brought a lighted area into view as they descended. Torches illuminated the bottom of the stone steps and a kind of antechamber hewn from the solid rock. Two Grolim priests stood in front of a plain black door, their arms folded. "Who approaches the Holy of Holies?" one of them demanded, putting his hand to his sword hilt.

"A messenger," Belgarath announced importantly. "I bear a message for the Master from the Hierarch of Rak Goska." He held the rolled parchment above his head.

"Approach, messenger."

"Praise the name of the Disciple of the Dragon God of Angarak," Belgarath boomed as he marched down the steps with Mandorallen and Barak flanking him. He reached the bottom of the stairs and stopped in front of the steel-masked guards. "Thus have I performed my appointed task," he declared, holding out the parchment.

One of the guards reached for it, but Barak caught his arm in a huge fist. The big man's other hand closed swiftly about the surprised Grolim's throat.

The other guard's hand flashed toward his sword hilt, but he grunted and doubled over sharply as Mandorallen thrust a long, needle-pointed poniard up into his belly. With a kind of deadly concentration the knight twisted the hilt of the weapon, probing with the point deep inside the Grolim's body. The guard shuddered when the blade reached his heart and collapsed with a long, gurgling sigh.

Barak's massive shoulder shifted, and there was a grating crunch as the bones in the first Grolim's neck came apart in his deadly grip. The guard's feet scraped spasmodically on the floor for a moment, and then he went limp. "I feel better already," Barak muttered, dropping the body.

"You and Mandorallen stay here," Belgarath told him. "I don't want to be disturbed once I'm inside."

"We'll see to it," Barak promised. "What about these?" He pointed at the two dead guards.

"Dispose of them, Relg," Belgarath said shortly to the Ulgo.

Silk turned his back quickly as Relg knelt between the two bodies and took hold of them, one with each hand. There was a sort of muffled slithering as he pushed down, sinking the bodies into the stone floor.

"You left a foot sticking out," Barak observed in a detached tone.

"Do you *have* to talk about it?" Silk demanded.

Belgarath took a deep breath and put his hand to the iron door handle. "All right," he said to them quietly, "let's go, then." He pushed open the door.

CHAPTER TWENTY-SEVEN

The wealth of empires lay beyond the black door. Bright yellow coins—gold beyond counting—lay in heaps on the floor; carelessly scattered among the coins were rings, bracelets, chains, and crowns, gleaming richly. Blood-red bars from the mines of Angarak stood in stacks along the wall, interspersed here and there by open chests filled to overflowing with fist-sized diamonds that glittered like ice. A large table sat in the center of the room, littered with rubies, sapphires, and emeralds as big as eggs. Ropes and strings of pearls, pink, rose gray, and even some of jet, held back the deep crimson drapes that billowed heavily before the windows.

Belgarath moved like a stalking animal, showing no sign of his age, his eyes everywhere. He ignored the riches around him and crossed the deep-carpeted floor to a room filled with learning, where tightly rolled scrolls lay in racks reaching to the ceiling and the leather backs of books marched like battalions along dark wooden shelves. The tables in the second room were covered with the curious glass apparatus of chemical experiment and strange machines of brass and iron, all cogs and wheels and pulleys and chains.

In yet a third chamber stood a massive gold throne backed by drapes of black velvet. An ermine cape lay across one arm of the throne, and a scepter and a heavy gold crown lay upon the seat. Inlaid in the polished stones of the floor was a map that depicted, so far as Garion could tell, the entire world.

"What sort of place is this?" Durnik whispered in awe.

"Ctuchik amuses himself here," Aunt Pol replied with an expression of repugnance. "He has many vices and he likes to keep each one separate."

"He's not down here," Belgarath muttered. "Let's go up to the next level." He led them back the way they had come and started up a flight of stone steps that curved along the rounded wall of the turret.

The room at the top of the stairs was filled with horror. A rack stood in the center of it, and whips and flails hung on the walls. Cruel implements of gleaming steel lay in orderly rows on a table near the wall—hooks, needle-pointed spikes, and dreadful things with saw-edges that still had bits of bone and flesh caught between their teeth. The entire room reeked of blood.

"You and Silk go ahead, father," Aunt Pol said. "There are things in the other rooms on this level that Garion, Durnik, and Relg shouldn't see."

Belgarath nodded and went through a doorway with Silk behind him. After a few moments they returned by way of another door. Silk's face looked slightly sick. "He has some rather exotic perversions, doesn't he?" he remarked with a shudder.

Belgarath's face was bleak. "We go up again," he said quietly. "He's on the top level. I thought he might be, but I needed to be sure." They mounted another stairway.

As they neared the top, Garion felt a peculiar tingling glow beginning somewhere deep within him, and a sort of endless singing seemed to draw him on. The mark on the palm of his right hand burned.

A black stone altar stood in the first room on the top level of the turret, and the steel image of the face of Torak brooded from the wall behind it. A gleaming knife, its hilt crusted with dried blood, lay on the altar, and blood-stains had sunk into the very pores of the rock. Belgarath was moving quickly now, his face intent and his stride catlike. He glanced through one door in the wall beyond the altar, shook his head and moved on to a closed door in the far wall. He touched his fingers lightly to the wood, then nodded. "He's in here," he murmured with satisfaction. He drew in a deep breath and grinned suddenly. "I've been waiting for this for a long time," he said.

"Don't dawdle, father," Aunt Pol told him impatiently. Her eyes were steely, and the white lock at her brow glittered like frost.

"I want you to stay out of it when we get inside, Pol," he reminded her. "You too, Garion. This is between Ctuchik and me."

"All right, father," Aunt Pol replied.

Belgarath put out his hand and opened the door. The room beyond was plain, even bare. The stone floor was uncarpeted, and the round windows looking out into the darkness were undraped. Simple candles burned in sconces on the walls, and a plain table stood in the center of the room.

Seated at the table with his back to the door sat a man in a hooded black robe who seemed to be gazing into an iron cask. Garion felt his entire body throbbing in response to what was in the casks, and the singing in his mind filled him.

A little boy with pale blond hair stood in front of the table, and he was also staring at the cask. He wore a smudged linen smock and dirty little shoes. Though his expression seemed devoid of all thought, there was a sweet innocence about him that caught at the heart. His eyes were blue, large, and trusting, and he was quite the most beautiful child Garion had ever seen.

"What took you so long, Belgarath?" the man at the table asked, not even bothering to turn around. His voice sounded dusty. He closed the iron box with a faint click. "I was almost beginning to worry about you."

"A few minor delays, Ctuchik," Belgarath replied. "I hope we didn't keep you waiting too long."

"I managed to keep myself occupied. Come in. Come in—all of you." Ctuchik turned to look at them. His hair and beard were a yellowed white and were very long. His face was deeply lined, and his eyes glittered in their sockets. It was a face filled with an ancient and profound evil. Cruelty and arrogance had eroded all traces of decency or humanity from it, and a towering egotism had twisted it into a perpetual sneer of contempt for every other living thing. His eyes shifted to Aunt Pol. "Polgara," he greeted her with a mocking inclination of his head. "You're as lovely as ever. Have you come finally then to submit yourself to the will of my Master?" His leer was vile.

"No, Ctuchik," she replied coldly. "I came to see justice."

"Justice?" He laughed scornfully. "There's no such thing, Polgara. The strong do what they like; the weak submit. My Master taught me that."

"And his maimed face did not teach you otherwise?"

The High Priest's face darkened briefly, but he shrugged off his momentary irritation. "I'd offer you all a place to sit and some refreshment, perhaps," he continued in that same dusty voice, "but you won't be staying that long, I'm afraid." He glanced at the rest of them, his eyes noting each in turn. "Your party seems diminished, Belgarath," he observed. "I hope you haven't lost any of them along the way."

"They're all well, Ctuchik," Belgarath assured him. "I'm certain that they'll appreciate your concern, however."

"All?" Ctuchik drawled. "I see the Nimble Thief and the Man with Two Lives and the Blind Man, but I don't see the others. Where's the Dreadful Bear and the Knight Protector? The Horse Lord and the Bowman? And the ladies? Where are they—the Queen of the World and the Mother of the Race That Died?"

"All well, Ctuchik," Belgarath replied. "All well."

"How extraordinary. I was almost certain that you'd have lost one or two at least by now. I admire your dedication, old man—to keep intact for all these centuries a prophecy that would have collapsed if one single ancestor had died at the wrong time." His eyes grew distant momentarily. "Ah," he said. "I see. You left them below to stand guard. You didn't have to do that, Belgarath. I left orders that we weren't to be disturbed."

The High Priest's eyes stopped then on Garion's face. "Belgarion," he said almost politely. Despite the singing that still thrilled in his veins, Garion felt a chill as the evil force of the High Priest's mind touched him. "You're younger than I expected."

Garion stared defiantly at him, gathering his Will to ward off any surprise move by the old man at the table.

"Would you pit your will against mine, Belgarion?" Ctuchik seemed amused. "You burned Chamdar, but he was a fool. You'll find me a bit more difficult. Tell me, boy, did you enjoy it?"

"No," Garion replied, still holding himself ready.

"In time you'll learn to enjoy it," Ctuchik said with an evil grin. "Watching your enemy writhe and shriek in your mind's grip is one of the more satisfying rewards of power." He turned his eyes back to Belgarath. "And so you've come at last to destroy me?" he said mockingly.

"If it comes down to that, yes. It's been a long time coming, Ctuchik."

"Hasn't it, though? We're very much alike, Belgarath. I've been looking forward to this meeting almost as much as you have. Yes, we're very much alike. Under different circumstances, we might even have been friends."

"I doubt that. I'm a simple man, and some of your amusements are a bit sophisticated for my taste."

"Spare me that, please. You know as well as I do that we're both beyond all restriction."

"Perhaps, but I prefer to choose my friends a bit more carefully."

"You're growing tiresome, Belgarath. Tell the others to come up." Ctuchik raised one eyebrow sardonically. "Don't you want to have them watch while you destroy me? Think of how sweet their admiration will be."

"They're fine just where they are," Belgarath told him.

"Don't be tedious. Surely you're not going to deny me the opportunity to pay homage to the Queen of the World." Ctuchik's voice was mocking. "I yearn to behold her exquisite perfection before you kill me."

"I doubt that she'd care much for you, Ctuchik. I'll convey your respects, however."

"I insist, Belgarath. It's a small request—easily granted. If you don't summon her, I will."

Belgarath's eyes narrowed, and then he suddenly grinned. "So that's it," he said softly. "I wondered why you'd gone to all the trouble to let us get through so easily."

"It doesn't really matter now, you know," Ctuchik almost purred. "You've made your last mistake, old man. You've brought her to Rak Cthol, and that's all I really needed. Your prophecy dies here and now, Belgarath—and you with it, I'd imagine." The High Priest's eyes flashed triumphantly, and Garion felt the evil force of Ctuchik's mind reaching out, searching with a terrible purpose.

Belgarath exchanged a quick look with Aunt Pol and slyly winked.

Ctuchik's eyes widened suddenly as his mind swept through the lower levels of his grim turret and found it empty. "Where is she?" he demanded wildly in a voice that was almost a scream.

"The princess wasn't able to come with us," Belgarath replied blandly. "She sends her apologies, though."

"You're lying, Belgarath! You wouldn't have dared to leave her behind. There's no place in the world where she'd be safe."

"Not even in the caves of Ulgo?"

Ctuchik's face blanched. "Ulgo?" he gasped.

"Poor old Ctuchik," Belgarath said, shaking his head in mock regret. "You're slipping badly, I'm afraid. It wasn't a bad plan you had, but didn't it occur to you to make sure that the princess was actually with us before you let me get this close to you?"

"One of the others will do just as well," Ctuchik asserted, his eyes blazing with fury.

"No," Belgarath disagreed. "The others are all unassailable. Ce'Nedra's the only vulnerable one, and she's at Prolgu—under the protection of UL himself. You can attempt *that* if you'd like, but I wouldn't really advise it."

"Curse you, Belgarath!"

"Why don't you just give me the Orb now, Ctuchik?" Belgarath suggested. "You know I can take it away from you if I have to."

Ctuchik struggled to gain control of himself. "Let's not be hasty, Belgarath," he said after a moment. "What are we going to gain by destroying each other? We have Cthrag Yaska in our possession. We could divide the world between us."

"I don't want half the world, Ctuchik."

"You want it all for yourself?" A brief, knowing smile crossed Ctuchik's face. "So did I—at first—but I'll settle for half."

"Actually, I don't want any of it."

Ctuchik's expression became a bit desperate. "What *do* you want, Belgarath?"

"The Orb," Belgarath replied inexorably. "Give it to me, Ctuchik."

"Why don't we join forces and use the Orb to destroy Zedar?"

"Why?"

"You hate him as much as I do. He betrayed your Master. He stole Cthrag Yaska from you."

"He betrayed himself, Ctuchik, and I think that haunts him sometimes. His plan to steal the Orb was clever, though." Belgarath looked thoughtfully at the little boy standing in front of the table, his large eyes fixed on the iron cask. "I wonder where he found this child," he mused. "Innocence and purity are not exactly the same thing, of course, but they're very close. It must have cost Zedar a great deal of effort to raise a total innocent. Think of all the impulses he had to suppress."

"That's why I let *him* do it," Ctuchik said.

The little blond boy, seeming to know that they were discussing him, looked at the two old men, his eyes filled with absolute trust.

"The whole point is that I still have Cthrag Yaska—the Orb," Ctuchik said, leaning back in his chair and laying one hand on the cask. "If you try to take it, I'll fight you. Neither of us knows for sure how that would turn out. Why take chances?"

"What good is it doing you? Even if it would submit to you, what then? Would you raise Torak and surrender it to *him*?"

"I might think about it. But Torak's been asleep for five centuries now, and the world's run fairly well without him. I don't imagine there's all that much point in disturbing him just yet."

"Which would leave you in possession of the Orb."

Ctuchik shrugged. "Someone has to have it. Why not me?"

He was still leaning back in his chair, seeming almost completely at ease. There was no warning movement or even a flicker of emotion across his face as he struck.

It came so quickly that it was not a surge but a blow, and the sound of it was not the now-familiar roaring in the mind but a thunderclap. Garion knew that, had it been directed at him, it would have destroyed him. But it was not directed at him. It lashed instead at Belgarath. For a dreadful instant Garion saw his grandfather engulfed in a shadow blacker than night itself. Then the shadow shattered like a goblet of delicate crystal, scattering shards of darkness as it blew apart. Now grim-faced, Belgarath still faced his ancient enemy. "Is that the best you can do, Ctuchik?" he asked, even as his own will struck.

A searing blue light suddenly surrounded the Grolim, closing in upon him, seeming to crush him with its intensity. The stout chair upon which he sat burst into chunks and splinters, as if a sudden vast weight had settled down upon it. Ctuchik fell among the fragments of his chair and pushed back the blue incandescence with both hands. He lurched to his feet and answered with flames. For a dreadful instant Garion remembered Asharak, burning in the Wood of the Dryads, but Belgarath brushed the fire away and, despite his once-stated assertion that the Will and Word needed no gesture, he raised his hand and smashed at Ctuchik with lightning.

The sorcerer and the magician faced each other in the center of the room, surrounded by blazing lights and waves of flame and darkness. Garion's mind grew numb under the repeated detonations of raw energy as the two struggled. He sensed that their battle was only partially visible and that blows were being struck which he could not see—could not even imagine. The air in the turret room seemed to crackle and hiss. Strange images appeared and vanished, flickering at the extreme limits of visibility—vast faces, enormous hands, and things Garion could not name. The turret itself trembled as the two dreadful old men ripped open the fabric of reality itself to grasp weapons of imagination or delusion.

Without even thinking, Garion began to gather his Will, drawing his mind into focus. He had to stop it. The edges of the blows were smashing at him and at the others. Beyond thought now, Belgarath and Ctuchik, consumed with their hatred for each other, were unleashing forces that could kill them all.

"Garion! Stay out of it!" Aunt Pol told him in a voice so harsh that he could not believe it was hers. "They're at the limit. If you throw anything else into it, you'll destroy them both." She gestured sharply to the others. "Get back—all of you. The air around them is alive."

Fearfully, they all backed toward the rear wall of the turret room.

The sorcerer and the magician stood no more than a few feet apart now, their eyes blazing and their power surging back and forth in waves. The air sizzled around them, and their robes smoked.

Then Garion's eyes fell upon the little boy. He stood watching with calm, uncomprehending eyes. He neither started nor flinched at the dreadful sounds and sights that crashed around him. Garion tensed himself to dash forward and yank the child to safety, but at that moment the little boy turned toward the table. Quite calmly, he walked through a sudden wall of green flame that shot up in front of him. Either he did not see the fire, or he did not fear it. He reached the table, stood on his tiptoes and, raising the lid, he put his hand into the iron cask over which Ctuchik had been gloating. He lifted a round, polished, gray stone out of the cask. Garion instantly felt that strange tingling glow again, so strong now that it was almost overwhelming, and his ears filled with the haunting song.

He heard Aunt Pol gasp.

Holding the gray stone in both hands like a ball, the little boy turned and walked directly toward Garion, his eyes filled with trust and the expression on his small face confident. The polished stone reflected the flashing lights of the terrible conflict raging in the center of the room, but there was another light within it as well. Deep within it stood an intense azure glow—a light that neither flickered nor changed, a light that grew steadily stronger as the boy approached Garion. The child stopped and raised the stone in his hands, offering it to Garion. He smiled and spoke a single word, "Errand."

An instant image filled Garion's mind, an image of a dreadful fear. He knew that he was looking directly into the mind of Ctuchik. There was a picture in Ctuchik's mind—a picture of Garion holding the glowing stone in his hand—and that picture terrified the Grolim. Garion felt waves of fear spilling out toward him. Deliberately and quite slowly he reached his right hand toward the stone the child was offering. The mark on his palm yearned toward the stone, and the chorus of song in his mind swelled to a mighty crescendo. Even as he stretched out his hand, he felt the sudden, unthinking, animal panic in Ctuchik.

The Grolim's voice was a hoarse shriek. "*Be not!*" he cried out desperately, directing all his terrible power at the stone in the little boy's hands.

For a shocking instant, a deadly silence filled the turret. Even Belgarath's face, drawn by his terrible struggle, was shocked and unbelieving.

The blue glow within the heart of the stone seemed to contract. Then it flared again.

Ctuchik, his long hair and beard disheveled, stood gaping in wide-eyed and openmouthed horror. "I didn't mean it!" he howled. "I didn't—I—"

But a new and even more stupendous force had already entered the round room. The force flashed no light, nor did it push against Garion's mind. It seemed instead to pull out, drawing at him as it closed about the horrified Ctuchik.

The High Priest of the Grolims shrieked mindlessly. Then he seemed to expand, then contract, then expand again. Cracks appeared on his face as if he had suddenly solidified into stone and the stone was disintegrating under the awful force welling up within him. Within those hideous cracks Garion saw not flesh and blood and bone, but blazing energy. Ctuchik began to glow, brighter and brighter. He raised his hands imploringly. "Help me!" he screamed. He shrieked out a long, despairing, "NO!" And then, with a shattering sound that was beyond noise, the Disciple of Torak exploded into nothingness.

Hurled to the floor by that awesome blast, Garion tumbled against the wall. Without thinking, he caught the little boy, who was flung against him like a rag doll. The round stone clattered as it bounced against the rocks of the wall. Garion reached out to catch it, but Aunt Pol's hand closed on his wrist. "No!" she said. "Don't touch it. It's the Orb."

Garion's hand froze.

The little boy squirmed out of his grasp and ran after the rolling Orb. "Errand." He laughed triumphantly as he caught it.

"What happened?" Silk muttered, struggling to his feet and shaking his head.

"Ctuchik destroyed himself," Aunt Pol replied, also rising. "He tried to unmake the Orb. The Mother of the Gods will not permit unmaking." She looked quickly at Garion. "Help me with your grandfather."

Belgarath had been standing almost in the center of the explosion that had destroyed Ctuchik. The blast had thrown him halfway across the room, and he lay in a stunned heap, his eyes glazed and his hair and beard singed.

"Get up, father," Aunt Pol said urgently, bending over him.

The turret began to shudder, and the basalt pinnacle from which it hung swayed. A vast booming sound echoed up out of the earth. Bits of rock and mortar showered down from the walls of the room as the earth quivered in the aftershock of Ctuchik's destruction.

In the rooms below, the stout door banged open and Garion heard pounding feet. "Where are you?" Barak's voice bellowed.

"Up here," Silk shouted down the stairway.

Barak and Mandorallen rushed up the stone stairs. "Get out of here!" Barak roared. "The turret's starting to break away from the rock. The Temple up there's collapsing, and there's a crack two feet wide in the ceiling where the turret joins the rock."

"Father!" Aunt Pol said sharply, "you must get up!"

Belgarath stared at her uncomprehendingly.

"Pick him up," she snapped at Barak.

There was a dreadful tearing sound as the rocks that held the turret against the side of the peak began to rip away under the pressures of the convulsing earth.

"There!" Relg said in a ringing voice. He was pointing at the back wall of the turret where the stones were cracking and shattering. "Can you open it? There's a cave beyond."

Aunt Pol looked up quickly, focused her eyes on the wall and pointed one finger. "Burst!" she commanded. The stone wall blew back into the echoing cave like a wall of straw struck by a hurricane.

"It's pulling loose!" Silk yelled, his voice shrill. He pointed at a widening crack between the turret and the solid face of the peak.

"Jump!" Barak shouted. "Hurry!"

Silk flung himself across the crack and spun to catch Relg, who had followed him blindly. Durnik and Mandorallen, with Aunt Pol between them, leaped across as the groaning crack yawned wider. "Go, boy!" Barak commanded Garion. Carrying the still-dazed Belgarath, the big Cherek was lumbering toward the opening.

"The child!" the voice in Garion's mind crackled, no longer dry or disinterested. "Save the child or everything that has ever happened is meaningless!"

Garion gasped, suddenly remembering the little boy. He turned and ran back into the slowly toppling turret. He swept up the boy in his arms and ran for the hole Aunt Pol had blown in the rock.

Barak jumped across, and his feet scrambled for an awful second on the very edge of the far side. Even as he ran, Garion pulled in his strength. At the instant he jumped, he pushed back with every ounce of his Will. With the little boy in his arms he literally flew across the awful gap and crashed directly into Barak's broad back.

The little boy in his arms with the Orb of Aldur cradled protectively against his chest smiled up at him. "Errand?" he asked.

Garion turned. The turret was leaning far out from the basalt wall, its supporting stones cracking, ripping away from the sheer face. Ponderously, it toppled outward. And then, with the shards and fragments of the Temple of Torak hurtling past it, it sheared free of the wall and fell into the awful gulf beneath.

The floor of the cave they had entered was heaving as the earth shuddered and shock after shock reverberated up through the basalt pinnacle. Huge chunks of the walls of Rak Cthol were ripping free and plunging past the cave mouth, flickering down through the red light of the newly risen sun.

"Is everybody here?" Silk demanded, looking quickly around. Then, satisfied that they were all safe, he added, "We'd better get back from the opening a bit. This part of the peak doesn't feel all that stable."

"Do you want to go down now?" Relg asked Aunt Pol. "Or do you want to wait until the shaking subsides?"

"We'd better move," Barak advised. "These caves will be swarming with Murgos as soon as the quake stops."

Aunt Pol glanced at the half-conscious Belgarath and then seemed to gather herself. "We'll go down," she decided firmly. "We still have to stop to pick up the slave woman."

"She's almost certain to be dead," Relg asserted quickly. "The earth-quake's probably brought the roof of that cave down on her."

Aunt Pol's eyes were flinty as she looked him full in the face.

No man alive could face that gaze for long. Relg dropped his eyes. "All right," he said sullenly. He turned and led them back into the dark cave with the earthquake rumbling beneath their feet.

ABOUT THE AUTHOR

DAVID EDDINGS was born in Spokane, Washington, in 1931 and was raised in the Puget Sound area north of Seattle. He received a Bachelor of Arts degree from Reed College in Portland, Oregon, in 1954 and a Master of Arts degree from the University of Washington in 1961. He has served in the United States Army, has worked as a buyer for the Boeing Company, has been a grocery clerk, and has taught English. He has lived in many parts of the United States.

His first novel, *High Hunt*, was a contemporary adventure story. The field of fantasy has always been of interest to him, however, and he turned to *The Belgariad* in an effort to develop certain technical and philosophical ideas concerning that genre.

Eddings and his wife, Leigh, currently reside in the Southwest, where they work together on these bestselling fantasy epics.

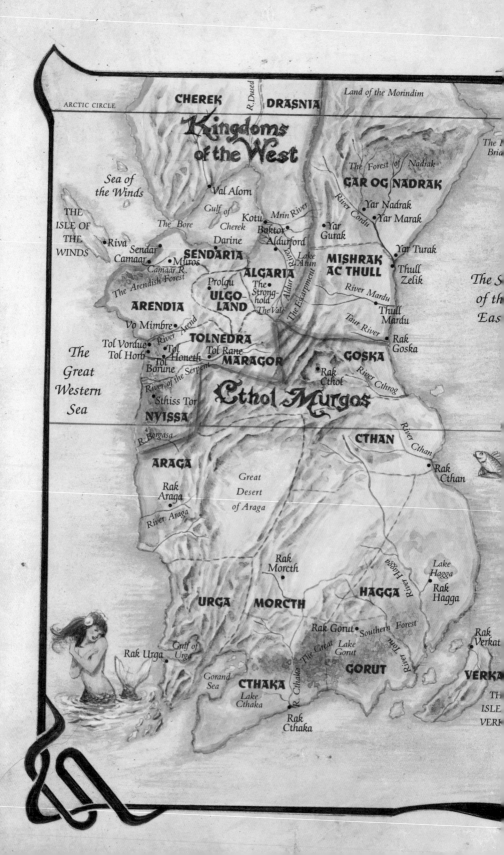

ARCTIC CIRCLE

CHEREK R. Dused **DRASNIA**

Land of the Morindim

The I
Bria

Kingdoms of the West

The Forest of Nadrak

GAR OG NADRAK

Sea of
the Winds

Val Alorn

Gulf of
Cherek

Kotu

Mrin River

Yar Nadrak

Yar Marak

River Cordu

THE
ISLE OF
THE
WINDS

The Bore

Baktor

Yar
Gurak

Riva

Darine

Aldurford

Yar Turak

Sendar

SENDARIA

**MISHRAK
AC THULL**

Thull
Zelik

Camaar

Muros

Camaar R.

ALGARIA

Lake
Alun

River Mardu

The S
of th
Eas

The Arendish Forest

Prolgu

The
Stronghold

Thull
Mardu

ARENDIA

**ULGO
LAND**

The Vale

Taur River

The Escarpment

Vo Mimbre

GOSKA

Rak
Goska

The
Great
Western
Sea

River Arend

TOLNEDRA

Tol Vordue

Tol Horb

Tol
Honeth

Tol Rane

MARAGOR

Rak
Cthol

River Cthrog

Tol
Borune

River of the Serpent

Cthol Murgos

Sthiss Tor

NYISSA

R. Borgasa

CTHAN

River
Cthan

ARAGA

Great
Desert
of Araga

Rak
Cthan

Rak
Araga

River Araga

Rak
Morcth

Lake
Hagga

River Hagga

Rak
Hagga

HAGGA

URGA

MORCTH

Rak Gorut

Southern Forest

Rak
Verkat

Rak Urga

Gulf of
Urga

GORUT

Lake
Gorut

River Tolm

VERKA

Gorand
Sea

CTHAKA

Lake
Cthaka

R. Cthaka The Great

TH
ISLE
VERK

Rak
Cthaka